Arizona Triptych

Donna Ashworth

Small Mountain Books
Flagstaff, Arizona

Copyright © 1999 Donna Ashworth
First Printing 1999
Printed in USA

Small Mountain Books
PMB #380
1109 S. Plaza Way
Flagstaff, Arizona 86001

Library of Congress Catalogue Card Number 99-096950

Library of Congress Cataloging in Publication Data
Ashworth, Donna
        Arizona Triptych/Donna Ashworth
        p.   cm.

        1. Flagstaff (Ariz)–History–Fiction
        2. Coconino National Forest (Ariz)–History–Fiction
        3. Lillian Wilhelm Smith, 1882-1972
        4. Women landscape painters–Arizona
        I. Title

ISBN 0-9630364-0-8

Front Cover Photograph

Sunset on Northern Arizona Ranch Country

by

Sherry G. Mangum

Flagstaff, Arizona

(Image has been digitally modified)

Production by : Northland Graphics

To Cynthia and Sheryl

With gratitude to

Scott Lederman, Cynthia Leigh,
Richard and Sherry Mangum, Mary Lou Morrow,
Amy Winter, and Kay Whitham

Louise Black,
who first mentioned Lillian Wilhelm Smith to me

and Sheryl Tongue who designed the book
and prepared the manuscript for publication.

Contents

Fictional and historical people mingle in these pages.

In Part One the people through whom the story is told, those who think and speak, are inventions of the author. They are:

> Jo, her mother and cousins, except for Lillian and Lina
> The Friendly family
> Ruby and her family
> Ada and Leah

There was a stuttering taxi driver in Flagstaff in those years, Earl "Bucko" Sisk, but Dennis is fictional. The U.S. Census for Arizona, 1920, listed a woman named Petra Armenta who identified herself as a laundress; in this story Mrs. Armenta is an invention of the author. Martin and Hilda Fronske and Wong Dew Yu (Dear Yu Wong June) were historical not fictional people.

In the 1920s the site of the Friendly ranch, part of the 19th century congressional land grant to the Atlantic and Pacific Railroad, was owned by the Atchison, Topeka & Santa Fe. When the railroad sections were offered for sale in the 1940s, they were purchased by Bob and Mary Chambers. Rita Gannon, daughter of the Chambers, granddaughter of Mary and T.A. Riordan, graciously offered the location as a setting for the fictional Friendly ranch.

Part Two is derived entirely from the books, records and memories cited in *Sources*, pages 538–541. It is as complete and accurate a biography as those materials made possible.

Stories go on, weaving their threads into other stories. Granddaughters of the women in Part One are in Part Three. Fictional characters are again those who think and speak. Occasionally they appear with real people, as in the scenes in which a fictional Meg talks with the real granddaughter of Wong Dew Yu and testifies in the courtroom of Judge Stephen Verkamp. The fire season of 1996 is related as it happened, but most of the names and identifying numbers of Forest Service personnel have been changed.

Lillian Wilhelm and John Wetherill in Tuba, leaving for Kayenta, 1913
Courtesy of Millicent Richardson and James E. Babbitt

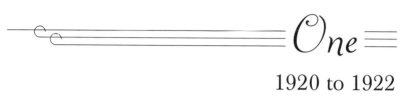

One
1920 to 1922

Dr. Damrosch said I might die.
That was hardly news. I assume
that everyone does, although there
may have been exceptions from time
to time. Who knows?

"No, no, Josephine." He had been our doctor since my grand-father, In The Family, so to speak. "I mean sooner than you might expect. Pulmonary tuberculosis destroys the lungs. One wastes away, sometimes quite rapidly. Tuberculosis is known as 'consumption' because it appears to consume one. You can see for yourself how drawn you look. Color not at all good."

Well, dandy. I had thought...the Spanish influenza epidemic had hardly ebbed. One couldn't forget *that* one, millions of deaths around the world. A persistent cough, a mild fever, crushing fatigue—it was the first diagnosis that came to mind.

Melancholia I put down to Nicky dying in France in the Great War, although to be honest, I'd have to say it was just as well. There had been laughs, and we had danced rather well together, but if he'd lived, he'd have been boiled to the ears most of the time and prob-ably drunk himself to death.

I was numb, of course. My gloves were beside me on his desk—very snappy really, chamois dyed cranberry red. Grandmother Boren had been aghast. "Josephine! *Red* for a widow?" I stroked them with one finger.

"Josephine, are you listening? I cannot emphasize too strongly the severity of this matter." Dr. Damrosch had the face of a Springer spaniel. "The tap drew off two pints of fluid full of bacillus. What remains near the bottom of your lungs probably has the consistency of vanilla pudding. However, people do sometimes recover. It would be advisable, I should say *imperative*, for you to leave sea level as soon as possible for some place in the West, some place with dry air and a high elevation. I have read that artists find Santa Fe a stimu-lating impetus to their work."

Thank you, no. If I were going to be sick and dying, I didn't want to be in an art colony, everyone painting green nudes. Exciting to *work* in, maybe, not to die in.

Dr. Damrosch had not asked my opinion about the needle he had inserted between the ribs in my lower back, but he did allow me choice in the matter of geography, which was good of him, I thought. In my experience, men of his generation weren't liberal about offering choice to women.

"Hart Merriam's sister Florence went out to Arizona nearly thirty years ago with a complaint of the lungs and came back cured. She is still living, actively, I might say, an ornithologist writing about birds. You would do well to consider Arizona. So long as you take the cure in some locale that is high and dry. Fresh air is required above all, good ventilation and exposure to sunlight. Rest. Perhaps a little mild exercise. And a great amount of wholesome food. Eggs. Eight large glasses of milk each day. We must overcome the tendency to become frail. You are too thin and run-down."

The man was out of date. It was fashionable to have the shape of an asparagus. "Emaciated," as Grandmother Bergman was fond of saying when she was pointing out what was wrong with the younger generation: bobbed hair, short skirts—to her mind quite scandalous.

I left Dr. Damrosch dazed by the news and stood in front of the building for some time, staring down at a Sidewalk of New York with no idea of what to do. One's mind is bizarre—I realized I was looking at the feet of passers-by. Trousers on the men were all cuffed, but no one was wearing spats. I couldn't think how long it had been since spats were fashionable. When I noticed a pair of button boots, I looked up to see the face above them: elderly, of course. She was the only woman in sight who was wearing a skirt that reached her ankles.

And where had all the horses gone? The street was crowded with black taxis, boxes on wheels with none of the elegance that carriages had once had. Odd what a death sentence does to one's eyesight—details were as strange and clear as if I had just emerged from one of Mr. Wells' time machines.

No doubt I was quite conspicuous standing there staring about me. I climbed up into one of the ugly black cabs and hid inside from the moving strangers on the streets. There was no clip-clop of hooves, which might have been comforting, just the noise of a rattling automobile.

In times of distress, where does one turn? I rode uptown between uncaring stone buildings to West 97th Street to see my mother, hoping she would be at home. Since my father's death she was usually out, being a volunteer, being a docent, being on committees here and there. Quite modern of her, really. "Volunteers keep the best of this country alive," she liked to say. Actually, I think she had waited thirty years for the freedom.

She had just come in. She looked marvelous, of course, all in pearl grey silk, fashionable down to the clocks on her stockings. "Do sit down, Jo. Sherry? Is anything wrong? You look a wee bit fatigued."

The room was a beautifully proportioned Federal decorated in a rakish variety of every style of the past forty years. A Tiffany lamp stood on a Craftsman table. Beaux Arts and Sheraton against Japanese and Gothic Revival—Mother was a fan of the arts, the more exuberant the better. She poured from a Waterford decanter into Art Nouveau glasses with stems that looked like moving seaweed.

I knew she would say the proper maternal thing. "Oh my love, of course you're concerned, it's serious. I'm stricken by the news." She raised her hand to her heart. "My only child. But there is something you can do, you see, you aren't entirely helpless. It's important when faced with a problem to take action." Action was her new motto; compared to the caution rampant among the aunts it was quite startling.

"Mother, t.b. can be *fatal*." It sounded bathetic once it had been said, full of fear and self-pity. Too embarrassing for words.

"I refuse to think about it in such bleak terms. Don't you do it either, Jo, it will only defeat you. The women in this family are long-lived. Concentrate on that. And look at it as an opportunity, dear: illness should make you aware of details you might have overlooked."

"I'm thinking of going out West."

"Oh, an adventure! I've always longed to see the West, so exotic. Of course you must go, despite what anyone says. Don't let them persuade you to settle for a sanitarium upstate."

"You wouldn't protest?"

"I'd go with you if I weren't up to my eyebrows with Lizzie Bliss putting pressure on the Met for an Impressionist exhibition. Honestly, I'm convinced most of those people think art is merely a form of archaeology, they're so enamored of all things ancient. But think of it! The West! You must write and tell me all about it." She settled into a Morris chair.

"I'd be alone as an *oyster* out there."

"Oysters live in—oh, I see what you mean, inside their shells. Well, that would depend on you, I should think. And if you need me, I'll be there in a wink." Since she had turned fifty, she'd been Little Miss Sunshine, the cousins were sure she had lost her wits.

I was fascinated by the West, of course; films on the silver screen about the Great Frontier were all the rage. "The Trail of the Lonesome Pine," "Arizona"—they'd drawn me to the theater. Me and half of New York. I never missed Will Rogers, so droll.

There were those paintings of the Grand Canyon commissioned by the Santa Fe. I longed to see with my own eyes whether Western air was that clear and brilliant, whether sky turned those colors at dusk. And then, my cousin Lillian had gone out to Arizona in 1913 with Zane Grey to paint landscapes and stayed, and I was quite green with envy. So I decided to hie me to the Baby State—for the sake of the infected lungs—to the highest place, a little town on the railroad line. I had loved Bertha Metzger's painting of the nearby mountains, although their name "San Francisco" had puzzled me.

When they heard the news, the aunts made horrified drawing room scenes. "There is nothing out there but snakes and tarantulas! Wild animals! Wild Indians, and you too small and thin to defend yourself! Uncouth cowboys! No Society at all!" Evidently I was guilty of a gross breach of something significant.

The men were too fascinated by chasing the Almighty Dollar to give it a second thought, or a first either, probably. I was rather hoping they would remonstrate, I was prepared to remind them that I was a widow with an income of my own and the right to vote for President, a modern woman. Nicky's father wouldn't have cared what I did: that man had all the personality of a turtle.

One by one the Grandmothers summoned me to tea. Great-grandmother Vogelin actually sent a note by her chauffeur, though the others used the telephone. Dutifully I pushed through a fog of fatigue to respond: one does not ignore grandmothers like mine.

Each placed me beside her, took my hand and patted it and said, "What's this I hear?" They went on to some variation of "I've always thought you such a clever girl, so talented. There will be no Art. You will waste all those years of training."

Great-grandmother Bergman seated me among the cushions of a Turkish cozy in an alcove and poured tea from a low table. She expected it would be enough to tell me that Arizona was quite out of the question and she would arrange reservations in a sanitarium in the Italian Alps. My stubborn refusal to budge offended her: she was accustomed to ruling everyone within reach.

Then on to Grandmother Scheffler's drawing room. She told me that as my mother was too frivolous to think of doing so, she would make arrangements for me to go to Switzerland, which was of course preferable to the Backwater of Arizona. Switzerland was close to Paris and Florence and Bayreuth. She would hear no dissent, it was settled.

The next day Grandmother Battenhausen recommended the Riviera for the sun. A tiny raisin of a woman, she was no less adamant than the others that I must not consider Arizona. "There would be no suitable companions for you there, whereas on the Mediterranean coast one can always find stimulating conversation." She smiled and patted my hand.

"I will definitely consider it. Thank you so much for your concern."

There is no freedom in a German family. I hear it's the same for Italians. My refusal to Listen to Reason marshalled the family's resources to prevent the escape of even one member from its collective rule. All during the weeks when the Palisades were red and gold, and Senator Harding was campaigning on a platform of "Normalcy," I fended off delegations from Cousins and Relations by the Dozens. "Jo, it's quite insane. Now more than ever German-Americans need to present a united front. Switzerland has fine sanitaria. It would be much more suitable."

They used every weapon. "Cousin Lillian went to Arizona and hardly comes back."

Between bouts of coughing and checking my handkerchief for drops of blood, I parried. "Lillian fell in love with painting it; you forget her show in Philadelphia last year. Alderman La Guardia was in Arizona until he was fifteen, and *he* came back."

"That noisy little Italian, how can you compare yourself to him?"

No one seemed to think tuberculosis gave me a right to tender ministration. I really thought they had forgotten the reason for the whole debate. They actually said, "Think of your mother. What if she should die while you're off on your primitive adventure?"

All through the Christmas season they treated me to one alarmed scene after another. It was swell, I've never been so exhausted. They sat in relays around my couch, talking, talking.

"There'll be no real theater out there. How will you live without theater?"

"Films are the coming art form. Please, Gertrude, don't look at me like that, it's too dreary." Gertrude's husband had been reported missing in action in France; some of the Cousins were of the opinion that it had been his only possible escape from her.

"Jo, it's bad enough that you look like a waif. You needn't act like one too." I wondered whether every family had a cousin like Gertrude.

*D*eath is a Big Issue, the biggest one ever has to face. Big when it is someone close, big when it is one's own. I did not want to allow the family to take charge of mine.

So on Monday, January 3rd, 1921, smoldering with self-pity, I decamped, alerting no self-appointed guardians. So weak I was barely upright, I took a taxi through bleak grey streets to the clamor and bustle of Pennsylvania Station and departed alone from the center of the universe. In my luggage were a folding easel and my paint box.

Money buys freedom and privacy, the two important luxuries. I had booked a mahogany-paneled stateroom with a double berth and a brass-fitted lavatory to be my cross-country home for nearly a week. Privacy has never been too ritzy for me. New York to Chicago by way of Philadelphia would be a day and a half, if we managed to make the usual forty miles an hour.

For half a day vegetation was so thick beside the tracks I could barely see out. I assured the solicitous porter, his white coat such a marvelous contrast with the warm dark tones of his face, that I really didn't *want* the berth made up. It upset his routine.

"You truly don't?"

"I truly don't. I need to rest, I've not been well."

"That sure is bad."

Bad? It was an *outrage.*

"You ring, now, any time you need anything. Between meals the chef could take a minute to whip you up some milk with eggs and mashed fruit. Shall I ask him?"

Dr. Damrosch would have approved of that. "Yes, please. Very thoughtful."

Through a day and a night I lay limp as a petunia, lulled by the rocking and swaying of the moving car, dozing, waking to watch Ohio and Indiana and Illinois slide past the window. Little towns, people moving about and sometimes gazing back at the languid Idle Rich while the train stopped for ten minutes to take on water and the conductor waited to shout "Bo-o-o-o-ard!" in rising syllables. The clang of the bell, the clack of wheels against rails speeding up, and we were off again in smoke and steam. Wagons pulled by horses went along the roads for all the world like a novel come to life. Lights came on in houses at dusk. It haunted me. What did they *do* with their lives in such dinky places?

Then Chicago's Dearborn Station, where the through car was switched to a different train for another 1,683 miles. The Atchison, Topeka and Santa Fe line, more little towns and farms, rabbits in the fields, the sun coming up on the unbelievable size of the sky of Kansas arching away to the horizon. I'd had no idea the world could look so large, it was quite liberating. I said it over to myself: "On the Plains through Kansas," matching the rhythm of the wheels beneath me, that mesmerizing sound inside a train.

I tipped the Santa Fe porter to bring trays of anything tempting from the dining car. The dear man always included a linen napkin and a cut flower in a vase. And I never changed out of my new plaid blanket robe—dropped waist and single button, very much the latest thing. The freedom not to put on day-time clothing was wild indulgence. Grandmother Scheffler would have had apoplexy: "So *unseemly*, Josephine. And cut from a blanket, not at all appropriate." But the robe was a comfort, and Doctor Damrosch had warned me not to take cold.

One morning I woke in anticipation of the Rocky Mountains off in the distance. I lay and watched for them as the train rolled along. Finally: dark blue shapes, a line of them all across the horizon. I thought at first they were clouds. Peaks shining with snow rising out of the plain, appearing and disappearing as the land rose and fell in pale golden waves. Gone again. There again. Delicate grasses blowing in the wind, leafless little willows in the low places. I hadn't felt so religious since I was fourteen.

To my shame, I very nearly cried. I didn't want to cough out my life onto a handkerchief in bloody drops. I wanted to live and paint huge canvases of those mountains, the promise of something glorious about to happen. How would one paint such clarity of air without old-fashioned realism? What would Cezanne have done with such landscape? What would Monet do with such air, such brilliant light?

The size, the *size* of the land. No wonder artists traveled West. The intoxication, the soaring joy! Too maudlin for words, really, but I was quite weak.

The porter came in with a lunch tray. "It's ten below out there. Wind coming right off Canada."

"How far away are those mountains?"

He arranged a setting on my little table, his marvelous black hands moving among the cloth and the flower and the plates

I was quite fascinated with the patterns they made. "Further'n you'd think. The big ones are a long ways from here."

I smiled like a dope the rest of the day, happy that the world held such country. How would one paint it to show the enormity? I decided that a low horizon line might do the trick, the lower third of the canvas. Sky rich with clouds. The whole seen beyond a fore-ground of grasses. Or—this was quite exciting—a huge painting in three parts, each panel framed separately, to convey the sweep.

We passed through little towns with Spanish names. The mountains were a purple so dark in late afternoon they were almost black against a pale sky. Then up through a narrow valley, Raton Pass to New Mexico, old snow glistening in the low light, and after that, huge emptiness mile after mile across the top of the world.

The simplicity of the scene was liberating. Was such luminous beauty typical? Perhaps I had been too hasty in rejecting Santa Fe. If I didn't like Arizona, I would come back.

At Albuquerque I woke and gazed out the window into darkness, hoping to see my first Indians. I had read that the women sold their wares on the platform, their skin taking the light in a marvelous way. Ridiculous of me, they had no doubt gone home at sunset.

Arizona at last, the shapes of distant buttes in the night. I imagined invisible Apaches watching from behind every shadowy hill. Danger is *so* exciting from the safety of a train.

Sun rose the next morning on land stark as the steppes—it looked as if it had *never* received any rain. Knee-high bushes threw long shadows across the ground. Now and then there were little towns the color of dirt.

Hours later, if I put my face close to the window, I could see a huge solitary mountain ahead, incongruous in that bleak land. The tracks pointed straight toward it. My destination? Oh, surely not! There were no trees, no real bushes, only a few winter grasses. It had a unique kind of beauty if one weren't planning to *stay*.

Mile after mile the train went on. What had I done? Defied The Family and crossed the continent for a desert? At least it was dry, that much was obvious.

The porter knocked to say I should dress and pack, we weren't far out. When I looked again, the big mountain was still ahead and there were purple-black hills out the window, piles of them, some with craters, and a few dark shrubs. Wearing my red coat and hat, I sat with bags and boxes, feeling very small and hopeless for the first time. Could I recover any health at all in such country? I wasn't sure I was up to it.

*A*t eleven o'clock in the morning, dizzy, sun at my back, I stepped down from my Pullman Palace car for the first time in days into Flagstaff, Arizona, at an astonishing 7000 feet above sea level, the elevation of the St. Bernard Pass. A ten-minute stop was barely time for the porter to see that all my trunks and boxes were around my feet, the conductor shouted "Bo-o-o-oard!", and the last contact with home jolted away without me into an icy wind, pistons stroking, whistle blowing. There was no snow on the ground, thanks for small blessings. I pulled my beaver collar up around my chin and ears, glad in that wind that cloche hats were in fashion. Also thinking I had carried Stubborn a bit too far.

I had never in my life stood alone under such an enormous sky. No doubt it's good for me to feel that wretched now and then.

"Taxi, m-ma'am?"

He was holding his cap with one hand, hunching his shoulders against the wind, and pointing toward a shining Model T sedan standing a few yards away. The passenger door was open, inviting. Clever of him. On the body was a painted sign: Shamrock Taxi. Shamrock? There were Irishmen in *Arizona*?

"Is it usually this windy here?"

"Yes, mm-mma'am, it is often." He didn't *sound* like an Irishman.

"Do you have a hotel?"

"Five. There's the Commercial across over there. Down on the nn-next corner is the B-Bank. Up the b-block from that is the Weatherford. All up-to-date."

He actually looked at my hat and coat and shoes. "You won't be wanting the Pine or the Ideal. Weatherford'd be b-best. It's farther from the tracks. They turned on the steam heat last month. Commercial is mmmmostly traveling gentlemen, salesm-mm-men and such. B-bank's the oldest."

"The Weatherford then." I hurried to the car and huddled inside, grateful that Ford had finally built an enclosed body with glass windows. What a gale! *Often*, did he say?

He strapped my box trunk to the running board and piled the bags into the front seat. "I'll come right b-back and get the wardrobe trunk, it'll be okay here."

Before he went around in front of the hood, he confided, "Won't be a mmmminute to get 'er started. Put alcohol in the radiator just this m-mmmm-m-" It was taking so long to get the word out he sounded as if he were humming. "-morning."

He cranked for a good deal longer than a minute, but finally all four cylinders caught and he jumped in and grasped the gas lever to adjust it. "She does real good at this altitude. Hits on all four cylinders mmmm-m-most of the time. Planetary transmission. Not often I have to get out and get under." I was prepared to say I was glad to hear it, but he let out the clutch and started off with such a lurch that I caught at the side strap.

Air was clear as good crystal, I could give them that, even in winter with a gale blowing. On one side of the street, such as it was, were the railroad tracks, with houses beyond and farther a smoke stack with no smoke. On the other was what looked like a row of saloons that had been converted to cafes by the Eighteenth Amendment. The very thought of alcohol made me queasy.

I saw no wild animals or wild Indians, and the cowboys riding along with such grace looked more unwashed than uncouth. Here and there along the street a flivver, a wagon, horses—actually, more horses than flivvers. Were those *hitching posts*? How archaic. Only one building taller than two stories. All were built of stone or brick. The rim of the little bowl in which the town crouched was covered with green trees that tapered toward the top—pines perhaps. Beyond, mountains towered above them. What a stage set!

"We got a Normal School, three b-b-banks, four churches not counting the ones in Mm-mill Town, five hotels, six doctors, and nine miles of sidewalk. Downtown's paved with b-b-b-bilthulitic just like in Chicago. We danced a Virginia reel right in the mm-mmmm-middle of this street on the Fourth of July after it was finished. One of the b-big attractions of the day, people came from all up and down the railroad line to join in. Pretty good town. Population's above three thousand now."

"Imagine that." Manhattan alone had a population of almost three *million*.

He drove with his head tipped back, the better for me to hear him. "I try to mm-mm-meet all the passenger trains. Ten a day, five going east, five west. You came in on Number Nine, did you know that?"

"No, I'm sure I didn't." I wondered whether, if *I* stammered, I would talk so much.

"It's usually the first one I get to the depot for. One and Four and Ten, it's not even daylight yet this time of year." He swerved around a corner. "Hope you like the Weatherford, it's only twenty years old. Jimmy Swinnerton stays there when he's in town. So does Zane Grey. President Roosevelt was there once. Mmmm-mister Hearst."

Was Jimmy Swinnerton the Hearst cartoonist who had been cured of tuberculosis and begun painting afterwards? That was encouraging. Zane Grey didn't impress me, he was married to one of my cousins. Despite his best-selling success and all that money, some of us, the younger ones especially, thought his sentiment too gauche for words.

Shamrock pointed out a doctor's office—I'd have to remember that. "Ahead's the telephone exchange and the Weatherford. Rent's five dollars a week and up. You staying long?"

"I'm hoping to find a room to let where I can live quietly for a while, perhaps in a private home." That sounded more plaintive than I had intended.

"That right? Mrs. Green has a room she wants to rent to a boarder. Mrs. Green on Verde." There was a pause. "I can come by this afternoon, let's see, about two o'clock, after Twenty-one comes in and before Number Two, and take you over to mm-mm-meet her."

"Yes, thank you." I'd have preferred to rest in a hotel room, gathering courage and other such resources. However, Seize the Moment, and all that.

With no traffic as impediment, he made a full turn in the middle of the street and pulled up in front of a three-story building of red stone, this one with a balcony railing on the second level and the oddest cone of a tower above the corner. "Here we are." He throttled down the sedan, killed the spark, got out and came around to open the passenger door. "Tell B-b-bert you want a room on the sunny side."

We made An Entrance into the lobby, he with important trips in and out carrying my bags, I walking as tall as possible, very Big City in my red coat with beaver collar and cuffs. The aunts had agreed with the grandmothers, of course. "Josephine, *black* for a widow." Cousin Gertrude had said I looked like a macaw. Gertrude tried too hard to be sophisticated, in my opinion. But the coat had suited my mood at the time. I had bought the red hat to match. I *liked* red.

Maybe it was rather splendiferous for Flagstaff: it attracted attention from the men idling around the stove and the man at the desk. He at least was not wearing a huge hat as the rest were. *Indoors*!

"Have you a good room on the sunny side?"

It must have been Bert. He was wearing a ring with a bluegreen stone—I couldn't take my eyes from it. Mrs. Astor herself wouldn't have worn such a gaudy ring. And Mrs. Astor wasn't one to stint.

"Yes ma'am, you betcha. Has steam heat. Only fourteen buildings can claim that so far. Turned it into the mains last month. Name?"

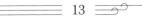

"Mrs. Nicholas Boren."

"Staying long?"

Shamrock bustled up. "I'm driving her this afternoon to see Mmmm-mrs. Green's room."

"Ah. Mrs. Green on Verde." They had both said that as if it were some kind of local joke. I missed the humor entirely.

"I have a cousin here, I think. Miss Lillian Wilhelm in Kayenta. May I send a message or make a phone call?"

Every man in the room began to laugh, including Bert. "Ma'am, there's no telephone line farther'n Tuba City, not yet anyway, not until the Navajos decide they want to put up the poles. Send a message'd take at least a couple days up and a couple back—road kinda wanders around in the junipers if it's passable, which it's not hardly this time of year. Spring's worse. You have to ford the Little Colorado wherever the bottom's sandstone unless you go by the Cameron bridge."

I resented the laughter. How was I supposed to know? "Is Kayenta in northern Arizona?"

"Yes, ma'am, but it's up on the Reservation. I guess you people from New York don't realize how big the state is." How did he know I was from New York?

In a sunny-side room taller than it was wide, I was so forlorn that I did not remove my coat or hat. For two hours, wearing them for familiarity, I lay on the bed exhausted, awash in self-pity. "Whatever am I doing here? I don't even know who I *am* in this place." I peered inside myself and found absolutely nothing, truly did not know who I was. Dr. Freud would have been fascinated, no doubt.

I wanted to bolt back to that stable of a station and board the first passenger train that came through no matter where it was headed. *Leave* that depressing little burg and the people in it to their wind. But I was too fatigued to move.

At two I struggled to my feet and went down the stairs to find Shamrock waiting, good as his word. "I swung by and told Mm Mm-m-mrs. Green we were coming. She's expecting us. It's only four b-blocks, thought I'd drive you past the big b-b-buildings. We can come b-back on Leroux so you can see the fine houses. Slow though. Mm-mmmm..."—he paused for a deliberate breath—"Marshall Neil doesn't like cars speeding. Scares the horses."

Big buildings—he meant *seven* additional two-story colossi. It was too quaint. In New York, buildings were so tall the tops were invisible from the street; pediments and domes and gargoyles and caryatids, you could see them only from another building.

"Here's Western Union in case you want to let the folks b-b-back home know you got here okay." Later, perhaps. At the moment I was thinking of going on to California and dying beside the Pacific.

"Babbitt B-Brothers. Oldest b-b-b-b...tall b-building in town, but it has steam heat. We've got seven thousand feet of underground mmm-mmains laid in cement, steam comes from south of the tracks."

He turned the corner, avoiding a slow horseman in the exact center of the intersection. "Now we're on San Francisco, named after the mmm-m-mmmm...Peaks. On the right's the post office, guess you'll need to know that one. B-B-Babbitts have the whole west side of the b-block clear to the garage, George Verkamp runs it. New M-m-mmasonic Temple on the right with lawyers' offices on the ground floor, County Court House on the far corner. Steam heat there too. That's the tallest building in town on account of the tower."

He was proud, the funny man, boosting two blocks of modest structures. You could say this for them: they didn't hide the sky. In New York you scarcely noticed the sky.

"County jail. Steam heat there too. Would you b-b-believe it? This here's the Ideal Hotel. In the flu epidemic they used it for a hospital. And Verde up ahead. Notice it's pretty level the whole stretch from town to here, no climbing or anything. I figured you'd like that, easier and all. You're a lunger, I guess."

"Lung-'er?" It sounded quite provincial.

"T.B. of the lungs. You didn't mm-mm-mention being a school teacher or a secretary and wanting to be close to work." It was a caution: don't assume all Westerners are dolts.

"That's M-m-m-Mrs. Green's place up there, that white one with the little rock wall around the yard. Summer vegetable garden on the far side."

With a flourish, he pulled the Ford into a full turn in the street, a showman to his fingertips. "There's M-m-m-mmm...Ruby Green waiting on the doorstep, b-b-b-big as life. B-been in this country since she was not much more than a girl."

She looked to be of an age with the grandmothers, but that was the only similarity. Lean and strong and brown from the sun, grey hair fastened back into a bun. The hem of her blue dress was blown back to her ankles. She was smiling. Great-grandmother Bergman's *pleasant* expression was a mouth that turned down and pursed at the same time.

Shamrock opened the passenger door. "Afternoon, Ruby. This is Mrs. B-B-Boren, come to see your room."

"Hello, Dennis." She came out to meet us, took my hand in both of hers. "I don't know if I could call such a pretty little woman 'Mrs.'"

There was no possibility of formality, I could see that. "My grandmothers call me Josephine. Almost everyone else says Jo."

"Josephine like the woman Napoleon loved?"

No one had ever put it that way, as romance. I very nearly cried. "I'm told it was quite fashionable at one time."

"Well, I shouldn't wonder. Your coat is such a fine color, red becomes you. I do like to see it on a woman with your dark hair. Come in, come in."

Dennis sat down on the big porch. "I'll wait out here, if you ladies don't mmmind."

There was a glass window in the front door, a staircase just inside, flowered wallpaper. "I'll show you the ground floor first, you'd be free to use the parlor and the kitchen. Player piano's new. I got it for company after my husband died. Just before he went, he deeded the ranch to my daughter and her husband, to save me legal trouble, you know. I don't have many piano rolls as yet." Her parlor was light and airy with tall windows, but I could imagine how it might be after sunset when the curtains were pulled against cold and night.

"There's no steam heat this far out yet. Furnace chimney connects with the room upstairs that would be yours, but I didn't brick up the fireplace. I do like an open fire on a stormy night."

The kitchen was as big as the parlor, big enough for a table that would seat ten or twelve at least. I didn't remember ever *seeing* kitchens in the grandmothers' houses.

"I still have the old wood-burning range. Seems like I've cooked on it all my life. My children are telling me I should get an electric for hot weather now that I'm not out on the homestead. They think the old stove will soon be a thing of the past, but I don't know if I want to learn a new way. There's comfort in what you're used to."

The room smelled of two loaves of bread that were cooling on a table. Afternoon sun through the west window turned it all golden. There was a rocking chair, yarn and knitting needles beside it. It was too quaint—I was feeling quite soppy, so I quite fell in love with it.

"I've spent years in this big old room. In winter we used to heat all our water on the stove and bathe in a Number Three washtub right here where it was warm. That was when we had to carry all our water in, before we got the city system. I've had Coffin and Wilson install a bathroom upstairs, all new modern fixtures, but maybe you'd like to try a sponge bath down here if upstairs seems cool to you."

A bath by the kitchen stove. Imagine! I didn't know such places were *left* in America. I also didn't know about a Number Three washtub. Did one stand in it or dip one's fingers?

We climbed to the second floor. "I had the upstairs done over after the children were gone. Took out walls and made two bedrooms into a big one the whole width of the house front." She opened a door.

"See, it gets morning through the east dormer once the sun is above the hill and evening through the west. This time of year sunlight most of the day comes through the south window."

Light *spilled* into every corner. Who would have thought a bedroom could look so bright in January? Air was still, that awful wind shut out.

"Furniture's from Sullivan and Taylor downtown." The room was a refuge—blue flowered rug, walnut four-poster bed, a rocker wing chair at a window—but spacious enough for anything I might want to add, like my easel if I felt up to painting. A table in the east dormer to hold one of her loaves on a colored plate with sunlight slanting across it—I could paint one composition after another in this room, something modern perhaps. But not Cubist, that was already boring, in my opinion.

Mrs. Green looked at me, smiling. "I just started advertising. I had in mind a single lady, a teacher at the Normal School maybe, who'd want a quiet room and meals in. A young widow who needs a home for rest would do just as well. You are a widow?"

"The second battle of the Marne."

She nodded. "War takes too many good men. So do a life of hard work and then old age. Too many women get left alone. Seems like we could figure out a better way, but I don't suppose we will."

Everyone was dying, all of us, all the time. I couldn't think why it had taken me so long to realize it. A better way than war and Spanish influenza and tuberculosis. A better way than dying of old age. It was too awful.

"It's sad, left alone in a big house that used to be full, so after my husband passed on I made a place where someone else might want to be. Life and talk here again. Why don't you sit down, dear? You look a little peaked all of a sudden. You are just a bit thin, you know."

January, 1921

Dear Mother,

A brief note from your wandering child, as in the old song, so that you can tell the family that of course you know where I am. I doubt they will send someone to fetch me back into the collective bosom, but one never knows—it might be best not to give them the exact location just yet.

I am stopping in what seems the pages of a book, the funniest little half-formed burg you can imagine. I cannot actually say that I decided to stay. It was simply that on the day I arrived I collapsed, went completely to pieces. Crossed most of the continent and could not go a mile farther. I curled into a big chair and cried and cared not a fig about dignity, I fear I was feeling dreadfully sorry for myself. Also too ill to care whether I died or where. Quite a revealing experience.

The most marvelous woman named Ruby Green simply took charge of me. I wonder whether you would like her. A taxi driver who brought me to see the room she had for rent, a wonderfully natural man named Dennis, was Ruby's willing ally. He hustled back to the town's best hotel, which towers a full three stories above the street, to fetch my bags while she put me to bed in a big four-poster. Between them and their round-the-clock humanitarian attention, I've recovered enough poise to sit up part of each day.

So here I am for the nonce in a big sunny upstairs room. Ruby has brought up pink geraniums for all the window sills. There is no snow, but the wind is punishing, so I called Dennis to drive his taxi to a store called Babbitts'—a mercantile and grocery store run by a ranching family—and buy a wool blanket for my knees when I'm sitting in a wing chair by the window. Ruby arranged to have a New York paper delivered by the open truck that brings her afternoon grocery order. Too thoughtful, really, I was quite touched.

Every morning before the Number Nine train comes in, Dennis brings milk fresh just hours earlier from local cows and delivered to Etter's Depot downtown. I pay well for the service, and why not? It's small town entertainment to see my milk arrive in a Ford taxi.

Don't worry about me. I am in the best possible hands in a really quite reassuring situation. There is as yet only the tiniest spot of blood now and then when I cough, an indication that things are not so bad as they might be. You may tell the aunts that I'm having an epic adventure in the West. While that's not absolutely true quite yet, I intend to work up to it.

More later,

Jo

*W*ind beats against the house and rattles window glass—usually during the day, as if there were some connection with the sun. Nights have been cold and quiet, except for trains, of course, but they don't wake me now that I'm accustomed. I've tried to keep the windows open as Doctor Damrosch advised, but even when I wear a cap to bed and huddle around two hot water bottles, I am simply too cold. It's not often that I'm roused by the night sweats that, lucky me, accompany tuberculosis.

Afternoons I've been sitting in the sun in the deep wing chair, wrapped in my blanket, taking what is prescribed as a "silent cure" and catching up on news of great importance. According to the papers there's trouble all over Europe: famine, unemployment, typhus, strikes in Austria, revolts in Ireland, twenty-five million starving Russians—what could one expect after a War To End All War? In Berlin 29,000 children are reported ill with tuberculosis— my, that makes me feel ever so much less afflicted.

I'm also reading back issues of the local weekly—all sixteen pages of it. The official paper of the county Farm Bureau, it carries a full page of brands and stock news, a regular column about farms and ranges. It likes to call itself "pert and chipper"—droll as can be. I am quite gratified to learn that City Clerk Clarence Pulliam has recovered from mumps. Pine tar and honey are recommended as a remedy for colds—what, I wonder, is pine *tar*? The chairman of the County Board of Supervisors and three other men went out to a place called Lee's Ferry with a new boat for the ferryman strapped to the top of the car. It's all too rich for words.

I see that the public library, which has been sponsored by the Woman's Club, is to be taken over by the city and placed in *one* room upstairs in one of the two-story buildings. They're all pleased about it. The bookstacks in the New York Public Library are in seven *levels* underground beneath the main reading room—oh my. I suppose it would be best to keep mum.

It has been discovered that loggers at Camp One near Volunteer Canyon have been making moonshine; they claim they produce it as gifts. There is no phone number in town with more than two digits. The cousins simply would not believe me.

Contract bridge is all the rage, but auction is coming into favor. The Flagstaff Woman's Club and the Shakespeare Circle are well-thought-of: "Never intentionally does one miss these social evenings," according to the Society Editor, who writes regular columns. There are "jolly" dancing parties every week, a dancing *club* with twelve couples, including three Babbitt pairs. I have not yet sorted out the Babbitts—there seem to be a great many of them. I gather the second generation is in full cry.

Yesterday afternoon as I was resting, the player piano down in the parlor erupted into "Alexander's Ragtime Band" and brought me to my feet. From the head of the stairs I looked down at Ruby, her hands gripping the piano bench, pedaling away enthusiastically as the keys moved by themselves. I might have expected *anything* else to be her taste, not rag. I sat down on the stairs to watch. She worked her way through "The Missouri Waltz" and quite amused me when she began to sing with gusto, "I Was Paddlin' Madeline Home." But when she launched into a lusty chorus of "Indian Love Call"—"When I'm calling you-oo-oo-oo-oo-oo-oo"—I fled to my room to avoid unseemly laughter.

If I'm not coughing these cold, windy mornings after breakfast, I sit in Ruby's warm kitchen drinking coffee from a Blue Willow cup, watching her bake and discussing the news. An old friend, an early pioneer named Hank Lockett, died early in the month of cancer of the throat. "He came a long way to end his days in Flagstaff, Arizona." Such a poignant thing to say.

Mayor Sam Quay is all for building a dam to make a place called Switzer Canyon into a lake. Editor Breen approves. Ruby is not convinced. "They say it's for flood control and a way to add to the water supply and there's granite formation in there so the lake would hold, but I'm not so sure. They'd have to divert the Rio de Flag into it, and you can see for yourself that so far this winter there hasn't been enough snow to fill a wash tub."

She spoke to Mrs. Armenta who was busy heating water on the stove and sorting clothes—Ruby had engaged her, "because of my boarder," to come in twice a month from her house south of the tracks to do washing, sheets and things. "Petra, are you able to get enough water in Mill Town to keep your work going?"

I wasn't sure how much English Mrs. Armenta understood, I had not yet heard her speak. Her answer was marvelous: her head tilted to the side, she raised her shoulders and her eyebrows and made a vague gesture with both hands.

Ruby must have translated. "Goodness knows we have problems about water around here, always have, Fred Breen knows that as well as anybody. But when he says, 'Let's come alive and have Switzer Lake,' I wonder who'd own the land around it." Mrs. Armenta nodded and twisted one side of her mouth, a very expressive cynicism.

If I were a part of this town rather than a spectator from Mars, so to speak, no doubt I would regard it quite differently. I might not be fascinated as a naturalist studying some strange new creatures. As it is…

February, 1921

Dear Mother,

I must admit I miss you and think of you often. Terribly old-fashioned of me, I know. Still, now and then I am reminded of your quite civilized attitudes, and I can almost hear your voice commenting on human foibles. There was an occurrence here last week I would like to have your reaction to.

I spend most of my days alone in my lovely bright room, reading and resting, hardly going downstairs except for meals with Ruby. She seldom says anything disapproving about anyone. I quite like it, it's restful. But the son-in-law (Fred) of her old friend Jim was arrested for a shooting last week, and she was upset. "Jim Lamport signed for a twenty-five hundred dollar bond, which shows what he thinks of the whole affair, and not just because Fred married Edith either. She was born here, and she's a fine woman, a schoolteacher. The whole family's standing right with him."

"Good for them," I said. I envied Edith her family.

"He isn't a native"—she meant Fred—"he arrived only about ten years ago, but he took to the country like he was here all his life. Anything that needs doing out-of-doors, he's your man. Been a Forest Service ranger for eight or nine years now, the first fire lookout on the Coconino, up on Woody Mountain a year before they put a telephone up there."

Mother, the story is too rich, the stuff of movies; you'd never read it in a New York paper. But it seems a little too Western. Tell me what you think.

Fred Croxen, thirty-three years old, rode out on his horse one morning to see a rancher named Charles Quayle—"a man prodigal in his threats to do serious bodily injury" to various people he'd had disagreements with, according to the local newspaper—and interrogate him concerning wood he was alleged to be cutting on land that did not belong to him and inquire about his grazing permit, whatever that is. (Ruby says it's becoming a contentious local issue: seedlings in the forest, just beginning to recover from severe logging, are grazed by livestock, thus inhibiting new growth.)

Croxen talked with Quayle in the ranch house, peacefully, and then rode on to the adjoining ranch of Quayle's brother, Arthur, to inquire about his grazing permit. That much was apparently routine in the life of a ranger.

At the brother's ranch there was some trouble. Arthur Quayle ordered Croxen to get off his place and never set foot on it again, a ringing line if ever I heard one. Ruby says the Quayle brothers have been "pistols," always quarreling with somebody. Fred Croxen had had trouble with them several times; Charles Quayle had frequently threatened to kill him. Sheriff William Campbell had warned Croxen to take no chances.

Remember, I'm taking the story from the newspaper. It was after leaving Arthur Quayle that Fred Croxen was in real danger. When half way back to Charles Quayle's ranch, he saw someone rushing a saddled horse from the barn to the house. Soon he heard a rifle shot and thought he had been the target.

As Croxen told the story at the inquest, "I saw that something was up and was afraid of trouble." Well, I should think so! He left the road, circling around. Quayle rode up in a bad humor, intercepting him and starting a 'calling down': "Look a here, I want you to quit running it over me. You trespassed me two or three times. Once was a deliberate lie. I'm going to make you cut it out—do you understand?"

Quayle stopped his horse, the reins in his left hand, and faced Croxen, who stopped his horse. They were fifteen feet apart. Quayle dropped his right hand to his trouser pocket, which is apparently a dangerous move in the West. Given his attitude and reputation, not to mention previous threats and the fact that his trouser pocket was where he always carried an automatic pistol, Croxen jerked a .38 from his belt—"I out with it"—and fired without aiming.

Quayle went off the right side of his horse, holding on to one rein, reaching for the rifle in the scabbard on the other side of his saddle. Croxen shot again, taking deliberate aim at Quayle's heart. As Quayle continued to move, Croxen shot a third time. Quayle fell to the ground face down.

Croxen loped away to the ranger station and telephoned to the sheriff and the Forest Supervisor, Ed Miller. The sheriff told him to go to the town of Winslow and wait. An all-purpose man named Dutch Lochman went to take over duties at the ranger station.

It seems to me a bit excessive—fourteen men set out for Winslow fully armed, "in case any emergency might arise." It's my opinion they didn't want to miss the excitement, but I am not well acquainted with such matters. Arthur Quayle loaded his brother's body into an automobile and he headed for Winslow as well. After preliminary investigation and a visit to the Quayle ranch, everyone came back to Flagstaff, where Jim Lamport signed a bond guaranteeing Croxen's appearance for the conclusion of the inquest. It is Ruby's opinion that Charles Quayle "as good as committed suicide; sooner or later men like that do one way or another." The coroner's jury evidently agreed—yesterday's paper reported a verdict of justifiable homicide. And I, well, I can't believe that such a real-life Western happened within a week of my arrival.

There seems to be dying everywhere I look. Not that I'm blaming Fred Croxen if the town doesn't. He was quick to react to what was no doubt a danger to himself, and I must say I admire both his skill with a gun and his honorable behavior afterward.

Maybe it's that the Great War is so recent—all those people killed to no apparent purpose. And the nasty little creatures that cause disease kill millions every year. I'm not saying this well, I'm afraid. It's that dying seems such a tragedy for all of us, and then to kill. . . . Tell me what you think. Am I being sophomoric?

As ever,
Jo

Except for the wind, which has kept me indoors, weather has been mild for the two months I've been here, with record warm days. "Wait for March," Ruby said all through January and February. "Big storms sometimes come in March. Right after Christmas in '15 we did have three days and three nights of snow that never stopped till there were more than five feet of it on the level. My, that was something! Buildings caved right in. Nobody could get around, we were all stuck at home.

"When clouds cleared off, temperature dropped to twenty-five below. My son-in-law would leave the house every morning before daylight with a bale of hay on the back of his horse trying to save some of the stock. He'd come back after dark and say, 'I found fifteen more froze.' My daughter says it like to broke her heart to see how hard he tried and all for nothing. They haven't quite recovered yet. But often we get the winter's biggest storms in March."

She hoped so. Drought, she said, was worse than it had been for twenty years; cattle and sheep were starving for want of grass, and that meant ranchers worried about losing everything. I hadn't thought of it that way. In the city, weather is an inconvenience that keeps one from going to hear Caruso, a dreadful bother. But dead livestock and bankrupt people...the West is a virtual education, no doubt about it.

Late one cold Friday morning I was sitting over a second cup of coffee when the kitchen door opened and a woman walked in. "Mama! Road's dry so we thought we'd come in and get some things. I've been baking so much to take advantage of the fire in the stove that I'm almost out of flour." She embraced Ruby. Behind her a man was helping two little girls out of their coats.

"Jo, this is my daughter, Emily." Pride shone all over Ruby's face. "The one I've been telling you about."

She was tall as Ruby, not impossibly older than I—healthy was the first word I thought: I was very aware of health. Rosy with the cold, open and cheerful, hair curling naturally around her face, she looked like a woman who could do *anything*. I felt quite envious. Also small, thin and completely incompetent.

"We've had news of you out on the ranch." She smiled at me across the room. "Mama has company again and somebody to cook for, was what we were told."

"And her husband Roger." He looked familiar, like every movie cowboy I'd seen, the clothes, the big hat he held in his hand. Strong nose. More a man of character than good looks, I thought.

"And her girls—Rose and Virginia." They were children: pretty and not yet marked by thought. But they'd been trained to good manners, they smiled without squirming and said hello politely before they hurried into the parlor to pedal the piano.

Coffee was poured, and there they all were, sitting around me at the table, talking news I barely understood. "Good weather for patching the spring box and cleaning the gutters."

"The girls have been trying to train their ponies to a ground tie."

"We'll send that heifer out on the spring sale, she's too mean to keep." It made me feel uncomfortably shy and an interloper too, living fraudulently in a house where I didn't belong. Which was true enough, I supposed, but I hadn't thought of it that way before.

With no signal I could see, Emily and Roger stood in unison. "All right if we leave the girls here for a couple of hours? We need to get back before dark. Good to meet you, Jo." And they went out into the town, leaving the children side by side on the piano bench, each pumping on one of the pedals.

Early in the afternoon their parents were back with a flurry of activity, more news exchanged, the girls buttoned into their coats. The house seemed quiet after they had left.

A comment from me was definitely in order. "Ruby, they certainly leave good feeling in their wake. I quite like them."

"Thank you, Jo. I'm glad to hear it." She smiled at me. "I don't get to see them nearly as much as I'd like to. Until you came, I felt lonesome to see them drive away. Times like that, the newspaper can be good company." The news and I—on an equal footing.

The *Sun* is weekly entertainment, she was right about that. T.E. Pollock is having an attack of lumbago, which in larger cities might be considered a rather private matter unworthy of public print. However, interspersed is News of General Interest. A contract has been let for construction of a 450-feet-long suspension bridge at Bright Angel trail; Ruby says that is in the bottom of the Grand Canyon. A man named Slipher at the observatory is lecturing on photographing Mars. Nestling in my sunny wing chair in the afternoons, I ponder whether every town has such a contradictory identity.

All day I wait for Magic Time, late in the afternoon when the sun almost touches the western hill. Light is brilliant, it *animates*, actually floods down the street. Every stone, every leaf, every wall shines, and I am lifted out of myself into outright enchantment. I move from one window to another to see it from different perspectives.

I agree with Kandinsky: colors awaken emotions in the soul. As the sun sinks lower, color changes by the moment and becomes soft, gentle, with smokey blue shadows, and then fades into a luminous afterglow. When there are clouds sliding past overhead, they are shades of pink and apricot and gold, shades I didn't know could exist in the sky. It's intoxicating, I soar into joy. There's a sense of Belonging which I don't even try to dispel. I've set up my easel and made pencil sketches from each window, but I honestly despair of getting the light right, the color.

Now and then without warning I plunge into melancholia. I can think of no reason to go on living and why bother? The voice of the earth *cries* with death. Perhaps illness is the explanation for such wild swings. Swell. I have the self-control of a yo-yo.

One evening, standing at the west window, I realized that a quarter moon was hanging just above the observatory buildings on the hill across town, perilously close. Though it meant trudging myself back up, I went downstairs.

"Ruby." She was in the kitchen kneading bread to rise through the night. "Do reassure me—what's the moon doing way over there?"

She dusted flour from her hands and stepped to the window. "Why, Jo." She looked at me. "The moon goes across the sky east to west every night. Just like the sun does every day."

I suppose I had read that. But I had never *seen* it.

"So do the stars."

Isn't the world full of surprises, though?

She was good enough not to laugh. "Everything travels but the pole star. It's a grand show. I used to sit with my children on a little hill out on the ranch and watch."

I would not have noticed in the city, what with lights and buildings and being in a taxi if I were outside at night. But we had often summered on the island, among trees, of course, though I could have seen movement in the sky if I had looked *up* for more than five seconds.

My sophistication chastened no end, I went out to stand in Ruby's yard for a moment, absolutely gaping. I am twenty-nine years old—*twenty-nine!*—and until this month I had never really seen the stars. I'd had no idea—there is not one blank space among the millions and millions, not *one*. They cover the sky with tiny dots of shining color, big, little, bright, dim. I smiled up at them like an idiot. To think I might have died without seeing the stars. What an upstart I've been.

Once a week or so in the afternoon I've heard a knock at the door and then a little voice. "I look a fright, I know, my hair's like moldy hay. But I just had to run over and tell you." Always the same thing.

Ruby invites her into the kitchen. "Ada, you came just in time. After your news, you can help me decide…" about spice for a cake or colors for an afghan, something she could do herself without a minute's thought. Frankly, Ada doesn't sound like a person you'd appeal to for advice.

Later I hear the voice going toward the door, saying, "I must get on home. I'm busy as a ticking clock." And a tinkly little laugh.

I watch from my window as Ada limps away, tiny and white-haired, her back bent, her left foot dragging a little. Finally, trying for casual, I ask Ruby, "Have you known her long?"

"I've known Ada since heck was a pup. My heart just aches for her. She raised a big family—those that lived—and did well by all of them. Now her husband's passed away and her children have moved to California. They send money every month so she can stay in her home, but most of it's closed off, she lives just in the downstairs bedroom and the kitchen, and she's so lonesome sometimes she has to find excuses to go visiting or cry."

Oh, swell. One more dumb mistake for Josephine. "She has trouble walking."

"When she was fifty or so she was herding cattle into the pen, ground was wet and her horse slipped. Fell on her leg and broke it in three places. It never did heal right."

"Does she live nearby?"

"Clear over in the West End. She tries to walk a mile or more every day."

That's more than *I* do. Heroic, these Western women.

"She's always been a game little thing. And fun! What a scamp. You should see how comic she looks when she crosses her eyes. I've wished I could do it from the day I met her. She does make me laugh, tries to pay for her visits that way, I suspect. She was reminding me just now"—she begins to smile—"of the time Leo Crane, the trader up at Keams Canyon, was reported killed by Indians. He absolutely denied it and demanded proof." Then she laughs so heartily that I laugh with her.

I try to imagine women of any age in my family crossing their eyes. "What was her news?"

"Little Henry Giclas found an old grandfather clock in an empty room, so he pulled the works out and took them apart and built a toy machine. It was Mr. M.J. Riordan's clock. Eli Giclas didn't know how to tell Mr. M.J. what that smart little dickens of his had done."

She is obviously delighted by the story. "It's as good as a play to watch Ada act it out. 'Now comes the good part,' she'll say, and she's laughing so hard she can hardly tell it."

I resolve to come downstairs to meet Ada next time she visits— Ruby assures me that local courtesy would not forbid. A woman who can make people laugh to fill her own loneliness is quite outside my experience. Besides, it would be a pleasure to know a woman who is smaller than I am.

*M*rs. Armenta is at the clothesline hanging out sheets. The afternoon is warm as a spring day with no wind, so I button my coat and pull my red hat down around my ears. "Ruby, I think I'll walk down to the post office." After all, Doctor Damrosch said 'a little mild exercise'." Wholesome food Ruby is taking care of; fresh air and exercise are up to me. I am feeling particularly well today, so I like the idea of venturing forth into Flagstaff on my own.

"I've written again to assure my mother that I am well cared for. Shall I ask whether there is mail for you?"

"Yes, thank you." Is it my imagination that she seems to look pleased with me? "What a good idea. I'm expecting Sears' spring catalogue."

Sun is warm on my face. Mountains soar up into a huge blue sky, and I am out of doors. I stroll, savoring the quite heady feeling of being a normal, healthy woman instead of a languid invalid. Of such small illusions is happiness made.

Property owners cannot agree on paving outside of downtown: for the first half block there is no sidewalk and the street has dried to dust. What looks like a cow–oh, surely not!–is ambling away from me along Verde, going home, one wonders, or merely exploring?

Dennis is quite right: it is an easy walk, not much up or down. Within half a block I reach the Court House sidewalk. Another block, and I'm across from the Babbitt building at Senator Ashurst's new post office, which shares its building with the Forest Service. Though it fits more loosely than it did in the Fall, I am feeling urbane in my smart red coat, my beaver shawl collar. I hope the hemline is not too high; apparently there are places where police are arresting women whose skirts are higher than three inches above the ankle or less than four inches below the knee. Of all the nonsense–fashion is beyond *police* control.

As I approach the post office, the door swings open and a *cow* comes out, pushed from behind. A man on the sidewalk laughs loudly.

"What's the trouble, Ed? Unwanted visitor?"

Ed pushes the cow onto the sidewalk. "Right in the office. Found her leaning against the Forest Supervisor's desk. How'd you like her in the County Attorney's office?"

"Naw, she knew what she was doing. Did you give her the grazing permit she was looking for?"

Cows wander into federal offices in this town! I should disapprove, I know, the aunts and cousins would, but I enter the building smothering laughter. I can see I should get out of my upstairs room more often. The West is too droll for words.

My letters posted, I cross the street and continue walking on the sunny side, noticing across the way a bank, a barber shop, a drug store, and something named the Confection Den.

I cross again opposite the Weatherford Hotel, pursuing adventure. There is a crowd of Solid Citizens in the middle of the block in front of the town hall, much shouting and laughing. In New York I would turn away; here I quite boldly stop to investigate the entertainment. But from several feet away, of course, it might be thought rude of me if I were to step into the group as if I were not an outsider and a complete stranger.

In the street are five elderly men, seventy years old, perhaps eighty. One is acting as referee of sorts. "Magistrate Gilliland takes this match at three out of five falls. While he's preparing to meet a challenger, we'll put two more Union Army veterans against each other, Ben Doney and Jim Milligan."

There is much cheering. "Give 'em room, folks. Before we're finished, we'll determine which of these worthy gentlemen has been least affected by advancing years."

They wrestle! They actually *wrestle*, two old men who are fiercely enjoying themselves, each struggling to force the other down. Men and women in the crowd call cheerful encouragement, and laugh, and applaud.

"Hold him, Jim!"

"Show these boys a thing or two."

"Good move, Ben, you can take him."

"A good man just gets better."

"My money's on that skinny one."

My mouth is open—I am quite entranced. It has been almost sixty years since the end of the War Between the States. They must have been mere boys. Imagine the uncles so forgetting their dignity? I laugh with the other spectators, hoping not to provoke my lungs to a bout of coughing. What kind of people are these Westerners?

The crowd shows no sign of losing interest, but I realize that I am droopy as an old rose. I don't feel at all well, and on top of that, home is three and a half blocks away. It will seem like miles, I'm sure.

I turn away and retrace, walking slowly, disturbingly weak. I walk past the Confection Den to glance in. It looks clean enough. Perhaps another day I'll stop to buy something that takes my fancy. Is there such a thing as an eclair out here? Or are Western pastries quite unique? I hope so.

Behind me I hear a shout and a sound of hooves. I turn to see a riderless horse coming down the street at a fast trot, its head held high to keep dangling reins off the ground. A man steps from the sidewalk, quite calmly grasps one of them and swings the horse into a wide circle to stop it. I see it coming toward me and, as fast as my fashionable shoes and hemline allow, take refuge in a recessed doorway, unfortunately not recessed quite enough for my comfort.

My face is inches away from the odorous side of the horse, which has come to a halt leaning resignedly into the wall. Pinned, I fear for my shoes, my beaver collar. A stirrup presses into my arm. I can see nothing but the flank of a horse in winter hair.

A hand reaches under its neck to retrieve the other rein, and a deep voice says, "Now just where did you think you were going?" Whatever these people are, they talk to horses.

Human footsteps approach, running, I think. "Many thanks, Matt. This critter gives me the slip every time I take my eyes off him. It's gettin' old. If he wasn't so good on the trail, I'd give'm to my worst enemy."

"He sure was headed somewhere in a hurry."

"He don't care where, long as he can leave me afoot."

Plaintively, I say, "Excuse me," just as the door behind me opens and I fall backward into the arms of a man who is good enough to catch me before I sprawl onto the floor.

"I'm sorry, ma'am, I didn't notice the fix you were in there for a minute." He helps me to my feet.

I adjust my coat and attempt to smile. "The smell was the worst part." But I am unaccountably shaky, struggling to breathe. Silly of me. "Is there…may I…"

"Would you like to sit down, ma'am? Here's a chair."

I'd rather *lie* down. "Would you call Dennis, please?"

"You're Mrs. Green's lodger?"

I can't think how he knew that–this is my first foray onto Flagstaff streets. He steps to the phone on the wall and cranks it. "Is that you, Hazel? Sometimes I can't tell between you and your big sister. See if you can locate Dennis and ask him to stop by the Western Union office lickety split, would you? Try the livery stable first, then the Commercial. Got Ruby Green's lodger here needing a ride."

Someone is in the doorway. "Are you hurt, ma'am?"

The man on the sidewalk says, "Here comes Doc Fronske. Hey, Doc, got a minute to see to a little lady in distress? She's been about squarshed by this horse a'mine."

After nearly two months in the refuge of Ruby's house, I meet within three minutes Matt, Buck, the Western Union telegrapher, and Doctor Martin Fronske, thereby doubling my social contacts in Flagstaff. I haven't exactly been a gadabout.

March, 1921

Dear Jo,

It all sounds entrancing! Oh, I know you're ill, but you'll soon get over that, I'm convinced of it, and then what adventures you're going to have! I'm quite envious.

Your natural questioning of death may well be sophomoric. At any rate, it's the kind of issue we tend to grow numb to as we get older unless we happen to be philosophers or theologians, who consider such things their lives long.

I remember how stunned I was when my grandfather died. I stood looking into the coffin thinking, "What is it, this monstrous force we call death?" When the minister put his arm around my shoulders and said, "Don't worry about your grandfather, he is in Heaven," it seemed superficial. I was twenty-three at the time and quite sophomoric myself.

Then my father died and my brother and my husband, and I was not the same woman afterward. Thank God I had no son to send off to war. My mother will go soon.

It seems to be a law of nature: trees die, even stars, I'm told. But yes, I agree. It is a never-ending tragedy. Is it the greatest tragedy, do you think? Ah well. How like you to raise such questions.

Little has changed here since you left. Things are horrible in Europe—hunger and unemployment and strikes and riots—and to make things worse, the Allies are talking of requiring fifty-six billion dollars in war reparations from the starving Germans as well as a tax on their exports and profits. I don't know how anyone could think such a scheme would work, and evidently Lloyd George agrees.

Police had to be summoned to calm crowds trying to get in to see Fairbanks in "The Mark of Zorro." Plans are afoot to censor motion pictures. I'm surprised they are taken seriously—the "movies" seem so ephemeral. A young German named Einstein suggests that there is a possibility of measuring the universe: that is far more worthy of attention, in my opinion.

The music world has some news. You remember hearing Mary Garden sing Melissande and Thais? She has been named director of the Chicago Opera Association, and there are those who are in a dither about it. A woman, you know, can't be satisfied with the vote, where will things go from here? I'm quoting my brothers. I can't believe we're in the same family. Paderewski has arrived in New York and announced his retirement as a pianist. Your grandmothers are virtually devastated about that.

They are still outraged that you ignored their dictates and went off to Arizona on your own. Each has spoken to me privately to inquire whether a threat to tie up your money in some way would bring you to your senses. I tell them I doubt it, which confirms their opinion that they should never have insisted that I marry your father, since his untimely death has obviously addled my always fragile wits.

I'm afraid your aunts and cousins have not forgiven you for "sneaking off" and traveling to the barbaric West against their advice. They are conspiring to refuse to correspond as a sign of their displeasure, a sore trial to you, no doubt. I confess I'm baffled by their desire for power. I've never felt it myself, and it seems to me little short of Medieval. How, in a democracy, they can still hold to such outmoded authoritarian attitudes is beyond me. However, since I am a minority of one, perhaps I am addled, as they claim.

When you left, I was up to my eyebrows in the Met's Impressionist show. It is lavish, a huge success. The rooms are crowded with people wondering how the French painters could have been considered shocking such a short time ago. Some Matisse and Manet and Degas works have been tossed in for good measure, to less approval. I like them, as well as the Picasso and Braque which I've seen, which confirms the family's conviction that I am quite mad.

The retrospective show of Alfred Stieglitz, forty years of his development, was what one would term a success de scandale. It quite marked his resurrection as a photographer; thousands attended. But I am afraid it intensified gossip about the romance he has been having with the O'Keeffe woman you met at the Art Students League: forty-five of the pictures were intimate images of her, some of them nudes with her paintings in the background. One hears as much comment about her as about him—it was an altogether bizarre debut.

Jo, I wonder whether you would mind an innovation in the way I sign my letters. You are the only person in the world who can call me Mother, and I love it, of course. But you see, Mother is not my name, only your name for me, and it feels awkward for me to use it in reference to myself. If it doesn't seem too modern, I would like to sign my own name. Tell me if it bothers you.

Are you painting again, darling? Do keep me informed.

Affectionately,
Lilly

P.S. Quite by chance I saw your cousin Paul Scheffler in the lobby of the Waldorf. He requested that I convey to you his admiration of your "spunk" and his envy of your Arizona sojourn. I gather he is not happy with the life his parents have planned for him and sees the West as an escape into freedom. I thought you would like to know that at least one of your cousins approves of you.

In mid-March there was a heavy snow fall on the nearby mountains—the Peaks, as they are called in quaint local idiom. Ruby said that would help the town's water supply until rains begin in July. When the skies cleared, there was a knock at the front door. From upstairs where I was reading about Harding's rejection of the League of Nations I heard a voice talking with Ruby—a rather distinctive rumble, ever so masculine.

"Been almost two weeks since I pinned her with Buck's horse. I thought I'd stop by and see how she is."

"Well, now, that's good of you, Matt. Come on in. Would you like to have a cup of coffee? There's some on the back of the stove."

"That'd sure hit the spot. Doc Fronske says she's not doing so good."

"That isn't your fault, she was sick when she got here. Poor little thing, she's not much bigger than a bug. I've been making her rest and giving her aspirin now and then and brewing up some Mormon tea for her every afternoon. It may not do her any good, but it can't hurt. Soon as I hear about somebody going below the Rim, I'll ask for some greasewood."

The voices faded into the kitchen, and I lay back in my wing chair and gave up trying to hear. I wasn't sure I—no, I couldn't quite remember what he looked like. With that voice he was no doubt short and thin—voices seldom match bodies. At least Fate has a sense of humor.

It was thoughtful of him to call, if that's what it could be labeled. A Call by a Gentleman in New York would have been conducted quite differently, *certainly* not in the kitchen. I smiled: the Grandmothers would not concede that he was a gentleman, but then, the Grandmothers were there and he was here. Twenty minutes later I heard him leave. Should I have gone down to thank him? Oh my, I realize that New York manners might not apply in Arizona.

Ruby had indeed been tending me. She carried a cup of pale tea up the stairs in the middle of every afternoon, made from a local bush with green branches—Emily had brought it. "Indians boiled it and made a medicine, I'm told. Settlers got the idea from them. There's some that claim it helps with one thing or another. I quite enjoy the taste, mild, a little like nuts. I put honey in it, some claim honey is a tonic for all kinds of ailments."

Doctor Fronske agreed that he'd never heard of Mormon tea being prescribed for tuberculosis, but it probably wouldn't hurt and if it did, we'd stop. He came to Flagstaff because of t.b. himself, and he's still thin as a stick, though a handsome man.

I quite like him: he's cheerful and kindly, German by ancestry. Ruby says he is thirty-eight or so and was an athlete when he was younger. Seven years ago he arrived in town from St. Louis, in time to be worked to exhaustion like the other doctors when the flu epidemic was at its worst.

I hadn't been in to his office, unless you could count the day I had stood in front of it watching two old men wrestling. I hadn't seen a doctor at all. That probably proves I'm too defiant for words. So a doctor was called for me, and I'm grateful. Doctor Fronske says he'll stop in every other day or so as long as I'm feeling weak.

I've made a point of going down to breakfast and supper—you couldn't really say it's Dinner, we eat in the kitchen. I try not to let

Ruby see how tiring it is to climb back up afterwards. My feet, which used to dance half the night, are ninety pound cabbages. Each. Thus are the flighty fallen.

To postpone stair climbing, I've been sitting with her and talking long after the evening meals are finished, she in her rocking chair knitting sweaters for grandchildren, I resting my arms on the table and looking at my hands.

She tells me stories of her life. "There wasn't a doctor for miles out there on the homestead. That poor little baby was so sick, and I was just an ignorant girl. I saw she could hardly breathe, and I picked her up against my shoulder and took off running, goodness knows where I thought I was going. My husband spied me from the barn and knew something was wrong. He was hard put to catch up with me, but he finally got me stopped and took her away from me till I could think again.

"My, those were hard times, when this country was young and so were we, which is a good thing, I guess. Youth'll get you through hardship you never want to do again. I don't miss it."

Loath to bring anything alien into that room, I am hesitant to talk about life in New York, so I tell her about Cousin Lillian. "She came out to Arizona in 1913 with Zane Grey's party."

"The writer, that Zane Grey? The stories about the West?"

"He has a new book out this year, but then he *always* has a new one out. He married my cousin Lina."

"Well, I never! I've read one of his books, that one about Rainbow Bridge. My son-in-law gave it to me for Christmas six years ago."

"*The Rainbow Trail*. Lillian did the cover and illustrations for it."

She laid her knitting aside and went into the parlor for the book. "Why, this is a nice picture, the people look alive. Your cousin is a good artist."

"She has an ability to make things look real; her first formal lessons were when she was six. The family thought her watercolors were simply marvelous. At twelve she was accepted into an adult drawing class at the Art Students League in New York."

"Her parents allowed a girl of twelve to take classes with grown-ups?"

"They arranged it. The whole family has been involved in art for generations. Lillian's father is an importer of china and glass. It's quite a distinguished branch of the family—artists, scientists, doctors, businessmen."

Was I being top-of-the-heap? I hadn't intended to boast, though perhaps I was. Oh, I'm sterling, I'm not above vanity occasionally.

"That explains it, then, her having such a background."

"You should see the flowers she painted when she was just a little thing. They all thought she would concentrate on flowers because women *do* so often in the East, it's considered feminine. But she always has cared about color more than subject. You can see it in her paintings. They're *about* color, they fairly glow."

I watched as she paged through the book stopping at the illustrations. "You shouldn't judge her by those, the publishers wanted something old-fashioned. In the paintings she does for herself color is bold, quite modern."

"To think Zane Grey has such connections."

"We've all thought for years that any success he's had as a writer was because Cousin Lina took over the business side with contracts and investments and taxes. She's good at it, and he seems happy to have her do it. She even edits before manuscripts go to the publisher, she was an English teacher. Why she let him change her name to Dolly, I've never understood. I refuse to call her that, although it's probably a losing battle. Most of the family isn't altogether pleased about the influence he's had on Cousin Lillian."

She looked up from the book.

"Bringing her to the Wild West. It's not as if she was a child. It's just that—she's known him for years and traveled with his expeditions and illustrated his books. He's an adventurer; it's hard not to be influenced by an adventurer who's rich and famous. It's been a long time since I've seen her paintings. I wonder whether they've changed because of him."

"Everybody you know influences you some way or other. You can't help it."

"The family gossips that Lillian with her connections was intended to be his passport into intellectual circles. But perhaps it's been an even trade—she's had his contacts in the West, the people he knows."

"He goes up around Monument Valley. All the adventurers there start from Kayenta, it's a little bit of a place, only a few buildings and corrals. She must know John and Louisa Wetherill. I'd say they're good contact."

"I haven't heard of them."

"Both Western-grown. They built the trading post at Kayenta a good ten or more years ago when this was still a Territory. Of course they're there for a living, but they're the kind of people who make you proud to be human, honest and hard-working, the best kind of Western folks. Louisa's a rare woman, to make a home in such empty country and keep the post going while John's gone exploring, looking for wonders no one knows about. He has the strength of an ox, though you wouldn't think it to look at him. She has a way with the Navvies, speaks their language like she was one of them. Mr. Grey did your cousin a favor if he introduced her to the Wetherills." She laughed. "I daresay she'd never met a woman like Louisa in New York."

It was a different view of Lillian entirely. "I envy her the health she has for traveling about painting the West. I've missed painting. Even if you're not proficient, it can take hold of you, life and color come right off your fingertips. It's the most satisfying thing. Perhaps now that it's Spring, I'll feel up to it again."

Ruby laid the book on the table beside her and took up her knitting again. "Well, I hope so. We've had artists coming through since I can remember on their way to the Grand Canyon or Monument Valley to paint pictures for the railroad. Louis Akin stayed a few years, built a house on the road out to Fort Valley. Most liked it, especially when he showed us his paintings. Poor man, he never made much money, though he painted such beautiful things. He died of pneumonia when he was only forty-five, because he was always in poverty, I thought. Once he tried to start an artists' colony up on the Hopi mesas and got only Kate Cory. She lived at Oraibi for years. There've been more men, but women have been here too. I'd be proud to have a painter living in the house with me."

Reminded of What's Important, I have begun to rest with determination. One needs a reason for going on. Isn't it fascinating: the impulse to *make*, to create, is so strong that even illness can't subdue it. Art is more than what one sees in museums.

Meanwhile I'm pursuing news of Arizona through the weekly paper. The man who owns the Weatherford Hotel says he will spend the coming summer building a road right to the top of the Peaks. Sixteen men with some mules to help are carrying long lines of cables on their shoulders down into the Grand Canyon for the Bright Angel footbridge.

Those things are close. From out here, New York is in Outer Mongolia, though I wouldn't breathe that to a soul. What will I think when I go back? If ever I recover, that is.

I am feeling much more chipper though. Ruby has suggested that, the weather being unusually mild, I might be up to a matinee at the Orpheum. Flagstaff society is gearing up for a series of dances at the new armory and a ball at Ashurst Auditorium. I probably couldn't manage that. The Woman's Club is sponsoring a five-day traveling Chautauqua concert—such a boon to small rural towns—guaranteed in Flagstaff by such go-getting local businessmen as Nackard, Pollock, Pulliam and one of the Babbitts, and she wonders whether an afternoon concert or lecture would be too taxing. But if I think I might enjoy sitting in the dark and watching Lillian Gish in D.W. Griffith's "Way Down East", billed as The Unexampled Wonder of the Twentieth Century, she'll reserve two seats and ask Dennis to drive us. There's a matinee this Wednesday.

I'd like to try. It's been a month since I've been out of the house—what fun to go someplace with Ruby. If that works out well, maybe I will attend one of the Chautauqua concerts. The *big* one will be a five-person orchestra plus a soprano, which is hardly the Met. But why not? If I survive Gish, I'll treat Ruby to the snazziest culture the town has to offer.

April, 1921

Dear Mother,

In March I over-did and spent a few weeks recovering, coughing up the most revolting sputum (no blood). Although I have days when I couldn't lift a hand and it seems The End Is Near, lately I'm feeling better, "on the mend," as Ruby says. Language here is different from that of the big cities Back Home—another wonderful phrase. Nearly everyone comes from somewhere else. Even Ruby grew up in the southern part of the Territory and traveled into this country with her husband to homestead when it was virtually empty, just after the railroad came through.

I see by the papers that a vaccine against tuberculosis has been developed, too late to help me. However, I've gained a little weight and now and then I feel so much improved that I've gone out a few times in the afternoon to stand across the street and sketch Ruby's house in pencil. I enclose the best one—you'll notice the sharp contrast between light and shadow, quite realistic.

I've also attempted a few pen sketches. I enclose one of my big room with sunlight pouring across it late in the afternoon. I haven't Cousin Lillian's facility that makes sketches look as if they would come alive any minute. But I'm rather pleased with the way I've rendered the wing chair, and I think the intensity of the Western light, even in an interior, is caught rather well. I've set up my easel and opened my paint box: I'm determined to essay the scene in oils, with myself in the wing chair, my first self-portrait. At half an hour each afternoon, when the light is just right, I might be able to do it without undue fatigue.

I didn't call on Cousin Lina when she came through in April, motoring east to Pennsylvania on these awful roads. I didn't even know about it until she was gone. The paper says she had a maid and a chauffeur with her, which was no doubt impressive for Flagstaff. I hope she found the trip to California stimulating.

Out here in The Provinces the big topic of conversation is the weather: a late frost in early April killed fruit in the little settlement of Sedona below a long system of cliffs referred to as "the Rim." Then two weeks after the Forest Service had all its fire lookouts stationed on mountaintops, a foot of wet snow fell. "Worth millions to ranchers," the local paper says.

Oh, all sorts of exciting things are happening. A frost last week "played the deuce" with gardens in town and Emily's garden out on the ranch. Imagine a killing frost in June! The town fire whistle blew twice in one week because two barns were ablaze.

Lowell Observatory was open to the public recently so all inclined could view Jupiter and Saturn. Ruby and I called Dennis to drive us up. There we stood in the darkened room, chatting with Wylmuth Case, the only art teacher at the Normal School here in town. The daughter of a state superintendent of schools, she has studied in Chicago and California and manages to fit a real art class into the industrial and teacher training which are her primary responsibility.

When it was our turn to look through the eyepiece of the giant telescope, I was stunned speechless, if you can believe it. Those distant planets were as clean and beautiful as anything I've ever seen. To think I had to come all this way for the opportunity. I still feel off balance because of such a double identity for the town, "out of kilter"—Ruby's expression.

I must tell you about a hilarious local custom, it's such a scream. Apparently most employees get their pay on Saturday near the beginning and middle of each month. Now that weather is warm, "pay day" is the occasion for a downtown party! Everyone who is anyone—men, women and children—congregate on two or three blocks of Aspen Street north of the railroad tracks. People who have cars park them along the street. Merchants keep their stores open, bakeries and groceries, drug stores, a place called "The Dresswell Shop." Babbitt Brothers building is aglow. A merchant the young people call "Uncle Billy" Switzer is out on the sidewalk; so are most of the others. People visit from car to car as if they were making calls.

Ever solicitous of entertainment for me, Ruby hired Dennis last Saturday night to drive us. We went early so that we could have a favored spot, parked just behind Editor Breen's sisters in front of the barber shop, and there we sat enthroned in a Model T taxi for two hours. I'm sure I met half the population. Nobody was on a toot as far as I could see—in a town this small no one could get away with it. Ruby introduced me to everyone who looked in: "This is Josephine Boren, my lodger." The windows were down, so people leaned in and offered strong welcome—men shake hands with ladies here, women offer their hands to other women—and asked, "How do you like Flagstaff?" assuming that I do, and "How are you feeling? Are things looking up?" It's so rich!

I'm sure the grandmothers would not have approved at all, but for me there was something quite delightful about the lights and colors, the throng of cheerful people, the open friendliness. Just before we left, I sent Dennis into a bakery to buy three chocolate eclairs, one each for Ruby and for me and for him too. I don't know when I've enjoyed a gesture so much. Such ebullience is, I've read, often characteristic of tuberculosis. Don't frown, Mother, we did not eat eclairs on the street.

Ruby and I have been playing checkers in the evenings. I can hear Cousin Gertrude saying, "Oh, poor Josephine," with relish, but really I quite enjoy it. Ruby plays with a ferocity I would not have expected and forces me to mind my moves. She gives no quarter. The window is open to soft summer twilight, breeze lifting the curtains. The click of the pieces, Ruby's small triumphant snorts when she takes one of mine, my moans of anguish when I make a blind mistake—it's all quite companionable. I've thought of buying a Silvertone radio receiver when I can be sure of reception, but I fear to spoil the mood with such tunes as "When the red, red robin comes bob, bob, bobbin' along."

You ask whether there is anything you can send. Yes, please: books. For most of each day I rest in my room, and it helps to have something to read. There are two shops here that sell books, but the selection is not as large as one might wish. I would like to have Edith Wharton's The Age of Innocence now that she's become the first woman to win the Pulitzer. And Main Street by Sinclair Lewis, it's recommended by the New York papers. You may imagine the books being received at the railroad station and delivered to my door by Dennis in his Ford taxi. Since I pay him handsomely, I am rapidly becoming his best customer, practically the mainstay of his business.

Thank you for your thoughtful answer to my thrashing to and fro on the mortality question. Some days I grieve so for humanity I can hardly bear it, how we struggle and suffer, and then we die. We always have, through aeons of time.

I've done a good deal of pondering on the puzzle you set: is death the greatest human tragedy? Now don't laugh—I'm going to be sophomoric again. No, I say, and countless victims of cruelty might agree with me. Poverty can be as great a tragedy. Life without love of some kind for something, and I'm sure I don't know how so illusive a thing as love can be assured. Artists of any kind, and those for whom craft is an art, who work through years unpraised, unrecognized and unrewarded—we have no idea how many of those there have been. I suppose I'm saying life can be *at least as tragic as death, and I don't want to believe that's a law of nature too, about which we can do nothing.*

Why do I carry on like this? Sentimental humbug, pretentious posturing, and quite out of date, it's embarrassing. Forgive me. It must be because I'm not well.

My greetings to Cousin Paul when next you see him, and thank him for his message.

As ever,

Jo

*D*r. Fronske said, although there's talk of isolating people who have it, tuberculosis is something of a mystery. A world-wide plague and all that, and we've known since 1882 that it's caused by a bacillus, and a vaccine has just been announced that uses serum made from a potato. A *potato*? But it is of no use to people already infected, and no one knows what medicine would work as a cure. Clear dry air makes the battle easier for the lungs, good food and rest easier for the whole body, and they do the trick for some people. Not for others. You don't know until the symptoms vanish whether you're one of the lucky ones, and then you must be wary of a relapse—arrested doesn't mean cured. We couldn't know yet. It was a good sign that I was not coughing up blood: whatever was eating away in there hadn't found a vein. There was hope. Meanwhile, was I sleeping with my windows open?

I was still back with that word Hope. I was not even sure what the word meant—look ahead and expect Something Wonderful perhaps? I couldn't recall such a mood except perhaps briefly when I was a girl. Peculiar that one syllable could burst upon me and reveal a vacuum so long-standing as to be a habit. How dreadfully unamusing.

Looking ahead to something wonderful was what the whole country roundabout was doing: anticipating the Fourth of July.

I gathered it had something to do with Flagstaff history, its founding or some such event—raising a flag on the Fourth. You'd have thought they *owned* the holiday, the way they went about it. And then, they all know one another, the town is so small—I suppose it is natural for them to celebrate as a group. I find it somehow endearing.

Plans were big news for weeks: two days of old-fashioned foot races and baseball games and bronco riding and a modern Ford Auto Race. (Bought from the Babbitt Ford dealership, I wondered?) For excitement, fires that started now and then out in the forest couldn't begin to compete, even fires fought by aviators in flying machines, the newest trick.

I had watched the European war. For me Organized Patriotism was useful as a wet cracker. But Ruby was good enough to include me in the preliminary hilarity. "Look at this, Jo. The Fords must have fenders. That's to keep the dust down, I suppose. Tops and wind shields may be removed, but passengers are allowed. Now what sense does that make?"

I leaned over her shoulder to read the *Sun* in the light of a Friday afternoon. "I don't suppose a passenger would crew like in a boat to keep the car on the track?"

"I wouldn't think so. But then, it wouldn't be like a horse race, would it? Or a buggy race. That's all I've seen."

"Maybe it just gives more people a chance to be in on it. Race judges will be Sam Sweitzer and Peaches Hock? A man and a woman?"

"Peaches Hock is a man."

I stood back and stared at her. "*Peaches?* His parents didn't name him *Peaches*, surely?"

"Remigius is his given name."

"The logic escapes me at the moment."

"Maybe he couldn't pronounce it when he was a tyke. I don't know how nicknames got to be such a thing around here. His father's name is Balthazar, but he goes by Balzar."

I went back around the table to my chair. "How droll. I'll never get over this town."

She folded the ten pages of the paper and handed them across to me. "Will you be wanting to go, do you suppose? We could invite Ada too. She knows stories that would loosen your eye teeth."

Was I up to it? My first thought was fatigue—tired, too tired to move, scintillating as a piece of toast. The second was a flare of anger. The fashion for romantic invalids went out with whalebone corsets, and I had no intention of becoming one of those tedious people who wear illness like a badge of distinction and won't talk of anything else.

"As we say in New York, I wouldn't miss it for the world. I'm not part of the dances and bridge games, but I'd be welcome for an out-door affair, wouldn't I?"

"Well, of course. Everybody's welcome, if they're sober."

"Should we pay the extra twenty-five cents for a grandstand seat?"

"Oh, yes. You don't want to be standing all day. The Third's a Sunday. Probably the Fourth would have more going on, if you think more than one day would be tiring. I'd better get out a couple of parasols. That sun can be mighty hot when you're just sitting and watching."

As an all-round celebration it was top notch. I wore a summer cotton frock I had bought in a moment of whimsy downtown at J.C. Penny's "Golden Rule" store, butter yellow with pale blue flowers, utterly unlike anything I'd ever owned. The grandmothers would have said it was suitable only for an Irish servant on her day off, but Ruby assured me it was hunky-dory, which I assumed was positive. Somewhat to my surprise, I felt carefree in the dress. If that made me Irish, well, fine with me.

We met Ada, her white hair a beacon in morning sunshine, at the entrance gate at the head of Beaver Street. Her hand went up in greeting while we were still half a block away in the taxi. I realized immediately that her yellow cotton dress matched mine in every detail. Oh my. In the East I'd have fled home in disgrace to change. To save her illusion of superiority, Cousin Gertrude would have said she was disguising herself as a garden or something equally cutting.

Dennis opened the passenger door and said he'd b-b-be around when we were ready to go. "Ada!" I was gay as a debutante. "We're twins. I'm honored."

She laughed on her whole face as if it were a delightful joke. "I feel smart as paint. I got mine in Girls and Children. Did you?" Then she crossed her eyes! The burlesque in that lined old face was so comic I nearly choked.

All day I stayed close beside her, ready to be so bold as to put my arm around her shoulder if the ground was uneven. Truly, I was not preening myself on being a goody-goody, too sweet for words. I was weak myself, but there was that dragging little foot of hers. Anyone would have done the same.

Four days later the *Sun* reported more than nine hundred paid admissions on the big day, and it was indeed a throng, any direction you looked—hot, happy people released for a holiday and ready for a high old time. Ruby and I put Ada between us in the grandstand because she had not brought a parasol.

"I never owned one in my life. My grandmother said she didn't care to see a burnt woman nor a burnt man neither, but I couldn't be bothered. Takes up your hands." Ruby smiled at me over her head.

She favored us with commentary. "The celebration was arranged by the baseball committee, so the ball games are featured. The little man, well, he's not as small as I am, but for a *man*...the pitcher for the Kingman team, he's Lefty Miller. Came here a few days ago with his brother who's in the cattle business with the Babbitts. Look how clever he is with that ball, and him left-handed too."

She knew them all. "The umpire is Maggie Pulliam. He was in balloons in France, the war, you know. I'm sure he'll be fair. He's city clerk and his father is a J.P."

Probably I looked as mystified as she'd have been in Manhattan. Through all the contests and races she made sure I understood. "Now in this hundred-yard dash coming up, two of the men are Navajos. I'm eager to see how they do, Indians are such good runners." Indians joining in? *Wild* Indians? I hardly knew what to think.

She could change subjects so fast it was dizzying. "There's Buster Raudebaugh with his hair grown in just fine. Not long ago his head was scalded with boiling water and he wore a bandage all around it, we were afraid he'd be bald as an egg. He's a sweet boy, I think, for all his pranks. See how the track is built up around the edges, slanted in so the racers will be safe? Heavy rain makes the field a pond. Many a boy has learned to swim here after a storm."

Behind us there was a commotion, someone bumping past others to reach an empty seat. A man, I thought, the voice was so harsh and querulous. "If you'd pull your knees in, a person could get *through*." I glanced over my shoulder and saw an irritated woman at least as old as Ruby, plump, white-haired, swatting at knees with her cane. "Takin' up the whole way is what you're doin'."

"Great balls a'mud, Leah, hold your horses."

"How do you know my name? I don't know you from Adam's off ox."

"Say, Leah, we'll all move down and you can sit right here."

"I want to sit there in the middle, not right here."

"Leah, let me stand up to give you room to get by."

With a good deal of fussing she settled in behind me. "People are so ornery these days."

Ruby turned and patted her knee. "Hello, Leah. It's good to see you."

Ada said, "A real pleasure."

"Who are you?" The old voice was loud.

"Why, your friend Ruby Green. You've known me for forty years."

"And I'm Ada Nelson. You've known me that long too."

"I have not. I never saw you before."

Ruby's voice was calm. "Well, it's good to see you anyway."

Ada: "You're looking real chipper."

I couldn't see Leah unless I were to turn around, but I could hear her anger. "I am not. How would you know? Get out of here, we don't want your sort." I hoped she wouldn't lay about her with her cane–I was first in the line of fire.

A young man standing at the end of the row called cheerfully. "There you are, Grandma. Gave us the slip smooth as wax, we've been looking everyplace. Mama wants you to sit with her."

"Oh, for crying out loud."

Seven people stood to let Leah pass, seven pairs of hands steadied her and patted her as she grumbled and insulted them. Seven faces looked concerned. Her grandson took her arm and led her slowly down toward the front seats as we all watched.

"I gather that was Leah."

Ruby nodded. "It's just a shame. There never was a better woman in this whole country, hard working, ready to help anybody who needed. Everybody loved her, and with good reason. It isn't right that she should come to this."

Sentiment was not Ada's strongest suit. "It isn't right what's happened to *any* of us. Lives should end better than they do."

"Amen," Ruby said. "Amen."

I could not think of anything appropriate to say. "People seem to take care of her."

Ada snorted. "They'd *better*. That's not the real Leah."

"I wish you could have known her." Ruby defended her old friend. "You'd have liked her."

Ada changed the subject away from Cosmic Injustice, and I went with her willingly. Who of us could contemplate that sort of thing for long?

"This three-hundred-yard horse race is a free-for-all, that means any age rider and any kind of horse. Buster Prochnow is a good guess to win it. He isn't much for school, but he's a good rider. Only thirteen, the oldest boy in that big family. That's his little brother Bob over there, see?" She pointed. "With that tow-headed Henry Giclas. What a pair they are, two burrs in a mare's tail. Probably grow up all right though. They have good parents.

"They say this pony race coming up will be half a mile. Oh my, is Val drunk, I wonder? He's always been loud and quarrelsome–I don't know what gets into some people. He'll be arrested if he isn't careful. We can't stand for drunks."

At noon when the four big cannons of Battery A fired forty-eight rounds, one for each state, she squealed and covered her ears, with never a thought for dignity. As far as I could see, age had injured and weakened her body and made it pitiful, but left her spirit unharmed. I wasn't sure I could say the same for myself at less than half her years. Ada was quite the corker, an example I vowed not to forget.

As the show went on, I was most taken with the bronco riding–I'd never seen such violence and danger. Even as I was watching, I thought of how I would describe it to my mother. The noise, the dust, the sweat on the horses, the strength of the riders and their bravery. They seemed to me the rarest kind of men, able to match such determined animals bone for bone and muscle for muscle. I was smitten by the exoticism of it all, I suppose, but they were indeed impressive, infinitely more so than the manicured men I'd met in drawing rooms in the East. I'm sure I was a little in love with all of them, right there. They were so different from *me*.

Ada was eager for the Ford auto race to begin. "Mr. Arches of Standard Oil in L.A. says he'll fill each tank with free gasoline up to ten gallons. That's handsome, I think. Peaches Hock is a good choice for a judge, though he's so young. He's a natural mechanic, that's what he did in the war. The Babbitts have him in their garage. He's a hero, did you know that?"

"I haven't heard about it." I knew I was about to.

"He was only seventeen, before the war, and he was in an auto race right here. Peaches was in the lead on a lap around the track." She used her crooked little hands to sketch the story in the air. "A man whose name I won't mention–he was just old, that's all, so he shouldn't be blamed–thought the race was finished when it went past him, so he walked out onto the track, slow, you know. He couldn't see any too well, either.

"Well, Peaches came roaring around the turn at twenty miles an hour and saw a slow old man right in front of him. Here comes the good part: he had less than a second to decide what to do. Run down a man older than his grandfather? Swerve into the crowd and hurt people? Or take his chances with the built-up bank? He made the choice that was most dangerous for *him*, quick as a wink he turned into the bank and rolled his car right over."

I had followed her hands. "Was he hurt?"

"No, not much, scraped up some is all. But naturally he was out of the race from that minute. They gave him the first prize anyway. The whole town agreed it was the right thing to do. *Almost* the whole town—you can't do anything without complaints from somewhere."

"And being judge today is another award?"

"I'd say so. To let him know we remember."

"That's wonderful, Ada. A wonderful thing to do."

"Sometimes we do ourselves proud. Sometimes we have no more backbone than a worm."

There were all of four autos in the race, what Ada described as "Australian pursuit." I gathered that meant a car was eliminated when it was passed by another, but I wasn't sure. When a man named Schmidt was slowed by a spark plug cap that flew off, Ada was much distressed for him. "Oh, what a shame! A shame!"

"You know him?"

"Just barely. But it's a shame."

A woman stepped through a hole in the wood of the grandstand and was carried out with injuries, and Ada was very nearly distraught. "Oh, how awful! I hope she'll be all right."

I hesitated to ask. "You know her?"

"Just barely. But I don't have to, do I? She's the new secretary to Mr. Dolan over at the logging company office. I hope it isn't serious."

With the things she knew, she should have been employed by the *Sun*. "There's a man in this town, I'm not mentioning his name, who's a *rounder*. Decent women and girls aren't safe with him. I wouldn't be his wife for anything." I will admit I was curious to know who it was, but I didn't ask.

By the end of the day I was fatigued by sun and excitement. That and novelty—it was such a new world, everything about it unguessed, that I felt awake down to my toes.

No doubt I was radiant as we walked back toward Beaver Street, although maybe I was merely flushed with fever. People smiled and nodded. Mrs. Armenta, walking with people I assumed were her family, waved to me. Men lifted their hats after they had greeted Ruby and Ada. I hoped it wasn't t.b. euphoria I was feeling, a surge that would fade before dinner time. I quite liked it.

A man in rough clothing–worn trousers of some tough fabric and a jacket that had seen better days–stepped in beside us to speak to the ladies. "Aunt Ruby. Aunt Ada. How's the day gone?"

They were his aunts? Ruby hadn't mentioned a nephew in town. Or was this another Quaint Local Custom? I very nearly asked before I remembered my place as a guest.

Ruby seemed comfortable with him. "Just fine, Matt. As good as any Fourth I can remember. I didn't see you riding."

"I'm gettin' to the age I think I ought to save my spills for work. I don't jump right up any more."

Ada agreed. "Isn't it the truth, though? Before you know it, you're creaky as an old door."

Ruby smiled. "The life you've led up to now has been spills a'plenty, I'd think. How's your little brother?"

"Last time I saw him he was all right, going up to Mexican Hat on some kind of wild goose chase. Wanted me to go too, but since Papa died Mama needs a hand on the place. Luke's not one for staying put and tending to chores, though I'm not sure he's up to adventuring either." He shrugged, rather ruefully, I thought.

"I should think your mother *does* need help. It's good of you, Matt, to see it. Give her my hello."

"I'll do that."

"Will she be moving into town this winter with Daisy?"

"She's talked of it. She gets lonesome out there with Papa gone."

"Well, tell her I'll be pleased to see them if they do."

"I will."

As soon as Ruby had spoken his name, I'd been looking at him, wondering if this was the man from last April, the one who'd caught the horse and pinned me in the doorway. His voice was deep enough to qualify. If so, I'd been wrong about his size–he topped Ruby by several inches and towered over Ada.

"Aunt Ada, if you get any smaller, you'll fit in my coat pocket."

"Where I'll ride snug as a pup with my head sticking out to see the world go by."

His face wasn't a matinee idol's, even a little crooked somehow, but he didn't look like someone pretending to be what he wasn't. *Real* was the word I thought. "And your lodger, Aunt Ruby, she looks like you've been taking good care of her."

"Why, where are my manners?" Ruby stopped and turned to me. "Jo, you remember Matt, don't you? You met him last spring."

I took my cue from Ada. "Just barely."

I am studying Flagstaff through its newspaper, trying to decide. The raw little town is entertaining enough to distract me from t.b. half the time. I *am* feeling a little better, and I quite like the few people I've met. But I haven't forgotten that when I arrived that cold windy day, I was thinking of going on to California or back to Santa Fe, either of which might be more sophisticated, have more art and music.

I'm not anxious to start all over, alone again in a strange place. On the other hand, I might never have another opportunity to explore the West—should I take my observation to a different town? I read the *Sun* for something that would help with a decision. Stay? Go? Oh my.

Big news "in these parts" is usually weather. Summer rainy season is welcome. Rivers, streams and lakes don't always contain water, and though several dams have been proposed, including one on the Colorado River, the underground topography creates "currents"—what a bizarre image—that make storage questionable. In mid-July we had a heavy rain that the paper called a "dandy," saying it "busted the drought wide open." Heavy rains through August filled water tanks and caused grass to grow high. Farmers began to worry about blight on their potatoes and the possibility that they wouldn't be able to harvest ripe grain because fields were so wet.

I quite enjoyed the rains while they lasted, loved the sound and the smell and even found the accompanying thunder exciting. They settled dust and cooled the air so that in late afternoon I could sometimes walk into town.

Once I went as far as a block south of the tracks to take my coat for cleaning at a laundry owned by a man named Wong June. Ruby says the story around town is that he worked for a time cooking for the men who were building the railroad, but she thinks he isn't nearly old enough to have done that. "He came here from Ash Fork on the railroad line, but that's no proof." She's heard that Mrs. Wong's name is Dew Yu. "Or Dear Yu, something like that. I'm not sure how the Chinese would say it.

"He brought her and their two oldest sons from a village in southeast China five or six years ago. It was against the Chinese Exclusion Act for people who weren't relatives of native-born to come into the country, so he hired Francis Crable—a lawyer, you know—to help him prove he was a citizen. She and the boys landed in San Francisco.

"We were all waiting to see whether she had bound feet, and some were disappointed when they saw she didn't. She wasn't much more than twenty, poor little thing, in a strange place, barely able to understand a word anybody said to her. I wished I had some way to let that woman know I felt friendly, not like some."

"Ruby, how uncommonly nice of you."

"But I would have looked like a giant to her, I'm sure, she's not even five feet tall. I've never seen her but three or four times. She's stayed close to the laundry—they live in a room at the back. I hear she's really the one who runs it, does everything by hand, even makes the soap. Her husband, well, he's often in the newsstand talking to other men. I should think she'd be lonesome if she can take the time for it."

The oldest son could have come for the coat. "Ben Sen, but everybody calls him Sam. He's sixteen now, speaks English because of going to school. They're all named Ben something—Ben Jun, Ben Fun, Ben Foy. The last two are just little fellows. Of course, if you want the exercise, you go ahead. It's a brand new building on the corner of Phoenix and San Francisco, nearly half a block long. They've just moved from a little bit of a place down the block on Agassiz right behind the train depot."

It was curiosity as much as anything. I wanted to see whether I would have looked like a giant to Dew Yu, but we were about the same size. Sam took my coat, smiling, courteous. She was working at an ironing table, a woman with a broad forehead and hair fastened back into a bun. There was a baby in a basket under the table, a child sitting beside it with a toy of some kind, with wheels. Behind her a boy of about ten was washing clothes in a big corrugated metal tub, scrubbing against a board. The room was different from anything I'd ever seen, warm and moist because of water steaming on a wood stove, and it smelled of soap. For a moment she looked up and met my eyes. I smiled and nodded, once for me and once for Ruby, trying to bridge a chasm, and she smiled back before she looked down again at her ironing. I walked home with the sensation that behind everything I could see there was a mystery that I hadn't suspected, lives I couldn't guess at. And people I would never be able to talk with. It wasn't entirely comfortable: I was Adrift on the Unknown. Terribly metaphysical, I'd have been embarrassed to tell anybody.

Despite my pleasure in the summer storms, I understood the term "under the weather" when it was applied to an old man named Al Doyle who has been ill. Ruby says Zane Grey has based characters in his books on Mr. Doyle, an old-time guide and rancher. I haven't met him. I wonder whether I would like to? It's possible he is "not ornamental," as Henry James said of Commodore Vanderbilt.

There was a "cloudburst" at Tuba City, according to the paper, but I don't know whether Cousin Lillian was there. I have no idea where she is, apparently she is always "on the go," as they say here. Perhaps at Mr. Grey's hunting lodge, described as "commodious," or at his house on Catalina Island off Los Angeles. The *Sun* says he's spending the summer there. If Cousin Lina is with him, the editor did not see fit to print it.

Every week brings an Event of Note. In late July a rancher at Rogers Lake to the west of town was brought in on the logging train with a badly inflamed appendix, but operation in the little six-bed hospital had to be delayed until a surgeon could travel up from Phoenix. The rancher, Jack Crabb, died of peritonitis—his appendix ruptured before the doctor could arrive. Given the difficulty of travel in this country, one takes a train, a connecting line between the Santa Fe and the Southern Pacific. The county Superior Court adjourned for Crabb's funeral, which is an indication of the status of ranchers here.

Some news I can garner firsthand. Emily's family is preparing to move into town for the winter so that Rose can go to school. Ruby said of course they could all stay here, but Roger's mother has been alone in her house for two years, and Emily said Dora would be glad for their company. "You have Jo, Mama. Dora needs us. She's pleased that she'll have Rosie all to herself most of the time for nearly three months. She's missed having children in the house."

"You'll keep Virginia out at the ranch through the fall?"

"This year we will. Next year she'll be in first grade too. I'll come in with the girls and Roger'll batch it. He says he feels lonesome already. I just feel tired thinking of the running back and forth and the moving."

How selfish of me: instead of thinking of Emily, I had been wondering how soon I would tire of the player piano if they were here.

October, 1921

Dear Mother,

I've been in Flagstaff two months short of a year now. I'm sure October is the best time, but perhaps that's because I'm feeling quite well and unaccountably cheerful, so much that I went to the new beauty parlor upstairs in the Babbitt Building to have my hair freshly bobbed. It was beginning to look shaggy by comparison with the wives of Flagstaff's "go-getter" businessmen. Flagstaff is agog with the news that a local man has won honorable mention in an art show in New York. The fact that it is actually Jamaica Bay and not Manhattan escapes them, and they are as proud as though it were. I don't suppose you'll be in Jamaica Bay, but if you are, you might stop by and look at "Woodland Path in Autumn" so I can sound knowledgeable. The artist's name is George Hochderffer. A Man of Affairs in this little town, he married a New York schoolteacher a few years back, goes east with her in the winter, and returns to Arizona in the summer to manage his cattle ranch. Ruby says George probably decided to take art lessons at Columbia and the Art Students League because he can't stand to be bored.

Does your sphere of attention include Jimmy Swinnerton who draws cartoons for the Hearst newspapers? He is apparently in and out of Flagstaff often for painting trips. Just recently he exhibited in Los Angeles—a group of canvases he has done of the scenery near here. I've not seen his work. Ruby says it is well-spoken-of by those who have.

In August Swinnerton came through with writers he wanted to introduce to the Hopi snake dance. (I'm told it is performed with live snakes, some of them poisonous, which sounds quite appalling.) The dance is a prayer for rain and, as Ruby said, it worked ahead of time. The half dozen men in his party experienced "cloudbursts," bottomless mud, and usually dry desert streambeds full of raging water four feet deep. The Swinnerton auto and others owned by T. A. Riordan, Charles Babbitt, and Billy Friedlein got through to the Hopi towns, but others were not so fortunate. One car was caught by rapidly rising water and rolled over and over downstream. The Sun said that roads were drowned as deep as the streambeds and fields were two to three feet under water.

Obviously, life for a landscape artist in Arizona is not always genteel. But Swinnerton came back with sketches he had made in the Hopi towns *and settled in to do a little painting before going on to the big Hearst cabin at the Grand Canyon.*

It is absolutely marvelous to feel rather chipper again, it makes me aware of things I once took for granted. Each afternoon I work at my easel a few minutes on the study I'm doing of my room. I'm trying for a modern effect—you'll be happy to hear it—concentrating on patterns and contrasts of the colors I'm applying, blues and warm yellow-browns. It gives me pleasure to wake up each morning and glance at the dormer to see what I've done and plan what I'll try later in the day.

Now the rains have ceased and given way to gorgeous autumn—clear blue skies and sharp frosts in the night. It's easy to feel connected to the seasons here, they seem so much a part of life. I enclose a little watercolor I did this week of trees in Ruby's yard flaming golden as captured sunlight. You'll notice that on the bottom I wrote Whistler's line: "Painting is the poetry of light."

As ever,
Jo

I *do* find life here wonderfully salubrious, I must admit that much. As my acquaintance lengthens, I become more engrossed by the activities that interest Fred Breen, the editor of the *Sun*. Sam Campbell, who keeps eighty hives of bees, takes a swarm from the gable at Sam Black's house, and I wish I had been there among the crowd that watched. (Ada says that "Honey" Campbell is a notorious bootlegger and bold as brass about it.) Doctor Fronske's wife, Hilda, presides at a meeting of the Shakespeare Club, and it occurs to me that if I were to live here permanently, I could join. I examine that idea. Ruby suggests that she might have a quilting bee this winter with Ada and Matt's mother, and I feel pleasure about the idea, though I've never used a needle in my life. I'm living in a book: everything is full of meaning. Superstitiously I try not to think of it, but now and then I can't help expecting that I might live after all. And that's too swell for words, if you ask me.

Probably The Family will be outraged, but I've decided I would like to stay on in Arizona through Christmas. The holiday social season in New York is beautiful, but I hate to jeopardize my health by returning too soon—"over-stimulus" is the term I can use to justify, and Doctor Fronske says to be wary of a relapse. I'll send gifts for everyone, of course, it would be unthinkable not to, but I'm planning for the people here too. I wonder whether Ruby would like to have a roll of "I Wonder Who's Kissing Her Now" for her player piano? I've tried pedaling it, but the effort makes me feel like weak tea.

Today is fine and warm. Through the window I can see Virginia, here for a few hours, helping Petra Armenta hang sheets on the line—she isn't really helping with the hanging, though Petra lets her think so, just handing up clothes pins when they are needed. Both are being very solemn about it.

Sun, which was often too strong for comfort in June, is now an affirmation, a blessing on my shoulders, balm on my soul. I've become too sentimental for words. *Nothing* bores me, nothing, except perhaps the effort to be flippant. If I stay much longer, will New York have me back?

I have decided to go down to Wong June's laundry to retrieve my dress. At first my route is straightforward, but one block north of the tracks I must maneuver to avoid passing pool halls. Ruby has taught it to me. "It used to be worse, we had to try to avoid saloons too. In the middle of the block, at the alley, cross over. That will take you past a card room, but it can't be helped. Just look straight ahead and walk tall as you can, and no one will judge you harshly." I wonder: has it always been hard work for a woman to be respectable?

A train is clicking and rumbling east, probably filled with raisins from California or something equally quaint. Waiting for it to pass, I hear a man's voice say, "Mrs. Boren, it's good to see you out again." He has come up beside me.

I look up at him. "Matt, forgive me, I don't know your last name."

"You couldn't forget it. The name is Friendly." He lifts his hat. Sudden light from the sun models the planes of his face, which looks as if it has not been shaved for two or three days.

I smile. "You're joking. That's made up, isn't it?"

"No, ma'am. Not unless my great-grandpa did it." He settles his hat, and his face is in shadow again. "I suppose somebody did once, and here I am stuck with it."

"I've heard worse."

"Me too. I've always been glad it isn't Surly."

A laugh explodes out of my chest. Not until now do I realize I haven't heard myself laugh freely for a long time.

"Or Backward," he offers. "That would be a burden. Warden would be pretty rough."

"You wouldn't like Straggler."

"No, I sure wouldn't. Name like Dandruff, I'd have had to hide from the other boys in school."

I'm enjoying the game. "Slippery? What about Glum?"

"Why ma'am, you have a real knack. Next time I have a litter of pups to name, I'll call on you for help."

The caboose slides past and the rails are clear, but I continue to stand there, liking his real face, his eyes and the weather lines that ray from the corners. I think he is well acquainted with the unsheltered country that lies around us for hundreds of miles.

"So I'll keep it. Friendly's not so bad, when you consider what it might have been."

People can change with acquaintance. Nicky was fun until I married him and discovered he had to be plastered to the ears to be interested in conjugal activity, which was *not* fun. But I think it might be safe to like this man.

"I'm just back from duck hunting at Rogers Lake. My mother said to me before I left in the dark yesterday morning, 'If you shoot straight enough to hit anything, I want you to take a brace of ducks to Ada Nelson and another to Ruby Green before you bring any home to me.' Do you suppose Ruby'd be disposed to roast a duck for dinner tonight?" He raises a burlap sack. "Fortunately there's enough for everybody."

"You shot them yourself?"

"On the wing. You ever clean a duck?"

"What does it involve?"

"Oh, a couple hours of smelly mess for fifteen minutes of eating."

"I could learn, I suppose." I have a quick image of Gertrude's horrified face.

"Wouldn't do that to you—the pin feathers are a real chore. So I cleaned the whole lot out at the lake and left the mess there."

I confess I was relieved. "I'm sure we should be grateful to you."

"You don't know the danger I went through to get 'em. There were twenty to thirty men from town out at the lake, firing in all directions. Doctor Mackey shot Joe Wilson, not on purpose, but it hurt just as bad. A twelve gauge pump shotgun with a charge of Number Four at close range can make a wound to remember."

"*Shot* him! How?"

I think he is enjoying himself–he raises his eyebrows and grins. "Now I been known to lie, but this here's a true story. They were in a little steel boat, Doctor Mackey in the stern. He reached for the gun and it caught, he can't remember how or on what, and discharged. Hit Joe in the hip. Doctor Manning was close by– Mackey's a dentist so he was glad for the help. It took a lot of us quite an effort to get Joe into an auto and bring him home. Cut the crowd down a bit."

It has seemed to me reading the *Sun* that every man in town, including Jim Lamport and several of the Babbitts, has been out hunting everything that moved–deer, turkey, lion–with humorous reports on who has brought in what. Tribal Ritual, I suppose. A man named George Bailey nearly drowned at Marshall Lake after his canoe went down under him and another hunter had to come to his rescue. I'm not surprised that someone has finally been injured in the melee.

"Well, Mr. Friendly, since the ducks were procured at Risk to Life and Limb, I could hardly refuse them. Do you deliver?"

"On my way right now. Tired of carryin'm."

"Please thank your mother for us."

"First thing. Hope you like'm."

I walk on to the laundry in no way diminished by the encounter. He's not on my social level, or at least whatever level I had in New York. Probably he knows nothing of music and art and books. Still, he is capable for his time and place. A Folk Hero, I shouldn't wonder. What an amazing place Arizona is, quite authentic.

October, 1921

Dearest Jo,

I was impressed by your watercolor of Ruby's house surrounded by autumn trees. Obviously illness has not impaired your spontaneity nor your eye for contrast. The effect is very immediate: I feel as if I'm standing there, preparing to walk through the welcoming door into the house that shelters you. It quite takes me into your life. Thank you.

Your news from the West continues to be fascinating. I am delighted to hear that your illness does not keep you isolated from all the fun. That would indeed be, as you implied in an earlier letter, tragic.

Since you feel that tragedy includes unrecognized artists, you might be pleased to hear, if you haven't already, that an exhibition of your cousin Lillian's paintings was held in January in Phoenix, which is in Arizona, I think. The news just reached me through the family. Apparently her work, all of it done in the West, was well received and reviewed with approval in the local newspaper. You had just arrived and were quite ill, so perhaps you did not know about it.

Your cousin Gertrude sent on to me a few lines copied from Lillian's last letter, which she has seen.

Some people like the snug enclosed valleys. Perhaps because of the years I spent among the tall buildings of Manhattan Island, I prefer the wide spaces, the distant view of mountains, and above all, the views from the tops of mountains. Three times I have ridden to the top of those grand Peaks. In the saddle 500 feet below the top in mid July our horses buried their warm noses into a ten foot snowbank. Leaving them in the shade of the pines at timber line, we'd climb the great volcanic boulder to gaze at last in breathless awe from this great height of 13,000 feet upon more of the earth's surface than one is privileged to see from any other point.

I assume Gertrude meant that to alarm me about the sort of activity you would undertake any day now. Instead I felt a happy admiration for Lillian. I didn't suspect she had it in her.

Unable to reach you, the family is conducting a campaign against me. They think it is ever so subtle. "Lilly, I don't know how you can endure the worry," they sympathize. "I'm sure I would go out there and bring her back where she can be nursed properly." My mother pats my hand and murmurs, "My poor daughter, bereft of the company of her child." I have given up trying to explain that you are doing very well in the West; they don't hear me.

Have you read that in August Enrico Caruso died suddenly in Naples after lapsing into a coma from an illness he contracted in New

York? Your grandmothers are devastated, of course and wondering how they can go on. So are the Italians. Their King ordered a special funeral service in Caruso's honor.

Englebert Humperdink, whose "Hansel and Gretel" opera you saw as a child, has also died. So has Saint-Saens; you remember "The Carnival of the Animals?" The grandmothers are saddened, but apparently they do not consider the loss of an occasional composer as significant as that of a tenor.

For most New Yorkers the big news seems to be that a film titled "Tarzan of the Apes" has come to the city. It stars lions, apes and other jungle animals, to the great excitement of the public. Rudolph Valentino is tres chic in "The Shiek.". I have not seen either of these films. Probably I will not.

I was stunned recently to learn that Joseph Duveen, the art dealer, had bought Gainsborough's painting "The Blue Boy" from the Duke of Westminster and sold it to H.E. Huntington for six hundred and twenty thousand dollars. Imagine! Duveen drives prices of painters dead more than two hundred years up and up by playing on the vanity of a few rich old men while superb painters who are still living languish in poverty and obscurity. There is no justice in the world of art.

England was terribly upset about losing a national heirloom to America. Duveen permitted a public exhibition in London just before it sailed, protected by a waterproof box, a steel box, an iron-bound case and two Duveen employees. The arrival of "The Blue Boy" was a headline story here, as was the news that Duveen had denied the Met permission to exhibit it on the ground that the museum was not "secure" enough. Can you believe the arrogance of that man?

He escorted it personally to the Huntington home in San Marino outside Los Angeles. The irony is too great, that a famous painting by an old English master should repose in a new house in California presided over by Arabella Huntington. I don't suppose it came through Flagstaff on the railroad?

Your cousin Paul came to call on me last week. Poor dear, such a handsome young man, so restive in his position at the bank. His parents are urging him to marry, and he fears it would be the final tie that would bind him to New York forever. He requested your mailing address so that he might write to you. "Arizona fills my dreams," he said. "Knowing it is there keeps me sane." Naturally I will do nothing without your permission. Would you mind if I were to give him your address, strictly confidential, of course, and allow him to read your letters?

Good luck on your painting.
Lilly

In the midst of life, indeed. Any direction I turn my mind there's death. In the New York papers I read of the arrival in Washington of the coffin bearing the body of the Unknown Soldier, and that set off a bout of secret sobbing, grief for all the men and boys dead in that stupid war and all the stupid wars. It's too tragic to bear. My own demise hangs over my head again. I had a sudden failure of pep early in the month, I don't know why, but it frightened me and sent me back to frantic resting. It's too depressing for words—all the color of life was at my fingertips and here I am lying in my room all day, betrayed by my own lungs. You would think men would be satisfied that all people die without setting about killing them wholesale to no good purpose. I truly suspect they enjoy it. Nicky *wanted* to go to war. He repeated all the slogans everyone else was using, but there was a barely hidden relish at the idea of killing with no moral punishment.

They kill *any*thing. During deer season Ed Babbitt saw seven mountain lions together, and ever since half the men in town have been clamoring to help the state predatory-animal man go after them. "Varmints" they're called, which I gather means some kind of nuisance. Ruby says cattle are money, and it's a question of how many lions ranchers can afford to have around. She also says Ed Babbitt is neither a liar nor a drunk, but she's never heard of that many lions in one place in her life.

Zane Grey, my own cousin's husband, kills for fun, as if it makes him feel alive. I am quite sure I would not care to meet a wild animal face to face, but when I heard he had hunted for two months and "got" only one bear, I was glad. A professor at the Normal School "got himself a trophy of the hunt," an old wolf that he's having mounted, and I was furious. He didn't even have the excuse of intending to eat the poor old thing, as I ate the ducks Matt brought to us or the quarter of a deer that Roger provided. He simply wanted to "get" it.

A man named Charles Miller has killed thirty-two bears and twenty-nine lions *this year*, and you'd think he's some kind of Epic Hero. They're all impressed about the tame wolf he uses for hunting. The Epic Hero killed its mother and eight little pups she was defending and saved the one to train. No one seemed to think there was anything dishonorable about that.

Last week he and half a dozen men from town went out after bear and came back with a four hundred-pound female their dogs had treed and a "giant" black male seven feet long that had been crippled by two shots in some earlier year and wounded by a grizzly, perhaps some time back—grizzlies have not often been seen in recent years. The cowardice of it, the senseless meanness, drives me to despair.

One night a man named Sandy Donahue was shot in the right thigh while he was walking along the tracks, no one knows by whom. Dave Joy, night watchman at the mill, found him.

Ruby was indignant. "Sandy was a saloon keeper, it's true, but hotel owner and fire chief too. There's no bad in him. Oh, he used to have fun, and he made things fun for the rest of us. He was a mainstay of this town. Now he's a penniless drifter."

"*Why*? Prohibition?"

"They say he used to drink a fifth of his own whiskey a day. But he was so generous to anyone in any kind of need it would warm your heart. Nobody was turned away. Maybe he was so good that he forgot to make a profit and ended up with nothing. It can happen. Now he's reduced to asking for money from old friends, and they're glad to help him because of past favors and past regard."

"Being penniless is no excuse, surely? Why would anyone shoot at a man who was just walking along?"

"Who's to say? I think some men are just glad to have a target."

It's not that they lack danger enough for excitement. In August there was a fire in the Ideal Hotel less than a block away from us—nobody noticed until the rafters had burned and the roof fell in. The whole third floor was destroyed. Last week with a strong wind blowing, the M.J. Riordan house south of the tracks burned when the family was away on a trip to Lee's Ferry. Fire started under the roof at noon, and men at the mill got there quickly to move the furniture out and help the town's new hose engine. Mr. T.A. Riordan said it was fine thing to see how a little trouble gets all the people together and takes attention from imaginary trouble. Why, then, doesn't it satisfy their need to hurt something?

I stay in my room until I can control such thoughts so Ruby won't see. I'm afraid to tell her how I feel, that causing death may be economic, but it is not glorious. Maybe it's an Eastern woman's point of view—I refuse to call killing "sport" or "honor." Killing to be killing is not heroic. I have decided I'm not in love with Western men after all, they seem not to see the wonder in the life all around them.

One morning in the middle of hunting season, something went wrong with Ada. A small stroke, perhaps, if there is such a thing. Creeping out of bed to face another day with whatever laughter she could muster, trying to sit up in the cold—oh, it's too cruel. She was able to lie back on the pillows and pull a blanket to her chin. Then she lay there expecting death until a neighbor noticed there was no smoke rising from her chimney.

We learned about it when Dennis came with my morning milk. Doctor Raymond had been to see Ada in his Packard Light Six and said it appeared to be an ischemic incident, whatever that is. The women from the church had already divided her day among them so that she wouldn't be alone. "She's in b-b-b-bed. Would you b-be wanting mmmmmme to drive you over to see her?"

"I'll go with you, Ruby, if that's all right. Would she mind? I couldn't bear to sit here and wait and wonder. Let me get a sweater." Climbing the stairs, I was so upset I could barely see. Ada deserves better from fate than she's had. It's *not* just being ill that makes me so rebellious.

We left Petra Armenta up to her elbows in suds. Yellow leaves were blowing through the air as we drove across the almost-finished Aspen Avenue bridge on the Rio de Flag, "the only up-to-date bridge in town," the *Sun* says. The house was square, red brick, with a porch the width of the front. Its wood trim needed paint.

Ada was small as a toy on the bed. The right side of her face looked rigid; her right hand curled into a little claw on her chest. Her voice was slow and careful, and no wonder. She could speak with only half her mouth. "…here…my friends." I didn't trust myself to talk—her friend, and I was so new to her life. The goodness of it.

"Sit... tell me news." What news could we have that she didn't already know?

Ruby had never looked so strong to me. I went to a straight chair against the wall, fighting back tears, but she pulled one to the bedside and took Ada's hand in her own. "Well, I'm afraid Al Doyle isn't doing well after that operation last week. They've sent for Lee."

"...orphan...all alone...five...poor little boy..."

"He's seventy-two now, I think."

"...no education...sent to a farmer...poor little boy..."

"Took off for the west right after the war between the states. Seventeen then, I think."

"...children living?"

"Three. Two have died."

"Sarah holding up?"

"I hear she is."

"...married..."

"I make it about forty-five years now."

Tears began to slide from Ada's eyes across her delicate cheeks. "Poor Sarah...hard for her." I could see the effort she made to speak with her lop-sided mouth.

Ruby gave no sign that she noticed. "Al hasn't been the most refined of men, but nobody can charge him with weakness—he's used his body hard. Lena will come soon as she can to be with her mother."

"...only one other man...alive...gang...finished the railroad...across the continent..." Her good hand groped in the air.

"Thirty-eight years ago. Seems to me you haven't forgotten the really important things."

Only the left side of Ada's mouth smiled. "...*people* well enough...good sign..."

"So it is. I expect you'll be able to be with us for Thanksgiving as usual."

"...this morning...low as a snake's chin...going to die... used to run like the wind...thought I did...looked forward to... it again...how good it would feel."

"Oh, wouldn't it though?"

"...looks like I won't...Doctor says...be there Thanksgiving... certain as sunrise. Lucky I'm..." She lifted her left hand and wiggled the fingers. "...hand I hold a fork with..."

It was later that day that I learned about the Big Game Hunter who had killed a mother wolf and eight puppies, and they became connected in my mind–Ada bravely wiggling her fingers and that man killing the helpless.

Al Doyle died the following Monday before his son Lee could arrive. The news hurt Ruby, I could tell, though she'd known it was coming. "Many people new to this country trusted Al with their lives. Jimmy Swinnerton. Zane Grey. And he brought them back safe. That's a good thing to be able to say about a man."

"It is. Yes, it is."

"There's some you couldn't say it for. It's a part of our lives gone. *I'm* older than Al was. Part of my youth gone." She wrapped herself around the pain.

I did something I've never thought to do in all my life–put my arms around a woman old as my grandmothers and a head taller than I am. Part of her past gone. I'd never even met him, but part of the past was gone for me too, part of a brave time. Who cared whether Mr. Doyle was ornamental?

His body was prepared for burial at the Babbitt undertaking parlor and then moved to the Federated Church for the funeral. Ada insisted that she would attend. "All I've done is sleep…you can see I'm buttoned…Dennis can help…not a block to go…carry me into the church…put me between you…"

We did as she wanted. I said I'd add the cost of Dennis and his taxi to my regular bill, but he wouldn't hear of it. "N-n-no sir. It won't take me a mmmminute. I'm going anyway." We drove down the block with Ada tight between Ruby and me in the back seat. She was pleased to be out again so soon, "fit as a fiddle," to hear her tell it.

The church includes most of the Protestant congregations of Flagstaff–not in a union except for the Sunday School but a *federation* which has one pastor and governing board but separate identities. Ruby explained. "There wasn't enough of any one group to be sepa-rate, so six years ago we got together with the Methodists and worked out an arrangement for all of us to meet in their building. We thought it made sense."

Ada nodded. "…different as mustard and custard, but… Christianity…no 'isms."

"How many groups federated?"

Ruby answered. "Methodist, Presbyterian, Lutheran, Baptist, Congregationalist, a few odds and ends."

Ada's voice was still slow. "The editor, oh *darn…*"

"Fred Breen."

"…said God's plan didn't involve…" She looked to Ruby.

"Technicalities."

"I liked that."

It was a handsome red stone building across the street from Emerson School, solid and secure with an ornate front window and a heavy portal. Light flooded into the sanctuary through colored glass onto masses of flowers. Ruby said she bet Al Doyle never would have guessed there'd be so many flowers for an old cowboy and so many people come to show what they thought of him.

Ada gestured vaguely toward a man at the back, and Ruby interpreted. "There's Wong June with his two oldest boys. They attend here regularly. Mrs. Wong comes sometimes with the babies."

We sat on wooden benches next to Emily and Roger and their girls. There was a piano for "Nearer My God to Thee," which everyone sang together. Reverend Zook was elevated only slightly above the crowd, just high enough so that he could be seen but not so high as to set him apart. And there was a sense of Community, of loss of one affecting all, that moved me almost to tears. I'm such a sap sometimes.

*T*hrough all the killing and dying, November was as pretty as any Ruby remembered. She had the oil furnace serviced and lit to be ready for the coming winter. Life goes on somehow, I suppose, despite all that death can do.

Ada improved daily. She was not walking, but the right side of her face was less spastic. Doctor Raymond said he was encouraged that her right hand was not so clenched and rigid.

One bright windless day we waited until Petra was hanging out towels and then strolled across town to visit and found that a grey-haired woman with a figure like a pillow had moved into the back bedroom. Ruby was not surprised.

"Well, Margaret. Settled in?"

"I am, and grateful to you for pointing me to such a comfortable place."

"Jo, this is Margaret Friendly, Matt's mother, moved into town for the winter. Margaret and I were pioneers together in this country close on to forty years ago."

I searched her features, looking for the honesty I thought I'd seen in her son's. I probably looked nearsighted, the sympathetic way she smiled at me. "And this is the little lady Matt pinned with Buck's horse?"

A man who had been leaning on the back door frame pushed off with his shoulders and came toward me. At first I had taken him for Matt, but the face was different and something about him, something in his smile or the way he moved, lazy and smooth—he's sure he's charming where women are concerned, I thought.

"And this is my other son, Luke. You haven't met, have you?"

"Not that I haven't wanted to." He bowed over me and took my hand and held it too long, staring intently into my eyes, sparking me like a movie lover. It was embarrassing, knowing his mother was watching. Was it a blush I felt, that tight feeling in my cheeks?

I turned to Margaret. "How's Ada?"

"Seems to me she gets better all the time. She'll be trying to get up soon, I shouldn't wonder."

"I hear voices down there!" A sudden clatter on the stairs, and a young woman bounced into the room, not much more than a girl really, with glowing skin and an unfashionably rounded body. "Aunt Ruby!" She embraced my landlady cheek to cheek. "It's been ages!"

Ruby returned the hug. "Daisy, you're beautiful as ever. It's good to see you. Good to know you'll be in town until spring, my boarder probably needs the company of someone closer to her age than I am."

With a smile that would blind a tree, Daisy turned to me. "You're Jo. Matt's told us about you. He felt like such a *dope* the day he pinned you with Buck's horse." When she hugged me too, I smelled soap and lavender sachet. "You're the lucky woman who's getting well on Aunt Ruby's cooking. You don't look sick at all, just modishly slender."

I couldn't help being charmed, she was so, well, unaffected. "I'm not sick all the time, not too often these days. The air and the cooking are doing the trick, I think."

"Is she bullying you too much? She can be fierce when she knows what's good for you." Daisy laughed as she talked—the words came out laughing. The grandmothers would have frowned at her lack of reserve.

Her mother touched her shoulder. "Now Daisy, stop your teasing. These ladies came to see Ada."

She danced—there was no other word for it—to the bedroom door. "Aunt Ada, look who's here!"

I settled into my chair smiling, and Ada noticed the reaction. "Daisy's fresh as morning air...lucky to have her in the house... spreads good feelings all around..."

When we had kissed Ada goodbye and returned to the kitchen, Luke was gone and Daisy was ready with fun, nodding as she proposed it. "Have you been anywhere yet? Before the weather gets cold, why don't Matt and I take you out to the cliff ruins in Walnut Canyon? I bet a cookie you've never seen anything like it. What do you think, Aunt Ruby, is she up to it? We could take Matt's Tin Lizzie and pack a picnic."

Ruby turned to me. "I think you might enjoy it, Jo, while the weather holds. It's only a few miles east of here, and the road's pretty good finally. People built their houses there hundreds of years ago, nobody knows who, Indians of some kind."

Spending a day with Matt and Daisy, what a swell idea. "Thank you, yes, I would like to very much. So kind of you."

Daisy clapped her hands."Yay! I'll talk to Matt, and we'll make plans. Do you like fried chicken? Corn fritters? Apple turnovers? We'll have such fun, wait and see." She said nothing about including Luke.

Ruby turned to Margaret. "Ada's been coming over for Thanksgiving several years now, her children being so far away and not likely to get here. Can we count on you two and Matt and Luke?"

"Emily and Roger will have their cows shipped by then?"

"They'll be there with their two girls and Roger's mother. There'll be twelve of us. Plenty of room at the table."

"And many hands to help."

I left that red brick house in a virtual tingle. I hadn't felt deprived, talking only with Ruby and Dennis and Ada and Doctor Fronske, but Daisy by herself was a social whirl. I was quite taken with her.

Ruby pulled my hand through her arm as we went down the steps. "That Daisy, it's hard to feel blue around her."

"Luke, though. It's as if he doesn't quite belong in the family."

"Margaret's had her share of worry about him since he was just a little tyke. Always in some scrape or other, nothing that put him in jail, you understand, just that, well, he needs excitement, I guess. Doesn't always know the right place to find it. Seems like almost every woman has at least one child who gives her heartache. I have a son—but you don't want to hear that and I don't want to tell it."

We turned east toward home, a long stroll away. "Why have they moved into town? To help Ada?"

"No, not entirely—they decided to get away from that isolated ranch—you just get to where you feel so shut in and lonesome. Snow can be up to your waist sometimes in the winter, not always but sometimes, makes it hard to get around, and no need to once the cattle are shipped. Matt will go back and forth. We used to do the same, many families did. It's hard to stay there through the cold weather. Margaret's as experienced as they come, but still…"

"They have friends in town?"

"Oh, lots. Different kinds for different reasons. Matt's are in the livery stable, Luke's in cardrooms and such places, I should think. Margaret and Daisy know everybody respectable, especially the ones who've been here a good while."

"I should like—well…"

She squeezed my hand where it rested on her arm. "You'd like Daisy to be your friend?"

"I've never known anyone like her."

"You couldn't do better. She has her sorrows too, same as all of us, but she keeps them to herself mostly. I'd say she'd be as good as any medicine you could find."

"I'm older than she is?"

"Once you're grown, age doesn't matter so much. Ada's ten years older than I am. You don't make friends by number, do you?"

$\mathcal{T}$he sky was massed with radiant white clouds. We rattled along over a rocky dirt road that followed the land between hills, east into morning sunlight. Matt and Daisy had packed a hamper into a little one-seater Roadster. I was euphoric: it was my first out-of-town outing, and I felt quite my old self, or very nearly, only a twinge now and then, too annoying for words.

Because I had seen photos of all kinds of adventurers, I had bought at Penney's store a pair of whipcord breeches that laced up to the knees. How was I to know? Next to Daisy's full-swinging riding skirt I felt rather a fool in them, as if I were costumed for a play. Appropriate clothing certainly varies from one place to another.

Clutching my sketchpad (one never knows what might turn up), I was squeezed into the auto between the Friendlies. Matt drove capably, I thought, not too fast or reckless and with only a hint of bravado. He quite confused me with talk of four cylinders and three-point suspension. Maybe everyone knows this, but I didn't—the

T was built for rough roads. It has high clearance and wheels that can bend at different angles. I gathered that was important.

At first Daisy sang and laughed and teased her brother, but when we had left town, she climbed over the door of the moving automobile and stood on the running board, her brown hair blowing in the breeze. It is not bobbed. I find the old-fashioned effect quite appealing.

I was alarmed, but Matt was matter-of-fact. "She likes to be out there, ever since she was a kid. I guess it means she trusts me to drive careful."

Holding to the windscreen strut, she talked quite gaily about New York City. "I've never been east, though I did go to California once on the train. What's it like? New York is different from here, from what I read in magazines."

How does one summarize the city for a girl who has never seen it? "There are definitely more people. Bigger buildings, bigger stores. Less sky—you can't see far, just down the street."

"I wonder whether I'd like that. Does it make you feel crowded and closed in?"

"I didn't think about it really, but I suppose it will when I go back. It was the *houses* that felt closed in, even though they're bigger than houses here."

"And the land was smaller?"

She had it exactly. "Yes, you're right. Smaller."

The light was so intense that every tree vibrated with it, every rock, and it was intoxicating. I could see for miles. In New York I didn't think of land as big or small or any size, just something on which things were *built*.

She didn't give me time to muse about it. "New York is the fashion center, they say. In the section on clothes, the Sears Roebuck catalogue calls the really smart things, the kind you would never wear to do any work in, New York styles. Even the daytime frocks look too spiffy to wear. The women must be wonderful to see."

"I suppose they are, and not by accident. They work at it, all of them."

Daisy giggled. "Every time I look at the mannish styles and flat chests in those drawings, I have to laugh at the thought of me with my bosom trying to squeeze myself into them."

Matt spoke from behind the steering wheel. "I laugh at the corduroy knickers and the blouses they call middy. And the underwear. What they call foundations."

"Oh, Matt, behave." Daisy paused to brace for a rough stretch and find a handhold on the inside of the car. "Are New York women clever and witty?"

I looked at the life I had left and saw it all too clearly. "They work at that too. Some are—Dorothy Parker makes it seem easy. But some confuse wit with sarcasm. My cousin Gertrude, for instance, is more insulting than clever and doesn't know it." The day was so wonderful that I didn't want to think about Gertrude. "Will it rain?" I asked Matt. "Those clouds are so huge."

"Oh, I don't think so. They don't look like rain. Maybe in a day or two."

I was impressed—I've not met any other man who could glance at clouds and predict rain two days away. "What is this place we're going to? Is it far?"

"One hour, and ten miles, and you're back almost a thousand years. You'll see. People built in the canyon and lived there a long time, and maybe seven-eight hundred years ago they went away and never came back."

Daisy spoke from the running board. "Sometimes if you're quiet, you can almost feel them, women calling to neighbors on the other side of the canyon. It's a beautiful place. I like to imagine the women looking up from grinding corn or making things they needed and seeing sunlight on the canyon walls or hearing a bird sing."

Matt was rather less lyrical. "The settlers used to come out here sometimes to hunt for things those old people had left—a sandal, pots, arrows—turn them up with shovels. Things kind of got out of hand, people brought picks and dynamite to find more. Some of the folks in town, Father Vabre and some others, tried to stop it. Then before the war President Wilson made the canyon a National Monument."

I did hope Daisy wasn't trying to dance out there, but I suspected that her feet were moving—the chassis was rocking. It made me queasy, but she seemed to have no cares. "Ten years or so ago a woman writer came out from the East and visited. Mattie Pierce has been there for nearly a coon's age with her husband, as custodians, living in a log cabin. She says that was the oddest woman she ever saw. Nice enough, but odd. She put the canyon into a book."

Sun came up in my dim brain. "I know that book! I read it!" We were going to the place Willa Cather wrote about in *Song of the Lark,* the canyon where the soprano rested from her life in Chicago in a little room—I remember how she said it—"in a wrinkle in the cliff" that made its roof and an everlasting floor. I couldn't have been more excited.

There was no hint of anything special ahead. Ground rose slightly, but I should think you could pass by the canyon a hundred times and never guess it was there. For centuries, until only forty years ago, the secret was hidden away. Matt drove right up to a log cabin among trees, pulled the throttle and spark levers up and turned off the key. I looked around for a clue and saw nothing much, except a break in the trees not far away.

Daisy hugged an older woman who came out to meet us and called her "Aunt Mattie." "How have you been?"

"Fair to middlin', I'd say. Always a little behind like a cow's tail."

"This is Josephine Boren, visiting in Flagstaff."

"Pleased to meet you."

Matt shook hands with Mr. Pierce. "How are things?"

"Oh, fine and dandy, Matt. Fine and dandy."

"Heard you had that Philadelphia scientist out here last summer."

"Yes siree. Doctor Colton'd been here before, back in nineteen and twelve. Wasn't his first ruin. Last summer he got serious with his survey. That man sure is interested in most everything."

"What'd you think of his wife, Mattie?"

"Well, she was a real intelligent little woman, real pretty. I liked her all right. But I couldn't tell if she liked *me*."

I could hardly listen to the pleasantries. There was something Cather had said about the sadness of the past, and the obligation to do one's best. I wanted to get to the canyon.

Daisy hugged my arm and laughed. "Look at Jo, she's on pins and needles to see it. Come on, we'll leave Matt to talk."

Walnut Canyon is a place one might create for old tales—four hundred feet deep, a sinuous stream bed at the bottom. The cliffs would make sense, I suppose, to someone who understood the forces that created them, but to me they were a chaos of shapes that had no connection, like the architecture of one culture resting on another, and another piled on that. The instant I peered down and along the canyon, I knew it as a place where a story should have happened.

And it did. Rock layers lie in stripes. Something—water or wind maybe, I don't know what—scooped out long shallow overhangs on either side. In the shelter they provided as far as I could see along the cliffs were stones cleverly cemented with mud to make walls for rooms, safe places to sleep dry and out of the wind.

I had particularly liked Cather's line about art being a device to stop life from running past us and away. I did some quick pencil sketches on the spot, sitting on boulders and using my lap as a desk. I hoped they would convey some of the wonder I felt. I was quite pleased with the dense cross-hatch shading I used for the door openings.

Matt and Daisy knew of a break in the canyon wall, and we clambered down to a place where those old people lived, hundreds Matt said. I think they must have been smaller than we are or didn't mind stooping: the ceilings are quite low, in many places blackened with soot from ancient fires. Matt said that the Pennsylvania scientist found evidence showing the people were farmers who grew corn and beans in the bottom of the canyon and on the plateau that surrounds it. Then they went away, and one only guesses where and why.

Matt and Daisy were most understanding: they gave me silence to sketch or to stand and imagine, to bring back to that hidden place images of the people who made lives there a hundred centuries ago. I rose out of my body—the oddest sensation—and moved into a vanished time, floated through an invisible boundary, and the past continued on into the present and the future. Quite bizarre, I'm sure I'll never be the same.

All those people went away, and they died. No one else came along to build there and hide their empty houses as in towns of long habitation, so it must be faced. No voices have been there for nearly a thousand years. If I had been alone, I might have cried.

And then, the sharpest shock, I looked up and saw Daisy slumped on a rock some distance away with an expression of utter grief on her face. Daisy, so alive, laughing and dancing, a picture of despair and unending hopelessness. Perhaps she was sad about all the people who have gone into death, but it looked like more than that. I've wondered ever since whether when she thinks someone is watching, she *acts* cheerful to hide feelings that are too painful to show. Daisy is a good deal more than surface, I think.

The mountain peaks looming ahead as we returned to Flagstaff in the afternoon had significance I had not noticed before. I suspect the huge spaces of the southwest echo with something sacred beyond every horizon, and I'd been so concerned with myself I hadn't noticed. I wonder whether Daisy and Matt and Emily, who have lived their lives here, Ruby and Ada and Margaret, who came as adults, have known all along and haven't had words to say it. Nor do I have a way to express it to them: I feel the worst kind of simpleton when I try.

All month Babbitts Grocery Department has been advertising ducks and geese, "everything for Thanksgiving that's available anywhere." The delivery truck driver has carried asparagus and oysters (both imported by train) and fruit for pies into the kitchen. Matt stopped by yesterday with two wild turkeys, freshly cleaned and plucked, and half a wagon load of wood split for the cookstove.

I think one has to take part to *be* part, a shorthand aphorism I've made up myself. "Ruby, I've never done anything but eggs in my life. And I don't want to be in the way of all you capable cooks. But I'll feel useless as a child if there's nothing to keep my hands busy."

"You can make up the turkey stuffing, it takes forever when I've got all the rest to do. I'll be grateful for the help. Sit down over here and fill this big pan with little pieces of dry bread. That should do the trick."

This morning Ruby is baking rolls and washing potatoes. Outside, sun is bright but air is cold. The wood stove has made the kitchen the best room in the house, full of the smells of food cooking. Emily will arrive any minute with her family. Ada and Margaret and Daisy will be here early. I am conscious of being an outsider, a virtual stranger among people who are old friends, although their manners are probably too kindly to remind me of it. I've chosen a plaid wool skirt and a sweater to wear, which would not be considered appropriate by the Family—it would be merely snappy in the East—but I fear I will be too swank for the occasion.

When ten people come through the kitchen door on each other's heels, I am safely ensconced in a corner from which I can see and hear and be ignored. Matt is carrying Ada, who waves and laughs, "Here I am...big as life." Which is big indeed. Ruby pulls the rocking chair into my corner and Matt places her carefully in it. I can see that part of my task is to keep Ada amused—I'm relieved to have her company. And her guidance: I do hope she'll warn me before I commit a *faux pas*.

Emily kisses Ruby's cheek—"Mama, another year." The men shake hands; the women tie on aprons. My attire is a touch foreign, but not *too* wildly so. Daisy comes to whisper, "I'm glad you're here."

Roger's mother, quite the prettiest older woman I have ever seen except for my mother, comes to our corner. "Ada, I can't tell you how glad I am to see you looking so well. You don't know how concerned we've all been."

"Thank you, Dora. You *always* look just lovely."

"And you're Jo, Emily has been telling me how glad they are you've come to live with Ruby." Having made our corner feel smug, she turns back to the work table and seems to know just what to do.

Ada whispers, "You can tell Roger's a rancher...hat line across his forehead...white above, brown below. Be there when he's eighty." Matt also has a hat line. I hadn't noticed before.

"Your real rancher...grew up in the business his daddy started...man I'd trust with anything...especially horses. Those boys grew up...in the saddle. Margaret says once Matt was only four... found him way out in the pasture lying sound asleep...back of an old horse. Seen it standing against a rail fence...climbed up and slid over...then it moved away and he couldn't get down. She says that's why he looks so comfortable on a horse...used to sleeping on one."

Luke leans against the table giving Emily the benefit of his charm, despite her bland reaction. He's as tall as Matt though not so rugged in appearance. The real difference between them is in the way they behave, in what comes from the inside. Luke is electricity barely controlled–I quite like the analogy.

He turns his head and smiles at me. "I'm ignoring our guest, the stranger that is within our gates."

He is so smooth, the way he crosses the few feet between us and crouches down to sit on his boot heels. "Mrs. Boren, we'll be neighbors until spring, and our families, so to speak, are close, and I am Friendly. Would you grant me the privilege of speaking to you by your first name?"

The bold thing! His older brother hasn't asked, and I've seen much more of *him*. In the grandmothers' New York it would be an impertinence. I am at a disadvantage, not knowing Western custom and not wanting to be an Eastern snob in front of everyone.

"I should hope all of you would." That seems a safe response. "Ruby and Daisy do. Please, as you said, consider me a friend of your family."

"I'll be happy to. A good friend and more than a friend. I look forward to our being better acquainted. Do you ride? Or would a spin in an old-fashioned buggy suit you instead?"

He is altogether too fast to suit my taste, Western or no. "We'll see how I feel when the weather warms again."

When he returns to the women around the cooking table, not to the woodpile where the other men are working, Ada taps my arm with her good hand and beckons me closer. "That Luke…all over the ladies like scum on a pond."

She catches me by surprise every time—obviously I don't think older people can still be funny, no credit to me. I laugh so loudly that Ruby and Margaret turn to look at us. Smiling at them, I lean toward Ada and whisper, "Do you suppose he practices in the mirror?"

"…tries it on his horse?"

In New York I wouldn't trust him with two pennies. Here in Arizona I don't know what to think. Oh my. I've had a rather limited exposure to the men.

They begin to carry in firewood to fill the box beside the stove and stack high near the parlor fireplace. Rose and Virginia have started to work their way through the piano rolls, and the men, going back and forth, sing along loudly, "Through the sycamores the candlelight is gleaming on the banks of the Wabash far away." Daisy seizes her brothers' hands as they go past and two-steps them to the door. I notice that Luke—who is not making many trips—uses footwork that is showy. Matt is more, how do I describe it, his dancing is honest as his face. When they have stocked both rooms, Roger comes in and hugs his wife and sings "Just cast a look in her direction. Oh me oh my, ain't that perfection?" into her cheek. She pinches flour onto his nose. Pies are ready to go into the oven, sitting in a row on the table. I watch Ruby and Margaret and Dora and Emily, wishing I could be so sure and easy at work preparing a holiday.

I'm not terribly good at drawing people, but I watch it all closely to remember it for a pencil sketch to send to my mother: "The View From My Corner of Ruby's Thanksgiving Kitchen." It will be about the goodness of Connections.

Ada's task is to keep *me* amused. "Daisy moves…sunlight on water…you should see Emily ride…prettiest thing. She has a mare she's trained…you'd think they were dancing. You know why? She never fell off. …you find out how hard the ground is…you get careful. Her girls ride…everybody does on a ranch."

I watch them and think of my big family in New York, arriving at the airless home of one grandmother or another for a holiday gathering. In my youth the food was German—goose and dumplings, strudel, the long tradition—prepared out of sight by cooks in some distant kitchen. Children were required to sit silent unless spoken to but were allowed to turn the pages of books while they tried to avoid the tension building in the parlor.

The adults could not leave one another alone. The year I was twelve Cousin Elizabeth was badgered and bullied because she was obviously in love with a perfectly nice young man who was a reporter for the *Times*. He was nearly penniless. His family had lost all their money. He had no business acumen. He had not attended a reputable college. He was obviously Inappropriate. I peeked up from the pages of my book to watch her face go from red to white. Finally her eyes looked dead. She married a man the family approved and became an invalid. I suppose it was her only escape.

Destruction is the easiest thing in the world. Still in my teens, I wondered whether my mother had been treated to such scenes. If there was a man she had loved once, she never mentioned it to me, but I could see there was no warmth in her marriage. I wonder whether it's possible for any of us to know our own parents. The family chose Nicky, and it was a crashing mistake, but my mother had no hand in it.

These Arizona people have something to do besides trying to rule one another, maybe that explains the comradely mood. Ada and I begin to sing too. "Now I ask you very confidentially, ain't she sweet?" Emily sings as she puts the pies into the oven. Daisy dances a tribute to them. It's too quaint really, too picturesque for words. I am quite taken by it all.

December, 1921

Dearest Jo,

I truly love your Thanksgiving kitchen sketch. It's better by far than a photo would have been: all the smells and music and cheerful bustle are there. What a flair you have for that kind of thing, all the better for being unexpected—you've always cared more for landscape, I've thought. I am overjoyed to see such talent in you.

I have decided to go to France in the spring. It is not entirely a coincidence. I have been thinking ever since you left of the fun we had in Paris when you were fourteen, also wondering what the war years have done to French painting, and when I read that Anatole France had won the Nobel for literature, it was simply too strong an impulse to resist. I come by such interest naturally—I was born the year of the Salon des Refuses, as I'm sure I've told you.

Oh, 1907 was an exciting time to be in Paris! Do you remember? England had just conceded France the right to be in Morocco, and there was a renewed interest in African masks and such. The restoration of Dreyfus had undermined even further the prestige of the Government and that meant the Academy's control of art. There was that wonderful retrospective of Cezanne's work, and the Steins had just bought a Matisse.

People were talking of startling changes in the canvases of Braque and Leger and Picasso—that painting of the girls of Avignon—and Duchamp's "Nude Descending a Staircase." Lyricism and charm, light and color were out, even the Impressionists had become passe, and the new Cubists were talking of form, of rigor in construction, escape from an order dominated by the past. The picture was suddenly an object itself, born of austerity and thought, not an imitation of anything else.

One's mind felt it had moved into a second birth, a future in which all things seemed possible. Your father had died two years earlier, if you'll recall, and I was on a trip that was intended to "assuage my grief" after the dutiful mourning. If the family had known what I was to find in Paris, I would have been held at home, I'm sure.

Such freedom, such rebellion! For a time every artist was undermining the foundation theories of every other artist, even their own theories. What a sensation it produced in America at the Armory Show in 1913. But then the war interrupted French life, and most of the painters were in the army or in England. Renoir and Degas died.

There are things to do here. There's talk of organizing a museum to acquire and display modern art, and I would like very much to participate. I can't bear not being in touch with France; I want to see for myself what they are doing. I do rather miss the color of the Fauves. In which direction are they all moving? Or are they all going in different directions?

I can't tell you how alive I feel at the thought that within a few months I will be standing before fresh paintings in studios in Paris, intoxicated by the smell of turpentine.

I'm on wings. Do rejoice for me, darling. Better yet, if you think you have recovered by then, come with me. It would be such fun to be in Paris with you, two women together sharing opinions.

Love,
Lilly

P.S I almost forgot: your cousin Paul is so grateful that you've given him permission to read your letters. They have been his only reality all month, he says. He is trying to draft something that might interest you but complains that his life is so dull by comparison that he can't think where to begin. Poor dear, I'm concerned about him, but I hesitate to interfere.

There's a maudlin poem that is much appreciated in Arizona.

> Out where the handclasp's a little stronger,
> Out where the smile dwells a little longer,
> That's where the West begins

It's too deliciously low-brow doggerel. At Brown's News Stand I bought Christmas cards that were printed with the lines and sent them off to New York to people who will think I'm being cleverly witty. No one will guess that I'm so awash in sentiment that I believe every word.

I am Up To My Ears in Christmas. It was the most sensuous of tribal rites for me from my first awareness, rich in sound and smell and taste and color, none of them available at any other season, ripe with meaning that comes only through the senses. None of my grandmothers could ever have known what magic their parlor decorations were, how they opened my spirit to the most intense fantasy.

All of this is dreadfully melodramatic, I know, and I would feel abject chagrin were I to reveal it to anyone. I reveled, I *wallowed*, in every nuance of the season. Because of the pageantry of that old northern European festival I learned all I knew of beauty. There was one fragile ornament that hung annually on Grandmother Scheffler's tannenbaum, perfectly round, a delicious deep pink, glittering with a golden tracery, that spoke to my little girl mind of love and goodness.

And all of that was *before* the gifts were presented. The books in their rich bindings, the dolls in their beautiful dresses, and one year a tiny flower of porcelain to wear on the finest of chains about my neck—nothing in this world can ever be such a fairyland again.

By the time I was fifteen, I could no longer find my way into that rapture, and I struggled in vain to re-capture it. For half of my life I've mourned it. Nothing that the city could offer, shop windows, bakery smells, music in lofty churches, nothing could provide the thrill. I thought Only the Innocence of Childhood, et cetera.

One must pass from receiving to giving! I know I'm not the first to discover such a banal truth, but that's what I've learned in this hardly-formed Western town, and Christmas is alive again. I've found that I love giving presents! The Family is full of people who say, "I would never use it," and hand back carefully-selected gifts. It's such a delight to think that won't happen here.

I've been on a spree. On the kitchen table I've poured through Ruby's catalogs searching for thrills to be delivered to the cousins' children: Lionel trains and Tinker Toys and Erector sets and Teddy Bears. There is actually such a creation as a Flossy Flirt doll with eyes that roll. How I laughed over that one—and then promptly ordered it sent to the little daughters of the cousins.

For the men I chose biographies of Henry Ford and Woodrow Wilson. For their almost-grown-up sons *Tarzan of the Apes* and Sabatini's *Scaramouche*. What fun! I hope the boys will have to hide to read them. The girls will be opening perfumed soap and books by Gene Stratton Porter, the women silk pongee bloomers and Zona Gale novels. Not one of them uplifting, I hope, just good stories. I've sent Edna Ferber to Gertrude; the two of them have much in common, if what I hear of Ferber's disposition is true.

For my mother I wanted something that would mean Arizona. "Ruby, she loves beautiful shapes and colors and designs. Is there anything created here, honest pieces done as honest art or craft, that a woman of discrimination would cherish?"

She looked thoughtful. "I don't know if I'd recommend the things most tourists buy. Let me see. There isn't time to go up to the trading posts for rugs. Babbitts might have something though. Oh, I know, I know just the thing. Nampeyo."

I was completely at sea. "What is Nampeyo?"

"Nampeyo is a Hopi woman from up on the mesas, the reservation, who makes the most beautiful jars and bowls and vases in the old-timey style in wonderful golden browns. She copies symbols on the pieces dug up by those science men. Or did, she's getting old now. She's famous though, very highly regarded. The Harvey company had her up at the Grand Canyon for a while demonstrating. We'll ask Matt if he knows where she is. Or Babbitts might have something she made. The shapes are very graceful."

"Perfect! Just what my mother would want. I don't know whether Nampeyo would be right for the grandmothers, but I can decide when I see."

Dennis came in one morning with a crate of items I had ordered for people here in town, and I've had delicious hours sitting on my bed and wrapping them. Sheep wool slippers for Ada and Margaret and Emily and even Dora, elaborate dolls for Emily's girls—I stroke their dresses and arrange the flounces—fleece-lined leather gloves for Matt and Luke and Roger and Dennis too. For Ruby I have warm slippers and piano rolls of "Beside a Garden Wall" and "Baby Face" and "If You Knew Susie."

I puzzled long over the catalogs trying to select a gift for Daisy. Since the day at Walnut Canyon I've seen no sign of distress on her face, but that one moment has haunted me. Perhaps books that might answer her questions about the world the daily trains come from: Mary Roberts Rinehart and Edith Wharton? Books have meant escape for me, but I don't know whether they hold such value for Daisy.

Finally I appealed to my mother for help, asking her to find for me in New York a pendant on a delicate chain like the treasure I once received for Christmas. This one should have a golden daisy on porcelain, hand-painted. It was the kind of request Mother cannot resist; she went right out to a jeweler and ordered exactly what I had in mind custom made. One of a kind. Since it arrived yesterday, I've been virtually crooning over it.

I am aglow in as many colors as an Arizona sunset with the fun of giving presents. When I read in the paper that for the second year food and clothing are to be distributed to families in need, momentum carried me completely overboard. I asked Dennis to go into Penney's to buy one winter coat in each size for boys and another full set for girls and deliver them anonymously to the Masonic Temple. Not only can I afford the expense, thanks to my father's will, I can't afford to miss the pleasure. That's not bleeding heart, honestly, it's pure selfishness. Take part, et cetera.

"Get the happiest colors you can," I urged, "but please don't tell who commissioned you."

"I b-b-b-bet they'll guess."

"Oh, Dennis, think of some way to keep it a secret. It would spoil everything if I were to receive praise."

"I'll send mmmm-my sister-in law. That woman is hard as old b-b-b-bread when it comes to secrets."

Of course, for a few days I was embarrassed about it, hoping it wasn't a stupid gesture. I don't really know anyone, not even a dozen people, and I'm isolated, playing Lady Bountiful out of a flush of tubercular intoxication. It's so easy to doubt oneself.

It wasn't until Dennis brought his sister-in-law's report of the excitement among the Masons as they discussed who should receive the coats that my spirits revived.

"Did they ask?"

"You b-b-bet."

"What did she say?"

"She said, 'Least said, soonest mended.'"

Today is Friday the 23rd. For three days early in the week there was snow mixed with rain, and Ruby and I spent all one stormy afternoon in Ada's kitchen with Margaret and Daisy, making old-fashioned fudge and fruit cake, and as Ada said, "having the *best* time." I can't think when I've laughed so much over nothing at all.

Dennis is coming soon to drive us to a little old church on south San Francisco Street to watch the community Christmas tree being set up. The idea came from the Women's Club, but the Forest Service selected and donated the tree. George Black's Lightning Delivery has brought it into town. It will truly be a community tree: Flagstaff Electric Light Company is providing illumination, merchants are donating tinsel and decorations, the Woman's Club will furnish bags of candy for the program that will begin at six o'clock on Christmas night.

In the newspaper editor Breen assures citizens it will be a "big get-together of the people," not a charity affair. All month school children have been learning songs and church choirs have been practicing; Professor Ridgley of the Normal School is preparing instrumental music. Rehearsals are being held all this week at the Orpheum Movie Theater. It's too quaintly old-fashioned for words, I love it. It's been at least two hundred years, maybe more, since New York was small enough for such an event.

Doctor Fronske and his wife have gone to St. Louis for the holidays. They have family there, of course, but how sad to miss all the fol-de-rol. Eli Giclas, who is in bed with the grippe, doubts he will be able to attend, but vows to get up for Christmas dinner. I'm so new to it all, to being *immersed* in pagan jollity, that nothing, no illness, not even coughing up blood, could keep me away.

Suddenly I'm crying. Who knows whether such a Christmas will ever be my lot again? This simply can't be normal, this quite insane up and down. I know I have a serious disease and I'm out here away from everything I've ever known, but something must be *wrong* with me. Alone in my room, I cry. Honestly, I'm such a dud.

*E*arly in January there was a heavy snow storm that downed electric light wires, a hardship for everyone—except old-timers who have lived here for years without electricity. A dozen autos were stranded on the road to a town called Williams, half a day's drive away when the road is bad. Travel was impossible in every direction, except on trains, of course. They were our only connection with The Outside World.

The *Sun* reported coasting on Observatory Hill and said that although there were some injuries, no one was maimed, a relief to all, I'm sure. The editor's whimsical view of events never fails. Ruby says he has been that way as long as she's known him, a dozen years at least.

However, in the falling snow a sixty-five-year-old man left town to walk ten miles or so to his cabin at Volunteer Canyon, lost his way, sat down against a tree and froze. Died alone, poor man. I didn't know him, but as Ada would say, I don't have to, do I?

After the storm, skies cleared but wind blew in a fury and temperatures dropped to below zero every night. The coldest was minus twenty, a record. Water pipes burst all over town. It was minus thirty-four at the base of the big mountain at the Experiment Station, where work is going on about trees, what makes them grow or something. The men have been excited about seedlings that are coming up all over the place. Swell for them, no doubt. Ruby said what a mercy, given the cold, that Mr. Pearson and his wife May had left the station for Albuquerque, and most of the scientists were gone.

I must admit, shameless romantic that I am, I liked the severe weather. Thanks to Matt and Roger, we had stacks of wood to keep a fire going in the old kitchen range. With drifts all around us, there was not much worry about water, although getting it took a good amount of time- Ruby said snow is mostly air and I learned by experience that she was right. We stepped out the door and scooped up a pan full, brought it in to melt down into almost nothing, kept at it all day, and managed to get by until our pipes could be repaired.

Pressed into squares, snow served in the ice box near the back door. Last summer we needed a delivery twice a week from the Babbitt ice house; this winter we barely need to empty the drip pan.

It felt good to be in the kitchen, cozy and *sheltered*. One thing I've learned in Arizona is how luxurious it can feel not to be dashing about all the time. Using snow pleased me no end, I felt like a pioneer. Ruby said that in Arizona you soon learn to make use of water in any form you can get it, you don't know when it might disappear on you. She'd lived too many years without city pipes to rely on them.

Dennis had his taxi in for repairs at the Babbitt garage, which is the Ford dealership, but we phoned orders for what we needed and markets delivered groceries by sleigh—on credit, of course, Ruby pays her bill twice a month. It was a comfort to know that a few blocks away Ada was safe with Margaret and Matt and Daisy; food was being delivered there too.

Every day or so, we called to inquire about them. That is, Ruby called on the phone that was attached next to the door on the kitchen wall; I listened to her end of the conversation. When she had hung up, she told me what had been said.

"Margaret's worried about Luke. He never came home last night, and in all this snow, she's afraid he got caught out somewhere. Matt's gone now to see if he can find his brother. It does seem hard on her."

As we heard the story, Matt brought Luke home drunk, and neither one would say where he had been or with whom or where he had found the whiskey. Margaret said it was good of the boys not to tell if the truth would have worried her all over again, but it didn't help a whole lot. Next she knew he might be arrested. Ruby said your child is always your child, no matter how old, and you can't help but care. I wouldn't know from experience, but I wondered whether my mother would agree. If she worries, she doesn't, as Ruby would say, *pester* me with it.

Of course Daisy made us laugh. You'd have thought she considered it her job to cheer everyone up. "Drifts are so deep, I'm thinking of making a slide from my bedroom window. What do you suppose Editor Breen would say? Imagine if all the neighbors did it and everywhere you looked there were grown women shooting out of upstairs windows and whooshing away."

Ruby and I decided we weren't quite up to so much fun, but we'd be happy to come over and cheer Daisy on. I wish I could be more like her: make the day sunny for everyone around me. Despite the furnace, our bedrooms were too cold to linger in and the parlor was so chilly we weren't interested in playing the piano. We lived in the big old kitchen, dashed for it in the morning carrying our clothes. Ruby taught me to bake cookies and finally a pie—I was ridiculously proud. Sometimes while she knitted, I read aloud from Mary Roberts Rinehart, whose latest book was selling well.

Ruby said since Mrs. Rinehart was famous she guessed it was time to become acquainted, and it was my opinion she would be a more entertaining author than the Sinclair Lewis novel *Babbitt* or Harold Bell Wright's latest sentimental opus. I had bought *Tish* and *The Circular Staircase* before the storm began.

"I've read them both, Ruby, and I'm dying to do them out loud. I think you'll like them. *The Staircase* is the latest craze, a mystery; it has a secret room, noises in the night, a midnight expedition to a cemetery, a veiled lady and two men in disguise, six corpses, and lots of fainting and restorative cups of tea."

"Goodness, it sounds rousing enough to get me through turning the heels on a dozen pair of socks. Read away."

I had whooping fun doing it, you can *act* a Rinehart book, and Ruby said it was better than a movie to hear me. She laughed out loud at the Tish stories—a fifty-year-old maiden aunt with surprising "enthusiasms." I could barely get the words out while I was reading about Tish driving a racing car: trying to find out how the gears worked, she side-swiped another car and threw it off the field, skidded off the track, turned completely round twice, threw a tire— and bumped home the winner, with the end of her tongue nearly bitten off. Ruby had to put down her knitting and wipe her eyes, she laughed so hard.

Tish was Ruby's kind of person. Reading to her I discovered how much I like women of any age who can laugh. For the past year I've been learning nice old cliches like that, so proud about it I've beamed like a simpleton.

To avoid boredom, we strove for variety in our kitchen routine. Ruby told me stories. "There never was a train through most of Arizona when I was a girl. I remember the first one I saw, I was twenty by then. My husband heard the A & P tracks had been built past the south side of the Peaks, and that would make it easier to ship cattle out to market. Nothing would do but we had to come up here and homestead. Land free for the working on it, he said.

"Everything we owned was in our buckboard. We finally got up from the Verde Valley and stopped out yon in the cedars to make camp for the night, with a canvas draped over a rope and pegged down so we could sleep under it. Next morning I raised on my elbows and looked out. Why, there was a train going by not far away! My first train—I laid there and watched till it was out of sight and thought I'd never seen anything so powerful that looked so puny under the sky."

My life was not nearly so full of events as hers, so I told her about Cousin Lillian. "Almost every summer for nine years she's traveled with Zane Grey, part of groups he put together, with a chef and even a valet, I'm told. Friends and relatives and secretaries. Guides. He travels too often, the grandmothers say, and what is he running from? Cousin Gertrude says it's an obsession, but Gertrude is a fan of the new psychology, and we all tend to ignore her, she can be such a bore about it.

"Grey goes to Florida or Catalina Island for the fishing—*drags* Lillian and her little sister and her cousin Elma along according to the family but leaves his wife at home. There's a good deal of unkind speculation about that. Usually he's been in Arizona for part of April. You have no idea how the stories have circulated—Lillian is going on a horse into a Howling Wilderness, Lillian had gone into a place no white woman had ever been before, Lillian was in mortal danger daily because of *That Man*. The first four years she came back to the city with stacks of watercolors, and there was a good deal of clucking and tisking over them but not much envy, at least from the older generation. We younger cousins didn't say what we were thinking—that we wished we could go too."

Ruby could knit without looking at what her fingers were doing. "I would have wanted to go when I was young. Your cousin doesn't travel with him now?"

"Sometimes. Just before the war she moved to Arizona to live year around, much to the alarm of the aunts and grandmothers. I think she's been painting down on the desert. She married a man no one knew a thing about, that was another outrage. But I've heard she still travels with Grey in the summer, all over northern Arizona. I don't know where she is. Maybe she's heard I'm here, maybe not. I suppose I could write to Cousin Lina and ask."

One windy morning when sunlight was bright on the snow outside the windows, Luke knocked on the back door and came in smiling like a salesman. "Aunt Ruby, you look younger every day."

"I do not. You must be losing your eyesight."

You'd have thought he didn't hear her. "Jo, there you are, lovely as ever. Did anyone tell you Aunt Ruby was our nearest neighbor out on the ranch? I practically grew up on her cookies." He took my book away from me and tossed it onto the table so he could take both my hands. "I can see her cooking has put roses in your cheeks."

If my face was red, it was because I was in a sudden huff. He was intense, I had to admit, and a woman finds that attractive. He looked straight into my eyes rather than off to one side. But he was obviously playing a part that he expected me to fall for. I am not sixteen any more, I know better than to be taken in. Did he think I was stupid?

I pulled my hands away with some difficulty and folded them in my lap. I did *not* simper or giggle for him. "I hadn't noticed."

He knelt beside my chair. "I've come to take you away for a dash across the country. Sun is shining. I have a sleigh and horses waiting at the livery stable and a brand new blanket from Switzer's to wrap you in. I promise to keep you close to me, warm and safe. Get your coat and hat, and I'll be back in two shakes. When you hear the bells, come running out."

His presumption was insulting, I was so angry I could not speak. Run out? *Oh!*

Ruby came to stand beside me. "She isn't well, Luke, and shouldn't be out in this icy air. Treat another woman to a ride in your sleigh."

He didn't seem in the least rebuffed. "When the weather is warmer then, Jo." He stood up smiling, graceful. "I'll look forward to it. Aunt Ruby, good to see you looking so chipper."

When the door had closed behind him and he'd gone off whistling to the gate, Ruby snorted. "I swear I don't know about Luke anymore. He was the sunniest little boy you ever saw. Now I hardly know him, the way he acts. He never learned it at home. His family's as good as any I've ever met, all of them nice as if they were split from the same piece of kindling. You'd have liked his father."

"I like the *rest* of them." The wonderful security of the big old kitchen felt fragile for the first time. Damn Luke and his invasion. The oily insult in his manner sullied me—I wanted to wipe it off.

"It's like something went wrong with him back about the time he was twelve or so. But likely he won't bother us after a few more weeks. Soon as spring comes, he'll be gone again. When there's work to be done out at the ranch, he'll be out of here fast as a dog can lick a dish."

February, 1922

Dear Mother,

Your invitation to go with you to Paris has thrown me into a quandary. Every day I'm of a different mood about it. It seems to me a major decision—and perhaps it is. Please forgive me for taking so long to answer.

There are reasons for and against. Flagstaff is not without painters, they come through often in pursuit of scenery. A few amateurs live here and offer lessons and paint when they have the time. But there is no sense in the community that art matters, none of the excitement that seems part of the very air in Manhattan. No museums, not a single gallery—no place one can go to see paintings or hear ideas. I feel an isolation that goes beyond being ill, as an artist, that is.

I would love to go with you. Of course I remember Paris in 1907—how could I forget the stimulus on every street, the passionate interest? Paris was the beginning of my desire to paint; whether it was art itself or the enthusiasm surrounding it I'm not sure. Ever since, I've tried to recapture the initial ecstasy. I wonder whether it's possible to feel so excited about painting any place but Paris.

I am deeply touched by your acceptance of me as another woman, not as a subordinate, a child. Your statement that it would be fun to be there with me and share opinions reduced me to awe: given the atmosphere of hierarchy within the family, you are indeed the rarest of mothers. I hope the compliment doesn't make you uncomfortable.

For months I've been considering the possibility of moving to Los Angeles or Santa Fe to see other aspects of the Western Frontier, also to be closer to art and music than I am here. But at the moment I'm in the middle of unfinished stories and unripe friendships, and I resist departing until I learn how they turn out. I realize that means I've come to care about a handful of people who of course don't have the claim on my loyalty that you do. Nevertheless, what happens to them seems important to me.

Flagstaff and the people I've met seem to be good for me. My health and general well-being have improved marvelously in the past year. However, Doctor Fronske thinks that I have not yet conquered beyond doubt the t.b. bacillus. There are still symptoms—chronic fatigue and lassitude, an occasional bout of coughing, rapid mood swings—and he questions whether a return to the heavier air at sea level and the contagion that flourishes in crowded cities would be advisable. He has sent a sample of my sputum to Phoenix for an analysis by chemists there.

Oh dear, what should I choose to do? Either way I will probably lose an opportunity.

I've decided that my health is the strongest argument, and I hope you'll understand that, much as I'm torn between polar opposites, it would be best for me to remain in Arizona a while longer. At least, that's today's decision. What is the date beyond which I can't change my mind?

Speaking of people, Daisy's daisy, the pendant you commissioned, couldn't have been more successful. She wears it always nestled into the hollow of her throat; I see her fingers reach to touch it often, as if she finds pleasure or comfort in knowing it's there. I like to see that little flower: it enhances her face and reminds me of your excellent taste. I do wish you could meet Daisy and the people I know here, I fancy you'd find them as fascinating as I do.

I am confident that Paul would think so too. I've still had no letter from him, but my sympathy goes to the man who was always my favorite cousin. He should simply get on the train and come out here.

Love,
Jo

*A*da is slowly recovering from her "ischemic incident." Her right arm works almost as well as it did before, although her face is still slightly asymmetrical. She can move herself from bed to chair, from one chair to another if they aren't too far apart. There's still a problem with walking because of the injury to her leg years ago—she says she's awkward as a cow on ice. Perhaps that too will improve as the weeks go by. Dr. Raymond says we can expect another incident, perhaps serious enough to kill her, though he can't be sure. We are concerned about her, we do everything that might be helpful, and we look at each other and wait. Waiting is not a strategy I would recommend to the Faint of Heart.

Meanwhile: the latest from the "wide-awake" little town of Flagstaff—that's what it likes to call itself. I don't consider it gossip, most of it, more like the kind of interest I would feel for the characters in a book. Gossip implies relish for the worst, doesn't it? I don't want to harm anyone, except perhaps Luke, and that's more a case of wishing he would go away and stay away.

It seems citizens with some go and pep are ordering parts to build radios. I don't know whether wide-awake includes moonshine whiskey, but moonshine is in the neighborhood. I read that Congress is debating Prohibition again—it's definitely an item out here. One cold day in January City Marshall Neil and "night sticker" Dave Joy raided a south side house that had been selling booze for thirty cents a drink and found a ten gallon still wrapped in burlap and hidden in a *tree*. The mash was located buried in a manure pile. Isn't that too priceless for words?

Doctor Fronske was not available to patients for a few days in late January: he was operated on in the logging company's Mercy Hospital—what a name!—for appendicitis. Remembering the rancher who died last summer, I was apprehensive to hear that nothing could be done until a telegram to Phoenix had brought Dr. Payne Palmer up on a train.

Dr. Raymond, the man who tended Ada when she had her stroke, was available but I suppose he hesitated to proceed alone. He is another person who came to Flagstaff with a case of tuberculosis, nearly twenty years ago Ruby says. He seems to be completely cured, or at least arrested. Apparently some don't recover, but enough do.

As soon as Dr. Fronske was up and about, we had what locals are calling The Biggest Storm Since 1916, three feet of light, fluffy snow in two days. Drifts werc ten feet high, temperatures well below zero. For two weeks Dennis drove a sleigh to provide taxi service.

After an eight-horse team pulling a makeshift plow cleared the middle of the streets, Matt rode across town to shovel us out. I did my part: I stood at the window admiring the way his body moves. But wind promptly filled his trenches and he had to do the job several times.

I've been here a year now. In many ways I wouldn't trade the experience for anything, but despite my decision to stay on, with every week I am reminded that I simply don't understand Western culture. We speak the same language—almost—and we have the same government, the same holidays and all that, but there are definitely differences, some of which I probably haven't noticed. I hesitate to express an opinion for fear I'll be violating some invisible convention, accepted and never thought about.

For example, the matter of killing animals—I do not understand the attraction for the men of shooting every wild creature they can find. They're so *proud* of it, every man who is anybody has several guns. Deer "season" is past, but it seems there's no end to hunting mountain lion; a female "six feet from lip to tip" was shot near Turkey Tank in January, another in early February near Williams by a fourteen-year-old boy who had only his dog for help. A government game hunter has killed all of eight lions recently. The other men heap praise on such great hunters; women and children admire them. Lions are dangerous animals, they all say, to humans and livestock, to civilization itself is the implication. Perhaps so, but I sense a thrill in the killing that goes well beyond the purely practical. Sometimes I feel as if I'm in the outer reaches of Timbuktu.

When the paper carried the news that reporter Nellie Bly had died of pneumonia, quite young, only fifty-four, I waited for Ruby's reaction. It seemed ironic to me that a woman who made the swiftest-ever solo trip around the world and conducted so many crusades for social reform was mortal like the rest of us.

Ruby was a pioneer in this country, with all the courage and work and hardship that went with it, and her friends were women whose daily lives were very nearly heroic in my opinion. To her, Nellie Bly was no Freak of Nature, merely a woman who could of course do brave, difficult things as well as most men. "All it took was grit," was what she said, "not muscle."

She was more interested in talking about the Supreme Court's rejection of the past when it upheld—unanimously!—the woman suffrage amendment. "It used to make me mad as a hornet that I could work a roundup and a branding, stick as long in the saddle as my husband, churn the butter and cook the meals and do the wash all the time in the family way, figure out the income tax when that came in as a law, but I wasn't thought smart enough or strong enough to vote. It never did seem fair to me." Knowing her is an education I could never have had in the city.

We aren't entirely benighted out here in the Wild and Wooly. We can't go downtown to see Fred and Adele Astaire or Al Jolson or Will Rogers, but within two weeks in February I could have seen Nazimova and Valentino in "Camille" or what was billed as The World's Greatest Motion Picture which cost—gasp!—over a million dollars to film: "The Four Horsemen of the Apocalypse," again with Valentino. An Italian immigrant, he was reported to feel that the part, an Argentine famed as a dancer of the tango, would make his reputation. I gather it has done so quite effectively. "Brooding emotion" is what critics are saying. My!

I say "could have seen." Ruby and I discussed reserving seats at the Orpheum for a matinee, but it was so cold and so much flu was going around that church attendance was down. We decided to stay home and entertain ourselves in the kitchen. "Make winter last a little longer," as Ruby said. "Soon it will be too hot to bake. Want to try a chocolate cake this afternoon?"

Every newspaper brought topics we could examine. Big Issues: paving the town streets, building a dam across the Colorado River in Boulder Canyon—Hoover and the river commission are due to visit— even the "open door" policy in China that Secretary Hughes wants. Ruby says she likes to "get down to brass tacks" on things. I'm not sure what that means, but I discover I like it too, as Ruby does it.

Sandy Donahue, the saloon owner who used to be such a favorite in the town and now is "down on his luck," has been suing Babbitt Brothers. If I understand the outline, they loaned him over seven thousand dollars because he was in debt and took deeds to his hotel when he didn't repay after several extensions. He wanted the action declared a mortgage so that he could redeem his property, and they refused, and he sued. In December a jury found for Sandy; in February a judge in Phoenix reversed the decision.

Both of us felt sympathy for Sandy, as the jury no doubt did. We hated to see a man who had been good to people lose everything, it didn't seem right. But he had been drunk a good part of the past few years, Ruby said, when he should have been tending to business. The Babbitts had been more than fair, and it wouldn't do the town any good for them to go under too. That was what was important to her: how the town would be affected. "Business has its rules, all big human affairs do, and Sandy should have known them."

We spent all one afternoon debating. I must say Ruby could keep a lawyer on his toes, she sees issues so clearly, but her heart is with what she calls "moral justice." We finally decided Social Order must be served, and we felt terrible about it.

One morning our phone call to Ada's house put us into the middle of a fuss that was going on over there. Luke had indeed found someone else to ride in his sleigh: his sister. It seems that at first light the day before he drove her at a fast pace seven miles out to Rogers Lake where he met some men who loaded boxes of something onto the back, and they barely got home by dark. Margaret said Daisy was near frozen and about to cry. Matt was being closed-mouth and grim, and she suspected Luke was transporting moonshine into town and wanted a woman along to make him look respectable. What a rotter.

He had gone off with his boxes the minute he had Daisy home, and he had not come back. They were all upset that he would use her, as Ada put it, "just to save his own worthless skin—he's about as attractive as a dead toad." Ruby agreed. "You don't put your family in danger, not if you're a good man. I swear I don't know what will happen to him, I feel just plain sad about it." There was nothing we could do except wait and see.

We passed the time as best we could. Zane Grey's latest book, *To the Last Man*, is about a feud thirty-eight years ago in Pleasant Valley fifty-some miles south of here. The Phoenix paper criticized it as inaccurate. Actually, the language was "got it wrong," "dust but not sand," "yanked it all out of shape." Mr. Grey is "a tenderfoot"—rather painful criticism for a writer who seems to pride himself on telling the West as it is.

When Dennis came by with my morning milk, we asked him to look in at the stationery store on Railroad Avenue and see whether there was a copy of *To the Last Man* for sale. He came back with one that afternoon, and we settled down to decide for ourselves.

It was my first Zane Grey novel. He said in the Foreword that life without idealism is not worth living, and he did write a rancher who told his son, "You're on the side of justice and right. Knowin' that, a man can fight a hundred times harder than he who knows he is a liar an' a thief."

But half the book is a love story and Ruby said the other half was about no Arizona people *she* ever knew. They talked like somewhere else. "Ah, now, yu'all cain't come thet on me. Ain't y'u an Injun? Ain't y'u a hoss tracker thet rustlers cain't fool? Ain't y'u a plumb dead shot? Ain't y'u wuss'ern a grizzly bear in a rough-an'-tumble?" It was fun to read aloud once I got used to hamming it up, and I made Ruby laugh. But I was embarrassed that an Easterner...

I suppose I'm an awful snob—I kept thinking, "Why didn't Cousin Lina edit such stilted lines out? He must have convinced her that Westerners really sound this way." I doubted that the best either of them could write would ever be Deathless Literature. Honestly!

After we had finished the last page, Ruby sighed and said, "No, he didn't get it right, like the paper said, but he wasn't trying to so you can't hold that against him. He was telling an entertaining story not writing a history book. I wish he hadn't made all the sheepmen drunken villains and called them the Hash Knife Gang, which wasn't true at all, and named the worst of them Daggs, who was a real man that I used to know. My folks were always cattle people, but I don't think he should have made the ranchers so good and noble. Way I heard the story was the cattlemen did the first killing. Still, I suppose you can't expect a novel to be true to the facts. True to life, maybe, but not true to the facts." The woman is amazing. Alexander Woolcott never in his life wrote a critique that tried so to be fair.

*E*arly March—wind is still bitter cold, but most of the snow has melted. Daisy phones to say that she and Matt are coming for a visit, just a couple of hours, if it's all right with us. They have a surprise, and we'll never guess. We doubt it has anything to do with Luke, he's living in a room at the Commercial Hotel as if he had all the money in the world. One can't help suspecting Ill-Gotten Gains.

Ten minutes later their Tin Lizzie stops at the back gate and Matt steps out. Daisy doesn't wait for him to open her door, she rushes up the walk and into the kitchen. "Jo! The most wonderful thing! Matt has a Nampeyo bowl for you!"

He cleans mud from his boots before he comes in, carrying something in his hand. "It's just a little one, one of the first she did in the old style. Not as big as the bowl you bought for your mother, but I thought you might like to have it."

She squeezes his arm. "Oh, he's so modest. You'd think he just found it somewhere."

Ruby takes the little bowl into her hands. "Why Matt, this is very nice. I should think it would be even more valuable than the newer ones. The Harvey Company would be glad to have it."

"I don't know. It was given to me as payment for services."

Daisy hugs me. "I haven't seen you for days. You know what he did? Back when the snow was melting, he went out to the ranch on his horse to see if everything was all right and how the overwinter cows were doing, and there were the Olsons in their old wagon trying to get into town with a sick baby, stuck in mud up to the axle. He spent hours helping them dig out and then brought the baby into town himself, wrapped in a blanket, holding it against his chest with one arm, because he could get it to Mercy Hospital sooner on his horse than that muddy old wagon could. I could cry, he's so wonderful." She smiles at him like a sunrise.

"That was a mighty sick baby, Mrs. Olson sure hated to hand him over. But he pulled through. Jim Olson came by last evening with this little bowl and wanted to give it to me for thanks."

Daisy clearly loves him, it's a joy to see. "He didn't want to take it."

"I don't need to be paid for a thing like that. Anybody'd have done the same."

"But Mr Olson insisted. He said he knew it was worth something, his father had traded for it years ago, but to them their baby was worth more, and he was in Matt's debt."

"Thing like that might get broken if you left it with a cowboy like me. I told him I'd put it in the keeping of someone who'd give it proper care."

Daisy is fairly bouncing. "That's *you*! We're all so proud of him."

"Oh, now." He gives me one of his nice smiles. "It wasn't all that much." The man is too good to be real, he must have come out of a book.

I cup my hands around the curve of the bowl, loving the way it feels against my skin, smooth and earthy, loving the golden color and the brown designs. "Matt, I'll be the caretaker, I can do that. But something like this belongs where it was earned. No matter how long I have it, it will always be yours."

Ruby puts her arm around my shoulder. "Handsomely said, Jo."

Daisy hugs Matt. "She's matched you."

So here we are, Awash in Sentiment, and nothing can be done except to pour coffee all around and uncover my most recent chocolate cake, which is received solemnly by Matt and praised fulsomely by Daisy. You'd think I invented motion pictures, she's so pleased with me.

"Guess what else, Jo. Matt has a friend he knows from when they were in the cavalry in France. The only man I know who's as good as my big brother."

Ruby has taken up her knitting. "That's Lewis Smith's oldest son?"

Matt takes another piece of cake—very gratifying. "The same, Jess Smith, out Kayenta way, works trips for John Wetherill."

"Maybe your cousin knows him, Jo." That brought my mind to a focus.

"He and his father have bought a flock of sheep thinking grass might be good after the winter we've had."

Daisy takes another piece of cake. "Matt's going to help them move the sheep. But when he gets back, it'll be time to go out to the ranch, if there aren't any heavy spring snows. Mama says to ask you politely if you'll come for a couple of weeks to stay with us before we bring the cattle on and the real work starts. You can sleep with me. If the weather's good, we'll take you to Wupatki. I hope you feel like saying yes."

Well! It sounds like the kind of adventure people come west hoping to have. Ruby is smiling at me. "It's a rare opportunity, Jo." I don't need to ask Dr. Fronske whether he thinks I should. I don't even say we'll see how I feel in a month or so. I say yes.

Daisy hugs me again. "Yay! We'll have the best time. Do you ride?"

"Ride?"

"A horse." Her face is suddenly cautious.

"Not yet."

"Yay!" She claps her hands. "Isn't she wonderful, Matt? Not *yet*! Give us a chance and I bet a cookie we'll make a Westerner of her."

Paris
March, 1922

Dear Jo,

At the risk of disappointing you, I am about to make a thoroughly banal remark. I hope I can trust you not to think, as your set would say, I've gone daffy.

Nothing is as it used to be! That's probably been true through all of human history, of course, and a cataclysm like the Great War—all the horror, the pointless death—was bound to change France. I'm embarrassed that I came over expecting Paris to be exactly as I remembered it, and I mourn the city I knew as a young woman. Or is it the young woman I was that I mourn? Who knows?

Even my ship, the Olympic, was different in subtle ways, furnishings, food, service. It seemed to me that the tableware had lost its luster. But Madame Curie sailed on the Olympic last year when she returned from her America tour, and I trusted Madame's two Nobel prizes. I should have remembered that intellectual achievement is no guarantee of taste. Not that the ship is inferior, don't misunderstand me. I should not hesitate to recommend it to someone who did not travel in the grand old days.

By the way, Madame has just been elected to the Academy of Medicine, the first woman to be so honored. Or is it the Academy of Science? One took her in and one refused to do so. I can't remember which is which, but it probably doesn't matter—French society has always been critical. Consider this example: there is a dance craze here, jazz, and tango music which everyone is wild about, and the old men carp that it detracts from postwar rebuilding. They seem to think everyone should be working. I'm glad to see that someone is enjoying life. The Russians are not: the town is full of aristocrats who have been stripped of rank and money.

About recent French art my reaction is a sense of dreadful loss. If I can judge by the paintings which I've seen, something bleak happened to the country's spirit during the war, although I'll concede that it just might be my spirit that is diminished. Well, naturally something bleak happened. But how in the nine years since the Armory Show could color and exuberance so thoroughly have disappeared? I have not visited all the ateliers, but every canvas I have seen is black and grey and ocher.

Except for American tourists, few people have money to buy paintings. I do resist the implication that art can flourish only in an ebullient economy, that art and money are connected, it seems so crass. That proves me the most hopeless idealist, I suppose. How long can a painter with no income survive with vision unless there is a market?

And there is barely a market. Durand-Ruel, the dealer who took up the cause of the Impressionists, and Vollard, who promoted Cezanne and Gaugin, are no longer influential. The redoubtable Kahnweiler— Picasso, Gris, Braque—has been virtually destroyed by government seizure and liquidation of his stock; he is German, you know, thus by strange reasoning, not a proper French dealer.

The Impressionists created a revolution of light, of beauty; I remember standing before them with every nerve thrilling. Life was suddenly wonderful. Then color for its own sake made art the most exciting of all experiences—Vlaminck and Derain and Vuillard and Utrillo and of course Matisse, so hungry for pure color—oh, they did make me feel alive. I came to Paris this time hoping, longing for a renewal of that ferment in my mind.

Freedom is in the air—freedom for American and English expatriates. The city is as warm with women writers, photographers, publishers, bookshop owners of all nationalities who have no husbands or children to hamper them. The American Romaine Brooks is finally a success after she fought through her youth to achieve it.

But Modigliani has died. Dufy is doing fabrics, Leger and Duchamp machines. Soutine's work is all writhing ugly colors and twisted red faces. Roualt lays a wide brutal band of black around every form. He has for years, of course, but somehow it seems more ominous now. Braque and Picasso are wealthy, no longer on the barricades—I cannot determine whether anyone is. Gris is ill and discouraged, Matisse somewhere on the Riviera. Gertrude Stein, who covered her walls with those wonderful Cezannes, is now living quietly. When Dada broke up last year, Picabia— remember how Stieglitz promoted him?—sneered his contempt for painting and those who respect it. The Independent Salon has barred his work.

It's so dismal, so disillusioned, I could cry. It will soon be April in Paris, and there is no lyricism, no spontaneity, no sheen. Art is a casualty of modern war. In growing despair, I've pursued a phantom through the galleries. *Was it only myself, young and impressionable, and my capacity to respond has worn away with age? It can't be true: in New York art seemed a cause worthy of dedication.*

Is Europe too worn out and wounded to produce art that Americans can look to for guidance? It occurs to me that leadership may have passed from the battle-scarred old world to the exuberant new one. Have you read anything of Mencken's? His claim for an American language distinct from England's and producing a distinct literature—that might apply to painting as well. Have we begun to paint in our own language?

I find I'm anticipating a return to New York to test my questions. It would be too ironic to have come all this way to learn appreciation of the art of my own country.

Love,
Lilly

P.S. Have you read Katherine Mansfield? I'm told she is here in France, desperately ill with tuberculosis, apparently having received no benefit at all from a sanitarium in Switzerland. It was wise of you, dear, to resist your grandmothers and choose Arizona.

On Monday two feet of snow fell out of a sky that was uniform grey above our little town. Snow continued to fall all week, and Ruby and I went on with cooking lessons in the warm kitchen. "What do you think, Jo? I'd say it's time you baked us a loaf of bread. You don't mind getting right in with your hands, do you? Bread dough just has to be kneaded if it's to come out right."

I tied on the apron that had come to be recognized as mine, feeling quite picturesque in it. In the East I had grown up in, the only people who wore aprons were servants. "Goodness but I'm learning to be useful. You must think I've been a complete dud all my life."

"Why Jo, I don't know how you could say that. You've brought the whole world into this house. Told me about things I never had time for, books and paintings and a kind of people I've never met, like your mother in Paris, France. I say the two sides ought to go together, but we've neither one of us had the chance, that's all."

"Oh, Ruby." I touched her arm and then, though my head was no higher than her shoulder, wrapped my arms around her narrow old waist. "You're the wisest person in the world. I love you, I truly do."

She pulled me close against her apron. "And I love you, Jo. I don't know what I'd have done without you this past year. I'd have been most as lonesome as Ada."

"It hadn't occurred to me that I might be giving anything to you, you've given me so much." I rested my head against her and tried not to cry.

"Well, of course you have. And you weren't even doing it on purpose."

We both laughed at that and moved apart, and I patted my eyes dry. "To do good without trying to—that's a new idea."

"The best kind of good, it seems to me. Now if you can learn to bake a decent loaf of bread, you'll be just about perfect. Ready?"

That big kitchen was my whole reality for weeks, but I didn't feel confined at all. Cold burned my lungs if I so much as stood in the open doorway, and I tried to hold my breath when I went out to scoop up another pan of snow. Though flu was finally letting up, Ed and Ray Babbitt were sick, so the *Sun* reported. Also Mr. and Mrs. Eli Giclas and their son Henry. A man whom the paper actually referred to as Skinny Jones had pneumonia. I was overjoyed not to have to be in society, to have refuge in Ruby's kitchen and her friendly company instead. Away with Society—I snap my fingers at it.

Dennis came by with papers and milk. The grocer's boy carried food from the delivery truck. Matt stopped in every day or so to inquire about our well-being and sample my latest efforts at cooking, so solemn in his approval that I blushed. To think I would feel pride in such a homely success as biscuits and gravy.

On Friday, Daisy arrived with snow flakes in her hair and, as Ruby said, roses in her cheeks. She said, "I saw that new-fangled snow plow down the street. It's plowing snow like anything," but there was none of the usual bounce in her voice.

Just inside the door she unwound a purple scarf from her neck and sat down to pull off her boots. "It's so good to have a wonderful place like this as an excuse to get out. Gloom is thick over on the other side of town."

Ruby hung Daisy's heavy coat on a peg. "Something's wrong?"

"It's Luke again. I could kill him the way he keeps Mama torn up. He came in this morning charming as you please and tried to get money from her. He knows what she's got has to see us through to the end of summer when we sell the cows, but he doesn't care." Tears flooded her eyes. "He's the most selfish person, all he thinks of is himself. A buzzard is nicer."

"Oh, Daisy." I rushed to her without a thought of decorum and put my arms around her. I don't know what good I thought *that* would do, it probably made me feel better than it did her.

She put her wet cheek against mine. "He looked around as if he was trying to see something he could take and sell."

Ruby put her arms around both of us. What a melodrama we made, like an opera, but Daisy's usually sunny face wet with tears was so tragic. Damn that wretched Luke, how could he?

"We don't know what kind of trouble he's in, gambling or women or bootlegging or who knows what. But with this slump, we have barely enough to take care of ourselves. Oh, Aunt Ruby, what if we...what if...Homestead Relinquishment..." She fairly moaned.

"Now, it won't come to that. Matt's too good a man to let the ranch go, you know he is. He's strong as a government mule. Your mother's too experienced."

"There are farms and ranches all over the place where people are trying to sell." It was true, I had seen them advertised in the *Sun*, For Sale Cheap. "They're talking of buying old John Clark's farm to build a high school, and his brother Asa is blind and can't help."

Ruby's very voice was a comfort. "Are you folks in debt?"

"No." Daisy pulled back and wiped tears away with her fingers. "No loans. No mortgages, thank goodness. With all this snow, grass should be up soon."

"This week's weather alone will be worth a fortune." Ruby handed her a scrap of cloth for blowing her nose, and another to me. "Good times look to be coming back—the saw mill's open already. I know last summer was so dry gardens couldn't be watered, but the range'll be in good condition this spring. You'll come through sure as home to the barn."

Daisy laughed at me, laughed with tears running down her cheeks. "Jo, look at you, you're crying too. Are you selling *your* farm?"

I was ashamed of myself. Some comforter. "Oh, I cry at every little thing lately. I'm a sap."

She reached out to brush at my tears. "I shouldn't have let go like that. It's Luke really. He scares me. It's awful when you can't trust somebody in your own family. Mama looks sick with worry, and Ada's mad as a little rooster sitting there in her chair, and when Matt heard about it he went off downtown with his face so hard and grim I hardly recognized him. What if he gets into a fight with Luke and his friends?"

Ruby's face looked hard too. "I'd put my money on Matt. But it isn't easy to wait and wonder, is it? I'm glad you came over here. Can I pour you a cup of coffee? There's good thick cream to go with it."

Later I stood at the window and watched Daisy trudge away down the street, her purple scarf the only color in the scene. "Ruby, is it really a serious problem, do you think?"

"The ranch or Luke?"

"Both."

"Ranching is always a gamble—water and grass and prices and disease and accident, every time you turn around there's something that could ruin you, and hard work's not enough. You hope good years will see you through bad ones. Of course it's serious, it's always serious. But I have confidence in Matt. The thing is, Luke could do something that will draw his brother in. Luke's the big problem, I think. It's lucky his father left everything to Margaret, he'd be likely to try to get control. It's a heartbreak when your child turns out bad."

"And I'm so fortunate, it's not fair." I turned to look at her standing at the stove, her hands busy as always. "Is there any way I could help them without hurting their pride? I don't mean to patronize. But they're so good. What could I do? Send Luke to New York to work for my uncles? He might shine in the city." I laughed to think of it.

She rested her hands and nodded at me. "That does you credit, Jo. You have a good heart."

"And bad lungs."

She smiled. "I'll think about it. There might just be something. Right now the best thing is to be a friend. A good friend is rare, as the world goes."

Since I left Ruby last week in Matt's flivver, I've done nothing but sketch one marvel after another—this country is fantastic Beyond My Wildest Dreams. The first revelation came barely out of town when Matt remarked that the hills and mountains on either side of the road were volcanos. I was All Agog. I'd read about such things, of course, and I knew about Vesuvius, but it was quite another matter to see volcanos in every direction, more than I could count. Matt said there were literally *hundreds* for miles and miles around. He has lived among them all his life, he was quite matter-of-fact.

I certainly was not. It's been centuries since an eruption, not during his lifetime, he said. Long enough ago for trees to be growing clear to the top of most of them. Nevertheless my imagination was much excited about how it must have looked when all this was active. We bounced along the road, fortunately not muddy, while my head swiveled. Some sophisticate I am, show me a few volcanos and I'm nothing but jelly.

He seemed to be enjoying my reaction. "We're getting around far enough now so you can see into the crater of the big volcano. Off here to the left."

At first I didn't realize what he meant, and then—"*That?* That's a volcano, the one way back there?"

The Peaks, the huge mountain I had first seen from the window of a train fifteen months earlier, the giant I had lived at the foot of and watched the top of through all kinds of weather rising above and behind other mountains, is one monstrous volcano. It didn't seem possible.

"They say there's a hot spot up there where snow melts off faster. I've never climbed it in winter to find out for myself. But you can see from here that the middle is hollow, a bowl, sort of, open to the northeast."

Morning light made the soaring peaks and the basin among them shine with a light that looked *within* as well as above, green and golden. I shivered with the thrill of it. "There's snow."

"Some years it never quite melts. City water comes from springs up in there."

"The water we drink? Cook with?"

He laughed all over his nice face. "It's gotta come from some-where."

"I suppose so. I just never thought."

"Took some doing to get it piped into town twenty or so years ago. Before that they used to have water carried in by the railroad in tank cars when there hadn't been enough rain or snow to keep the springs running."

We drove between two big volcanos and turned off the road, east, I thought, though my sense of direction is usually dependent on street signs. "Thought you might like to see Emily and Roger and the girls, see the ranch house Ruby and her husband built. It's not far, you can see the roof straight ahead."

"These mountains *tower* above it, that one goes straight up!"

"Breaks the wind some. They don't get much sun in the dead of winter, but close to the slope they catch run-off before it gets out into the flats–Mr. Green set up a whole system to hold rain. In this country houses have to be built where there's water. No city pipes out here."

There wasn't another house in sight anywhere. "No neighbors either, I notice."

"It's hard to live isolated like this unless you have family, some kind of company. You could go crazy. People get into town as often as they can."

The little house certainly looked as if it had been built years ago–wood with a stone chimney–and then added onto a room at a time, but it still was anything but expansive. Beyond was a barren immensity; that is, it looked barren and there was no question that it was immense. I prepared myself to save my comments for the land-scape, and then I stepped down from the Ford and turned around.

There was the big volcano, with a partial view into the crater. I could hardly be courteous long enough to say hello. I laid my sketch book on the hood of Matt's Ford and drew that astonishing side of the mountain with its open basin so I could do a painting of it later. To think Ruby looked up to it every summer day for fifty years! No wonder she became so strong and wise. I felt exalted, quite Beside Myself. Who would have guessed that a volcano could be so beautiful, so inspiring?

"This is fantastic, like something out of myth. A legend. A home for gods."

Matt was pleased. "Hopis say kachinas live up there, not gods exactly–how would you say it?–sacred beings, teachers, oh shucks, *kachinas*. But I'll bet not one person in a thousand looks at the mountain and sees that part of it, the sacred part." He nodded several times. "Good for you."

Emily seemed as delighted as Matt. "You make me see it like new, Jo, like discovering it. I've lived with it all my life, and I guess I never thought it was anything out of the ordinary. It's just always been there."

"Look at the colors in this light! What is it like in late after-noon?"

"It turns shadowy and mysterious sometimes. Blues and purples. Sometimes just at sunset the whole mountain turns pink—that's nice."

My mind went feverish. If I were to stay in Arizona, which isn't outside remote possibility, I could paint the Peaks from all sides in all seasons. Maybe I could set up my easel on Emily's porch and paint them in all kinds of light as Monet did the facade of Rouen Cathedral. Set up *ten* easels and move from one to another as the sun moved or weather changed. I could quite cheerfully do that until I'm eighty, I'm sure, and never miss New York.

"How much time did it take?"

"The mountain? To grow, you mean?" Matt smiled at Roger. "Don't she ask good questions? I'd say a long time, millions of years maybe and then a long time for some of it to wear away."

"Do you suppose the earth shook? Was there a roaring noise?"

"I'd say so, wouldn't you, Roger?"

"Oh, no doubt about it. Looks peaceful now but she had to be a rip-roarer once."

Matt said, "Since you're interested in volcanos, we ought to backtrack a couple miles and go past the lava flow between Sunset and O'Leary."

Which we did. There was a primitive kind of road that led to a perfectly symmetrical cone with rusty orange around the top—that accounted for the name Sunset. It too had a crater that was visible until we drove close. Then suddenly: a whole valley filled with jagged black lava in amazing cracks and slabs and lumps, hard and cold. Matt stopped to let me get out and touch it. "It's rough to my fingers."

"Sure is. You couldn't walk on it without cutting your shoes to pieces. I tried it once when I was a kid, and that was enough. Over here's an ice cave. Sometimes in summer we come and chop some pieces out to keep our food cool for a while. There's not as much ice, though, as there was when my parents came forty years ago."

"It looks as if all this happened day before yesterday. Does anybody know?"

"Nothing definite, though we've had some guesses. A long time ago, like centuries. That scientist who comes out here from Philadelphia, Doctor Colton, wants to work on it. I've always been curious, I hope he does. It's practically in my back yard, you might say. I got some books once by mail, but they didn't help much."

He smiled and shrugged, modest as could be, but I looked at him with new interest. An Arizona cowboy who reads mail-order books on geology—well! How's that for breaking simple notions?

Through jolting miles we wound between dark volcanic hills in every direction. I didn't bother to count. It was eerie, not dead so much as alien, as if it had nothing to do with humans. Not that trees and shrubs do either, but this was different. I could have been looking at the surface of a planet that had never known people of any kind.

Matt gave me snippets of information. "Notice the ground is black with cinders and ash. There's over a hundred square miles of it, north and east. Maybe that's the way the wind was blowing." An ancient wind.

Farther on, land stepped down in long flat levels from the Peaks into a huge valley, and the view opened to the umpteenth spectacle of the morning—a spreading landscape green in the foreground and then rosy hues and blues that shaped themselves and stretched away under the sky into an unimaginable distance. Matt pulled on the brake lever. "That's the Painted Desert. Quite a sight, isn't it? Little Colorado River's out there somewhere, though we can't see it."

Having exhausted all my superlatives, I sat wordless with an electric thrill. Put New York city down in that country and it would be dwarfed, but who would want to? I looked back into a past old beyond imagining and saw where human ideas about beauty might have come from. Space—air gleaming with light and color.

Matt's voice was quiet. "I always stop here for a minute. Seems like it's never the same twice."

I turned and realized he was looking at me, not the distant colors. Wanting to see, what? That I cared about it too? I couldn't find words grand enough to say what I felt, but he nodded as if he were satisfied and let the clutch out and drove toward a land where all myths were surely born.

The black cinder road wound between volcanic cones and red earth slopes and fantastic forms off to either side. Trees were shorter and shorter as we drove along—nearly round in shape and dark green, Matt called them junipers—and there were little bushes he named as rabbit brush. His voice barely rose above the sound of the auto engine. "Trees don't get in the way of your eyes out here. But it's hard country for cows, can't run enough on it to make money some years. Guess we trade cash for the view."

"*Run* them?" I had wild visions of daily stampedes.

"That's just a way of speaking. You don't want to get cattle excited, it isn't good for them. You like to see them lying down, that's when they're comfortable. 'Run' really means put them onto the land and let them wander, as many head as the range can carry without overgrazing." He was using words I only partly understood.

"Some years we have three hundred fifty cows with their calves, maybe two-fifty long yearlings, a few bulls. And the horses, of course, they'll eat twice as much grass every day as a cow will."

"That seems a lot of animals to me. How much land do you have for that many?"

"With fee land, state and BLM lease, forest permit and what we own ourselves, around forty thousand acres."

"Forty *thousand?*" That seemed enormous, a royal estate.

Matt laughed. "Plenty big when the range is good and there's lots of grass. Probably will be this year. Dry years it can seem pretty small. Water is what counts, it's more valuable than land."

"Well then, how much water do you have?"

"There's springs Papa developed right near the house, that does for us. Fed by snow melt on the Peaks, I'm told. For the cattle some seasonal seeps, and on the northeast corner our boundary goes right down to the Little Colorado, though it's quite a distance with sparse grazing for a cow to walk. In a drought it's easier to truck water up to tanks. Rainy seasons there's puddles all over the place. Papa taught me never to ride or drive through a puddle. Spoils them for the stock."

He shook his head. "Growing up I was always getting lessons. We'd be out on the range and he'd say, 'Suppose your horse gave out and you were stranded right here. What's the shortest distance you'd have to walk to get to water?' Sometimes it'd be a full day's travel. Man or boy, you could die quick in this country if you didn't know such things. I got so I could figure it in hours pretty close."

I admired him enormously; imagine knowing such arcane things. "How far are we from water now?"

"About five minutes." He grinned. "To the house. Here's where we turn off."

There was no sign of a building. A black slope rose in front of us. Matt pointed. "Got a basalt cap, an old lava flow right over our heads. Goes for miles. Highest spot on the ranch." He steered a track that curved among the junipers.

The house when I first spied it looked pitifully small and plain under that looming volcanic ridge, weathered boards with a wooden porch. Smoke rose from the chimney. But behind us the Peaks were visible, and off to the northeast the Painted Desert shimmered like a fairyland. As we drove closer, I saw that a canyon cut down between the ridge and the house and exposed blocks of red stone below the dark basalt.

"Pa built the house on that point above the canyon. He said it was the most beautiful spot he'd ever seen, he planned the windows so every one would have a view. Then he figured out how to pipe water from a spring right into the kitchen so Mama wouldn't have to carry it."

With that, the house was modest, not plain, and courteous in that splendid landscape, a place for habitation not for show. When Matt cut the engine, there was space and silence and the peace of plants growing. I was nearly numb with the wonders all around.

Daisy came bouncing out to meet us and opened the car door. "Here you are! We've been waiting lunch for you. Did he stop and show you all his favorite places and talk your arm off about them?"

"Oh, Daisy. I couldn't have imagined. I'm...he...you're so *lucky*"

"Aren't I though? We've been cleaning all week getting ready for you." The smell of baking bread came through the open door.

Inside, horse shoes that had been made into hooks for hats and coats were fastened to the wall. Hand-made chairs stood around a big wooden table. Colored curtains hung at the windows; colored calendar prints were on the walls. I loved how comfortable it looked, how honest and hard-working.

Margaret was at the big wood stove pouring hot water into a basin. "Welcome, Jo, come and wash off the road dust while Matt brings your things in. And then we'll eat the soup Daisy cooked in your honor, almost as thick as stew, and the bread she baked."

After lunch Daisy fairly ushered me around the house. "We've got three rooms, the big one for cooking and eating and talking, and two bedrooms off to the side. One for Mama and this one for you and me. Do you like my grandmother's quilt? Matt and Luke have a sleeping room fixed up for themselves in the feed shed. The outhouse is over there, see? Papa built it above a fissure in the edge of the canyon—just like he said, rain run-off washes it clean. I hope you won't mind it."

"A water closet, indeed, and with a view. How could I mind?"

The wonder of that forty-five mile drive from Flagstaff had worn me out—the very thought of doing anything made me ache. For two days everyone was thoughtful and let me sit in the shade and fed me huge wholesome meals I couldn't finish. Daisy arranged little shows.

"This young man is a week old," she panted, her arm around the neck of a struggling calf; a cow was calling from behind a fence. "Feel his nose, it's so soft." It was velvet, much to my delight.

"Matt says he'll show you how he throws a rope if you won't cheer." He looked skilled and graceful, neatly dropping the circle of his rope around any object I proposed, including his sister and his mother, and I laughed but I did not cheer, though I felt like it.

Daisy seemed to know the ordinary things that would be a delight to me. "Sit still and I'll ride Caliche around you like I was herding steers." She was a marvel to see, feminine and strong and sure and so economical of movement that I couldn't see her signals to the horse.

At night lying under the quilt her grandmother had made and listening to her breathe, I thought how happy I was to know her and Matt and Margaret. The contrast with The Family was preposterous. I wondered for at least the hundredth time what my mother would think of them.

This morning at breakfast—early sunlight coming through the windows and across the room—I announced that I had been a slug long enough and I was ready to Venture Forth. Daisy looked at me closely. "You sure? Well then, yay! Matt, can we get everything done fast and drive over to Wupatki?"

He raised one finger as he drank the last of his coffee. "Easiest thing in the world. You want to come, Mama? Daisy can hang on anywhere."

Margaret smiled. "If these girls'll help, I'll make up picnic sandwiches out of that pot roast I cooked with juniper berries. We can be ready in an hour."

And here we are, Daisy and Margaret and I, standing under an enormous sky and looking across at an ancient Indian ruin—Wupatki, the most magical place I've ever seen. I am clutching my sketchbook to my chest but making no move to use it. I can only look. I had no idea until ten minutes ago that Flagstaff is in an enchanted land.

We're on the edge of a broad shallow canyon, a "wash," Daisy calls it, with the Painted Desert stretching away on our right and on the left the same black slope with its volcanic top like old ramparts. Pure magic is growing right out of a rocky ledge—the remnant of a large red-rock building, deserted, silent, empty, and absolutely beautiful. It hadn't been visible until we were almost upon it. I fear I'm in danger of Waxing Rhapsodic on every occasion, like some literary English lady traveler, but really, this place coming on top of the past week has pushed me over the edge. Perpetual enthusiasm will probably be my fate.

Daisy hugs my arm and shivers. "Isn't it amazing? We thought you'd appreciate it." Except for singing birds, it is so quiet that I can hear a breeze whispering in the knee-high bushes all around.

"Who...who did that?" I wouldn't be surprised by any answer.

"We think maybe ancestors of the Hopi, but no one knows. There are hundreds of buildings all around here, seriously, *hundreds*,—this is the biggest—and they were all empty and half crumbled by the time the first white people arrived, just before the Civil War. They were empty when the first Navajos came long before that. Hopis have some stories, but no proof."

There are standing walls built meticulously of small slabs of reddish rock. "It's the most beautiful building I've ever seen anywhere. Why was it abandoned, does anyone know?"

"We just guess. Maybe not enough water."

"Someone, some people, built this and just walked away from it?"

"I guess so."

"But they must have known it was gorgeous. Look at the stone work, it's so careful."

Matt is standing behind us. "Sure they did. Proud of it, I'll bet. Stood back and looked at it and said, *That* oughta please the wife."

We turn to laugh at him, and Daisy points to a horseman coming slowly from the east. "Look, Matt, there's Peshlakai. Or is it Clyde, I can't tell so far away."

"Peshlakai, I think. I'll go on and talk to him."

I can't distinguish any detail at that distance. "Who is it?" The man looks so picturesque on his horse in this huge wilderness. "A cowboy?"

Margaret sits her comfortable body down on a flat stone. "An old Navajo."

"An *Indian*?" Alarmed, I look around for a safe place to hide. "Isn't he...I mean, should we run? Why is Matt walking toward him, to keep him away from us?"

Margaret laughs, but it's kindly. "He lives right near here with his family, has for fifty years from before there was a Flagstaff.

They're our neighbors, no harm to anybody. Old Peshlakai's been to Washington twice and talked to the President. He's probably coming to be sure we don't misbehave or take anything."

Daisy squeezes my shoulder. "You should see your face, Jo. Poor thing, you're really scared, aren't you?"

"Outright panic is more like it. But I'm calming down." I feel like a ninny, believing in Wild Indians.

Margaret pats the stone beside her. "Come sit and rest a minute, why don't you. If you'll think about it, that house across the way was built by Indians. They know about beauty, some say it's the way they think. See how straight and true the walls are, still, after who knows how long? They used the ridge itself for a foundation and some of the walls. See how it's all mingled together? That was clever."

Daisy is perilously close to the edge of the wash. "You should see the rugs Clyde's wife weaves. Sally's an artist. Peshlakai makes fine silver jewelry."

Margaret stands, graceful for such a plump woman. "Matt'll likely be a while, they'll get to talking about grass or water or something, sheep. He'll want to know if the people have heard anything about Doctor Colton's plan to have the government take over the whole area and protect it. Why don't we go on and look around?"

We negotiate a kind of trail, circling to approach the ruin from the head of the ridge. I watch where I put my feet, but Daisy goes dancing on ahead. She is amazing, she and her mother both. No doubt Ruby knows Navajos too and didn't think to mention it. I feel an absolute ignoramus.

I stop to breathe and turn to Margaret, who is behind me. "What did you mean about protecting the area. From whom?"

She seems content for the pause. "From whites mostly. It's enough to make you sick, the things some people do."

"Why would anyone want to harm such a lovely place?"

"Money mostly. Old Ben Doney was coming down here prospecting every winter from thirty years ago. He was sure there was a rich mine around somewhere, and when he didn't find one, he came into the ruins and dug up old pots and jewelry and scraps of woven cloth and such and took them back to town to sell. Had quite a collection finally. He even found the body of a baby. And another time a dog and a parrot."

I'm disgusted. "Did he sell them too?"

Daisy has come back to us. "I wouldn't be surprised at anything Ben Doney would do, for money or otherwise. You never know whether to be mad at him or laugh."

Margaret smiles and shakes her head. "He's eighty now. In 1917 he tried to enlist. Said he could shoot as well as anybody, and he was peeved when they wouldn't take him because he was too old."

"He says he fought in the Civil War. Matt says he's never stopped since."

"There was a time when he knew this whole section better than anybody. When that professor Fewkes wanted to investigate, he hired Ben as a guide. But there have been others who've come out here to destroy and called it fun. In my book, that kind of person has the brains of a walnut."

I have to laugh at her image. "What's the protective plan?"

Margaret has found another rock to sit on. "That Antiquities Act that Congress passed twenty-five years ago didn't stop a thing. Doctor Colton thinks a bill making this all a national monument, would mean a caretaker or a superintendent or something. Old Peshlakai and his sons try, but they can't do it all."

We go on slowly, looking at everything. Daisy says Matt's guess is that once there were four set-back stories. Maybe a hundred people lived here. Most of the rooms are full of rubble where walls and roofs have fallen in, but enough detail is visible for me to respect the hands that did the building. We climb up onto a section that must have been a third story and look out across the expanse of the Painted Desert. I envy those forgotten people who lived here in such beauty—red walls against a blue sky and the colors of the land. Did it make them kindly?

Perhaps Margaret is thinking the same thing. "A good number of folks must have lived here and lots more in the country round about. Quite a community. If they were like Indians now, they got along all right. No way of knowing, of course."

Here and gone. It's too overwhelming. A baby. Families. Vanished. Walked away into a colored past, a time beyond counting. I concentrate on the view and then on the masonry work.

Matt catches us up. "He didn't know about Doctor Colton's bill. He says Ya-ta-hay to you, Mama, Daisy. And he says hello to you, Jo, and welcome. Or the Navajo equivalent. Next time you come he'll shake your hand."

Daisy says, "That's a little joke. Navajos shake hands because they think whites expect it." It isn't such a joke for me, I have never touched an Indian.

"Well." Matt becomes a tour guide. "Have you seen the two circles and the blowhole?"

Later, sitting on a huge flat block of stone that has broken off the canyon wall and tumbled down, we eat Margaret's picnic and the others rest while I open my sketch book and draw. My chest feels full of the glory of this ancient place, more impressive by far than the ruins of Imperial Rome because they are alone, not crowded by new buildings, a new city. The years seem clear and invisible as the air. How do I put that into a sketch? I'm sure I will dream of this day for a long time. I'm like that, I'm afraid. And in love—in love with this land.

Driving back to the ranch when the sun is low over the Peaks, we decide not to turn off to go to another old building named Wukoki, a Hopi word, Matt says. We can save that and go another day. Another day. I am quite startled to realize that this week is the first time in nearly a year and a half that I've looked to the future and said, "Yes. I'll do that."

May, 1922

Dear Mother,

I've received no letter from you since March, six weeks ago, when you were being disappointed about current French painting. Thinking that you might have returned to the exotic island of Manhattan, I'll address this letter to your apartment. If you have stayed on in Paris for the spring shows and shopping, it will be waiting for you when you come home. So much has happened that I want to write while I have the details straight.

First, I'm feeling remarkably well. At this altitude, activity makes me short of breath and Doctor Fronske is still not confident that my lungs have healed completely—the tests in Phoenix hint at remaining bacillus. But my appetite is excellent, ravenous actually, I'm sure I've gained five pounds this month. I'm absurdly chipper and cheerful, and I haven't had a day of fatigue all week. Yesterday Ruby and I went to the Orpheum to see Douglas Fairbanks in "The Three Musketeers" and loved it.

I mailed a letter to you addressed to your hotel in Paris describing my first two weeks out on the Friendly ranch with a few sketches of it and of Wupatki. If you had sailed before the missive arrived, no doubt it will be forwarded, so I'll not repeat my effusions. Matt took it into town to mail and carried another to Ruby, telling her that I had been invited to stay another two weeks to see the cattle driven from lower ground near the river onto the higher range and that I was having such a marvelous time I had accepted. She sent back word that the house was too quiet without me, so she had brought Ada in to stay a while, but she was glad I was enjoying ranch life.

There were a few cold, snowy days in Flagstaff in late April, not surprising anyone, I'm told, but the elevation of the ranch is two or three thousand feet lower—imagine!—and our weather was radiant. Daisy and I spent part of every day in the saddle. That's right, your big-city girl, on a cow horse. She gave me a little old mare named Piñon and with Matt's help taught me how to ride it in the Western working style, which requires reins in the left hand and leaves the right free for roping. So far I have not attempted that, but who can tell? Lately I seem to be quite bold enough for anything.

I wore one of Daisy's riding skirts, altered with a belt so it would not slide off over my hips. She was all curves and grace—I'm afraid I looked like a lampshade. We offered up Peals of Laughter getting the skirt belted in. Matt and Margaret smiled when I walked out into the kitchen, but I fancied I looked almost native. Thank goodness Cousin Gertrude wasn't there to give me her opinion.

A Western saddle is large enough to live on almost, too heavy for me to lift onto the back of a horse. So Matt did that part and pulled the cinch tight and all the rest of getting ready to ride. Though he and Daisy assured me that I didn't have to fear being bitten, he put the bridle on for me too—a horse's teeth look very large when I'm looking straight at them.

All the Friendlies, even Margaret, can swing into the saddle in one smooth motion, but I could not even get my left foot into the stirrup or reach high enough to pull myself aboard—they laughed and led Piñon to an old stump so that I could use it as a mounting block. Margaret said, "We taught Daisy to do it that way when she was just a little girl. She learned on Piñon too." Which made me feel more like a child than I already did.

I had daily lessons for a week on the flat ground around the corrals, which were built with crooked juniper sticks—"stays" Daisy called them. Piles of dry "tumbleweed" had been blown against the fences by winter winds. Matt was pulling them off a few at a time and setting fire to them. "Don't want them burning on their own, could take out all the fences."

There's a large bump built into the front of a Western saddle, a "horn," they call it, which is perfect for a novice to hold onto. You can be assured I did so every time we moved faster than a slow walk. On the third day I learned how to kick Pinon into a trot and, with Daisy beside me on Caliche just in case, I went bouncing along holding tightly to the horn with my right hand. As we went past Matt, he shouted, "Hold 'er, Newt, she's headed for the pea patch!" and I laughed so hard Daisy put out a hand to steady me.

It would be indelicate of me to mention the places where I was stiff and tender from those lessons, but I'm sure you can guess. From on top a horse's back is broader than it looks from the ground and the leather saddle is harder. I discovered bones and muscles I didn't know I had. For the first week I had to hold onto something after dismounting until my legs steadied. But Daisy was patient, and I was persistent: I wanted so much to learn to ride.

One day—after I had learned to get on and off Pinon without the stump—Daisy and I rode north to the ancient house at Wukoki, an hour or so east of Wupatki, out in the red land where there are few cinders or even volcanic cones. We carried lunch on the backs of our saddles and didn't see another person the whole day. I went into transports all over again about the beauty of the country. Far on the horizon were shadowy monoliths of stone, the edge of Monument Valley, Daisy said. In the foreground, rock layers lay in thin red sheets every place rains had cut shallow cracks into the earth. Daisy has "heard tell" that the rock was once sand on the floor of an ancient ocean. "My grandma didn't doubt it, doesn't the Bible say there was a flood over all the earth? Matt thinks there's a scientific explanation."

I looked into each red crack as we passed it and watched the distance eagerly for the first view of Wukoki. It had been there all along before I recognized that the vertical line the same red color as the earth was a wall.

The house is on three levels, built so cleverly on a sort of undercut pedestal in the middle of a sunken bowl that I couldn't tell where the natural rock left off and the constructed walls began. After centuries of silence, half of them are still standing, such was the skill of those ancient masons. It's the most hauntingly beautiful place, with a vista—miles and miles all around—that seemed to mean more than I could guess. The Peaks are visible on the southwestern horizon, rising up out of the earth, piling up ridges on hills and lines swooping to sharp points against the sky and all of it curling around and falling down again into the crater hundreds of feet below. Directly opposite is the great expanse of the Painted Desert.

Leaving our horses patiently waiting, we climbed a rickety, handmade ladder up through a cleft in the rock. Daisy was a wonderful guide; she taught me to see what I was looking at. "You can tell it was safe from attack: you couldn't get beyond the overhang without tall ladders, the ground is fifteen feet down, the outside walls have almost no windows."

"Who would have attacked?"

"Nobody knows. This part used to be at least three rooms tall. See the holes where poles were fitted in to support the floor above? Here and here, see? and where the connecting doors were. I'll bet a cookie this section over here was another room—there's a corner—maybe three more rooms. There might have been a dozen rooms all together."

"Could they stand on the roof? That part is like an observation tower."

"Isn't it though? Wupatki is at the base of that black volcanic mesa, the same one that's behind our house. I think people on the roof of Wukoki could have seen people on the roof of Wupatki, maybe signalled to each other."

The walls are two feet thick, skillfully laid with the kind of natural blocks that are still scattered all around and joined with mortar of gritty red mud. Without Daisy I might not have noticed nine curious little holes no bigger than my hand that slant clear through the north and east walls, out and down at an angle. "You can see the ground outside. Isn't that something? Matt thinks they were meant to let air in but not rain or wind. The walls that have fallen might have had some too. Aren't they clever?"

On a magnificent platform larger than any of the rooms—Daisy said she thought it was a place where the people worked or just sat on warm days—we hung our feet over the edge and turned our backs to the sun, eating our lunches, resting in the breeze. For minutes at a time we just sat and looked and listened to the silence.

Daisy bet another cookie that it "used to be a lot noisier with all those people around—you can almost hear their voices." We tried to imagine that we were those old people living in that wide beauty, talking idly and finally personally.

It was my fault, I suppose. "Matt is such a good man, the kind any girl would jump to marry. Handsome, strong, dependable. Why is he still single? Did he have someone once?"

"There's been a girl now and then who's looked at him like she was interested, and he looked at one or two, it seemed to me, specially after he came back from the army. But even if you count all the people for miles around, there aren't really many, not enough for a good sample. I guess he never saw one that he wanted."

"How old is he? Not that it's any of my business."

"Thirty next month. I'm sure Mama wonders sometimes if he'll ever get married, but she doesn't say. The ranch couldn't support another family."

It was pushy of me, I know, but something about that beautiful place made me feel so soft and happy that restraint just drifted away into the air. I forgot courtesy entirely. Daisy said that Indians think asking questions is bad manners and they avoid answering them. Sometimes you can't find out what you want to know. But we weren't Indians, so it was all right.

Things come at one out of the past here. I told her about Nicky, whom I hadn't mentioned until then, and about the aunts and grandmothers. "Sometimes I had the sensation I was living without air. I wonder whether they felt that way when they were young and then as they grew older behaved in the only way they knew, as if their minds were trapped in something sticky and invisible."

Daisy seemed amazed. "I never guessed. All the things I read, well, New York shines in my mind. I dream of going there. Sometimes I feel imprisoned here and I'm just wild—I long to get out and see what other places are like, any place different from Flagstaff. I'm afraid I'll spend my life without seeing a single new thing. I could cry it's so frustrating."

So that explains the look I saw on her face that day at Walnut Canyon. Isn't it too sad and ironic? I feel liberated in the very place where she feels trapped. Oh, we humans are a funny race.

She told me more about herself, how unattractive she feels because she is not fashionably thin, how devastated she was when her father's horse fell on him and he died days later of his injuries. "His heart was damaged. They told him he could never live at this elevation again, and he said he didn't want to live anywhere else. I think what the doctors said killed him as much as his horse did."

We were long hours out of sight of any building, no roof between us and the sky. I doubt I'll ever be the same. I know I won't. Being in Arizona has made a different person of me. And I'm quite enjoying the woman I think I'm becoming.

I don't know when I've ever written such a long letter. I hope it didn't weary you. But the past month has been as significant as anything in my life, and I wanted you to know about it.

Love,
Jo

P.S. You've told me the family is refusing to speak to me as an expression of displeasure, so I don't know how I can get a letter to my own cousin. Please, Mother, will you see Aunt Lenore and try to get an address for

Lillian? It would be too sad to miss her if she should come through. As for Cousin Paul, I thought of him every time something happened at the ranch. What in the world is keeping him in New York?

The Friendlies—Friendlys?—were the best of hosts, too agreeable for words through the month I was at their ranch. Every day I looked across the Painted Desert and felt peace in my soul. I did not know that Cousin Lillian was out there somewhere, riding through that country on a horse. When I returned to town, I was appalled to learn that she had come in with Zane Grey just two days after I had left. If only I had written to her, we could have arranged a meeting. I'd have been proud to introduce her to Ruby and Ada and Dennis and the Friendlies.

The Grey party was here a few days, at the Weatherford Hotel, "outfitting," the *Sun* said, for a trip to Kayenta and Rainbow Bridge. Four horse-wranglers and Lee Doyle, son of the old guide who died last year, went with them. Matt said he thought one of the wranglers was his friend Jesse Smith.

The editor referred to Lillian as a "talented artist and illustrator particularly adept in portrayal of our scenery and of Indian life." She stopped in at Breen's office while she was here. He used the occasion to mention the "hundreds of artists who are drawn to Arizona for its powerful color." Maxfield Parrish was here for quite some time in 1902; I didn't know that.

Three weeks later they were back—with material for a novel, Mr. Grey said—the day Daisy and I were at Wukoki. He offered five hundred dollars for a year-old wolf Charlie Miller had, although heaven knows what he intended to do with it. Fortunately someone else had already bought it.

After a week Grey went on to Catalina Island, but Lillian stayed a few hours longer to attend a Chautauqua lecture. I don't know where she went after that. The *Sun* said she "makes her home on the Kimoworo ranch near Phoenix." Ruby says it's hot there this time of year.

Now we're back to normal, which includes more upset about Luke. He has disappeared. Matt and Daisy came into town for supplies yesterday and stopped by to talk. They can't find him, and no one seems to know a thing. Their immediate worry is, should they tell their mother?

Every fragment of news seems like a clue. Eighty gallons of corn mash and "everything but a still" were found in a cellar a quarter of a mile from the house on the Piper ranch. Could there be a connection? Matt doesn't think so, but Daisy wonders.

A lawyer named Harben who had recently moved to town and been made assistant county attorney was found unconscious on a stone wall half a block from us the last night anyone remembers seeing Luke. Harben had left his office late, apparently in good health, and walked down the street. Two ladies going home from an Eastern Star lodge meeting said that near the W.H. Switzer house they saw him stumbling down the street groaning. Twice he fell before he collapsed onto the wall. They reported it, and Harben was carried into the court house, but by morning he was dead. No one knows why.

Doctor Fronske did an autopsy and reported that he was mystified. Stomach and kidneys were sent to Phoenix chemists, who found no trace of poison. The coroner's jury decided death was from unknown causes, but Matt and Daisy looked at each other when I told them about it. Ruby's eyes were on her knitting. The silence in the kitchen frightened me.

Ada, in her quirky wisdom, saved us all. "Well, if worry isn't contagious as wet paint! Now you've got me doing it. Let's see, that skeleton that was found half way down the trail at Walnut Canyon last week with no clothes on and a bullet in its head, you don't suppose that could have been Luke did it, do you? It had to been years ago, but it could have been Luke, couldn't it? The Nolan barn burned out in Doney Park last Saturday with two horses in it. Said to have been a spark from the house chimney, but what do you think?"

Ruby's accustomed to Ada, she caught on first. "There were three women through here hiking coast to coast. Mighty strange, if you ask me." She hadn't looked up from her knitting, but I could tell.

Matt was solemn. "Half a hundred Texas and Oklahoma farmers running from the boll weevil are going up to Houserock Valley. Determined to homestead despite what anyone can say about that country being all rock and sand. A thousand more coming. Luke was likely the one who talked them into it. Least he could have done was tell 'em not to take their women and children yet."

Daisy's eyes were alive. "Who do you suppose talked the Central Bank baseball team into calling themselves "The Moneygrubbers?"

"Couple of forest fires this week."

"There's flappers in the news."

"Somebody had the hare-brained idea of building a cabin up on Woody Mountain for the lookout man to use. Be sissies up there next thing you know." We were all smiling by then.

"I couldn't tell you how, but Weatherford's toll road up to the top of the Peaks looks like it might even get finished. Probably Luke trying to open up the area to tourists."

"Some more Chinese wives came in on the train last week. Could it be Luke sent them?"

"Maybe he's gone off with Zane Grey."

Ada topped us all. "There's an election coming up. I can't wait to see if Luke's running for sheriff to replace Billy Campbell." With that we were all laughing at our own jokes. "That Luke," Ada said, "he's more fun than a barrel of monkeys."

Daisy knelt beside her chair and hugged her. "Aunt Ada, you're the best thing that ever happened to this town."

Ruby nodded. "If it hadn't been for her, we'd have all quit and gone back to Texas after the first hard winter."

She loved the attention. "I'm little for my size, so I needed to develop what talent I had."

Ruby laid aside her knitting. "What do you say we finish off Jo's apple pie so she can make another one?"

So life goes on in our little town. Editor Breen worries that we are facing water famine, and nothing is being done. Tom Pulliam is elected mayor. A circus comes through town. Miller's dogs tree a man and a woman near Mormon Lake, and the man denies he is a bear. Dave Joy resigns as night marshall, probably because the job kept him from drinking after dark, Ada says.

In the East Lillian Russell, "The American Beauty," dies and the news does not touch me. Once I would have cared, but what matters is not the other side of the continent, it's the Here and Now.

When Cousin Lina, "Mrs. Zane Grey," motors through on her way to New York without stopping to see me, I am hurt. Perhaps she really did not know I was here, after all I'm younger than she is by almost a decade, and I have no famous husband. She can't keep up with everyone. But my family's effort to punish me with isolation, mean and stupid to my mind, is emphasized. Daisy would never treat me so.

The same week tragedy in town shames me into forgetting myself and my petty problems. A twelve-year-old boy dies in Mercy Hospital, his face burned to a crisp. At six o'clock on Tuesday morning he had wakened to find his house on fire from a defective flue in the kitchen stove and hurried his eight-year-old sister outside into falling snow. Trying to save his two-year-old brother and his mother, who was frail as a ghost, Ada said, he chopped through a door with an axe to no avail. Neighbors alerted by the fire alarm found him standing barefoot in an inch of snow, crying down his ruined face.

What is Lillian Russell compared to that, or Cousin Lina, or my hurt feelings? What does it matter that the Leupp Indians won a baseball game against Flagstaff? *Baseball!* How trivial.

Sam Beeson's little son found a dynamite cap and hammered it with a rock. The explosion took off the tip of his thumb and the index finger on his left hand, blew pieces into his body, damaged his eye. Ross Fuller crawled into the den of a lion and shot her in the face, held her paw and squeezed it as she died, and then took her five kittens because he wanted to sell them. I begin to tremble as I read the paper.

I turn to Ada and Ruby but can find no words. "I know," Ada says very softly. "I know. Sometimes life seems about as pointless as shaving an egg and you wonder why we try so hard to go on with it. Seems like the only thing that gets us through is propping each other up. Just barely."

That gallant withered little woman. Her children dead or gone. Her legs next to useless. She's seen years of tragedy and outrage. Go tell all the left-over European monarchs: nobility is not external. She's as good a teacher as I've ever had. Following Daisy's example, I go to kneel beside her and put my arms around her. She pats my shoulder with her good hand, and we prop each other up as best we can.

*T*he year circles around and we come back to where we were before: which means that the Fourth of July was here again. Have I actually been in Flagstaff so many months, a turn and a half of the calendar?

The town celebrated for four days. They took the holiday *seriously* with so much ballyhoo they attracted attention from Far Afield—there was a press correspondent here from the Los Angeles *Times* wandering about with a pencil and a little notebook. I hope he did not present us as a bunch of rustic hicks with quaint country habits, but I would not be surprised at anything.

It was the opinion of the Chamber of Commerce that the celebration was the best in years—such a crowd that there were no vacant seats for any event and hundreds of people were standing. Everything went smoothly because the Knights of Pythias were in charge.

I knew of the order, which has been around since the Civil War with quite admirable intentions. How could one quarrel with such lofty (albeit unattainable) goals as universal peace based on friendship and generosity? If it all sounds old-fashioned, well, the order takes its name from the brotherly-love story of Damon and Pythias. Somehow I did not expect to find Pythagorean philosophy on the Arizona frontier, which is further proof of how narrow my perspective was in the cosmopolitan metropolis. We were all so modishly cynical after the war, so sure of our superiority. It seems quite sad to me now.

Brotherly love did seem the order of the day. Tuesday's parade through crowded streets included a splendiferous variety. Ruby and Ada and I watched from the Shamrock Taxi, and I loved every minute. Battery D of the National Guard went by on black horses; twenty children from south of the tracks carried the flag. There were mounted cowboys *and* Indians, the fire truck, Rebekah women and Camp Fire Girls, military bands.

And the large entries! For Babbitts Dry Goods, Peaches Hock drove a limousine full of women. An Arizona Lumber and Timber wagon carried a log cabin. The Babbitt Trading Company truck, decorated with rugs, featured an old Navajo man beating a drum and a woman weaving. Hopis making blankets and baskets were on the float for the Moenkopi trading post. I'm hopeless, I tingled through every hour of the morning—it all seemed so happy and inclusive—and sometimes I laughed aloud. Ruby and Ada said they were as "tickled" by me as by the parade.

The crowd was a good show too. People called out to the riders, who waved and made jokes. A doctor named Miller was wearing a high silk hat. Two mounted policemen rode back and forth to keep order, not that there was much need. Any direction I turned my eyes held something that delighted me.

There was rain for an hour on Wednesday afternoon—"like clockwork," Ruby said, every July 4th—but for most of the celebration skies were brilliant blue. The horse races included many Indians, and to everyone's jubilation, Flagstaff's team won the baseball tournament.

For me, the most fascinating spectacle of all was the Hopi dances at night on Railroad Avenue. Ruby urged me to see them.

"Would you be wanting to go down tonight and watch, Jo? You won't see anything like it anyplace else in the world, and you might not be able to get up to the mesas, it's such a long hard trip."

The sidewalk was crowded with spectators, and I took my place among them not knowing what to expect, standing close to Ruby for reassurance. She was a brick. "There'll be a whole big family from the reservation—Shipolovi and Mishongnovi and Shungopovi."

"Can they leave when they want to?"

"The reservation? Well, of course—it's a home not a prison. They've danced up at the Grand Canyon and here and there around the state, along the railroad line but other places too. For money, you know. Last year when missionaries tried to stop the dances, a teacher at Tovea took some Hopis to Phoenix to show officials it was mostly religious."

"The dances are their religion?"

"Most are, the visible part of it. But not these. I expect they'll be social dances, Buffalo or Butterfly or some such. The kachina dances couldn't be done away from the villages where they belong."

Before I could ask all my other questions, there was a rhythmic kind of sound from behind us. People stood aside for a line of Hopis to come onto the street, the men with rattles and bells tied to their legs. That explained the rhythmic sound: it was made when the men walked. They were wearing headdresses of buffalo skin with horns attached. That is, I *assumed* it was buffalo—how would I know? Some carried drums, those at least I recognized.

As they took their places in lines, Ruby bent to speak quietly to me. "The girls are all ages, eight up to about twenty, all unmarried. Married women don't do these dances. I don't know why exactly, it just seems to be something that isn't done. I think they're supposed to be dancing opposite their nephews, but maybe not since they aren't dancing at home. I don't understand all of it. I don't think anybody on the outside does."

In their hands the girls were carrying ears of corn or sticks with feathers attached. Bracelets and hanks of yarn were on their wrists, feathers on their heads. Their eyes were hidden by some kind of coarse hair strung on a thong tied across their foreheads. All quite foreign to my experience.

The drummers began to beat a pulse for a chant that I thought hypnotic. But *dancing* would not be my word for what the lines of people were doing, it was more a matter of stepping vigorously from one foot to another to the beat of the drums. That made the bells and rattles part of the music; I rather liked the effect.

Ruby bent to me again. "As I understand it, the song tells about little boys growing up to be good runners who wake up in the morning and run to the springs for a bath. The girls are supposed to grow up to be beautiful and choose their husbands well."

"I like it. Does it seem soothing to you?"

"Yes, always. I'm glad you see that. Hopis are good folks, in my opinion, peaceable, hard-working farmers, religious through and through. You wouldn't expect their dances to be violent."

One more lesson in Educating Jo. I could understand why peaceful Indians and restful dances wouldn't have much appeal for movie-makers, but I did think the usual presentation did not have to be so one-sided. Most movie-makers were New Yorkers transplanted to Hollywood, filming their own opinions, I suppose.

The dancers withdrew to one side and another group came in. Ruby was pleased. "Oh good, it's the Butterfly Dance. I like this one."

The girls were wearing hair bangs over their eyes as before and the same straight black dresses and silver bracelets, and in addition tall wooden boards on their heads, painted with symbols and surrounded by feathers, the whole edifice strapped on with a leather harness.

Ruby explained: "Those tablets on their heads represent rain clouds and sunflowers and butterflies and what not. For some dances the men wear tablets but not this one. Those are eagle feathers in front and back."

"My! Why are those—what are they? animal skins?—hanging from the belts of the men?"

"Fox. I don't know why. Just that Hopis often dance with reminders of other creatures. Notice that both girls and men are holding little sprigs of fir, that's to represent life, I'm told. The men have soft white eagle feathers in their hair."

I could make little sense of what they were doing. They lined up in two rows, and when the drums began, moved in a slow deliberate step and then followed around in curves. I would have been lost without Ruby.

"Watch the pattern they dance, it traces the shape of growing corn and then the tassel. You can see it once you know. I'm told it's hard to learn because they have to make changes all at once at the right place in the song. But it's so pretty."

I came away from the evening knowing little more about Indians than I had before, but I could say that Hopis at least seemed to include the entire world in their religion—rain and plants and other creatures. I wondered if they included me as well.

I enjoyed the thought, even though theirs was so distinctly different from any religion I had known of. One plus in my sojourn in Arizona has been the realization that there are many ways of living and thinking, and one might be no better than another. I'm practically a genius to have discovered what everyone else has known all along, I'm sure.

Through July there was rain almost every afternoon. I looked forward to it: pure white clouds that appeared by noon and massed until they turned dark, wind and thunder and brief sheets of rain that left evening air cool and sparkling clean. It was quite refreshing to the spirit. Wild flowers began to bloom along every wall and in undisturbed corners. They wait for summer storms, Ruby said.

For all the rain in town, what she was hearing was that there hadn't been much in the country roundabout and stock tanks were low. There had been over a hundred fires so far in the forest, most due to lightning; the home of Mr. Salas, whose wife had recently died, was struck and burned. "We need longer water mains, that's obvious, but most of all we need more rain. Snow last winter wasn't enough to make good range, though we hoped so at the time. And Roger says the spring market for cattle was not satisfactory."

I was learning to worry with her rather than looking on from the outside. My friends were likely to have troubles if more widespread storms did not develop soon. My friends—I liked thinking those words. Friends: people you trust and care about, people whose difficulties you share. People who add to you, who make your life bigger.

July, 1922

Dear Jo,

I was fascinated by your tales from the Friendly ranch. It was the sort of experience I had hoped for you. That such people have taken you to their hearts is a compliment, I think. I like them from afar.

Your cousin Paul agrees. He tells me he is carefully preparing his departure from the bank. A few more months, he says, and then he'll bolt for Arizona.

New York feels familiar for my weeks away, and yet somehow strange.
I wonder whether I have changed more than the city has. Pablo Casals
has taken up conducting at Carnegie Hall in addition to performing
brilliantly on his cello. A Shakespeare folio has recently been sold for the
astonishing price of $9,000. The coming theater season will feature the
Barrymores in three of the bard's dramas, as well as two plays by Eugene
O'Neil. All of it seems quite distant somehow, perhaps because your
letters from Arizona are so immediate, perhaps because I was so shaken
by my failed pilgrimage to Paris.

As I promised in my communication from the City of Light, I have
been on a quest through the streets of Manhattan, going from one gallery to
another in search of paintings distinctly American. That may be a
chimera, the obsession of a parochial mind. In a few galleries one has the
impression of a hotbed of uninhibited exploration, but from what I have
seen so far, I would judge the island to be for the most part Stieglitz
territory: the Modernism which he has promoted for so long is everywhere,
and he has the last word in most debates, probably because he is so forceful,
so (dare I say it?) so German.

All of this is wonderful for the career of Georgia O'Keeffe, the young
woman whose name is still linked with his, and for others whom he approves
of or deigns to acknowledge: Dove, Marin, etc. I can't say that I like the
man—he simply will not stop talking—and that aversion no doubt
influences my reaction to his artists.

Permit me a disclaimer. I am not young and struggling nor a
practicing painter, merely an enthusiast (I resent the word dilettante)
whose money is important to the livelihood of such struggling painters. I
feel that I myself am somehow under attack, that Stieglitz regards me only
as an archaic mind that he will enlighten if I allow him. Is it surprising
that the attack seems to me to be violent and unjustified? Lizzie Bliss has
just paid the sensational price of $21,000 for a Cezanne still life; she speaks
of forming a museum of modern art with her collection as a nucleus. Ought
Stieglitz to be alienating her and others like her?

I'm afraid his near-abstractions, no matter how emotional he says they are at base, are too intellectual for me. I may be outmoded: I hold that art should speak to the heart as well as the eyes. Impressionism was built on the science of optics, I know; Matisse's paintings were nearly geometric planes. But I felt—with my entire body—when I looked at them, and that was part of the excitement. Thomas Moran said once that the Cubist attempt to express the intellectual in the form of art was something that could not be done. I am coming to believe him.

It may not be the fault of the painters at all. New York seems to me almost as scornful of sentiment as Paris, almost as disillusioned about life made empty and faith destroyed by that monstrous war. It could be that an art based purely on mind is the artist's escape from the feelings that betrayed us into meaningless death. Everywhere I hear of a "revolt against the tyranny of the middle class." I was not aware that middle class outlooks had any influence: perhaps painters need a direction for generalized anger.

There may be light at the end of this particular tunnel. I am on the trail of a movement of pure color and recognizable forms centered far from New York. Apparently for the past five years there have been annual exhibitions here in the city prepared by the Taos Society of New Mexico. I did see the first at the Milch Gallery when it was here and was unenthusiastic. Though the technique was superb and the subjects exotic (Southwestern Indians), I thought the paintings romantic, sentimental, narrative illustration in the 19th century style, so I did not visit subsequent shows. I've since seen reproductions in Scribner's magazine and have continued to feel that the modern movement has not yet reached Taos.

My friends tell me I should give New Mexico a second chance, especially Santa Fe. They are intrigued, as am I, by the possibility that a truly American art may come out of the deserts of the West. What do you think, darling? I am tempted to board a train as you did and travel to Santa Fe to see for myself.

Would it be possible for me to continue on to Arizona to see you? I am considering making the trip to coincide with something called the Santa

Fe Fiesta, which is held early in September. Might I visit Flagstaff thereafter? I would so like to see you and meet your new friends.

Love,
Lilly

August, 1922

Dear Mother,

All here are excited to think that "Jo's mother" might actually come to visit, even Dennis, who is planning to polish his taxi so that he can transport you through the streets in high style. Ruby says she would understand if you were to decide that the Weatherford would be more comfortable, but she would be honored to have you as a guest here on Verde—she is "spiffing up" the spare bedroom. Petra Armenta has the clothesline full of sheets that have been in the closet for ever so long. Ada is shaking out her wardrobe, washing and ironing, so you will not have a bad impression of her.

I'm touched that they are all so eager. I've talked volumes about you, of course, praising you to the skies—which is high indeed in Arizona— and I want them to like you, want you to like them. I remember how supercilious I was at first. Now I fear to have the town laughed at by Know-it-all Big City Types, and I am finally aware that they might feel the same. You are exquisitely courteous as well as accepting of all sorts of people, and I know you wouldn't patronize them. That they trust you not to do so moves me deeply.

Early October is the most beautiful time of year here: storms have receded; leaves are impossibly golden; skies are brilliant blue. Nights are cool, but days are warm and sunny. I'm so happy you'll be here then. You will, won't you? It would be a terrible let-down if you were to decide not to come.

When Matt and Daisy were in town this week, we told them the news, and Daisy was as excited as the rest of us. She is a whirl of ideas about events and outings, places we can show to you, things we can do. "Jo, I'll clean the whole house, and you can come to the ranch for a few days. We can take her to Wupatki for a picnic and—what do you think, Matt? Can we round up some cattle so she can watch?" Matt smiled and said it would be "easy as one, two, three."

I can barely wait to bake a chocolate cake for you—imagine! —and walk with you around town and introduce you to Dr. Fronske. Don't bother to bring formal clothing, just comfortable things you can do something in, if you have any.

I'm dying to hear what The Family has to say about your proposed expedition. It hadn't occurred to me before—has any one of them except Lillian and Lina ever traveled west of Chicago? I'm also eager to hear your comments on the painting being done in Taos. I was aware of the exhibits in the city and was dubious. First: the painters lived far from New York—which we all knew was the center of the western hemisphere. And then, they had formed a colony, which I understood as a group clustered closely for mutual stimulus and the comfort of shared interests. I was uneasy about the possibilities for artistic incest and jealousy in such dependency. It did not occur to me that my definition of "colony" might also be a description of the situation of artists in Paris.

In anticipation,
Jo

To Paul: I can understand that it would be more difficult for you to break away than it was for me, your responsibilities and all. But perhaps you could accompany my mother and tell the family you are doing so to offer her your protection against the danger that would surround her here?

Cousin Lillian came through town again recently. The *Sun* reported early in the month that Jimmy Swinnerton was here with his wife for his annual visit and went on to Kayenta for an unprecedented gathering of artists. Rudolph Dirks and George Herriman, both syndicated cartoonists from New York, were also with him. The paper said it's his custom to bring friends every year to show them the wonders of Arizona.

It sounded quite exciting. Maynard Dixon, who paints Western landscapes in oil, and his wife, a photographer, followed them a few days later. And *then* New York illustrator and landscape artist W.R. Leigh and his wife arrived and left immediately for Kayenta. Lillian was with them; the editor referred to her as a "talented artist" and said she planned to stay with the Wetherills for a month.

Apparently they were all there, by plan and arrangement, to vacation together for two weeks until the Hopi snake ceremony at Hotevilla—as I understand it something to do with snakes gathered from four directions, washed and purified and released to carry prayers for rain into the earth. We learned of the date only when an old-time Indian trader named Lorenzo Hubbell came into Flagstaff and told Fred Breen.

I must confess to feeling rather hurt and left out. Probably Lillian still has no idea I'm here—how could she? After all, I've tried to keep my whereabouts confidential.

I would rather go into Indian country with Matt and Daisy than with a group of strangers, no matter how notable. At the dances there was apparently a large crowd of visitors from Flagstaff— Hotevilla is closer than the other Hopi towns—and I might have found they interfered with what I could see. Ruby says staying through a dance on a hot August day might have been altogether too much for me. Nevertheless, I was in a bit of a pout. But I'll get over it: I'm big as all outdoors, a phrase that means more here than it did in the city.

I was as excited as anyone when an aeroplane came to town at the end of August. First it landed south of the railroad tracks on a field east of the Normal School. "Think of it," was the conversation on the sidewalks, "fifty years ago you came into this country on a horse, forty years ago on a train, twenty years ago in an automobile if you could stand the roads, and now you could come in the air!"

Due to worries about noise and "that thing" falling out of the sky on people's heads, the plane moved out to Babbitt Pasture north-west of town to fly stunts for the entertainment of the crowd and— such excitement!—passengers could go for a ride at fifteen dollars each. Ada says those who went up couldn't stop talking about it, "flapped like wash in the wind" was her way of describing them.

I've come to feel a part of what goes on. When more rain than usual fell in June, I rejoiced with everyone else; I worried when less than usual fell in July. Heavy clouds soaked the Inner Basin and left snow on the top of the Peaks, and I too was relieved for the assurance of water in Ruby's kitchen. Petra's first grandson was born, and I sent cunning little blue shirts. And I grieved for an old man named John Clark who came into this country forty-five years ago, cutting his wheat for the last time: soon a new high school will stand where his farm is, perhaps a city park as well, if citizens vote bonds to buy the land. Will anyone remember in coming years what once was on that ground and the man who owned it? Probably not.

Luke came back, "naked as a shorn sheep," Ada said. I loved the image, though he wasn't really without clothing, just without money. He boasted at the livery stable that he had to help his big brother with the roundup. Ruby said he was way too early for that and it was obvious to everybody he didn't have any place to go where he wouldn't have to work or he wouldn't have come home.

I couldn't believe he would do much besides just get in Matt's way and eat Margaret's cooking. Thinking of how distressed Daisy must be, I was frustrated to be in town where I couldn't offer help or comfort, *anything*. It's agonizing to worry and be unable to take any action, what we would have called in the city "a bum show."

It must be as painful as anything that can happen to a family, to have a bad person in it. Sick and leaden, wanting to do something to right the situation and unable to find anything. Ruby says Navajos know: it's a real insult when they say, "He acts like he doesn't have a family." I hoped Margaret wasn't thinking it was her fault somehow, that Luke would have been different if his upbringing had been different, though it was obvious to everyone that wasn't so.

Ruby and I talked about it. "She loved him, you see, when he was a baby and a child and a boy. You don't get over that tender feeling. It's easier for you and me—we can get mad because we're farther away."

"It isn't at all nice of me, Ruby, but I wonder if it would be better if he were to die."

"No, she'd still grieve and think of him every day and cry every night. If he went away and never came back, she'd feel just as bad. It's the love, it gives you more chances for sorrow than you can count."

She lifted her chin and tightened her mouth. Suddenly I remembered what she'd said once, that she had a son she didn't want to talk about. "Oh, Ruby. Oh, I'm sorry."

Tears stood in her fine old eyes. "One way or another, you lose them. That's the way it is."

"You haven't lost Emily; Margaret hasn't lost Matt and Daisy."

"The babies they were with their arms soft around your neck, you always lose that. Even if they grow up to be good people, even if they stay close, you miss the babies they were. But listen to me go on." She turned her back to dry her eyes. "What do you say we walk over to Ada's?"

I don't know when I've felt more Elemental Anguish, but a light touch was obviously the thing. "I know, let's call and tell her we'll stop at the Bon Ton Bakery and bring a fresh pastry and have a tea party."

She smiled. "The very thing, Jo. She probably needs cheering up since getting around is so hard for her. Looks to me like we all do, but you and I can fool ourselves we're doing it for Ada."

*O*ne warm morning at the end of August I answered the phone to hear—I couldn't believe it—Cousin Gertrude's mocking voice. "Well, Jo, I've found you. You're fast, but not too fast for me, if you recognize a double *entendre* after all this time in the sticks."

The last person I'd have wanted to talk to…how in the world?

"I'm half a mile away at a quaint hostelry called the Weatherford Hotel. A stuttering taxi driver told me where you might be located. He was so proud of himself and so pleased to know I was your cousin. What a bumpkin."

Dennis was *not* a bumpkin. Nobody had known where I was, except my mother…

"Would you like to know how I found you? It wasn't your mother, if that's what you're thinking, she's been inscrutable as a Chinaman. I employed a little detective work. Clues put together. And intuition. When that peasant with the taxi stammered that he'd b-b-b-b-been the first to m-m-m-m-meet you when you arrived, I was hard put not to cheer. What a triumph!"

I felt sick—Gertrude in Flagstaff with her jeering sarcasm, examining my friends and laughing about them, it was too unpleasant for words. "What do you want of me?"

"Why, to see you, of course. I'm on my way to renew an old acquaintance in California, and I stopped off to visit my cousins, although the buffoon with the taxi tells me Lillian isn't here. He offered to drive me immediately to the house where you're living, but I fear I'm too fastidious to accept local domestic hospitality. What a thought! Tell me, do—the taxi man revealed that your landlady was a cattle rancher—does she wear boots like a man?"

I had learned through painful episodes not to be drawn into Gertrude's meanness. "How long do you plan to stay?"

"Only overnight, I'm afraid. I doubt I could tolerate this country inn longer. Civilization certainly has been slow to reach the Baby State, hasn't it? The last outpost of frontier, resisting modern times fiercely as a middle-aged virgin. It's too rich for words, I wouldn't have believed it if I hadn't seen it for myself." She laughed, *so* superior. Ada would have said trying to teach Gertrude to be nice would be like trying to teach a rooster to lay eggs.

I turned to look at Ruby and saw that she was watching me with concern on her dear old face. Not in a million years would I have introduced Gertrude into Ruby's house and watched her catalogue every detail, building entertaining stories for recounting back in New York. "I'll join you downstairs in the hotel dining room in an hour. It's in the basement."

"That *is* thoughtful of you, Jo, to spare me the embarrassment of not knowing what to say. As it is, I'm policing my vocabulary. I'm not sure how many words the local yokels know." And then that sneering laugh again.

I hung up without saying goodbye. "Ruby, it's too awful. My cousin Gertrude, the nasty one, she's invaded the Weatherford."

"She would be welcome here."

"No she wouldn't, you'd hate her." Peeved, I plunked down on a kitchen chair.

"I doubt that."

"The best thing you could say would be that she was another experience you'd had because of me. I wouldn't think of putting you through it. You or Ada or Daisy or anybody I care about."

"I've seen pretty much all kinds in my life."

I sighed. "The thing is, Ruby, I would be ashamed of her and afraid you'd think less of me."

"It would take more than a cousin, I can tell you that. Don't fret, it'll all come out in the wash."

I went upstairs and pulled out my smartest summer frock, blue linen with blue buttons. I had brought it from New York. It was probably wildly out-of-date already, but so what? Gertrude would laugh at anything I wore, she always had—it was her way of proving she was in the know. Drawing on my stockings, I fumed. That high-hat *snob*. Critical was her only approach to people. She'd made every cousin in the family miserable since she'd been twelve.

I called for a ride with Dennis to save my shoes from dust. He was so proud of himself that he had helped her to find me. "First thing she did was mmmmention your name. Well, you coulda knocked me over with a feather. Your m-mmm-mother coming and then your cousin stepping down from Number Nine. Never a dull mmm-mmoment around here."

He fairly sprinted to open the passenger door when we arrived at the stairs that led down from the sidewalk to the Weatherford's restaurant. "You enjoy your lunch. Maybe I'll just hang around to see the reunion."

"Oh, Dennis, there'll be nothing to see. No glad cries and embraces. Probably she'll be half an hour late, she usually is."

I had been waiting long enough to remind myself that I was no longer the girl Gertrude had tormented so often, when she made An Entrance into the dining room that attracted every eye, which was what she wanted, I'm sure. Her frock was chocolate brown, tasteful enough, but her cloche glittered and twinkled above penciled brows and a brilliant mouth; her shoes were equally scintillating. She paused in the doorway long enough for all to observe the effect, then flung out her arm and cried, "There you are, Jo, at long last!" and advanced on me, her hat reflecting the ceiling lights. I couldn't imagine wearing such a thing in August—she'd be overheated in no time.

She bent to kiss my cheek—her perfume was overpowering—and waited imperiously for the waiter to pull out a chair. I thought she was overdoing the Wealthy Sophisticate a bit. Her husband's death hadn't left her *that* affluent, though added to what she received from her father's estate, it enabled her to indulge all manner of bizarre whims.

"Well." She settled herself with a good deal of commotion. "I must say you're looking healthy as a farm girl, not at all what I expected. I do believe you've been turned away from death's door, at least for the moment."

"I may have." The waiter, whom I didn't know by name, thank goodness, placed menu cards before us.

"Then why are you still hiding here in a wilderness? Surely you could come home to the sidewalks of New York." She'd always had an artificial laugh; it seemed unusually irritating just then.

"When my doctor says it's safe."

She leaned toward me and spoke in a loud whisper. "Do you trust any doctor who would live in this place?"

"Oh, Gertrude." I had to shake my head. "You remind me of how far away I am."

She drew off her gloves and opened her bag—also glittering—to pull out a package of cigarettes. "Do you mind?" She fitted one into a brassy holder. "I've taken up the habit." She barely acknowledged the waiter who appeared with a match. "Now do tell me what you find to do in such a dinky burg." She exhaled a great cloud of smoke. "You can't possibly enjoy it."

Something naughty came over me. "Well, let's see." I leaned back. "There are Indian dances. Cattle to herd. Long hours on horseback across open country. I stay quite busy."

"Jo, you don't know how I sympathize. Here you sit in last year's fashion with your hair shaggy and your nails short, telling me about a life of hardship, and you don't complain. By the way, I'm not sure that color is good on you, now that you're brown as a pushcart peddler."

I actually laughed, seeing her clearly, oh *very* clearly. "What do you suggest?"

Another cloud of smoke. "Well, not anything too bright, you'd look like an Italian. Black always did make you sallow. White would emphasize the tan. I wonder about peach. Definitely not pink, you'd look quite childish."

"I'll consider peach. Does the family know you're here?"

"Heavens no! It's the most delicious secret. I didn't tell a soul what I had deduced about your hideaway. Later I'll inform everyone I've seen you and how you look."

"I'm sure you will."

"But not until I return. I'm dying to see their reaction. I can just picture it." Another laugh: she was looking forward to causing shock waves. Goodness but Gertrude did enjoy herself.

The waiter came with an order book and stood waiting. Gertrude dismissed him with a gesture and leaned in confidentially. "That man looks Chinese to me."

"He is. Several eating places in Flagstaff are operated by Chinese."

"Is the food safe?"

I decided not to tell her the cook was no doubt Chinese too. "Much of it comes in on the trains."

"That's a relief." Another cloud of smoke. "I wouldn't want to reach California with an upset tummy."

Without looking around, she beckoned oh-so-casually and the waiter came at once. He'd been watching her, everyone in the room had. In a voice louder than it needed to be, she ordered oysters, the most expensive item on what she referred to as the *carte du jour*. She was putting on quite a show.

I rather wished she could be less flamboyant. "Tell me, Gertrude, is there family news my mother may have missed?"

"Your grandmother Scheffler has been keeping to her room for days at a time." Grandmother's room was large and lovely, full of books and paintings—it looked out onto a garden. I could see that she might stay in it as a way to escape the attention of people like Gertrude. One of the advantages of getting older ought to be that one can quite calmly refuse to put up with certain people any longer.

"The rumor is that she's devastated by your disappearance. Really, Jo, I don't understand your mother, I'd think she would summon you home to see her mother one last time." No scruples, Gertrude had absolutely no scruples.

A man stood from a table in the corner and moved toward us. Luke—I hadn't noticed him before. His shirt had definitely just come from a haberdashery. "Jo, I haven't seen you for weeks. You're looking bright as a new penny."

I can't say I was overjoyed. "I'm surprised, I thought you'd be out on the ranch."

"Business in town." He turned to Gertrude. "The word has spread that one of your family is among us."

I sighed. "Gertrude, this is Luke Friendly. Luke, my cousin, Mrs. Voss."

She extended her hand. He took it gently; he didn't know that she was not likely to break, not Gertrude. "A very charming cousin, I must say," and gazed intently into her eyes. He'd already had time to evaluate the rest of her.

"Is this one of the dangerous Western men I've heard about?" She had that much right.

"Ma'am, I'm dangerous only to men who would do me ill, *never* to a lady. May I join you for a moment?"

I thought he was disgusting, but Gertrude fairly simpered. "Please do, Mr. Friendly, I hardly expected to find such courtesy on the frontier."

He wasn't bad looking, if you didn't know him. I tried to see him as Gertrude might: an exotic figure of romance, a chivalrous cowboy, a knight of the frontier—in other words, a trophy.

"*Mrs.* Voss? I'm surprised to hear that such a lovely young creature is married." Ada would have said he was like a fly around jam.

"My husband died in France, Mr. Friendly." She dropped her eyes in artificial sorrow, and I saw her as he might: dollar signs all over her, a remarkable opportunity.

She mentioned stopping off on her return trip east, "for a day or so." He hoped she would do the town that favor. She expressed a desire to see something of this fascinating country. He would consider it a pleasure to serve as her guide. I looked from one to the other, annoyed with both of them, and a quite wicked idea occurred to me. Gertrude and Luke—it was such a delightful picture that I put my napkin to my lips until I could control myself.

If only she would take him back to New York with her…if only he could avoid spoiling everything… It would get him out of town and (probably) keep him out of jail and (perhaps) relieve his mother's anxiety. As for her—well, I couldn't think of anything Gertrude deserved as much as she did Luke. She'd get her money's worth from him and make him work for it, but even she would realize his motives sooner or later. As Ada would say: Luke was sincere as a Bible salesman.

Santa Fe September, 1922

Dear Jo,

I am reeling under the impact of new sensations in a place quite foreign to me and loving every minute. Travelers rhapsodize about the light in Italy, in Greece; they pale by comparison with New Mexico. The space, the color, the Spanish-Indian culture—I am alive to my fingertips. Do rejoice for me.

On the westbound train my excitement grew with every mile—by the time we had climbed into New Mexico, I was ecstatic. The light was brilliant, no doubt due to the elevation and the dry air, and the land that swept away to towering mountains with Spanish names, all that land with nobody in it, well, you must have experienced a similar intoxication. For a woman who has lived her life in quite different conditions, it was a revelation very nearly religious. Superlatives are inadequate; words cannot do justice.

At Lamy Junction sixteen or so miles to the west of Santa Fe, I descended with my luggage. There is no track to the capital city except a spur to carry freight, but I had been told to expect as much and cheerfully allowed myself to be bustled into a funny little autobus for transporting. With tourists becoming ever more frequent, it is a routine form of conveyance. Away from confining railroad cars, I was part of the quite incredible space.

Almost hidden in the vast land, overwhelmed by surrounding mountains, Santa Fe came suddenly into my awareness. Some say it is sleepy. I disagree: I find it fascinating. First, it is much older than Manhattan, older even than the Massachusetts colony, and formed by several diverse influences, so that a newcomer from the East feels alien. One building after another has no visible roof! Cathedral bells ring through the transparent air. I've frequently wondered: am I still in the U.S.A.?

My hotel, named La Fonda, is suitably exotic, a design by a local firm incorporating elements of Spanish adobe and Indian communal— fluid lines, softened corners, dark ceiling beams. I'm told it's being referred to as "Santa Fe Style." I find it beautiful, now that I'm accustomed. From my window I look out across the trees in the old-fashioned town square to the Palace of the Governors, which is a modest one-story, anything but a palace, and the new Fine Arts Museum, also adobe pueblo in style, the patron agency for artists. Both the palace and the museum display paintings. Quite without knowing I was doing so, I had established myself almost at the center of New Mexico art.

I have found what I came looking for! On my first day, after a breakfast of ingredients I could not pronounce, I strolled across the plaza to the Fine Arts Museum and walked into a crowd of scurrying artists busy hanging a show to coincide with the Fiesta, artists who live both here and at Taos. Trying to stay out of their way, I looked about and felt the old thrill, the kind I've known in Paris. Color! Life! Beauty! Joy in the landscape—I was entranced. Not by all the canvases, but enough, enough.

As I was resting in the patio (such a civilized concept, the patio), the most charming woman came to introduce herself and sit beside me. You'll never guess. A former editor of Poetry magazine—you remember, Frost, Sandburg, Pound—who came to New Mexico seeking a cure for tuberculosis: Alice Corbin Henderson. A fortunate meeting for me; her home is the center of the local artists' circle. She knows everyone, seventy-five resident painters, another two hundred or so in summer, and she has introduced me.

Through her, I have been received in an old, mud-plastered house on Canyon Road, the home of Olive Rush, a marvelously versatile artist— she is off in Nebraska at the moment, but her studio was open so that one might see her work—and the new Santa Fe style house built by another painter recovered from tuberculosis, Carlos Vierra, dean so to speak of the artists here. (I thought of you, of course, meeting an artist who has recovered from t.b. in this climate. There's hope!) Also scores more people, some of whom have recently moved into picturesque dwellings, where they hold weekly showings of their work.

My meeting with Alice Henderson was fortunate for them as well, especially for Josef Bakos, William Shuster, Fremont Ellis and Sheldon Parsons: I've been buying paintings greedily from them, and from others as well—Rush, of course, I like her landscapes and one must encourage women. I see Cezanne in their work, the Fauves and Expressionists—and no wonder: many trained in New York schools—but the primary influence is New Mexico's monumental landscapes and clarity of air and undiluted color. I'm having the canvases shipped east on the railroad.

Alice Henderson is of the opinion that I've brought more encouragement than local artists have seen all year. (I wonder: also more money?) At the Fiesta, ancient but re-established three years ago, I bought two paintings and several drawings offered by local Indians, who had organized a fair to take advantage of the Fiesta crowds. Quite exuberant, I went back and forth between dancers in the plaza and Indian booths, finally choosing the most distinguished rug, which I'm having shipped home, and several pieces of silver jewelry, which I'll bring to Arizona so that you may see them.

Reluctant to leave this magical place, I have been persuaded to stay until the end of the month. My new acquaintances have offered to drive me seventy-five miles north to Taos for a Fiesta there and a visit to the art colony. They say I'll find both the little town and its art somewhat different from Santa Fe, older, more traditional and definitely more remote. It's wonderful to have an excuse to remain a few more weeks.

And then, Jo, I'll return to Lamy Junction and proceed to Arizona for a different kind of experience. To quote Dickens: "What larks we'll have."

With anticipation,
Lilly

P.S. Paul said your suggestion that he accompany me was the most exciting temptation he's had for years. His arrangements are in a particularly delicate stage at the moment (He is shifting funds about to protect them from his father's outrage) and he fears to leave even for a week. I reminded him of the Gordian Knot, and he confided that he dreams of buying a ranch and wants to insure he will have the money. Or perhaps, he said, he could meet someone experienced like Matt who would allow him to buy in as a partner. I find that a most intriguing idea, and I told him so.

I read the newspapers anxiously, wondering what my mother will think. The town has voted for bonds to buy John Clark's hundred and sixty acres—I doubt that would interest her. Neither would the news that a Japanese farmer named Matsumato is harvesting lettuce from his thirty acres on the Pump House Ranch and shipping it to New York. Asphalt streets are coming closer. We can be assured that Verde will be paved before the first snow; Ed Raudebaugh has already laid concrete curbs and gutters. She will not be impressed unless underlying rock must be dynamited as it was when work was done last month on Birch. If that happens, perhaps we can arrange to be out at the Friendly ranch during the noisiest part.

I hope she will not consider Flagstaff too bucolic for words after Santa Fe. I seize on the information that Harold Colton, the scientist from Pennsylvania, is proposing that a museum be founded to preserve relics and antiquities retrieved from such ancient houses as Wupatki, if there are any left by now. Editor Breen approves the idea and suggests it be turned over to the Woman's Club. Apparently the ladies are considered the logical source of support for scientific as well as cultural affairs. Would my mother find that interesting?

She will be here during the annual blood sport in the forest. I fear I can't hide that from her. Three weeks ago a forester from Albuquerque, Aldo Leopold, addressed a meeting of the Flagstaff Game Protection Association at the court house. That was his topic: game *protection*. I simply do not understand what is meant by the term—I'd have thought exactly the opposite was what everybody had in mind. Ruby seemed to notice nothing amiss, so I hesitated to bring the matter up.

Arizona has hunting seasons and licenses and something called a "bag limit." She laughed heartily when I asked whether that meant what would fit into a sack of some sort and then explained kindly. Nevertheless, I am embarrassed: I seem to be unable to straighten it out in my mind. What is a public shooting ground? My impression is that the ninety members of the Association shoot *everywhere*. Leopold advised the establishment of refuges and game wardens as New Mexico has to fight "game hog menace," and I am completely baffled. Hogs are a menace? Or are they game?

Last week Zane Grey was here, apparently without Lillian, saying, "No place in the West calls to me as does the broad and magnificent stretches of open country in Arizona." His purpose was to "outfit" with Lee Doyle for a bear and turkey hunt. I don't wish to sound petulant, but it simply does not make sense to me to love a place and try to kill everything in it. There must be something missing in my makeup, since so far as I know I'm the only one to feel this way.

My mood is particularly sullen because of an event reported in this week's paper. With so many armed people out in the forest —the telephone directory would be but a partial list, according to the *Sun*— a twenty-six-year-old man was shot and killed by his best friend who mistook him for a turkey. Light was poor at dusk. The dead man was tying his shoe lace; his friend, who had been hunting separately, shot at a movement he glimpsed. Though it was a mistake, it was a stupid one committed by a man so anxious to kill something that he did not take basic care. Ruby thinks so too.

I definitely will not tell my mother about it when she arrives on tomorrow's train. I'm particularly anxious that she see the good in this country I've learned to love. I know she would not make the kind of jeering comment I could expect from Gertrude. But what would she think?

Speaking of Gertrude, she never did get to California. Before we had left the Weatherford basement that first day, she and Luke had made plans to meet the following morning. He would call for her, he said. Would she prefer to drive out to Walnut Canyon in an automobile or (here his manner turned confidential) in an old-fashioned horse-drawn equipage? I was appalled to think of the desecration those two narcissists would inflict on the spirit of that place, but Gertrude distracted me.

"Oh, make it horse-drawn—how nostalgic. Do you own one yourself?"

"It will be no trouble to hire an equipage at the livery stable."

"You must allow me to bear the expense...no, I insist. Since the outing is to be for my entertainment and you'll be taking time from your duties, it's only fair. And that I compensate you for your time."

I was sure Luke had never intended to pay for anything, but he can't have expected the terms of their relationship to be established so easily and so early. He made the briefest of protests before he capitulated, ever so gracefully. "Until tomorrow then, Mrs. Voss." In no time they'd be on to first names the way things were progressing.

Gertrude barely touched her oysters. "Jo, you must help me to shop. I haven't the faintest idea what costume would be considered suitable or where to buy it. I count on you. There's no point in trying to pass myself off as a Westerner, nor do I want to look so dowdy as all that. Is it possible to be *chic* in outdoor clothing around here?"

We flitted from store to store until all the town knew I was a party to my cousin going off with Luke for a day. She chose corduroy knickers which buttoned at the knee, walking shoes, a tailored shirt embellished with a man's tie. I could see from the way she preened before the mirror that she adored the figure she made.

"You'll need a hat with a large brim."

"Whatever for?"

"Sun can be brutal at this altitude."

"But will it complement the ensemble?"

"Would you prefer a sun-burned nose? Red and peeling?"

Preoccupied with herself, at no time did Gertrude ask to meet my friends or see the life I had in Flagstaff. Finally she dismissed me, and I fled home full of news of the day.

"You should have seen them, Ruby, each thinking how to outsmart the other, it was too rich for words."

"But this could be dangerous, Jo."

"For which one? It's a perfect match, double justice."

She looked at me earnestly while she thought about it and began to smile. "Since you put it that way, I can see the possibilities."

"Isn't it a scream? Let's walk over tomorrow and tell Ada."

Next morning after I had explained Gertrude and done a few imitations, Ada laughed until she was wiping tears away. "And nobody can blame you, no matter what happens. You had nothing to do with it. And which one would you warn?"

"Isn't it too hilarious?"

"Jo, some news is dry as an old saddle, but this will keep me chuckling for weeks. Both of them thinking they're so clever." She began to laugh again. "Nobody nice will be hurt. Oh, I do so love to see people get what they deserve."

"But mum's the word."

"Oh my yes, we mustn't let on—either one could be scared off in a minute. Thank goodness I've got the two of you. This kind of secret could make me bust wide open if there was nobody I could talk to about it."

It wasn't exactly a secret. Luke took Gertrude to dinner at the Weatherford that evening, and Gertrude paid. They drove the buggy up Mars Hill to Lowell Observatory, and Gertrude paid. They took an auto down the Oak Creek road into the canyon, and Gertrude paid. In no time the whole town knew about their jaunts, according to Ada, and talked of it endlessly. There were those who thought Gertrude should be warned off and didn't know what to do since it should be up to me, and I ought to know about Luke if I was ever going to.

Petra told me with much head shaking and furrowing of brow that Luke was "*no bueno por nada.*" I was touched by the anxiety in her dark eyes. "*Senora, no bueno.*"

Ada was having a high time. "I just smile pretty as you please and nod. Butter wouldn't melt in my mouth. Soon as they turn their backs…" She crossed her eyes so comically I choked. "This is the best story I've watched for years."

All three of us hoped Margaret and Matt and Daisy wouldn't hear of it too soon, but the fifth day (Luke and Gertrude had gone out to Mormon Lake to watch the hunting) they walked into the kitchen the picture of distress, prepared to Do the Honorable Thing and save Gertrude from a broken heart.

"Even out on the ranch we heard about it," Matt began, "about Luke romancing your cousin, and we're pretty upset."

"Why?" How could I tell them I was prepared to see Luke go into life-long servitude?

Daisy was touchingly agitated. "Oh Jo, you don't know Luke. He's so selfish, I'll bet a cookie he isn't able to care about anybody but himself, he never has been yet. What if he's just after her money?"

"Just?"

"Well, yes, money is nice, but what if she thinks it's *her* he wants, then she'll be terribly hurt."

Margaret was the one who mattered if what Ruby had said about losing children was true. It was her *son* we were discussing, after all. I set a cup of coffee on the table in front of her and eased into a chair, deciding how to begin.

"Luke is a handsome man with polished manners when he wants to use them." She smiled with her mouth, grateful for a compliment about him. "He's strong, he moves with assurance, he can be quite charming. Think how he looks to Gertrude. Has he brought her out to the ranch?" All three shook their heads.

"You might feel differently if you'd met her. Suppose she wants him because of the sensation he'd be in the city? How impressed her friends would be if she were to come back with a real Western cowboy? And Luke might enjoy playing that role, being admired by all and sundry. He might be very happy the rest of his life. Maybe he'd be better at it than anything else he could do—it might suit him."

Ruby had brought cream from the icebox; she was watching me. Matt was watching his mother. Margaret's eyes didn't leave my face. "He'd be comfortable and well cared for and definitely well dressed, she'd see to that. Maybe she'd take him to Europe." I glanced at Daisy. "Luke would be a *phenomenon* in Paris, ladies would fall in love with him in droves, I should think. He'd thrive on it, and the only work he'd have to do would be to keep Gertrude proud of him."

I was actually managing to convince myself it was the best thing that could happen to him. Daisy was wavering. "Jo, you're so good, to see what it could mean to Luke. But what about your cousin?"

"That's the thing. She too cares about no one except herself. There isn't room for much in her head except how she looks to other people—her clothes, her hair. She'd wear Luke like a piece of jewelry. They'd both be getting what they want."

"That's not a real marriage."

Ruby put an arm around Daisy's shoulders and squeezed. "Course it is, and better than what some people ever have. It might not be what *we* would want, but it isn't up to us to decide for others."

Matt smiled slowly. "Might keep Luke too busy to get into trouble." He was a better man than his brother, I thought, about a thousand times better. He'd want to make his own life, not circle around someone else's.

It took an hour to persuade the Friendlies that I was in no way alarmed for my cousin and to relieve their honest hearts. They never did laugh with delight as Ada had, but they too agreed to watch how things developed without trying to interfere. Daisy sniffed, "Luke's a grown man, I *think*. It's up to him what he does as long as he doesn't shame us. Maybe we'd be relieved if he did move to New York to be a rich woman's husband."

Matt was cautious. "Hasn't even been a week yet. I haven't heard that anything's gone that far."

With both people wanting the same thing, it went far and fast. At the end of the week, Gertrude boarded a train going east, not west, and Luke went with her. She telephoned from the Weatherford as he was helping Dennis to tie her trunk on the running board.

"We went out to that run-down ranch yesterday to tell his mother, such a dumpy woman, but I thought it was good of him. The sister certainly lacks style, doesn't she? Anyway, I'm dying to show him Manhattan and show him *to* Manhattan." Her laugh was high and excited. "We'll be married soon after we reach civilization. The cousins will love him immediately, I know. I'm not sure about the Grandmothers, but he'll win them over, he's such a prize."

Well, how nice for Luke. Who else would have considered him a prize? I couldn't wait to tell Margaret she'd said that. And I did hope Daisy was dancing in delight. It was too rich.

It's certainly true that one satisfaction about having news is telling it. Ruby and I walked to Ada's house as fast as we could and were pleased that she hadn't heard. "I've been right here all morning. Luke a prize, that's funny—I never saw two people so eager to take on problems. Sit right down and tell me all about it so I'll know something the others don't. Flagstaff'll have fun with this story for years."

It was her opinion the town would never see either of them again. "Jo, you'll have to tell me what you hear about Luke in New York, please do. I hate it when stories stop all of a sudden."

What a swell way to look at life: stories unfolding.

While Ruby phones her grocery order, my mother sits at the kitchen table drinking coffee with thick cream from one of the blue willow cups and reading the *Sun*. I am busy in my apron, kneading bread and watching her covertly.

"Jo, I understand finally what you've been writing about all these months." She looks up. "A man out hunting deer shot off one of his own *toes*. How extraordinary. Two other men went off with bows and arrows, which I'd have thought out-of-date for a century or more, and each of them killed a lion. The sheriff has been in a gun fight with horse thieves. I feel as if I'm in still another foreign country."

Things have been lovely since yesterday when she stepped down from the AT&SF car in her silk stockings and modish silver shoes—strap across the instep—to face my embrace and Dennis' grin and curious inspection from a crowd of men lounging about the station. I was so proud of her, a lady to her glove tips despite her sojourn in Santa Fe.

"So this is Dennis, my daughter's virtual life-line all these months. I'm pleased to meet you at last." Not a hint of condescension. "And this is Flagstaff. I had no idea the mountains were so close."

To his credit, Dennis had his own kind of courtesy. "Welcome. It's an honor for us." I suspected he had given thought before hand to a greeting on which he would not stammer. And he didn't say a thing about Gertrude—I'd been afraid he might.

As she had twenty months earlier, Ruby was waiting outside her house. "I heard the whistle as the train left and knew Dennis would have you here in two shakes. And here you are. We like Jo so much we know we'll like you too."

Each offered both hands to the other. Each offered a comradely smile. "I feel I know you so well. Please call me Lilly." "Please call me Ruby." Dennis and I stood side by side beaming like a couple of full moons. Mother was eastern elegance, every detail of her clothing quietly correct, her ashes-of-roses hemline not too short, not too long. Ruby was in the blue cotton dress I knew so well and everyday shoes, her grey hair in a bun, and she was a lady too. Arm in arm they turned to the house talking of train travel and yellow autumn leaves, and I followed true to form, Awash in Emotion. The whole scene was almost more goodwill than I could encompass.

Through the window I saw Ada watching, waiting her turn in her Sunday-best dress. When I introduced her, she was irrepressible as always. "Look at you, how pretty you are. Plain as the nose on my face where Jo gets her stylish ways."

To my delight, my mother answered, "I've heard that pretty is as pretty does. If that's true, you must surely be the most beautiful woman in the world."

Ada clapped her old hands and laughed. "You turned that compliment around in the blink of an eye—a woman after my own heart." Mother would never have a nicer tribute.

With one continuous grin, Dennis carried her bags upstairs to the spare bedroom—cleaned, Ruby said, "to a fare-thee-well." Mother was ushered into the kitchen for her first cup of Arizona coffee, she and Ruby and Ada chatting like old friends about the differences between East and West. I was silent spectator, recognizing that women whose lives had been separated by a good deal more than miles could be so instantly compatible. It had to do, I thought, with being able to see outside oneself to the reality of another soul: one more lesson to be tucked away under the heading of Educating Jo.

Because Ada couldn't climb the stairs, I stayed in the kitchen with her when Ruby went up with Mother to show her to the bedroom and the modern bath and help her to unpack. Ruby offered the privilege to me, but I was pleased by the warmth between them and declined to interrupt it.

Ada watched them out of the room. "She does you credit, Jo. I didn't see the cousin, but your mother makes me think even better of you. That's one of the few things parents can do for their grown-up children."

"Ada, you're teaching me to be wise—surely that's another."

"See," she smiled, "see how much you're like her."

Doctor Fronske stopped by in the afternoon to be introduced. The grocery delivery man came in to "meet Jo's mother." Not until after supper, after Dennis had come to drive Ada home, did I have my celebrity to myself in my room, virtually glowing about her comments as she stood before the painting on my easel.

"But darling, it's too wonderful! You've definitely developed a stronger feel for composition—I'm impressed that your off-center placement of the tree works so well against these features back here. The color would hold its own against anything I saw in New Mexico."

We settled in to talk, I perched on the foot of the four-poster bed in my blanket robe, she in the wing chair. "What a wonderful place. Such warm people."

"It's not Santa Fe."

"No, but why should it be? Neither places nor people can be identical."

"I've been waiting to hear your opinion of Taos."

"Oh my, Taos. Enchanted. Timeless. The most spectacular setting you can imagine—magnificent, panoramic vistas. Remote, you understand; one approaches on a narrow steep road through a frightening canyon, and finally there's a very old Indian pueblo plus an adobe Spanish town, much smaller than Santa Fe, no electricity. And the buildings—stunning. They're made of mud, plastered annually, mud mixed with straw. When that brilliant sun is on them, they shine golden. It's the most magical effect."

"How long did you stay?"

"Four nights in another La Fonda; it was once a store. Not nearly so impressive as the hotel in Santa Fe, but adequate," she laughed, "if one were not too demanding. As it too opened onto the plaza, we were at the center of everything."

"Did you see the Fiesta?"

She pushed her slippers off and curled her legs under her robe, quite an artless movement, I thought. "It was wonderfully colorful and exciting, a Spanish carnival and Indian dances with names like Corn and Sun Down. I felt uncomfortably ignorant; it was so removed from my experience that I needed explanations for everything. Quite a different world."

"Yes, I know. Humbling, isn't it?"

"Probably beneficial." What a contrast she was to Gertrude.

"Did you meet artists?"

"Several. Most live on a hill with a view down Taos Valley. There are no galleries, so one sees paintings in the studios. I was received affably, but I find that one usually is if one has money." She smiled. "Excuse my cynicism. And then, Mabel Dodge has been there for several years. In Santa Fe they say she chose Taos because she wanted her own domain."

"Mabel Dodge, the woman who worked on the Armory Show? Who held a salon on Washington Square?"

"The same. A noteworthy salon." A hearty laugh. "A catalyst for people who termed themselves movers and shakers. She's breaking her chains, she says, and beginning anew. She entertained us quite graciously one cool evening and talked endlessly of paradise and utopia, aesthetic needs, spiritual hunger, and all that. The original art colony was solidly established by the time she arrived, but she seems to be casting a wide net, hoping to expand it."

"Did you like the Taos paintings?"

She answered slowly "What shall I say? As I expected, the painters are virtuosos in the realist style, detailed and authentic, anecdotal—very marketable. For a time most of them were at the National Academy or the Art Students League: I confide that for me the only quality that distinguishes them from Nineteenth Century academics is that their subjects are southwestern Indians. I hate to say it of people who are working so sincerely, I truly do, but I still must judge the paintings, well, exotic and very capable illustration but neither challenging nor inspiring."

"I rather thought you'd react that way. I felt the same about the Taos paintings I've seen: enviable technique—I wish I had that skill—but an older style. Landscape is usually background for the figures."

"The jest in Santa Fe is that its art colony was founded by painters who were discouraged by the conservatives in Taos and fled. I did buy a Hennings, a bit in the passe fashion but so colorful, and a Dasburg, though I thought it rather pictorial." Another laugh. "I was charmed away from my prejudices."

"Good for you. I want to see the paintings that did that."

We talked like two chums until midnight, laughing, covering The Family, art and music news. I told her the whole story of Gertrude and Luke—"What a mimic you are, Jo. That's Gertrude to a T."—and she thought it too delightful. "My first thought is that each will make the other miserable. Luke might be back within the year. But perhaps not. I hope Gertrude has her money tightly invested."

"I hope Luke doesn't lose his looks. Speaking of cousins—tell me about Paul. Is he really serious about breaking with the family and transplanting himself, or is he procrastinating?"

"I think he is quite determined. He's always been deliberate and prudent: it's in character for him to remove his estate from his father's control and do so in slow steps so as not to arouse parental alarm. Paul will arrive in Arizona fairly soon, I expect, with the means to realize his dreams. I must say I admire him."

"I've said nothing to the Friendlies about his buying in as a partner; I don't have any idea how they would receive such a proposal, although I gather money for wells and windmills would make an important difference for them. And much as I like Paul, they may not prove compatible. But it would be an intelligent move for him—ranching amounts to a good deal more than writing checks. And the Friendlies are in need of cash. Paul's money and Matt's experience might be a good combination."

"From what you've written about Matt, I would think he'd be the kind of man we could trust to treat Paul well. We must wait and watch, I suppose, as you say you all did with Gertrude and Luke. Ada might agree that this development too is as good as a show." Until last night I had not realized how much I liked my own mother.

And now she sits in the kitchen—wearing a plain shirtwaist and a tailored skirt and looking elegant even in that—reading the *Sun*. "I notice the paper is Republican."

Ruby hangs the telephone in its cradle. "Right from the beginning. The state usually goes Democrat, but Fred Breen doesn't budge. Nothing weather-vane about him."

"I can see that he's anything but narrow. On the same page he reports that an old mule in a stall broke a rancher's arm and then goes on to discuss a new star cluster discovered by C.O. Lampland of Lowell Observatory and Professor Shapley of Harvard. Quite an informed presentation—it defines parsecs and confides that the known universe is now two quintillion miles bigger. The editor assumes a catholicity of interest among his readers. I believe you did say that, Jo."

"It's an amazing town." Clever of her to recognize it so soon.

She lowers the paper. "Ruby, I've read that women are beginning to work in astronomy here and there. Are there women on the staff at Lowell?"

Ruby takes the question with her usual precision. "Women? The only one I know of was Miss Leonard, she used the telescope and worked on writing up the information, doing drawings and things like that. Regarded as a pioneer in what they call planetology. She's been gone since Mr. Lowell died five or six years ago."

"She left when he died? Was that considered odd?"

"The *day* he died. The biggest part of her job was as his personal secretary, she traveled with him everywhere he went for twenty years. Mrs. Lowell lost no time in getting rid of her."

"Ah, yes, I see. There must have been gossip."

"Some. He'd known her for ten years before he married Constance. But there never was any evidence of anything done wrong, at least none that I know of, just people speculating."

"She was a formally-trained astronomer?"

"Not that I heard of. She was in astronomy societies in France and Mexico. Mr. Lowell sponsored her, I was told—he was the one who trained her."

"I sense a dramatic story there and a good deal of emotion."

"That's probably true."

"In addition to the science."

Ruby smiles at her. "That's probably true too."

"Are there any women who are trained scientists in town?"

"Gracious no, I'm not sure we'd know what to do with them. Miss Leonard, you see, was secretary to a man, so that was all right."

I rub my hands to dust the flour off. "I'm ready to let this bread rise. Shall we three go on a walking tour? I told Ada we'd bring lunch to her house at noon. She's very excited."

"Will it be acceptable to appear on the street dressed as I am?"

"Oh, Mother." I cover the dough with a towel. "Far more acceptable than Gertrude was in her sequined cloche. Right, Ruby?"

"Let me take off my apron, Lilly, and I'll be proud to be seen with you on every street in town knowing that folks will be watching from windows. Maybe Ada will feel up to walking back with us a block or two to get in on the parade."

So we stroll out into an October morning, and the first person who approaches to be introduced is old Skinny Jones. Mother exchanges the usual pleasantries with him, but as we walk on, she turns to Ruby. "What an extraordinary thing, you actually call him Skinny to his face."

"Everybody does. We always have, suits him, don't you think?"

Mother laughs. "Yes, obviously; he looks to be fashioned of sticks. Does the poor man have a legal name?"

"He must have, I'd think, but I can't remember it off hand."

Mother hesitates. "Skinny is distinctive, I suppose."

"He's been a carpenter in town since heck was a pup. When Lowell put in the telescope in 1894, Skinny helped build the dome."

For two days Flagstaff's light and color were intoxicating and its citizens warm and hospitable. Hilda Fronske stopped us on the street to invite Mother to attend next month's Shakespeare Club meeting as a guest. "We've hesitated to bother you, Jo, fearing that your illness would make Society burdensome. Perhaps you'd care to attend as well?"

Mother had been accepted immediately, while I was still probationary, but I didn't pout. In fact, I was tickled that her qualities were so apparent and not at all averse to having *entree* because of her. In Manhattan one's family was accepted without question as a guarantee of good behavior, a guide to what one might prove to be.

For two days, I showed Mother the places I knew: the post office, the Confection Den, Wong June's laundry, Dr. Fronske's office. Most of both days we sat in the kitchen and talked with Ruby—to ignore that would have been to lose the best part of my months in Flagstaff.

Mother was interested in everything. "Ruby, please enlighten me. The *Sun* reports possibility of a dam on the Colorado River; in the East I read nothing about it. Is this something new?"

"Oh my, no. There's been talk of it since the Bureau of Reclamation started in 1902."

"Are there good reasons for such a dam, do you think?"

"Depends on where you are. This country up here in northern Arizona doesn't stand to get much benefit, all we've got is deep canyons along the river. But down south, well…"

She dried her hands and sat at the table. "You have to understand what water means in the West. We've usually got practically none and most of the time it looks like we'll have to close up shop. But now and then we've got too much all at once, like when heavy snow up in the Rockies fills the river and floods farm land, especially down around Yuma. That happens off and on, scares the socks off people who think it'll turn California into one big lake. In 1916 the Southern Pacific thought it would lose its railroad bridge, water was so high. Now, those people want a flood control dam."

Mother laughed. "An understandable position."

"And we'd like to have a good source of irrigation water. All year long Flagstaff gets less rain than some places get in a day. We'd be glad to have some of the Colorado if anybody could figure out a way to get it here. We're interested in this talk about a dam over in Boulder Canyon, but we don't expect it would affect us much.

People upstream in flatter country, what they call the Upper Basin, think they could profit by a dam built up there."

"What does this man Hoover have to do with it? He was in Santa Fe when I was there. Isn't he out of Washington?"

"Secretary of Commerce. He's chairman of the commission that's trying to work out an agreement between seven states. Good luck to him. Getting seven western states to agree about water would be quite an accomplishment."

"Water is that important?"

"Worth more than gold."

The third morning Matt arrived in his Ford to drive us north to the Friendly ranch. "Daisy's so excited she can't hold still, finally Mama put her to scrubbing the floors to keep her busy. We've all been looking forward to you. Daisy'll sleep in with Mama—hope you two don't mind bunking together."

"Not in the least." I could tell from her voice that Mother had liked him from the first moment, work clothes and all. "Jo has told me so much. I'm sure I'll enjoy everything."

We had agreed that October being a busy time for ranchers, two nights would be a proper visit, and we loaded the back of the Ford with groceries Ruby had suggested. "Margaret won't let you pay for your food, but when you live so far from town, it's always welcome when visitors bring something to help out. Good manners, you know."

I was agitated, wanting my mother to see in the volcanos and the Painted Desert the wonder I had seen. She didn't disappoint me. "Oh, the grandeur! The enormous *size*! It makes one feel larger, don't you think? And blissfully alive."

As the shortest, I sat in the middle of the auto trying to keep my legs out of the way while she and Matt conducted a spirited dialogue literally over my head. They had agreed to use first names, at least *she* had. "Such glorious weather, Matt. How long will it hold?"

"You're here at the best of the aspen color, it'll be gone by the end of the month. But blue skies and bright sun usually last almost to Thanksgiving."

"And what is it that you'll be doing with the cattle during that time?"

Such a talent she had for conversation. I hadn't noticed before, too young, I suppose. From all appearances, she concentrated solely on the person she was talking to, which is a trick that could be learned, but as a result she also knew just what to say. I was very impressed—a gratifying feeling.

I had hoped she would recognize the goodness of the little
wooden ranch house with its magnificent views and not notice how
small and plain it was, but there was barely time for her to see it
before Daisy came bouncing down the steps to greet us. "Yay! You're
here!" Margaret was behind her on the porch. When I introduced
her, Mother set me another Good Example. "Margaret, I've been
anticipating talking with a woman who lives a rancher's life. I've
never for one day been so quiet and isolated as you are here. I hope
we'll have an opportunity in this beautiful place to discuss how it is
for a woman."

"Most of the time I'm too busy to notice." Margaret smiled.
"And having a family I don't feel lonesome. You know, Lilly, nobody
has ever asked me that before. We can have a good talk about it."

Daisy turned and hugged me, whispered, "Bet a cookie they do.
Your mother is wonderful." Matt went off to live a rancher's life, and
no one thought to ask him about it.

There was so much to show and only a few hours to do it all:
the spring, the corrals and pens, the calves, the golden eagle soaring
above the ridge. Most important to me—the colors of the land at
sunset. We sat on the porch and watched the final brilliance.

"You're right, Jo. Magic Time is a good name for it. I've never
seen a painting so inspiring; how would one begin?"

"I tried when I was here in April, evening after evening. I
learned to see each detail clearly, but I never did capture it to my
satisfaction. It might take a lifetime to produce one true canvas."

And then the rising blues of dusk while the cliffs far away across
the desert still glowed with light—we could only gaze in awe. Daisy
talked about the dreams she'd had as a child sitting just there.
"Sometimes there were whole cities of fairies in the pink layers. I
made up stories about them." Matt leaned against the porch rail and
listened to her. "I used to beg my big brother to ride over there with
me, but I never told him why."

"Farther away than they look. But we could have done it if I'd
known it was so important." His voice was enough to send shivers
all over a dope like me. So did the smile Daisy gave him. She didn't
notice Margaret standing in the doorway, waiting to summon us in
to supper.

The next morning after breakfast, Daisy and I left Mother and
Margaret cheerfully chatting over the picnic lunch they were packing
and went off to the corral to saddle three horses. That is, Daisy
saddled and I did as she told me.

"Now hand me that blanket. Mama says it's only a little over an hour to Wupatki. Sometimes riding makes her back hurt, but she thinks she'll be all right. She isn't trying to impress your mother."

"*I* am. Wait until she sees me on Piñon, she'll be proud of me, I hope. Gertrude would say I looked like a circus monkey."

"From what I saw of Gertrude that day they came out, I can't imagine *her* on a horse. Oh good, here comes Matt with our mothers. It's so nice of him to take the whole day to go with us. Some men would say they didn't have the time."

Mother and the lunch settled comfortably with Matt in the car, Margaret majestic in the saddle, we started out on a blue and gold morning with no wind at all. Matt drove as slowly as he could, but that was faster than our horses could walk, and he soon left us behind. I was glad for the silence. Glad too that Mother would have her first glimpse of Wupatki without a distracting crowd. I wanted her to see it, see what it was, not just be polite about it.

In that wide, beautiful land, clear under its brilliant sky, a peace settled on my chest and lasted all day. I was content with the rhythm of the horse, the warm comfort of the autumn sun, the company of my friends. When we came up to them at Wupatki, Mother and Matt were sitting on a red stone and gazing across at the old building. Mother turned a face to me that looked as if she'd just seen a vision and spread her hands as if to say she had no words.

We stayed for hours. All of us, even Mother, clambered over the rubble that choked the rooms, exclaiming and explaining. Mother: "But this is a national treasure. Why have I never heard of it?" Daisy: "I used to ride over here and try to decide which direction I'd have gone if I'd been those people who left." Matt: "Toward water." Margaret: "It must have been different a thousand years ago. This country barely supports the Peshlakai family now, and we figure there were a hundred times that many in all the ruins."

I saw details I hadn't noticed the first time, like the reddish volcanic hill to the northwest, its crater clearly visible. Like the blocks of stone that had fractured off all along the wash—there was building material everywhere. It was a shock to realize that the rock-strewn mound I had thought was part of the ridge was actually walls that had fallen and melted upon themselves; my back prickled to think that buried under the rubble must be more rooms, more masonry. Some of the standing walls sagged and leaned, dignified but ready to collapse. It was too awful—someday the old building might disappear altogether.

Mother bent to pick up something small from the ground. "Look at this. There are stripes on it, definitely painted. What in the world…"

"Sherds." Matt was a trove of information. "There used to be lots, all over the place. The big ones, especially if they could be pieced together so you could see the jars and bowls they used to be, were carried off."

"By…?"

"Pot hunters. They were all over this country, pretty well got the easy ones."

"There were so many pieces?" She rubbed the sherd between her fingers.

"Too many, I think, too many to be accidents. Sure pottery gets broken, but not everywhere. I've wondered if the old people did it on purpose."

"Why would they have done that?"

"I don't know. Maybe they couldn't carry much, didn't want somebody else to use them. Maybe a religious reason. I don't know."

We sat on a rock as big as a house to eat our lunch and gaze about us. Mother and Margaret became engrossed in a conversation about living close to Indians ancient and modern. "Another way of looking at the world, would you say?"

"You can learn a lot, if you can get past your own way and stay still and listen. It doesn't come to you all at once. A lot of things you never really thought about, like why you look at somebody who's talking to you or whether you show respect to other creatures or what the sun means to you. Things like that. You see yourself and wonder."

"One might be better for doing so."

"And then there's the question of time, of what it is. You're definitely part of it."

"It moves through you? You're on its line?"

"Something like that."

Matt lay down on a flat stone, put his hat over his face and went to sleep. Daisy and I talked softly. "I don't think I would ever want to leave this country if it were my home."

"I couldn't leave it *forever*, I'd be so homesick I'd waste away. But Jo, think how thrilling it would be to go someplace else and then come back and discover it all over again. You'd want to wrap your arms around everything you saw."

I looked out across the enchanted miles and knew what she meant. "It would be all the better for the contrast."

"That way you'd never get tired of it. *You* could do that, go to New York once a year and then come back here. I hope you will, Jo."

"Then I would never have to say goodbye."

"You know what I wish? I wish that you and Matt…" She glanced at him to be sure he was asleep and whispered. "I know he isn't a clever man from the city. But he's so good. And he needs somebody to love, everyone does."

My face tingled—I thought not from the sun—and my throat felt tight. What a swell reaction. "The woman he loved would be the luckiest woman in the country. But he hasn't said one word to me, Daisy. He's kind and helpful, and he smiles, and that's all."

"What's wrong with him? Maybe he doesn't believe you would love a cowboy, you know so many rich city men. I'll bet a cookie he thinks he wouldn't measure up. And after Luke ran off with your cousin, he must be wondering what you'd think of him. Jo," she hugged my arm, "let's see if we can reassure him. If you're interested, that is. Are you?"

I searched wildly through my dull wits for the proper answer. It would be embarrassing to say yes and find out *he* wasn't interested. "I could love a cowboy—if he were a cowboy like Matt."

The rest of the day I watched how he walked and climbed, how he laughed with Daisy, how his face looked when he talked with my mother, how strong his arms and shoulders were under his shirt when he cranked the Ford. But he never once spoke to me with anything but the courtesy he always showed. I was just a Friend of the Family far as I could tell. Rats.

Well, what *did* I want? Since it seemed I was really going to live after all, what did I want? I was out of the habit of thinking ahead.

That night Mother and I, lying in the dark under Daisy's quilt, turned toward each other and whispered. Just as I was feeling sleepy, she said, "Jo, I've been thinking. When your cousin Paul comes out here to meet Matt, he's going to fall head over heels in love with Daisy."

It was in the air, everyone was talking about it. "I've been thinking that myself. I can't imagine that he wouldn't, she's so gloriously alive and beautiful and cheerful and loveable and Western. How could he resist?"

"…the kind of girl Paul needs to soften the control he keeps on himself."

"I can't wait to see it. If he's not besotted with her immediately, I'll kick him."

"But would he be good for her?"

"If he loved her, he would be. And Mother, in winter when most of the cattle were gone and this place was cold and there wasn't much to do, he could take her all over the world." I shivered with the thought. "Imagine taking Daisy to Hawaii, what fun it would be. She'd love it. Daisy to Brazil, to Australia. *He'd* love it. And he'd bring her back in the spring."

"We must definitely arrange a meeting. It would be all to the good—two very nice people."

"Let's do it as soon as we can."

"But we mustn't appear to be managing things. Paul's had enough of that from his parents."

"Wait and watch."

"Exactly."

"What fun."

I couldn't tell her of my conversation that afternoon. Matt was steady, smiling, reliable and apparently not besotted with anyone, me in particular. My money could be a help to the ranch, as much perhaps as Paul's, but he probably wanted someone taller, someone stronger. A woman who could saddle her own horse. I would be no more useful on a ranch than a Pekinese.

*M*argaret, I can't tell you how pleased I am to have met you. I've so enjoyed my visit." We were standing at the foot of the porch steps.

"Come again next Spring, Lilly, before work gets heavy around here, and maybe we can teach you to ride a horse the way we did Jo."

Arizona sunshine was bright on my mother's hair. "I would consider it the adventure of a lifetime. Perhaps you would consider coming east to visit me in New York. It would be a rare treat to have you as my guest and show you the sights."

Daisy was beside me watching their farewells—I felt absolute electricity as she waited for Margaret's response. It was slow. "Now, that's a brand new idea. I'd never have thought of that. Oh my, me in the city."

I couldn't tell whether it made her nervous or excited. "She's at the center of everything, Margaret, and there's a guest bedroom in her apartment. She would be a marvelous hostess."

"I'm sure she would be. It's a wonderful invitation. Just give me time to get used to the idea." Daisy seized my arm but said nothing.

"Certainly."

"I'll sure give it some thought." She looked at Matt, where he stood beside the flivver. "Imagine. After all these years…"

He nodded. "Wouldn't you say you've earned it?"

"I don't have the right clothes for a big city."

Mother's courtesy was impeccable. "You'd be all the better for not looking like everyone else. But you may be sure I'd see to it you had clothing in which you felt at ease."

"Well, I'm disposed to accept. But I don't want to rush into it. Maybe next year…"

They left it at that. Daisy and I hugged and said, "See you at Thanksgiving or before." Privately I had resolved to invite *her* to New York when I went back, if I went back.

Seated between Matt and Mother, I scarcely heard what they were saying—volcanos and cattle prices, horses, windmills—for thinking of what I would show Daisy: Central Park and Fifth Avenue and Coney Island, the libraries and museums and galleries and concerts and restaurants the city offers. Daisy would make old New York shining new.

All the way to the jagged black lava flow I thought about that, excited as a puppy. And suddenly I could see quite clearly how absolutely selfish I was. Ever since I'd arrived in Arizona, all I'd thought of had been myself: not once in twenty-one months did it occur to me that I could give Daisy what she wanted most, not even when she told me about it that day at Wukoki. All I'd thought of was what she was giving me—the world had been a mirror in which I'd seen only myself. I was so ashamed I could hardly bear it.

Flagstaff looked cozy when we finally came within sight. Forty-eight hours had not changed the white house on Verde; it stood dear and welcoming. Matt lifted our bags out of the Ford, and I rushed through the kitchen door. "Ruby! Ada, you're here!" I embraced one and then the other. "And Petra." I hugged her too. "We had a marvelous time."

Ada kissed my cheek and said I was appealing as apple pie. Ruby looked concerned. "Lilly, there's a telegram for you—the first I've ever seen—from New York City. The boy delivered it this morning. I do hope it isn't bad news."

I stopped still with the sudden change of everything. "How did they know…?"

Mother took the envelope from Ruby and loosened the flap. "Paul. I told him in an emergency he might reveal that he knew how to reach me."

A moment was enough. "Yes, it's from Paul. 'Doctor says your mother's heart failing and advises immediate return.' Well. Rather a lot to put into ten words."

"Lilly, I'm so sorry."

"Thank you, Ruby." She sighed. "Would it be possible to phone the depot from here?"

"I think so, I've never tried it."

"I'll need the first available compartment on an east-bound train. We won't have done all the wonderful things you had planned, Jo; I won't have time to meet Emily and her family. I'm sorry."

I was buffeted between what I wanted and what I knew I must do. Petra had stopped working to watch me. "Two compartments, adjoining if possible." My little raisin of a grandmother in her lovely garden room, of course I must go. Death again, always near, always lurking just out of sight. I'd almost forgotten.

Mother smiled vaguely, half her mind hundreds of miles away. "Are you sure? She wouldn't want you to endanger your health."

"I can come back soon. May I, Ruby? If I pay my room rent for six months and leave most of my things in it, may I come back as soon as I decently can?"

Ruby put her arm around my shoulder. "Your room will be right here for you, just like you'd walked out an hour before."

My voice was shaky. "I'll miss you. I'll miss both of you. And Petra too. Will you be all right?"

Brave little Ada. "…like an empty sack. But we'll be at the depot when the train pulls in, if Dennis'll allow it."

Matt, standing by the kitchen door with his hat held against his belt buckle, stepped aside so that Ruby could use the telephone. Mother said softly, "Jo?"

The instant I met her eyes, I knew what she meant. "Daisy."

"Do you think…?"

"Matt!" I went to him and put my hand on the hand that held his hat. "Would it be possible for Daisy to come with us? As my guest, of course." I was rather rushing and unable to slow myself. "She could share a compartment with me, share everything, there'd be no expense to you at all. I'd have her back by Spring at the very latest."

"Well, now, hold your horses. You're not going to want her around if there's sickness in your family." He glanced at Mother, "Or worse."

"Yes, I do. I will, I'd want Daisy around for anything. You saw that it was my mother's idea. Oh Matt, please let me do this."

"She'd like to, I know. It would be the best thing that could happen for her."

"Spring at the *latest*. If you're worried about her, I won't let her get ten feet away, ever."

"That's not it."

Ruby turned from the telephone. "There are two compartments open on Number Twenty-two leaving at 6:25 this evening."

Mother sat down at the table. "That will be fine."

It was urgent. "Matt, that's only six hours, barely time to get to the ranch and back."

He smiled suddenly. "She'd never forgive me it I didn't get her here in time to catch that train. I'll have to tie her down to keep her from bouncing right out of the car."

I very nearly hugged *him*. "I won't go without her, we can take a later train if we have to. Tell her not to bother five minutes about packing. We can buy anything she needs, we can go shopping in New York. Oh Matt, you're the best man in the whole world."

When he had closed the door behind him, I slumped into a chair, exhausted. "Too many changes of emotion today, too fast. I shouldn't have to pack more than two bags, there's no need to do it at once."

Mother's voice was tired. "I must send a wire to Paul to ask him to meet our train." She looked at me and smiled. "To meet us and Daisy. I suppose we can do that on the way to the train. Shall we tell Dennis we'll need him?"

Ruby was still at the telephone. "I'll do that. And we haven't any of us had lunch yet."

I said, "I want some of Ruby's bread in Ruby's kitchen."

Mother agreed. "So do I. And Ruby, may I make a suggestion? No, go ahead and call. Something just occurred to me. Jo, here we have two women without much responsibility except to one another." Ruby was listening, her hand on the phone. "And they've been very good to you." Ada's eyes went from one to the other of us.

I matched her solemnity—I knew where she was headed. "They have indeed. I'll feel terrible about leaving them."

"Good to me as well. What shall we do to express our gratitude?"

"It would have to be something huge and grand."

"Have you any suggestions?"

"Oh now." Ada protested. "We're the ones in debt to you. Jo's made life worth living, hasn't she, Ruby?"

"That she has. She doesn't owe us a thing."

I continued to look at Mother. "I can think of one thing good enough."

"Would they come, do you suppose?"

"I suspect they're a stubborn pair. If we were to send the tickets…"

"…and 'spiff up' my guest bedroom…"

"…and promise no work unless they wanted to…"

"It wouldn't hold a candle to Arizona."

"But they might."

Ruby came back and sat down beside Ada. "You two aren't fooling me a bit. I know what you're up to." Ada said, "That's right. We aren't dumb, you know," and crossed her eyes.

Mother blinked and smiled and leaned forward. "I don't know what awaits me at home. But I would consider it a great honor if both of you were to visit me in New York as soon as I'm in a position to entertain you."

Ada looked at Ruby. "They sure went at it the long way around, didn't they? What do you think? I've got a hankering to see the Statue of Liberty."

"You know, I've never seen an ocean my whole life."

"Neither have I. There's that Broadway I've read about. The whole shebang. I wouldn't mind, would you?"

Ruby smiled at Mother and me. "It's a right handsome invitation, Lilly. We might just take you up on it."

"If the good Lord's willin' and the creek don't rise."

"Goodness, I was about to call Dennis." Ruby went back to the telephone.

Ada looked years younger than I'd ever seen her. "Wait till I tell *this* news around town."

Two

1882 to 1972

Her life was a novel—adventure and love, art. Also, as in a novel, struggle and loss. The story began in Manhattan with a large family and prestigious art schools. In the middle was a Zane Grey plot: Eastern woman comes to Arizona, discovers a huge fantastic country, marries a noble cowboy, and rides on trails most people only dream of.

She painted constantly through seventy years and earned her living doing it but did not achieve an enduring reputation. One reason was all too familiar: she was a woman when serious artists were assumed to be men. Then there was the home she chose: most of her career was in thinly-populated Arizona, which the rest of the country considered a cultural desert. Fickle fashions in art explained the rest. The vogue for landscapes, as for most paintings of recognizable subjects, went into a long decline after she moved to the West; the theories that had formed her work were over-ridden by waves of modern styles. She died two months short of ninety in poverty at the Arizona Pioneers Home in Prescott, her work already fading into the past.

*T*he initial fifteen years were promising. Of distinguished German and Swiss-French ancestry, she was born in 1882— as a little town named Flagstaff was being established in Arizona Territory—and named Lillian Emily. Mama was twenty-two-year-old Lenore Louise Bergman, the daughter of a caterer

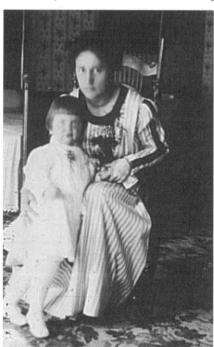

Lenore Wilhelm and her daughter
Courtesy of Sharlot Hall Museum

who had studied in Paris and Rome, who had founded a business on Manhattan Island and in 1881 sold it to legendary restaurateur Louis Sherry. More, she was a grand-niece of philosopher-mathematician Baron von Leibnitz. A parlor pianist, an enthusiast of opera, Mama had gone to school in Switzerland and married an established man sixteen years her senior. Probably she expected her life to be a social success. Any woman in her position would have.

Papa's background was a family from Gottingen in Germany. A painting by a great uncle hung in the Dresden Museum. Henry Theodore Wilhelm was the

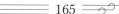

Henry Wilhelm
Courtesy of Richard Williams
Nephew of Lillian Willhelm

son of a doctor whose father had owned a farm in lower central Manhattan where Cooper Union college had been built. For many years Papa's prosperous company, Wilhelm and Graef, imported fine china, glassware, and *objets d'art* and sold retail from a store on Broadway. During the Cleveland presidency it furnished chinaware to the White House.

When Lillian Wilhelm was born into a long-gone world, most of the ships docked along the lower end of the island used masts for sailing. For two years the Metropolitan Museum of Art had been established on the 5th Avenue side of Central Park, but there was no Dakota apartment building and no Waldorf-Astoria Hotel. Brooklyn Bridge and the Statue of Liberty had not been completed; neither had Saint Patrick's Cathedral nor the Flatiron Building. All vehicles in the cobblestone streets of the city were pulled by horses, even the street cars that ran on tracks. The Wilhelms lived in a solid three-floor-and-basement brick house faced with brownstone on the corner of Manhattan Avenue and 123rd Street, across from Hancock Square, a short walk northwest of the lakes and trees of Central Park. Two blocks away Morningside Heights rose two hundred feet above the houses down on the plain. When she was five years old, Morningside Park was established and construction began up on the Heights for a huge cathedral overlooking the slope down to the Hudson.

Separate from tenements and the Bowery and throngs on the Lower East Side, her neighborhood looked more like a town than a city. There were no crowds and few buildings between Central Park and the river. An occasional horse-drawn wagon or carriage was the only traffic past the brownstone row houses with their elevated front stoops. Bicyclists had Broadway almost to themselves.

Mama and 7-year-old Lillian with Richard, Arnold,
Theodore and Henry in 1889
Courtesy of Richard Williams

During Lillian's first fifteen years, five boys were born to
the family. Cooks and maids, a seamstress and a governess
tended to household details, which left her free for such mischief
as sliding down banisters with her little brothers. She was out
on the street pushing the current baby in a carriage during the
early hours of what became the Great Blizzard of 1888, when
the city was paralyzed by drifts that reached as high, it was said,
as twenty feet.

*A*t six she drew a cup and saucer unusually accurate in perspective for a child so young. Or was it a sketch of her governess at age ten? It's impossible to be sure—the first attempt by other people to preserve details on paper was eighty years later. At any rate, with his background in art, her father decided that his daughter was precocious and hired a private teacher. He may have been quite proud of her.

Her early sketchbooks show that she had an ability to "capture a likeness," to represent things as they were, which was still regarded as a virtue in an artist. Through her youth, she pleased parents and teachers by concentrating on flowers, a proper subject for a young lady. Not until she was nearly an adult was it apparent that it was the *colors* of flowers that appealed to her. Color became a major element in her art.

To put her in context: Lillian Wilhelm was one year younger than Pablo Picasso, a generation younger than pioneers Claude Monet and Paul Cezanne.[1] Two years before her birth Mary Cassatt had been elected to the Society of American Artists. The year after she was born, Edouard Manet died. His "Luncheon on the Grass"—which had caused the first scandal of revolt against the official Salon of the French government—had been exhibited twenty years earlier. The Philadelphia Academy was gossiping about the uproar that had exploded when Thomas Eakins had dared to treat female students as he did the young men—shocking: allowing them to paint nudes. When she was eight years old, Vincent Van Gogh shot himself.

But Lillian wasn't trained to the scandalous *avant garde*. In art America was half a century behind Europe. The National Academy of Design, founded in 1826 by Samuel F.B. Morse on the model of the Royal Academy in London, was the focus of the New York art world. Considering itself "conservative of the best," it discouraged innovation.

Nevertheless, art was in the throes of the first real revolution since the early Renaissance. It had been assumed for centuries that good painting was idealized human action with an inspiring

---

[1]And five years older than Wisconsin-born Georgia O'Keeffe (1887–1987). With the possible exception of Grandma Moses, O'Keeffe was to become the most widely known American woman painter of the twentieth century.

message from history, fable or scripture. "Correct" choice of subject was essential. For young artists, raised on romanticism and originality, the situation was ripe for rebellion: over several years the Impressionists of France had been developing a style that concentrated not on subject but on manipulation of paint with color placement, optical mixing, and the effects of light and shade to translate onto canvas what their eyes saw.

By the time Lillian began to study, Impressionism had become the most popular kind of painting in America, short brush strokes and bold color harmonies the most popular style among American artists. Even Frederick Remington, the ultimate narrative action realist of the late Nineteenth century, experimented with light and color in his Nocturnes. He was still painting horses, of course, but not always at full gallop in noon sunshine.

*M*ama had three sisters—Adele, Augusta and Elsie—with children of their own, and Lillian had many cousins: Roths and Reeds, Schwarzes and Schedlers and Battenhausens. Except for such scraps, the story of her childhood was lost with the 19th century. But we've read the books and seen the movies; we can imagine. It was very different from a childhood in Arizona, where she would spend two-thirds of her life.

When most towns in America were still small, Manhattan was facing its urban problems. The old horse cars for transportation were replaced by trolleys that ran on both sides of Central Park and in 1892 by elevated railway lines—there was an El station near the Wilhelms' brownstone house. A fire house and a public school were in the neighborhood. Downtown on the lower east side, there were a thousand people crowded into each acre; fewer than one hundred per acre lived on the northwest corner of the big park.

In 1894 when she was twelve years old, Miss Lillian Emily Wilhelm was enrolled at the Art Students League of New York, which had been founded nearly twenty years earlier for "Ladies and Gentlemen who intend to make art a profession."[2] The

---

[2] A twenty-year-old schoolteacher in 1907, Georgia O'Keeffe enrolled for a class at the Art Students League.

League provided traditional academic training for a host of artists who achieved twentieth century reputations. To gain admission, students were required to submit specimens of their work. All were enrolled at first in Antique classes to draw from casts of classic sculpture before they were allowed to register in a Life class with a living model.

At that time classes were not offered to children; however, obviously gifted teen-agers, those who seemed to have by-passed preliminary stages in their development, could be admitted to adult instruction. At twelve, Lillian qualified.

The Art Students League was in mid-Manhattan, on East 24th Street a block from Madison Square, a section filled with businesses, hotels and churches in buildings of brick. Elevated trains and trolley lines ran into the area from the Wilhelm home down both Ninth and Madison avenues, providing easy access even for a twelve-year-old.

Cousins, 1896
r to l: Lillian, Eda Schwarz, Henry Wilhelm, Richard Wilhelm,
Carl Schwarz, Theodore Wilhelm, Carl Schedler, Arnold Wilhelm,
Bertha Schedler, Elma Schwarz
Courtesy of Richard Williams

All evidence told, she lived through a comfortable child-hood. In 1897 Columbia University moved into buildings up on Morningside Heights within view of her house. The neighbor-hood was still quiet and residential; there was little carriage traffic on the tree-lined dirt streets, which were ideal for bicycling down the middle. The few street lamps were gas.

O n New Year's Day of 1898, fifteen-year-old Lil (she was Lil by then) began a diary, resolving to "be a little less selfish and try and please Mama more than I did last year." An intense, emotional, intelligent adolescent, she poured out lofty ambitions in Victorian sentences: "As before me is spread my new diary, each page spotless and pure, so have I an outlook on the new-born year, and hope to leave each day as unsullied as the pages of this new book."

Despite being bright and privileged, she was normal enough, puzzled by square root, interested in snowfights and bicycles and walking to Public School No. 10, laughing with "chums." The "brainless chit-chat" of "shallow, empty" girls irritated her. Almost every weekend she walked a block to Sunday School at her family's German-centered Reformed Church of America.

She recorded visits to art galleries and the Museum of Natural History, to matinees to see Sheridan's "School for Scandal," "The Girl of the Golden West," "The Merry Wives of Windsor." In the company of family she attended lectures illustrated by "magic-lantern" stereopticans with three-dimensional views: lectures on Italy, sculpture, recent tendencies in American art. She was a bookworm—she said so herself—who concealed novels in her apron in cooking class: Jules Verne and Walter Scott, *Adam Bede*, *Ramona*, *Quo Vadis*. (Her aunts pronounced *Quo Vadis* "very immoral and unfit for a girl.")

With people telling her she had "a real good solid talent," she made a drawing of a third-century Roman emperor for her father, another for her grandfather. Everywhere she saw subjects: the pages of her diary were crowded with thumbnail sketches of streets, the bend of a knee, faces—"I endeavor to read character at a glance; in the art I aspire to this will be of the greatest aid."

A page from Lillian's diary
Courtesy of Sharlot Hall Museum
Prescott, Arizona

*I*t had been a time of optimism that didn't last, for the Wilhelms and for countless other families. Papa's importing firm had been hard hit by the Panic of 1893 and the resulting recession, and he was much worried about business. Mama was ailing. By March of 1898 they were looking for a less expensive house away from the city, Hampstead perhaps or Ridgefield Park. Like any fifteen-year-old, Lillian was dispirited by the thought of leaving her friends—"my very being rebelling." Nevertheless a sign on the front of their big brownstone near Central Park read "To Let."

Her parents favored a "dreadfully dilapidated" property they had found on a little hill in Clifton, New Jersey, a mile and a half from Passaic. Lillian liked a tower room that looked out over the rural view and would be "lovely as a studio." There were cherry trees, a cow, chickens, a garden, black currant bushes. War with Spain was declared, she wrote, but "even though nations be abattle, things go on as usual." The first load of household furniture went to Clifton in early May; in the week of Lillian's sixteenth birthday, the move was complete.

Because she was expected to graduate soon from school, her grandparents invited her to stay in their house in Manhattan. She thought it lovely of them, but there was tension. Aunt Gussie told her she was too reserved and dreamy to be popular, and Lillian spent hours lying on the floor of her room, crying. For a month she saw her family on weekends and traveled by train and ferry back to a city she was finding noisy.

She feared that she had "not an atom of dignity" in her makeup, but an elocution teacher had observed: "I have often noticed that you strive to do better than others; you do not like to be superseded." Ranked first in her class, she wore a graduation dress of white dotted Swiss to deliver a valedictory.

A realistic world lies before us, but to us it seems idealistic, like a mysterious city seen from a height, with its sunshine and success for those who choose wisely and persevere. Of course there will be trials—the shadows of life which we must expect and overcome... Classmates! [She stepped forward and spread her arms.] We part today...God speed you one and all. Farewell!

Her grandfather accompanied her to the station with her luggage, and then she was free to be "a heathen" for the summer in Clifton, playing croquet, climbing in a big maple tree, wading in the brook, taking long walks. She started a bug collection and added a bat and a snake to it. There were kittens, a guinea pig, a dog named Bismarck—until her father protested the slur on the memory of the Iron Chancellor, but recently dead. On rainy days she embroidered or darned stockings; sometimes on sunny days she worked in the garden. At night she looked for stars with the aid of an atlas.

She detested the "Gretchen" hair style her mother liked for her, long braids coiled around the top of the head. First, it left a big funny space at the back. Second: "I am not German, don't want to be, as long as there is an ounce of American blood in me."

In the city, she had sometimes been given charge of her younger brothers, especially little George, walking them out for airings or sitting with a book while they played in a park. Sometimes she was so distracted by their behavior, she confessed to her diary, that she boxed their ears. In July, with no warning in the pages, she reported:

> *I have a sister (of all things!)...Oh dear! dear! at this late hour...it seems quite improbable.*

The baby was named Claire. Lillian found her to be a lovely little thing who examined her own fingers and as the months went by learned to crawl and stand. Big sister Lil was expected to walk George in his perambulator and take Claire too out for airings and found to her frustration that growing responsibilities limited her time for art or for anything personal.

*D*uring the year and half of residence in Clifton, the family situation went from bad to horrible. Mama, not yet forty, was sorely tried by it all: she could not find servants whom she could keep more than a week, and work in the house, the kitchen, the garden, not to mention care of seven children, was simply beyond her. Frequently unwell—"miserable, pale and hollow-eyed"—she fainted at intervals. "Poor dear bothered Mama," Lillian wrote in September, "always something new to bother her."

More and more of the household tasks were given to the older daughter. Soon Lillian was cleaning and cooking. Once she "danced up and down the lawn in the misty lovely moonlight." In late October she went for Halloween pumpkins in the pony cart. She was "a perfect hoyden" in the first snowfall. When Theodore Roosevelt was elected governor of New York, "dignity was cast aside" and she cavorted with neighborhood boys around a bonfire. Late at night she read *Deerslayer, David Copperfield, Ben Hur, Lorna Doone, Puddinhead Wilson.*

But increasingly her days—so she told her diary—were taken up with working, working, working, in her kitchen apron until nearly midnight. She declined invitations to visit friends, knowing that she was needed at home, and felt she had to steal time to write to Lina Roth, a second cousin whose grandmother lived in another brownstone neighborhood on the corner of 79th Street across from Central Park.

Cousin Lina was enrolled at the Normal College back in New York, studying for a career as an English teacher. The relationship was:

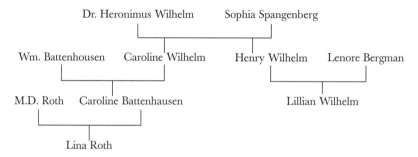

Courtesy of Richard Williams

Lillian called the years between sixteen and twenty her "Time of Trial." Sometimes Claire was ill or fretful: "I bore her screaming as long as I could in sheer desperation, pressing my throbbing temples with one disengaged hand." Mama was often critical, angry and sarcastic. After Lillian helped the older boys make a canoe, she put George into it, tucked up her skirts, and splashed up and down the brook pulling him behind her. Mama told her she was a tomboy, "a great stupid awkward girl."

In those years of the family trouble, she knew "sorrow and tears, terror and mental strain…repression…the bitterness that early experience left on my soul like a heavy weight."

I am wretched again, alas! Heartsick and homesick for the old life, the city life—the life with a purpose. We live a busy life here— oh yes, we work, and hard too. I suppose I am not yet old enough to be fascinated by this living for the children—I'm too selfish. Good God—I cannot! I love them, but is there not something beside the everlasting trifling—why not live for Science—for Art! My brain seems to nearly burst at times when I think of something new, and weird and strange—ache to get my pencils, but am bound by the little creatures on my lap. It is a grim relief to shed bitter tears when I'm alone—oh I am burning to shake off all the trammels of conventionality and stand—alone-free and for Art!

*P*apa, **fifty-five years old**, was having no easy time of it himself. He had a new store on 42nd Street—one with twenty foot ceilings—and the family wished him success, but business was dreadful. To get into the city and home again, he rode a train, the Weehawken ferry, and horsecars, coming in tired late at night. The oldest brother, Harry, went into New York to help him in addition to caring for the animals in Clifton, milking and "choring," but Papa was so sick over business that finally he "worried himself into prostration."

It upset Mama, whose symptoms of hysteria became ever more varied. The fainting spells increased in frequency and lasted longer. Moaning and weak, her teeth clenched, she would say, "My heart! It's stopped beating!" When Lil escaped household duties for a visit to friends in a city thronged with Rough Riders returned from the war, a telegram from Papa—"Lillian, come home quick, Mama sick"—brought her rushing back to discover that her mother had recovered. At noon one day Mama exclaimed abruptly, "Lillian, I am going to Europe!" Lillian feared for her mother's life: "Were it not for will and determination, she might long ago have succumbed." [Mama would live another fifty years.]

On a Thursday, to ease her mind, Lillian "ran to the tower, opened the dear old paint box, neglected two years, hastily sketched a head on the canvas and began to paint." She hoped that a course of study was before her, that she could develop "the one talent I possess and produce the pictures and fancies that crowd my brain, and make me worthy of my name and family."

But Papa caught his foot on the carpet in the dark, fell backward down the stairs and broke his arm and several ribs, bringing his horror-stricken daughter hurrying to light a candle. "His groans were most awful to hear." For weeks he was in bed with pain in his chest, and business deteriorated still further. "Pneumonia set in." It was feared he might die from internal bleeding. He was very dejected.

She wished her younger brothers "had more heart, were loyal to their work." They were good, but "shirkers," and she was "nearly desperate at times to make them move from their apathy."

One day the boys came running for big sister Lil: Arnold had fallen from a tree and they feared his back was broken. She "flew to the grove and saw them trying to lift him," gasping through white lips, "I'm not hurt." The injury was only a wrenched shoulder, but Baby Claire was teething, and Lil was at her wit's end by then with her own hysterical symptoms. Chronic toothaches, blinding headaches, violent pain near her heart—she blamed it on being weak, worn out, run down, and hopeless about getting away. Her grandparents told her she should go to work to earn money for the family and provoked a storm of tears. She was seventeen.

Finally it was too much for everyone. Papa gave up his store on 42nd Street, requested a loan from a friend for a new start, and took an office in the Madison Square House farther downtown on 25th Street, across the Square from the big Dewey Arch. His affairs seemed to progress. Mama went into the city several days a week to seek an apartment so that she could watch Papa's health and spend two or three hours with him each day in business. And Lillian was "ready to leave this hated place" and say "a lasting farewell to horrible '99."

During the first week of January of 1900, glad to return to New York, she took George and Claire to Grandma's until Mama and the rest were through with the moving. She felt they were received ungraciously—"taunting words" rang in her ears. But an apartment that would suit was soon found, and they settled in to try once more.

Already there were changes. Streetlights were still gas; hansom cabs pulled by horses plied up and down. But elaborate apartment buildings were going up west of Central Park, and the old neighborhood was becoming drab. "Luisa's house which once commanded so lovely a view of the Hudson is now wedged tightly between lofty apartments. Great buildings have taken the place of the white house on 83rd Street and made Ada Gardener's little frame dwelling, where five years ago we used to gather the sweet climbing roses and drugged peonies, sink into insignificance."

[She couldn't know that a hundred years later the uptown street on which she had been young would be part of Spanish Harlem, a walk away from the Cotton Club and the Apollo Theater. A neighborhood bar would be built into the street-level floor of the "lovely" home she hadn't wanted to leave.]

*F*or three years after the return to Manhattan, Lillian left her diary blank—too busy, perhaps—and there were only hints and fragments of what she was thinking and doing to fill the gap.

During the last months in Clifton she had told her diary, "Mr. K willingly promised he could have me for Normal College." Papa had said no. "He knows not, or does not realize my ambitions." A resume compiled years later by friends included a statement that at the age of seventeen she was a teacher at Normal, a school for young ladies that became Hunter College. Lillian said nothing about it in the diary.

Across the Hudson near the Clifton house, the town of Leonia had long been a leisurely retreat above the bluff of the Palisades. Painters Durand, Cole and Bierstadt had built studio shacks there. In the 1890s Leonia developed as a collection of art colonies. Foremost in the group was Charles S. Chapman, member of the National Academy and teacher at the Art Students League, who was reputed to be America's best interpreter of forests in oil. With Harvey Dunn, also of the Academy, he founded an art school which operated until 1917.

Lillian said later that she had studied with Charles Chapman and Harvey Dunn and at the Leonia School of Art— but probably not during 1899 or she'd have written of it in her journal. In the first decade of the new century she may have gone back and forth across the Hudson on a ferry, as her father had done, to travel to the short-lived art studio in New Jersey. No evidence was left to confirm.

So we look at what painting was in those years and guess at influences. She came to maturity at the turn of the century in "The Long Afternoon of American Culture" at a time when tradition and polite society ruled the visual arts, which were idealistic and lyrical, observant and realistic, concerned with technical skill. The older painters had died; a younger generation trained in Paris was coming along. American Impressionism had already been captured by Eastern academies and prosperous culture. John Singer Sergeant was the ranking painter, but the best *known*—Maxfield Parrish and Charles Dana Gibson— illustrated popular magazines.

*O*n New Year's Day of 1903, twenty years old, Lillian began to write again in her "dear old half-forgotten diary." The year had ended in tears. They had had great trouble all along, but it might have been worse.

> *There is so much to say that I will not attempt tonight to give even a faint outline of all my future plans and past happenings. Only this—that I feel each year, each season brings me nearer that glorious goal—artistic ability and the only path is knowledge. Brains for thought—heart for soul. Hope in Providence and much work—may that be the food for the coming year!...I owe a great deal to myself, chiefly education, of which I cannot have enough...The very fact of being in competition with active minds is exhilarating.*

Her time was still engaged with house work and tending children—Claire was not yet five years old—and she wished Mama could find a maid who would stay longer than a few days. When weather allowed, she pulled George and Claire on a sled to a snowy park. A man near her age said that she had been "bringing up all those boys," over-worked and harassed as if she had the responsibility of a married woman.

But most of the pages were crowded with talk of the Academy: she had become a student in the School of Fine Arts at the illustrious National Academy on Amsterdam and 109th street—the Central Park neighborhood again—and was feeling ecstatic about it, alive, full of hope. [There is nothing in the record that reveals how the tuition was arranged] When in March she was advanced without warning from drawing plaster casts in the Antique class to human figures in Life class—*not even on probation!*—she went along the street smiling, fearing she looked foolish and not much caring. She would work nearly every day at the Academy for at least four years, perhaps as many as ten, modeling with pencil, pen, charcoal, watercolor and oil.

For nearly a century painting, especially with watercolors, had been considered a genteel accomplishment for a young lady. Daughters of upper class families were taught to draw and paint as they were taught to sing and play piano, as adornments. It was widely believed that women were not truly creative, that they created passively and unconsciously, that they could not be tough or intellectual. What they created was "low" not "high" art, parlor skill only, most acceptable as decorative design—as in flowers painted on china plates. Not until the middle of the Twentieth Century were women taken seriously by most critics.

Despite that discouraging climate, women artists in the late 19th century were active professionally, painting and sculpting; art, along with teaching, writing, and nursing, was one of the few respectable occupations open to women. Sarah Miriam Peale, who was frequently referred to as "America's first truly professional woman artist," had died only recently, in 1885. Cecelia Beaux, already forty-eight years old, was being compared favorably with John Singer Sargeant. In 1902 she had been elected to the National Academy and painted—in the White House itself—a portrait of Mrs. Theodore Roosevelt and her daughter Ethel. William Merritt Chase, one of the country's leading artists, was calling Beaux "the greatest woman painter of modern times."

Lillian sketching at an easel
Courtesy of Museum of Northern Arizona
Flagstaff, Arizona

When he ignored accepted wisdom and allowed the best training available for his daughter, Papa could have hoped for a career in painting for her or at least help for the family finances, which were still shaky. Each time he moved his business location, the streets outside were torn up for construction of the new subway or the sewer, and he was forced to move again. He encouraged Lil to turn her talent to money: "Papa wants me to paint Easter cards for Dempsy and Carroll, pray I may be successful." He took her gilded glass designs into the office to show to exporters and to dealers who sold to New York's wealthy.

*S*he confided what she was thinking occasionally in 1903, the year of the Wright brothers' first flight at Kitty Hawk. Later she blackened paragraphs or cut out whole pages with a knife, keeping her secrets from anyone who might read the diary. But she left this entry written at 9:30 in the evening of June 25th:

> *A long day passed, like all others, in constant running and watching and labor. I felt discouraged, rather out of temper and choking it down went out just now into the yard, the one spot where one can stand at night under the stars and speak one's thoughts to one's own heart and Him who watches over us. No wonder there, at this repetition of what I have so often done, that my thoughts should rapidly turn to that one being that I have been en rapport with for so long—years!—and as I breathed a prayer for that one soul which still exists for me as the highest and dearest ideal I looked intently toward the Great Dipper, that grand constellation—as if in answer to my pleading came a flash— a shooting star. I felt suddenly at peace, as if that answer prophe- sied—what shall I say—a meeting? When an interest is as spiritual as this that is not even to be desired—not necessary— merely the feeling of a dear Presence is what I wish most to retain and will I feel sure. An inspiration!*

Was it Victorian religious sentiment, or had the aspiring artist of twenty-one felt a Love From Afar for someone over the past three years? It can be read that way and indeed, whether she had time for it or not, she had earned a measure of good- ness. But she gave no clue to a name or an identity.

Again, we look at sketchy evidence and wonder. Three years earlier her cousin Lina, vacationing at an inn where the

Lackawaxen joined the Delaware River, had met a handsome, intense, moody dentist from New York who had escaped the city for a weekend with his brother. His name was Pearl Zane Grey. Lina was seventeen; he was twenty-eight. He had kissed her the day they met and had been courting her ever since.

Zane Grey was all his life attractive to women; he thrived, he said, on their attention, needed it. "Friendship for girls ...[kept] something alive" in him. Although he held old-fashioned standards for other people, it would not have been out of character for him to have courted Lina as he glanced at her cousin, hoping to win her admiration.

In 1903 Lillian told her diary that she had received a circular advertising *Betty Zane*, a book which Grey had recently published with money furnished by Lina. The two girls, only a year apart, were friends, but love is often immune to convention, especially in idealistic young women. Because of what was to happen later, it's tempting to speculate that Zane might have been Lillian's "dearest ideal" when she was twenty-one. Only speculate: despite decades of gossip about a romance between them, the conjecture was louder than any offered proof.

Entries for 1904 were erratic. Most were about classes at the National Academy. She went to a ball, wearing a made-over dress and Mama's opera cloak, and danced more than at any time in her life.

The new century balanced between past and future, looking both ways. Her youth was ending; maturity was just ahead. How could a young dreamer tell what *that* would be? There was terrible worry about Papa's business. He had moved to a parlor

Lillian dressed for a ball
Courtesy of Museum of Northern Arizona Flagstaff, Arizona

floor and basement on Fifth Avenue—two doors above the bank and opposite Delmonico's—and offered stock to the public. Construction of the city subway had interfered again, and a crisis was at hand, she said, for which they must all steel themselves.

Cousin Lina had a modest inheritance. She offered to "invest" it in Zane Grey, who longed to leave dentistry, where he had felt out of his element, and try his luck as a writer. In November of 1905 they married. The honeymoon journey included a stop that was to affect Lillian's life eight years in the future—the Grand Canyon and a four-day visit to the rambunctious little cattle and logging town of Flagstaff in Arizona Territory. Grey would be part of Lillian's life until she was nearly fifty.

*H*er relationship with her mother became ever more strained as she outgrew adolescence. She continued to live with her parents, who had moved to a respectable brick house on Aldus Street, in the southwest Bronx near the river and the road out to Westchester. Three theaters were just around the corner; there was easy access to the city on trains and the newly opened subway system.

But home was "the scene of anger" and "hostilities" in which Papa and the boys got no dinner and Lil (she was still Lil) resorted to "subterfuge to get my way without argument, necessary alas under the circumstances." Mama was often "in a nervous state, furious, unreasonable." People who knew Lillian later in Arizona were aware that she did not sympathize with her mother's social interests, which put pressure on Papa to pay for expensive clothing.

Corsets and collars were stiff, as was public morality. Lillian spoke of pressure from all quarters:

> *...forever harping on the marriage question, which meanwhile I care not, dare not, will not consider. And then the sordid viewpoint repulses me. Mine may be too ideal, but it pleases me, who am after all the main person concerned.*

Her only intimate view of marriage and motherhood was of her mother's frustration. And it would have meant the end of her ambition: a career—anything other than domestic—was unthinkable for a married woman.

On August 21st of 1906 she began another diary, what she called a "good convenient late-learning journal." She needed a place for confidence: just that day a woman, "shocked," had termed Lillian's request to use her daughter as a model "your disgusting proposition." She wrote about daily work in life classes at the Academy, of playing tennis, bicycling, swimming off Coney Island, of family—grandparents and aunts and uncles and cousins, her father, her brothers.

But she mentioned her mother only when she sold art work: "Ma took check and will say nothing about it meanwhile." Mama wanted money "in the worst way."

Doggedly Lillian tried to earn those checks, "ready cash, alas so indispensable." In August, starting out hopefully with samples, sometimes visiting fifteen firms a day, she walked all over the business districts trying to place a series of greeting cards she had designed—cupids, harvest cornfields, witches. Usually she was received courteously and met some encouragement but also outright refusals—"not in style," "cannot use"—and many suggestions that she come back in a month. "Forlorn hopes yet not deserting me, nay, never," she walked and walked. For the first time ever she ventured onto Wall Street down toward the tip of the island, stealthily consulting a guide book to avoid getting lost. "My prices low," she told her diary, "yet I hope to do well with them once I get started."

She was twenty-four by then. Sometimes she was reduced to her "last cent" and took anything that was offered: coloring photos, working on catalogues and, yes, designing flowers for use on china plates. "Work now, Lil," she told herself. "Work. It's up to you."

*T*here was **urgency in her struggle:** in addition to her money worries, she was in love, a love far more intense than her "spiritual interest" of 1903. And it was a secret. Valentine's Day six months earlier had been "the birth" of her soul when she had "slipped from enfolding arms" and "the full glory of the meaning of life first dawned on a mind…that had no inkling as yet of the joy so exquisite that it amounted to pain." The evening of March 26th was also significant, but she didn't say why.

Was he the "dear Presence" whom she had held as a high ideal three years earlier? There's no way of knowing. The enfolding arms were not Zane Grey's—he was not yet back from his honeymoon on Valentine's Day. Discrete even in her diary, she referred to the man only as "C," and described him: "big, broad, the firm chin and straight yet tender mouth, the eyes understanding." Merely to see such a man in the subway caused something to wind itself about her heart until she could scarcely breathe. He may have been associated with the Academy: she told him, "Call me Lil. Everyone calls me Miss Wilhelm there."

She did not say why her love must be concealed from everyone. With a "precious package of letters," she crouched by a window, her thoughts "flying, oh so far." Going downstairs at ten to lock the outer door, she stood looking at shining stars with her arms outstretched, "longing, expressing the dearest wish of all…when will we take that path together?" Late one afternoon standing in half light by a window, she told a friend "a little of the soul struggle and the joy" she felt. But not everything, oh no.

Then for a month she did not write in her diary, and when she returned to it in late October, the handwriting was smaller and more cramped. Something had happened—it was over. "The flame has turned to ashes, the light of a countenance beloved vanished into mist…the glow remains."

Ah, girl, these are sad days for you. The despair and humiliation in me are only to be overcome by an overmastering desire to be cheerful. Where none suspect I am able to mask my "knife of flame." With nothing to do but wait and hope for happiness— someday.…Work is a panacea and destroyer of all sorrowful thoughts.

There was little mention of her cards after that and more attention to painting at the National Academy. Instructors told her one of her pieces was the best of the year and awarded her the coveted first: "Miss Wilhelm! You've got Number One!" She attended a performance of "Pagliacci," went to museums to copy paintings and to Low Library at Columbia University to find a book. Soon she was speaking of "the everlasting dreadful cards."[3]

---

[3]The brilliant colors of aniline coal-tar dyes had revolutionized illustration and advertising. In the winter of 1910–1911 Georgia O'Keeffe, having tried commercial illustration in an effort to support herself with art, decided that her work was merely conventional and that there was no tradition of successful women artists. She gave up painting for months.

On Christmas morning Lillian lay in bed thinking.

The year has been so eventful, fruitful too in many ways. It has added more to my character I believe than all the other years. More that is wholesome and loveable, I know, for has not the sweetest and dearest influence permeated every hour since the first wonderful amazing month. Now become a song without words, a soul without clay, an ethereal spirit that beckons on to finer realities, higher aims, nobler thoughts, to visions of a life far from the mart and the struggle of man, to the serene peace of the hills!

*H*er diary stopped soon after that entry. She would be in New York seven more years until the first trip to Arizona drew a line across her life, but almost no evidence about those years remained—the kind of gap frustrating to a biographer. There were people for whom art was as necessary as air. That she went on painting through years of struggle would indicate that she was one of them; probably she continued to study at the National Academy.

She wore her skirts to the floor and her long hair arranged with pins on top of her head: bobs and flappers would not be fashionable until the '20s. Although horses still dominated, there were many of the new automobiles on city streets. Construction had started on Pennsylvania Station.

1907 was the climactic year of European immigration. Nine million immigrants in a decade changed New York beyond recognition. Theodore Roosevelt was President until 1908, and America was in love with his daughter Alice. In 1909 Peary reached the North Pole, so he said, and made adventure fashionable. William Jennings Bryan, William Randolph Hearst, Booker T. Washington, Andrew Carnegie, Thomas Edison, and Helen Keller were in the news.

At some time in those years she moved into another brownstone at 13 W. 70th Street, across the street from one of the gates into Central Park, but nothing was said about whether she was living alone or with her parents. She was still studying, still painting. In February of 1907 she was teaching somewhere, but the name of the school written in her diary was illegible when anyone finally got around to reading it. She spoke of "naughty girls" and five hours a day and "teaching as training."

In the spring of 1907 she was on the Academy's nine-person Selection Jury for a student exhibition, honor as well as responsibility for a young woman. She evidently thought so—she kept the gallery list the rest of her life. Five of her paintings were hung in the show, all landscapes: sunset and early evening on the Harlem River, twilight on College Heights, "The Knoll." An occasional fragment, a clue here and there, were all that remained in her papers.

"Inspiring" subject had been discarded by American Impressionists by then in favor of light and color. William Merritt Chase was fighting conservative ideals. But European innovation in painting had not ended with the Impressionists: experiments with color and form by Cezanne, Seraut, Gaugin, Van Gogh, Matisse would take European art into independence from natural representation. They were little known in America.

In 1908 eight men in revolt against the National Academy, the "Ashcan" artists, held an exhibition of work in unfinished style about disorderly city life that broke the genteel spell of the Academy. Probably Lillian saw or at least heard about the exhibit at New York's Macbeth Gallery. Newspapers were full of headlines: the public flocked, critics were hostile, and the Academy was outraged for the most part.

Heading the *avant garde*, photographer Alfred Stieglitz maintained a small gallery on the top floor at 291 Fifth Avenue, a mile and a half south of Central Park, a brief subway ride from her address. Two months after the "Ashcan" show, Stieglitz mounted an exhibit of masses of form in high-keyed, saturated color by thirty-nine-year-old Frenchman Henri Matisse, who was urging painters to *paraphrase* nature in simple pure color, not "copy it stupidly." Saying "I paint objects as I think them, not as I see them", Spaniard Pablo Picasso was shown by Stieglitz in 1911. So was Russian-born painter Max Weber.

*Z*ane Grey was never far away. He and Lina, whom he had renamed Dolly for reasons of his own, lived in an old farmhouse on land they had bought with her money at the confluence of the Lackawaxen and the Delaware, where they had met. But in efforts to sell articles he had written, he sometimes traveled into New York on the Erie Railroad which ran close by the house. Again, it would not have been out of character for him to have entertained his wife's cousin while he was in town and his wife was three hours away by train.

He quite frankly told Dolly that he did not know the meaning of love and that no woman could hold him for long. In letters to Lackawaxen he mentioned "lady friends...another crazy woman in love with me." At the least he would have wanted Lillian's admiration—he was like that.

For years William "Buffalo Bill" Cody's synthetic Wild West Show had been a sell-out success wherever he took it. In March of 1907 the handsome old showman, back from his last European tour, opened in Madison Square Garden, racing into the arena each day on a white stallion, accompanied by Sioux on horseback yelling and waving rifles above the feathers of their magnificent "war bonnets." There were covered wagons pulled by mules, four hundred horses and twenty buffalo in what Cody called his "educational exhibition." It was full of action and drama; spectators became so aroused they felt they were part of the show.

Fascinated by Western myth like almost everyone on the Eastern seaboard, Lillian was in the audience one day. Her escort, she said, was cousin Dolly's husband. Together they arranged permission for her to sketch in watercolor Sioux and

Arapaho with names like "Spotted Weasel," "Iron Cloud," and "Bear Shield." She considered the faces more interesting than those of the rich young ladies whose portraits she had been painting.

By contrast with 19th century art, her Indians were not romantic near-naked savages. Their bodies were slight, merely indicated, their jewelry sketched, but their faces received careful treatment. Although she accepted the usual stereotypes of her time, she painted Indians as people.

Lillian's portrait of an Indian
Courtesy of Museum of Northern Arizona
Flagstaff

Lillian in a canoe
*Courtesy of Museum of
Northern Arizona
Flagstaff*

Grey was in New York with Dolly's encouragement to talk with a white-bearded Westerner named Charles Jesse Jones. After a lecture describing wild game in Yellowstone Park, "Buffalo" Jones received the neophyte author in his hotel room and took a copy of *Betty Zane* to read. The result was an invitation to travel—on the last of Dolly's money—into the Arizona Strip in the summer and rope mountain lions. That trip was to transform Zane Grey into a best-selling novelist, one of the most successful of his time.

After his return from Arizona, his stories *The Last of the Plainsmen*, *The Heritage of the Desert* and then *The Riders of the Purple Sage* established him as a writer of the West and launched him onto the stage of a nation hungry for exotic romance. Lillian, visiting at the house in Lackawaxen and canoeing on the Delaware River, listened fascinated to Grey's tales of Arizona.

*D*uring one of his early trips to Arizona, Grey had met tough old Al Doyle, who had been buffalo hunter, miner, freighter, cowboy, rancher. Doyle had settled in Flagstaff where he and his son, Lee, accepted occasional commissions to guide visitors. At some time over the next three years, they told Grey about the Navajo Reservation and traders John and Louisa Wetherill at Kayenta, a trading post near a spring on the southern edge of Monument Valley.

Descendants of people who had begun to move west generations earlier, the Wetherills were pioneers born and bred. Both families had reached the Mancos Valley in southwest Colorado in 1879–1880 when John was fourteen and Louisa Wade was two—children who could scarcely remember any life other than hard country where danger was always waiting and courage was a necessity. Through years of prospecting and ranching and exploring and trading to the Navajos, they had come to know the Four Corners country and the hardy people who had come into it to homestead. Better yet, they knew the Indians who had lived there for centuries and the customs that governed their ways. [They must have seemed quite a find to an Eastern novelist who had made his reputation by telling tales of Arizona.]

Grey was intrigued by stories about a giant natural arch which the tribe called Nonnezoche–The Rock Rainbow That Spans the Canyon or something that translated like that–in the uninhabited country behind Navajo Mountain near the Colorado River. John had first seen it in 1909.

Navajos had told Wetherill that the arch was a holy place created long ago by a sacred nature person, watched over by sentinels of Talking Rock, dangerous for them to approach. Unless they knew the proper prayers, so sacred that it was dangerous to repeat them aloud, death was the punishment for passing under it and attempting to return. Did not rainbows across the sky retreat so that humans could not go under them? The Navajo who had told Louisa about it was One Eyed Man of the Salt Clan, but he had died soon thereafter. The Dine did not attempt to impose their religious beliefs on others, but they were uneasy about visits to the arch.

Nomadic Paiutes were old in the country, a thousand years perhaps, not so old as the Anasazi, but older than the Navajos. A Paiute, Nasja Begay, had agreed to go to the arch with Wetherill as guide in 1909 for combined parties headed by archaeologist Byron Cummings and surveyor W.B. Douglas, and Wetherill had come back safely to the trading post at Oljato.

His imagination fired by the story, Grey wanted to go to the secret arch himself. John Wetherill preferred archaeologists to adventurers. However, he had guided five groups into Bridge Canyon since 1909. Grey persuaded him to take a novelist in spring of 1913.

Aeroplanes were still uncommon anywhere and unreliable at best; there was no question of flying over that convoluted country. Experiments in color photography had been conducted since 1861, although there was no commercial development as yet. Grey had illustrated *Betty Zane* with pen and ink drawings and *The Last of the Plainsmen* with photographs, but the stone rainbow was a different situation entirely.

Planning a sequel to *The Riders of the Purple Sage*, he invited his wife's artist cousin to go with him into an outright wilderness. His publisher, he was confident, could be persuaded to purchase paintings for his novel, even paintings by a woman.

Dolly had two small children, the baby less than a year old—it was out of the question for her, of course. And she was needed in the East as her husband's editor, agent, and business manager. She was too valuable to the enterprise to go jaunting about Arizona. Lillian was not married though; she could go.

When she accepted, her family thought she was "loco," but the baby, Claire, was already fourteen, and family responsibility was waning. Her imagination had been whetted in 1911 by Buffalo Jones' 101 Ranch Show at the Waldorf Astoria. The West! The exotic land of romance![4]

Victorian opinions about a young woman's behavior were still in force: to travel unmarried and unchaperoned in a man's expedition would have been altogether too daring. So her pretty, lively first cousin Elma Schwarz, eight years younger than Lillian, went along to preserve proprieties, at least for the public. (See photo, page 169)

*I*n mid-February, around the time they left Manhattan, an exhibit organized by the American Society of Painters and Sculptors opened in an armory building to show the work of new American independents and the daring art being created in Europe, where artists had moved beyond Impressionism to something even bolder. Their paintings were constructed on theories that color builds volume and solidity, that color is structure, that there is a *logic* of color. Matisse had attempted to simplify painting on rational principles; colors, he said, achieve identity only in relation to one another. The French held that a painter "cannot be too submissive before nature" and abandoned perspective for the idea that a painting should not be an imitation of anything else.

It was a huge collection. Rooms in the armory were crammed to the ceiling with 1300 works, one-third of them from

---

[4]Georgia O'Keeffe had spent a few months in the West by then. In the summer of 1913, after a winter of teaching art in a public school in Amarillo, Texas, she worked as a teaching assistant at the University of Virginia.

Europe. The impact on both painters and the American public was profound. The artists feared that their rebellious work was tame by comparison with the French. Public reaction was hostile. "A harbinger of universal anarchy" was one of the kinder terms used by the 300,000 people who viewed the exhibition in New York, Chicago, and Boston. Other comments were: "…a lunatic asylum… a gospel of stupid license and self-assertion…a farce." Lillian left New York with all that ringing in her mind and crossed the line that separated her from the first third of her life.

*H*eaded away from art scandals and toward Navajo country, Grey took his party first to Long Key in Florida, where he had fished for "powerful and savage…watery denizens" the two previous winters, then to Texas and on by the Southern Pacific railroad to southern Arizona, the setting for his recent novel *The Light of Western Stars*. Fourth in size among the states with 113,810 square miles, Arizona ranked near the bottom in population, behind even the ten square miles of the District of Columbia. In 1912, just a year before the trip, it had been admitted to the Union as the 48th state.

Grey's group left the Southern Pacific in Phoenix and transferred to the "Peavine"—a branch railroad which wound among the hills through Prescott to Ashfork—then changed again to the Santa Fe for travel to Flagstaff, as close as they could get by train to their destination. In April sunshine they set out on horses. A few hours out of the little town, trees disappeared, then so did shrubs and bushes, until there were only grasses and rock, and they rode in a vast rolling plain punctuated here and there by ancient volcanic buttes.

Visibility in New York had been limited to a street, a block. In Arizona it seemed infinite. The sky was three-fourths of the landscape and cyan blue. Except for wind and the click of the horse's hooves on stones, both the land and the sky were silent. Along the way there were houses of stone which had lain deserted for centuries.

They rode through fantasy—strange shapes, broken knolls, mud mounds striped in color, a long line of rosy cliffs far ahead. Air was transparent; light was part of the earth. Everything in that fierce, aloof country was new to travelers accustomed to the temperate scenery of the East. At night they made camp under a sky solid with stars that were cold and clear. Sunrise began to appear in the land scores of miles distant. Wind blew gritty dust. Clouds advanced from half a day away. Late in the afternoon when light was brilliant, blue shadows grew in the cliffs and streamed down the rocky eastern sides of hills.

Arizona was beyond any definition of aesthetics, beyond anything human. It was tougher than pretty, bigger than beautiful, hard and spare and demanding. And Lillian was old enough to recognize it for what it was.

Weather was warm compared to April in New York. The party reached a bridge over the red sandstone canyon of the Little Colorado River, filled with spring run-off—Navajos called it Red Water Wash—and moved on through another long day's riding past cliffs colored in layers to an isolated Babbitt Brothers trading post: Tuba, named for a Hopi man at Oraibi. Built in 1870, the post was run by Sam Preston, a Babbitt partner-manager for twenty years by then, and by his wife Laura. Nearby were communal buildings abandoned six centuries in the past and dinosaur tracks unimaginably old.

Twenty years later Lillian described the first part of the trip on Phoenix radio station KTAR.

I was initiated into my life in this blessed land by a four hundred mile horseback trip, accompanied by a chuck wagon with supplies. We left Flagstaff to penetrate into the shimmering beauty of the Painted Desert region. Only one automobile had ventured into the first hundred miles of those sandy wastes, and every sandstorm obliterated what roads there were. Our dear old guide, Al Doyle, who showed me how to ride like a cowboy so that the long twenty-five and thirty miles that constituted the day's loping and trotting would not too greatly tire me, showed me to a place at the end of the day where I could paint, and try—and oh how I tried—sometimes to the point of tears—to interpret the divine beauty of those sunsets.

Today the first lap—to Tuba City—of that never-to-be-forgotten awakening to the wonders of Arizona is made in two hours, over a splendid road, whereas it then took us three and a half days.

They renewed supplies and then, with John Wetherill heading the party, the huge volcano near Flagstaff still visible behind them, they moved on north-eastward toward Kayenta,

l. to r. Sam Preston, Joe Lee, John Wetherill, and Lillian
at the Tuba trading post in 1913
Courtesy of Millicent Richardson and James E. Babbitt

three more sunsets away. A day out of Tuba the volcanic peaks
were gone, and the endless sweep of the horizon began to close
in. Finally they were riding in a broad valley—Klethla—formed
on the south by dark dunes. To the north were sandstone cliffs
that were salmon-pink at sunrise and changed through the day
as the sun moved.

For two days, dipping now and then into cross washes, they
rode beside a mesa that stretched out of sight and watched the
sandstone cliffs, closer now, as they seemed to surge up out of
the earth in a great curve. Where the two met, the mesa with its
dark trees and the beautiful sandstone, the party scrambled
down through a pass where there had been a marsh not long
before. The route had been used by explorers and recently
improved by Wetherill and his partner, Clyde Colville.

Suddenly there was a country even more fantastic than
what had come before: red stone towers of stunning shapes and
sizes that receded far into the distance. Navajos called it
Clearings Among the Rocks. To the north stood the dark
basaltic spire of El Capitan (Agathla—Much Wool) soaring 1300
feet above the plain. To the south cliffs stretched in a long, dim
line. Elevation was 5700 feet, more than a mile above sea level.

When he arrived in Kayenta that April, Zane Grey was forty-one years old. Lillian was nearly thirty-one. Later, he described the sandstone trading post in his novel *The Rainbow Trail*: "…the edge of a steep slope leading down into a valley vast in its barren grey reaches…two squat stone houses with red roofs, and a corral with a pool of water shining in the sun."

Kayenta (Big Spring) was near Todanestya (Where Water Runs Like Fingers Out of a Hill). The three-year-old Wetherill home was sheltered from the wind in a sandy hollow; water from the springs reached it by gravity flow. Probably Grey's party slept as they had for five nights, under the stars, outside in the yard.

Lillian was only five years younger than Louisa Wetherill, but their lives could hardly have been more different. Western-born, Louisa had grown up as the daughter of frontier settlers Jack Wade and Julia Rush near the rugged San Juan Mountains in southwest Colorado. In 1896 at the age of nineteen she had married the son of a neighboring rancher. By then John Wetherill was an experienced explorer and self-taught archaeologist who had excavated in Mesa Verde with his brothers. In Utah's Grand Gulch he had looked at clues and decided that three distinct cultures had once lived there. [Later investigators decided that he was right.]

For thirteen years Louisa and John had shared the sparest of shelter among Four Corners Indians. With their son Ben and a daughter, Georgia Ida, they had lived six years at Ojo Alamo in New Mexico, a trading post just north of the silent pueblos at Chaco Canyon. (John's older brother Richard had excavated at Chaco since 1895, at the giant ruin with a Spanish name—Pueblo Bonito.) When Ben was ten and Georgia Ida was eight, they set up a post in Utah south of the Colorado River at isolated Oljato (Moonlight Water) in a low, dirt-roofed cabin built of juniper logs.

In 1910 they had moved into tents and wagons at Kayenta and begun to build again. By then John was an experienced guide for scientific parties. Fluent in the intricate Navajo language, Louisa was well on her way to recognition as the first serious amateur collector of Navajo stories and sand paintings as well as local herbs and plants. Lillian Wilhelm and Louisa Wade

Wetherill were to be friends for the next thirty years, which probably said a good deal about both of them.

*A*fter a pause at Kayenta, the party set out again. With them were George Morgan and Mormon cowboy Joe Lee. All were mounted on Wetherill's horses; supplies were carried on pack animals. Wetherill knew the way into the torturous canyon of the sacred arch, but some Indians resented intruders into their country, horses needed looking after at the end of a day's riding, and local people needed employment, so he planned to meet Nasja Begay along the way.

They rode out of Kayenta past the spectacular Organ Rock monocline and into the great sprawling maze of the Tsegi (Rock Canyon), moving between high walls of buff and salmon that restricted the view. Miles and miles, no order to any of it, undercuts and overhangs and bas-relief arches, into a branching side canyon with an entrance so inconspicuous it would have been easy to pass by, and finally they looked up to an enormous south-facing alcove in the sandstone cliff where a silent building was hardly distinguishable from the rock behind it—Betatakin (translated as some variation of High Ledges House, House on the Edge, House on a Rock Ledge). Wetherill had first seen it only four years earlier.

No one else was there; no one had lived there for six hundred years. Except for the sound of the wind, Betatakin was silent. When the Easterners climbed up to the ledge, they found handprints of long-gone people on the walls.

The ancient rock that was the bones of the land looked softer late each afternoon as the sun sank low. Sleeping in blankets and eating spartan provisions cooked over small fires, they traveled on through eroded rock and naked earth of the Tsegi to other empty houses at Keet Seel (Broken Pottery) in sandstone that was a thousand feet thick at that location. Lillian discovered among broken shards on the floor of the cave a piece of pottery made by a woman who had been dead for centuries. Fascinated, she wrapped the "fragment of antique art" carefully in her neckerchief and carried it away.

Then it was up onto a windy plateau, down into labyrinths of narrow sandstone canyons, across shifting sands, acres of pebbles, ledges and rock-strewn taluses. The U.S. Geological Survey called the area "the most inaccessible, least known and roughest part of the Navajo Reservation." They struggled around the great dome of Navajo Mountain (Navajos called it Head of Earth Woman, sometimes Enemy Hiding Place or Enemy Mountain because the U.S. Army had maintained a heliograph there) and over treacherous billows of stone, the Slick or Bald or Bald Head Rocks. Grey, ever dramatic, re-named them "The Glass Mountain."

Veteran of many treks, archaeologist Neil Judd, who had been with the 1909 group of surveyors, called the route "the most trying I have ever experienced." W.B. Douglas, struggling over the Slick Rocks behind Wetherill, had said, "This is one trail that no woman will ever take." [In the four years since, *six* women had made the trip with no untoward effect.] Later in the summer of 1913 Theodore Roosevelt described the "toilsome" country as a contorted wilderness of twisted valleys in which humans were like pygmies.

*T*here were fifteen miles of rough country yet to cover, country cut by deep canyons. Finally, Navajo Mountain looming behind them, they approached the hidden arch. Grey described a stream bed of bare stone that was treacherous for the horses, rock-strewn and cactus-covered ledges, a ragged iron-lined amphitheater, sunset rimming the walls. Tired, he glanced behind at the straggling party–Lillian and Elma, Joe Lee and Al Doyle–with "admiration for their gameness and glee for their disheveled and weary appearance." Finally he could only drag along with his eyes on the ground. And then–

> *I saw past the vast jutting wall that had obstructed my view. A mile beyond, all was bright with the colors of sunset, and spanning the canyon in the graceful shape and beautiful hues of the rainbow was a magnificent natural bridge.*

Only sparse vegetation grew near, yucca and bunch grass and stunted piñon. Concealed in a deep canyon six miles south of the Colorado River, the solitary sandstone arch was massive– 275 feet long and 300 feet high, 33 feet wide at the top–yet it was dwarfed by the canyon walls. Grey and his Eastern companions thought they understood why it was considered worthy of Navajo prayers. For centuries it had stood silent and alone, hidden, a thing of grandeur that needed no human viewers to reinforce its power.

Nonnezoche the stone rainbow
Courtesy of Museum of Northern Arizona
Flagstaff

"The Indian Who Prayed to the Rainbow
Bridge and Would Not Go Under It But
Climbed the Cliff and Went Around."
Courtesy of Museum of Northern Arizona
Flagstaff

At night, the cliffs looming black against the stars, they built a fire and camped on the hard Kayenta sandstone on which the rainbow rested. As foreigners, they were perhaps safe to do so. Nasja Begay sat silent at a distance, watching. Later Lillian painted a watercolor portrait of him.

*S*eventy years earlier an American named John Rand had invented the collapsible tin paint tube that made outdoor work in oils possible, but oil paints dried too slowly for trail work. Through the ten days that the Grey party stayed near the arch, Lillian sketched with pencil, ink, and watercolor, "painted like mad," and produced the initial work for illustrations of Grey's next novel, *The Rainbow Trail.*

Her work was purchased by Harper and Brothers for the going rate: $40 each for three paintings, $50 for the jacket illustration or frontispiece. The book was issued in August of 1915.

The cooperative relationship between Lillian Wilhelm and Zane Grey was to last more than fifteen years through trips around the West. The only woman who worked with him as illustrator, she furnished paintings for other Arizona books. In 1915 she sold his publishers a cover and three illustrations for *The Border Legion*—again $170. Later she furnished a painting for the cover of an edition of *The Last Trail*. Scenes from *Under the Tonto Rim*, *The Call of the Canyon*, and *Wild Horse Mesa* were used in promotions.

Slowly Arizona and the people Lillian met influenced her work. For her the West was a long pushing beyond the boundary of the easy and the already done. She said, "It is human nature to be lured into adventure by the unfamiliar and unknown," and spoke of "the magnificent material Arizona presents to the artist, each day revealing new beauties and new inspiration." In vast Western spaces she took herself into changes she could not have imagined. Her training had been in Eastern schools during a time of ferment when a dozen European post-Impressionist movements were breaking traditional concepts. However, at the age of thirty, she saw the landscape and the people of Arizona, and hues she couldn't have painted out if she'd wanted to came into her life.

Over the years her work left fashionable theories behind in the East in favor of the southwest's brilliant light, clear air, and rock-solid land. Her subjects were not small intimate "corner-of-the-garden" or "cozy-forest-nook." She painted the size of Arizona: "I love the mountain tops."

In northern Arizona, she was a contemporary of open air painters Jimmy Swinnerton, Maynard Dixon, Gunnar Widforss, Mary-Russell Ferrell Colton. And Kate Cory, twenty years Lillian's senior, who had arrived in Arizona in 1905 and lived seven years in Hopi villages. Like them, Lillian painted the broad sweep of the land. But they were all too widely separated and too individual to have much influence on each other. By the very nature of the vast country, the artists of the Colorado Plateau could not be called a school.

Northern Arizona attracted them, men and women alike. Pennsylvania-schooled Mary-Russell Ferrell Colton, recently married to a University of Pennsylvania zoologist, also traveled through Navajo country in 1913 and returned at intervals through the next thirteen years. For the rest of their lives, her career and Lillian's ran parallel—but different, very different. Lillian reacted to the trek into Rainbow Bridge by deciding she needed more training: "The beauty of Arizona and its great spaces made me feel how necessary it was to continue my studies." She boarded a train for the East, resolved to work on understanding color, its relationships, balancing and counter-balancing, contrast and harmony. Her teacher was Arthur Wesley Dow, influential author of two analytical teaching texts.

Aware of the revolutionary painting of Europe, Dow prepared his students for early abstraction: "Beauty is not Representation," he decreed, and insisted that painting should be two-dimensional patterns of color rather than illusions of reality. Using his five composition principles (opposition, transition, subordination, repetition and symmetry), he urged harmoniously spaced linear design and abstract balance of shape against shape, dark against light, solid against void to produce arrangements of light and dark instead of what he thought of as the traditional tyranny of realism. His dictum was that "space art is visual music" which could be taught by strict rules. He presented it to students who included Georgia O'Keeffe and Max Weber.

However, on trips to the Grand Canyon in 1911 and 1912 Arthur Dow had found that his meticulous color theories did not entirely work on Western landscape. When Lillian studied with him, he was back in New York revising his ideas.

She returned to sea level in the East to find that the Armory Show was still a scandal. The notorious exhibition had been a shock which encouraged artists away from what came to be considered by critics as "outworn" styles. Shape and color in painting had become more important than what they represented. Ideas about art were in violent flux.

American painters increasingly took their lead from the flat planes of Matisse, from the Fauvist "color for color's sake," from Cezanne's conviction that color was not "decoration." As collectors began to buy abstract art, Cubism became fashionable, realism was submerged, the market for academic painting was wrecked, and critical attention to landscapes went into a long decline.

For a hundred years there had been a tradition of landscape painting in America. The West had been treated with the atmospheric realism of Henri Farny, the action realism of Remington and Russell, the romantic realism of Moran and Bierstadt. Artists of the *avant garde* in the East called it "illustration" and "narrative." Artists and residents of Arizona countered that geography, atmosphere and culture should make their own styles of art from region to region, an argument that was largely ignored by the Easterners. The authority of Paris and New York remained dominant for decades.

The year 1913 was a turning point for American painting and for Lillian Wilhelm's career. In the middle of an artistic controversy that would boil throughout the twentieth century, she avoided academic realism for the next few years, but not because she lacked the skill to do it. There was ample evidence in her sketchbooks that it was easy for her—and what else had the conservative academy been teaching her? For twenty years of study in New York she had been praised for realism.

Trends themselves rapidly became formal rules. In her paintings, especially in oil, she tried to make the new rules fit her talents, her training, her affinity for landscape, and her subjective inclination. Then and later, she ignored the "classic" modernism that moved toward abstraction, but it would be years before she painted in a style that seemed comfortable to her. Louisa Wetherill, a Westerner who liked pictures that looked like something she could recognize, said of Lillian's oils during her early Arizona years, "She can do better than that."

Lillian's pencil sketches of Louisa Wetherill's parents
Courtesy of Harvey Leake
Great-grandson of John and Louisa Wetherill

*I*n the spring of 1914 Europe was building toward a war that was to make life difficult for German-American families like the Wilhelms and for the Germans who dominated New York's music. The public mood made them hesitant about taking a public role.

Zane Grey had his own reaction to the war. A volatile personality, he reacted to war, to criticism, to all kinds of events or to nothing at all, with black moods: "I am a man beset by fears, hounded by a dreadful and fatal possibility, a bitter and terrible catastrophe."

In those years depression was not recognized as an illness that should be treated. Everyone including the sufferer considered it weakness, whining self-indulgence, something to be ashamed of—which made matters worse. Add to that the insecurity chronic in people who pull their work out of themselves, always doubting its value. America's most popular novelist was often nearly paralyzed by his own emotions.

Grey reacted to depression with constant movement, incessant adventuring, hunting, fishing, sailing, setting up half a dozen different places to live. In 1914 he escaped to the West with another entourage which included Lillian and Elma.

His party was a week crossing the continent by the Atchison Topeka and Santa Fe railroad. One day there were mountains ahead, and they climbed from the plains to the transparent air of New Mexico's high desert. After crossing the Rio Grande at Albuquerque, they had occasional glimpses of color in distant hills and passed old black lava flows and mile after mile of sandstone cliffs, the sculptured red sandstone of the previous summer.

It's likely: Lillian gazed out the window of the rocking train in growing excitement, trying to ignore the talk of the others. Finally she stepped down at Gallup amid its low brown hills, and there was the sky again and the brilliant light of the Southwest. The elevation on that high plateau was 6,500 feet.

The Easterners left the train at Gallup; they arrived some days later in Flagstaff, according to the newspaper. Details of the ride were not preserved in any of the usual archives, so we have to guess about their route. [Western history is full of guesses, even when the story includes people of note.]

Perhaps it was Al Doyle or his son Lee who had come east from Flagstaff to meet them at Gallup with horses and

Lillian with her horse and Al Doyle
Courtesy of Museum of Northern Arizona
Flagstaff

wranglers, a chuck wagon, and gear which would make them all comfortable through two hundred miles of riding and camping. Grey admired them both: "To Al Doyle I owe more of the Western atmosphere of my books than to anyone. He was a treasure mine of memories and he could talk...Despite his long and rough career, he was a gentle and kindly man, the most intelligent pioneer I ever met and of an upright and splendid character." In Lee, he said, "I have found much that was so splendid in the father."

Groups riding west from Gallup used the National Old Trails Highway, a primitive wagon road that followed the railroad tracks and the shallow Rio Puerco along the 35th Parallel. The first night they slept between sheer sandstone walls and the next morning moved out into the open freedom of Arizona, freedom that could lift a heart cramped by family tension and New York streets.

The difference was profound. New York was theaters and museums and galleries and libraries, the gathered communal treasures of Europe and the American culture that had grown out of them. Arizona's culture had grown out of the land. Its stunning space was clean and quiet, powerful, personal.

The country near the New Mexico border was low and brown—even in spring the sparse vegetation was barely green along the Puerco. Fine sand from surrounding formations washed down into the slow watercourses of Northern Arizona and became saturated where underlying layers prevented drainage. The result was quicksand which mired and sometimes swallowed horses and the wagons they pulled. On one occasion, so it was told, a steam locomotive had fallen off a bridge and sunk out of sight. Even when the beds looked dry, they were likely to be treacherous: in 1853 Lieutenant Amiel Whipple had been dismayed when his mules sank up to their bellies in the sand of Lithodendron Wash, dry at the time. Knowledgeable travelers were wary.

But the sky was huge, the land spread off into infinity, and Zane Grey was avid for any experience he might turn into a book, willing to turn aside to find it. Two days of traveling west through open country would have taken him and his people up a lonely track that wound across the bentonite of the ancient Chinle Formation and into another of Arizona's wonders: tree trunks lying along the ground four feet in diameter, sometimes ten. As much as 125 feet long, they had turned to colored stone more than 150 million years in the past.

There was rudimentary access; travelers who were willing to get off the Santa Fe cars and hire horses could ride to the site. But as tourists had increased in number, so had would-be entrepreneurs interested in turning the ancient trees into money. Chunks of wood had been hammered to pieces. Large logs had been dynamited by people searching for crystals; wagonloads had been hauled to a mill built nearby, crushed into abrasives and shipped out for commercial use. Irreparable damage had been done before President Theodore Roosevelt had, eight years earlier, established the ancient fossils as the Petrified Forest National Monument.

*T*here was still a week or more of riding ahead before they could reach Flagstaff, on down the Puerco to its junction with the Little Colorado near Holbrook, another day to the little settlement of Winslow, where all the old trails converged because of Sunset Crossing, the one place in many miles where a rocky ledge from bank to bank made the bottom of the Little Colorado firm enough to provide a safe ford. Most of the people who traveled through that country did so on the comfort of railroad cars, but compared to the Slick Hills that Grey and his group had struggled over a year before on the way to Rainbow Bridge, the Old Trails Highway was an easy road. Sun was at their backs in the mornings; the San Francisco Peaks at Flagstaff were visible from seventy-five miles out.

A day's ride farther, to the west of Winslow, was a strange 600-feet-deep hole in the plain, nearly round, nearly a mile across, with a 200-feet-high rim. Away from all the old travel routes in country that provided no water and no shelter, it had not been discovered until 1891, when a prospector had stumbled onto it, picked up lumps of what he thought might be iron in the rubble around it, and sent them off to a mining company for assay. Some of the few people who came by to see it called it Coon Butte; others said it was a hollow mountain. The occasional scientist who arrived wondered whether it was volcanic in origin. Just five years earlier an engineer named Barringer had prepared a paper in which he had argued that the crater had been created by the impact of something extra-terrestrial, a meteor, for instance, but such a huge meteor hole had never before been found, and most authorities dismissed his theory.

Zane Grey loved that sort of drama and the stories that could be built around it. The crater would have seemed to him worth what locals called a look-see, even though the detour complicated travel.

The problem would have been that between the hole and Flagstaff was a sudden narrow canyon 250 feet deep with precipitous sides. Lt. Edward Beale, exploring with camels, had called it "a chasm in the plain that prevented passage of wagons." Whipple had decided it was impossible of descent and named it Canyon Diablo. Until the railroad came through in 1882–83, everyone had gone around, all the way to Leupp on the Little Colorado, thirty or so miles out of the way.

Travelers sometimes loaded their wagons onto flat cars at Winslow and rode across the canyon on the railroad bridge, which the Santa Fe had expanded in 1900 to include an additional track. In 1913 a highway crossing was begun near Two Guns, but it wouldn't be finished until October of 1915. Grey's party had options for crossing Canyon Diablo in addition to the Leupp detour, but they left no word of how they might have accomplished it.

*F*rom there details were verified by newspapers. In Flagstaff Grey identified Wilhelm and Schwarz as his "nieces," and then, guided by Lee Doyle, they sought the best possible contrast to their long dry ride from Gallup: the rushing water of Oak Creek, deep in its canyon. Sun was hot, but they were cool under the moving shadows of oak and white-barked sycamore. Pine and fir trees climbed slopes that soared suddenly into colored cliffs.

Grey's group could have descended into Oak Creek Canyon with a chuck wagon to carry their gear. In 1902 the Munds Road/Verde Cut-Off had been broadened to become the Schnebly Hill Road so that the handful of settlers in Sedona could drive into Flagstaff to buy supplies or to sell produce. In July of 1914 a dirt road good enough to drive an empty wagon over was completed the length of the canyon.

Grey stored the image. Six years later he would use it as the setting for *The Call of the Canyon*, but in 1914 he had other places to go. Retracing a familiar route, the party climbed out and away from Oak Creek, left Flagstaff behind, and returned to the colors of Monument Valley, the friends of Tuba City and Kayenta. (The Wetherills were missing their daughter, 17-year-old Georgia Ida ["Sister"] who, after years of learning from now-and-then tutors was away at a convent school.) When the Eastern travelers returned to Tuba from their visit to Kayenta, Sam Preston proudly drove them into Flagstaff in his new-fangled automobile.

That summer they were all over the landscape. After Flagstaff they went to stand in awe on the south rim of the Grand Canyon, which had been created a National Monument in 1908 by President Roosevelt. The view left visitors numb; ten miles wide, a mile deep through formations laid down long before there were dinosaurs, it seemed timeless. But the rim was not what it had been only a dozen years earlier. Although access roads for autos were ungraded dirt, the railroad line from Williams that had been completed in 1901 had brought it into a new era.

People who had lived in the canyon four thousand years earlier were long gone and so were the explorers and prospectors who had been a rugged part of its recent history: "Hermit" Louis Boucher was no longer there; John Hance had left his cabin and his ranch, though he could still be seen around the

El Tovar, entertaining tourists with tall tales; Pete Berry guided a tour now and then out of his Grandview Hotel and into wild canyons. But almost three hundred people were year-around residents and there was a school for children of Bill Bass and a few other families. The Kolb brothers were setting up shop. Even some of the tough old pioneers had automobiles.

There were few tourists in 1914 to distract Lillian from whatever it was that she thought, few compared to the hordes of later years. She was there just in time. Tourism was growing–water was brought to the hotels in railroad tank cars to support it. There was talk of improving the dusty roads. John Muir had been a visitor, so had Gifford Pinchot, John Burroughs, C. Hart Merriam, and President Roosevelt. Irvin S. Cobb wrote that to see the canyon was to "realize what an entirely inadequate and deficient thing the human imagination is." Any who cared to do so could sit quietly on a bench to watch the sun set in undisturbed silence. A tourist herself whether she realized it or not, Lillian took advantage of the closing opportunity to feel alone with the age, the size, the shape and color.

*T*he Wetherills joked that guiding Zane Grey was "like moving a house plant," but travel through the rock-dry, forbidding landscape of northern Arizona was an exercise in endurance and forbearance for anyone who tried it in the early years of the twentieth century. Adventurers had to expand to fit the country, to rise to it. One wonders what kind of person she was becoming, that New York woman, that she willingly went there so often. She claimed to have bones of iron, but still…

Was it quality of life in Arizona that drew her? the light, the land, the space, escape from New York and Mama and pressure to marry? Perhaps the Navajos and Hopis: how could any people not be beautiful who lived free amid the shapes and colors of that vast expanse? Added together it was probably what she had said before–"I am burning to shake off all the trammels of conventionality and stand–alone–free and for Art!"

There was enough variety for a lifetime of exploring. In late spring of 1915 Grey and his entourage rode northwest from Gallup through scrubby piñon-juniper, small as ants in that broad, colored country, to a trading post on the banks of Ganado Wash. Artist Maynard Dixon, who had visited in 1902 and 1906 and was there that summer, said it was "a solid mud and stone bastion, almost a fort, with barred windows and heavy double doors and ready firearms in every room." The walls were lined with books; floors were covered with Navajo rugs.

The sixty-two-year-old trader, "Don" John Lorenzo Hubbell, had been there since 1872 as a self-described "merchant, father confessor, justice of the peace, judge, jury, court of appeals, chief medicine man, and de facto czar," looking after Navajos demoralized by their confinement at Bosque Redondo. Born in New Mexico on land granted by the king of Spain to his mother's family, Hubbell had been described by adventurer/journalist Charles Lummis as "…a mild, blue-eyed person whom no desperado would tackle; the courtliest of men, the most generous…"

Lummis went on: "All along that strange bald country are men worth knowing; for the frontier is the hardest test of manhood." Hubbell was "the dean of the grizzled veterans… patriarch and prince of the frontier." Patron of Navajo rug weaving and silver smithing, Don Lorenzo had become a magnet for all sorts of travelers—explorers, artists, writers, scientists—who counted the man himself as significant as the scenery and came to sit around his large dining table for the talk.

[One wonders what that authentic Western hero thought of Zane Grey and his cavalcade of relatives and secretaries and personal servants. And what Lillian thought, seeing Grey set next to such men as Hubbell and Wetherill and Doyle.]

*I*t takes time to re-make a life. Through four years Lillian returned from the West to Manhattan, which was defined by the East River and the broad Hudson, the Harlem River and the Atlantic. There was water everywhere; there were trees everywhere, walls of vegetation right to the water's edge. The highest point on Manhattan was Morningside Heights, a low ridge along the Hudson—low, that is, compared to the cliffs and spires of Monument Valley that rose a thousand feet. From the top of the Heights one could see all the way into Central Park, a mile or more at least.

The northeast had a three hundred-year-old history of European settlement that had erased most evidence of the original people except for words left as place names. Clusters of colonists enclosed in river valleys, turned inward upon themselves, had tended toward introspection and preoccupation with the opinions of their neighbors. Cities along the coast turned toward Europe.

Spanish presence in northern Arizona was *four* hundred years old, but it had made little impression, even in architecture. A score of Indian tribes, although reduced in number, lived on land designated as their own. There were open miles sharp in the clear dry air and people who knew how to live in them. It couldn't have been more different from everything Lillian had known.

Zane and Dolly Grey had moved into a two-and-a-half story house that had been built by his brother on the west bank of the Delaware at Lackawaxen. At Dolly's invitation Lillian painted friezes of stylized Navajo and Hopi and animal figures above the windows and the fireplace in the rooms which Zane used as his study.

Sometimes days were damp and grey, windy and cold, and rain dimpled the Delaware or mist hung above the water. Sometimes the hillside across the river flamed with autumn leaves, and sun rose from downstream, and Canadian geese flew upstream honking. She could launch a canoe into a wider river than most Navajos had ever seen.

The Greys remodeled the old farmhouse into a cottage for the use of secretaries and their families; the Wilhelm cousins stayed in it occasionally. Sixteen-year-old Claire was at Lackawaxen visiting her cousin Lina in the summer of 1915 while Grey was meeting Lorenzo Hubbell and fishing the Pacific waters off San Clemente.

That was the year he hired another secretary, a striking seventeen-year-old brunette named Mildred Smith. A "special friend," she would remain with him through his trips to Florida and Arizona, California, New Zealand and Australia. She and the Wilhelm sisters, companions on those travels, were to be in touch the rest of their lives; the Wilhelm family knew the three to be good friends.

Maybe there was nothing illicit in Grey's relationship with "the girls." He spoke of their "value" to him, but he was decidedly outnumbered, to his occasional frustration. Sometimes they sided against him or fussed among themselves or made so much high-spirited noise in the middle of the night that local ranchers disapproved. Dolly feared that he tried to keep their hearts and souls in bondage, and she was probably right, but on the issue of romance, hints and speculation—always more fun—took the place of solid evidence.

Dolly served as his editor and agent, responsible for putting the novels into final form and for the sales and contracts and royalties that funded travel which usually left her at home. She felt badly neglected and told him so. In turn he called her vindictive, hard, satirical, mean, unjust, a fiend, a *German*, [worse even than the New York critics of his books] and said, "I'd rather go to Hell than stand your scorn and bitterness and discontent any longer." But she was compensated for her role: by a partnership arrangement, half of his considerable income belonged to her. In their letters mutual anger alternated with expression of affection. The marriage lasted forty years, until his death.

*Z*ane Grey, frequently off fishing somewhere, was only one part of Lillian's life in the East. Perhaps in the winter season of 1915 she and her mother were in attendance when Toscannini conducted the orchestra at the Metropolitan Opera for the last time. Perhaps in 1916 she saw Geraldine Farrar slap Enrico Caruso resoundingly during Act I of "Carmen," to the delight of suffragists. Papa, always such a vigorous man, would not have been with her: he had suffered a stroke which restricted his movement. He was over seventy by then, his business struggles behind him.

The Wilhelm daughters were royally entertained by Zane Grey. During part of the summer of 1916, Claire and Lillian were with his party at Avalon on Catalina Island, where he was trophy fishing. Experienced, they sometimes traveled without him: on August 25 the Flagstaff newspaper published the following note:

> Miss Lillian E. Wilhelm, Miss Claire Wilhelm and Miss Mildred Smith, all of New York, arrived in Flagstaff Sunday. The Misses Wilhelm are cousins of Zane Grey, the famous author who has written so much of Northern Arizona, incorporating it in some of his best books. The ladies have made trips to the Indian country with Mr. Grey a number of times. They have been visiting for a couple of months on the coast and expect to visit the Moqui snake dances this year.

Lillian was at the Tuba trading post during the season that year as "a guest" of Laura Preston, who had married Sam Preston in 1904 and lived at the post since 1905. Laura had a reputation for a straight-laced firmness on moral matters; her attitude toward Lillian was always that of a warm friend. Therefore there were women across the plateau who refused to believe rumors about an affair between Zane Grey and his wife's cousin. If there had been any carrying on, they said, Laura wouldn't have stood for it.

Lillian was at Tuba in 1916 long enough to volunteer the supervision of art classes at the school, supplying Navajo and Hopi children with materials and encouraging them to extend their sketches beyond rug and sand painting designs. The children were natural artists, she said, who needed direction more than instruction.[5]

Again she returned to New York for a winter of study, painting, concerts and exhibits. Maybe she saw movies—in 1916 twenty-five million people a day in America were paying to see "the flickers." Probably she saw little of Zane Grey: he was sunk in another of his black spells. "A hyena lying in ambush," he called it. That the temperature was below zero for days and coal nearly impossible to buy didn't help.

*T*he weather triggered Lillian's decision to abandon the east coast for southwestern sun. Later that year after another painting and exploring season, she moved permanently to Arizona. She stayed in touch with her brothers and sister and traveled East now and then but established herself as a resident in a new state and stayed for the remaining years of her life.

She described it as "the home and mecca of beauty lovers from all over the earth." Years later she told a radio audience:

> *My trip in '13 was of only a few weeks duration. The beauty of Arizona and its great spaces made me feel how necessary it was to continue my studies—but in summer time the Navajo*

---

[5]In 1916 Georgia O'Keeffe began her long liaison with photographer Alfred Stieglitz, who maintained a pioneering gallery in New York to show contemporary art. His initial sponsorship of her work was to prove the most important factor in the success of her career, which was to be such a contrast to that of Lillian Wilhelm.

Reservation lured me, and the hospitality of Arizonans moved my heart. By 1917 New York meant only a fine background, and a month away from Arizona seemed wasted.

It was a fateful decision. What was developing in Europe or New York did not seem pertinent to painters entranced by the land around Taos, along the Pacific coast, across the Colorado Plateau. Why come to the West if they were not to paint what they saw around them? Art historian Ruth Westphal was to say, "Many of the most promising students of New York's Art Students League in the early 1900s guaranteed their own extinction as acknowledged American artists simply by boarding a train that carried them West." For years "American" painting existed within East Coast art colonies.

But Lillian couldn't know at the time the long-term effect of her move. She began to spend her winters in the mild desert climate near Phoenix, a small agricultural center fifty years old, not counting ancient Indian settlement. Its population varied with the seasons. Houses in higher elevations were not insulated, so for thirty years people from Flagstaff who could afford to winter in the desert had done so. Snow-weary fugitives from the Northeast were discovering it.

On about the latitude of North Africa, Phoenix enjoyed winters that were comparable to spring in some other cities. Warm sun was a balm on shoulders almost every day. It was never, even in December, so far to the south as to seem to have sunk away. The shortest days were ten hours long, not so brief as they had been on the Hudson. Often in January coats, jackets, even sweaters were not necessary out of doors. It was all too wonderful to be real. She called it, "…a land of opportunity for those whom the rigors of severe climates drive into the southwest and a place of heavenly sunshine for those who have time to rest and play and enjoy summer activities while in other parts of our country folks shiver and freeze."

Water, so often a flood in other climates, was scarce in the desert, essential to any life at all. Eight hundred miles of canals carried water from the Salt River to irrigate the cotton and alfalfa fields and citrus groves that carpeted the wide valley. Ditches controlled by headgates brought water to lawns; a Town Ditch ran through the middle of the community.

Because of its winter weather and ambitious management of the river, Phoenix was growing fast, new ways elbowing out the old ones. There were about 25,000 people and 11,000 autos; hitching posts still lined the streets for farmers and Indians who came into town in buggies and wagons. Horsecars ran on seven miles of paved streets, where the Adams Hotel was a local model of elegance. South of town in the Riverside Ballroom public dances were held.

On mountains of rock that rimmed the valley outside the irrigated fields there were plants with strange names and stranger shapes—towering saguaro cactus, whips of ocotillo that bore leaves only after a rain, cholla that looked soft when the sun was behind it and clung painfully to legs and fingers. In spring the desert was glorious with golden blossoms on prickly pear cactus and lacy palo verde trees.

It too was different from Manhattan and as enticing to an artist as Navajo country. The bare mountains turned soft and red at sunset; clouds in the sky were radiant with colors. One could be outdoors for long hours to put it all on canvas: for a painter interested in color and landscape, the desert of southern Arizona was its own kind of liberation. Two decades later Lillian said:

> For four years I lived on Camelback Mountain where I saw each day at sunrise and sunset the crags of mysterious Superstition Mountain, the undulating hills, rising to the impressive Four Peaks on the horizon line, the foothills, the blue peaks of the Macdowells. The whole glorious sweep invites one to revery.

The official record and the papers Lillian preserved were sketchy, full of gaps and questions. She had friends in Arizona for whom there was a frustrating lack of evidence: where did she meet them? And what was she doing on Camelback Mountain? Possibly during those four years she was sometimes a guest in a little adobe house, the home of Jessie Benton Evans, who had come to Arizona not long before from Chicago, Paris and Italy. Evans owned forty acres at the base of Camelback where she held regular salons. Probably Lillian had met her—they were both professional painters in what was still a small community.

*I*n **November of the year** she moved to Arizona someone appeared for whom there was no warning a biographer could see, of whom there was no previous mention in the census, city directories—nothing. A thirty-four-year-old spinster, Lillian Wilhelm married a man named Westbrooke Robertson. The marriage lasted only five years; later she removed everything that referred to Robertson from her papers. Whatever her reasons for marrying him, she erased him afterward, rendering him invisible as far as she was concerned.

Most of the people in Phoenix had come from somewhere else. Seventy-five years later Lillian's nephew remembered an impression that she had met Robertson in the East, and he does look Eastern in the one photo that Claire preserved. Maybe Lillian married him there too: in a legal paper she said that it had been in Maricopa County, but there was no listing in the

Westbrooke and Billy Etsity at Tuba, 1917
Claire Carlin Collection
Courtesy of Carolyn Timmerman, Zane Grey's West Society

office of the Clerk of the Superior Court, no "hard file" which could be examined. She left a note that she knew a woman named Nancy Robertson who lived on West McDowell but no explanation about who that was.

In 1918 cousin Elma was with Zane Grey on the Tonto forest with "a companion", in 1919 with "a friend" [another cousin? Claire perhaps?] In August he wrote to Dolly that he had received a letter. Lil's husband "has been transferred to some little desert station in New Mexico, all because he was patriotic and the agent at Yuma is pro-German. All her nice comfortable home, the garden she had toiled in, the chickens, she had to leave." Were the station and the agent agricultural? Indian?–there were Mohave, Apache, Yuma and Cocopah in the jurisdiction. Grey didn't say.

In September he wrote from northern Arizona, "Lil is here today. She looks fine and happy." He didn't mention Robertson. The Flagstaff newspaper, reporting her passage through town, said she had arrived from Crown Point, New Mexico, a small town northeast of Gallup in barren country just off the Navajo Reservation.

Two photographs of Lillian in her albums were labeled "New Mexico 1918–1919." Navajo rugs hung on whitewashed

Lillian in New Mexico
Courtesy of Museum of Northern Arizona Flagstaff

walls. There were a rocking chair, a wood-burning stove, an easel. But no image of Westbrooke Robertson.

Claire and Elma were in Grey's party again that year, as well as his brother Romer with his wife, and so was a young woman named Ackerman from Middleton, New York. Al Doyle was along as "pilot." Their purpose, according to the newspaper was "to make a trip into the Indian country." A photograph of three of the women wearing broad-brimmed hats and sitting on the bank of the Colorado River was evidence that they went down a trail into the bottom of the Grand Canyon.

Deep in the Grand Canyon
Claire Carlin Collection
Courtesy of Carolyn Timmerman, Zane Grey's West Society

*A*lways **there were changes.** Zane Grey had become established as a *Western* writer. In 1918 he and Dolly moved to California with their three children, leaving the Lackawaxen house in Pennsylvania where Lillian had painted Indian designs in the study. It remained in their possession as a place to visit when they were in the East, one of many houses, cabins, and fishing camps which were established by the restless writer.

As the dreadful European war came to an exhausted end, an epidemic of influenza spread throughout the world, reaching the Navajo Reservation by way of Gallup. Soon smoke was rising from burning hogans where people had died and which could no longer be lived in because of chindi, understood by Anglos to mean ghosts. The reservation itself was under quarantine. The yard at Kayenta filled with Navajos who had been stricken. The whole Wetherill family was ill—Clyde Colville went out every day to bury people. When the sickness finally ebbed, three thousand Navajos had died. Deaths in the family of Nasja Begay, the Paiute who had been on Grey's first trip to Rainbow Bridge, had left only a child alive.

Lillian was of an age when death begins to impinge. In March of 1919 her father, seventy-five years old, succumbed to his third stroke. A full-page obituary in *Pottery, Glass and Brass Salesman* described him as a Mason, one of the oldest retail merchants in the china and glassware business in the country and one of its finest judges, who had made twenty-three trips to Europe during his heyday in search of goods. A final paragraph was painful.

> Personally Mr. Wilhelm was, to all outward appear-
> ances, an unfailing optimist. He always saw the bright
> side of things and was always looking for better times
> to come. He was never known to complain, no matter
> how hard the blows of adversity, and his sunny
> disposition won and kept for him many friends who
> stood by him even in his darkest days. It was only after
> his death that his private diary was found revealing
> how deeply his soul had been charred by his reverses,
> for even his family knew little of what was going on
> beneath his apparently cheerful exterior.

The Wetherills were aware that Lillian had been fond of him; probably she went east for his funeral. When Papa died, no more horse cars moved on tracks through New York streets that were thronged with immigrants. Delivery wagons were still pulled by horses, but every intelligent veterinarian was rapidly converting to a small animal practice.

A year earlier an old friend, contralto Alice Mandelick, who had married millionaire manufacturer John Haldane Flagler, had died of influenza. Later a hint remained in Lillian's papers that Flagler had proposed marriage to her and offered her a ring, possibly when she was in the East for her father's funeral, perhaps in December of that year when she and Claire were at Long Key with Zane Grey—the Flagler hotel system was involved in the Long Key Fishing Camp. Lillian was thirty-seven years old at the time. Such a marriage would have made a profound difference: Flagler owned a yacht, a house on Park Avenue, a farm in Connecticut. But he was over eighty, and she was already married. That he did not know about Westbrooke Robertson raises even more questions. Apparently the elusive husband was not with her—did he play so small a role in her affairs? Was he never mentioned by her family—was he *that* invisible? She claimed to have provided her own support with the sale of her paintings during the years of the marriage and implied toward its end that Robertson had no occupation.

*O*f 111 films of Zane Grey's books, 68 were set in Arizona. Jesse Lasky, who with Samuel Goldwyn and Cecil De Mille had "discovered" Hollywood, produced 53 of them. In 1919 *Desert Gold, The Rainbow Trail, The Light of Western Stars*, and *The Riders of the Purple Sage*, were being made into silent movies. Lillian and Claire and Elma and Mildred witnessed the whole exciting process. Grey was adamant that films should follow his books faithfully and insisted in contracts that they be shot in the places he had described. The result was that he personally traveled with Lasky's film crews, re-visiting scenes of earlier adventures. So did "the girls."

The movie treks made quite a difference for the economy of Kayenta. John Wetherill rented horses to Lasky at the rate of two dollars a day. Once he charged $1800 for the use of fifty horses for eighteen days. Lasky said "thousands" of Indians were employed as extras; "hundreds" of people arrived from Los Angeles. There were nine guest bedrooms by then at the trading post, with accommodations for only eighteen people ($1.50 a day for each room), so tents were pitched outside around the post.

It took everybody Louisa could muster to feed the crowds. Breakfasts were in shifts, technicians and laborers when morning was barely light, actors and directors at a more leisurely hour. Tables were everywhere; dishes were constantly being washed; lunches went out onto location. The moviemakers were billed thirty dollars per day for meals.

Watching the movie-making did not require all of Lillian's time. In February of 1920, having

Lillian and Claire at Lackawaxen
Claire Carlin Collection
Courtesy of Carolyn Timmerman,
Zane Grey's West Society

produced sufficient Arizona paintings, she exhibited them somewhere, a gallery perhaps, in Philadelphia. A month later she was living in Phoenix and riding a horse to the tops of Camelback Mountain and Squaw Peak for the "revelation of the wealth and fertility of the valley." In May she and Claire visited the Lackawaxen house briefly and heard the news that Grey was buying land under the Mogollon Rim for a hunting lodge he planned to use occasionally.

*A*rizona's population in 1920 was 334,162—a growth of 130,000 over ten years, most of it in Phoenix and Tucson, where modern street cars ran on electric overhead lines. National prohibition of the manufacture, sale or use of alcoholic beverages had been in force for a year, and flagrant resistance to it was growing. Thanks to a constitutional amendment, women could vote in national elections, even flappers who wore their hair and their skirts scandalously short.

Lillian painting
"When the Desert Is in Bloom"
Courtesy of Museum of Northern Arizona
Flagstaff

In January of 1921 Lillian showed oils and water colors at the Berryhill store at the corner of Washington and First Street in Phoenix. The purpose of the show, which included Kachina dolls, necklaces, moccasins, relics, mementoes and souvenirs which she had gathered, was publicity for Grey's novel *The Mysterious Rider*, which was issued early in the month.

She told a reporter who covered the opening: "I believe the country in the northern part of Arizona to be the most colorful in the United States...I have become very fond of [Southern Arizona]. Of course it is quite different from the Navajo and Hopi country, but it offers fully as great opportunities for the artist, and I look forward with pleasure to future work on the great desert country here in the Salt River Valley."

Later the gallery of Miller and Sterling in Phoenix, which showed her work through the decade, included three of her paintings in a collection of Arizona artists. "Surprise Valley", painted as an illustration for *The Rainbow Trail*, was on display. So was a study of a Hopi Kachina dance. An oil of Rainbow Bridge had been bought by Zane Grey on his recent visit to Phoenix, but he allowed it to remain in the collection until after the exhibit closed.

By August she was back at Kayenta, visiting the Wetherills, with whom she had become close although they were as unlike as East and West. Their daughter, Georgia Ida, sixteen years younger than Lillian, wrote letters to her when she was traveling. Georgia Ida rode bucking horses; Lillian was an

Lillian (l.) and Louisa Wetherill at Kayenta
Courtesy of Harvey Leake

aristocrat as far as the Wetherills were concerned. Friendship between the women persisted despite their differences.

There was a catholicity in her associations. In Flagstaff a few women painted as a hobby. Emma Verkamp, wife of David Babbitt, had learned as part of her education to do small delicate things like flowers on china. Her sons Raymond and Joseph married girls who were more ambitious about art, although they did not attempt professional status. Rose (Mrs. Ray) exhibited her work occasionally. At some time during the '20s Viola (Mrs. Joe), who began to paint in the middle of her long life, bought at Miller and Sterling two small watercolors which Lillian had done in Indian country and took them home to Flagstaff. Thirty years later Viola bought from Alex Brody, son of a Territorial governor who was associated with the Museum of Northern Arizona, a hand-made wooden frame for a single bed on which Lillian had painted Pueblo images in bright yellows and oranges and blues— apparently for a child's room.

*T*here was hardly a part of Arizona that Lillian did not know, sometimes as a visitor, sometimes as a resident, through the six decades she was in the state. For twenty years she lived off and on in towns in the Salt River Valley— long dirt roads apart, separated by farms. In January of 1922 she bought in her own name twenty acres of citrus grove in Scottsdale near the Arizona canal, a mile north and east of a cluster of buildings—all there was of the little town. Money to buy the "ranch" was borrowed from her family, perhaps from Zane and Dolly; two years later they mentioned a note, a mortgage, a debt she was repaying.

Near the Pima Reservation, the Scottsdale section had been subdivided in 1895. After a land boom in 1914, 10,000 acres were under cultivation, most in citrus trees. There was a school, a bank, post office, general store, newspaper. Population was about five hundred; roads were unpaved. One-story frame houses were surrounded by rows of trees that would have looked exotic to a woman from the north Atlantic coast—orange and grapefruit and lemon trees, green with glossy leaves all year around, golden with fruit. There was a small house in the grove on her acres. For the next fifteen years, as a property owner, she used it as her legal address no matter how far she traveled.

In the transparent air of the Salt River Valley, snaggle-topped mountains were incised against the sky. Camelback was only four miles away from Lillian's citrus "ranch" with Squaw Peak and the Phoenix Mountains behind it. The Macdowells were ten miles to the north; South Mountains were sixteen miles on the other side of the valley. The Superstitions, thirty miles distant, were clearly visible.

*I*t was a year full of events. There was travel, of course, and adventure. Much of it began at Kayenta. At the trading post in April she met Charles L. Bernheimer, who was outfitting for one of his exploring expeditions. She was there with a Zane Grey party that included his brother Romer; a pair of friends from Catalina; Lee Doyle, Jack Way and W.F. Wallace of Flagstaff; Con Sullivan from the Grand Canyon; and George Takahashi, Grey's personal cook. (Dolly was in California struggling with income taxes.) After a rest of several days, they went to Rainbow Bridge "on a trail never ridden by white men" with Wetherill and his son Ben, twenty six that year, as guides.

Sixteen-year-old Louise Anderson from Grey's Ohio home-town made the whole trip. She described quicksand, an impossible trail, "a terrible hill miles and miles straight up"–the usual reaction to that country–and said that Grey placed Lillian in the center of Surprise Valley and instructed her to paint the four directions.

Grey was riding his "great horse, White Stockings…fire in his eye," which the Doyles had stabled for him over the winter. It was his eighteenth trip to Arizona, the third to Kayenta, the second to Nonnezoche. Surveyors had begun to approach the arch from the Colorado River by then, not an easy venture. Wetherill's new trail made Grey's hair stand on end, so he said: a perpendicular and barefaced wall, peaks and parapet and ramparts cleaving the sky, a gateway between two high grey walls, slopes that were bare and smooth and steep. The great arch, which he had not seen since 1913, was "a masterpiece of nature," mysterious, triumphant, austere.

Several years in the future, Lillian remembered:

> *[After 1913] I was a member of three other expeditions with Zane Grey to the Rainbow Bridge…I also went once with Ben Wetherill's outfit. I am told I am the only woman who ever made so many trips into this wilderness of rock and sand.*

*B*y the 1920s the reputation of the Wethcrills was as magnetic as that of Lorenzo Hubbell—people arrived from all over the country. In the first week of August, 1922, a hard-drinking cartoonist for the Hearst newspapers, Jimmy Swinnerton, arrived at Kayenta with his wife. Trained in techniques of landscape painting at the art school maintained by the San Francisco Art Association, he had recovered from tuberculosis in the Mohave Desert around Colton, California. In 1909, the year when John Wetherill first saw Rainbow Bridge, Swinnerton had made an initial foray into Grand Canyon country. Since 1914 he had been a frequent traveler in northern Arizona to gather images for his sensitive landscape paintings.

He often brought as many people to meet the Wetherills as Zane Grey did. In 1922, preparing a cartoon series featuring Indian children ("Canyon Kiddies") he arrived at Kayenta with a few friends from Los Altos, where he lived, and two of the nation's best-known cartoonists, Rudolph Dirks ("The Katzenjammer Kids") and George Herriman ("Krazy Kat"). A week later Maynard Dixon, whom Swinnerton had known since art school days, arrived with his wife, photographer Dorothea Lange. Then a courtly New York illustrator named William Robinson Leigh showed up. A railroad-sponsored artist, Leigh had been painting in Arizona since 1906, had finished an Oraibi canvas in 1917. While they waited for the announcement of the Snake Dance at Hotevilla, the artists rode into the Tsegi on Wetherill horses to see the ancient houses there.

Lillian was at Kayenta in that remarkable gathering from the day they arrived. In the guest book she painted a desert watercolor; Swinnerton did several "Canyon Kiddies" panels; Leigh drew in ink a horseman exploding out of the page; Dixon painted a rider on a hilltop with northern Arizona spread out behind him. It was a record that collectors coveted in vain: the Wetherills held onto it. No notes were kept of the conversation around the dining table, where Louisa sat at the head in front of the kitchen door.

Like 2000 other visitors, Swinnerton and his friends watched the Snake Dance on August 26; perhaps Lillian was with them. Though the others went back to Flagstaff, she stayed on at Kayenta for another month. Mildred visited for a week in early September.

After that Lillian took a few days to travel into the vast, rocky desert of the northwestern corner of New Mexico to see a mystery the Wetherills had known for years. It was so remote in time and place that it was almost beyond comprehension—the massive masonry buildings, three hundred or so of them, in Chaco Canyon.

Chaco had been at the center of a culture gone so long that no one could decide exactly what it had been. Obviously organized: witness the skill of the builders, the roads and canals and platform mounds and signal stations, the shaping of the land itself. Travel to the site on the edge of the San Juan Basin was a three-day ride each way from either Gallup or Farmington: fewer than two hundred tourists had mounted horses to make the effort.

It was enough to put New York into new perspective: the structures in the broad New Mexico canyon had been deserted for three hundred years before the first settlement on Manhattan Island. Standing inside the ruined walls and looking across the plaza, Lillian painted Pueblo Bonito, a four-story communal structure of 800 rooms and thirty-two circular pit kivas of different sizes. The surrounding country was various shades of New Mexico brown with none of the spectacular reds of Monument Valley; the old pueblo was also brown. She solved the problem of color by painting Bonito at dusk with stars just appearing in the sky and shadows of purple, blue and lavender.

In September or October of 1922, nine months after Lillian bought the citrus grove, Westbrooke Robertson disappeared suddenly after telling a neighbor that his brothers had married wealthy women and he resented having married a poor one who expected him to "squat on twenty acres." He was "quitting for good." As Claire told it later, Robertson expected to be waited on hand and foot and demanded much service.

The deepest wounds, the most profound embarrassments, are hardest to talk about: Lillian never mentioned him in later years, except to say that he had been "a mistake." Since the days when she had masked her "knife of flame," she had learned to hide behind an impassive face: one can only guess at what she felt about those five years to have eliminated Robertson so thoroughly. He vanished out of her life.

*T*ales of heroism have a broad appeal. Grey looked at men of the West and used their example to touch an American nerve and create a stereotype which the world took to its soul. John and Louisa Wetherill appeared under other names in four of his Arizona novels: *The Vanishing American, The Rainbow Trail, The Lost Pueblo, Captives of the Desert.* Al Doyle, somewhat sanitized, served as one of his fictional models for what was to become the western hero. In Arizona for a bear hunt in 1921, Grey had visited Doyle shortly before old Al's death from cancer.

Doyle's son, who had worked with his father, became Grey's agent in Arizona for horses, hands and supplies, outfitting expeditions and hunting trips from the Doyle ranch on what was known as Upper Oak Creek Road. Claire, described by her family as "a live wire," said years later: "Lee Doyle's daughter Lana was a friend of mine while I was a teenager traveling with my cousin and his entourage on the many trips he took gathering material for his work." Like his father, Lee Doyle was also the Zane Grey hero—cowboy, woodsman, rancher. Most of the time he preferred the company of a horse and a couple of friends.

One of those friends was a man seven years younger, a good-natured cowboy named Jesse Raymond Smith who, it was said, served as a pattern for Grey's fictional characters Brazos Keene (*Knights of the Range, Twin Sombreros*) and Pecos Smith (*West of the Pecos*). If Jesse was indeed the model, Grey saw him as a paragon of honor, courage, and practical intelligence, a man of "cool and reckless insouciance" who could kill when he had to but was nonetheless honest and upright and protective of women. A dead shot, he had "an uncanny instinct for recognizing dishonest men" and a modest sense of humor. In no time at all, he began to play an important part in Lillian's life.

Jesse Smith had been born in 1886 in Colorado to a family that had traveled west from Iowa in covered wagons to the mining towns near Denver. With his father, Louis, he had trailed a herd to Montana at the age of sixteen, captured 6000 wild horses in Nevada at twenty. In the Western tradition of good stories, he was to tell through the rest of his life that when he had been sixteen, Buffalo Bill had invited him to go to

Al, Jess and Ned Smith
Courtesy of Harvey Leake

England with the Wild West Show and his mother, Inez, had refused permission because she had feared he would learn bad habits. When he was twenty-three, the Smith parents with a daughter, Janie, and their sons Jesse, Albert and Ned, had moved from Cortez, Colorado, to northern Arizona.

At least once Jesse had worked a roundup for Jim Ramer on the huge OW ranch a long day's ride on a horse north of Pleasant Valley. A big man, Ramer wore a pistol on his hip and carried a rifle on his saddle and did not hesitate to use them. The kind of man Zane Grey liked to write about, he held open house for all who cared to stop and played his fiddle for dances. In 1917 he sold the OW to a former Hashknife cowboy, retired, and died seven months later at the age of sixty-seven.

New York author Porter Emerson Browne described Jesse Smith in words fit for publication:

I plead guilty to quite a bunch of everything wild that comes to the thrill hunter of real honest-to-god wild west. Not that I am a bit snakier than the average real cowhand, broomie chaser, bronc buster or general prowler in the large, unclosed spaces—men that have come or gone or that still linger. I was and am merely one of them, always hunting new thrills in the land where the bronco pony and wild cow are always ready to match the cowboy in a battle of speed and wits.

I've had a lot of fun in my time. Catching wild mustangs on the seamy side of Nevada scenery is fast work and dangerous. Dragging these old moss head steers out of the brush in rough country is no labor for invalids. Stepping aboard the hurricane deck of fifteen or twenty mean broncos every day for a couple of months is good fun too, even if it does shake your hair loose, and I've seen sixty hours in the saddle many a time with a bunch of cattle in wind and snow and drift and the danger of stampede.

There was a rumor that somewhere on the Navajo Reservation he had a son who lived with his mother's clan. Such gossip has ever been easier to tell than to verify.

Jess (l.) and Jot Stiles
Courtesy of
Mary May Stiles Bailey
Daughter of Jot Stiles

In June of 1917, two months after the United States entered the European war, the 29-year-old cowboy, deciding he was "too antique" for more wild-horse chasing, had "bought a pair of flat-heeled shoes, learned to walk," joined the army down in the southern Arizona border town of Naco, and "become one of the fifty thousand Smiths in Uncle Sam's A.E.F. outfit."

By 1919 he was back in the state after two years in France as a Sergeant 41 with the Engineers. Five feet eleven inches tall, Jesse Smith had brown hair and eyes, heavy eyebrows, a ruddy complexion. According to the Army, his character was "excellent." He had no war wounds.

Browne again, speaking for Jess:

I bought a bunch of horses and headed for Navajo land to swap with the Indians for blankets and jewelry. While thusly engaged I signed to star as a dude wrangler in Wetherill...headquarters at Kayenta, for the famous Rainbow Bridge trips.

My first job was a trip into Utah to buy pack animals and saddle stock. I finally made a deal for a bunch of forty mules which were in the bottom of Hack's Canyon. The trip in there after them and rounding them up was anything but tame.

He also signed on with the Aztec Land and Cattle Company, which owned the storied Hashknife brand, to break horses around Winslow and work cattle drives. That much alone put him into the company of legendary men. He liked to tell about the day his dark-haired father, brown from years in the sun, visited camp while he was gone and pitched in to help with branding. The foreman called Louis Smith "the best damn Mexican cowboy I ever saw."

Jesse Smith (l.), Hashknife cowboy, watching Clair Haight stir beans
Courtesy of National Old Trails Museum
Winslow, Arizona

He was better than a Zane Grey novel. In 1919, he and his father were at Kayenta, probably as trail hands, in the company of Herbert Babbitt and Mr. and Mrs. George Babbitt, Jr. With his brother Albert, fourteen years younger, he worked for John Wetherill on several of the grueling Bernheimer exploring expeditions that struggled around Navajo Mountain from 1919 to 1923 into country that until then had been declared impossible.

Charles L. Bernheimer, a wealthy New York businessman with a craving to explore blank spaces on the map, had become interested in the southwest because of Zane Grey's novels. With John Wetherill, the Smith brothers, and Zeke Johnson of Blanding, Utah, he and Earl Morris, representative of the American Museum of Natural History, found all the scenery a man could want.

> The view was appalling. On every side yawning, rocky throats, bare of vegetation and probably 600 feet deep, opened before us. Beyond these funnel-like gorges were humps, tubercles, and whalebacks, a veritable sea of them, gray and bare; beyond them a narrow vein-like crawling green thread was discernible. That was Navajo Canyon...There was no turning back, and ahead of us was a steep descent over slick-rocks, with occasional sharp bends and narrow ledges, one quarter of a mile or more in length. Fortunately the wind had chiselled delicate wavelets into the rock surface. This somewhat improved the footing, but the descent was steep and staggering, with nothing to hold to in order to prevent slipping. There was no time for faint-heartedness. No one dared to be dizzy. A scare among the pack animals meant disaster. To stop to think was impossible.

Bernheimer described himself as "tenderfoot and cliff-dweller from Manhattan," John Wetherill as "pathfinder and pathmaker." Al Smith was a "faithful and reliable daredevil," cowpuncher, cook, athlete and "good all around man." Jesse, who was with him in 1922 and 1923, he termed a "fearless and determined" scout, packer, horse wrangler and understudy to John Wetherill.

> After our cavalcade reached the Rainbow Bridge we divided–Johnson, Al Smith and I with the horses and mules, returned over our new Red Bud Pass [they had

Navajo guide Shadani and wrangler Jess Smith (r)
1921 Bernheimer expedition
Courtesy of Albert E. Ward

used dynamite to open it wide enough for their mules to slip through] to Painted Rock Camp, preferring this to a trip of nine or ten miles through deep sand and unknown conditions, which Wetherill, Morris, and Jess decided to undertake afoot. Their intention was to travel downstream through Bridge Canyon to the point where it joins Forbidding Canyon as far as they could go.

As explorers, they gave some thought to the names they put on the land: No Name Mesa, Cliff Canyon. Their camps they christened Rough Trail and No Good and Hardboiled. Their clothes were abraded to shreds by the sandstone defiles they wormed their way through. Apparently they enjoyed it all thoroughly.

*F*or the past ten years Lillian had traveled with such men. In July of 1923 she went again past Navajo Mountain to the rainbow arch with Ben Wetherill, who was at home in that country. She called it her best bridge trip. Three travelers from Chicago, two of them women, were on the trek, as well as

Elizabeth and Marion Wetherill, daughters of John's brother Richard.

The oldest of the five Wetherill brothers, Richard had been ambushed and shot at Pueblo Bonito in 1910 at the age of fifty-five. His wife Marietta had moved with her children to Cuba, east of Chaco Canyon, and then to Sanders over the border into eastern Arizona. Elizabeth was twenty-four and Marion sixteen the year their cousin took them on the difficult trail to Rainbow Bridge.

Zane Grey was on the Reservation later that summer while Lasky was filming another of his books—Grey and assorted guests from Hollywood, Avalon, New York and California, as well as Lillian, Mildred, and Grey's cook George Takahashi who carried a puppy. Jesse and Al Smith and Ben Taylor led them and a dozen or so mules to Nonnezoche, Lillian's second bridge trip of the summer. She drew a sketch in the visitors book that had been established at the base. They tried to reach Wild Horse Mesa (Kapairowitz Plateau) a hundred miles north of Kayenta but were stopped by the Colorado River in flood.

Apparently Lasky relished the challenge of shooting in Navajo country: Monument Valley, the Tsegi, Navajo Mountain.

> Camps were established at intervals for 200 miles across the reservation...Every available truck and touring automobile and nearly all the horses in Northern Arizona were pressed into service. They made many of their own roads across the trackless wastes.

> Trucks were constantly breaking down due to the terrific strain under which they operated...Several thousand dollars worth of camera equipment almost went down in quicksand on the way back from one location eighty miles out in the desert. Blinding sandstorms occurred frequently, after which the six cameras had to be taken apart and cleaned carefully...It rained at least once on most of the days...Electrical storms disturbed some members of the camp.

> A village was built on the desert ninety miles from Flagstaff. Delays were caused by the difficulty in getting

lumber fast enough. One Flagstaff mill turned its attention to our orders for several weeks. A hundred carpenters worked on this construction undertaking.

One of the biggest jobs of all was the building of (a full-scale replica of) the cliff dwellings at Keet Seel in the Tsegi Canyon 185 miles from our supply base, Flagstaff. It meant transporting 24,000 feet of lumber, or approximately 20 tons, by truck to Kayenta and from there by mule back to Tsegi Canyon, twenty-eight miles away. Twenty tons of cement were carried in the same way as well as every last nail, hammer, can of paint, tapeline, and everything else. A mule can make the round trip in four days.

Joining Wetherill in support of Lasky's efforts, Lee Doyle worked as location manager, furnishing horses, trucks, lunches for hundreds of people. Jesse Smith was employed as packer and crew for camp and trail tasks and as head of the pack train. Lillian said she spent twenty-seven days in the saddle with him looking for locations for the movie version of *The Vanishing American*, for which Doyle furnished 1000 horses.

Residents in northern Arizona watched it all and formed opinions that might have surprised the Easterners. They mimicked Grey and laughed about him around campfires and continued to tend what they considered his cavalcades. He was "heavy-handed", they said, when it came to getting something he wanted. [As far back as the Hopi, Arizonans have been sensitive to Eastern manners.] Some judged Lillian as pretty but "a typical Eastern woman" who thought she was superior to ordinary Westerners. Her years after the age of sixteen had not been happy or privileged—far from it. But her experience had produced a woman very different from themselves, and Arizonans were inclined to read that as a feeling of superiority. The Wetherills said, "She was a lady."

Billie Williams, seventeen-year-old daughter of a trader, thought Jesse Smith was "awfully nice." Cowboys, she said, were "sure good men, splendid, down-to-earth, honest, kind, well-mannered—the kind of men who made the earth." They "treated women like paper dolls." Jesse Smith was "a wonderful fine western cowboy…the kind everyone admired."

Lillian
*Courtesy of Museum
of Northern Arizona
Flagstaff*

In December of 1923, charging desertion and non-support, Lillian filed for divorce from Westbrooke Robertson, which put her outside the pale of respectable society as it was in those days. Her attorneys advertised to find and notify him, but no one had heard from him except a man who said Robertson had gone to "San Antone." Mildred Smith, who appeared as a witness, testified that she had lived for several weeks in the little house in Scottsdale and could corroborate Lillian's testimony. In May of 1924 the divorce was granted by Maricopa County Superior Court.

She immediately married Jesse Smith. According to Billie Williams, "all of us were stunned." [One wonders what Mama had to say.] She was 42; he was 36.[6]

Porter Browne described Jesse's proposal:

I met her during my rambles, and one moonlight night on the sandy slope of a pinnacle of the Painted Desert I slipped up on her affectionate side and fooled her into consenting to trot along life's old trail with me in double harness. And she's always ready to go anywhere any time if only I give her time to get her paints together.

According to a note Lillian left later in a copy of Grey's novel *The Vanishing American*, the proposal was at Organ Rock south of the San Juan River on the western edge of Monument Valley, no where near the Painted Desert. But poignant nonethe-

---

[6]In 1924 Georgia O'Keeffe married Alfred Stieglitz, who was a generation older than she was. He had traveled west of the Hudson only once, twenty-four years earlier. He never did so again.

less: so ephemeral a human arrangement as marriage contracted at a remnant of silt deposited hundreds of millions of years earlier by a Paleozoic sea.

*A*n outline for what they did and where they were during the next thirty-five years can be laboriously constructed from brief references in newspapers, memories of people who knew them, an occasional official document, a few letters. In combination they make a story as episodic as beads on a string. A few clear patterns emerge—art, adventure, friends, Arizona, and always the two of them together—but the details are as hazy (and sometimes implied) as those of Lillian's youth.

In July Lillian and Jess were in Kayenta; so was Mildred. And then they all went off on a new trip with Zane Grey. First to New York, where streets were full of high black boxy automobiles and only policemen rode horses—Grey said it was a wonderful, terrible place. He was half bewildered, shocked by flappers and Flaming Youth.

Then north to Nova Scotia, where they looked at a schooner that was for sale; Grey, always a fisherman, wanted one for deep-sea adventure. Dolly was alarmed about the expense when she heard of it. By fall the Smiths were back in Arizona, at least part time in Lillian's house in Scottsdale. A skyscraper was completed in Phoenix that year, the ten-story Luhrs Building, which was visible for miles across the valley.

There were new developments for their friends in Navajo country. Almost from the beginning John Wetherill had recognized that Clyde Colville was good with the business details necessary at a trading post—better, in fact, since John tended to give merchandise to needy Navajos—so he left that responsibility to Clyde and concentrated on lucrative tourist/guiding/movie tasks. Sometimes as many as four parties at a time, outfitted and guided under Wetherill supervision, went out from Kayenta, most of them during the summer season when northern Arizona was free of snow.

Louisa had made a reputation among academic archaeologists with her knowledge of Navajo culture, history, language and use of north country plants. In autumn of 1924 she was invited to lecture at the University of Arizona in Tucson. John went with her.

They decided the southern desert would be a fine place for a guest ranch during winter when activity had wound down at Kayenta. In October they signed a ten-year lease for the La Osa ranch south of Tucson on the Mexican border, planning to use it mid-October to mid-May. An old thirty-two room adobe casa, pasture for fifty head of horses, eucalyptus trees and lawns—it was picturesque enough to satisfy visitors who yearned for exotic winter adventure in the Southwest.

Jess and Lillian went south to see La Osa and offer what help they could to the new venture. Horses, mules and wranglers traveled down from Kayenta to provide for hunting parties and long pack trips. Some lasted weeks, all the way from La Osa to Kayenta, twelve miles a day, limit of ten persons. Ben led one on a four-month, 2000 mile trip that required a pack train of thirty-five animals.

*I*n December the Smiths went back to northern Arizona for an episode that was to become a classic in range management. The background was complex, as usual. Hunters had been taking as many as five hundred mountain lions a year from northern Arizona forests, nearly eradicating them. Domestic livestock had grazed on the range heavily. Several seasons of ample rainfall had encouraged growth of grasses and forbs, and deer had responded by reproducing rapidly, often with twins. As a result the deer herd, estimated at 3000 on the North Rim of the Grand Canyon in 1900, had increased to at least 20,000 by 1924, or 50,000—opinions varied—well beyond what available forage could support. Complete destruction of browse plants was predicted, with deer starving by the thousands.

The Secretary of Agriculture appointed a committee which recommended the immediate removal of half the deer on the north Kaibab. An attempt to trap and transport them had failed. Of ten captured, only one deer had reached the railroad line alive, and it had promptly died. Flagstaff's George McCormick proposed a "sensational" drive of up to half the deer on the North Rim, at least five to ten thousand, down into the Grand Canyon. (There was some gossip that he knew the route because he had driven rustled horses across the canyon on it.) The starving deer, some at only two-thirds their normal weight, were to swim the Colorado River and climb up to the South

Rim, where a special hunt authorized in Washington would have thinned the resident herd. Arizona Governor Hunt agreed to pay $2.50 for every deer delivered to the new range.

There was much controversy about the plan and months of meetings with game wardens and forest supervisors. Everybody had an opinion: the Izaak Walton League, Stephen Mather of the National Park Service, the governor, the Phoenix Gazette. Jimmie Owens, a veteran North Kaibab lion hunter who had contributed to the problem, said it wouldn't work, but nobody listened.

It was a scenario tailor-made for Zane Grey, who sketched out a story in which the drive would be the main episode and squabbled with the Hearst newspaper chain for exclusive literary rights. Financing was arranged from Lasky's film company in return for exclusive rights to film. If the government would issue a permit, he said, a copy of the film would be furnished for educational purposes.

Around 150 to 200 cowboys and Navajos—who refused to attend unless they were paid their two dollars a day in advance—were promised for the drive, which was planned to be completed in six days. Three miles of six-foot drift fences were constructed. Deer were to be baited by bushels of apples, potatoes and chewing tobacco.

Horses furnished by Lee Doyle descended the Tanner Trail, swam the Colorado and climbed up to the North Rim, herded by Doyle and Jesse Smith. According to Flagstaff's *Sun*, Jess and Lillian had traveled up from Scottsdale for the occasion. Among the crowd of Flagstaff men, loath to miss the excitement, who took their automobiles across the river at Lee's Ferry and positioned themselves to watch were Coconino Forest Supervisor Ed Miller and ranger Dutch Lochman.

Game Warden Jack Fuss crossed the canyon with Jimmie Babbitt and a few other men and twenty-seven head of pack horses. It was a miserable four-day trek: cold and snowing the whole way, and the food was inedible. The saddles, Fuss said, were just about cold enough to stick to. He predicted that if McCormick did manage to get any deer into the canyon, he would lose two-thirds of them on the trail.

The drive had been planned for early November when water level in the river would be low, but complications had slowed arrangements and it was not until December 12 that everyone was on hand. As Jimmie Owens had warned them, it was a complete failure. Ed Miller and Dutch Lochman looked the situation over and went back to Flagstaff just before heavy snow reduced visibility to fifty feet and temperatures to well below zero.

On a Tuesday morning a ten-mile-long line of mounted cowboys and walking Navajos combed through the forest from eight miles back ringing bells, blowing whistles and banging on tin cans. Initially they frightened five thousand deer toward Saddlerock Canyon. But order quickly disintegrated into a rout. Drivers could not see each other in the snow and thick brush. The Indians, who were cold and walking fast, got well ahead of the horsemen.

As the line tightened, deer charged not down the trail but between the Navajos and *toward* the horsemen, broke through the line and jumped the fences. Cameramen could see only blurs. Not one deer was sent down into the canyon.

"It was a world of experience," returning men told the editor of the *Sun*. "Deer cannot be driven or herded. It just can't be done." Buck Lowry compared deer to the American people: "They can be led and baited quite easily, but can't be driven with any degree of success." Inveterate hunter Zane Grey advised that it would be best in the future not to kill so many mountain lions.

An estimated forty percent of the deer on the North Kaibab died of starvation during the winter of 1924–1925.

Six weeks after the fiasco, on the morning of January 30, 1925, the three-masted schooner "Fisherman" cleared Balboa, Panama, after sailing from Nova Scotia where Grey had bought it. With the usual large group including Jess, Lillian, Mildred, Elma, and Claire–who had married a radio pioneer and broadcasting executive–he set sail for a four-month ocean voyage. "The girls" wore nearly identical white middy blouses, long white skirts and white hats with navy blue bands–very nautical.

They sailed out to the Galapagos Islands, then back to the Mexican coast. Lillian painted watercolors to illustrate Grey's book about the trip, *Tales of Fishing in Virgin Seas*, which was published in 1925. Jess, who said he was "employed" for the

"The girls" on a Galapagos island
(l. to r.) Mildred, Lillian, Claire, Elma
Claire Carlin Collection
Courtesy of Carolyn Timmerman, Zane Grey's West Society

trip, fished with Grey's sophisticated equipment and was photographed with a large marlin, which may have been quite heady for a life-long cowboy.

They finished the voyage north at Avalon on Catalina Island, twenty-six miles from Los Angeles out in the Pacific, which Lillian had visited in previous years as part of fishing expeditions. Population was 1500 in winter, five thousand more in summer. Five years earlier William Wrigley jr. had used part of the money from his chewing gum fortune to buy the entire 76-square-mile island. He had already built a home high above the bay, a yacht club, a tower that rang chimes four times an hour, and a baseball field where his Chicago Cubs could train in the spring.

For nearly a decade Grey had visited Catalina for the fishing in deep water off the western shore. Although he still had the Lackawaxen house and was building another in Altadena on the mainland, he had bought one of Avalon's building sites, a narrow, steep-sided ridge three hundred feet above the water across the bay from Wrigley. He proposed to construct a Hopi pueblo on the property. The reasons for that particular style might have seemed puzzling, but Zane Grey was wealthy as the result of an estimated fifty-six million readers around the world, and he did what he wanted to do. [That fifty-six million did not include the family of T.A. Riordan in Flagstaff. T.A. forbade his granddaughters to read Grey's novels: "They aren't literature."]

At Avalon, passengers from *Fisherman* were treated to an examination of the site, the blueprints (approved by Dolly), and the initial stages of construction. All kinds of experiences went with being in the party of a celebrity. One that would be of value to the Smiths ten years later was an introduction to William Wrigley and his son Phillip, who was twelve years younger than Lillian, six years younger than Jess.

At some time during that peripatetic year, the Smiths met another celebrity, a novelist who was a rival with Zane Grey for popularity and sales, Harold Bell Wright. A man of sincere religious belief, Wright had moved to Tucson in 1916 hoping that the dry desert air would cure his tuberculosis. Author of *The Mine with the Iron Door* and *When a Man's a Man* based on his travel in the Baby State, Wright had recently published *A Son of His Father*, an Arizona novel with a first printing of 600,000. Critics deplored a sentimentality that made Zane Grey "seem cold and hard," but Americans read his books eagerly for his affirmation of goodness and practical, non-sectarian Christianity.

The Wetherills met Wright in no time. After he had built a complex of hacienda-style buildings in the desert east of Tucson, he bought 20,000-acre Los Encinos ranch near La Osa. And he too knew movie people: Samuel Goldwyn, Victor Fleming, Sol Lesser of Paramount, and Jesse Lasky. When parts of *A Son of His Father* were filmed at La Osa, Wright was there to watch. Lillian and Jess signed the guest register in December.

*A*n enlisted man at Naco on the Mexican border in 1917, Jesse Smith had met Jot Stiles, whose uncles and father had come to Arizona from Texas in 1904 with the Hashknife outfit. The two Westerners became friends.

In northern Arizona after the war, with a wife and three children, Jot Stiles formed a partnership with Jesse to manage the Babbitt Trading Post under the blue skies at Tuba City. On the outskirts of the little settlement, the post was a big stone building; at the top Sam Preston had built a windowed octagon to let in light. Adjoining was a long, low stone building for the "guest ranch."

Ten years earlier Lillian had been a guest of Laura Preston there. After a separation from Sam Preston [who was acquitted in a notorious murder case and then died], Laura had moved away. In 1926 she married Walter Runke, Superintendent of the Western Navajo District. That was not the end of her friendship with Lillian: it would last another forty-five years.

Jot Stiles, who had grown up on the southern edge of the reservation, spoke the Navajo language and understood enough of the culture to stay out of trouble. For years people laughed as they told about the winter day when an old man standing with the group around the stove in the center of the post "keeled over" onto the floor. Navajos fled through the door to get away in case the old man had died, but Stiles knew the danger as well: a building in which there had been a death would be unusable because of chindi. No Indian would come near it. Stiles vaulted over the counter and grasped the unconscious man. Navajos joked that he was so fast he nearly beat them through the door. The old Navajo, it was said, recovered from being dragged out and dumped into a snow bank.

Smith and Styles decided to split the job where they could. Jot devoted most of his time to the Indian trading part of the business and to care of the livestock. Jess took responsibility for tourists and sight-seeing expeditions; he called it "an ex-cowboy's paradise."

They named the guest facility Shekayah, "my home" in Navajo. There were a lobby, a kitchen and dining room, bedrooms for tourists, all in a line. Lillian decorated the buildings with her paintings of Indian country; handwoven Indian rugs covered the floors. Jess and Jot printed business cards identifying the post as Tourists' Headquarters and a folder describing it as "The Gateway to the Best of the Rest of the

Lillian painting "Sunshine on the Tsegi"
Courtesy of Museum of Northern Arizona Flagstaff

West." With photographs of Coal Canyon, Nonnezoche, Betatakin, a Kachina Dance, and Lillian painting in Monument Valley, it was designed to entice Americans who were beginning to vacation in the West.

> Shekayah Ranch—a home for travelers—in an oasis on the Painted Desert. Set in the wide, open spaces on the Navajo Reservation, you will find a rambling house of thick stone walls, with home comforts and modern conveniences. Rooms are large and airy, well furnished. The dining hall has a southwest exposure, with a view of the distant snow-capped San Francisco Peaks. A large lobby furnishes a delightful place for music and recreation, and fresh vegetables, milk and 100 percent pure spring water are to be appreciated in a desert resort.

> Good trail and pack horses will be kept at the ranch. The visitor may enjoy short daily rides which offer surprising changes of scenery—from the nearby Hopi village, where these industrious and clever people live and work and dance their weird ceremonial dances; the mesa's edge, with its vista over many miles of Painted Desert, and dinosaur tracks in solid limestone—to week-long tours in hidden canyons, cliff dwellings in great caves, the magically beautiful country around Navajo Mountain, the famous Rainbow Bridge, and Monument Valley.

*I*n January of 1926 Lillian received a letter from the wife of Harold Bell Wright alluding to a visit she and Jess had made to the southern border of the state, a painting that had been sent, and a proposed visit to the Reservation. At the end of April Jesse heard from Wright: "Thanks for your good letter with the copy of the letter from your brother. (Al was by then working at the Grand Canyon.) I wish I could start within the hour to explore this wonderful country of his."

And then there was a paragraph about a rift with another novelist: "I am sorry to hear that you and Mr. Grey have agreed to disagree. I do not know him but knowing you as I do I find it hard to believe the difficulty is of your making. However you will probably arrange to live and enjoy life without his favors." As the Smith family understood it, the cause of the quarrel was Jesse's anger: he charged that Grey had taken stories he (Jess) had told about his experiences and claimed them as his (Grey's) own to enhance a reputation as a virile outdoorsman, clear dishonesty in Jesse's cowboy opinion.

Later in the year the Flagstaff newspaper included a sketch of Lillian's in a report of a strange event:

> ...at Tuba City there appeared a richly colored double halo around the sun and three brilliant mock suns or "sun dogs" bright as the actual sun, and an inverted halo or rainbow, reaching to points north and south of the zenith, the outside more brilliant than the inside—all the warm colors of the rainbow.
>
> The phenomenon was seen in the heavens last Monday afternoon at three o'clock by a small group of people at Tuba City, among them Mrs. Lillian Wilhelm Smith of Shekayah Ranch and Porter Emerson Browne, novelist and playwright who for several months has been a guest at Shekayah.

The Flagstaff newspaper mentioned visits by the Smiths several times. The little town among old volcanos—on the rail line, headquarters of the Babbitt company—was the logical place for a trader to go for supplies.

That year her portraits and landscapes of Arizona were part of the fifth annual California Watercolor Society exhibit. When she showed her paintings in the Arizona Federation of Women's Clubs Biennial Council Art Exhibition, she was in the company of Kate Cory, Jessie Benton Evans, Gunnar Widforss, Ron Megaree, Flagstaff's Stanley Sykes, Claire Dooner of Prescott, and Marjorie Thomas of Scottsdale.

By then Lillian must surely have met Mary-Russell Ferrell Colton, who was six years younger and all her life considered "artist" to be the word which defined her. Harold and Mary-Russell established a permanent home in Flagstaff in 1926 on land they had bought from C.J. Babbitt out on the Fort Valley road.

The move to Arizona changed the course of Mary-Russell's career, as it had Lillian's. She continued to exhibit her paintings in the East as a member of "The Philadelphia Ten" and became an organizing influence for the arts in Flagstaff, but her focus gradually moved toward northern Arizona Indians. Alarmed by the loss of Anasazi antiquities to institutions in the East, the Coltons joined with local people to establish a society that would form a museum for northern Arizona science and art, Indian as well as modern. Mary-Russell wanted it to be a cultural center, an "intellectual apex" for the whole area.

*T*here was a blur of activity in 1927. In January three of Lillian's paintings—Rainbow Bridge, sunshine on the Tsegi, and Kayenta Ridge with Agathla beyond—were hung in the lobby of Flagstaff's new Monte Vista hotel. The local newspaper, reporting the event, described her as "an ardent interpreter of the beauties of northern Arizona" and declared that the paintings were "attracting much admiring attention and favorable comment." As was Lillian herself—she was a guest at a dinner meeting/astronomy lecture/musicale of the Business and Professional Women's Club in the Monte Vista's dining room. Speakers were from Lowell Observatory: C.O. Lampland and V.M. Slipher, whose wives were also guests. And an old friend from Tuba City lived in town, Laura Preston Runke, who had joined the Federated Community Church four years earlier.

In February Jess, working to the northeast out of Cameron to plot and construct a new road to Tuba City, riding through another trackless waste where vegetation was measured in inches, came upon something that puzzled him until he bent down for an examination. Lying out across the ground was an unsuspected group of ancient trees turned to stone ages earlier, some barely visible in the sand. Until then, they had been unnoticed by Anglos.

When the news got back to Flagstaff, three of the Babbitt men rode out to investigate and returned with samples of mineralized wood. The *Sun* gave Jess credit for the find and promptly named it the Sunset Petrified Forest. West of the better-known forest, east of Cameron eight or ten miles, it extended "away from the road as far as one can see" with new "combinations of tints and textures."

Jess' local fame was followed closely by grief. His parents had recently moved to Oljato. Their daughter Janie and her husband John Taylor and five children—Jack [often called

"Tuffy" because he wasn't], Jessie, Glen, Inez ["Tiny"] and Albert—had taken the trading post there, the one that had been established by the Wetherills.

In April Louis Smith died "due it was thought to heart strain," the editor of the *Sun* explained, "received three weeks previously when Mr. Smith had worked from 9 o'clock in the morning to 4 in the afternoon trying to start his car, which stalled 13 miles from Kayenta on the road to Red Lake." Sixty-five years old, a big rugged pioneer of pioneer parentage, he had been in the best of health, of remarkable physique, "accustomed to use his superb strength without stint." But there had been a "searchingly cold wind" that day as he walked back to Kayenta. A pain in his chest had forced him to remain in bed for several days before he was moved to Tuba City, where Jess lived and his son Ned was employed by the Reclamation Service, and then on to Prescott. Jess and Lillian and his third son Al reached him there before he died, leaving Jess with the knowledge that families tend to thin out over time.

He and Jot Stiles were friends and partners, suited by their lives and experience for the trading post job, but their families were not compatible in the close contact of the Tuba post. Porter Emerson Browne, speaking for Jesse, hinted at sharp maneu-vering—"When I woke up the cards had been stacked against me; the jack pot was a good one, but I didn't even have openers, so I was forced to a showdown, and that little game was over"—but Browne may well have been guilty of literary license.

At any rate, some time in May or June there was a dissolu-tion of the partnership. Jot Stiles bought a half interest in the Red Lake Trading Post from Johnny O'Farrell and became a partner with the Babbitts a second time. The Smiths moved into town for the summer, maybe to a room in the Monte Vista Hotel—Jess received another letter there from Harold Bell Wright.

*F*reed from duties, they had a grand time. The Flagstaff newspaper told readers they were making Flagstaff their headquarters between interesting trips. Roads all over Arizona were terrible, unpaved and often ungraded. A driver with any sense carried water and a shovel as necessary items in travel equipment. But Jess was capable and Lillian was game,

Lillian
Courtesy of Harvey Leake

and they went everywhere, across miles and miles of country
that was bigger for having so few people in it. And oh, the sky!

They had a kaleidoscope of friends. For a while in February
they visited the Wetherills at La Osa. In early June they were in
Phoenix with Cleo Wilson, the widow of a pioneer and prominent citizen who had died in 1906, and Lou Ella Archer, a
woman who was familiar in local society, such as it was in those
years. Born in Minnesota, Archer had come to Phoenix with her
parents in 1900 to live in an uncle's house, Palm Villa, on
twenty acres at the northeast corner of Central and Thomas. A
graduate of Phoenix schools and a college in the East, Archer
had just returned to live in Palm Villa, a "landmark" quite
different from Lillian's twenty acres in Scottsdale. She had
achieved a reputation as "one of Arizona's most outstanding
and prominent writers and literary authorities" for her poems
and reviews in newspapers. [Her brother Shreve achieved a
reputation as one of the founders of the manufacturing firm
Archer-Daniels-Midland.]

Fleeing the desert's summer heat, the Smiths returned to the
Monte Vista in Flagstaff to meet Lucy B. Motley of New York.

The *Sun* called her "a friend of Mrs. Smith who has never been in this part of the country though she has lived many years in England, has toured the continent and otherwise traveled extensively." With Alice King, another friend, they drove Mrs. Motley to see the Grand Canyon.

Proud of the spectacular show they could offer to Eastern visitors, they took the long road back to Flagstaff, bumping along on a rough track through the high desert to Cameron, then on to the serene ruins and petroglyphs around Wupatki, still as breathtaking as they had been fifteen years before on Lillian's first trip to Arizona. Only four years earlier President Coolidge had designated the area a national monument.

There was another day's motoring past wide vistas of the Painted Desert, volcanic cones and cinder hills to the tumbled lava beds around Sunset Crater. Less than a thousand years old, the crater and its jagged black basalt flow would become a national monument in 1930, after locals became alarmed by the news that a movie company was planning to dynamite it in order to film the resulting landslide.

Life had not been easy for Jess' mother Inez, a tiny woman with dark eyes. There'd been hard work, loss of babies, the frequent "moving on" common to the frontier, the kind of thing that doesn't always make a woman strong. She had not recovered emotionally from the death of her husband, with whom she had had a close relationship, and her grown children were concerned that she seemed to be increasingly unstable. It had all finally been too much.

Jess and Lillian tried to entertain her with a seven-week driving trip to Colorado that included two of Janie's children. Their route went through the Navajo reservation by way of Mexican Hat to Grand Junction, a jolting camping adventure on the rough Western roads of the day. When they toured Rocky Mountain National Park, construction had not yet begun on the eastern section of Trail Ridge Road; they crossed on narrow old Fall River Road, expanded years earlier from an ancient route up Fall River Canyon. [Charles Lindbergh flew to Paris that year, which wasn't easy either.] Lillian carried a large Kodak camera for making photographs of scenes she might want to paint later.

After several weeks visiting relatives near Denver, they returned to Arizona by way of Mesa Verde and Ship Rock. There was a painting stop near Lukachukai on the Arizona side of the state line. Then they jounced along across Navajo land to Oljato to drop off Inez and her grandchildren.

In that huge empty country the Smiths were constantly in company. The next move was south to Kayenta to see the Wetherills and listen to the story of their first airplane ride. In April a two-seater from Scenic Airways had landed on the flats near Church Rock. John and Louisa had gone up separately with the pilot to see from the air the land they had entered by wagon little more than a decade earlier.

Their daughter Georgia Ida, who had married in 1921, returned frequently with her girls. Johnni Lou was four years old by then. Lillian's namesake, two-year-old Dorothy Lillian, had been born in her grandparents' home in 1925. Lillian had painted birth announcements for each of them. Through her childhood, Dorothy would remember, "We were always happy to see Aunt Lillian and Uncle Jess come to Kayenta. He was the kindest man we ever knew. She was self-willed and eccentric and lots of fun."

*I*n August the *Sun* noted the Smiths' return to Flagstaff: "Mrs. Smith brought home a number of delightful water color sketches made in remote spots of interesting desert scenes. Several done in the Lukachukai Mountains are especially charming and Mrs. Smith will reproduce them in oil. Several of her oil paintings hang in the lobby of Hotel Monte Vista. Mr. and Mrs. Smith will make Flagstaff their headquarters, making trips from here to various points, Mr. Smith on business and Mrs. Smith carrying on her art work."

The newspaper also noted that on August 19th they were dinner guests of Alice King at the Monte Vista.

Leo Weaver, who liked to joke that he had missed being born in Arizona by two years, had built the first guest ranch in the state dedicated strictly to catering to tourists: the Flying W at Wickenburg. An ambitious, likeable, gregarious man who never did anything small, he had recently bought the old Joe "Hooky" Fisher homestead on the Schultz Pass road to run it as a summer guest "home," with polo and Arabian horses. He and his wife Nell welcomed visits from Lillian and Jess now and then, but not as paying guests—"they never had any money."

The following year the Wetherills gave up the lease on their La Osa guest ranch near Tucson. It had been popular but not lucrative enough to repay their investment in improvements. For another dozen years they concentrated on the summer season at Kayenta.

In September of 1927, just before the winter season started, Lillian painted in the Flying-W guest book a small watercolor of a stagecoach arriving.
Courtesy of Henry Giclas and Marie Stilley

The Smiths were constantly moving, driving slowly through Arizona's glorious open country. At least twice she painted the San Francisco Peaks. In the late 20s—between 1:30 and 3:00 a.m.—she did an eight by eleven inch oil in blues and whites of full moonlight on the cliffs of Oak Creek Canyon. Her paintings were again displayed for sale in the lobby of the Monte Vista Hotel—photographs made at the time showed them hanging on the walls. After a purchase, she promptly brought in a replacement. The *Sun* described her as "an individualist...well-loved by Flagstaff people."

In October, wind was growing colder in northern Arizona and snow threatened Oljato, where Inez Smith had spent the summer's end with Janie. Ned drove his mother to Flagstaff; Jess and Lillian took her back to Scottsdale for the winter.

Lillian was never much of a housekeeper, according to her in-laws. They knew Jess thought she was wonderful, but they were uncomfortable with her. Under stress of being a guest in someone else's messy home, Inez Smith's emotional condition continued to deteriorate until the day she went outside with a bottle of kerosene, poured it over herself, and set it afire. Jess, seeing a "tower of flame" through a window, knew what it was and shouted, "Oh my god!"

Through succeeding decades, members of her family lived with the memory of her death, sometimes in silence. What could anyone have said that would have been adequate?

*D*uring desert months of light and mild temperature Lil— she was always Lil to her family—transferred her sketches into oil. Constantly at her easel, she believed that work was close at hand for everyone who could find it or become conscious of it.

> *For the artist in music, literature or art a world lies open, but one should not rest when the impulse is there. It takes work, and plenty of it, to accomplish these things, exhausting effort and often sheer muscular effort, but it is worth it.*

Work was a panacea as well as a calling: her family was slowly growing thinner too. Papa was gone. In 1927 her brother, Dick, whom she had tended and nursed and pushed in his carriage, died at less than forty years old.

*F*or more than a decade, remembering the designs she had seen on potsherds at Betatakin and Keet Seel, she had tried to interest Eastern manufacturers in producing a line of dishes, to be named Shekayah, that would incorporate six patterns from Apache and Hopi baskets, Ute beadwork, Acoma and Aztec pottery, and Navajo rugs. The Eastern manufacturers felt that Indian art was of little interest to Americans: "The entire idea was so new," she said later, "the designs themselves so entirely different, that they required some time to become familiar with the idea." When they did, "it was so truly American that it appealed strongly."

Two patterns were produced late in the 1920s. Navajo dishes in brown and black were made by Leigh Pottery in Ohio with Lillian's name on the back in gold script. A yellow Apache

Hopi pattern (l.) and Navajo pattern (r.)

basket design came from Lamberton Scammell; some were made in Bavaria. They were introduced in 1928 at the Arizona State Fair and were later exhibited at the National Pottery Show in Pittsburg, where they were recognized as "the first authentic effort to bring archaeological beauty into line with utility." It was indeed a first: Mary Colter's better-known Mimbres designs on tableware for dining cars on the Santa Fe's "Super Chief" were produced in 1936, nearly a decade later. (Colter had by then designed and furnished Harvey Company hotels and restaurants along the Santa Fe line and six structures at Grand Canyon.)

*O*n their travels **Lillian painted,** with the unfailing help of her husband, who insisted she be allowed to work without distraction. "I had learned that she would go any place, any time, where there was a chance to paint a picture." That included Arizona's most famous attraction: the Grand Canyon of the Colorado River.

In those years there were 147 miles of roads in the national park, 167 miles of trails and 96 miles of phone lines to be maintained, in addition to construction of camp grounds, cabins, warehouses, etc. The cross-canyon Kaibab trail had just been completed with a bridge spanning the river. Despite "unsatisfactory" access roads, visitors totaled over 175,000. The Superintendent referred to "a large force of men required."

One of those men was Albert Smith, who was at the new Pasture Wash Ranger Station, thirty miles west of the El Tovar

Hotel on an ancient Indian trail that had been widened in the 1890s by local residents. Not on a regular scenic route and "practically impossible for visitors," the remote station was a working camp with a cabin, a barn and corrals, used almost exclusively by horseback park employees to maintain the road, the Bass and Havasupai Point trails, which weather damaged every year.

In 1928, on lonely roads described in official reports as poor, bad, and wretched, Jess and Lillian dodged their Studebaker between the branches of cedars and spent three intoxicating months with the plunging vistas along the South Rim. She painted several small canyon pictures and two large ones, "Strength" four feet long, and "Silence" three by five feet. She described a painting trip to the Great Thumb, a plateau of sedimentary rock that protruded into the canyon west of the Kaibab Plateau which formed part of the North Rim. Together they forced the Colorado into a wide curve.

> We left Grand Canyon [Village] in our big "Studie" loaded with food, bedroll, water cans, easels and canvas, etc., went out on the Hill Top road, but turned right on a road that went along the rim of the Great Thumb. There Albert met us with two riding horses and a pack horse, an Indian (Havasupai) having helped him bring them from Pasture Wash. We camped that night close to the car, and the next morning left with the pack horse for the west side of the Great Thumb, a 20 mile ride. My first glimpse of the gigantic panorama was overwhelming , but I am always ready to tackle anything that Jess selects as a picture subject. He has an uncanny perception in that direction.
>
> He chopped out the heart of a huge old cedar tree, anchored my canvas with nails and ropes. We ate supper, and dropped into our camp bed rolls. It was about 4:30 a.m. in the first dawn-light that I heard the campfire crackling, and before the sun came up Albert and Jess were on their way, Albert to return to Pasture Wash, Jess to water the horses at the only water hole on the Great Thumb, fifteen miles from where we were camped. The vast panorama staggered me. I sat for hours studying it, trying to decide what part of it to put on my canvas, then went to work, and made the most careful drawing possible, all with the brushes. About 5 o'clock I suddenly became frightened, wondered if Jess would find me, and in my panic thought of a smoke signal. At a

safe distance from my canvas stood a big cedar tree. I hastily gathered dry twigs and branches and started a fire close to it. As it began to burn the smoke rose several hundred feet straight up in the still air. It was so quiet that a raven flying a hundred feet above me made the only sound, its wing feathers scraping each other.

Presently Jess appeared. He was greatly amused at my naive thinking that a man who had followed as many trails as he had would not find me without a smoke signal. He was hungry and tired, but slept only a few hours when he decided the thirsty horses must go back to the water hole to relieve their need. This was the procedure the entire time we were there on the Rim. Miles and miles of riding for Jess, and thousands of strokes of the brush for me.

Later I learned from members of the Geodetic Survey that no other white woman has ever been known to go within twenty miles of my spot on the Rim.

Four or five days later Jess carried the canvas [3 feet by 5 feet] on the toe of his boot and led a pack horse along that rough terrain (there was no trail) the twenty miles to where our Studie was parked. It was scratched by brush but not badly. But oh what an effort that was. His share in the picture I feel was as much as mine.

*T*he decade was coming to an end with optimism all over the country. In New York construction started for the Empire State Building and Riverside Cathedral. In Phoenix the Westward Ho and Biltmore hotels were nearing completion, as was a new county court house. Jessie Benton Evans' adobe house at the foot of Camelback Mountain was metamorphing into Scottsdale's first resort–Jokake Inn. Zane Grey's pueblo house on Catalina, more than twice as long as it was wide, over-looked the casino that Wrigley was building down on the shore. In Flagstaff, Lowell Observatory received shipment of a 13-inch lens for a telescope which, the staff hoped, would enable discovery of a suspected planet somewhere out beyond Uranus. Downstream from Lee's Ferry, a new bridge across the Colorado opened access to the North Rim. A Forest Service fire lookout tower overlooked the Great Thumb.

Lillian's life seemed increasingly promising. With the cooperation of women's groups, support for the arts had been organized in Phoenix. She was one of the first members of the Fine Arts Association, founded in 1925 as part of the Phoenix Woman's Club; she and Jessie Benton Evans were listed as "professional members." In 1928 when the Arizona Artists' Guild was formed, she was a charter member. The two groups shared space in what became the Art Center at 45 E. Coronado. [Formal art organizations were not exclusively female: Lillian's friend John Halstead, who had also studied at the National Academy, was a member of the Artists' Guild.]

The American Artists Professional League was organized in New York in 1928 by associates of the National Academy and "dedicated artists of stature" for the few painters, sculptors and graphic artists who still worked in traditional realism. She was accepted into membership. In May of 1929 fifty of her paintings were on exhibit under the sponsorship of the Arizona Museum, newly opened in Phoenix after ten years of organizing effort by Elizabeth Seargeant Oldaker, an artist trained in Europe and California.

Summer brought more rough Western adventure. She descended the narrow path into a remote branch of the Colorado drainage two waterfalls south of the river. A handsome people, the Havasupai, lived there between red-rock walls and watered their fields from a milky blue-green stream. Busy with watercolor sketches, Lillian was told she was the first white woman to hike into Havasu but neglected to mention who she went with.

She and Jess traveled again to Oljato. On July 12 the Flagstaff *Sun* reported:

> Mrs. Lillian Wilhelm Smith of Scottsdale, well known artist in oils and china painting, will spend the summer just across the border in Utah, where she will visit relatives and do sketching. She finds the summer colors particularly delightful for subjects in that section during July and August. Mrs. Smith has traveled extensively and painted wherever she went so that her exhibits show a variety of subject and treatment.

In September she and Mildred, two of Grey's children, his brother, a few Flagstaff and California friends, and George Takahashi went on a trip with Grey to "Segi, Kayenta, Monument Valley, Noki, Paiute, Rainbow Trail, Surprise Valley and Nonnezoshe." Grey termed it "simply epic"—they were all sick with some kind of stomach complaint. Marjorie H. Thomas, "widely-known Western artist" whose mother was daughter of a prominent Boston family, was also on the trail. Thomas, who had trained at the School of the Museum of Fine Arts in Boston, had arrived in the tiny settlement of Scottsdale in 1909, had been there more than a decade before Lillian arrived.

But optimism was becoming ever more difficult in Jess' family. Five years earlier his younger brother Al had married a schoolteacher named Henrietta Phelan. Brother Ned was at Kayenta in the middle of September, driving Al's wife and children from the Grand Canyon to visit Janie at Oljato, then going back to Red Lake where he was cutting wood on contract for the Park. Only twenty-nine years old, Al was showing the first symptoms of a progressive neurological disease, probably multiple sclerosis. Within a few years the youngster who had been a reliable daredevil and good all-around man on the Bernheimer expeditions—fluent in the Navajo language, appreciated for his Dutch oven cooking, trainer of mules deemed too intractable for Fred Harvey's dudes—would weaken until he was bedridden.

Zane Grey's Arizona adventures were also coming to an end. In the Tonto Basin Lillian painted Indian designs around the fireplace in Grey's hunting lodge, just before he stopped hunting. Angry about refusal of a request for a special permit to hunt bear out of season, he left Arizona in a huff, never to return. The state had been ruined by motorists, he complained; the Grand Canyon was "a tin can gasoline joint." Furthermore, the Navajos were doomed, the beauty and romance of their lives were dead. The acutely sensitive novelist did not take rejection calmly.[7]

*A*rt on the Colorado Plateau was still, as it had been for the better part of a century, a matter of individuals painting alone, with little professional contact, and that was a challenge to the impressive energy of Mary-Russell Ferrell Colton. She and her husband had accepted responsibility for the

---

[7]In spring of that year Georgia O'Keeffe, who had spent the previous decade with Stieglitz in New York, paid a brief visit to Taos, New Mexico. For the next seventeen years she was to be in New Mexico only during the summer.

new Museum of Northern Arizona and set up its first collection in the Flagstaff Women's Club building west of downtown on Aspen Street, across the Rio de Flag from Emerson School. Children walking home in the afternoons often stopped to look at the Indian bowls and baskets displayed in cases—the staff regularly cleaned their fingerprints from the glass.

Planning a show of Hopi art for the next year, Mrs Colton organized the museum's First Annual Arizona Artists Arts and Crafts Exhibition. Artists, "both from the north and from the south" were invited to submit original work which could be sold from the show. Cash prizes were offered.

"Arizona Artists" opened on July 8, 1929, with a reception and tea in the lecture room of the Women's Club building. Flagstaff's George Hochderffer had hung three paintings, Stanley Sykes two, but most of the thirty-two canvasses that were displayed by thirteen contributors had been painted by women. Mary-Russell was there, of course, with two oils and a watercolor. Prescott was represented by Kate Cory, Ada Rigden, and Claire Dooner-Phillips. Paintings by Gertrude Young and Louise Norton had come up from Tucson. Della Shipley of Winslow had sent two. Artists from Scottsdale were identified as Lillian Wilhelm Smith, Jessie Benton Evans, and Marjorie Thomas. Lillian submitted oils of Rainbow Bridge and Havasu's Navajo Falls (priced at $250).

The Arizona Artists exhibition closed on July 29 with optimism, hope for the future. Ten weeks later the crash on Wall Street changed the market for artists as surely as for everyone else. Lillian was forty-seven, a little over half through her life. Women who knew Jesse Smith said of him, "He was the husband every woman longs for. He took care of her, protected her. When they were camping, he did everything to make her comfortable—piled up rocks to form a tub so she could take a bath." But even a Western hero could not fight down an adversary like a world-wide economic collapse. Years of increasingly hard work were ahead.

*E*conomic implosion was not immediate. For a year or two it was easy, for many people, to ignore what was happening as businesses disappeared slowly—and with them the jobs they had provided. Finally one of every four men was unemployed; millions of people had no income. Fear was tangible. Anyone who lived through that time could verify the fear.

Most American artists had worked alone, essentially on speculation: life for them had always been a gamble. Lacking unions or the strength of Actors' Equity and the Federation of Musicians, they saw their incomes plummet as their sales evaporated. In April of 1931 galleries in New York began to mount unemployment fund exhibitions.

Shocked, trying to find a popular market, artists turned to styles that seemed more relevant, more *American*, than the non-social Modernism of the exciting revolutionary years. Thomas Hart Benton termed abstraction "an academic world of empty pattern." Ben Shawn said, "The French school is not for me."

Submerged through the seventeen years since the Armory Show, painters of "old-fashioned representation" returned to prominence. Debates about nationalism held the attention of people in academies and studios and galleries, with resulting problems for curators building a collection for the new Museum of Modern Art. The few artists who continued to work in abstract styles met hostile reaction.[8]

The first museum devoted exclusively to American art, the Whitney, opened in 1931 while the latest trend in criticism was taking hold. Realism was back, social realism this time, which was not the same as the "traditional" realism supported by the Artists Professional League. The American Scene was expected of artists: farms and factories, city streets, working people. Critics approved satire, political propaganda, improvement of society and anecdotal paintings that "expressed the spirit" of the country or reminded worried citizens of home and supper in the kitchen.

Max Weber, who had lived in Berlin and in Paris, was saying, "…the very physical features of the country of a people determine to a large degree the character of their art." Edward Hopper spoke of the qualities indigenous to American art as being "in part due to an artist's visual reaction to the land." Despite such talk, the land was usually no more than farms in a painting's background.

---

[8]Georgia O'Keeffe's giant flower paintings were criticized for "social irrelevance," she herself for "exaggerated individuality."

Modernism had not been a comfortable style for everyone; neither was Social Realism. Landscapes produced in the Southwest, in New Mexico and California and Arizona, were not part of what critics were calling "the American Renaissance." Lillian Wilhelm Smith, who had concentrated on her personal views of Arizona and Indians, found herself even more outside art's shifting main current than before.

She was not the only artist who ignored dogma in art criticism—others all across the West held to their own ways of seeing. Often that vision left humans out of the picture entirely. Jimmy Swinnerton had not studied in the East; his desert-scapes ignored the Eastern mode for social significance. Californian Maynard Dixon had for years been saying of his sojourn in New York: "After listening to exploiter Stieglitz expatiate and observing so much cleverness and futility, I was glad to quit that stale-air existence and come West." It was brave defiant talk, but Western population was sparse. In Phoenix, artists were selling their paintings of the state's scenery door-to-door.

*T*hrough the Depression Lillian and Jess, like the rest of the country, struggled for their own support. In the orange grove in Scottsdale they had a home and agricultural property, more than many people could claim. However, financial collapse had spread into a planet-wide web. Citrus farmers in southern Arizona, dependent on sales elsewhere, were hit as hard as everybody else. The Scottsdale bank, serving a population of 2000, closed in 1933; so did the Chamber of Commerce.

President Hoover expected that things would be back to normal soon and warned workers about the dangers of socialism. His administration was criticized as too cautious in response to the crisis. Thus in 1929 and 1930 under the Reconstruction Finance Corporation it gave emergency money to the Forest Service for construction projects, roads and so forth. The funds reached into rural areas all over the country; in the West they made a significant difference for some people.

Going into the decade, Jesse Smith, a strong man in his early forties, was hired to work summers for the Prescott National Forest. During the Depression the Forest Service was reliable employment for a certain kind of Western man, the kind Theodore Roosevelt had described as having "bark on" like healthy trees. Since its beginning in 1905 the Service had sought "rope, ride, and shoot" men who could take hardship for granted, alone or with others, and work effectively under any conditions nature might put in their way. The wild horse project in Nevada, the Bernheimer expeditions around Navajo Mountain–Jess had been doing that sort of thing all his life. If anybody was a man with bark on, he was. His idea of dressing up was to change his khaki work clothes for a red and black Pendleton shirt.

Most useful for the skills he had been honing all his life, he was practical, good with tools and horses and people, experienced with solving outdoor problems. He would have been considered too old, unless there was an emergency, to fight the fires that swept through the forest every summer threatening mines, summer camps, private clubs, and cabins, sending great plumes of smoke up into the clear air.

When his job called for it, he dressed in uniform pants, shirt and tie. For daily tasks–construction of trails, phone lines, fences, campgrounds, and repairs to storm-damaged roads around Crown King in the Bradshaw Mountains–he wore Western working clothes. Lillian's friends called him a "forest ranger," the term the public used for any man who worked in the field. It became, within the agency, a specific designation for a career professional, a graduate of a university program who had a degree in forestry, but "ranger" retained its public definition: any out-on-the-land employee, even a seasonal.

The office for Forest Supervisor Frank Grubb was in Prescott. The Smiths came to know the town in Arizona's central highlands where three creeks met. [Towns in Arizona were always by necessity situated near surface water.] It was a little over 5000 feet in elevation, a little more than 5000 in population, if you included the 876 people at Fort Whipple seventeen miles to the north. Prospectors and miners, cowboys, sheepherders, and Yavapai Indians thronged the four miles of paved streets.

The eighth largest town in the state, Prescott was proud that it had been the capitol of Arizona *twice* (1863–1867, 1877–1889) before the railroad came south from Ashfork on its way to Phoenix. When Jess and Lillian arrived, it was a summer resort that boasted a shaded Plaza two blocks long and a four-day rodeo named "Frontier Days" that dated back to 1888.

The alluvium on which Prescott was built had been deposited after the age of the dinosaurs. Looming around the little town were granitoid mountains and buttes that dated back millions of years before that. The mountains limited Lillian's view somewhat—in Prescott she couldn't see quite so far as from other places in Arizona. But she could see far enough: there too the sky was always clear as glass and cyan blue and infinitely high.

She had always worked, all her adult life, but no evidence was kept in her papers that she had a long-term arrangement with an agent or gallery. Often she sold directly to people who liked her paintings, avoiding commissions, seeing to the dogged work of promotion herself, and in doing so she became a thorough professional. She had gained valuable knowledge about the art business since student days in New York.

For a creative artist in any field, self-promotion can rob production time and erode confidence, but she talked optimism:

> Of course there's a practical side to life. We all know disappointment, worry and grief—no human can escape—but even as beauty passes, so these things pass, and it helps us so much to hold to the happier thoughts.

William Wrigley, whom the Smiths had met on Catalina, had bought the elegant new Biltmore Hotel on the desert north of Phoenix. During winters from 1930 through 1935 Lillian served as hostess and artist-in-residence for the art shop in the lobby at the Biltmore. Her corner was indicated with a decorative grill and backed by a wall of plate glass looking onto an enclosed court. Reporters called it "a riot of color" filled with her paintings and dishes, which they described as "incredibly old patterns of enormous significance, steeped in the lore of a race of considerable antiquity, which have lost none of their intrinsic charm in the conventionalized adaptations." When commissioned, she painted landscapes, portraits of guests and Wrigley family members.

The Jot Stiles family had bought a service for twelve of the Navajo tableware. Porter Emerson Browne said her china would be taken out of his house over his "prostrate form." Maie Bartlett Heard, wife of a leader of the Phoenix elite, was a philanthropist, a collector of Indian art, a moving spirit in the

Phoenix Fine Arts Association. The Heard Museum which was
her great interest was nearing completion in Phoenix. Maie
Heard bought a set of the Apache basket dishes. She wrote to
encourage Lillian to concentrate her effort: "We have many
artists who paint Indians," she said, but no one who had
produced Indian tableware. Thirty years later she reported that
she never missed a chance to serve tea on Lillian's dishes.

Late in the 1940s Goldwaters department store carried her
brightly colored adaptation from Hopi baskets of symbols for
prayers to bring rain. She named it "Whirlwind." Applied to
"fine Flintridge China," it was available as a set (dinner, salad
and bread-and-butter plates, cup and saucer) for $15.50 or singly
as collector's pieces. Lillian was sometimes in the stores to
promote sales.

*E*very art show was an opportunity, and she took advantage.
Mary-Russell Colton's second annual Arizona Artists
Exhibition in July of 1930 included fifty-four paintings by
twenty-eight artists, almost doubling the show of the previous
year. There were still few men represented: Nils Hoogner of
Chambers, D. Paul Jones of Santa Fe, and Ole Solberg from
Flagstaff had joined Stanley Sykes and George Hochderffer.
Though many of the women were new, Mary-Russell and
Lillian were on the gallery list again with two oils each. Claire
Dooner Phillips (another student of Arthur Dow's) and Ada
Rigden (wife of a rancher) sent their paintings from Prescott for
a second year.

Publication in books was a new form of promotion for
artists. After the Grand Canyon trip in 1928 Lillian had traveled
around the Colorado Plateau with Lou Ella Archer. Working
together, they built up material for two books that combined
Lillian's paintings with Lou Ella's poems in praise of southwest
scenery. Capitals for each page of poetry were Lillian's Indian
designs. Her landscapes were in the brilliant colors which she
had used all her life—Monument Valley with a saffron sky,
Canyon de Chelly in rosy pinks, Walpi in the blues and laven-
ders of twilight, shades of maroon in the shadows around
Rainbow Bridge, a lavendar and orange Betatakin. [Georgia
Ida Wetherill hated that one: "not realistic," she said. Her
daughters' opinion: "That teacher (Dow) nearly ruined her."]

The collaboration on work that was personal to both Lou Ella and Lillian cemented a friendship that lasted for years.

Lean times were fastening onto America, but Archer had important contacts: their books, *Canyon Shadows* (1930) and *Sonnets to the Southwest* (1931), were handsomely published by the Los Angeles *Times* to sales that were more modest than the women had hoped but under the circumstances better than they expected. Archer included a sonnet dedicated to Lillian:

In the Thirties there was less time for adventures in the northern part of the state, which had made the previous years among the best of Lillian's long life, but she and Jess traveled when he wasn't working. In the summer of 1931, they were among the guests at Tuba City, where they knew two men who were fixtures in northern Arizona history. Leo Weaver had resigned from management of the Monte Vista Hotel, where they had sometimes stayed, and taken charge of guest entertainment for Johnny O'Farrell. Then managing the Tuba trading Post for the Babbitt company, O'Farrell would be a Babbitt partner for forty years and become a part of Navajo country history.

Visiting in Tucson, she painted an oil dated 1931: "Casa de Bienvida, El Encanto Estates," the home of W.J. Young. At the turn of the century Young had founded near Tombstone the Courtland Mine and produced one million dollars (dollars as of 1900) worth of copper. [How did Lillian meet him? Again, no answers were preserved in her papers.] His U-shaped Pueblo Revival house in El Encanto Estates was new in 1931; four years after she painted Casa de Bienvenida, Young died.

*T*wenty-five years earlier she had walked the streets of Manhattan trying to sell her greeting cards, trying to earn her livelihood with art. She was still at it, moving through business in the West. Painting was what she knew. As she had said when she was twenty-three, "Work now, Lil. It's up to you."

She began to save newspaper clippings that documented determined activity in all directions—more beads on the string. There was a letter from Gumps in San Francisco saying that the prestigious store would be pleased to work with her on Indian designs. Her Shekayah chinaware was shown at the Palace Hotel on Market Street. Through 1931 and 1932 the Paul Elder

Gallery in San Francisco exhibited the chinaware, twenty-five of her oils of the Southwest and seventeen of her watercolors, "both figures of Indian life and pure landscapes."

In 1931 she entered the Phoenix Women's Club Art Exhibition with two watercolors and five photographs. (Mary-Russell was also in the show; so were Jessie Benton Evans and Ada Rigden.) She submitted five landscape paintings to the third annual Arizona Artists show at the Museum of Northern Arizona. That year her chinaware traveled in an exhibition of pottery sponsored by the General Federation of Women's Clubs–to Massachusetts, West Virginia, New Jersey, Indiana, Alabama. Her watercolors were shown in Florida. When the American Artists Professional League held its initial exhibition in Prescott, her work hung on the gallery walls.

Arizona had established an annual Territorial Fair in 1905 and changed the name to State Fair in 1912. From the beginning it included a Fine Arts Division under the auspices of the Phoenix Woman's Club. Original work–paintings in oils and watercolors and pastels, photographs, ceramics, sculpture, china painting–was shown in the Woman's Building after a Jury of Selection had approved them. Over the years Lillian entered annually and received six first awards, three seconds, and several mentions for her paintings and dishes. "Hohyana Kachinas" dancing in a plaza won a first prize early in the 1930s.

In May of 1932 Archer and Smith were featured as guest speakers on the KTAR radio program "Society Column of the Air" to discuss the books on which they had collaborated. In July Lillian exhibited a fourth time at the Arizona Artists show in Flagstaff with a first in watercolor and another first for her Shekayah dishes. The whirl of self-promotion was evidence of her developing business sense–and of Depression-era need.

*T*he working climate for German artists was being destroyed. Through the 1920s they had painted irreverence, anarchy, emancipation [again] from the cultural past. In March of 1933 when Adolph Hitler became Chancellor of Germany and assumed full power, he promptly began an assault on books by "Jews and radicals," burning them in public bonfires. With influential writers and scientists on proscribed lists, artists too became political outlaws. Finding it difficult to buy paint and canvas, painters were obliged to join the Nazi Art Association which controlled all aspects of culture.

The party opened two exhibitions of painting in Munich, one of approved "German" art, the second pieces of "degenerate" modern art shown so that it could be ridiculed—Impressionists and post-Impressionist paintings, 20,000 of which had been confiscated from museums. Viewers flocked to see the modern pieces and so ignored the government choices that the whole affair became an embarrassment to Nazi propagandists and was quickly closed.

Since 1919 the Bauhaus had been teaching "modern" theories about design in art and architecture, about the inter-relationship of all arts, about housing based on mass manufacture—all kinds of ideas that were anathema to minds pre-occupied with grandiose romanticism and ruling the entire world. Gestapo officers closed the Bauhaus in 1933 and scattered its teachers into exile. Artists who did not care to glorify past culture were not wanted in Germany.

Wassily Kandinsky went to Paris, Paul Klee to Switzerland. Hans Hofmann, already in America, was joined by Josef Albers and architects Mies van der Rohe and Walter Gropius. Marcel Duchamp and Max Ernst fled Europe just before war was declared.

A wave of artists escaped to France and hiked across the Pyrenees or boarded ships at Marseilles. It wasn't that they were longing to be assimilated into an American culture that they considered raw and unsophisticated and still reeking of Puritan influence: they wanted to avoid extermination.

At the last possible minute American heiress Peggy Guggenheim, who had been assembling a representative collection of their paintings, shipped them across the Atlantic labeled as household goods. The flood of European art into the country increased pressure for innovation on American painters, sculptors, architects and graphic designers.

In the positions they achieved at Yale, Harvard and Black Mountain College, the emigrees changed the appearance of American cities and the paintings that hung in their "International" buildings, an influence that reigned with barely an audible challenge for the next quarter century.

In Arizona smaller towns like Prescott and Flagstaff, where business had never needed towering skyscrapers of the kind that suited Chicago and New York, the straight-line style of the Bauhaus exiles had limited impact. A few Santa Fe painters became interested, those who had tried painting New Mexico's landscape in techniques reminiscent of Cezanne, but in Arizona intellectual theories about visual art were received more kindly by transplanted Easterners and college art departments than by any long-time residents who might still be buying paintings.

Lillian had maintained her connections to the East and sometimes traveled across the continent for visits. She had to have been aware of the influence of Europeans on big city tastes; she may have been weary of the successive tsunamis that roared through the art world. Her paintings, especially in water-color, became ever more realistically lyrical.

Widely considered elsewhere as a cultural backwater, at best a slow eddy, Arizona—where shape and color were what could be seen in all directions never completely abandoned romantic realism. There was no way of knowing that within twenty years shifting American population would begin to alter western landscape beyond recovery and make the representa-tional paintings that spanned the state's first hundred years into historical records.

*A*s it did often in the Twentieth century, political stability was coming unraveled. There was a Third Reich in Germany. In China Japanese troops advanced south of the Great Wall. America was pinning its hopes on Franklin Roosevelt's New Deal: the banking act, the farm credit act, all the monetary and relief legislation. Roosevelt's new Civilian Conservation Corps set out to employ a quarter of a million young men in "useful public work" in the nation's parks and forests under the supervision of 24,000 LEMs—Local Experienced Men. Working out of tent camps, the C.C.C. built roads, trails, public campgrounds and recreation sites, telephone lines, fuel breaks, guard stations and fire lookout towers, anything the national forests could plan to keep its consignment of city boys busy.

Jesse Smith had been doing harder work than that all his life—it was a job made to order for him. The Forest Service assigned him to Company 882 F-33-A as a CU-7 Foreman, Technical Personnel. Tent houses for the 847 young men he worked with were set up first at Walnut Creek near Prescott, then moved to a Turkey Creek site near Mayer twenty miles to the southeast. For smaller projects there were "side" camps.

In and out of the office, about town, living in camps, building with stone and concrete and re-bar to put firepits in place, and bath houses, picnic tables, toilets, garbage cans, pipelines, foot bridges, reservoirs—it was just a matter of working through the details. The slow patient day-to-day tasks of ordering nails and lumber, of painting, excavating, requesting iron work from the shop, of supervising men and carpenters, mules and trucks, boys in crews—what was that to a man who had worked the Bernheimer expeditions?

Jess was all over the Prescott Forest. There was a hiking trail to carve around Thumb Butte, improvements to be made at the county fairgrounds, pasture fences to build at Mayer and Wolf Creek and the Crown King ranger station. Wooden lookout towers were replaced in 1934 by new metal structures at Mount Union, Horsethief Basin, Mingus and Tower Mountains.

He wasn't all work, of course. Sometimes he took a few hours between fixing shovels and hunting fence posts to play poker with the other men. In winter he often drove south to Scottsdale, to the Biltmore Hotel to see Lillian's "exabition."

Proud of her work, Jess called her "my little artist." He was always on the watch for scenes that might suit her, places no one had depicted before. In the 1932 KTAR speech she mentioned a situation he had arranged for her after the fire season ended.

> Last November it was my privilege to live for weeks in a little cabin on the top of a huge crag on the summit of the Bradshaw mountains. In a 40 foot fire tower next to the cabin, I felt like an aviator hovering over half of Arizona. A huge canvas received the impressions and emotions of that experience.

> Range after range to the Mexican line near Yuma were my special scene, although in every direction other marvelous subjects for pictures presented themselves. Five miles from another human being, this silence and aloofness from the fast moving world was a never to be forgotten experience. A retreat into the wilderness that still abides.

The tower
Courtesy of the Museum of
Northern Arizona
Flagstaff

When storms came, clouds later drifted out of the deep canyons below my mountain top. Once a lacy shred of cloud rising gossamer-like between me and the setting sun changed to gold lace with rainbow iridescence, a sight so beautiful that I longed to share it with the whole world.

In more than half a century as a resident of Arizona, she lived a story that touched every part of the state and one after another of its institutions. In the spring of 1933 fifty-five of her paintings were shown in Phoenix under the sponsorship of the Arizona Museum. In July, occupied elsewhere, she did not enter the fifth annual Arizona Artists show in Flagstaff.

She was near Prescott during those years, and Prescott had a women's club that was the oldest in the state—the Monday Club, which devoted a good deal of attention to educating its members about art. Ada Rigden and Claire Dooner Phillips were on the club's Fine Arts Committee; Kate Cory, who had studied at New York's Art Students League and exhibited in the 1913 Armory Show, was a speaker at meetings. In October the art committee decorated the club house "in a most artistic manner" as a studio "featuring the paintings of Lillian Wilhelm Smith." Tea was served on china designed by the artist. Lou Ella Archer's poems were read, and Lillian told the story of their travels in the Southwest as she sketched "the scenic wonders of this locality" for her illustrations.[9]

*L*illian never learned to drive. On her painting and selling and exhibiting trips around Arizona, Jess was at the wheel during the months when he wasn't working for the Forest Service. In their flivver they became acquainted with the Hassayampa Trail, a long drive from Phoenix through

---

[9]Through 1932 and 1933, when Lillian Wilhelm was promoting her work every way she could think of, Georgia O'Keeffe was hospitalized with depression and a psychoneurotic breakdown brought on, it was assumed, by Stieglitz's heavy-handed control of her life and her career.

Lillian and Jess
Courtesy of Arizona Historical Foundation,
Arizona State University
Tempe, Arizona

Wickenburg and Congress Junction, then up the escarpment called Yarnell "Hill" and across Peeples Valley to Prescott. It was the most direct route to the northern part of the state.

The road through Black Pass, described as one of the best in Yavapai County, had recently had some of the kinks taken out, but it was still a miserable, crooked track. From Peoria to Rock Spring, along New River, the Agua Fria and Bumble Bee Creek, it wound around hills at the foot of the Bradshaws to Mayer and on to Prescott, narrow and rutted, painfully slow. That is, it was a typical Arizona highway: spectacular scenery—space and unpeopled miles that could set passengers to thinking of years not so long before—all paid for with fatigue and motion sickness. Jess was stationed at the CCC camp at Mayer; they knew Black Pass too.

Although the two-lane stretch from Tucson to Nogales was oil-surfaced by 1928, roads all over much of the rest of the state were still dirt, little more than the primitive trails that miners' wagons and stage coaches had established. Drivers planning to go off the main-traveled routes around Phoenix and Tucson still carried shovels with them for digging out of sandy washes. In hot weather over-heated autos with their hoods up lined steep climbs, which drivers spoke of with awe: Yarnell, Oxbow, Fish Creek. Experienced motorists in the desert waited until the sun was down and left in the cooler nights, and they always carried water.

In 1921 the state highway department had printed the initial issue of a monthly newsletter named *Arizona Highways* to inform the motoring public about conditions. Maps included keys that

identified established roads as paved, graveled, graded, dirt and
"inquire locally for conditions." In the early Thirties a mere
3000 black and white copies of the little newsletter were printed
each month.

Travel was improving slowly: through the hard-times
decade the state hired out-of-work men and gave them shovels
and brooms for road construction and maintenance. Gravel was
gradually replaced by oil surfaces with sub-grade and seal coats
and then with "high type" cut-back asphalt.

*A*fter 1929 neither of the Smiths, certainly not Jess, did
much adventuring with Zane Grey, who preferred fishing
off Tahiti from his schooner to travel on land. In 1931
Dolly informed him by radiogram that his money was gone, he
owed $103,923 in income taxes, and he needed to come home.

The Depression hit Grey hard. By 1933 his bank accounts
were overdrawn; his movie contacts were going bankrupt;
employees who had worked his fishing trips in Tahiti were
threatening lawsuits and bad publicity. Still, he mattered: his
books about adventure and love and nobility of character were
a refuge for spirits seared by money worries, and his house on
Catalina Island was a retreat for people whom he cared to invite
to laze slow delicious hours looking down on boats in the little
bay.

Long silver swells out in the sea danced with light as the
sun rose. Breakfast was in a glass-walled alcove or on the terrace
with its half-circle view. At mid-morning the bay shaded from
blue toward pale green in the shallows and color soared upward
to the deep green of the hills and a brilliant blue sky. Ridge tops
shimmered in noon light; sea air blew through the long hallway
that ran the length of the house.

The world softened as sun sank to the western ridge tops.
Then lights along the shore reflected as broken bands of color in
the water, and music from the ballroom in the casino floated up
the hill. Sometimes a rolling fog filled the valley, hiding red tile
roofs down in Avalon, huge ships on the horizon, and mountains over on the California coast. The house usually stood
above it. Fireplaces warmed cold windy evenings.

Mildred Smith was no longer with Grey; she had left in
1930 with bitterness and acrimony on both sides. Lillian visited

Catalina sometimes and painted a Navajo yei figure above the fireplace in the study, a Hopi design above the fireplace in the big front room. She had contributed such designs to three other houses which Zane and Dolly had set up, patterns she had learned from blankets and pottery and sand paintings. Her contribution to curtains was a tall stencil of a kachina to be painted onto cloth.

When she boarded the ferry which took her back to the mainland, she probably felt the same pang at leaving Catalina that others have felt. Despite the romance of it all, Zane Grey left the island after a disagreement with the Tuna Club, which had disallowed his huge marlins as record catches because of the weight of the line he used. Worse was the lack of privacy—tourists treated his home as a public facility, climbed the hill and peered through the windows, walked right in and used the bathroom. He kept the house, but he moved away, moved on.

*W*illiam **Wrigley, who owned the whole island,** died in 1932. But his son Phillip, trained in every phase of the Wrigley business, was ready to take over. During the Depression, when other companies were cutting wages, he raised them and anticipated federal programs with income assurance and pension plans. Lillian stayed on at his Biltmore as resident artist.

Life-long cowboy Jesse Smith was in charge of the hotel's Indian room during the winter seasons at least by 1933. For a woman in her early fifties who was accustomed to roughing it on the trail, and for a man who had spent his life out-of-doors with horses, those years of careful upper-crust hotel work must have been tiring—smiling, always smiling, no matter who was in front of them.

Georgia Ida and her daughters, living in Mesa, occasionally visited the Biltmore art shop and the Scottsdale orange grove. The girls were impressed by the clutter in the

Lillian at the Biltmore
Courtesy of Museum of Northern Arizona Flagstaff

house: stacks of paintings, some of them taller than children, crowded every room, with paths between them. Lillian didn't seem to be overly concerned about the confusion, they decided, but then she was an artist, and they had always considered her an aristocrat.

She was still trying to be optimistic, at least on the surface:

To keep the joy of living uppermost in our minds through the complications of modern life takes great enthusiasm and a profound appreciation of the privilege of living in one of the loveliest parts of the world. After twenty years of earnest effort to interpret the color, atmosphere, and native life of Arizona through my brush, I still feel as if life cannot be long enough to depict all the glorious panoramas, the wide spaces, the hidden loveliness that reward the searcher of new fields within our state.

*A*rt was the unifying theme of her always shifting life; the lovers' partnership with Jess was the core of the second half, a span of years so fragmented that it needed a core. Sometimes they were apart—she was busy with work and people and organizations. Sometimes she painted alone for days. But always Jess was at the center.

In the Biltmore's summer off-seasons, he worked as a "ranger" and Lillian was everywhere, scrambling to stay credible, showing her work, speaking to women's clubs in Arizona and California about Arizona's Indians with her photographs and paintings as illustration. In 1934 she entered a Prescott scene in the Phoenix Woman's Club annual show, placed six paintings and her tableware patterns in the Hesla Company store in Prescott, and spoke on China and Indian Art and German Art for women's clubs around the state.

After an absence of one year, she exhibited four paintings in Mary-Russell's sixth Arizona Artists show. One of the oils dated from her movie expedition days: "On Location in Marsh Pass." Mary-Russell's comment on the plight of a painter could have been spoken for Lillian.

It does not seem a generally accepted fact that the artist must eat. True, there is a literary fallacy to the effect that the hungry genius produces the really inspired work of art, but take it from an old painter (lately fallen into a soft job as Curator of art in a museum) three meals a day is stimulating to genius…Remember

*the artists and the craftsmen of our state who contribute to your
pleasure by their talent. Help us to give them what encouragement and assistance you can afford. Many of you may look upon
it as a luxury, but should its color and beauty disappear
completely from your lives, existence would be drab.*

Alert to possibilities, building a reputation, Lillian was
involved with an array of art organizations. In 1935 her work
was hung in shows at the Charcoal Club and the Fine Arts
Association in Phoenix and in the Artists' Guild show at Pueblo
Grande. At one point she was president of Verde Valley Art
Association.

South, middle, north—she was all over the state. When the
seventh of the Museum of Northern Arizona's annual art exhibitions was organized, she sent four paintings. But the Coltons
and their small museum staff were moving from the Woman's
Club into a new building out on the Fort Valley Road. There
was no space adequate to hang an art show; the seventh exhibit
was the last.

For another twenty-five years roads across northern
Arizona's Indian reservations in the northeast quarter of the
state would be little more than wandering unreliable tracks.
Colored photography had not yet reached the sophistication
that made magazine reproduction feasible. *Arizona Highways*
printed no color landscape photos until late in the decade, when
editor Raymond Carlson began to buy the work of an immigrant photographer named Josef Muench. Not until 1943 would
color define the magazine.

Lillian moved into the vacancy—her canvases and watercolors were a revelation to Arizonans who hadn't the stamina or
leisure to travel. On December 19, 1934, she used her paintings
to illustrate a lecture at the Heard Museum on "The Beauties of
Havasupai Canyon" and was introduced as "one of the few
people" ever to hike into it.

A booster of the state for artists, she praised it in her
lectures.

*Our clear revealing sunshine brings to light many of the happier
forms of self-expression. Our very soil is rich with an invitation to
create—clay in the creek beds and red and ocher and cobalt in the
rocks…How rich we may feel in this beautiful environment.*

*O*rganized government support for artists began soon after the inauguration of Franklin Roosevelt in 1933, when his administration had begun organizing work relief. In April of 1935, after bitter debate in the Senate, a bill establishing the Works Progress Administration was passed and signed. As part of WPA the United States supported and subsidized an arts program that was unprecedented in any nation: Federal Project Number One was a "white collar" program designed to provide work for artists in easel and mural and poster painting, sculptors, architects, photographers, writers, musicians, as well as people experienced in theater and those who could arrange and preserve historical records. And why shouldn't there be a Federal One, they said—artists needed an income as much as manual laborers; the arts were as much the concern of an ideal government as business and agriculture.

Between 5000 and 6000 men and women equipped by training, experience and ability were employed by the federal art program, men like William de Kooning who, with his busy brushstrokes and thick paint, had helped to create Abstract Expressionism and to bring the center of the art world from Europe to America.

Private organizations served as cooperating sponsors and contributed money and materials. In 1936 a series of national and circulating exhibits was organized, initially at the Museum of Modern Art. The first Municipal Art Exhibition in New York was held in the newly-opened Rockefeller Center in 1936 under the sponsorship of Mayor Fiorello LaGuardia. Galleries began to appear in the West as parts of community art centers.

In many states Federal One was the responsibility of the director for women's work. That suited the prevailing opinion that organization of the arts in general was properly a task for women of wealth and leisure—the Junior League, for example, which was committed to developing the potential of women and improving communities through the action of trained volunteers. It gave nationwide support to Federal One, often by art exhibitions.

The fashion, some said the *cult*, for mural painting had arrived from Mexico just as the Depression had set in. Before the Federal Art Project, few murals had been commissioned. But there were all those post offices and schools and hospitals and courthouses that had been built during the boom of the Twenties with blank walls that could be decorated by artists who needed work. FAP set groups of them to the cooperative task of producing huge frescos in public buildings.

Arizona had a small population and not many applicants who could be certified by the project. Despite the difficulty, by November of 1937 fifty art centers had opened around the state. Before the program ended there were more than a hundred. Kate Cory painted detailed landscapes that recorded vegetation in various parts of the Arizona desert and in Boulder Canyon before the dam was built. People who worked in hand crafts participated too, copperworkers and potters and Navajo weavers.

There was no evidence that Lillian was ever part of the program, an omission that might have been significant. Perhaps her income put her just outside its reach. Perhaps having a working husband was a factor. Perhaps something in her character—what the Wetherills called "aristocratic"—caused her to resist joining.

*A*lthough the national economy was still deeply depressed, the Smiths left their positions at the Biltmore Hotel at the end of the 1935 season and returned to a kind of life that was more congenial. Travel amid big country and colorful people resumed, primarily in Arizona as before.

She had connections everywhere. Radio was the biggest commercial entertainment in the country, and the KTAR appearances had introduced her to radio men Howard Pyle and Arthur Anderson in Phoenix. Her sister Claire's husband, Phillips Carlin, was general program director of NBC. Claire and her daughter Virginia, who were visiting "Aunt Lillian" during the winter of 1934-1935, were at the Grand Canyon to watch the first NBC Easter broadcast.

In 1929 Flagstaff had inaugurated an annual 4th of July All-Indian Pow Wow, which attracted people from tribes all over the northern part of the state. They drove into town in wagons and trucks and camped in City Park, crowded into every available space, cooked their food over fires. Navajo women hung rugs from ropes strung between the trees and draped them over the tailgates of trucks. Jewelry and all kinds of crafts were displayed for sale along the road.

The Pow Wow lasted four days. A parade started at eleven o'clock each morning; after dark there were ceremonial dances lit by camp fires. The big events were the rodeos at 1:30 each afternoon in the stadium at the park. There was bronc riding, of course, and steer riding and calf roping and bulldogging, with saddles and boots and cash as prizes. Tourists who crowded the bleachers liked the wild cow milking, tug-of-war games between women of different tribes, Hopi stick-and-stone races, and the sack pull that the men played from the backs of fast-moving horses. When Lillian proposed a broadcast from the Pow Wow in the summer of 1936, her friends recorded the first all-Indian program to be presented on radio.

She was fifty-four, still working hard at her life-long profession. In 1936, *Wonders of the West* by writer and newspaper columnist Oren Arnold included seven full-color plates of the paintings by Lillian which Lou Ella Archer had used in her books of poetry, and the *Arizona Republic* reported another painting session in the fire lookout tower.

> The past week has seen the return to Phoenix of Lillian Wilhelm Smith, well known artist, who has spent the past several months in the vicinity of Crown King intently at work on a panoramic view of the mountain ranges as seen from a 40-foot fire tower up the mountain from the town, at an altitude of 7000 feet. During the weeks she worked on the painting, Mrs. Smith saw no one except Mr. Smith, who is in charge of a forest service project in the area and who first brought to her attention the magnificent view from the mountain fire-tower in this almost inaccessible region. The picture includes much of the southwestern portion of the state, showing Minnehahah Flats, Vulture Peak near Castle Hot Springs, Hassayampa river, the Harquahala Mountains and the Chocolate Mountains near Yuma as well as the surrounding Bradshaws, and the artist has imprisoned the changing lights of mid-afternoon as reflected upon this beauteous area, upon her canvas. She has entitled her work "Blue Beauty of the Bradshaws."

Busy, always busy. If she was wearied by the unending effort, she did not complain publicly when her work found no buyers. The bird's-eye firetower painting was displayed at the Hassayampa Hotel through several years, unsold.

*A*n amateur painter born in Colorado, Walter Bimson had come to Arizona in 1930 to assume the presidency of Valley Bank and Trust Company. Through the Depression years he bought paintings by struggling and unknown Western artists and used the walls of each bank branch as a showcase where they were hung. In April of 1937 Lillian noted in her accounts:

> *Sold "Hopi Women Threshing Wheat" to Walter Bimson for $125. It's a picture I'm not ashamed of although not considered one of my best and am glad W.B. has it and thankful for the financial help.*

These Hopi women were threshing their wheat with flails as in Bible times, then throwing the grains into the air to separate the chaff which blew away—a most primitive method, and of great picturesque value to the artist.

Bimson's support was welcome to the state's artists. In 1937 the Phoenix Fine Arts Association was an influential sponsor of the Federal Art Center which had been established under the auspices of Federal One—that helped too. But Depression hard times went on and on as if they would never recede; Lillian's dogged self-promotion also went on and on. There was some success—a painting of the Superstition Mountains was sold to an Eastern manufacturer.

Her brother Arnold was employed by New York publishers Grosset and Dunlap. In a deal arranged in 1937, lithographs made from twelve of her paintings were printed by his firm for the last Zane Grey publicity campaign. She listed the subjects:

Surprise Valley	Superstition Mountains
Navajo Falls in Havasu	Oak Creek Canyon
Rim of the Tonto	Hohyana Kachina (Hopi Hair Dance)
The Navajo Home	A Ga Thla near Kayenta
Wilson Mountain	Rainbow Bridge
Wild Horse Mesa	Monument Valley

Grosset and Dunlap held copyright on the lithographs until 1941, during which time it cooperated with Whitman

Publishing Company to make the paintings into 250-piece jigsaw puzzles.

*J*ess' brother Al, who had made seven trips over the grueling trail to Rainbow Bridge, had become paralyzed from the waist down. With no definite diagnosis, his family struggled to find the reason: he never drank coffee or alcohol, but there had been a fall off a trail with one of Wetherill's mules—could he have hurt his back? In 1935 Jess took him to Prescott to consult a chiropractor, hoping that might help. In March Al died there, and his body was returned to Flagstaff. Jess sent a Navajo runner to locate an itinerant preacher everyone knew as Shine Smith (not a relative) to conduct the funeral service.

Al was buried in an unmarked grave. His wife Henrietta had spent the last years of his life working for Louisa at Kayenta. Deaf after quinine treatment for typhoid fever five years earlier, she was bitter, left with four children to raise, unable to pay for a stone of any kind. She sought relatives who would help by taking her nine-year-old daughter. It was a side of the Old West that Zane Grey did not write—what it could do to people, to families, how unforgiving it could be when the strength of youth was gone or the mind was tender or luck was just plain bad.

The years were not kind to the Smiths. Louis and Inez and Al were gone. Henrietta was desperate. Arthritis disabled Janie's husband John: they left the trading post at Oljato and moved to Kingman. One of their sons would be killed in World War II; another would be a suicide; a third and their daughter Inez ("Tiny") would die of cancer.

*A*rizona was immense, great stretches of it apparently empty of humans. There was variety enough for twenty lifetimes of exploring. In mid March of 1937 the Flagstaff newspaper reported that Mrs. Lillian Wilhelm Smith, "well-known artist of Mayer," and Captain and Mrs. Garland J. Parrish of Prescott were in town on their way to visit friends and a relative of Captain Parrish in Tuba.

In April she and Jess were in Flagstaff with Mildred Smith, who had been visiting them for two weeks and was ready to board a train going west. Mildred was described in detail by the *Sun*—a scenarist and playwright, former literary secretary to

Zane Grey, author of a little theater play that recently had enjoyed a three months uninterrupted run, associate for several years with one of the biggest studios in Hollywood.

On a long sightseeing and camping trip they had driven through scrubby piñons and junipers on the old stage coach road from Montezuma Castle, past the station under sycamores on Beaver Creek which had been abandoned the year of Lillian's birth. A red cliff gradually spread as the view opened through hills with hints of vivid sandstone waiting for erosion to expose it. Then there were layered and colored walls that stretched for miles and they drove into the tiny community of Sedona at the mouth of Oak Creek Canyon. It had long been considered a sacred place. Though there was evidence of human presence since 8000 B.C., in 1937 only a few families lived among the redrock cliffs, no more than two hundred people.

Mildred was ecstatic about the beauty of the colored strata, the soaring formations. A New Yorker living in California, she said that Arizona was of all places the nearest and dearest to her. To her mind, Sedona was a new wonderland.

Her enthusiasm was contagious. On that day Lillian "quite lost [her] head and heart to the red cliffs and ivory ramparts," and wanted to live in that beauty and paint it. The scenery was accessible from dirt roads across the Verde Valley to Prescott, and an improved road down through the canyon was nearly finished. The creek offered swimming and fishing; the climate was mild the year around; hunting and horseback riding were unlimited; C.C.C. men were building camping and picnicking facilities.

Grasping for income to stay alive in the Depression, Arizona ranchers had begun catering to guests, who were welcomed all over the northern part of the state—Rimrock, Beaver Creek, Chino Valley, Wickenburg, Payson, Skull Valley. There were fourteen such accommodations around Prescott. Even the reservation advertised: Chinle accepted visitors. The Wetherills had ten rooms for tourists at Kayenta. (The gambit was not always successful. Leo Weaver lost his guest ranches at Wickenburg and Flagstaff to the Depression.)

There was no electricity at Sedona, no telephone, no well, only one little store, but surely it was an ideal place for a guest ranch. Jess was the perfect host, experienced with livestock and people. A spot was available in a sheltered park on the site of the first patented homestead, the historic ranch which had been the home of Carl and Sedona Schnebly. Oak Creek ran through it. A wooden-planked concrete bridge at the end of the old road up the hill to Flagstaff spanned the creek on the property; an irrigation ditch led to an orchard. From a knoll where the Schneblys had built a house with lumber hauled down from Flagstaff, the view stretched for miles in all directions, past Bell Rock and Coffee Pot Butte, into the mouths of canyons, up Schnebly Hill, around to Wilson Mountain—named for a man killed by a bear fifty years earlier.

Since 1916 George Black and his wife Stella had owned the land, which had changed hands four times since homestead status. In 1919 a fire had destroyed the wooden house Carl Schnebly had built, with a loss to the Blacks of $3000. They were interested in leasing the ranch to someone else.

There was civil war in Spain. In Germany Hitler had broken the Versailles Treaty and re-occupied the Rhineland. Denounced by the League of Nations for his annexation of Ethiopia, Mussolini had withdrawn and entered into a Rome-Berlin axis. Peiping and Tientsin had fallen to the Japanese, Shanghai was under attack, and South China was suffering a naval blockade. There were purges in Stalin's Russia—trials and executions of high-ranking officials—and open warfare with Japanese troops on the frontier between Siberia and Manchukuo. Obviously, the international situation was ever more dangerous, but the American economy had improved somewhat during Roosevelt's first term. A European war might make it even more robust.

Lillian was fifty-five years old; Jess was forty-nine. They decided to take a chance, sold the house in the citrus grove in Scottsdale which she had owned for fifteen years and staked the money on a second Shekayah. They would be there for what she would call "ten wonderful years."

The Flagstaff newspaper, reporting on the new venture in Sedona, described Jess as "big, loveable and easy-going." Lillian was "a sympathetic landscape and portrait painter" who had "contacts in art and literary circles both east and west." The editor confided that several of her paintings had sold in the East over the past year and that she had been "receiving letters from prominent and wealthy people all over the United States expressing cordial interest in her guest ranch plans."

They took possession in autumn fruit-picking time. Brilliant sunshine illuminated colored cliffs and the golden leaves of trees along the creek. Sky was an arch of intense blue thirty miles wide. There was color everywhere: the very ground was red with iron oxide. Piñons and junipers were deep green.

A season of decay, storms and growing cold and darkness in the northeast, autumn in Sedona was a time of radiance. Yellow leaves still hung on the sycamore trees at Thanksgiving. Of all changes of the year, autumn was the most intoxicating.

Jess, working for the Forest Service twenty miles away near the Verde River, managed time to build a few detached cabins. Lillian supervised the transformation of the ranch. Fields and orchards were improved to provide vegetables, fruit and dairy products. Adjoining an existing stone house with a big fireplace, she built a rock-wall dining room, plastered it in a soft rose color to echo the surrounding cliffs, and painted Indian designs in the interiors. Large windows faced in all directions. Her Shekayah china was brought in for serving meals.

There was so much hope. A new kitchen and store room went up. An experienced ranch cook, Dora Sessions Lee of the Verde Valley, was prepared to offer food more cosmopolitan than a cowboy's menu: "potatoes cooked any way in the world just so you fry 'em" and rare beef: "Just cripple 'er a little and drag 'er in." She found Lillian pleasant and easy to work with, "sweet, utterly delightful."

They planned to attract girls from twelve to sixteen for summer riding, swimming, hiking, art classes. Rates would be $100 for one month, $175 for two, $250 for three. Accommodations were offered to adults at $25.00 per week.

Winters were mild at that elevation. Their leaves finally gone for a season, the oak and white-barked sycamore trees made intricate patterns against cliffs and sky. Shadows turned dark up the canyons.

Sometimes clouds hung overhead like a roof, filled the valley from rim to rim, hid the tops of the cliffs and settled into fog that erased all the colors of the red rock. There were nights when wind whined and snow whirled around the rock house, and the world was shut away. Jess carried in wood; he and Lillian sat together in front of the fire, its light soft on the rosy walls.

Storms never lasted long. When clouds lifted, the sandstone buttes were dark and wet, white with snow on the north and east sides, and ice formed at the edge of Oak Creek. On the first warm day, every hillside was alive with sounds of snowmelt trickling down to the creek. Lillian could paint it all in comfort from the windows of her rock house.

Mildred Smith was a guest for a couple of weeks the first summer in 1938. Arnold's wife and his son Dick were at Shekayah for two months. Nearly sixty years later Dick reminisced:

> Lillian was in the process of trying to improve on it, but it was pretty rustic. The cabin we stayed in was one of two or three. Then there was the stone house—with kitchen, dining room and living area at the front end of it. There was an adobe saddle house and store room west of the stone house. The horses were pastured in the field south and west of there. We would walk back east to Oak Creek in the afternoon for a swim...The ranch remained pretty rustic while Lillian was there due to lack of help, time and money.

Sometimes there was afternoon rain on hot summer days, sometimes Oak Creek was a rampaging torrent which was entertainment to watch. Nights were open to the sky and the light of the stars. With only kerosene for lamps, the country was dark and neighbors invisible.

They never had room for more than ten visitors at a time, but thanks to hard work and constant entertainment and a year-around welcome, the Sedona Shekayah attracted guests, and the Smiths managed to get by. They provided camping and picnics with cowboy cooking, hunting and fishing, swimming and hiking and riding in the wet green smells of the creek and the canyon. Lillian lectured on Arizona with her lithographs and china as illustration; they were offered for sale to guests.

Entertaining and feeding guests and keeping them happy was hard work. But there was time for friends and painting, time for beauty. Lillian loved the Sedona years.

Flagstaff was only thirty miles away. On a Tuesday afternoon in November of 1937, described as a "well-known artist," she spoke at a meeting of the Flagstaff Woman's Club on "her personal reaction to the three different types of country in Arizona—the desert, the cultivated sections, and the mountains" with her paintings as illustrations.

In August of 1938 she was back in Flagstaff for a tea in the Episcopal parish house that opened a two-day exhibit of paintings by Lillian, Mary-Russell Colton, Rose Babbitt and her sister Margaret Walsh, who was on the faculty of Arizona State College in Tempe. The local newspaper referred to the exhibit as "an outstanding social event of high interest" for which more than one hundred invitations had been issued. Mrs. Babbitt had contributed landscapes, Miss Walsh kachina dancers, Mary-Russell six canvases of northern Arizona desert landscapes. Lillian's paintings were eight watercolors of lower Oak Creek Canyon and Sedona.

But her exposure was state wide. In 1937 *Arizona Highways* magazine had become daringly modern when it used colored photographs on the front covers of some issues. Black and white art photographs began to appear in the state's magazine by 1938. In 1939, under the titles "Arizona Sketch Book" and "Wheels Through the West," it published prints of Lillian's paintings, including the one of Walpi by starlight, in the February and June issues. For those months her paintings were the only color pictures in the magazine.

Jess did what he could to help his wife in her painting, choosing spots where she could set up her easel. For twenty years he had wanted her to paint the Verde Valley from Mingus Mountain, a place no one else had used, with the red rock canyons and the Peaks in the background. She completed a canvas of the scene, describing it as

> ...the wide flung vista of the Verde Valley, rich with archaeolog-ical treasures...its backdrop the red rock walls that break to lead one into lovely Oak Creek Canyon. The rim above, darkly forested with tall pines, for miles, is crowned with the heaven reaching San Francisco Peaks near Flagstaff.

*T*he years in Sedona went on. It was so quiet. There were the sounds of water in the creek and wind through sycamore branches, now and then a voice somewhere, only an occasional auto and very seldom an airplane. Sedona was beauty and space and peace of the kind that inspired an artist who had eyes to see it all.

In spring fruit trees were in bloom and there were horses in the pasture. Light was brilliant. Birds sang. Grass and leaves on sycamores by the creek were tender green. On clear nights the stars were so bright one could see by their light to walk to the corral.

Lillian turned fifty-seven, sixty, sixty-one. Always an artist, she continued to work at her easel when she could find time and exhibited new paintings and those that had not yet sold—in Florida, in Los Angeles, in Phoenix at the Art Museum, the Pueblo Grande museum, and Fred Wilson's Trading Post. For several years she sent paintings by bus to the Arizona State Fair, figures and landscapes in oil and watercolor, and continued to receive prizes.

The two sons of Jesse's brother Al—"out of hand" going into puberty according to their hard-pressed mother, who had been supporting her children by doing laundry on a wash-board—lived at the Sedona guest ranch through most of the 1940s. Jess introduced them to people as "The Cough Drops" (the Smith brothers) and they liked him, but they resented it that Lillian expected them to help around the place with work they considered much too hard, do their own laundry, "shift for themselves," wear clothing that was worn and torn, and they were no happier than most teen-agers are with home and authority. It can't have been easy for anyone. The older, Louis, joined the Army Air Force just after his seventeenth birthday. Two years later his brother Jesse enlisted in the Navy.

*A*merica was at war. Though tires and gasoline were rationed and there were no more expeditions going out from Kayenta, Sedona meant isolation for the Smiths no more than the Tuba Shekayah had. Lillian was never without human contact, no matter where she was.

In 1941 Bessie Elda Hazen, a successful painter and an art instructor at U.C.L.A., was met at the railroad station in Flagstaff by a former student, Catherine "Kay" Henson, who had taught art in the Flagstaff high school and married Prescott artist Ray Manley, a cousin of Jessie Benton Evans. As they drove down Oak Creek Canyon on a road being prepared for paving, headed for the Verde Valley, Kay Manley mentioned Shekayah and Lillian Wilhelm Smith. Why, she and Miss Hazen were old friends! Manley turned into the guest ranch for a reunion between the two older women. She would see Lillian through to the end, years later.

In 1921 a group of women in Oakland, California, had formed a service club for women and named it Soroptimist, a word derived from Latin (soror = sister, optima = best). In the

20s and 30s it evolved into an international federation dedicated to the economic advancement of women of all creeds and colors. Membership, a cross-section of executive women actively engaged in business and professions, was by invitation. Chosen for "their individual qualities as well as their status in their chosen area of work," they sponsored a wide range of projects to improve the lot of women and girls throughout the world.

The Flagstaff Soroptimist Club, the second in Arizona, was chartered on April 22, 1942, with eighteen members, all identified by occupation: a court reporter and a court clerk, a doctor and a doctor's office manager, nine business women, the town librarian, a horse breeder, secretary of the college board, an orchardist, and Lillian Wilhelm Smith, who was listed not as manager of Shekayah but as a painter in oils who had illustrated Zane Grey's works.

Guests included Justice McAllister of the Arizona Supreme Court and Judge Mangum of the County Superior Court, Mayor Joseph Waldhaus and Postmaster George Babbitt and Monica Nackard of the Business and Professional Women's Club, as well as Soroptimist officials, national and Southwest Region. There were sixty individual place cards painted with Arizona scenes by the artist member, who had crossed the new Midgley Bridge and driven up through Oak Creek Canyon with Jess to attend. Mrs. Joseph R. Babbitt complimented her on them. Justice McAllister welcomed the Flagstaff club to "the enchanted circle of outstanding women in history." The group's initial project was a study of taxes as they affected local conditions.

In February of 1944 the Flagstaff newspaper, full of news about war loan drives and ration coupons, WAVEs and WACs, reported under "Social, Club and Church News" that the Soroptimists at their regular luncheon meeting at the Hotel Monte Vista had heard Lillian talk about her Shekayah dinnerware. She showed several pieces of strongly-colored pottery modeled of Catalina clays; the reporter especially liked the bowls. Porter Emerson Browne and Zane Grey were quoted in praise of both lines.

In May her painting of the entrance to West Fork in Oak Creek Canyon (the locale for Zane Grey's *Call of the Canyon*) appeared on the cover of "American Soroptimist," a national magazine with international circulation. The editor reported: "From the windows of her ranch home she has captured the beauty of the canyon as the sun and shade revealed the striking pattern and unbelievable accent of color that is Arizona. [Her] flare for powerful treatment of design is matched only by the delicacy of her brush in a mass of intense and vivid color. Her portraits have gone to many states, to France, England, Germany and South America. Her paintings have taken prizes in many parts of the nation."

She knew all kinds of people. In 1943 surrealist painter Max Ernst, who had helped to found the Dada movement in Cologne, was a guest at Shekayah for three months with his artist wife, Dorothea Tanning. He described it as "a camera-sharp place…where heat bounced like coiled springs off the burning red rocks." She spoke of "a blue [overhead] so triumphant it penetrated the darkest spaces of your brain…Even the stars shed perfume with their light."

Shekeyah's guests included a San Francisco woman who referred to the Smiths as "wonderful, adventurous people, a soul-mated pair." They told their visitors they had never been happier and had less. War was raging around the globe, in Africa and Asia and Europe and the Pacific islands. Jews all over Europe were in death camps. Japanese-Americans were in "relocation centers." Survivors of the tragic Dust Bowl migration were singing: "Come on, you Okies and Arkies, let's go git Japan—we taken California, and we never lost a man." The Smiths lived with sycamores in the colored landscape at the mouth of Oak Creek Canyon. There were friends. There was love. They could claim more reasons for happiness than many people at the time.

Finally the war ended and with it gas and tire rationing. From June through September of 1946 people from Arizona and New Mexico and California, from Mississippi and Minnesota and Michigan and Texas and Ohio signed the guest register at a showing of Lillian's paintings.

In September of that year Producers-Actors Corporation moved into Shekayah for five days to shoot scenes for a movie which it copyrighted as "Gun Fighters." It was an ironic place for that particular story. Based on *Twin Sombreros*, a novel by Zane Grey that had been issued in 1940, it featured Brazos Keene, who was supposed to have been modeled on Jesse

Smith. Colorado was Grey's setting for the book, but he was no longer around to insist on fidelity.

Producers-Actors paid a total of $475.00 for the use of the ranch yard. Its crew changed a wall, added a lean-to, pruned a few trees and dug up three small poplars, balled them, and replaced them after shooting. Starring Randolph Scott, directed by George Waggoner, the film was released by Columbia in 1947 to an unenthusiastic reception.

Still painting and exhibiting despite all the visitors, Lillian was "active," according to art catalogues.

I feel so sorry for those who say there is no work. It is there, if we can but find it or become conscious of it when it is close at hand. For the artist in music, literature or art a world lies open— but one should not rest when the impulse is there. People say, "I always wanted to paint—to write—to sing." It takes work, and plenty of it, to accomplish these things. Exhausting effort—and, often, sheer muscular effort—but it is worth it.

*A*rizona artist **Louis Akin had died** the year of Lillian's first visit to the state. A heart attack had killed Gunnar Widforss in 1934, leaving only a handful of the pioneering painters of the Plateau. Al Nestler was still alive; so was Jimmy Swinnerton. Kate Cory, twenty years Lillian's senior, had been in Prescott since 1912. In 1941 Mary-Russell Ferrell Colton, who had been exhibiting with the Philadelphia Ten since 1911, stopped painting. After that year, there were no more shows in the city where her art career had begun, and slowly she became reclusive.

We live among the dead and they among us. In 1929 Flagstaff saw in the *Sun* that an auto accident had killed Leo Weaver's wife Nell. Lorenzo Hubbell, paralyzed by a stroke, had died at Ganado in 1930. Georgia Ida Wetherill had been killed in an auto accident in July of 1935. A heart attack had finished Zane Grey in 1939 when he was sixty-seven years old. Stella Black, wife of George Black when the Smiths leased the old Schnebly ranch, was dead of tuberculosis.

Good friends fell away during the 1940s; "died" became a familiar word. Harold Bell Wright, who had published nineteen books in forty years, died in 1944 in San Diego. John Wetherill, bothered by his heart, died in July of 1944 in Ashfork, on his way by train to sea level. His partner Clyde Colville died four months later, and the sandstone house at Kayenta was looted, sold, burned. On September 18, 1945, Louisa Wetherill died in Prescott at the age of sixty-eight.[10] Ben Wetherill was gone within the year. Arizona artist Maynard Dixon "passed over," as they said, in 1946.

Losing people and places is a painful part of growing older. Lillian's brother Arnold died in 1943 after a heart attack. Dolly Grey had sold the Lackawaxen house in 1945. In 1947, the year electricity became generally available in Sedona, Lillian and Jess lost their Shekayah home. After Stella's death, George Black had married again, a schoolteacher named Sallie. For five years there was a flurry of legal action on the section where Shekayah was situated, warranty and quit claim deeds, transfer back and forth of parts of it between George and Sallie, sale of parts to other people.

The general opinion was that Sallie, a small woman who always wore a long black dress, was demanding and difficult to deal with—frankly, a ferocious reputation. When she entered her bank in Flagstaff, it was by appointment, and an official met her at the door. Because of an irregularity in the contract, she took control of the old Schnebly ranch and reclaimed it for sale to a relative. In those years after the war Arizona was dealing with a rapidly growing migration into the state. The Community of Sedona had almost 350 residents already, and the land was more valuable as real estate every month.

Ellsworth Schnebly, whose mother Sedona knew Lillian, said: "Lillian and her husband were worked to death and robbed by Sallie Black, who had leased them her property for a guest ranch but who beat them out of all that her husband earned while working on another job." Probably they were naive about business—her family thought so. Al's widow referred to one "pie in the sky" idea after another. But they had lived at Sedona for more years than at any other place since childhood. They did not recover from the loss.

When they drove away from Sedona, another line was drawn across Lillian's life. There was almost as much time left

<hr>

[10]In 1945 Georgia O'Keeffe, 60 years old, settled the estate of Alfred Stieglitz and made a permanent move to a property she had bought in New Mexico.

as the years she had spent in Manhattan, but the best part of her life had been the freedom of the middle, and it was gone.

*J*esse Smith was sixty years old in 1948, no longer useful to the Forest Service. Lillian was sixty-six. It had been a long time since either of them had looked young. With the citrus grove in Scottsdale a decade in the past, they had no home of their own.

Their financial numbers were not reassuring. Social Security dated from 1937 when the average hourly wage was one dollar. In 1948 the monthly Consumer Price Index expense for food, clothing and medical care totaled $83; the median wage in 1949 was $877 annually. For his work from 1937 to 1950, Jess received Social Security checks that averaged $343 a year.

Lillian had always been self-employed. From Social Security she was receiving less than one hundred dollars a month. Although she had recently accepted a $500 commission for a painting to be placed in a Phoenix home, her oil paintings were usually priced at a bare $50 to $275. There was no choice: they had to continue working as long as they could.

After the loss of Shekayah, they lived a few miles away in Boynton Canyon. Then Jess worked for a time as manager at Dr. Carlson's ranch on Oak Creek and as manager of the Oak Creek Lodge. The war was over. Gas and tires were no longer rationed, so they moved frequently. His sister Janie owned a motel, also named Shekayah, in Kingman; they visited there for a reunion with brother Ned and went to see Dolly in Altadena.

The family of her childhood was fading. In 1947 and 1948 her brothers Harry and Ted, both in their sixties, were buried. On a Friday night in January of 1948 her mother, eighty-eight years old, thirty years a widow, died after a long illness at her home in the Bronx. Some of her dreams had been realized: the obituary in the New York *Times* described her as a patroness of the Metropolitan Opera and a member of Liederkranz, a distinguished German-American musical society.

Lillian went East to visit what family she had left and wrote to "Jess darling" that she was painting a set of six watercolors and visiting with Dolly, who offered to take care of "grandfather's cuckoo clock and Father's lovely big picture" at her house in Altadena. She ended, "More tomorrow, sweet. Ever devotedly, lovingly."

Claire's children thought Lillian was "the loveliest gentle person." They "adored Uncle Jess." So did Al's children: Bobbie, younger than "the Cough Drops", liked to put her head against his chest and listen to the rumble his voice made coming "out of his boot tops" and savor the smell of him—wool, cigarettes, and sometimes whiskey. [Prohibition had long since been repealed.]

But even heroes cannot escape time and sickness. On a Monday in July, while Lillian was in California visiting Dolly, he had major surgery in the little hospital at Cottonwood in the Verde Valley. It was ominous for a man of sixty, no matter how fearless and determined his adventures had been and maybe more discouraging because his body had always served so well. Lillian rushed home on a train to be with him.

They needed money more than ever. In 1949 she listed the location of a dozen of her unsold landscapes to be shown at a Hospital Benefit. It read like a summary of thirty-five years: eastward from Fossil Bay at the Grand Canyon, a view from the North Rim with the Peaks on the horizon, "Silence" from the South Rim, the Temple of Sinawava in Zion Park, three views of the San Francisco Peaks, an old desert road, the Superstition Mountains, Navajo Falls in Havasu, Walpi, Monument Valley, Oak Creek from the Sedona Bridge.

*E*verywhere in Arizona there were mountains on some horizon, often in range beyond range. Aldo Leopold had called the southeastern corner of the state a country of "mountain islands" separated by fertile valleys. It was a jumbled land where rock formations spanned two million years.

Some were places of legends that had excited imagination for a century. Near the town where Jess had joined the army thirty-three years earlier were the Dragoons on the eastern side of the majestic sweep of the San Pedro River valley. Apaches with Cochise had held out there as long as they could in the Stronghold, as it came to be known.

At the north end of those mountains the Amerind Foundation sat in a grassy dell circled by porphory boulders, shaded by oak and mesquite and cottonwood. A private and non-profit research facility with adjoining museum and art gallery, the Amerind had been founded in 1926 and incorporated in 1937 by William Shirley Fulton and his wife Rose Hayden. A native of Waterbury, Connecticut, a graduate of Yale, Fulton had visited

Lillian and Jess at Amerind
Courtesy of Arizona Historical Foundation
Arizona State University
Tempe

Arizona off and on from 1906. Wealthy with money from patents and a brass foundry, he had retired finally to devote himself to recovering the story of ancient native populations.

In 1931 Fulton had bought a 2000-acre ranch in Texas Pass and built a cluster of pink Spanish-Colonial buildings roofed with red tile. Rose, daughter of a mining engineer who owned the Copper Chief in Jerome, raised and trained quarter horses on the ranch. At slightly less than 5000 feet elevation, it was a refuge of peace and beauty as well as an institution of learning.

In 1950 Jess, an old cowboy who needed a job, answered an Amerind employment advertisement, and the Smiths moved again—into accommodations on the grounds. Hired to do general light work, Jess drove a tractor, went into Dragoon for mail, mended fences. The Fultons' fortyish daughter Liz liked him: he was nice, he was quiet. Lillian painted the surrounding landscape.

Liz "adored" Lillian and considered her a friend, wrote to her for years: "When are you two coming for that visit?" Rose Fulton bought five watercolors that Lillian had painted of Indians long before in New York and the oil of Hohyana Kachinas that had once taken a first at the state fair. It was hung in the Amerind gallery with paintings by Jimmy Swinnerton, Frederick Remington and Arthur Wesley Dow. W.S. bought one of her oils, "Verde Valley," and presented it to the institution.[11]

The Smiths did not stay long at Amerind, only a year or two. In 1952 Lillian wrote a letter to an old friend in Prescott, Congregationalist minister Charles Franklin Parker, to say that they had made a complete change. They were living in a house on the OW cattle ranch—on a hill in the middle of an open grassy park surrounded by pines and oak—with a long view of the Canyon Creek valley. "Jess' love for this place is so great (he has dreamed of it since he first helped gather cattle here in his twenties) that I agreed to everything just to give him this opportunity to manage his dream ranch."

Once Apache country, then homestead land, the OW had been enlarged years before by Jim Ramer, who brought 4000 head of cattle onto a range that totalled—once he had acquired assorted homestead rights and grazing permits—100,000 acres. Hashknife and Graham-Tewkesbury names were part of its history; so were Will Rogers and Clark Gable. Sold and sold and sold again, acquired by a bank after World War II, the OW was owned by seven Phoenix businessmen, including Walter Bimson, J.E. Kintner, also of Valley Bank (an old friend from Tuba City days) and Frank Snell, pre-eminent attorney.

"Everything" meant working twelve to fourteen hours a day sometimes. After completing their employment agreement, the Smiths realized that the businessmen expected them to "take

[11]No longer even a half-year resident of New York, the husband who had promoted her work no longer living, Georgia O'Keeffe was out of fashion during most of the 1950s. Through the decade she showed her work only three times. The New York Times referred to her as "an enigmatic and solitary figure" in American art, primarily of historical interest.

A view from the OW manager's house
Courtesy of Susan Olberding

care of us just like at your guest ranch." "It was a whale of a blow," Lillian wrote to Parker, "but I agreed, for Jess' sake."

From the roomy house they lived in, there was a view from every window of horse and cattle pastures irrigated from the creeks that circled around them, of cloud shadows on wooded hillsides, of a pegged barn that could hold a hundred tons of hay. It was a place of peace and pastoral beauty that seemed made for an artist's hand.

The families and their guests arrived on week-ends expecting clean beds and good food. Lillian could serve as a hostess—she had done so for years—but it was hard work. Sometimes one group of visitors going out met another coming in. She did not complain: "Jess made sacrifices for our gamble in Sedona in order that I might live in beauty there those ten wonderful years." The owners were appreciative, "but Jess and I have worked harder than we did at Sedona." She was seventy years old. His taxable income for 1952 was $227, for 1953–$340.

Another thing Zane Grey had not written about was the slow death of hope as time goes on. Jesse Smith was only sixty-three, but his health was ever worse. He had to leave the OW.

By 1953 they were back in the Verde Valley, and Jess was again in the Cottonwood hospital for surgery. He was in great pain. Lillian's youngest brother George, was the only one of the five still living. He wrote:

> *You both have had more than your share in everything. I do hope you and Jess will soon be able to get a place where you will both be happy and won't have to work so hard. I'm proud to have such a fine brother-in-law. You and Jess are much too good to have those things come your way. I always will say if anyone had a sister like I have they will be very proud, as I think the world of you and a great deal of Jess. I've not forgotten how you were ever since I was four years old.*

*T*he **Consumer Price Index** had risen by six points over the past five years, beginning a long, steady climb. Jess had no income for 1954 and 1955. Needing money, as always, Lillian continued to offer her paintings where they might sell. The year of her husband's second surgery there was a one-artist exhibition at 19 East Coronado in Phoenix, three buildings up the block from the Art Center in the offices of the Symphony Association. Her life-size portrait of an Indian was hanging in the lounge of the YWCA as part of the State Federation of Women's Clubs collection.

The year after she left Sedona she had painted walls in the children's wing at the Flagstaff hospital as "artist member of the Soroptimists." In 1953 and 1954, cooperating with the Women's Auxiliary of St. Joseph's Hospital in Phoenix, she did murals in the sunny semi-circular children's recreation room in the pediatric ward. Six small panels between the windows were of different parts of the state: Oak Creek country, Cochise County, desert saguaro, palo verde, ocotillo, and forest pines. On the walls beside the doors were two wider views, one of a coast village in Mexico, the other of a Pima Indian village.

Mildred Smith, married to a man connected with the movie industry, had retired to a house on the Schnebly Hill Road in Sedona. The Smiths, her friends for nearly thirty years, lived not far away in Clarkdale, then in Tolleson and back to Cottonwood, and through it all Lillian tended her contacts. In December she supplied paintings in oil for a "second annual" show at the Phoenix Art Center Annex, including canvases which had not sold over the years: Rainbow Bridge in shadow

Lillian with her paintings
Courtesy of Museum of Northern Arizona
Flagstaff

with sunlight beyond the arch, "On Location with Paramount" in Marsh Pass at Tsegi, Havasu Canyon in 1929, a portrait of Jess in western dress, and "Silence" of the Grand Canyon. Later the exhibit moved to the Symphony Association's rooms for a two week showing.

Newspaper coverage of her work called her "romantic," which was accurate enough. She had been part of American art's revolution away from the idealized realism of the academy and into a heady new freedom. Avoiding the mathematical and mechanistic lines of Modernism, she had stayed with color and Western land and adventure on a frontier with few inhabitants. At the age of seventy-one she was still working, still living with her cowboy. "Romantic" in any of its definitions was not an inappropriate label.[12] In public statements she sounded notes of old-fashioned idealism.

---

[12]Toward the end of the 1950s Georgia O'Keeffe's work became fashionable again. When the Metropolitan Museum mounted an exhibit titled "Fourteen American Artists," an entire room was given to her paintings.

The artist still at work
Courtesy of Arizona Historical Foundation
Arizona State University
Tempe

Art is a grand thing to live with. Arts of all kinds, poetry, music, painting, writing, and most important of all, the art of living, of living wholesomely, graciously, unselfishly. All these arts are interrelated. Some form of self-expression is essential to us all for real happiness—and granting the necessity for material security, for money to pay our bills, to keep the wheels a-rolling, yet without art and without love, life is rather a poor thing.

eople she had known continued to drop away. Leo Weaver died soon after she left Shekayah, Sedona Schnebly in 1951, Dolly Grey in 1957, her long service to her husband's career ended. In 1958 Kate Cory died in the Pioneers Home in Prescott. After forty years in Scottsdale, Marjorie Thomas had returned to the East. Mary-Russell Colton had faded into what was probably Alzheimer's disease.

The world empties for most people as they grow older; it did so for Lillian. And Jess obviously would not be with her much longer. In the winter of 1958 he was a patient for two months at the big white Veterans Hospital at Fort Whipple.

Established in 1864, the fort had been named for Brigadier General A.W. Whipple, who had been in Arizona in 1851 as part of a boundary survey and again in 1853 directing the railroad survey. Its original purpose as a defense for settlers against Yavapai Indians had long since been forgotten; by 1960 it served primarily as the site of a Veterans Administration hospital.

The strength that Jess had always had was gone, and so was his role as the one who took care of things. In March of 1959 his condition justified moving him back into the Veterans Hospital. From the chaplain at Fort Whipple Lillian rented a tiny house on Beach in Prescott, a short street close to the Sharlot Hall Museum, so she could be near him.

The Wetherill grand-daughters, Johnni Lou and Dorothy Lillian, were both living in town. When they could manage it, they drove her out to visit her husband. She was often alone, writing affectionate letters to him on days when she could not see him.

Rational to the end, he was bedridden, finally on oxygen. "It's those cigarettes he's smoked all his life," his wife said. "They're killing him." But like her father, she did not show her feelings; she had hidden them since she'd been twenty.

At 12:55 on a March day in 1960, seventy-three years old, Jess died. Son of people who had traveled to Colorado in a covered wagon, World War I stable sergeant, roper of wild horses, friend of Lee Doyle and John Wetherill, he left America while John Kennedy was using television to campaign for the Presidency. The death certificate listed causes of his death as rupture of an abdominal aortic aneurysm, carcinoma of the prostate gland, and pyelo nephritis. Lillian placed among her papers a small watercolor sketch which she labeled "view from the window of the room where Jess died" and a letter identified as "last letter from Jess." He had signed it, "all my love and a million kisses, ever your lover."

Four days later he was buried in Prescott's National Cemetery in the silent company of other veterans of the Great War, all of them in straight rows. Thumb Butte reared against the skyline. It had come down to that for a good man—a square stone in the grass.

Jesse R Smith
Sgt 41 CO 20 Engineers
World War I
September 4, 1886   March 18, 1960

Most of us die in vain, and there isn't much we can do about it. The trick is to avoid *living* in vain. People of all kinds felt admiration, respect and love for Jesse Smith—evidence that he passed that test, if evidence be needed. Claire wrote in tribute to him, "He could not give [Lillian] much materially, but he gave her love."

"Because they were so good to Jess," she donated a large painting of Rainbow Bridge to the Veterans Hospital, where it was hung in a lobby. Two paintings were given to Yavapai Community Hospital. Walter Bimson bought a watercolor landscape she had painted years earlier in Havasu Canyon. There were a few canvases remaining, but the work of her life began to fade.

The Mountain Artists' Guild had been organized in 1949 from the Prescott Art League; she joined it the year after her husband's death. The Guild mounted a show of her work at the public library in Prescott the next year.

Friends said Lillian, was lost without Jess. She stayed on in Prescott, at first in the little rented house on Beach, and was listed in the 1963 city directory as "householder." She liked Prescott. It was "a jewel-like town nestling among the encircling hills." Sometimes in the 1960s she visited Claire in Connecticut and they talked

The last portrait of Lillian
Courtesy of Museum of Northern Arizona Flagstaff

about their years of travel, but she no longer enjoyed going East. Her family, what was left of it, recognized that she was "a true convert to the West."

*T*he Russian satellite, Sputnik, had opened a new age in 1957; manned space flight had followed four years later, and the race was on. Americans were preparing to land two astronauts on the moon. Lillian's world was disappearing. There was no more talk of a schoolgirl's "mysterious city seen from a height, with its sunshine and success for those who choose wisely and persevere."

Claire Dooner Phillips died in 1960, Ada Rigden in 1962 at the family ranch near Prescott. In 1963 Mary-Russell Colton was taken to a private hospital in Phoenix as a resident patient. A year later W.S. Fulton died at Amerind. In 1967 a fire at the Zane Grey house in Altadena destroyed manuscripts and memorabilia. Rose Fulton went in 1968; so did Lou Ella Archer, eulogized as a major benefactor of the Humane Society's Tempe animal shelter. Dora Lee Sessions, Shekayah's cook, died in Prescott in 1969. After a heart attack, Jimmy Swinnerton was living in a convalescent hospital.

Lillian knew a few people in Prescott—Kay Manley whom she had met twenty-five years earlier at Shekayah, the Wetherill grand-daughters and Charles Franklin Parker—and she managed to live alone for four more summers, smaller and narrower and darker than summers had been in her adventuring days.

Sometimes Georgia Ida's daughters took her out for picnics so that she could paint. Always she called Dorothy Lillian by both names—"it was special." But she was not the woman she once had been. Becoming senile, they feared. Definitely of uncertain mind. They went in regularly to clean and dust and discovered that emotions hidden through the years had been written onto scraps of paper and placed between the pages of her books. Criticism of her mother as "spoiled and selfish," for instance.

They were surprised by one slip on which she had confided that she had not been born in Manhattan at all but in Germany on one of her father's buying trips and that, having seen Germany begin two ghastly wars, she was ashamed of it. Always secretive, she had kept it hidden throughout her life.

When the Wetherill girls visited again to dust, the pieces of paper were gone from the books.

Finally they began sprinkling talcum powder in the tub so that they could tell whether Lillian had bathed. When she was eighty-three, she fell and broke her left arm, and that was the end even of the illusion of Arizona freedom. Johnni Lou and Dorothy Lillian, both in their forties, had known her all their lives. Taking charge, they moved her into a modest nursing home where they hoped she would be comfortable.

In 1966 Walter Bimson bought for $750 "The Blue Beauty of the Bradshaws," and Claire wrote to acknowledge the sale.

> *Thank you for writing and for the check which I'll use in the interest of my sister. Am very happy you decided to purchase the painting.*
>
> *The last time I was in Prescott Mr. Sam Head, attorney, thought it advisable to handle some of my sister's affairs since her mind is not as sharp and retentive as it once was. Accordingly he drew up a Power of Att'y.*
>
> *Physically my sister Lillian seems to be in good shape but is very forgetful. She has been living for the past couple of years in a private nursing home where apparently she is happy and well cared for.*

Laura Runke had gone on from her Tuba City years to be elected Flagstaff's first councilwoman. She was of a different opinion about the nursing home. After visiting Lillian, she returned to Flagstaff upset. "I don't think she's getting enough to eat," she told friends. "She's cold." She solicited warm clothing from everyone she knew and went back across the miles to Prescott with boxes of donations. In gratitude Lillian gave her old friend the painting of the Verde Valley viewed from high on Mingus Mountain.

Johnni Lou and Dorothy also became alarmed but discovered that they had no authority to extricate their elderly "aunt." Without Jess, she was afraid to move, afraid of change, afraid of the matron. They wrote to Lillian's sister and asked for help.

In May of 1968 Claire visited Prescott and found the situation not what she had thought. Still outraged three years later, she described it in a letter to Walter Bimson:

[The] home was the nearest thing to a Dickens scene that I know of. Lillian was robbed right and left there. Much of her mail was confiscated and through their neglect of her she suffered malnutrition. [Her meals were slid along the floor on a tray through a barely opened door. "Here, eat this."]…Lillian's friends were barred from seeing her and she was pathetically brain-washed. This was all heartbreaking to me…We knew none of this until we finally walked in on it unexpectedly, on our trip west. My husband and I lost no time getting her out of there. We actually kidnapped her.

The owner insisted that two of Lillian's remaining paintings had been gifts, and Claire was so anxious to get away that she didn't argue.

On May 17, 1968, one day after her 86th birthday, they moved Lillian into the Pioneers Home high on a hill above town. A three-story brick building a city block long, it was the only institution of its kind in the United States. In 1909 the state legislature had authorized it as a shelter for Arizona pioneers and disabled miners at least sixty years old who had lived in the state for thirty-five or more years. Lillian obviously qualified. From its windows there was a view of the Loma Prieta Mountains to the southeast; off to the northeast loomed the San Francisco Peaks, sixty-five miles away. They had been part of her life for more than half a century.

She would live at the Pioneers Home as a paying guest for the years that remained of her life. Claire sent money from Connecticut each month to the Yavapai County Board of Supervisors to pay for her care and began to spend winters in Green Valley south of Tucson, from which she could visit now and then.

The Fulton's daughter Liz went to see Lillian at the home. Kay Manley became a good friend, taking the shrunken little artist out for a day occasionally to paint—always on her birthday. Lillian would say, "You don't know what this means to me." With so much else gone, she did not lose her sight. Manley saw her once sitting in a low rocking chair, reading aloud from a book by Zane Grey and identifying passages she said she had contributed—"I gave him that." Example: the name "The Land of Marching Rocks" in *The Vanishing American.*

Lillian (l.) and Kay Manley
Courtesy of Museum of Northern Arizona
Flagstaff

Her work was not entirely forgotten: those people who still cared did what they could to perpetuate her reputation as an artist. In 1968 the Pioneer Art Gallery in Prescott held an exhibit of unsold oils, watercolors, and lithographs. The Carlins took boxes, paintings, and a trunk of Lillian's water colors to Manley, who spent months matting the watercolors, framing the oils, photographing and pricing them. A one-woman exhibit was held by the Mountain Artists Guild with a reception for Lillian. Money received from the sale of paintings contributed toward her support at the Home.[13]

Beginning in 1968 the Museum of Northern Arizona began to build a modest collection of her oils and watercolors. In April of 1969 Walter Bimson bought a fourth painting, an oil of Oak Creek Canyon. In June of 1970 there was a letter from Washington signed by Barry Goldwater under a United States Senate letterhead:

> *Just by accident I discovered that you were living in Prescott and I just wanted you to know that my prayers are yours for your comfort and happiness. I still treasure those plates you did for us so many years ago and I can assure you no one will ever equal their beauty or artistry.*

Lillian had been born when there were no automobiles or airplanes anywhere. In 1970 the Beatles' records were selling gold, and hippies were in full cry. There were two women generals in the United States Army. America was preparing an earth-orbiting space station.

Eisenhower's interstate highway system, first proposed in 1954, was spreading 900 miles across Arizona and changing travel beyond the recognition of old-timers. Some roads across the Navajo Reservation had been hard-surfaced between 1950 and 1960, the road to Tuba City in 1964. There was pavement to the property that had been the Sedona Shekayah; it was being developed into Los Abrigados resort and the adjacent shops of Tlaquepaque. Lillian's rock house was retained,

---

[13]The O'Keeffe mystique grew steadily through the 1960s. In 1970 the Whitney mounted a major retrospective. Acclaim and recognition increased, as did awards, but so did media attention. She herself became a commodity: there was as much public interest in her as in her paintings. She began to receive mail and visits from strangers, unwelcome phone calls.

surrounded by resort buildings which closed off the once spectacular view.

Her Sedona home would change until she would not have recognized it. Probably she would not have felt out of place in the hotel that her guest ranch became—she was in and out of expensive buildings all her life. But would she have preferred the unending noise, the cars and guests and staff? There would be more people working at Los Abrigados after it opened in 1978 than the whole population of Sedona had been in the 1930s.

If only it had been possible for her to revoke the final years to dance up and down the lawn in misty moonlight. Walk along Manhattan streets smiling because she'd been promoted. Ride twenty-seven days in the saddle with Jess looking for movie locations. Wake to winter sunrise on the cliffs of Sedona. Stand free and for Art.

In early February of 1971 she was ill and her heart was weakening. Fifty-eight years in the past she had slept in blankets on the punishing trail to Rainbow Bridge, a different place each night. At the age of thirty-five she had uprooted her life and replanted it across a continent. She had changed her residence often through the years. Near death, she was upset when hospital staff moved her to a different room.

During her last hours two weeks later Kay Manley, at her bedside, said, "You will be seeing Jess before long. Won't that be wonderful?" Lillian replied, "Thank God!" Her story ended on February 22.

Mary-Russell Ferrell Colton died two months later, Laura Runke in October of 1972. Mildred Smith died in Sedona in 1973.

*A*rt was not what it had been in 1913 when the Armory Show had set American painters on the pursuit of mass and color. Andy Warhol was featured at the Whitney in New York the year Lillian Wilhelm died. The paintings of Andrew Wyeth had recently been collected into a major show.

Everything was different. A Women's Art Registry was serving as a clearing house. Women Artists in Revolution demanded equal space for paintings by women in the Whitney annuals. Gestural art, Environmental art, conceptual art, technological art, electronic, action, op, pop, kinetic, minimal were the new mirages. The sale of a Velasquez painting for $5,524,000, a Titian for more than $4,000,000, had made headlines.

The time of Lillian's youth was long gone. Arthur Dow and his formulae were footnotes in art history books; except for O'Keeffe, of course,[14] only a few academics remembered the names of the students he had once prepared for abstraction. Zane Grey's novels were still read, though it had been decades since they had been on best seller lists.

But interest in paintings of the West had grown in a crescendo, a sudden giant popularity unlike anything known to the history of art. The eleven art museums in Arizona acquired extensive collections. Prices of paintings underestimated and neglected during the lifetimes of the artists increased, as did attendance at exhibits.

In Sedona an art center was established in a barn to provide facilities and programs to the growing population. Cowboy Artists of America had been organized in 1965. A painting from Lillian's time at Dragoon, "Desert Candles of the Lord: When the Yucca Are in Bloom in Old Cochise," was on sale in 1996 at the Biltmore house in Phoenix for $4000.

*S*ervices for **Lillian Wilhelm Smith** were at Prescott's Chapel of the Garden on Pleasant Street with a eulogy by Charles Franklin Parker. Her ashes were placed in the grave of her husband in Veterans Cemetery at Fort Whipple. The following week Dr. Parker wrote "Time for Concern" in his newspaper column *So it seems to me.*

> *A pioneer society seeking to carve a civilization out of the frontier is too engaged in its own process of survival to give much concern to the poets and artists who inevitably come to be a part of its life. These people come, write their songs, paint their pictures, but their portrayals of the land and its people often are not appreciated until later generations rise and in due time, seeking their own understanding of their past, rediscover those who depicted the lives of their fathers. It has ever been so, and Prescott and Arizona have mirrored this pattern of societies everywhere.*

---

[14]Prices for O'Keeffe's paintings continued to rise. When she died in 1986, blind and nearly a century old, her estate was estimated at thirteen million dollars.

Somehow, this came vividly to my mind this past week when we buried Lillian Wilhelm Smith, artist of the pioneer years of Arizona's twentieth century. Lillian came to this great country first to illustrate the writings of Zane Grey, who then was capturing the imagination of the American people with his many books of western life. Her brush captured vividly in oil and water color the characteristics of this great land—mountains, canyons and desert. In our opinion she was a fine artist but many of the years through which she lived were difficult years economically for the American people and this fact, coupled with the fact that Arizona was still within the first early years of its founding, never brought to this fine artist the recognition locally to which she was truly entitled.

The same was true of Kate T. Cory who, like Mrs. Smith, came from New York and training from the Art League of that city, but a time will come, if it has not already arrived, when the work of these two excellent pioneer artists will be acclaimed, and we urge the Prescott Fine Arts Association to begin now to accumulate works of these two artists who marched in the vanguard to bring cultural appreciation to this community in order that their work and their spirit may serve this community for all the years yet to come, and the ruggedness of the land presented in their landscapes may remind us, too, of the ruggedness of their own characters as they helped to bring a concern for the cultural even into the heart of a pioneering society.

Three

August, 1996

Vultures were circling above
Woody Ridge, visible against the sky
from road 231 as it passed through
Mill Park. A fawn killed by coyotes?
Archery elk season had opened at dawn
on Friday—it might be an elk wounded
by a bow hunter too lazy to track it
and finish the job. She hated it when
she came across one of those.

If it was an abandoned throw-down camp with garbage and dirty Pampers, she'd look for any ID and report the slobs to Meg. All summer she'd driven around the south end in a Forest Service rig, looking for people she could talk to about being careful with fire and packing up trash before they went back to the city. Some of them cleaned the site better than they'd found it. Others had closed down their brains when they turned off pavement. She was tired of coming on a camp site and finding garbage tossed everywhere, spoiling a perfectly nice place. It made her mad enough to spit *tacks*, as Grandma used to say.

Road 535 faced across open meadow and open air, right toward the vultures—she estimated they were three miles away. She'd have to go and look, it was part of the patrol job, but after the rains last week, Mill Park would be boggy. A one-ton truck with a 200 gallon water tank mounted on the back was heavy in mud, and dual rear wheels weren't much help if the mud was deep. She turned around and drove back to the two-track that took off on high ground. It was a horrible road but hey, at least it would be dry.

Jake Holding was supposed to be bow hunting close to where Woody Ridge dropped off. He'd left after work on Thursday so at first light he could be in position for a kill. She could do without running into him, he'd be furious because he didn't have his elk yet after four days and ready to take it out on anyone in sight.

For weeks he'd boasted around the station, jeering at men who went out in groups with rifles, and getting away with it because he was the engine boss. "Hunting isn't some boy scout picnic. You want to be a real hunter, you go by yourself. Only a fool who's dumb or drunk goes after elk in a crowd."

One thing you could say about Jake, he knew how to make work miserable for other people. That awful day last week when her truck was in the shop, she'd had to double up with him to respond to a fire at L.O. Pocket. He drove like a maniac, hit bumps hard, skidded around corners and fishtailed in the gravel. Finally she said, "Jeesh, Jake, slow down." He set his mouth in a hard line and drove even faster.

He'd been on her case all summer, criticizing everything she said on the radio. "Did it occur to you that it wasn't your place to request Engine 3-4? It's up to the dispatcher to decide who's going to be sent out to assist you on a fire."

"I'd just left them building fence at Fernow. I knew they were close."

"I *said*, you ask for an engine if it's too much for you, but not Engine 3-4 or anybody else in particular." Then he turned and strutted away and left her standing there wanting to throw something after him.

The engine people had told her that every now and then Jake got it in for somebody like a brain spasm and never let up. They were glad it wasn't one of them this year. Next season it would be somebody else who'd want to kill him.

The road was dry but so rocky and rutted that she was jolted, even at ten-fifteen miles an hour. Land was fairly flat with open little meadows deep in grass and sunshine. Basalt cap in there, probably from the Woody Mountain vent a couple of million years ago, that explained the shallow-rooted pine monoculture. Good country for elk, which was probably why Jake had put in for Unit 6B.

Hardly anyone camped back there. Most over-nighters stopped on the edge of Fry Park where they could see a long way. Or Fry Canyon— what a jammed-up mess that place could be on weekends. It looked as if only one vehicle had driven in since last Thursday's storm: raindrops had made tiny pits and wiped the road clean for a while, but there was one set of tracks in the dirt.

All those little trails that took off to the left had tricked her before— she stopped to look at the map. She should be close to Black Tank by now, where that big blow-down pine nearly blocked the road. Her wheels spun as she put the truck in gear and started on. OK, there were blue paint slashes on the trees; she was into the state timber sale. And there was Black Tank, full of water. Above the trees she could still see the vultures.

It really was peaceful, land dappled by sun and shade, birds singing. Not spectacular country where you could see for miles or where earth fell away at your feet into a canyon. Just nice, the forest alive and breathing. She liked the smell of the air through her open window. Probably the section had been hammered by loggers eighty years earlier, but they'd left more trees than in other places, yellow-brown giants that grew far up into the air, so strong only the smaller branches moved in the wind.

Big cumulus were already piling high, but they might not mean an afternoon storm, the bottoms weren't flat and black yet. What a job, driving around in the forest and taking care of it. Only five more working days though, and she'd be in class. She'd already given notice: available on weekends through hunting and wood-cutting season if they wanted her, but Monday to Friday she'd be at NAU all day. Jake had sneered about "stinking students" who couldn't last out the season. OK, fine. She was going anyway.

She bounced past Bob's Tank, close now to whatever the vultures were interested in. They were just above the trees ahead, graceful, resting in the air on their big wings, tip feathers up. One set of tire tracks went on ahead of her.

Through the trees she could see a patch of red, the side of a pick-up truck—it looked like Jake's. He said he wouldn't have anything lighter than a half-ton so he could carry elk home. Maybe that was what the vultures were seeing, part of a dead elk. Jake could be off somewhere bringing the rest in, even *he* couldn't carry a whole elk alone. The tracks in the dirt turned right to the truck.

You didn't want to be out in the open if you were alone with Jake. She stopped and locked the door before she heard the flies, all over the mound of a blue sleeping bag on the ground beside the truck. Then the horrible stink hit and went to the back of her throat.

She got the window rolled up fast. Oh god, the smell, heavy in her mouth. She coughed and couldn't get it out. Flies were thick on the sleeping bag, crawling on a head—she could see the hair.

Her hands shook as she fumbled the mike loose from the radio and pressed the key. "Flagstaff…" Her voice broke. Wait, she needed the map. Her fingers were numb—the map fought being unrolled. "Flagstaff, Patrol 3-4."

"Patrol 3-4, Flagstaff."

"Requesting law enforcement and, uh, and a coroner. My location is 20 north, 6 east, uhm, hold on—section 33." She stopped to control the shaking in her voice.

"What's the nature of the problem?"

"I have a fatality here involving a Forest Service employee." They'd all know who it was; he'd told people at the station where he'd be.

"Copy. Don't disturb the scene."

No chance she'd go near *that*. "I'll hike back and flag the way in."

She took a roll of pink ribbon, held her breath, threw open the door and slammed it as she took off. When she was back along the road with both trucks out of sight, she sat down on a fallen tree and hugged the pain in her chest. Not for Jake, turned into a horror. It was just—it was death. She didn't want any more death.

Her grandfather had been young and strong in photographs, but he faded into defeat and frailty and death after he'd lost his ranch to the bank. She wished she could buy it back and put him there again with Grandma, and everything would always be the same as it was when he was fifty.

*A*t her desk in town Meg was finishing paperwork. It had been the week the public went crazy in the forest. Files were piled on her desk.

Six hours of sleep all weekend. She'd no more than cleared off two lost children, envelopes with addresses in garbage left at a throw-down campsite, and a fight between drunks at Bonita campground than she'd dealt with money stolen from a fee box. At Harding Point there'd been a report of someone firing a machine gun. Fun, she was in touch with humans at their best. At least she wasn't city PD, that would be worse.

Other districts had requested help from forest law enforcement. Three teenagers had shot up a market at Munds Park—the sheriff needed blockades on both ends of road 240. A shot had been fired through a tent at Blue Ridge Reservoir. There'd been trouble at Cave Spring, campers refusing to move.

Ugh: preliminary investigation and securing the scenes, talking with witnesses, taking evidence and photographs, issuing citations, all in full uniform with silver badge. It was the reports that wore her down, pages and pages, hours at the computer—synopsis of incident, statements from suspects, witness attachments, and no room anywhere for humor.

It wasn't that she was a wimp. She'd spent three summers on patrol, one on helattack, two on an engine and two on a Hot Shot crew: she was a tough westerner. But she did like a laugh now and *then*.

The Forest Service was big on integrating women—they'd suggested last summer that she apply for law enforcement training, and she'd been flattered. It would make her the first woman law enforcement officer on the forest. She'd gone out to the ranch and talked with her mother at the kitchen table.

"I've been reading up on it. The Forest Service has had to protect people and resources right from the beginning—the first rangers wore badges and guns. They could arrest violators of grazing and logging regulations, moonshiners during Prohibition, people who started fires, even shoot to kill in defense of human life."

"I remember a case right around here, your grandmother told me about it. The ranger was not charged, as I remember. Cookies?"

"Sure. Now the big problem is crowd control. Phoenix has grown until there's so much recreation use of the forests that local sheriffs can't handle the problems."

"I can believe it."

"We've got about a thousand Law Enforcement Officers nationally taking care of federal regulations, most of them transfers from Fire. For twenty years there've been some women doing the job."

Her mother had sighed. "There's a new breed of people out there, people who don't *work* around here. Milk?"

"Please. What do you think? Is it an off-the-wall idea for me?"

Mom had paused, still holding the milk bottle. "Well, I'll give you my initial reaction. I've always thought you have a gift for making life delightful for yourself and everyone around you, like my mother did. It's a rare talent. Maybe you could walk into a situation and de-fuse it, who knows? What that kind of thing would do to *you* is what concerns me, whether it would damage you, make you hard and cynical—people vary in their reactions to all kinds of things. I don't see you as a cop."

"I don't think it's a cop job exactly."

"I know, luv. And I don't doubt you're strong and smart and brave enough to take on trouble. But I wonder whether you'd be happy as an *enforcer*. Did they think you could do it just because you're six feet tall and you could shoot straight by the time you were ten?"

"Somebody has to do it."

"To coin a phrase." Mom had returned the milk bottle to the refrigerator.

"Somebody else, not me?"

"Meggie, it's up to you. The job would be an education, that much is certain. Education is not to be sneezed at, it's a way of growing. But some of the things I've learned I'd rather not have known."

"We'd be in a terrible mess if there weren't some kind of order."

"Now we're talking philosophy?"

"Yeah, like lots more money, I'd be a Forestry Technician GS 462."

"If you take it, I'll watch with real interest. You might run away the first week, you could last for years and never miss a joke, might even be good at it. You won't know until you try, won't know that about yourself."

So she'd filled out the forms and gone through the background/criminal history investigation with no thought of the hours of desk work she was letting herself in for. Or of packing a sidearm everywhere she went. The job was so *serious*.

Nine weeks of training at the federal center in Georgia. Firearm qualification had been a snap. And take-downs: "Your foot goes here. Now, confidence! That's right. Lean into it." But not much had been said then about LEMARS paperwork.

> The Law Enforcement Management Reporting System (LEMARS) is designed to provide management with a means to identify and follow law enforcement activities. It will provide a method to record and analyze incidents involving violations or suspected violations on National Forest System lands. The use of LEMARS is mandatory.

That meant #53001 for incident reports, #53004 for violation notices, #5309.11 for preliminary investigation reports, #5100.29 for fires—half a day of paperwork for every day in the field. But it wasn't same old, same old; she couldn't complain of boredom. And after eight years in Fire, doing everything as part of a crew, she relished the independence. She worked for the Washington office, not the district ranger.

Men standing in the hall were complaining about Jake. "It's taking him a while. How long's he been gone now, four days?"

"He said he'd be home by Saturday night."

"Monday morning he'd have the head in for a shoulder mount."

"If he *didn't* get one, he'd never admit it."

"Come in here with another big story."

"You'd think he got drawn for bull in 6B because he was the best bow hunter in the state. That's a *lottery* with an eighteen per cent chance."

"There were only eighty permits in 6B this year."

"That doesn't prove anything. He was lucky, that's all."

"Coming in here bragging that he got a tag. Can you see him taking an *antlerless* tag?"

"That sumbitch pisses me off."

"He kills everything in sight—bear, lion, javelina."

"He's good though. Last winter he got four pheasants with arrows."

"Goes after squirrels, pigeons, rabbits, quail, even sparrows and prairie dogs."

"Gets 'm."

"So what? Anybody can kill. It's easy."

"Hunting's one thing, hell, we all do it. Killing everything in sight is sick. I say there's something wrong with him."

Jake was a terrible supervisor. He pushed the people who worked for him into a corner, shamed them in front of everybody, left them with no place to turn. No wonder they resented him. She'd heard him say on the radio, "Your orders were…" as if they didn't have brains enough to make decisions in the field. Once he'd even called the husband of a girl on one of the engines to complain about her. Everybody on the station had been incredulous. What had he expected, for crumb sake?

"He had three Bonus points for not getting drawn since '93. Gave him an edge, that's all."

"Remember last year he was out there anyway hunting for poachers and collected a cool thousand for getting one arrested and then bragged about it?"

"Didn't even try to keep it anonymous."

"Reported buddy hunting too."

"Make that three hunters mad enough to kill him."

Not only that, he was obsessed with perfection and his own image, documented everybody else's mistakes, especially if he thought they made him look bad. He was cheerful sometimes, even charming, but part of him was cold and scheming and another part was hot-tempered and violent. You never knew what to expect when you said good morning. Sometimes a flash of mean, sadistic even. That Jake, he was a swell bunch of guys.

"I tell you, I wanta punch him at least once a day."

"Somebody ought to."

"Won't be me. He's strong for an old guy."

"He's not so old, not over forty."

Duvenek ambled by; she saw his long thin body pass the door. "You guys still at it? You take Jake on, you'd better work out a few months first. He can bench three hundred. Be easier to shoot him."

There was silence until Duvenek had gone on down the hall. "Somebody just might one of these days."

"Too many chances out on a fire."

"Don't think I haven't thought about it."

The forest radio at the back of her desk clicked and came to life. "Flagstaff, Patrol 3-4." Josy out on patrol. "I'm requesting law enforcement and, uh, and a sheriff. My location is 20 north, 6 east, uhm, hold on—section 33."

Out in the hall somebody said, "Where Jake was gonna be."

Sherry was dispatching. "What's the nature of the problem?"

"I have a fatality here involving a Forest Service employee."

She laid her pen on FS #5309.11, point away from her, and keyed the button on her mike. "Flagstaff, 3-4 is responding."

"Copy, 3-4. I'll be on the phone with the county."

Great, some weeks the world seemed to go bonkers. Her digital camera was still in her truck; so were the equipment for casting tracks and picking up fingerprints. She sighed, packed her laptop into its padded case, and buckled on about thirty pounds of gun belt. "Never be unarmed," they had told her in Georgia. "Even off duty on your own turf, you need to be armed. Officers have been assaulted and killed." She picked up her notebook and the keys to her truck. With a county mountie coming, she probably wouldn't need to request support from another LEO. One thing she hadn't had so far was a body. No drug bust, no dead body, and nobody had shot at her. Whoop-ti-doo.

*J*n the lookout tower on Woody Mountain, Sarah notices the vultures. They've been around all summer, gnarly black birds, sometimes three dozen at a time. Sailing on the wind or perching in a snag with their wings held away from their bodies. In June she filled a sketch pad with drawings from every angle. Once she even put out a pound of hamburger on the ground so she could see them from above. They glided down through her clearing but didn't land to take the meat even when it had been there for three days. Finally it disappeared in the night. Randy said maybe a skunk had taken it, that should keep her paying attention. He didn't think a coyote or a lion would come so close to the cabin without Venn barking her head off.

She looks around for smoke, all around the wide circle, watching shapes slide past her eyes. When you're looking for smoke, there's no need to scan up into the sky...the land and just above the land.

She wishes she could find one. Now that she knows what to do, it's exciting to be the first to call it in and keep her voice calm. "Flagstaff, Woody Mountain, small white smoke at 171 degrees, seven and a half miles. Mexican Pocket." She loves it when she sees a fire...

On the last Monday morning in May the Mount Elden lookout had called on the forest radio. "Can you tell me if there's something going on northeast of you near the Arboretum? I see a small white smoke in there."

"I have a blind spot northeast of me."

"OK, then I'll call it." The reading from Volunteer lookout crossed Elden's line at a point less than a mile away.

For two hours she listened to the voices on the radio. To Jake..."Flagstaff, can we order a Ranger with a bucket? We won't be able to get engines in here on this ridge."

A Ranger was a state helicopter equipped to drop one hundred gallons of water on a fire. Randy had explained...he said she was his personal newbie. She could see the helicopter coming from the airport with a big orange bucket hanging beneath on a cable. The pilot was told he could refill it by drafting from the pond at the Arboretum.

She couldn't see the water released from the bucket...it all happened out of her sight behind the mountain...but she heard the voices. "Let 'er go!" That was Jake on the ground...his call number was 3-34.

"Ranger, 3-34. Next time work a little farther to the north out toward the edge."

"Roger, will do."

She had known Jake only a little more than two months, and she was impressed by how competent he sounded. "Ranger, 3-34. Open your bucket about six seconds earlier."

"I'm coming in right over the top of the yellow shirts."

A pause. Then, "Cut loose! Bull's eye, Ranger!"

Randy was on the fire too, with his engine, laying hose, Jake had called for it. "We'll need help with the mop-up. We got a lot of heavies in here." Randy says it's kind of fun spraying 60 PSI with that big hose.

Jake requested a county deputy "to come in and look at this." She was shocked at what they said when the deputy arrived. "Where do you want her?" A *woman* deputy on a fire?

Jake didn't seem surprised. "Have her follow the hose-lay from the road."

"Sending 'er up."

Then Jake went back to the pilot, who said, "I'll be coming in blind over the rock face, so say when."

"I'm in place. Go ahead, I'll catch you with a mirror. Line-up looks good. Cut loose!" It made her feel excited and alive and stuff to hear him. That's how it was at first.

A drawing pad is open flat on the firefinder. She's putting yellow into the tips of green pine branches with her colored pencils. And a touch of pink. She puts pink in everything for what it does to the other colors.

There are always *always* dark shadows inside trees. Landscape colors are a challenge to do in pencils...smoke on a fire is fun to do in a watercolor wash, dark green of the trees thinning to white...the white is paper, of course.

There was snow on the Peaks in April, and an icy wind was blowing. She'd climbed the tower seven times carrying things she wanted to have up there through the summer. A raven sped past on invisible currents, again and again, not moving a feather that she could see. Aspen trees around the north side of her mountain were white against the green pines. She thought it was so *rad*, the coolest, most inspiring place she'd ever seen.

She looks down on Rogers Lake...she looks down on almost everything. On May mornings before the water in the lake sank out of sight and left pale yellow meadow, it reflected the sky...and upside-down trees along the far shore. Clouds in the water changed the blue, made it more delicate. In the afternoon it shone like a silver sheet with dark tracery where wind ruffled the surface. At sunset there were warm colors in the water. Randy says, "To visual creatures, light is reality.

Pretty heavy, philosophy as physics. And the other way around, physics as philosophy." He sings, "I've looked at light from both sides now."

The water sank away too early, Randy said, things didn't look good. There hadn't been much rain last summer. Winter had been dry, only five inches of snow. Wind never stopped, and that dried everything out. Stock tanks were empty. She wondered what the animals would do with no water...

Trees in the distance are the color of blueberries, reflecting no light, just pulling it into themselves. But the new aspen leaves of May weren't dull, glossy yellowgreen...every day they were darker. Budding oak leaves were red.

Since high school art classes she's tried to do landscapes but her paper is never big enough. Here there are other problems. If you want to go by rules, mountains sixty and eighty miles away can look real...you fade the colors and blur the edges. But if you do it too much that's kind of cheating Arizona, making it look like someplace else. Atmospheric perspective as Leonardo saw it isn't like the dry Arizona air you can see from a firetower. Color is muted a *little* by distance. It never turns completely grey unless there's smoke from a fire some-where.

As soon as she hears Josy, she knows...it's where he said he'd be. She steps across Venn stretched out on the trapdoor to look at the map and trace the legal with her fingers. Down the ridge south of Black Pass at the end of the road. He said he'd throw a sleeping bag down half a mile beyond Bob's Tank, but he wouldn't be there long, he'd get his elk in *no* time. It has to be Jake. They're sending a sheriff and Meg Pederson. Josy is flagging the road. It's Jake dead down the ridge.

She had worked back to Black Tank, knotting pink flagging ribbons onto branches within sight of each other along the road. It wasn't the most pleasant walk she'd ever had—a raven flapping away from a tree had made her jump.

She'd seen the top of the head, flies thick on what was his face. She coughed, gagged, retched. The smell was still heavy in her throat, but hey, at least she hadn't eaten lunch yet.

The hair had looked like Jake's, short and blonde, but she'd been too hasty about the identity because it was Jake's truck. Some investigator she'd make. The best she could say for herself was that she hadn't poked around and disturbed clues.

She had noticed the tracks coming in though, Jake's probably. Nobody else had come by truck along that road, another half mile and it would dead-end. The bag hadn't looked torn by an animal. No sign of a struggle—he was just lying there. She looked at the dirt: there were no footprints behind her except those of her fire boots. She hoped law enforcement was hurrying, wished that smell in her throat would wear off.

Now that she was half a mile away, the morning was calm and beautiful again. Elk tracks crossed the road—two elk, she thought, going for grass or water or a favorite place to lie down. There was something lame about the thought of death in such smiling country, even the death of a man who had come to kill. Everything killed something—it was necessary—but she didn't like to think about it.

She'd been there when her grandfather had died, with her hand on his chest, and felt his heart slow and stop. Just *stop*. After twelve years, she still couldn't accept that such a thing could be. Maybe death seemed more outrageous from the outside, she hoped so. Maybe from the inside it seemed perfectly reasonable.

It was another hot day; no wonder the body back there smelled so bad. There was a soft breeze. High pressure had moved in behind the storm Thursday—on its way out now. She tore off another strip of flagging.

There'd been a wind advisory Thursday night, even after the rain had stopped. Trees in the yard had thrashed around. She'd stood outside separating the sounds and trying to keep them apart so she could count them until Walt had laughed at her and called her Nature Girl. She'd driven all the way to Ashfork to calm down.

Someone or something could have come up on Jake without waking him because the wind was so loud. The moon had been full Thursday night, with no clouds—it would have been easy to see the truck, the bag. She tied ribbon around a sapling.

"Next season it'll be somebody else who'll want to kill him." Everybody knew how he'd been harassing her—she had known where he would be, everybody did. Would they suspect her because she'd found him? Jeesh. Even dead he'd go on making trouble.

*M*eg killed her lights and siren when she turned off pavement. A cloud of dust would follow her the rest of the way. Driving through town she'd gone over in her mind what she should do so she wouldn't have to think when she got there. On the scanner she heard the county sheriff's office dispatch Len Bailey.

If Josy's fatality was a murder, it would be somebody else's jurisdiction and out of her hands, but she'd be expected to maintain liaison and assist in the initial investigation: securing and searching, making properly identified photographs, keeping field notes with an area map. Mostly she was supposed to prevent damage to forest resources, but she could cooperate in felony proceedings, serve search and arrest warrants, enforce laws, conduct investigations—things like that.

If it did turn out to be a Forest Service employee who was the fatality, there'd be a case report in duplicate to write for the LE supervisor. But if it was *murder* of a Forest Service employee, which form would be required? Oh frabjous day.

Half an hour of driving a little too fast took her to Mill Park. She stopped and keyed her mike, hoping Josy had pulled the hand-held before she left her truck. "Patrol 3-4, I'm at Mill Park. What's the best way in?"

"I came in on the two-track that turns east just before you get to Mill Park. It's dry and passable, but it's rocky. Keep coming southeast for a couple of miles. And Meg, you might want to avoid the tire tracks in the dirt if you can."

"In your estimate they're evidence?"

"No. *Lack* of evidence."

The whole forest was listening. "Josy, go to crew." Now the whole forest had switched channels.

"Patrol 3-4 on crew."

"What is it about the tire tracks?"

"There was that rain Thursday. When I came in, I figured only one truck had come in since then. I think it belonged to—to the fatality. Now there are my tracks. That's all I've seen while I've been walking."

"Nobody's ahead of me?"

"Just me. I thought maybe if you could watch for any tracks that I might have missed, we could stop everybody before Black Tank and walk them in. That's about a mile from, uh, the fatality."

Good for her, she wasn't mentioning names, a definite no-no. "Tracks are clear enough for evidence from there?"

"Affirmative."

"Be there in a jiffy."

"Take your time, it's an awful road."

It was an awful road, all right. Ten miles an hour was the best she could do, and there was hardly a minute to look at the tracks. She could see what Josy meant—the rain had left dirt looking as if it had been raked. Where one set of tracks didn't over-lay the other, she stopped and got out to look. She could identify Josy's by the rear dualies. The others were deeper, as if they had been made on a wet road. It looked like both trucks had gone through only once, but she'd let Detective Sergeant Bailey make that call.

Twenty minutes later she spotted Josy ahead in her green uniform, dark hair tied up under a cap. She came around to the driver's side.

"You know what, Meg? I think it's Jake Holding, but I didn't go close enough to be sure. He smells pretty strong."

"You didn't investigate?"

"I left my truck and ran."

"That's good." She pulled out camera and notebook and a roll of yellow flagging and slammed the door. "Will you stay here and hold the troops until I photograph the tracks?" Didn't she sound professional though. "I'll call when I've secured the scene."

"Sure."

"It's a mile?"

"About. Maybe more. You'll see prints of my fire boots. I didn't notice anything else except elk."

$\mathcal{D}$own at the lake two miles away tiny trucks speed along the road raising plumes of pale dust. She tells Venn, "Law enforcement is going out to the ridge. There's a fatality and Josy is flagging the road." She begins to cry. She's so relieved, so *relieved* that Jake is dead.

She goes back to the paper, wiping tears before they can spoil the drawing...beyond the green pines with yellow in the branches, the lake as it was in May at sunset. Three blues, lavender, pink and yellow with a little orange, just a touch because it could bring the lake too far forward.

She knows she should be sorry Jake is dead. He was kind at first, last April when she started work on the tower. Once in June he came by to take her with him to scout where elk bedded down at night, close to water, he said, the forest was so dry. He was a good outdoorsman.

Randy told her that Jake was a bad supervisor and most people didn't like him. He was buddies with *his* bosses, with the FMO and the lead clerk...anybody who could help him get what he wanted. But when it came to lowly firefighters, it was one damn dominance display after another. "Chew your face right off your head." Randy knows a lot of old songs.

But she thought maybe Jake would be her Jesse Smith, and she drew his hands in pen and ink to show how strong they were. He was nice at first and made her laugh. When he took an engine strike team to a fire near Kingman, she worried about him...

She was six maybe, sitting in the rocking chair in Beste's bedroom, using her whole body to make it go...She liked to sit there and look at prints of Lillian's paintings on the walls. *Rainbow Bridge* the colors of candy, *Walpi* blue and purple by starlight. Wonderful paintings alive with color.

Beste was her own special name for her grandmother. "I had a *bestemor* of my own. It's Norwegian." But the end of the word was hard, so she just said Beste.

Through the door she heard Beste at tea with her friends. "You know she was Zane Grey's mistress."

"Martha, you don't know that. You shouldn't bear false witness."

"Well, you know how men are."

"Yes, and I know what love is for a woman. I'll not speak ill of what a woman does for love." That was Beste.

"He didn't take her along on all those trips for nothing."

"She was his wife's cousin."

"Oh, for heavens sake, Alice, that doesn't mean anything. He was handsome and famous and adventurous. How could she have separated him from Art and Arizona?"

"There never has been any proof that I heard, just gossip."

"It didn't look good."

"That's no proof of anything."

Beste's voice again. "If there was a romance, then good for her, I say. I hope she was blessed by it."

"And Martha, Jesse Smith met her on those trips, he would have known if anybody did. He and Lillian went on traveling with Mr. Grey after they were married. Jesse Smith was a good man."

"Jesse Smith was as good a man as there ever was. He could do anything—except make a lot of money." Somebody laughed.

"So much the worse for Lillian."

"There never was a better man to his wife. Money's not the measure of a good husband."

"That's true, Louise. He was a hard worker. Many a man didn't see the crash coming. Many didn't face it with his disposition."

"There used to be gossip that he was a Navajo."

"I don't believe it. He could speak the language, the whole family could a little, but that's no proof."

"I heard he had a Navajo wife and a son who was a code talker during the war."

"I wouldn't be surprised, a young man who lived up there all those years, it would be no more than you would expect."

"These days a man would be proud to have a son who was a code talker."

"I was told his mother killed herself in front of them, in Lillian's house. Walked into the room with a pistol and put it to her head and pulled the trigger. Was that true?"

"I heard rumors of something terrible, but I'm not sure that was it."

Lillian's name caught her attention, but the rest of the conversation didn't mean anything…it was someone Beste knew a long time ago, the painter of the colored pictures.

"I bought the lithographs because Lillian needed the money," Beste had told her. "I've never been sorry. It cheers me to look at them first thing in the morning and know that a woman could be so alive, so in love with the world."

She watched Beste's face the rest of the afternoon, looking for a clue to color. What other reason for painting was there?

*L*eaning against the truck, Josy watched Meg stop down the road and bend over with her camera to her eye. They had known each other a long time—their great-grandmothers had been friends.

Sun was hot. She moved into shade and sat down on pine needles. The hand-held came to life. "Flagstaff, 3-4 on the scene." Meg was there already, with that awful smell.

"Copy, 3-4 on the scene."

"Patrol 3-4, when Bailey arrives, it's up to him if he wants to come on in his truck."

"Copy. I think I hear him now." She stood and brushed off the back of her uniform pants.

Detective Sergeant Bailey, not too old, forty something, was wearing a brown uniform and a heavy belt full of weapons and such. Advised that Meg had examined and photographed the road, he decided it wouldn't do any harm to drive closer. "Climb in, I'll take an initial statement.

No time was wasted in pleasantries. "Start at the beginning and give me every detail you can think of."

He was driving the rough road faster than she had. Holding to the door handle, she talked about the vultures and tire tracks on the road, only one set, no footprints. He could see for himself up ahead. The flies, the smell, the top of a head visible.

"Did you approach any closer?"

"I left my truck where it was and *ran.* There was a nauseating smell."

He stopped as soon as a patch of truck was visible through the trees, maybe an eighth of a mile away, and walked on in. Meg was tying flagging across the road, watching the ground as she went, a bandanna across her lower face. It probably wasn't doing much good.

OK, she sat on the ground under a tree and watched Bailey fit a mask over his mouth and nose before he walked up to Meg and spoke to her briefly. Stepping carefully, he went on to the sleeping bag and bent over it, took his radio off his belt. She'd *told* them somebody was dead, but hey, he had to see for himself.

If they didn't want her to move her truck, it was going to be a long wait. She dug the heels of her fire boots into the duff, turned the lugs on the soles out. Vultures were still circling. What could she think about that wasn't too depressing?

School maybe. Just being on campus again after ten years had been a huge step. She'd pulled into a Visitor Parking space in front of Old Main. She loved that original part: the old red sandstone building, steps that went up to the street, trees with sunlight filtering through them. None of it had changed since she'd dropped out.

She'd gone to windows in the Administration building and asked questions. No, there would be no problem about credits since she'd be enrolling as an undergraduate: transcript would be internal. Yes, she would still be able to file her application. She hadn't said anything to Walt about it—he'd jeer at her for being an over-age student. She'd left the papers and catalog in her truck at work, not because she'd been trying to hide it from him, not exactly. Just—she'd been excited, and she didn't want him to spoil the feeling.

*B*ailey had handed her a roll of red and yellow tape, it probably wouldn't contaminate the scene if she tied flagging to the trees fifty feet back. "That ought be be far enough. Don't walk any place else. Watch every step, look for cartridges, hair, footprints. Tag anything that looks suspicious. You got tweezers and baggies?"

"Back in my truck."

"Never mind, we'll get more people out here. Here, I've got an extra mask. Doesn't do a whole lot of good, but better than nothing. Takes me days to get the smell out of my nose. I don't know why. You get photos here yet?"

"A few of the scene from this position, the truck, the clearing."

"We'll do the body, get the head from every angle before we unzip the bag."

"Ok by me."

She'd found not a single footprint, no trace evidence, nothing. Bailey was wearing a white paper mask over his nose and mouth. He passed close enough to say, "Looks right now like the cause was one shot to the head." Law Enforcement was more fun than a barrel of cookies.

One shot to the head. After a rain storm someone had come up quietly and fired a bullet into the brain of a sleeping man and walked away without leaving footprints? That kind of ground—half an inch of pine duff on shallow soil with underlying basalt—not favorable for tracks, but she must have missed something.

Even inside the mask, the smell was sickening. The only bodies she'd seen had been in coffins in mortuaries, looking like painted wood. This one, what she could see of the face was black and swollen, hard to tell whether it was Jake. It was a relief to back off, as far as she could and still be professional, and make notes for a LEMARS report.

People in an official vehicle arrived, parked behind Bailey's rig and walked in. He told them to stay back until he'd finished looking the ground over. They were complaining about the road before they got their masks on.

She walked her flagging again, carefully, looking to either side as she went. Nobody said not to. She stopped now and then to shoot the scene from different angles and noted the position in her log. Again, no footprints. There had been rain, there should be footprints. Not even a chindi carried a pistol, did it? There had to be some human sign left somewhere—something she wasn't thinking or seeing. She looked for moccasin prints, for pine needles scuffed up. Nothing back in the trees, out in the road—nothing.

She noted the time in her log, listed procedures she'd taken, and sat in shade to think. Amazing what happened to a body when vital processes stopped.

Josy came up carrying her fire boots. "You know what, Meg? I walked in the trees instead of on the road, and I could do it the whole way with hardly a mark."

"Have a seat. Stepping on rocks and pine needles?"

"Where I could. And I put my feet down softly. I don't know if I could do it by moonlight."

"On wet ground."

"Right. Is it Jake?" She sat down and pulled her boots on.

"Probably."

"Dead?"

"No doubt about it. Not merely dead, most sincerely dead."

Tightening the laces: "Could you tell what killed him?"

"Bailey says it appears to be a bullet in his head."

"Jeesh. Any clues?"

"*I* didn't find any."

"Meg, he's been giving me a hard time all season. Do you think I'll be a suspect?"

"Everybody at the station will be a suspect. Everybody who knew him. He wasn't exactly Kermit the Frog."

"What a mess. Bad influence goes on and on, you notice?"

"Here comes Bailey."

There were wet crescents under his arms. He sat in the shade and pulled his mask down under his chin. "Damn, it's hot. You find anything, footprints, trace evidence like hair, fiber? Shells?"

"Not a thing."

"Neither did I." He fanned his face with his notebook. "I can't figure no tracks around the body, it looks like close range. There's gotta be a clue somewhere, killers almost always make a mistake. But you know what they say: a crime scene isn't a crime scene after it sits a couple of hours. Wind can mess things up."

"An empty shell might look attractive to a wood rat."

"Now, I didn't think of that. Or the weapon was a revolver—those babies hold on to their evidence. Listen, we won't need you here from now on. As a cooperating investigator, you're welcome to stay if you want to, but it won't be pretty. We're ready to open the bag, which will be seeping with body fluids. Bound to be maggots hard at work. But you can stay if you want to."

That was more death than she was ready for at the moment. "Thanks for the invitation—I think I'll pass."

"I don't blame you, I never get used to it. Also, you're entitled to be present at the autopsy. Probably be late this afternoon. Ever seen one?"

"That's a show I've avoided so far."

"X-ray and toxicology, if indicated. Microphone above the table for a voice record. With the head wound, there'll be an incision, scalp peeled clear back, top of the skull cut away, maggots lifted out of the brain—their stage of development will help to establish time of death—then the torso opened."

"Bailey, are you trying to make us sick?"

"Most people get sick their first autopsy. All right, I won't expect you. Don't notify anybody, I'll get next-of-kin from your office clerk and assign an officer to inform the family personally. What I'd like is for you to make a list of people at work I should interview, his friends, folks who didn't like him, who knew where he'd be camping, anybody you know who had a fight with him."

"It'll be quite a list."

"Not popular?"

She shook her head.

"Well, do what you can. A murderer is usually someone known to the victim." He grunted as he stood.

"O.K."

"I don't want to move that big green rig until we're finished. Could you take..." he glanced at Josy's name plate "...Ms. Kirkman back to town with you?"

"Sure. No problem." They both stood and brushed pine needles from their pants.

"You can probably bring her back to get it in the morning. Can you do that?"

"Somebody can."

"Fine, then. Thanks for your help. I'll be talking to you tomorrow."

*T*here's a locked gate at the foot of Woody Mountain. For more than four months Dad hasn't been able to surprise her by coming up to see what she's doing. At home he gives her privacy when she's working because he knows he shouldn't bother an artist. The rest of the time he's always at her with things she should do instead of what she's doing. Years ago painting became, like, a refuge, a place she could be free in. Homework was a refuge. The *bathroom* was a refuge. At least there was a lock on the door.

For five years she hasn't been able to sleep without pills, some non-prescription stuff from the drug store...without them she lies awake in the dark, four, five, *six* hours, growing more and more tense. Last winter Dad found the pills and took them away because he said she'd be addicted first thing she knew. She didn't *care*, she couldn't face nights thinking about what a fool she was. She bought more pills and kept them in her pocket always so he wouldn't find them. At night she put them under her pillow in case he came to search her room when she was asleep.

This summer she's gone home on her days off to do her laundry, but she can leave early because he agrees that she should get through the gate before dark. She hasn't felt so free since she was a little girl.

On clear afternoons she can see the rosy colors of the Painted Desert far to the east. Small clouds above it are pink on the bottoms...reflected color. South down the ridge is the apricot of the tops of the Oak Creek cliffs. Violet-green swallows speed past on the wind with a sudden silver shine when they wheel in sunlight. A Western tanager the shades of oranges and lemons flutters among the oak branches, golden against olive green. A raven sits in the pines looking at the cabin and *saying* something.

Hummingbirds perch on the cabin lightning rod or the guy wires for the tower. When they turn their heads, they flash like rubies. Randy drew a diagram and explained interference colors, a breaking up of light in striations in the feathers.

"It's the same principle as beetle's backs and flies eyes," he said. "Trust me. I'm a college boy, I know everything." He has a Forest Service key, so he can get through the gate.

It was December. Randy came up to her room to tell her the district would need a new lookout for the Woody Mountain tower next summer. "I'll help you with the application and introduce you to Mitch."

She looked out the west window across the roofs of Flagstaff. Lillian had done two paintings from a fire tower. "Dad won't like it."

Randy sprawled in the big chair. "He won't be able to say you can't because he'll know right where you are all the time. I carry a crew radio so I'll hear you every day. Shit, Sarah, you're twenty already. I can see you now, an old lady with a cane still on five dollars a week allowance." He sang, "When I get older, losing my hair." Half the time he thinks in songs…

Low sun lit the NAU dome. "He says he's helping me be free to paint without worry about money."

"That's bull, and everyone knows it but Dad. He wants to go on running things. We've got an engine foreman like that. Engine specialist." His voice was heavy sarcasm. "Jake's so anal about being in charge that nothing gets done. We've all learned: don't think, sit down and wait for orders. That's what you call a management style. As long as Dad goes on telling you what to paint and how to do it, he'll do the same thing to you."

It was true. Dad said not to waste her time with anything but oils, which was where the career was—nobody buys watercolors. She thought of Winslow Homer, but she didn't say anything. She knew he'd argue that Homer's watercolors didn't really sell until he was dead, and he was thinking of her career. There's no defense when you have a lawyer for a father, you know?

"So how about it? It's perfect for you. It's not hard physically, you're up to it. You'd be busy when there was a fire, but the rest of the time you could paint. Tell you what, I'll give you Venn for the summer for company, she'd be bored around here anyway." He grinned at her.

She could talk to Randy more than she could to anybody. She didn't really have any friends.

"You wouldn't make enough money to live on your own. He'll realize that. But you'd have a few thousand to buy things or go places he won't authorize. Get your tongue pierced and a stud put in…" he made his tongue clumsy "…so people will look at it when you talk. You'll be way rad."

They laughed. She would never get away with it.

Dad was coming up the stairs. "Hey, you two. Dinner's on." Randy jumped up. "Okay." She whispered. "I'll try it."

He came close and bent to her ear. "We'll keep it secret for a while. All God's chillun need secrets."

There's nothing on the radio about Josy's fatality. It's like that when they all get "on the scene." A boy fell a hundred feet off the rim on Memorial Day, and the radio *swam* with messages about multiple compound fractures and a climbing crew and a helicopter, and there were appeals for speed because of a life-threatening situation. But when all responding units had arrived, there was no more traffic about it on the radio.

"What are they doing down there?" She sits on the floor and rubs Venn's head. Venn shifts a little for a tummy rub.

Beste chose the name. "My bestemor had an elghund too. She called it Venn, Norwegian for 'friend'."

"Jake was so proud of his hunting bow." She pulls on a fuzzy ear and bends to confide. "It isn't *nice* of me to think of myself. I *shouldn't.*" The dog's tail hits the floor twice. "But now I can keep the mountain forever if I want to."

*A*t least when Josy was driving, the steering wheel was there to hold on to. She'd tried conversation, but it was difficult given the way she was bouncing around. What a relief to get back to the main road and stop clutching the door handle.

"Aaarrgh. Is that smell stuck in your throat?"

Meg nodded and screwed up her face. "Like an oily film. Seems to me the dead animals I've smelled weren't that bad."

"Was Bailey getting off on letting us know we hadn't seen the worst part?"

"Definitely makes a death significant, I'll say that."

"Some days are just made to live in memory. I can hardly wait to see what comes next." They turned north toward the Peaks. "Probably fill us with awe and delight."

"Well, one thing is easy, anyway. I have to stop by Woody Mountain and pick up Sarah's time report. I couldn't get to it over the weekend and Lee was urgent this morning. It'll only take a few minutes. Do you mind?"

"No problem. My motto is, 'Do all you can to help the payroll clerk.' Next to Mama and Grandma, the most important woman in your life."

Josy leaned her head back against the seat. "I used to wish Jake would be transferred because he made the job so miserable. But with everybody a suspect, things are likely to be even worse."

"Whoop-ti-doo."

"I don't envy you having to draw up that list." She sat up abruptly. "Meg, I've heard Jake bragging about Sarah, you know, nudge nudge, wink wink, hinting that he could go up and see her any night he wanted to. Will she be a suspect too?"

"Crumb, I'll have to include her. How long has she known him?"

"Just a few months, since the season started. I was there the day she came in for her radio and binoculars. Jake was all charm and good humor, obviously trying to make an impression."

"I don't think I've ever seen her."

"I've been picking up her time all summer, I've probably talked with her more than anybody else has."

"What's she look like?"

"Average size. Thin, frail-looking. Kind of all over light brown: hair, skin, eyes. She wouldn't stand out in a crowd. She has these cunning little hands though, I can't stop looking at them."

"What do you think of her?"

"Well, you know, at first I thought she was as bland as she looks, quiet, shy, not—not very animated, not interesting."

"Beige through and through."

"Right, that was the impression. But she's an artist—she showed me some of the drawings she's made up there. She uses very bright colors. And she looks as if she cares what I'm saying, sort of concentrates on me, so I've sat there in the tower half an hour at a time telling her about Walt. I like her, what I know."

"What was she doing with Jake?"

"Maybe she wasn't doing anything—you know how men lie to each other about sex. But he can be, *could* be, appealing sometimes, especially if you didn't know him very well."

"I've seen that. He turned his charm on me once. Like a sticky bun—I wanted to wash my hands afterward. Yuk."

They drove in silence for a minute, climbing up onto the ridge, probably an old basalt formation. She wished she hadn't said anything. "Meg, look, look at the road."

"What?"

"There aren't any tire tracks. You can see it got rain on Thursday and nobody's gone in or out, there aren't any tracks. She didn't leave the mountain all weekend."

"Didn't drive out, anyway."

"Above the gate we can look for footprints to see whether she walked out."

"She could have stayed off the road."

"It's a good four miles cross-country down to Black Tank. Four back. It would have taken her all night. Wind was *howling*. I can't believe a skinny kid, an artist, would do it. She'd have had to leave the mountain as soon as she got off work and stay away from roads."

"There was a moon."

"Could *you* do it?"

"The question is, could *she*? I'd like to climb the tower with you when we get there."

Southeast and in her area, there's a white smoke. Hurrying, dreading the sound of another lookout's voice, she dumps her sketch pad and pencils off the firefinder...rotates the sight...lines it up on the smoke, counts the marks twice to be sure she has it right. Maybe no one else has *seen* it yet.

In April and May she spent hours learning the landscape. Every hill, every road. She knows exactly where the smoke is, and it's easy to decide on the map how far away. She can't *believe* no one has called it yet. Clearing her throat, taking a deep breath, she picks up the mike.

"Flagstaff, Woody Mountain. Fire Flash." The other lookouts will all be looking around saying "Where?"

"Woody Mountain, Flagstaff."

"Small, white smoke. 145 degrees, 30 minutes. Seven miles. East of I-17 at Kelly Canyon." It's a beautiful smoke, strong and full, probably an abandoned camp fire, it's so close to a road.

Now they've seen it. Crosses come fast through the radio. "Elden, cross, 200 degrees 30 minutes." "East Pocket, cross, 40 degrees." "Kendrick, 158 degrees 30 minutes." They can all see it, but it's, like, *hers*. Flagstaff dispatches Engine 5-4 and the water tender. 5-34 says he's responding. So do 5-33 and Patrol 5-4. When they arrive, it won't be her smoke any more.

If Josy is too busy to come up and get the work time report, she'll call it in by radio tomorrow...it won't be a problem, there's no overtime. "Base eight," she'll say. Randy taught her that. "No harm sounding like you know more than you do, long as you're not working on the car."

At 16:30 Venn begins to whine. She hears a truck coming up the road through the oaks and looks down...green with a blue and red light bar on top, Randy calls it "the cop package." She can see that two people are inside. She can't see heads...the driver turns around behind the cabin and comes back to park under the tower. Josy gets out of the passenger door, looks up and waves...

*M*eg was breathing hard as they neared the top of the tower stairs. "And I thought I was in shape. Hold up a minute. Is there a chair up there?"

Josy stopped to rest on the fourth landing. "I never get used to it. We're at eight thousand feet. Maybe that's part of it, you think?"

It certainly was a different forest when you got above the pines. The sky was three-fourths of it, clouds and the miles of shadows they made. The Peaks were glorious, all those mountains to the north–they stopped her eye. Town amounted to hardly anything; the dome at NAU was the biggest building there.

"I didn't realize we'd be up in the death zone. Sarah must be Wonder Woman to climb this tower every day."

Josy's breathing was noisy too. "I don't know, she says she comes up ten minutes early in the morning so she won't be puffing when she goes into service."

"Good strategy."

Sarah pulled open the trapdoor above their heads. The instant impression was young, thin. Hair in two long braids. The voice was small. "Hi. Wait a minute, I'll step across the hole so there'll be room for you to come in."

They crowded into the tiny room, and Josy lowered the trap door. "I came by to get your time so Lee won't chew me to pieces." Bright and cheerful, playing the part naturally. "I couldn't get up here yesterday. This is Meg Pederson."

She reached across the firefinder to offer her hand. "Sarah. This is really a small duty station. But what a view. How far can you see?"

Sarah's hand was a little softer than she liked, even in a woman. "It's Jake, isn't it?"

"What?"

"The fatality. It's Jake, isn't it?"

"Why do you say that?" She hadn't expected to be on the defensive, not so soon, gimme a minute here.

"The legal. It's where he said he'd be, past Bob's Tank near the end of the road. It's Jake, isn't it?"

No point in lying. She sighed and pulled her note pad from her shirt pocket. Supposed to keep informed notes with details to refresh her memory "on what transpired."

"It probably is Jake. We don't have positive ID yet."

"How?"

"It looks like he's been shot."

"Who?"

"We don't know."

"He's so proud of his bow. He made it himself out of wood. It's recurved."

"You've seen it?"

"He brought it up here to show me."

She wanted to maintain control of the interview, if possible. "Do you have a bow?"

"Oh no. I have a pistol Randy bought for me." Sarah looked at Josy. "Jake came up sometimes to tell me what I'd done wrong on the radio. Supervisor's job, was what he said. Sometimes he'd talk about himself for a few minutes."

"Hey, that must have been loads of fun."

Control, if possible. "Do you have it here? The pistol?"

"It's in the cabin. Randy said I have to be able to protect myself."

"May I see it?"

*J*osy stayed in the tower to watch for smoke while Sarah and Meg went down to the cabin for the pistol. Cumulus clouds were beginning to merge across the north and turn dark on the bottoms—there might be a storm soon. It was wonderful being up in the air surrounded by weather, miles and miles of air and weather. Wind was fresh through the tower windows.

Little volcanos in all directions—look at them!—the newest rock in northern Arizona, hinting at faults and vents deep underneath. All deposited on top of layers that were millions of years older. On the Colorado Plateau earth history was everywhere you looked and everywhere you went. If you knew anything at all, you couldn't ignore it.

Clouds were really closing ranks over there and getting dark, it looked good for a storm. With no warning at all, a bright flash of lightning stabbed down out ahead of the clouds right into land still in sunshine. Then there was another strike—fast, like a rattlesnake.

She picked up Sarah's binoculars and focused them to her eyes. There wasn't any smoke visible out there. What was she looking at? She adjusted the firefinder ring, peered through the sight, checked the map. Hart Prairie! She hadn't realized the elevation on the prairie was so high.

Through the binoculars she saw another strike hit a tree. There was no smoke, maybe it would take a minute. She'd never been on a fire tower to see a storm and look for smoke. What fun!

Cloud shadows were creeping south across Rogers Lake. Thunder behind her. Turning with the binocs at half mast she saw that a light rain was falling above the golf course at Forest Highlands.

Then there was the Mt. Elden lookout's voice on the radio. "Flagstaff, Elden. Fire Flash."

What? She'd been *looking.*

"White top smoke in Schultz Pass. 327 degrees. Four miles."

She turned toward the Peaks. There it was. It had probably been there all the time. Just like life: while you were watching one thing, something else was going on behind your back.

She shouted down to the open cabin door. "Sarah!"

Meg appeared, holding a big baggie with what looked like a pistol in a holster, Sarah behind her. Both faces were looking up.

"There's a smoke in Schultz Pass. And lightning in two separate places. What shall I do?"

Sarah started for the tower stairs.

$\mathcal{M}$eg takes the pistol away down the road and off the mountain, and Sarah's glad. She's never liked it. Meg doesn't seem to think she's a serious suspect.

If she's called in for questioning, Dad will have a good lawyer, one of his friends to represent her, so she won't face it alone. But she hopes it won't go that far. She doesn't want him to have any reason to keep her from being independent. She's always done what he wanted, mostly, and that's won his praise...he says she's exactly the kind of girl he wants his daughter to be. He's proud of her...

Sometimes when she isn't home, he goes into her room and searches drawers, books, her paint box and sketch pad, to be sure she doesn't have anything he disapproves of. She hates it.

She's appealed to her mother for help and gotten no where. "What's Dad *looking* for? I don't have any privacy at *all.*"

"Oh, Sarah, he's just trying to be a responsible father. If you don't have anything bad, you have nothing to worry about."

"Mom, he even goes through my *tampons*! I can tell by the way he leaves the box."

"Don't shout, Sarah, it isn't ladylike. He thinks he should take time now and then to be sure he's guiding you into goodness."

It feels more like he wants to *own* everything. It's made her hide from him in her mind. The cabin on Woody Mountain is the first place she's ever had that's her own.

Under shadows the forest is almost black, but where there's space between clouds, sky's brilliant blue. Light stabs down and turns the drab pines into green flames. How could you convince a painter from someplace like Pennsylvania that the horizon miles away could be so clear and sharp? Sixty miles south Baker Butte is hidden behind dark rain.

People on Engine 3-2 have knocked down the Schultz Pass fire already. She wants to tell them that a black storm cell is coming toward them across the top of the Peaks, but maybe they can see it for themselves. There's a straight thick band of colors, not a bow, a *band*, above Mt. Elden, violet on the bottom and orange on top. Why isn't the spectrum bending? It doesn't make sense.

It sounds funny, but it's during storms that light can be best for color. The spring drought before rains came was hot, visibility was a hundred miles, and every line was clear and brilliant. But the light was hard and colors seemed to, like, *cower*.

It isn't just that Dad has to be in control of everything *she* is, he has plans for Randy too. "I have plans for my son. It's law school for him and then a place in my firm." Randy is interested in biology, but Dad doesn't ever really look at him, to see what *he* wants. He doesn't care what Randy does as an undergraduate. "Take whatever you want. It's grad school that counts."

At the dinner table Dad insists on debate…to sharpen skills, he says, and he criticizes what he calls "specious thinking." It's painful to sit there and listen.

It's like he waits for a chance. Randy was in a good mood one evening at the dinner table. "Today the wildlife biologist had this cool, three-foot-long stuffed trout. He was going up and down the hall with it showing it to everybody. It had great big brown eyes, and it was covered with fur. 'See, that's what we need,' he said. 'Fish with fur and big eyes. The loveable Bambi look. *Then* we'd get the public interested.'"

Late sunlight angling through the south window just missed Greg Hull's painting of the Grand Canyon. She laughed, imagining the big furry trout, and so did Mom. Dad laughed too, let Randy have his joke…then he asked. "Interested in what?"

"Oh, you know."

"No, tell me."

"Fish as living creatures. Worth saving instead of just worth catching. It's not glamorous being a fish specialist, especially if you're trying to save bonytail chub or something like that."

"Save?"

"From being killed off, rubbed out, erased. Fish have their place in ecosystems, just like any land animal. The trouble with fish is, they live in water." He put down his fork like he was tired.

"That's bad?"

"Out here in the West, water is all involved with agriculture and domestic use and legal rights and development and recreation. Ideas about biodiversity and conservation of native species, especially non-game, tend to get overlooked. All that fuss about releasing floods into the Grand Canyon: do you think they'd have done it just for fish?"

Dad sat back in his chair and looked interested. He loved a discussion with Randy. "Now, tell me what you mean by non-game."

She was sure Randy could see a challenge coming but wildlife meant a lot to him. "Creatures people don't try to kill for sport, or what they *call* sport. They might kill chipmunks or lizards or something like that for fun, but they wouldn't call it sport. I guess game is something wild that you'd eat and non-game isn't. An elk is game. With river fish, trout are game. Bonytail chub are "trash," especially if they're in the lake or reservoir where you're trying to catch trout. It's a question of human use."

"Do biologists object to sport fishing?"

"They wouldn't get anywhere fighting the Recreation sacred cow. And they like to eat trout as much as anybody. They just think other fish should be there too. *Need* to be there. A lake is an ecosystem that requires biodiversity as much as any forest or meadow."

"Do biologists object to human use?"

"It wouldn't do much good."

"Correct me if I'm wrong"...Dad said disarming things like that... "it's my impression that here in the West most lakes and reservoirs were created by humans."

"That's true." Randy's face began to look, like, *set*.

"Created for human use, to provide water for homes and farms. And electricity. What's wrong with providing for those?"

"Look, Dad, you're not going to get me to say that human needs should be ignored. Ecosystems are too complicated for simple answers, although that's are what we all provoke each other to. I won't even say that if there weren't so many people, there wouldn't be so much need. That's another discussion. Let's stick with fish and whether we should recognize their role independent of our opinions about Bambi eyes."

Dad's smile was huge. "Good! Good for you. Insist on following the original line, don't get diverted."

Randy ignored the praise. "It's hard to relate to fish, one to one, or any other way. Dolphins smile. Fish don't. In fact fish don't have much of *any* expression, now that I think of it."

"Hard to imagine being friends with a chubb?"

"Exactly. Did you ever hear about the rotenone poisoning behind the Flaming Gorge Dam on the Green River?"

"No." Dad's smile was fading. "No, I don't think I did. Rotenone is a South American poison?"

"They dripped it into the river at several points on tributaries to kill off native fish so that there wouldn't be competition for the rainbow trout they wanted to stock. Practically sterilized the water in a huge system. It was a notorious bungle in the 1960s, had all kinds of consequences that weren't foreseen because they didn't know enough about river ecology and, more pertinent here, they thought one particular species mattered and the rest didn't. They didn't consider *fish*. When you start calling living organisms trash, you don't just do ignorant things, you do damn *stupid* things."

That patch of sunlight had moved beyond Greg Hull's painting. She looked at Mom's centerpiece, seeing the curve of the bowl and light on it, the shapes and colors of the flowers…tried to escape what she heard into what she saw.

Afterward Randy came up to her room and stood in front of the west window, looking out across Flagstaff.

"Sarah, it's bull, the my-son-the-lawyer. Every human cell contains three to six billion nucleotide pairs. Synthesis takes place at the speed of two amino acids per second, constantly for countless enzymes in every cell. There are two times six thousand seven hundred ways of shuffling genetic divergences."

She wasn't sure she understood all of that, but she thought she got the idea. It *was* boggling.

"Do you see how huge the differences are between individuals? It's awesome. Nature loves diversity, makes as many kinds of beetles as possible, for example. Why is it that people don't? Why do people try so hard to make everybody into copies of themselves?"

He jerked his arm into the air. "It's murder, that's what it is. If he could, he'd kill nine-tenths of what we are, and he still wouldn't get what he wants. It can't be done. Shit. It sucks."

She was afraid he might cry. "Everybody who tries to force what people *are*. It's wholesale murder. We should treasure the differences between us." Then he grinned and began to sing "You'll do it my-y-y-y-y way."

"What do you think?" Before they had made the first turn on the road, she was anxious for Meg to say Sarah was safe from suspicion. "Is she a cold-blooded murderer?"

"Guess I'd put her pretty low on the list."

"Above me or below me?"

A brief grin: "I'll put you together. Crumb, maybe I should make two lists, one male, one female. Are there any other women you can think of who'd have motives?"

She thought about it as she was unlocking the gate and waiting for Meg to drive through so she could pull the bar across the road and lock it again. Back in the truck, she thought aloud. "He was really a jerk to Karen when she said no the third time he asked her out. Harassed her, assigned her the dirtiest work. Wouldn't speak except to give orders on a fire. She transferred to Blue Ridge this season. You know, all he did was prove to her she was right."

"OK, Karen. Anybody else?"

"All the women on engines hated him. Didn't you? Jill after he called her husband to tattle. Jeesh! Myrna on Elden has been reporting safety hazards for two years and can't get his attention. The lookout over on O'Leary was furious, she showed up the first of May to complain that there was no water up there, no propane, no lock on the door, and a window was broken, and Jake told her lookouts were low on his priority list."

"He didn't play favorites."

"No, he treated everybody shitty one way or another. Cheap bully. I don't know of a man on engines who didn't despise him. He was good on fire, I'll give him credit for that. But he acted like he was the only grown-up in the shop and the rest of us were pre-adolescent. I don't have to tell you, you worked for him two years."

Rogers Lake was up ahead, the grass bright green through the trees. "You notice I don't work for him any more. I couldn't handle being that mad all the time."

The meadow looked scenic with all those cows grazing and the clouds beyond, outlined in gold by the sun. Over the ridge ahead, the Peaks towered dark and mysterious, partly obscured by rain.

"You know what, Meg? I just thought. Jake's job is going to be open, and Bob Dalton on Engine 3-1 will be a prime candidate for the promotion. He's really been frustrated lately. He's had eight years on engines, and he knows fire and he can do everything, including politics and paperwork, and I've actually seen Jake arrive on a fire Bob is handling just fine and say, 'First get a line around it,' like Bob was a newbie or something."

Meg sighed. "Motive is the first question when you have a murder. In this case that includes half the known world."

Lightning stabbed into the hill ahead. There was a heavy roll of thunder and a few drops of rain appeared on the windshield. She watched the road. By now there'd be gossip and suspicion all over the station. Everybody would have clues to offer to distract attention from themselves. Innocent people would feel threatened. "Meg, this is going to be really ugly. You know?"

"I'll bet a cookie, as grandma used to say." It was a sort of private game they played, quoting their grandparents.

*B*ack in the office the first thing she did was call the Coconino Law Enforcement supervisor to report and ask for direction. "It's a forest employee dead as a fencepost and the county has the investigation. Do I file a 6309.11? A case report? A cooperative law enforcement activity report? An investigator's report? What?"

"Yes. All the above. In full, in detail. You might be in court about this. Criminal Proceeding."

"Oh, Raleigh." He'd done her two-month field training himself, she liked him.

"Yeah, I know, it's a pain. But you got a homicide. You'll need a clean paper trail or a slick lawyer'll be all over you."

She sighed. "OK. Shall I tag the lookout's pistol and lock it in the safe or give it to the county?"

"Both. Put it in a box and lock it up right away. You'll need to establish chain of custody. Get yourself a witness signature if anybody's still around. Call the sheriff's office to notify that you have it. Let Bailey pick it up himself."

"Photographs?"

"Download photos into your computer as usual with a dated summary of the subjects and approximate time—right now while you remember so you'll be able to do an ID later. Don't forget the cable connection." The first report she'd done alone, she'd lost her photos because of a mistake with the cable.

"An area map?" Her head had sunk to her desk.

"Yep, eight by ten. Copy and keep a set with your reports. Ask Bailey if he wants one. Also give him copies of your reports. Send some to me too. Got any other material evidence?"

"Not yet."

"Get it all done before you go home if you can. The sooner the better. Far as I can tell, you haven't made any major mistakes so far. Get a signed statement from Josy about discovering the body and visiting the lookout. Write down everything, signed, dated, witnessed if applicable. As usual, hand-carry final copies to me for review and approval."

There was sudden thunder; rain began to hit the sidewalk outside. The storm they had outrun at Rogers Lake had caught up with her.

She hoped the lights wouldn't go out—she had reports to do. The LE handbook:

> The Cooperative Law Enforcement Activity Report provides a means to evaluate problems regarding the protection of people and their property and to monitor cooperator performance. Cooperative law enforcement agreements will be measured in patrol units; that is, 4 person hours of patrol equal one patrol unit.

She'd joined the Forest Service because she wanted an active job out of doors, for crumb sake. She finished the last of the paper work and called home. There'd been no fires on his district during the afternoon, maybe Hill had been able to leave the office at 17:00. Maybe he'd have dinner started.

"Nothing for you to pick up, darlin'. I'm building my award-winning chiles rellenos. They'll be coming out of the oven when you get here. You're allowed a Negra Modelo."

"Yay." She let herself out of the deserted building. Half a day shut in an office bent over a desk wasn't what she'd had in mind. "Where's that happy little girl that used to be me?"

Low western sun shone through a break in the cloud—brilliant light poured through. But the storm wasn't finished yet. More lightning flashed to the north. During dinner, thunder crashed and rolled in all directions. He'd heard her go out on the call from Josy—she'd been waiting to tell him about it.

"Definitely Jake?"

"Hey, you've surpassed yourself on the rellenos this time. It didn't look much like him anymore, but I'd say so, yes."

"And no evidence, no clues?"

"Not a Twinky wrapper. Not unless Bailey found something after I left."

"Any sign of something stolen?"

"His bow was still in the gun rack on the back window."

"What do you think?"

"Now this is just a guess. My bet would be Peter Pan. He could fly. OK, a small man, somebody Jake had humiliated who had to do something to save his pride but couldn't take him on in a fight. Somebody with woodcraft enough to find him cross-country and thin enough to walk light. Duvenek made that silly crack about shooting, and he's skinny enough, but he's too tall to have a grudge against the world."

"Seconds on the chiles? He wouldn't have done it."

"Maybe not. Sure, seconds. Ed Osborn hated Jake and wanted his job, but he's too physical to kill him like that. Tomorrow I think I'll wander out to the engine shop and choose the smallest crewman there for my prime suspect."

"Hey, Ms. Equality, why not a woman? From what I've heard, Jake was impartial, he insulted all genders."

"I just don't see a woman doing it. The women hated him, but they didn't have egos on the line. I mean, women have egos too, they're just more likely to handle the problem differently. File a harassment suit. Charge him with rape. Hit his reputation or his career. Shoot off his balls." After the day she'd had, it felt good to laugh. After the *summer* she'd had...

When the dishes were washed, they stripped off their clothes, turned on the shower, and stepped into the tub together. She liked that part of the day best, after they had soaped, standing under the hot water with their arms around each other. She closed her eyes and leaned her head against his shoulder, the insides of her arms against his back, feeling peace, breathing the moist air, washing the smell of Jake's corpse out of her nose.

"Your brother would say this is an immoral waste of water. I'd say we're using it for a very good purpose."

"My brother is an environmental Puritan. He has a twisted idea of waste—his wife probably never has any fun. By the way, I laced those rellenos with a strong aphrodisiac."

She pulled back and laughed at him. "Get outa here."

"Really. Feel anything yet?"

*T*he cabin is only eleven feet by fifteen on the inside, really small, but Sarah loves it. In nice weather it opens to the whole outdoors. She hasn't lit the propane lamps. With Venn alert beside her, she sits on the doorstep, hands clasped around her knees, watching lightning flash...when it's sky-to-ground, thunder booms, like, in a *unity* of sound...but when she sees cloud-to-cloud streak behind the tower, she leans forward to listen carefully. She's sure the sound *follows* the bolt, traveling across the sky in the same path.

Dad wouldn't approve of her sitting in the open doorway in a storm. If she were at home, he'd tell her to come inside and close the door. If she were slow to move, he'd pull her to her feet. She'd go to hide in the bathroom, angry and ashamed that she couldn't defy him.

So she'll never *tell* him. People who disapprove and criticize and try to control everything, you just don't tell them.

When lightning passes and a soft rain is falling, she closes the door and changes into her big pink t-shirt. Being in bed with covers pulled up to her chin, especially with rain and wind outside, feels safe. The world in her mind can be as colored as she wants it to be. She's always happy when she's in bed with a storm outside.

She likes to sit in the dark on the doorstep of the cabin, looking up at millions of stars. This summer, away from city lights, she's discovered stars, how thick they are everywhere in the sky. Dad would never let her go walking after dark. "You don't have sense enough to avoid danger, Sarah." So she's never really seen them…

Randy says there are an estimated million billion *billion* planets in the universe. She knows the stars are so far away she couldn't reach them in her lifetime, but they seem so close, part of her neighborhood. Maybe when Lillian came here, or when Beste was little, people could see how many stars there were from their backyards. Most people go their whole lives now without having the chance. She's lucky…

"He telleth the number of the stars; he knoweth their names." Until now she didn't know how awesome that would be.

$\mathcal{T}$here's a band of morning gold showing between the trees. In the cold air she can hear a train ten miles away rumbling up the grade out of town. Only five more days to wake up on her mountain, then classes will start again. She registered last Spring…on her day off last week she'd picked up the class schedule…

Venn is standing at the door, waiting to go out. Oh, and *lightning* last night! There might be fires burning already. She throws back the covers and finds her slippers before she remembers that Jake is dead.

In front of the cabin windows she sets out corn and dry dog food for ground squirrels…poor soft little things. In June Randy said if it didn't rain, they'd starve. She likes feeding them, having them close enough to watch. It's hard for the squirrels when there's no rain.

She needs to get up into the tower, there might be smoke. On the fourth day of the season, in April, she learned that lesson. The day before had been *painfully* cold with thick low clouds and a southwest wind blowing at forty miles an hour, according to the wind meter. She thought no one would be camping or hiking in such weather and it was *crazy* for a lookout to be shivering in a tower that shuddered and thumped and howled.

But next morning by 08:00…Randy had her using military time for Fire talk…there was an escaped camp fire with thick white smoke at Chimney Spring and another in Fay Canyon.

What surprised her was the heavy smoke south on Wilson Mountain, white with some brown in it, near the top of a steep slope. Hikers wouldn't have been up *there*, would they? Wind the day before had been making too much noise for her to hear thunder, but she hadn't seen lightning anywhere...it was *April*, there was never lightning in April.

Three lookouts could see the smoke. It was so high that motorists were reporting it on cell phones. The dispatcher in Flagstaff had sent two air tankers, an air attack plane and a lead plane toward Wilson Mountain...air restrictions for private planes were imposed in a two-mile radius. The district Hot Shots and the Blue Ridge Shots drove to the Sedona airport—from there helicopters shuttled them up to the top of the mountain.

Grass and trees on seven acres were burning. The crews put in a quick scratch line, and fire burned right over it...tankers dropped slurry, and fire crept through it. By noon the smoke had barely diminished. There was worry that when air got cold at night, smoke would flow down into Oak Creek Canyon and people would complain and stuff.

So this morning she hurries to finish breakfast and get up into the tower. After last night's storm there might be fires everywhere. A cold wind is blowing...there are lenticular clouds *stacked* above the Peaks.

The trap door is heavy slabs of wood. With her arms she can't lift it up over her head and back against the wall. In April she learned to climb up close under it and put her palms against it and then straighten her knees and walk the door up.

She waits for Venn to climb in behind her, closes the trap door against the wind and looks around carefully, all around her circle. No smoke's showing yet. Maybe when the air warms, sparks will come to life in the wind. She keys the mike.

"Flagstaff, Woody Mountain in service. Wind southwest five to ten. Precip .21."

"Copy, Woody Mountain." Celeste is in the office today.

Her raven has already flown down to take the food Venn left in the dog bowl. It looks *huge* compared to the hummingbirds. Visibility is at least eighty miles, close to a hundred maybe. Morning shadows are long.

For some reason district crews and engines and patrol people aren't coming into service on the radio, she listens for Josy but doesn't hear her. She wonders whether they've moved Jake yet...she didn't think of that yesterday, like, how they would move him. How many people would it take? Poor Jake, he would hate it to be so helpless.

Anyway, *she* can move. Tomorrow and Thursday will be her days off, and she'll have to go into town to do laundry and take a shower.

She's glad the days are shorter now…maybe Dad won't expect her to stay to dinner.

Beste's house was only three blocks down the hill, on Verde. She could go there whenever she wanted to sit and look at Lillian's paintings of Surprise Valley and the Bridge. Her paintings weren't dark and brown like some old paintings of the West or hard primary colors like some new ones. They didn't say look how clever this artist is. She loved the feeling for the land she saw in the pictures.

When she was fourteen, Beste told Dad about how she had liked Lillian's paintings for years, ever since she was practically a baby. So he bought Jim Babbitt's book on Rainbow Bridge so she could read about it. At dinner he had her describe it for Randy and prompted her if he thought she was leaving something out. All winter she thought about the trip. How hard it might have been for a woman from the city but how thrilling to travel through a land where people never went.

Dad got into it, as always. Probably he thought he was doing something wonderful for her…he decided to take the whole family to Rainbow Bridge. Not days and days on a horse the way Lillian did, riding and struggling over the land and being heroic. Up Lake Powell on a boat and back to Wahweap in nine hours. She could have cried.

The night before, they stayed in a hotel with television and bathrooms and views of the lake. Sunrise on the water and the far cliffs was beautiful, but there had been no dam, no lake when Lillian was there. They ate breakfast in a restaurant with big windows that curved around them…shut off from the air and the sounds Lillian knew. Then they went pounding up the lake on a noisy power boat with sixty-five talking people lined up in rows all facing the front. The boat captain was a young woman who made jokes on the intercom and drove them into side canyons. That was okay, she hadn't been expecting John Wetherill or anything and she was glad to see a woman could do it without anyone complaining. It just injured her dream…

They sat in sunshine on the open upper deck. Navajo Mountain was visible most of the way. Dad was very happy, talking the whole time, informing…geology and early explorers. He had spent a lot of money for the tickets, but he never gave her silence so she could try to find Lillian.

Rainbow Bridge was in sight before the tour boat docked. Around a bend in the lake and there it was, curving against the sky in sunlight. A place of power so beautiful that her throat got tight.

From the boat the bridge looked smaller than she expected. You could walk right up to it on a boardwalk and a smooth path…noise…colored shirts. Laughter. Cameras everywhere. A woman with white knees said, "Is this all there is to it?"

Hundreds of people came there every day with their motors and their cameras…made the arch trivial, no more sacred than Disneyland. For tens of thousands of years it had been hidden and solitary…Navajos wouldn't talk about it.

Now tourists looked at it a minute and took a few pictures of each other and got back on the boat. It hurt so bad she couldn't say anything…

"*H*ey, Henry. How you doing?"

"Pretty good, Josy. How 'bout you?"

"OK, I guess." Skinniest Navajo she had ever seen. You wouldn't think to look at him he could work a fire as hard as he did. Climb out of his engine and start cutting line without a word and still be digging when everybody else was sitting down. The tip of one of his fingers was missing from roping horses out on the res.

Usually she went to her truck first thing in the morning and put her lunch box on the seat before she came in to look at the board. Her truck had been sitting out by Bob's Tank all night. Oh jeesh, she didn't want to spend the day doubled up as somebody's passenger.

"So Henry, it's quiet in here." Most days at eight in the morning, sounds were bouncing off the metal walls and the high roof of the shop, and people were doing things to tools and engines or talking or walking around or filling out paperwork. It was kind of pleasant, all the activity of getting a new day started. On a usual day through the big double door you could see sunlight warm on the ground, and outside was bright with green trucks and yellow fire shirts. Government: people working. "Where's everybody?"

"Meetings. You're supposed to be over at the fire office."

"Why? What's going on?"

"The ranger says fifteen minutes from everybody. She wants to shut down the rumor mill right away if she can."

"Good luck. I mean, she's right, but imagine no gossip around this place?"

"And nobody's supposed to talk to reporters until we know more."

"That's another case of it's easier to say than enforce. Can't turn your back on an order, grandpa used to say; you've got to stand right there and watch or they'll go on doing it their own way."

"Anyway, patrols at the fire office. Engines over on the other side of the shop. There's a sheriff here."

She could have guessed. "Didn't take him long. What are *you* doing?"

"Waitin' to tell people where to go. Clerks and archaeology in the ranger's office, timber and range and wildlife and recreation in the conference room with Meg."

"How nice for morale. Gonna be another great day, I can tell."

"Pretty serious." He put an arm around her shoulders for a moment. She was surprised, she'd never known a Navajo to do that for sympathy. "It was Jake?"

"'Fraid so, at least so I'm told. I didn't get a close look. I guess everybody knew by the time they went home?"

"They heard you on the radio. They thought that's who it was. Pretty serious in here."

"I'm not sorry I missed it. OK, might as well stroll across the parking lot and join the fun."

There were only four people on the district assigned to driving patrol, out of what had been fifteen—budget cuts had them down to a skeleton crew. The other three patrolmen were standing in the hall outside the fire office looking out the window. The door was closed.

"Hi, guys. How's it going?"

Abby's face was tight around the jaw. "A county detective's in there with Mitch, but nobody tells us anything."

Evan was his usual cheerful self. "You could have left him there and saved everybody all this trouble. It's not as if anybody cared."

"The thought occurred to me last night."

"Don't be a smartass, Josy. We're gonna have cops up the ying-yang until they decide to slap one of us in jail."

Abby ignored him, which was the best thing to do if you could manage it. "Is Jake really dead?"

"So I'm told, I didn't make the ID."

"Shot?"

"So they say."

"An accident?"

"I don't think so."

"Murder?"

"You know what, I didn't get close enough to see much."

"Do they know who did it?"

Evan ratcheted up. "We *all* did, obviously. If they knew, would we be standing out here like a buncha fuckin' school kids?"

Shaeffer turned from the window. "Hey man, chill out. Pull up a chair, Josy. I'm glad it wasn't me that found him, must not have been any fun."

"I could have done without it. The smell was the worst part."

"Any sign of a struggle?"

"Nope."

Evan just couldn't stop. "You tryin' to play cop, Shaeffer, is that it?"

"You don't want any details? Too tough to be curious? You're relaxed this morning–you got something you'd rather nobody talked about?"

Gawd. She pulled a chair out of Duvenek's office, sat down watching cars go by out on the highway. Why wasn't she surprised? She'd said yesterday a murder wouldn't exactly bring out the best.

Abby shifted to stand beside her. "You should have seen the shop yesterday afternoon. People coming in from the field wanting to talk– was it Jake? Without knowing a thing about it, they all assumed somebody had killed him, like they'd expected it. They wanted to know who had the most reason, who hated him the most, and they started remembering things. But nobody was sorry the least bit. It was gruesome."

They all turned when the office door opened and Mitch looked out. "Hi, Josy."

"Morning, boss."

Bailey came out. "OK, Mitch, I'll be back in a minute. Which way's the ranger's office? Morning, Ms. Kirkman, get any sleep?"

"Not much."

"I didn't either, my first body. Hang in there."

Yeah, right. You know what? It wasn't too encouraging.

*J*ust before she graduated from high school, Beste invited her, her alone, to lunch at the old Clark house. They sat in shade on the porch in the spring breeze. Vines softened the straight lines of the bricks. "Have you and your parents talked about what you're going to do now that high school is, as they say, behind you."

Actually it hurt to talk about. She spread her napkin on her lap. "I want to go to the San Francisco Art Institute. It's wonderful, Beste. Less than a thousand students, only nine to a teacher. It's *awesome*."

"Butter for your bread? I've read of it, the oldest school of art in California. What's the tuition?"

She hesitated. "It's expensive. Almost sixteen thousand a year."

"Housing on campus?"

"No. No dorms. I'd have to rent an apartment."

"And you want to go away from home and be your own person?"

"Oh, *yes*, Beste. It would be so exciting."

"But…?"

"But Dad says no. He says NAU's the best place for me, and I'll live at home. He went to campus and got a catalogue. He's chosen my *classes*. Underlined the major requirements. He's very excited about it."

"Well. That does sound like him."

"Dad says I'm too young to leave home yet."

"You are young, it's true. Younger than you know."

"He says once I have a bachelor's we'll talk about it."

"Yes. Well. I thought he might. Well." Beste stroked her water glass. "I'm not sorry you'll be here a little longer. You will remember what I said about individuals?"

"Yes. I will."

"There's something Georgia O'Keeffe wrote that you might find useful. I'll copy it for you."

That was when she really learned about Georgia.

> I grew up pretty much as everybody grows up and one day seven years ago found myself saying to myself–I can't live where I want to–I can't go where I want to–I can't do what I want to–I can't even say what I want to. School and things that painters have taught me even keep me from painting as I want to. I decided I was a very stupid fool not to at least paint as I wanted to and say what I wanted to when I painted as that seemed to be the only thing I could do that didn't concern anybody but myself–that was nobody's business but my own.

$\mathcal{T}$he conference table was lined with range and wildlife and recreation people. Meg sat at the end–a stand-up performance was not her style. "OK, guys, let's get to it. Carol wants to shut down the rumor mill if she can, so I'll tell you what I know and what I don't. You've heard about the body on Woody Ridge yesterday afternoon?"

Heads nodded. "Tentative ID is Jake Holding. That's based on documents in the wallet, registration of the truck, personal items like a recurved hunting bow, but we can't release a name until next of kin have been notified. So until then, no positive name, OK?"

Nobody looked particularly guilty, but how did she know what guilt looked like? "Cause of death was apparently a single gunshot to the head"–she didn't say 'while he was asleep on the ground.' "We won't know definitely until we get an official report. The jurisdiction is county, so until they pass their findings on to us, all we can say is 'tentative' and 'apparently' to our curious friends and families and any reporters who track us down. Got that?" She hoped it was the right tone.

"'Least said, soonest mended' is old as the hills. Probably half our grandparents said that, and it's still good advice. Say as little about this as you can, and be sure that little isn't inference and assumption. Please. Soon as we have anything, I promise I'll tell you. Scout's honor." She held up three fingers and got a few smiles.

Connie supervised the Rec unit—they joked that her middle name was "Crisis Management." Everybody knew she'd had no use for Jake. "Nobody would guess suicide, but is there a possibility? Accident?"

She wanted to say it right. "I saw the body, and it didn't look like suicide or accident to me, but the only part I saw was the head. I can't say murder: I don't have enough info yet. I'd like to know too, but crumb, I can't say for sure."

Duvenek's long legs tended to sprawl even when he was serious. "Find any clues?"

"*I* didn't. I can't speak for the county. Sergeant Bailey is here, by the way, said he'd try to get around to everybody if he could. You can ask him, if you want to."

The ranger rounded the corner into the room, the only woman on the district, except for the receptionist at the front desk, who came to work in a skirt every day. Bailey was with her. She began to talk without looking at her LE officer, who was supposed to be in charge of the meeting.

"This is Detective Sergeant Bailey, the officer handling the investigation into yesterday's death on the district. I want you to pay careful attention to what he has to say." She was also one of the few who wore make-up. "If I hear of anyone fomenting unsubstantiated rumors, any talk beyond the sheriff's office information, I'll take it very seriously."

Oh, for crumb sake, these were grown-ups, Carol didn't have to be abusive about getting co-operation. Most of them really had tried to cut the woman every inch of slack they could, it was tough to move into a job that had been done by men for seventy years and know everyone was watching. But Grandpa would have said, "Who does she think she is, the Queen of Sheba?"

Bailey walked around the table and stood beside her chair. "Ms. Pederson has told you what we know at this point? I don't have any secrets." He smiled down at her, at all of them. "We're going on the indication that the dead man was someone you all knew, but we won't confirm that until later this morning, so for now we'll ask you to be as hesitant as we are with a name. Will you work with me and keep speculation to a minimum? Over the next couple of days I'll try to talk with you individually when your work won't be interrupted. Maybe you'll have some detail that will help me do *my* job. Thanks ahead of time."

He was probably saying the same thing in every room, but he made it sound sincere, a good-guy show. She could learn from watching him. So could Carol, but she probably wouldn't.

"Ms. Pederson, could I visit with you once I've met everybody? Say, half an hour from now in your office? Get the formalities worked out, won't take long."

"No problem."

"Good. See you all later."

Carol turned and left the room and Bailey followed. "I guess that's all we have to say right now. Thanks for your patience, I appreciate it. And I'm not suggesting that anybody tattle, but if you do know anything that might save us all a lot of anxiety, I'd be grateful if you'd pass it on. Not accusations or even guesses, I know you wouldn't do that. Just facts, OK?"

Within fifteen minutes two of them had stopped in her office to say they'd heard Duvenek say "Be easier to shoot him" and ask whether that's what she meant by fact.

Sarah wonders if it would mean anything to Randy, that quotation Beste gave her. If it would help. She doesn't think it's good for him to have to resist Dad all the time with no help. He told her once about an Aberts squirrel that was found dead with its teeth fastened around the bars of the cage it had been caught in…she thought it reminded him of himself.

Just before the season started, while she was still living at home, Dad was at him one night at dinner about whether rights of the federal government to legislate about wildlife had precedence over state rights. "As I understand it, a state controls by such agencies as Game and Fish the taking of wild animals within its borders."

"The feds have to have some jurisdiction, Dad. Animals aren't good at recognizing lines on maps. What are you going to do about migrating birds, for instance? Fish in rivers?"

"I'm talking about law. You're talking common sense."

"It's not the same thing, I guess."

"Well, we want law to be consistent with reason, but if you're going to get anywhere with an appeal, you need to argue statute and previous opinion."

She could see Randy, like, pulling his mind around. "Ooooh-kay. I'll see what I can do here. Uuuh. There are some limitations on state control, all right. In the 1920s there was that big deer drive on the North Rim."

"*Hunt v United States*, 1928, Hunt was the governor. State against federal, went to the Supreme Court. Very good. What was the decision?"

"It was Arizona's worst example ever of game mismanagement. Big blooper. Still referred to in forestry texts. No thanks, Mom, no more."

"I mean how was the case resolved?"

"Uuuh. It was on national park land, wasn't it? Decision was for the feds because it was a question of protecting public land from over-grazing, so responsibility for the deer belonged to the feds. Wildlife as property, state or federal, is a concept that's kept everybody debating through the 20th century."

"Exactly right." Dad was beaming.

"I seem to remember that around the turn of the century, it was pretty well established that there was a constitutional basis for the argu-ment that wildlife, that is, life that's non-human and non-domesticated, was a public trust not individual property so Congress could legislate. I don't have the names of laws or anything. No cases to cite."

"How about examples?"

"Examples. Well, there were wildlife reserves early in the century. Congress regulated killing game birds and fur-bearing mammals because the states couldn't do it alone. Had something to do with the Interstate Commerce clause in the Constitution."

"The Lacey Act, 1900."

"Couple of Supreme Court decisions not long ago?"

"Right. You're doing fine."

"Yeah, well, I *have* been a little interested in wildlife."

"Spent some time in the library, I suspect."

"Yes, sir. About 1918, Justice Holmes..."

"Oliver Wendell Holmes."

"...argued that wild birds, especially migratory birds, aren't possessed by anybody and thus aren't owned by anybody and thus the states can't claim title and thus the feds can protect them."

"That's about right."

"The Supreme Court has ruled several times that states don't have exclusive authority. Didn't Holmes say that state title is a slender reed to lean on?"

"He did."

"After a lot of fights over state's rights, federal authority over wildlife was established in some situations. That case thirty some years ago about killing deer in Carlsbad Cavern National Park was another one that said the feds could control wildlife to protect the land. Even if all they were doing was trying to figure out how to do it."

"Cited *Hunt* as precedent."

"Yeah. But challenges and appeals are still going through the courts. You wouldn't believe the number of challenges and appeals. I take that back—you probably would."

*I*f there were more than two people involved, you couldn't do *any*thing in fifteen minutes. It was nine o'clock before Fire was back in the shop and ready to scatter. Hang on, Mitch had said, and he'd drive her down to get her truck. Josy sat on the table next to her lunch box, swinging her boots.

Engine 3-2 was based at the station ready to respond to fires near town, and the crew did maintenance to keep busy. Randy came in from the middle room whistling. Preparing to sharpen fire tools at the grinder—he was wearing a leather apron and goggles pushed to the top of his head.

"Morning, Randy."

"Morning." He unplugged an orange extension cord and began looping it across his hand and around his elbow. "They tag your truck as evidence?"

"I wouldn't be surprised. Potential weapon—you never know until results come back from the lab."

"Right. Appearances can fool you. Science, that's what you need, not jumping to conclusions."

"Hey, you know, there's something I've been wondering about." It probably wouldn't hurt to ask. "Does Sarah have some trouble walking? Usually we just sit in the tower and talk, but now and then I've thought maybe there was a faint limp or something."

"She does, yeah, a little. Makes her self-conscious." The smile faded from his eyes.

"Was it an accident? Tell me if you don't want to talk about it."

He looped a final twist around the cord and leaned against a post. "No, it's not a secret. When she was ten she had tuberculosis in the tibia in her right leg."

"In the *bone*? I never heard of such a thing."

"It's apparently more common in lungs, or used to be anyway, but t.b.'s a nasty bacillus. It can grow in soil and hang in the air or get into food and water. We never did know how she picked it up. The doctor our family goes to had never seen a case, so he didn't diagnosis it at first. It's called osteomyelitis when it invades a bone."

"What does it do?"

"In bones it makes a hole, dissolves a cavity. Does the same thing in lungs, so I'm told, but there you can cough up the pus it produces.

When it gets into a bone, it destroys surrounding tissue until it reaches the skin and discharges. In early years treatment was surgical—they cut to allow drainage. Patient usually didn't survive."

"Jeesh! *Yuk*! That's awful!"

"My parents were afraid she was going to die. She was in bed for a year on all kinds of front-line drugs with long chemical names." He swung the wrapped cord against his leather apron.

"And she was cured?"

"Apparently t.b. isn't cured, just arrested. The bacillus can encyst and be isolated but if conditions are right—mal-nutrition or serious stress or unsanitary conditions—it can break out and start gnawing away again."

"Is that why she limps?"

"The tibia is weakened because of the hole in it, or so I understand. And a fraction shorter than the other one. I think my parents have been too protective. Tried to keep her away from physical activity because the bone could break. Dad wouldn't let her hike or do any sports; until high school she wasn't allowed to walk to school. For a long time her outdoor activity was sitting on the deck in the shade. She grew up pretty much alone except for the family."

"Oh, no fair. Poor little kid."

He sang, "All the lonely people, where do they all come from?"

She smiled. "It's good she has the lookout job then. It gets her outside without big demands. She can do whatever she feels up to. Does she have any trouble climbing the stairs or going down?"

"Not that she's mentioned. She uses a backpack so she'll have a hand free for the rail. Well, gotta get back. Good luck, hope they release your truck."

She sat there alone in the big room, swinging her feet. First chance she got she'd tell Meg about Sarah's leg. *That* ought to eliminate her from any list of suspects, not if she'd have had to walk miles through the forest at night. Good. She didn't want the killer to be a woman.

There was a wonderful story way back in her family about two women who grew to be such friends, different as they were, fifty years different, that there was a kind of love between them. That was when love didn't always mean sex, and for another woman it didn't mean you were lesbian.

She'd been told the story all her life. "You were named for the woman who came to Arizona from New York because she had tubercu-losis. She rented a room in your great-grandmother's house, and they became friends. When the t.b. was cured, the New Yorker returned to the East, but she came back and stayed on with your great-grandmother right until the end, and then she married Meg's great-uncle."

She heard that story over and over when she was growing up and never got tired of it. It wasn't sappy or anything, but her throat got tight when she thought about people being friends years ago, and her name coming to her from someone who was only a memory. The past was never dead. It got longer all the time, always going on, always continuing into tomorrow.

*M*eg had been up since before sunrise on a rescue below Devil's Chair on Mt. Elden, a hiker who'd fallen and broken a femur. Search and Rescue had pulled her off a wall when she was in high school, but this guy had needed saving twice since June. Crumb, what was the point of living if you didn't learn anything?

The scanner was on Flag PD frequency, some kind of situation at the coffee shop on the Fort Valley road with traffic re-routed, several units on the scene taking shelter behind a wall. Something about a suicidal man holding hostages, expected to come out and surrender, keep the helicopter back. There was apparently a fall victim in Jack's Canyon, the Long Valley LEO was on it and DPS Ranger 3-2 with a long line. A wreck of some kind down at Blue Ridge.

It was easier to deal with illegal woodcutters taking green oak, vandalism at Elden Pueblo, violation of a road closure by bikers. Except that the men always thought it was ever so cute to read the name plate pinned on her right pocket—it clearly said Law Enforcement—and call her Meg, as if they didn't have to take her seriously. The ones who disgusted her most called her a tree pig, a terribly clever joke they'd just thought up. It was apparently hilarious to refer to her nine millimeter Sig as artillery. It wasn't a joke: semi-automatic, fired two or three rounds in a couple of seconds with little recoil.

On her belt she also carried two extra magazines, a twenty-six inch ASP collapsible baton, pepper spray, and handcuffs in a holster. LE was a laugh a minute, to coin a phrase.

Twice she'd started on a list for Bailey and chucked it. OK, gotta be done. At the top of the screen she typed: "Nobody liked Jake Holding. Some of the district staff didn't hide their anger, even hatred; others may have kept their feelings to themselves." She moved the cursor, deleted "their" and "them" and inserted "our": her name should be on the list too. "Every one of us (40 in Fire alone) is a possible suspect. A list of the more likely follows."

She made two columns under her initial paragraph—Men and Women and underlined the headings. Best thing to do would be to work fast in no particular priority without thinking that she was making a Most Wanted poster, but she was looking at the wall. She really couldn't say who was most likely, least likely. Finally she deleted her headings and typed: "All the people on district Fire, including patrols and lookouts; people on other districts cannot be excluded."

She'd retrieved a copy from the printer down the hall before Bailey appeared in her office doorway. "Sorry, it took longer than I thought it would. Talkative bunch of people."

Careful of his gun belt, he sat down heavily in the extra chair. "Whoosh! It's official: Jake Holding. Single gunshot to the head, penetration, trauma to the brain. Sometime Thursday night. Close range, no more than three feet away, probably from a pistol held by someone standing. Bullet's gone to the DPS lab."

"Well."

"No other sign of violence. Pooling of blood in the body indicates he was lying on his left side and never moved—about what we figured. So it looks like there's no question of criminal intent, and we've got a homicide. I sure hate the paperwork."

"Yes." Investigation of a felony was not her responsibility—he must have a reason for keeping her informed.

"I can't figure how somebody could have stood no more than three feet away on wet ground and not left a print next to the body. Damndest thing I ever saw. The team found a blond hair on the flag line you stretched, probably yours, but DPS'll analyze it. A lotta animal hairs— wouldn't be surprised if they bagged a few to keep the microscopist on her toes. No trace evidence of the perp on the ground, on the sleeping bag. That rain last night's gonna make it damn near impossible now."

She nodded. She doubted that Detective Sergeant Bailey, sworn and commissioned career peace officer who had passed both written and oral tests, was as folksy as he seemed.

"Got a list of prime suspects for me?" He took the paper from her. "Well! He must have been quite a guy. We'll see where they all were on Thursday night. I'm gonna need some help, I'll talk with my lieutenant and your Special Investigator. Any place you think we should start with these folks?"

"Fire, but most of them have gone out into the field already, won't be back until late afternoon. You could ask Mitch to call some of them in early. Engine 3-2 crew is stationed here, you could start with that. Lookouts are always in one place, if you want to get them out of the way. You'll enjoy the roads up to Elden and O'Leary. Get a Forest Service key before you go: locked gates to get through."

"Thanks. We already got a statement from Kirkman. I read through your report on the lookout on Woody Mountain."

"You got up early."

"Some days I'm tempted to retire so I can sleep in. What's your size-up on her?"

"Sarah? Unlikely, but there was gossip about a possible relationship with Jake. Unconfirmed."

"What about you? You got an alibi?"

"The early part of the evening–I was out on a false alarm at Fry Lake and it would have been easy for me to swing by Black Tank afterward. I got home before midnight. My husband can confirm that, but he's Fire on the Mormon Lake district so he's a possible suspect too. He and Jake have–had?–the same job on different districts, and there was no love lost."

"The plot thickens."

"So they say."

"Now, Raleigh says you've got a pistol for me?"

She stood. "It's in the safe."

Bailey pushed with his hands on his knees to help himself up. "Good, good. Pleasure to work with you. You're doin' fine."

"Thanks. Compliments are good for your health, as Grandma used to say." What advice would Grandma have had for a law enforcement officer? Something funny, probably, she was a one-woman party right up to the last farewell.

*L*ate in the morning Venn begins to growl. Her raven is, like, *threading* through air between the pines without moving a muscle. The Bronco is white with a light bar on top. She can see only parts of the man inside as he turns around behind the cabin and comes back to park. Thighs. A shoulder. He looks broad. When he gets out, she sees mostly the top of his head...thick hair, dark with some grey in it. He climbs heavily, each foot on a step shakes the tower.

Venn begins to bark. She takes a grip on the collar and opens the trap door. "It's all right, Venn. It's all right."

He climbs into her little room breathing hard, so big he fills one whole corner. Venn moves her nose up and down his leg...smells his shoes.

"Morning. Len Bailey." He stretches out his hand and shakes hers. "County sheriff's office." She can see it on the name plate on his brown shirt. His hand is as big as two of hers. There's a pistol on the big belt he's wearing.

"I'm Sarah Findlay. Take that handle there in front of you and close the trapdoor, will you?"

He drops the door, and she's closed in with him. His face is strong and, like, *fleshy*.

"Let me look around. Helluva view. Is that Lowell Observatory?"

People always ask that when it's perfectly obvious if they'd just look. "The Naval Observatory. They measure distances between stars, I think. Lowell is over there just above town. See the tops of the domes?"

"Oh, yeah. Of course. Town looks pretty small from here."

Venn lies down and sighs. "The lights are beautiful at night. I come up sometimes after dark to look at them. You don't realize when you're down there how many *colors* the lights are."

"You're not up here at night usually?"

"I'm in the cabin on the ground. Would you like to sit in the lookout chair? It's the only one I've got."

"With the driving I do, it's a pleasure to stand now and then. How long do you stay up here?"

"Usually eight hours a day. Longer if there's special fire danger. Sometimes ten or eleven. This is my first year." She sits on the window seat and curls her legs up...realizes she's trying to fold her shoulders around her chest and sits straight.

"How'd you get the job?"

"My brother helped me. He works on an engine at the Peaks ranger station, earning summer money."

"Randolph Findlay the Third. Met him this morning. Big, sandy-haired kid."

"Yes." He's already questioned Randy.

"What do you do in the winter?"

"School. I'm a graduate student at NAU. In art."

"That makes you about..."

" Almost twenty-one."

"You always wear sunglasses up here?"

"The light is so bright it hurts. My eyes are important to me."

"I see what you mean about the light." He folds his arms and leans against the window. Makes himself comfortable. Smiles. "How'd a little girl like you get such a big brother?"

She doesn't like being called a little girl, but he's probably trying to seem friendly. "My father is big. My mother isn't."

"Better than the other way around, I guess. So your brother helped you. You get along with him?"

Sergeant Bailey's trying to gain her confidence, she can tell. "My father's an attorney. He sees so much that's bad, he's very strict. We're the only children. Randy's two years older than I am."

He smiles. "I know your father, by reputation mostly. Hard man on a case. Never occurred to me what it would be like to be his kid."

"He tries to be a good father. Hard on a case, like you said."

He laughs. "I'll bet. I'll bet he is. So you and your brother learned to help each other."

She can tell he's leading up to something…she's seen Dad do the same thing, one question at a time, at the dinner table. "Sort of. I guess you could put it that way. Sometimes there were little things we'd keep between ourselves. Once he got home late from school, and I didn't tell. Or he hid something for me so Dad wouldn't find it."

"What was it?"

"A watercolor I really liked. So Dad wouldn't throw it away. He says I should do oils because that's where the money is."

He grins. "Where'd he hide it?"

"I'm not telling."

He laughs again. "Good for you. Is it still there?"

"Yes."

"Well, good for Randy. He takes care of you?"

"Dad takes care of me. Randy's you know, a *friend.*"

"This Jake Holding who was killed, was he your friend?"

"I've heard he didn't have many friends."

"Why was that?"

"The way he treated people."

"How was that?"

"I didn't see him with other people much. I've heard he bossed them and shamed them. The guys who worked under him. Women sometimes he tried to be charming to. But that's hearsay."

A smile. "He was charming to you?"

"Part of the time. When I saw him."

"Part of the time he bossed you and shamed you?"

"It was, like, the way he was."

"That's what I'm hearing everywhere. He have any enemies?"

"I…I wouldn't know. I don't see other people much."

"I talked to his father last night when he identified the body. I hate that part of the job, the family. Tough man, the old fashioned kind. I gather he loved his kid. Only child."

"That's too bad, I guess." Her voice breaks. Oh no, she's crying. Venn raises her head and looks up. She puts her hands over her face.

"You're pretty upset. Did the guy mean anything to you?"

"*No*! I just, I was thinking about *my* father, about fathers. Oh, *wait* a minute, let me blow my nose." It feels good to speak up for herself. She takes as long as she can to dry her face. "I'm sorry. Dad says men don't respect women who go to pieces."

"Hey, the world gives you plenty to cry about. Do it myself."

"You *do*?"

"Sure."

"Thank you."

"Look, Ms. Findlay, I'm trying to get some idea about who killed that man. Can you help me?"

It's the best she's liked him so far. "I only met him last April when I went into the station to get a radio and binoculars and stuff. That makes about, let's see, four months. I hardly ever talk to anybody up here all alone. Randy. Josy on patrol. Jake was, like, my supervisor. He came up sometimes to see how things were going."

"And he was rude and mean?"

"I thought he was pretty bossy. It was insulting if he thought I was doing something wrong. Probably no one is ever mean to *you*."

"Not often."

"You're lucky. You're not short and skinny."

He smiles. "Are you afraid to live up here alone?"

"Only of people."

"Is that why you had a pistol?"

"Randy bought it for me. He said I had to be able to defend myself and I ought to learn to shoot. He came up after hours a couple of times to teach me. I hate that gun…it's so noisy." She doesn't tell him she thought of using it on herself.

"If it isn't the weapon we want, we'll get it back to you."

"Whatever."

"It's registered to Randy. Shall we return it to him?"

"Thank you." Tears are running out of her eyes again. She wipes at them with her fingers. "I'm sorry. I don't mean to cry."

"No problem. Now, Ms. Findlay, there's one more thing. Do you spend the nights up here?"

She's feeling shakey, hears it in her voice. "I live on the mountain. On my days off I go into town, but I come back up before dark."

"What about last Thursday night?"

"Thursday?"

"There was a lot of wind that night."

"It's been *awful* lately, sometimes it scares me. Tearing through trees making a horrible roaring noise. When it's like that Venn whines and howls and I sit on the floor of the tower with her. I can't believe—that trapdoor there? Sometimes gusts actually lift it enough so when it drops it makes a loud thump. That's a heavy door."

"So I see. What was your wind speed?"

"It's been clear off my anomometer. I estimate at least fifty. Myrna on Elden has gusts of eighty. Randy says that's VFW."

He raises one eyebrow.

"Very Fucking Windy." Maybe she shouldn't have said that…old people can be weird about swearing. Randy says one generation's swearing is the next generation's slang.

"Good precise scale."

"I hate wind. Especially when you have to brace yourself and hold on to your clothes and it's, like, something alive and evil. The only bad thing about this job is the way the wind blows so much."

"Did you go walking Thursday evening?"

"*Walking?* On windy nights I fill all my water containers from the pump and shut myself in with the windows closed. In still air that doesn't move."

"Have any visitors that night, sleep-overs or anything?"

"No, I never do. I don't know who would come."

"Nobody camping on the mountain?"

"I didn't see any. Strangers can't drive above the gate. I've never seen a camper up here."

"Did Jake Holding come up after work last Thursday?"

"He told me a few days before that on Thursday right after work he was going down to a place he'd picked out so he could be up and ready to hunt at dawn."

"Did you know where he'd be camping?"

"He told me. He said it was the best place on 6B."

"So you knew where he'd be?"

"He showed me on the map."

"You didn't hear a gunshot that night?"

"Lately I've heard people target shooting down at the base of the mountain, but I wouldn't think I could hear anything that far away."

"Did he ever say someone had threatened him?"

"Threatened *Jake?* I'll bet no one would have dared. And he wouldn't have told *me.*"

"No, I guess not. Well, Ms. Findlay, I'll know where to find you if I have any more questions. Sorry I upset you. That wasn't my intention."

She rather likes him now that it's all over...he is nice enough. She wonders what kind of father he is.

District fire people are finally coming into service...she still hasn't heard Josy on the radio. There's no smoke anywhere, but prime burning hours are coming up. She looks around her circle carefully, avoiding Black Tank down the ridge. Where Jake died. She doesn't want to look there. She wonders what happened to his bow...

A car has rolled into a ravine on Long Valley district. Can Highway Patrol pull it out? Probably, you know, with a cable, but it will take a while. Stand by, they say. She likes that term.

At 11:50 she sees thick smoke coming up from behind Woody Ridge. At last! She reports it..."White top smoke at 169 degrees thirty minutes. The base is blind to me so I can't give you an accurate distance, but it's probably on Highway 89 somewhere north of Vista Point."

Myrna on Elden calls the smoke at 212 degrees. Vista Point reports it. Someone with a car phone says it's three miles south of Forest Highlands houses, so practically *every*body responds. A fire upwind of structures worries them all...politics, Randy says. "You don't wanna lose it. Makes the Forest Service look like a bunch of nincompoops. Voters who watch their houses burn are mad, for some reason." If Jake were still alive, he'd probably be driving fast to get there first and take control.

*T*hursday on her day off she'd try to get out to the ranch–she wanted to talk with her mother. Her career conditional year would be up soon–she ought to decide before her next firearms qualification course and before she was taken on as a permanent.

It would be embarrassing to back off: all that money had been spent on training her. She'd either have to go back to Fire or leave the Forest Service, and it might be seen as admitting a woman couldn't handle the law enforcement job. It wasn't that so much, she could do it. So far she just didn't *like* it.

Last week in addition to general patrol–she turned back through her log–she'd had unauthorized livestock where they shouldn't be, an aggravated assault, firewood cutting without a permit, a Satanist cult that had sacrificed a gopher, four people trying to set up residency in the forest. A Davy Crockett wannabe: she drove up on him bending over a little black bear he'd shot, cutting off its paws as trophies and he'd threatened her with the knife. She'd pulled her baton and smacked it out of his hand. Stink, she wished she'd broken his arm too.

She tried to keep a tidy desk, but sometimes she couldn't remember which stack she'd put a paper on. The local address Schaeffer had given her this morning, an envelope he'd found at a trashed-out camp site, where had she put it? She'd have to go to the address and serve a citation. Great—another new friend. Most of the people she cited didn't see her, they saw her uniform.

She no more than found the envelope than Sarah came on the radio with a fire. White top smoke on Highway 89 north of the vista—in there ten-to-one it would be an escaped camp fire, human caused, requiring LE investigation, her thirty-first so far. The Mormon Lake LEO was still at Devil's Chair. "Flagstaff, 3-4 is responding."

She drove up the circle onto the overpass and turned south on I-40. Best route was to I-17, leave it at Fort Tuthill. Driving was better than paperwork, but it didn't stop her wondering whether everyone she knew had shot Jake Holding.

She remembered Grandpa's solemn face: "I'm only a tenderfoot New Yorker"—after fifty years as an Arizona rancher—"but I thought 'he needed killing' was practically a legal defense in the West," and Grandma laughing and smacking a kiss on his bald head. "Paul, bet a cookie you've been reading novels again." They had so much fun together, those two old people, it was good to watch.

He protested, "I thought it was part of The Code of the West—get rid of people likely to harm the populace. Good idea, it seems to me."

"It wasn't in the statutes, but with a well-known trouble-maker it wasn't hard to convince a jury."

Hill's voice came on the radio. "Flagstaff, 5-34 on the scene. Escaped camp fire, quarter acre on the ground. It spread until the car was fully involved. Keep everybody coming. And we'll need Law Enforcement for traffic control." The smoke above the ridge was black and thick, sure sign of a car burning, but mixed in was white and thick—grass probably.

She loved hearing Hill on the radio, being on a fire with him. Their jobs were different, but it was a kick that they overlapped at some places. It would be sad if work made them strangers to each other. And they understood: she knew the reason when a fire made him six hours late coming home, he knew when she worked half the night on holiday weekends.

Stink, she was on call twenty-four hours. Memorial Day they weren't even home at the same time—he had back-to-back fires; she had missing people and shooting in camping areas and wrecked cars and ATVs romping around in wet meadows. They'd left notes for each on the kitchen counter.

"Flagstaff, 5-34. We've got a Mercedes here completely destroyed. We're going to need a tow truck to haul out what's left of it."

"Copy, 5-34."

Well, whoop-ti-doo, wasn't every day she had a Mercedes in her report. Hill would have turned it into a story by the time he got home.

Grandma and Grandpa would have liked him, the three of them'd have kept each other laughing. Hill would have liked them. Crumb. Stink. Maybe someday somebody would explain death to her, what it was and what it wasn't.

The ranch was half empty without them. She remembered how Grandma had sat on the porch steps with her when she was little and turned the Painted Desert and the Ward Terrace cliffs into magic places. "See there, just a little to the left of that blue shadow? I'm sure that's the door to a beautiful house. But we shouldn't go over there, you know. It would vanish before our eyes if we did."

"Why?"

"Because magic is like that. When you get close, it hides by looking ordinary. Isn't that amazing? This ridge behind the house could be *full* of magic, goodness and love that we can't see because we live right next to it. You never know where it is. So you know what I do?"

"What?"

Grandma had bent her head and whispered. "I act as if it's everywhere. What else can I do?"

"Could you try to talk to the magic?"

"It's very secretive."

Grandpa sat down and put his arm around her. "Magic is where your Grandma is. Take a look at that face if you don't believe it. She's been magic for me since the day I saw her get off the train with my cousin Jo, pretty as a picture and so excited. I knew right away magic was part of her, she plain shone. That didn't mean I was so smart: everyone could see it. You can, can't you?"

The highway ran through a state section for a mile. Trees ought to be thinned in there, they were prime for a wildfire—spindly, close together. Worse yet, upwind from that fancy gated subdivision. A cigarette flicked out of a car window on a Red Flag day and there could be a blow-up that would run right over the golf course.

District 5 LE was on the radio. "I've been released from the incident on Devil's Chair, I'll be responding down 89 south."

There was not much smoke on the road, no visibility problem, but traffic was backing up as motorists tried to see what was going on. Laurie was waving them on, Green fire trucks were visible back among the trees, an empty place next to the Mormon Lake Hot Shot bus. "Flagstaff, 3-4 is on the scene of Incident Five."

She wore her hair pinned up when she was in uniform. She eased her hard hat on, trying not to loosen anything. Everybody had to have a hard hat, even the press, no one was exempt. Over her uniform an extra large fire shirt, that was mandatory too—after eight years she was used to the smell.

*J*osy hadn't once grabbed for something to hang onto—Mitch was a better driver than Jake, smarter. He didn't have to pull out of a skid or a fish tail because he didn't get *into* one. On washboard stretches he drove slower; on the hill west of the Arboretum he geared down before the truck began to shudder.

"You know what, at least I won't ever to have to ride with Jake again. I wonder if he drove that way when he was alone, or if he liked to scare people to prove he was in charge."

Mitch was a decent kind of man. She liked him, sometimes he made her laugh. "Jake should have got through that phase by the time he graduated from high school. *I* did. That's when I realized it's only in movies that fools don't get hurt."

"Yeah, well, it was obvious he had a kink in his rope, as grandma used to say."

"I guess I didn't see that side of him."

"No, you wouldn't have."

He slowed enough to take the S curve approaching Rogers Lake without sliding on the gravel. "Cattle are still here, I see. I'm always afraid I'll run into one. Accident reports are a pain."

She looked at Woody Mountain, to the tower on top. Sarah was up there—she'd heard her go into service. Poor thing, a weak leg and a lonely childhood, confined in a little tower. It would be good to go up and check on her next time there was a chance.

They drove the next three miles without talking, and that was OK. You didn't have to talk *all* the time. She watched the pines go by. Sympathy got her into burdensome situations sometimes. That was probably how it had started with Walt. She'd felt sorry for him: he seemed so isolated, more intelligent than most people. He was really alone because he was so negative and critical, but she didn't find that out until later.

Mill Park was coming up. "You'll need to turn left soon, before we get into the open. That will take us right to the site."

"They moved Jake's truck last night."

"Long as they took the body too. Jeesh, what a job that must be."

And there she was less than twenty-four hours later, on the same rough two-track through the same peaceful forest, heading for Bob's Tank. There was a mess of tracks on the road.

Sarah's voice came on the radio. "Flagstaff, Woody Mountain, Fire Flash." She felt herself go alert.

"Woody Mountain, Flagstaff."

"White top smoke at 169 degrees thirty minutes. The base is blind to me so I can't give you an accurate distance, but it's probably on Highway 89 somewhere north of Vista Point."

Myrna's voice followed. "Flagstaff, Elden, cross, 212 degrees."

In her truck she kept a map on the seat beside her so she could locate fires and the quickest road into them. Mitch's was behind the right sun visor. Before she could unroll it, Flagstaff had plotted the smoke on the west side of 89 and dispatched Engine 5-1. Hill Pederson was responding too.

"That's near the Fry Canyon road, my response area, automatic dispatch."

"Relax, you'll get there. You want to stop and get your truck or go with me and come back later?"

No question—she was tired of being a passenger. "I should take my truck. My fire gear is in it."

"Is that you up ahead between the county rigs?"

She could see a glimpse of Forest Service green through the pines. "That's it, right where I left it."

Two men were back among the trees, walking slowly and scanning the ground with what looked like some kind of electronic device, fluorescing for hair or something? Still looking for evidence, after all these hours.

"So this is the shooting site?" He turned his truck around before he stopped. "See you there."

She held her breath and hurried just in case. Inside with the door closed, she picked up her notebook and wrote current mileage into it: for the next few hours mileage would be charged to the fire. When she had the engine running, she raised the mike to her mouth and keyed it. "Flagstaff, Patrol 3-4 in service, responding to Incident Five."

*W*ork in colored pencils is *personal,* at least to her. She hasn't had a course…Dad vetoed a class in art pencils. So she's read books, and this summer she's trying to learn by what she does on her own.

To her, pencils are quiet and clean. They don't smudge or smear. She loves to sit on the windowseat by the hour with a drawing pad propped against her knees stroking in thin layers of color almost transparent so that previous colors show through. It's hypnotic. She feels *serene* in the slow careful movement. Mixing colors on the paper by layering…starting with the palest because pencil can't be lightened, just blended.

She's doing a drawing she calls "Woody Autumn," but the mountain isn't in it at all…just the view. She's used three sheets of paper to sketch the panorama that stretches across the north from Kendrick past the Peaks to Mount Elden. The horizon line is below the middle of the page to suggest the size of the sky. In the foreground are aspen trees, parts of them, not the bases or the tops but enough of the middle for lots of white trunk and yellow leaves. The mountains aren't framed by trees. Seen *through* them.

The sketch is finished. At the back, the far-away sky, the base blue among the trees is in. Now she's working with green, layering it with the lightest of touches. She doesn't know why she likes green over blue for the sky, she just does. The leaves in all tones of yellow will go on last, in chalk so they'll *flame.* If it turns out, she might have all three sheets framed separately but hang them side by side, a drawing in three parts like a triptych…and give it to Beste.

*D*own through Fry Canyon Josy had watched for vehicles driving away from the fire location–part of her job was to note descriptions and license numbers of possibles–but there hadn't been a single one. She'd heard on the radio several units reporting that they had arrived on the fire. Flagging was already tied to a tree on the highway, so she didn't have to do that. Or figure a size-up: Hill Pederson had already called it as a quarter of an acre.

She could see a huge billowing smoke from a mile up the road. Black–that meant something serious on fire, a car probably, since there were no structures anywhere near. And lots of white: grass burning. No inclination, pretty much straight up, so there wasn't much upper level wind on it.

From the pavement she saw a dozen green fire trucks congregated back among the trees. Cars were beginning to pull off onto the shoulder.

You know what, there'd be a traffic problem if too many collected and worse trouble if people started walking in to see action. It was exciting—they wanted to see for themselves—she could understand it. But they got in the way and they didn't realize there was danger even with fire personnel around.

She knew the spot, a little throw-down camp site not far from pavement. There was a parking place next to Meg's truck where she wouldn't block access. She backed into it so she'd be positioned to drive out immediately if there was need.

"Flagstaff, Patrol 3-4 on the scene."

"Copy Patrol 3-4 on the scene."

She wore fire boots and NOMEX pants every day, no delay there. Peeling off her uniform shirt, she threw it onto the seat of the truck and buttoned a yellow fire shirt over her t-shirt. Du Pont guaranteed NOMEX wouldn't sustain flame. She hoped Du Pont was right. Her hard hat and fire pack and belt were in a side compartment behind the cab. Fastening those on, she opened the second compartment where she kept sharpened tools and pulled out her combi shovel-and-pick. Stood a moment to check air movement on her face, steady from the southwest about five to seven. Well, *okay*.

"5-34, Patrol 3-4, I'm near your crew bus."

"Come on in. Take the west flank and scout for spots. Don't get too far ahead of the crew." West flank, the foot of the ridge—a heads-up place. If wind changed direction, fire could run uphill or spot out to the side and trap people. She hoped the crew boss had put a lookout of his own somewhere on higher ground.

Meg was crouching with her camera at the obvious point of ignition—a ring of small stones charred on the northeast side where wind had blown fire into the grass. It widened to take in a furiously burning car, totally involved, fifteen feet away.

Jeesh! Talk about *ignorant*. Fire was burning beyond the car, around it, all on the ground, flame length about a foot. Hot Shots in fire shirts and hard hats were digging a direct line a few feet back; engine crews were spraying water from hoses. Your tax dollars at work, friends, activity everywhere.

She circled the heel where Meg was and walked up the line past all the bent yellow backs, ten feet out. Despite yesterday's rain, the dirt looked dry. Late in the season like that, grass was turning yellow. Potential there. She'd have to be heads-up for a wind change—fire could make its own wind that might turn squirrely or change direction.

Ten feet farther out, she walked back, eyes scanning, then toward the front again where smoke was thicker among the trees. Shafts of sunlight stabbed down here and there, patterns of light and shade in the air. She tied her bandanna across her nose and mouth.

It was noon—sun would have been nearly overhead in June, but it was lower at the end of August. Going north up the line she stopped often to turn and crouch down so that any small wisps of smoke would show up with sunlight behind them. You could spot them several minutes earlier that way before they got established.

The ridge was so close she must be almost on top of the Oak Creek fault. Rocks exposed on the surface were confusing, basalt and sedimentary jumbled together, here and there a few that might be meta-morphic. You could expect faulting to move rocks around, but she couldn't read it. Maybe after a few advanced geology courses it would be easier to recognize the ground she walked on.

With each trip up the line she was farther away from the yellow shirts. The burn must have been more than an acre by then. For an hour, until the crew had containment, she walked a grid. Finally, Hill called her in. Dirty and smelling of smoke, she hiked back to the burnt-out shell of the car.

She unclipped the canteen from her belt and drank from it, dried her mouth on her sleeve, probably smeared soot on her face. Meg was standing with two teen-agers of the "young male" variety while one of them talked on her cell phone. He didn't look at all happy.

Meg had moved off among the trees to her truck and sat there with an open laptop, typing her field notes. Oh, ouch, the paperwork. The Forest Service ran on paperwork, couldn't function without it. Probably the whole world did—*schools* certainly did.

Two boys stood like whipped pups, as grandma used to say, watching grown-ups who ignored them. Busy turning over blackened duff and spraying, turning and spraying, looking for pockets of fuel.

Sarah sits at window level with her drawing board on her knees. Light colors are supposed to go on first, then darker over them, then darker. But she remembers Georgia O'Keeffe. I was a very stupid fool not to paint what I wanted to"—and she feels rebellious. If it doesn't work to put the light on last, at least she'll be able to say for *herself* that it doesn't work.

Outside the window, sky is beautiful, just a few small clouds so far that might turn into a storm later. She feels quite happy.

She became in love with art the year she was so sick and couldn't go to school. Dad had carpenters build a bay window in the east wall of her bedroom so Mom could have sun to grow begonias and violets, all colors of flowering plants for her to watch. "Oh look, Sarah, the pink geranium has buds on it. Maybe tomorrow they'll open." Mom made special things to eat, thick soups from scratch, awesomely-good-for-you cookies, custards with crinkly brown edges.

When Randy came home every day, he read to her for an hour from the hobbitt books. Dad said, "If this isn't family values, I don't know what is." He came to sit with her after dinner and told her stories about history and law and politics, people and what they had done. Dad knew lots of good stories.

It was Beste who gave her art. When she could sit up against her pillows, Beste brought books from the libraries, big heavy books with glossy paper and pictures of paintings, all kinds, old and modern.

She liked the people who painted northern Arizona, Akin and Swinnerton for colors that made her tingle they were so beautiful. Merrill Mahaffey wets his canvases, pours the paint, uses an air brush and stuff like that to do the Grand Canyon and places. Alan Peterson does paintings with air in them.

And books about women painters. She could look at O'Keeffe's red New Mexico hills over and over for a long time, letting her eyes move across them. Bonheur and Cassatt bought big houses with the money they earned. O'Keeffe bought two.

Frida Kahlo limped from the time she was nine years old and the other children made fun of her. She grew up to be a famous painter in Mexico. Her pictures were strange, but that didn't matter…neither did her leg or what happened to her in an accident. She said she lived because she had painting to live for.

When Beste brought a lap table and a sketch pad, she could spend all day drawing if she felt like it, the flowers in the window or copying paintings in the books. Dad hired an art student from the university to come in three times a week and give her lessons. For a whole year Dad didn't tell her what she was supposed to do.

She was happy that year she was so sick. Everything around her was beautiful… everyone was kind and loving. Later when she was well and could go back to school, she missed how beautiful and loving it had been.

*J*osy had been released from the Mercedes fire at 14:00 about the time Meg had finished typing her notes, so they'd stood a few minutes talking between the trucks while she took off her fire gear.

"I guess you couldn't say it would have been *impossible* for Sarah to walk all that way and back in one night, but it doesn't seem likely?"

Meg was becoming more careful every month. "I wonder how long it would take to do it. There was a full moon and if she knew the terrain and stayed on fairly level ground…"

That wasn't what she'd expected. "Do you want to prove she did it?" Her hard hat and fire pack went into the side box.

"I'd rather prove she *didn't*. I was just thinking."

"Did you finish your list for Bailey?"

"To do it right, I'd have to include every person in Fire, all the engine and patrol people, lookouts, the Hot Shot crew and everybody else on the district including myself, and then start on the other districts. That would keep Bailey busy."

She unbuttoned her smelly fire shirt. "Mitch?"

"I can't see him doing it."

"Neither can I. He wouldn't have needed a gun. Did Bailey ask you what you thought?"

"Crumb, I wouldn't know who to point at."

"Yeah, neither would I. Well, on with the Smokey Bear act."

She pulled away from the truck cluster onto the highway, waved at the Mormon Lake LEO who was keeping traffic moving, opened her lunchbox and unwrapped a sandwich with one hand. So late in the day, she couldn't cover her whole patrol area—there wouldn't be time for much more than a survey along 231. And a few campers she should check on before she headed in.

Long as she was going up the Fry Canyon road, she ought to swing into Howard Pocket and look at last week's fire off the rim of West Fork. She was supposed to verify three consecutive days with no smoke before it could be considered out. Yesterday she'd been distracted before she could get there.

Come to think of it, that had been Jake's last chance to shine. It was a good thing he made the most of it. Three days later he was dead.

Scott on East Pocket had been the only lookout who could see smoke for the first hour. She'd been close by at Crater Sinks when his report came on the radio, so she'd been the initial unit to arrive. She'd tied flagging at the road and walked two hundred feet toward smoke that barely showed above the trees.

Her size-up was "one lightning-struck snag burning a third of the way down an inaccessible rock face." When Engine 3-4 came in, Henry peered over the edge: "How 'bout we just let it burn?"

But 6-4, up in an Air Attack plane, said sparks and debris were falling and starting grass down in the canyon. His opinion was that without climbing gear the snag couldn't be reached from above or below. By the time Jake got there and took command, three acres were on fire in scattered places and it was obvious some action had to be taken. Henry said, "Maybe so."

In no time Jake had three dozen people responding, Buck and Henry laying a hose to the canyon rim and spraying foam from above. Then he requested the dispatcher to send him experienced rock climbers who had gear with them. He ordered the helicopter from Green Base with a long-line bucket, plus a water tender to set up a dip station in Fry Park with a portatank. "Start a crew up West Fork with fire tools."

He sent her out to the side with a hand-held radio to watch for spots: "If the wind picks up, there'll be potential on top. Every fifteen minutes take the weather, RH, wind speed and direction. Keep an eye out for incoming lightning cells that could affect the wind and warn me in plenty of time to pull back." Jeesh, she could quote the training manuals too. Obviously nobody except Jake had a brain.

Buck walked the engine to within twenty-five feet of the edge, which was a piece-a-cake hose lay. The pilot flew over to re-con and said, "Looks like you got a fun one there." Two climbers arrived and started looking for a belay station. Air Attack circled and offered advice. All the Fire overhead were driving out from town to watch the show.

Finally there was a crew down in West Fork fighting grass fire and building a berm to contain the snag when it burned through and fell. The helicopter made thirty-two bucket drops with trips back and forth from Fry Park. It was Jake at his best, all over the place coordinating a complex operation. Not that it did him any good, but he didn't know it at the time.

She stashed the sandwich wrapper in her lunchbox. The first half mile of road 536A was a pain, narrow and rutted, but once she got into Howard Pocket the basalt cap was gone and she started down onto the Kaibab limestone, which was porous, and it smoothed out. Occasional reflectors were nailed to the trees—the wildlifers must have been there one night during the week surveying for owls.

She loved that part of her area. There were huge old yellow pines and white firs and oaks thirty feet tall. Different underlying earth changed vegetation types—you could tell without looking down that soil had changed. Sunlight filtered through different kinds of branches. White limestone rubble was exposed here and there.

In late June at a tank she'd seen three bull elk with huge racks. But it was bear country, surrounded by canyons—she almost always caught a glimpse of a cinnamon-black. Once she drove up to a tank and a bear stood up on its back legs to decide what she was—a classic posture she'd never seen except in photographs. Every time she went into the Pocket, she wondered if it had been named for old Bear Howard.

She parked where her own flagging was tied in the trees, took an apple out of the lunchbox and hiked through waist-high ferns to where ground began to fall away into West Fork and Casner Cabin Draw. The view from there was open to miles and miles of country. Shadows were growing on the south and west cliffs.

Last week standing there watching for spots, she'd decided the canyon walls were Toroweap Formation, white gold, obviously ancient sand dunes with all that cross-bedding. Maybe Coconino sandstone, but she thought probably Toroweap, upper paleozoic, two hundred and sixty-five million years old. It was eroded into rounded palisades and buttresses and fingers of rock with fir standing green against the white all the way down, growing anywhere they'd found a toehold.

The cliff she was looking at had been formed on the shore of an ocean that had receded millions of years ago, before Pangaea broke apart, long before volcanos erupted around what would be Flagstaff.

*H*er computer in its case, her camera stowed, she headed back toward town. A tubercular leg did put Sarah in a different light. The investigation wasn't up to her, but she couldn't help thinking. The county had probably taken a soil sample, not that it would be worth much if there were no shoe prints. If you wore all plastic clothing, it might not leave any threads. The weapon: Sarah had been so ready to hand over her .38, it probably wasn't the right one. There were about fifty thousand places in that country where a pistol could be hidden— stock tanks, rock piles, animal burrows, dead and down snags—they might not ever find it.

The radio was broadcasting an Attempt To Locate: white male, six feet four inches, tattoo on his left arm. In a motor home with a three-year-old boy. Armed and dangerous. She pulled off on the shoulder and wrote the details in her log in case she saw a tattoo through a window.

She could patrol a couple miles of forest on the way back. No point going up through Fry Canyon, Josy'd be doing that, but she could swing by Tule Tank and Garden Spring to see whether transients had set up housekeeping or end-of-summer campers were up to mischief. She didn't like to think about the Labor Day holiday.

She turned off pavement and bumped carefully over the track that wound between the trees. There was a tidy camp at the tank, a family by the look of it—a trailer, a couple of tents. A big screened umbrella tent for getting away from flies, table, lounge chairs, playpen inside. A small boy saw her coming and ran to the trailer—a man and woman came out and hurried to the road, waving. With luck they wouldn't want anything more serious than a look at a map.

"Flagstaff, 3-4. I'll be out of my vehicle at Tule Tank."

"Copy, 3-4."

"Afternoon." She stepped out of her truck. "I'm Meg Pederson, Peaks District Law Enforcement." It was a pair of worried faces that approached her.

"Are we ever glad to see you. Our daughter's been gone a couple of hours, and we're worried sick. She's only twelve." They both talked, interrupting, keeping her looking from one to the other. "She loves to hike and be alone in the forest. Nobody's driven past in the four days that we've been here, so we told her she could go on short hikes if she kept to the roads and didn't stay gone for more than an hour. Maybe we shouldn't have? But you can't keep your kids on a leash when they get bigger."

"I know what you mean." It probably wasn't the time to mention that transients were sometimes a problem in there. "You don't want to teach them fear."

"Back home I used to wander in the woods for hours. It was one of the best parts of growing up. I'd hate for my kids to miss that. I think it's healthy."

"I used to be out all day. It makes me mad to think things have got so bad that freedom may be dangerous."

"She's never been gone this long before. After an hour I started driving the road to the north all the way to the city wells, just got back, but I didn't find her. I was getting set to go out again. You came in from the south, did you see her? She's wearing shorts and a red shirt."

Not hard to imagine their sick fear, she was feeling it herself. "No, but then, I wasn't looking. Does she mind going uphill?"

"Climbs everything in sight like a mountain goat."

"I've got an idea where she might be—there's an old road not far from here that goes up through the pass. It hasn't been used by cars much for years, but hikers take it sometimes. Tell you what, I'll go and see if I can find her up there, it shouldn't take me more than half an hour. If I don't meet up with her, we'll call out county search and rescue and locate her before dark. Would that be all right?"

The woman began to cry. "We're so grateful. We didn't know what to do." The little boy began to cry.

"You hang tight here in case she comes back. What's her name?"

"Kristin."

"I'll be quick as I can."

As she drove away, she keyed her mike. "Flagstaff, 3-4. Be advised I'm going to be looking for an over-due hiker. I'll get back to you within half an hour if I need help."

"Copy, 3-4. Standing by."

When she was twelve, the old Black Pass road would have been exactly where she'd have been. She drove back until she found the turn-off and headed uphill in low. Stink but the world had gotten nasty.

When she'd driven as far up the old road as she dared, she hooked a radio on her belt, locked the truck, and began to climb. Tragedy in the making was getting to be too big a part of her life, too much in her mind. At the first turn she stopped and used her binoculars to scan ahead. Rocks, trees, more rocks and—she was sure it made her heart jump—a spot of red, a person, a girl sitting in the middle of the road.

"Flagstaff, 3-4. I've spotted the over-due hiker in Black Pass. I'll be climbing up to her."

"Copy, 3-4. Keep us informed."

She moved slower than she needed to, not wanting to cause alarm. The girl watched her come. From twenty feet away it was obvious she'd been crying.

"Kristin? My name is Meg. Your parents asked me to look for you. They've been worried. Are they ever going to be glad to see you."

"I twisted my ankle."

She sat on the ground and kept her voice calm. "Loose rock?"

"It rolled. I didn't fall down or anything, but my ankle twisted."

"Trying to keep your balance, that's happened to me. Congratulations on your reaction time. Does it hurt to walk on?"

"I tried." There'd be more tears any minute.

"May I see it?"

It didn't look too bad, not broken, maybe not even sprained. "Well crumb, you don't have any strange colors to show your brother. If I help you up and keep my arm around you, will you try to hop down to my truck? It isn't far."

"Are you a peace officer?"

"Sure am, darlin', peace, that's a very good word. Now, don't put any weight on the foot that's hurt and I'll pull you up easy. That's it. Hold on, I'll get over to the useless side. Lean into me and take a step with the good foot. How does that feel? We can call for a stretcher if we have to, but it'll give your parents longer to worry. What do you think? Can we get down this hill three-legged?"

It hadn't been much more than half an hour when she buckled a seat belt around Kristin. "Flagstaff, 3-4. I have the hiker, returning to Tule Tank." It was the happiest she'd felt for a week. If only helping were a bigger part of her job...

Kristin's father lifted her from the law enforcement truck; her mother hugged both of them. Everybody was crying, including the little brother and the baby over in the playpen. What a dandy ending, the kind she liked the best. "The closest hospital is in Flagstaff if you'd like to have her examined. There are a couple of walk-in clinics in town too."

"We can't tell you how grateful we are. How can we thank you?"

"No need—I'm grateful to *you*. So much of my job is ugly that it's a pleasure to have something good in my day."

"Well, without you, it might have been. We won't forget you or your name."

"Speaking of names, may I write yours in my log for the report? And your address? Paperwork's a major part of my job. I wonder what Superman would have been if he'd had to file reports."

She got away before *she* began to cry and drove on north toward Garden Spring. "Flagstaff, 3-4. I'm clear of the incident at Tule Tank. Everything is Code Four."

Back to the radio: a man in a grey car had taken a shot at a Phoenix DPS officer and fled, believed to be on the Coconino. Near Munds Park there was an accident with head injuries, request for helevac. Gun shots had been reported at the Blue Ridge reservoir. A nine-year-old girl was missing at Sunset Crater.

A car had gone off a bluff above the Verde River and was stranded in tree tops—the driver was saying there had been no sign to warn him. When she pulled into the station, she saw Bailey's van in the parking lot. Also Raleigh's.

*M*yrna on Elden is on the radio saying that she has a smoke. There it is in plain sight over at the party pit behind the old dump. She pushes everything off her lap. By the time Myrna has finished reporting, she has a cross ready. The smoke is already turning grey. Engine 3-2, first on the scene, says a quarter acre is burning on the ground. She hopes they'll say whether anything is burning besides grass. White usually means grass and grey other stuff.

It won't be as dramatic as the one early last week…she'd loved that one. At 15:25 Thursday Myrna had come onto the radio. "Flagstaff, Elden. Fire Flash."

Startled, she'd looked up. Where? Not five minutes before she had looked all around her circle…

"Elden, Flagstaff."

"Small white smoke at 238 degrees, seven miles, north of the railroad tracks on old Route 66."

That was in a huge blind area for Woody Mountain. She couldn't see a sign of smoke, with the binoculars or without. She checked Elden's reading on her map, just to be sure.

Five minutes later Elden's smoke report was "tripled in size, strong southwest wind driving it toward Observatory Mesa." Flagstaff dispatched a Hot Shot crew, three engines, a water tender and two dozers. The Air Attack plane took off from Pulliam Field. A police helicopter pilot said he was in the air nearby and he'd go have a look.

She's especially supposed to watch for smoke around Lowell Observatory because it's an important place and it's just above the railroad tracks where transients build fires sometimes. But she still didn't see anything. Finally, ten minutes after Elden's call, there was a tiny wisp of top smoke. She couldn't tell where the base was, it could have been anywhere, blown by the wind. By that time the Volunteer lookout had crossed it and Patrol 3-2 was almost there.

Suddenly thick white smoke, like, *billowed* up beyond the top of her mountain. Patrol 3-2 said half an acre was burning, trees were torching, and it was climbing the hill to the top of the mesa. Kathy on Air Attack ordered two slurry tankers and a lead plane.

People were arguing on the radio about how they could get the dozers and the big engines across the railroad tracks and up to the fire. "Can we walk the dozers through the Tunnel Spring underpass?"

"Send everybody up to the A-1 Mountain road, we can get them in from there."

"How about across the top of the old A-1 burn?"

From the Air Attack plane Kathy was telling them that they had three acres burning with spots a hundred yards ahead. Jake requested two more engines and a water tender to go up to Lowell Observatory and stand by. Air Attack and the helicopter began to look for roads the engines could use. Two television news crews arrived, Jake told Laurie to tie in with them. By 16:00 the Ranger 3-6 helicopter had arrived with a bucket, but there was no place close where it could be filled. A lead plane for the air tankers was ten minutes out…smoke was rising high into the sky. It was nearly 16:30 before a big white plane with a red nose, red tail and wingtips droned over her head…coming from Prescott. It followed the lead plane circling around and around, lower and lower, for what seemed like a long time. She traced it with her binoculars…it was the first tanker drop all summer that had been close enough for her to watch. Another tanker was circling above, waiting. The Air Attack plane was off to one side.

A heavy cloud of orange-pink appeared below the lower tanker and fell out of sight behind the trees. Within *seconds* it was gone. Randy says it's very heavy mud, and you have to get out of the way if you don't want to be hurt...also wet and slimey...nobody wants to be hit with slurry.

*R*ounding the end of Fry Lake, Josy headed north, feeling edgy. What had happened to her life? It had started so Dick and Jane, in Flagstaff in an old house that had been Grandma's. On a deep double lot in a treesy neighborhood, it had a front gate and a tire swing. She'd walked half a mile along quiet streets to Eva Marshall school, named for the town's first schoolteacher back in 1883. Then on to Flagstaff Junior High and after that a block over to the high school. There was no Wheeler Park yet, but the long strip of Thorpe Park was only two blocks from home with Mars Hill behind that—once she'd pulled a red wagon over there with wood in it for building a fort.

The big argument in town in those years was whether that Texas land corporation should be allowed to develop the Snow Bowl with condos and chair lifts and a new lodge. Some people argued that what was there already, all of it, should be removed and the mountain left to Alpine-type skiing, and everybody in town had a strong opinion. The Indians didn't want *anything* up there, of course.

None of it had touched her really—she was too busy winning hand-fuls of blue ribbons for track. Fifteen years later her parents and Aunt Virginia were dead and she was living with a critical grump and worrying about being a suspect in a murder.

"Flagstaff, Elden, Fire flash." She pulled over and waited to hear the location. When Myrna read out the degree from Elden and the distance, when Sarah had radioed a cross, she opened her map and traced the lines with her finger. Before the dispatcher had figured the township and range, she knew exactly where it was. An abandoned camp fire behind the old dump where high school kids partied.

*F*rom her tower, clouds always look so soft. The ones piling up above the Peaks are already black on the bottom...west they spread as far as Kendrick and at least 180 degrees across the north and east. Overhead is still clear, but there's a good chance of an afternoon storm. She hopes so.

It was so dry the first part of the summer all over the southwest that the Coconino Hot Shot crews were sent off to other forests and Indian crews were brought in to fill their places. There were nineteen

Red Flag days because of high wind. The engines were all on overtime, day after day. Lookouts stayed in their towers instead of going down for lunch...Jake extended them all until 19:00 for fear of a late fire getting started. The view was softer and more beautiful as sun was getting low, but sometimes it felt like the day would go on forever...

Bunches of pretty little mule deer with big ears were all over the mountain. Randy said they were looking for grass and water. At Anderson's feed store in town she bought a hundred-pound bale of alfalfa hay and pushed it out of the back of her truck down in her clearing, off in the trees where Jake wouldn't see it. She put a big basin down there too and kept it full of water. A few days later she counted eighteen little hollows on the slope where something had scraped out places to lie down.

Just because you can't save *everything* doesn't mean you shouldn't try to help what's close around you. At least she could try to make the top of her mountain a place where animals didn't starve. Randy called it Sarah's Ark. "Remember that lions might come in two-by-two too. When you're feeding deer, you're also providing food for predators."

After the forest was closed in May, she went twenty-five whole days without seeing smoke. The second week in June, a *month* early, clouds built up all along the eastern sky. On June 13th rain fell all afternoon. Her precip was nearly half an inch, more for the day than any other lookout on the forest.

But through May and June the Coconino kept restrictions in effect... no vacationers in the forest. On weekends she could hear secretaries and stuff going into service for "Closure Patrol." At night sometimes a plane flew above the districts, looking for illegal campfires...probably it made Phoenix people mad that they weren't allowed to come and camp anyplace they wanted. But what else could you do? If you let them run free, they'd burn the whole forest off.

*A*ll that work waiting on her desk and in her computer, and Meg was leaning back in her chair looking out the window at the trees across the parking lot—trying to decide. Maybe she'd made a mistake trying to be a law enforcement officer, and she didn't know. The stress never let up.

The women in her family had been Arizona for four generations. And ranchers, out-door horse and cattle women. Grandma had been beautiful on a horse when she was eighty; she said she'd got it from her mother, great-grandma Margaret—Meg had never known her. Anyway, they'd all been able to do hard ranch work plus house and children, become healthy and wise on it. Wealthy was grandpa's New York money and Aunt Jo's too; Grandma said it had made all the difference.

She'd grown to be tall out at the ranch, training horses, working calves—it had been play for her. Sometimes they'd had a family rodeo, and she'd won events as often as her brothers had. She could read weather, shoot her horse when its legs were broken, walk twenty miles crying to get home. On top of that: predict fire behavior, make it out safe through blinding smoke, give emergency treatment to friends who were hurt on a blow-up.

And now she was meeting creeps all day, people who thought she was some kind of joke. Maybe she'd thought law enforcement would be a challenge, fun even, because that's what everything had been for her. It wasn't fun.

What she'd learned to like when she was a child was the flowers that bloomed on tough plants at the ranch, free under the Arizona sky, responsive to seasons and what they brought. Flower families that endured for centuries—survived storms and drought and fire and the teeth of animals. Plants like that had character.

Her great-uncle Matt had taught her what grew in the hard, dry ground at the ranch: names of cactus; how to distinguish between mustard and pea families; which were in the rose family and how she could tell; how to recognize the five kinds of sunflower that grew on their land. She learned when each bloomed and where, how they smelled, what their defenses were. Which plants the Hopis used and for what. Her favorites were the bright yellow marigolds that grew no taller than six inches and smelled like lemons.

"You need to be able to distinguish between these two, Meggie, they're right here together—purple loco and pink penstemon. Look close now. What family is this?"

She examined stems, leaves, flowers. "Pea?"

"Ah, you make an old man feel like a good teacher. Pea it is. This one's the purple loco, and it's toxic, but not unless you eat it, which cattle will do. They get addicted to it, and often it kills them. We're ranchers. We pull up loco when we see it."

"So our cattle won't die."

"But the root can go down a long way, so it's not easy to eradicate. We keep trying."

"And we don't eat it either."

"No, no indeed."

"OK, I won't."

"Now, this pink penstemon, is it in the pea family?"

He didn't have children of his own, so she tried to make him proud of her. "I don't think so." She looked up at him. "Is it?"

"Snapdragon, you can tell by the flowers. It grows a little bigger than loco, and the flowers are rosier. Doesn't bloom quite so long in the summer. And here's the important thing: it doesn't grow anyplace else, just here near Sunset Crater. It's our special flower."

"Do we pull it up?"

"Do we?"

"I hope not."

Since grade school she'd been bigger than most of the boys her age, stronger too, better with horses, a better shot. But what she held in her mind were the flowering plants.

The radio: the Mountainaire Fire Department had found what was left of a big party from last night on road 235, an untended camp fire out of the ring and two intoxicated teen-agers who'd tried to escape in a pick-up truck. Mountainaire was calling for a deputy and 5-4 to set up a road block at the Howard Draw intersection.

The campground host at Ashurst Three was calling for help, some kind of marital problem out there. She didn't move: it wasn't her district, not her area of response, and she wasn't in the mood.

"3-4, Flagstaff." *Stink*! "Are you available to respond?"

Maybe most jobs were done by people who didn't feel like it. "Affirmative." Maybe there'd be children she could take out of range of their parents. "I'll be on my way."

*T*he old dump had been covered with dirt years ago and planted to grass, but people still brought garbage there. Josy wound through the pines on a one-track past a broken-down couch and an old refriger- ator, plastic oil bottles—piles of nasty stuff everywhere she looked.

By the time she arrived, Engine 3-2 was on the fire in a claustrophobic little clearing, just finishing a line around the grass that was burning. It hadn't spread into the trees, but some kid strong like ox/smart like tractor had carried in a few heavy logs from quite a distance and piled them into the ring. They must have been smoldering all night.

Warren shouted, "Hey, you're just in time. You want to use the drip torch, the chainsaw, the hose or the Pulaski?"

"I have a choice?"

Jill straightened her back. "She missed the grunt work, how come she gets her say on the fun part?"

Randy loved to tease. "You want the saw, Jill, is that what you're trying to say?"

"My turn, isn't it?"

Warren grinned. "Go to it then. I'm feeling plumb puny anyway."

She pulled her fire gear out of the side box. "I'll take the torch."

"You got it. You know where it is?"

"In the back."

It made sense to backfire and burn out fast—they'd be on overtime as it was with all those heavies. Their drip torch was icky, all eighteen inches of it so battered and oily you could hardly recognize it as cast aluminum anymore. She could tell when she picked it up that she wouldn't need to fill it. Good. Mixing one-third gas and two-thirds diesel fuel made fumes she'd just as soon avoid.

Unscrewing the ring cap, she flipped it to turn the nozzle outside, screwed it down again and opened the vent cap. The wick was wet and yukky. Early on in her job she'd learned that any fire fighter worth her salt carried a lighter—she fished in a pocket. All the wick needed to catch was one spark and there she was, walking the line, tipping the torch at intervals and dripping liquid fire onto dry grass.

Warren pulled the heavies apart with a Pulaski hoe and piled them loosely so Jill could cut through them without rocking the saw. She stood over them, feet braced, pulled the starter cord, and began bucking burning logs into foot-long lengths while Randy held the engine hose ready to foam any flying sawdust that might catch. When Jill had a few rounds bucked off, Warren tore them apart with his hoe and Randy foamed the shreds.

After the grass had burned itself out and smoke was gone in the logs, all four of them leaned against the engine for an hour, watching to see whether anything would come to life again.

After the noise of the saw and the smells of foam and diesel fuel, it was pleasant to relax and watch tree shadows reach across the ground and know you were doing your job. Right away Warren got into the murder. "That must have been some experience yesterday, driving up on the body. Glad it wasn't me. How'd you happen to be back there? Want some water from our communal canteen?"

"Thanks. Vultures. I was ready to be mad about Pampers."

Jill was wiping off the saw. "Well, guys, are we all suspects? I'd hate to think they didn't take *me* seriously."

Randy leered at her. "Don't worry about that, little lady. As for me"—he sang—"Call me Mr. Guilty, Mr. Guilty, that's my name."

Warren sighed. "Isn't it the pits? First we have to put up with Jake, and then we're suspects. Not you, Randy, you'd have *sung* to him until he gave up the ghost. But take away a job at the top, and everybody below stands to move up. If Dalton gets Jake's job, do I move up to 3-1? Or Buck? Or Ed Osborne? It would probably mean a raise in grade. Isn't motive the first thing they ask?"

Look how they were all thinking about themselves. "He's been giving me a hard time all summer, and I've bitched about it to everybody. You know what? I wish I'd kept my mouth shut."

"I've thought it though."

Sun is backlighting the western mountains, when Venn begins to bark. A man walks up the road alone, a bow hunter probably, all camoed up...his face is blackened and he's wearing clothes dyed with patches of dull green and brown like Jake wore when he was off duty. Also, the man is carrying a bow, that's the best clue.

She pulls Venn inside...closes the cabin door and locks it. Standing back so he can't see her, she watches him. He looks around at the cabin and the clearing and disappears down the southwest slope. She hopes he won't come back. Jake would have jeered at him, hunting from the middle of a road...after sunset... smoking.

At dusk she's lying in bed reading about Mary Cassatt. When Cassatt told her father she was serious about being an artist, he said he'd almost rather see her dead. He thought women were unreasonable and deficient in good sense. The book says Mary was frantic to escape to Paris, where art *mattered*. Her father took her there after she had been in art school in Pennsylvania for five years. *Took* her, decided where she would live. Women still wore big skirts and crinolines...the Civil War was only just over. But she was twenty-two, she could have gone to Paris without her whole *family*.

There's a faint splashing in the rain barrel, and she goes out to see what it is. A hummingbird is in the cold water, beating its wings.

She bends over the rim and scoops the poor little thing up in her hand. Its eyes are open, but it lies unmoving on her palm. So tiny. She curls her fingers around it and holds it upright. Water drips out of her hand. Through soft feathers, she can feel the tiny heart beating.

The thing to do is to get it dry. In the cabin she wraps it in a washcloth and holds it in her hands and breathes on it. It watches her but doesn't struggle. She hums softly to it.

When she carries it to the door, light is almost gone from the sky. She opens her hand so the bird can go home, but it flies to her right shoulder. When she raises her hand, the bird jumps to her third finger knuckle. Awesome!

*D*riving back to the station, she took her time, gassing up for morning, washing road dust off the truck. It had to be ready to go out again before she could leave it at the end of the day.

Sun had set and street lights were coming on. That was OK—late meant less time with Walt, less chance for him to complain. Criticism *accumulated*. Every word carried the weight of all the words that had been spoken before.

It was a long drive out to Mountainaire, but she was in no hurry. Walt probably didn't realize that knowing he'd be mad didn't make her want to hurry home; it slowed her down. She drove through neighborhoods, alone in the dark inside her car.

When she was little, her mother had pointed out an old house on Verde. "Your great-grandmother used to live there. When I was a child, that's where we had Thanksgiving. I don't know who lives there now. It was a long time ago."

She drove by sometimes, slowly, when she was feeling down, just to look at it and imagine what it had been like to live there. She hadn't the nerve to knock on the door and introduce herself and ask if she could come in to see it.

She'd never told anybody that she drove by the old house and tried to imagine her great-grandmother—it was private, missing what she couldn't even remember. Dusk was a good time to do it. She wound through old streets and looked for a time that wasn't there anymore. Curtains were still open in the kitchen, and she drove slowly, looking at the lighted windows. You couldn't see the past. Traces of it were inside you, but you could never see it, the way it was, the rooms, the people.

At the house she had grown up in she turned the corner. Once she had climbed those trees, proud that she could go so high. People had called her a tomboy. Old Emerson School was already closed by then— she'd been fourteen when it was torn down, and that part was gone. The Woody Mountain wells were in, so nobody worried about water the way her grandparents had. In wet years they'd drive out from town to see whether water in Lake Mary was up to the spillway yet. The new hospital hadn't been built; the ranger station was still up on Knob Hill.

Her sophomore year in college—thinking she'd major in geology and focus on her own country, northern Arizona—her parents and Aunt Virginia had been killed by a kid speeding, and that changed everything. Everybody was gone except a brother in California, and the house sold, and she felt so lonesome all the time she couldn't have cared less about tests and grades—she just stopped going to school. Ten years, and she hadn't got over it. Maybe she never would.

*H*er gun belt had its own place beside the kitchen door. She'd laid it there, checked to be sure the pager was on, Leatherman closed, holster for the handcuffs snapped. They'd discussed the day through dinner, dishes, shower.

No matter how she'd tried to keep the conversation light, it always slipped into grim and greasy. "Definitely the Forest Circus around the station this morning. Carol all over the place trying to keep a lid on, Bailey all over the place fishing for alibis."

She'd pulled out a kitchen chair and imitated the big Sergeant sitting down. "Whoosh!" Folded her hands across her stomach. "I'm canny and experienced, but I'm gettin' old and tired. No need to watch what you say around me." She'd thought she'd done the voice rather well. "By the way, he asked me where I was Thursday night."

Hill had looked up from the dishwater. "You? *Why?*"

"I've had max firearms training. After two years working engines, I disliked Jake as much as anybody. My movements that night aren't documented except in a log I could have fudged. I might have had reason to think he'd be a threat to you if a promotion job opened up."

"To *me?* That's absurd."

"Crumb, half the people who knew the late lamented must have wanted him removed whether they said so or not. And he was stupid enough to tell them where they could find him asleep. There's no reason why I should be crossed off."

"Or me, I suppose."

"Revoltin' development, isn't it?"

In the shower they'd stood quiet under the hot water. Toweling off, she'd told him about Kristin and her parents. "I was heroine of the hour. Coming after the stupid kids who'd destroyed a Mercedes, it was downright reassuring."

He'd put his bare arms around her bare waist. "How'd a nice girl like you get to be a cop?"

"Funny you should ask."

Lying together in bed reading, their shoulders touching, was balm for the spirit. She rested her book on her chest, and he turned his head to her. "What?"

"I'm wondering how long it would take to walk from Woody Mountain to Black Tank in the dark."

"That brain of yours is always working, isn't it? Why don't you try it? Privately on your day off. That shouldn't step on any official toes."

*A*ll night the tiny bird sleeps safe on her hand in the late moon-light that comes through the window, while she's careful to hold it steady. They make no sound to each other. She feels blessed…

In the morning she opens the door, and the hummingbird flies away into the sunlight. When she sees Randy, she'll tell him about how it stayed all night with her, on her hand. He'll make a joke, but he won't think she's making it up.

Wednesday is a day off. After breakfast, after dishes are washed and the bed is made, she carries her laundry basket out to the car…goes back for keys, list of things to do in town, art books that are due at the library. She hopes Dad won't be home until late…

When the letter came in March that she had the lookout job, he bought a little Toyota truck for her to use. It's her first car. She goes down the road in low gear, slowly…she always lets Venn run ahead of her all the way to the lake.

One morning in June, going around a curve on the southeast side, she saw something small standing in the road. Something that folded its legs and lay down…a fawn! A tiny fawn with spots on its back! Excited, Venn ran toward it.

She jumped out. "Venn! Venn, *no*! Come." Venn turned and came back to her. "*Good* dog. Good Venn. Stay."

She couldn't drive right over the little thing. It didn't move as she walked toward it, but its huge brown eyes looked up at her. She searched around the slopes for the doe, there had to be one watching somewhere back in the trees, a mother alarmed by the sight of this human walking toward her baby.

She gathered it into her arms, legs still folded under it, and care-fully lifted it up against her chest. Only a few steps, just enough to move it off the road, and she knelt in the dust and set it down as softly as she could. She couldn't resist stroking just for a moment the curved bone that shaped its head.

She was glad hunting season hadn't started. On the way home that night, she looked to see that the fawn was gone…

It's been a bonus all summer that she and Randy have the same days off. Alone like she is, there are always so many questions. No one gave her any training, just handed her a radio and sent her up, but she'd had Randy. "I can't figure out what all those numbers mean." "What's the difference between a Red Flag Watch and a Red Flag *Warning*?" "Nobody told *me* about being in restrictions. What does that mean?" "That smoke yesterday was so dark, what was burning?" This week she wants to know who told Bailey to come up and question *her*.

*N*othing was turned on yet—lights, computer, brain—when Bailey appeared at her office door. It was 08:01, for crumb sake. "Sergeant, you must have been up before sunrise."

"Just about. I was hoping you'd have a minute."

"Sure, anything to put off paperwork. Sit down."

It was too early for a whoosh. "Thanks. This case is cutting into my sleep, I was hoping you'd have some ideas."

She opened the blinds and pulled out her desk chair. "No easy solutions?"

"Damndest thing. A quarter of the office and almost half the fire people have no alibi. That includes four of the lookouts. The man on East Pocket referred me to his dog. 'Ask ol' Blue here,' he said, 'he was right with me all night.' He and Woody Mountain said they knew where Holding would be, he'd told them. All four said they were alone Thursday night, staying out of the wind. By the way, you were right about those roads: my back still hasn't recovered from the trip to Elden. The O'Leary road like to scared me out of ten years growth."

"Sometimes slides close it." She watched him.

"Whee, I'm glad I didn't know that at the time. Some of the engine people said they'd had too many hours on fires to do any socializing, went home and went to bed. Kirkman left late and drove to Ashfork and back—working off tension about her boyfriend, according to her. Duvenek claims he was working on his car in the garage, but he's not sure the neighbors noticed. Williams says she spent three hours in her jacuzzi playing jazz tapes, reading a book and drinking mint tea—I give that one first prize for creativity."

"People do sometimes have private spaces in their lives."

"I do too. Thursday night my wife was in Phoenix and I enjoyed having the house to myself. I've got no alibi either."

"So you were hoping I'd have something to say about...?"

He tore a page off his notepad, leaned forward and handed it to her. "Here's the list of folks with private spaces. It's gonna take us a while to check whether the people who say they had company really did, but I thought maybe you'd have some comment, like this guy's unstable or this woman's mad all the time, things like that."

Twenty-five names, seven of them women. "I've known some of these people for a long time. Some I haven't met, there's not much contact between Hot Shots and office staff, for instance. Few of us see the lookouts. I told you Duvenek's comment about shooting. Josy thinks Evan Franklin is hard to get along with, but I can't say that from personal experience. She's a long time friend—our families go three generations back—I probably know her better than any of them. Stink, Bailey, could you say positively whether *your* friends are capable of murder?"

"To tell you the truth, I couldn't even say positively that *I'm* not, given the provocation."

"Well, Jake was big-time provocation. I hated him—I notice you don't have my name here." The paper was shaking in her hand.

"Now, hold on a minute, making you mad wasn't what I came in here for. I just wanted to talk."

She didn't look at him. "Did you ask Raleigh what he thought?"

"I did, he pretty much told me the same—he's as baffled as I am. We can't find a thing to go on. Yesterday we went through Holding's apartment looking for evidence of drugs—you get an execution-style killing it's the first thing you think of. Zip. Booze and a regular arsenal of arrows, but no drugs. By the way, we're fairly sure the lookout's .38 isn't the murder weapon. I agree with you, she's unlikely. Nobody in your shop can corroborate a relationship with Holding, just his bragging."

"You *asked?* Damn it, Bailey."

"Wait now, wait." He held up both hands. "I didn't mention any names, I just asked if they knew of girlfriends and a couple of the guys said he'd bragged about the lookout. That's all."

"The worst gossips I've ever known have been men, especially if it's sex and they can hurt somebody." She jumped up and stood at the window. "Excuse my back, Bailey, but this hornet's nest is getting to me."

He came to stand beside her. "I sure got off on the wrong foot here this morning. Will you take an apology? I'm not accusing anybody, and making trouble for women is the last thing I want to do. That includes you."

> In carrying out the investigation, do not make the suspect
> aware of suspicions until such time as sufficient facts have
> been gathered to support criminal or civil action.

"OK. Give me ten years, and maybe I'll calm down."

Jovial, that was the word, a jovial laugh. "I hope it doesn't take that long, I was beginning to like working with you."

She turned and glared at him.

"Wrong thing to say?"

"Crumb, Bailey, next you'll be calling me 'little lady'."

His laugh sounded sincere enough. "Never."

"Look, let me tell you something. I'm not trying to do this job the way a man would, I don't want to, and I don't see why I should. Is there any reason I can't still do just fine?"

"None I can think of. My wife'd have my head—she says, 'Cut me in half, Len, and you cut yourself in half too.' No, you don't have to act like a man, I'd rather you didn't."

"Most of the women who worked with Jake didn't want to be alone with him. He didn't make passes at me because I'm taller than he was, which probably saved me from cutting his balls off, but I saw the way he treated the others, and I'll tell you something else, it was sick. I'll work with you, it's part of my job description, but if you want to poke and prod at women who are trying to…to do their jobs and put up with shit-head male attitudes, you'll have to do it without me."

"Ms. Pederson, I'm getting a bad rap here. I came to see you because I think a woman's perspective is not only valuable but necessary. We're not all shitheads."

"That much is true." She admired his skill. "There's too many of you, you can't all be alike." She smiled, a half apology. "But give us a little credit—what would you think of a woman who didn't have enough spirit to be mad?"

"Not much." He shook his head. "I mean it, I like working with you, and I hope we'll get along."

"OK. OK." She put out her hand. "Well said. We can if you won't expect me to fink on my friends."

"It's a deal." He shook her hand. "And I promise I'll put my name on the list of no alibis. I didn't know the dear departed, but if I had I might have shot him myself. I'll get my little paper out of your sight."

"No, leave it. I'll give it some female thought and let you know. Sorry I was so touchy—you're trying to do your job, and I've got a lot of what's called baggage."

So he went off down the hall. She tried to work on her Kristin report, but those twenty-five names got in the way. Finally she bolted, took her gear out to the truck and drove off to patrol. She shouldn't have been so angry with him, he hadn't really said anything. And she hadn't been exactly forthcoming, she hadn't mentioned that two weeks ago she'd arrived in the morning and found a photograph of Hill on her desk with pins stuck into the eyes.

The Mercedes and Party fires were on the board after Josy's name, and the Howard fire hadn't been erased yet. If she planned right, she could get to Howard Pocket at lunch time—she'd brought her geology book on Oak Creek Canyon, just in case. It had been about thirty hours since Jake's body had been carried out of the forest.

"Morning, Josy."

"Morning, Shaeffer, Abby. What's up?"

"Another day on the Coconino."

Abby sighed. "My district is swarming with campers, practically elbow to elbow. We can call it "dispersed" if we want to, but some of them don't disperse themselves at all."

"They think they're safer in clumps." Shaeffer laughed. "Square miles of open forest, and they set up little trailer towns."

The adze on her Pulaski needed sharpening—she'd carried it in from her truck first thing and leaned it against the wall for the Engine 3-2 slugs to take care of. "Hey, it's just as well—we don't ruin *everyplace* that way. You should see Fry Canyon."

"Friedlein Prairie is a zoo. So is Schultz Pass."

Abby snagged a book of contact notices from the box on the desk. "Tell me about it. I cringe every time I turn off 418 at Little Spring. One thing I won't do for fun in the summer is go camping."

"You know what? There are places on my district where nobody ever goes. 'Course they're twenty miles off pavement and dead end."

"Right. I've got that too, and I'm not telling anybody where they are." Abby was right—don't tell if you want to save it.

"What's this, group therapy?"

"Hey, Buck, how's it going?"

"Can't complain."

"What's on your schedule today, Buck—same old, same old?" It was just social noise, but social noise was important on any job, no matter what supervisors thought.

"Same old fence building. Hope for a fire dispatch in our AOR. Been quiet out there lately. I almost said 'dead.'"

"That's going to be a loaded word for a while."

The DG computer held her work reports—there was yesterday's fire time to enter. She logged on with the name of Grandma's mare, Shili'i', which meant horse in Navajo, Grandma said. Henry had seen it one day and smiled at her. "Pretty good, OK."

She had an old photograph of Grandma on Shili'i' with her two little girls beside her on ponies—Aunt Virginia on Litso, which meant five cents, and Mom on Sinda'o, one cent, penny. Their names and the names of the horses were on the back in graceful writing. They all looked so young and pretty and alive.

She'd barely stood up from the computer when Myrna's voice stopped movement in the shop. "Flagstaff, Elden. Fire flash." Everyone stood waiting to hear the numbers.

"Elden, Flagstaff."

"Small white smoke. 202 degrees. Six miles."

Close enough to be possible. People moved toward the wall map, everyone but Henry, who went on re-doing his fire pack. "Not on us."

Buck traced a line on the map with his finger. "Damn. Score another good guess for the Navajos."

Dalton leaned in beside Buck. "That's where we had the Lonetree fire last year, right on a road."

"Engine 3-4 wasn't on that one."

She remembered it. "Neither was I. But I was on Woody Mountain getting equipment numbers for inventory, so I went up into the tower and watched a while. I don't often have that perspective on a fire. Hill was there before I got to the top, half an acre crowning in heavy fuels, and he started ordering everything available. Hand crew, helicopter, dozer, hose cache—breathing heavy into the mike. In no time the smoke was big and black and two acres."

Abby had been close enough that day to respond. "I was there, god, the confusion. In the city limits, we must have had a hundred people. City battalion. City brush crew. *Four* aircraft."

"It was a Red Flag day. Wind up in the tower was blowing twenty. I was watching for sparks across I-40."

Shaeffer protested. "That was a mile *away*."

"Hey, I've seen a strong wind make fire jump both lanes on I-17. There were three agencies, weren't there? I remember radio confusion— city crews were operating on channel one, shouting orders. One of the copters couldn't get Victor frequency."

Buck turned from the desk. "And three of the aircraft had the same ID numbers. Helicopter 3-36. DPS Ranger 3-6. Tanker 3-6. *Max* confusion." He stepped back and bumped into Evan.

"Watch it." Good old Evan. "Watch your fuckin' back."

Buck didn't look at him. "*You* watch who you stand behind."

"Yeah?" Evan was already shouting. "For a prime suspect you're fuckin' cocky."

Heads came around—Evan didn't notice, or maybe he did. "You think we don't know you spent the night alone out at the Fernow cabin Thursday? And the rest of the crew came into town?" His face was red.

"You're crazy." Buck's hands were clenching. Warren and Dalton stepped in closer, ready to calm things down—Evan didn't seem to see.

"You think we don't know you were only ten miles by road from where Jake was shot? Mr. South End himself, you know every part of that district, you could easy have parked off in the trees by Kathy Tank and cross-countried. I saw your face when Jake was telling where he'd be. This gives you a shot at a promotion, doesn't it?"

She thought Buck was going to hit him. Henry warned, "Sheriff."

And there was Bailey standing in the doorway. "A shooting affects everybody different, in my experience." He walked in and stood between Buck and Evan. "Like to talk with both you men, one at a time. Morning, Ms. Kirkman. Any place private around here?"

"Try the weight room. Through that door."

"You first." He nodded at Buck. "And you," he looked at Evan, "I'll get to you in a minute. Why don't you just sit down right here and wait."

Evan sat at the table and didn't look at anybody. They all fled outside to the engines. After a minute of embarrassment: "Whoo! What was *that* all about?"

"Damned if I know. Evan's got a burr up his ass these days."

Dalton shook his head. "Man, I tell you, if they're looking at promotion for motive, they'll be coming after *me*. Yesterday Mitch told me I'm acting engine specialist for the rest of the season. I'm not too happy about it, under the circumstances."

"Then you're in position for an appointment. Good luck. Who's getting your job?"

"I don't know, Warren. Maybe you? Maybe Buck. Maybe Randy. Hell, that'll make all of us suspects. Maybe they'll fly it, they ought to."

"Far as I'm concerned, Evan should be at the top of a suspect list."

Henry said, "That Evan, he's a good man. But not today."

One Saturday afternoon in early May Sarah stood in her tower and watched a huge black smoke *boiling* up over the shoulder of Mt. Elden. Jake was first there, of course...he said three acres were burning and fire was crowning in the trees. An active power line and four neighborhoods were threatened, order air tankers.

Practically everybody in Fire on the district was dispatched. So were Crew Seven and three Indian crews, Navajo and Hopi. Voices in the Flagstaff office were, like, *brisk*.

Within an hour more than 150 people were responding to the staging center, which was at Mary's Cafe on the highway. Two dozers, two water tenders, city fire trucks were on the way or on the scene. An Air Attack plane was overhead, two helicopters were trying to help with bucket drops, a lead plane was coming. Jake was asking, "Do we have an ETA on those tankers? We've got fire a quarter mile from structures."

She thought he sounded just really rad, organizing the whole confusion. "Put a hose lay up the east side. Keep a lookout for spots." "Water Tender 5, support Engine 5-1." "Flagstaff, we've got dozens of cars congesting our entry. Out on 89 north is also a problem, can we close it? And we need structure protection, fire is within two hundred yards of houses. Call police and Doney Park Fire Department."

It was *awesome* to hear him. "We'll chase it down the east side and try to pinch it at the head." "Flagstaff, we need a couple of miles of hose delivered right away." "Flagstaff, we need power in this line cut off, it's arcing in the smoke." "How soon can we get those tankers? There's fire in backyards now." "Laurie, we've got citizens walking in to the head of the fire. Your job is to keep them out."

Three big air tankers flying out of Prescott droned over her mountain...but smoke on the fire was so thick they couldn't get under it. Couldn't see a thing and didn't want to drop a load of the heavy slurry close to the head for fear it would land on houses and smash them.

People were cleared off the Mt. Elden Trail and out of the trailhead. The arkies working at the Elden Pueblo ruin were worried, and Jake said, "We've got a dozer line in and a hose lay, you should be all right, but get your vehicles out of there." Then Randy radioed that media people with cameras had slipped through the line and were hurrying toward the head of the fire, right where it was most dangerous. Gas in the nearby pipe line was cut off. Dead trees in the old burn had caught, and fire was moving uphill.

Another hour, and there were voices on the radio calling themselves "Deputy I.C." and "Operations" and "Division A" and "Division B." More than four hundred people were fighting a fire that had already burned three hundred acres. Because wind was so strong, the point of origin was clear, and Law Enforcement was looking for clues.

The cause turned out to be "two young males playing with matches." Randy said it was too bad they couldn't put boys into deep freeze until fire season was over for the year, it would be cost effective. The district was telling reporters it might charge the parents $900,000 for suppression...

She wanted to hear Randy's stories about it, but on her next day off his engine was on a fire. Then there was that wild one north of Kendrick Park that jumped the highway in a gnarly wind and burned eight thousand acres, twelve miles of fence on the Babbitt ranch. Air Attack was talking about a solid wall of fire in the trees, blowing out. Twenty crews and five air tankers and three contract dozers were on order.

Randy's engine was there, she heard his voice say they were on the hccl of the fire. They fought it for a week. By the time she saw him again, the fire in east side neighborhoods was old history, and he talked about the one north of Kendrick Park.

"It was the biggest fire the Coconino's ever had. Eleven hundred people…it was really crankin'. Moonscaped both sides of the highway."

When she opens the service room door, Randy is waiting for her. He doesn't have Forest Service quarters, so he lives at home. Dad says it wakes him up to have the phone ringing all hours of the night or the pager making noise and Randy getting dressed in a hurry and leaving…it looks to him as if Randy isn't in control of his life. Randy says that's true, he's not.

He stands and talks while she sorts laundry into the washing machine. "Did the county mountie come up?"

"Yesterday. I told him I hadn't known Jake long. *You?*"

"Same thing. But Jake had been bragging that you were his personal lookout. I told Bailey I didn't think so, Jake was just bullshitting. He wanted to know if I had ever threatened or fought with anybody who had mistreated you, if I threatened Jake for bragging about you. I said it was the first I'd heard of it, he never said that around *me.*"

To think Jake had turned her into a joke in the shop…he was *disgusting.* "He asked if Jake had enemies. Meg took your pistol. Did Dad say anything to you?"

"He read about the murder and asked what I knew. Everybody at the shop is a suspect. They're all scared and mad at each other. Like kids, tattling and accusing. Yesterday was crazy, we all got questioned."

"Are you a suspect too? Oh, Randy."

"No more than anybody else. They'd all been bitching about him. I gather the county is frustrated because they can't find any clues, not a hair, not a footprint, nothing—so they're just vacuuming around, picking up everything that's loose, which they wouldn't do if they really had anything. Know what *I'd* do? Sweat everybody."

*M*eg was out of the office, driving north on 89 at the speed limit, but that wasn't fast enough for half the people on the highway. They rode her bumper, fidgeted back and forth, passed at the narrowest opportunity and in general irritated her no end. Might as well patrol along road 418 north of the Peaks. No doubt she'd find a law enforcement situation or three—people seemed to think the minute they left pavement they were in a primeval wilderness where no rules applied.

She nearly missed the turn onto 418, to the annoyance of the red truck behind her, which had to slow down. She felt no sympathy. "Bet you kill yourself in that crate."

"3-4, Flagstaff. Your location?"

The radio could always grab her. "89 North, turning onto 418."

"Disregard. 5-4, 6-4, respond to the Oak Creek Vista, a complaint about multiple violations. Your contact will be 6-52."

She'd missed that by being twelve miles too far away. Yay.

Rain shadow there northeast of the Peaks made for a dry forest, juniper, an occasional yellow pine but mostly blackjack. It was amazing how fast everything could change. One minute noise and road rage, the next tree shadows across a dirt road and 20 MPH. Tension drained out through her fingertips and evaporated into the dry air.

She wasn't paid to ID wildflowers, but it would only take a minute, close to the road, and she wasn't sure what that one was over there. She hunkered down—Grandpa had loved that word hunker sun warm on her back, a white noise of breeze in pines. For her twelfth birthday Great-aunt Jo had done a set of ten wildflower paintings to hang in her room, little watercolors that showed the whole growing plant.

"Matt chose the subjects. We spent days while you were in school riding out to find them and sketch them in the proper setting."

"They're wonderful. I wouldn't have wanted *picked* flowers."

"I thought not. If you can identify each one, I'll know I'm not a dud."

"Pink penstemon, it's a snapdragon."

"See Matt, she pointed to the rare one first."

"Loco weed, it's poison. Fetid-marigold—the Hopis make a die from it. They use this bee plant as a pot herb." She looked up at Uncle Matt.

"Right."

"Sand sunflower, wild zinnia—it's a sunflower too. Globemallow, slimleaf lima bean, twinpod—that's a mustard but it doesn't look like it. And Apache Plume is a rose."

She'd hung the paintings where she could see them from her bed. When Aunt Jo died, she looked at them and cried. Slowly they turned into company, reminders of being a child and the generation she'd been lucky to know.

Back in the truck, driving along, she felt better. She hadn't been fair to Bailey, he hadn't really said anything wrong. Next time she saw him, she'd apologize again.

Ahead on the left she saw blue up on a steep slope and took her foot off the gas. They didn't hear her coming, four teen-age boys with their backs to her, trying to muscle their Scout off a pine tree where it was broadsided. My my, the radio on too. And a rear tire flat.

At full stop, she found the license plate with her binoculars. "Flagstaff, 3-4, will you run a 28, 29 for me on an Arizona number?"

While she waited for the computer check, she watched the boys heaving, shouting at each other, trying to move a truck uphill. No question what had happened, the evidence was plain in the tracks on the slope. 4WD, they'd headed straight up, radio probably blasting. Fifty feet and the wheels began to churn up cinders and throw them out behind, and the driver had gunned his engine until the tire went flat tearing at lava rock. The minute he took his foot off the gas, he slid backward out of control. The Blazer was smack on the uphill side of a pine, passenger door deeply dented. She opened out her camera and made a few action shots.

"3-4, Flagstaff, that comes back 29 negative," and Sherry read for the whole forest to hear the name and address of a man who lived in town, William Ida Lima Sam Oscar Nora. Mr. Wilson, you've got a surprise coming.

"Copy. Thank you."

The boys finally saw her when she pulled even with them and stopped. Four statues in identical poses, staring. She shouted up at them—one reached in and turned off the radio. "Which of you boys is the son of Scott Wilson?" A hand went up slowly. "Could I talk with you down here, please?" Best to separate the responsible party from the group, it forestalled bluster.

Working to free his father's car hadn't done his new Dockers any good. "Morning. Registration of the Blazer is to Scott Wilson. That's your father?" He nodded. "You were driving?" Another nod—from the look of his face, he probably couldn't grow a real beard yet. "Your name, please?" Ah, Scott junior.

"Can you pull us out?"

"Not out of *that* situation, I can't, you're going to need a wrecker with a long cable." His face collapsed. "Yeah, it's tough, but I'm afraid you're in for it. Do you have a valid driver's license? That's good. How about a credit card? Hmm. Do you suppose your father has a credit card?"

"I don't want him to know."

"We never want Dad to know, but you won't be able to hide this one from him. Look at that door."

He sagged. "Shit."

"You're not the owner of the car. Without a credit card, I can't call a wrecker; any company in town would say no. So Scott, you're going to have to call your father, have him arrange for the wrecker and meet it out here."

"Shit. Shitshitshit."

"Yeah, deep. Here's my cell phone."

From ten feet away, photographing the slope, she could hear Scott senior shouting. Deep shit indeed, big learning experience.

"OK, Scott, now that we've got that squared away, there's one more thing. You've torn up the slope big time, as you can see from here. You're looking at a gully that will erode deeper every year. And that tree will be pretty well torn up by the time the wrecker gets you loose. So I'm going to write you an official citation for damage to the natural resources of the forest. Carries a minimum fine of two hundred and fifty dollars."

"*What?*" He screamed and actually pulled at his hair.

"It could be worse. You're a juvenile, so it'll be state court not federal." It was her opinion that getting away with it was no cure for the ignorant arrogance of youth. It made arrogant adults who still thought they could get away with it.

*N*othing like tension to start the day right. Josy turned off pavement onto the Woody Mountain road. Trouble certainly brought out Evan's worst. She wouldn't want to be on a fire blow-up with him—he'd probably lose it entirely.

This thing about Jake was wearing her out, all the overtones and undercurrents and worry, fear. Last night she'd gone to bed early and curled into a ball.

Walt had stood in the bedroom door and laughed, that sneering laugh when he was going to be superior. "Ah, the fetal position. I thought you were a grown-up by now."

She didn't really care any more what he said—that was his mistake. Hers was that she *had* cared.

"Job too much for you, little Arizona girl? Why don't you quit and stay home where it's quiet. I can take care of you."

Oh sure, no money of her own, completely at his mercy. He'd make the most of that. Last winter she'd put her pay check from the Snow Bowl into common funds, but he made more as an environmental engineer than she did, and when he thought she was spending too much for groceries, he shouted, "It's *my* money."

"Come on, get up. I want you to proof this report I'm writing. You're working yourself up for no reason." What he needed mattered, what she needed didn't. Not really an equal partnership. "Look, I'm getting sick of the job shit. I don't need this."

She turned her back to him. There was no way she'd tell him what had started it all—he'd rage and insult her and say it was her fault. He was the *last* person she could go to for help.

He stretched out on the bed and pulled her toward him. "Come on, Sweetie, I'll make you forget it."

She didn't even feel the fury coming, it was just there. "*Stop* it! Power games may make *you* horny, but not me." Men must think women could be wildly aroused in half a second.

He jumped up. "I can't believe this crap." He called her a frigid bitch and shouted that she'd be up a creek without him—she was a drop-out with no degree—and slammed out of the house. Fine with her—it was a relief to have him gone.

Sky was still mostly clear, but there was a chance for afternoon clouds, maybe a storm. It was good to be driving alone, things were so stressed. Evan was trying too hard to put blame on Buck—it made him look suspicious. Ever since she'd left the shop, she'd been trying to think whether there'd been some scene or other between him and Jake that might have festered. She couldn't remember anything different from the complaints they all had, but that didn't mean there hadn't been. A lot of things could happen without anybody noticing—it was a big shop with rooms all over the place.

Probably not a single person had seen the way Jake was hitting on her last season. By August she'd made it a point never to be anyplace near him unless other people were around. He'd ask to be served like it was supposed to be a turn-on, and tell her to do things for him. "Hand me that wrench." "Bring me some coffee." "Get me some batteries."

"You're closer to it than I am, Jake, and I'm busy." Maybe some girls fell for it— she didn't. "No more slavey time, Jake, get it yourself." But he went on with it for weeks, blocking her way when she tried to get past him, like muscle was romantic and women were just dying to be domi-nated. Creep.

Rains had settled the dust a little. She left pavement and headed toward the old dump. Yuk. For three days she'd have to go into the Party fire, through all the garbage, and check it for smoke. At least she could get it over with early.

She made a quick circuit around the perimeter of yesterday's fire for a visual check. Nothing. Held her hand above what was left of the black logs and felt no heat. Got the Pulaski and turned them over, raked through the coals. Nothing.

Trees were so close together she couldn't see more than twenty feet into them—there was a creepy feeling that somebody was watching her. Transients? It was close to the interstate. She kept looking around and didn't see anybody, but the feeling stayed with her. She hurried back to her truck, stashed the Pulaski way too fast, climbed in and shut the door.

Out of the trees she turned south toward the Arboretum. Somebody she didn't know on the radio was requesting Law Enforcement from the overlook across from the canyon vista point. "Illegal campfire, shooting, littering, inebriation, the whole nine yards." The dispatcher started the Mormon Lake and Sedona LEs in that direction. Best to gang up on a drunk who was waving a gun.

Sarah doesn't ever have much mail. Most of it is, you know, bulk. She knows Dad throws away catalogs he doesn't think she'll be interested in and stuff from banks offering credit. She's seen them in the wastebasket. Sometimes she takes them into the bathroom and locks the door and looks…it's, like, a kind of secret defiance. Usually she doesn't care about them, it just makes her mad that he has to *control* everything. He does the same thing to mail for Randy.

Sometimes when she's in town for the day, she spends time in her big room upstairs. She likes looking out her window and seeing her mountain. Today the house feels like a *prison*. It's big and expensive and the neighborhood up on the hill is nice…Dad chose it because it was close to his office downtown…but she feels like running away from it.

Through high school Dad came in every morning to wake her up. He'd wiggle her foot and say, "Beautiful day. Raining, but rain is beautiful." Or snowing or cloudy or whatever. She would sit on the side of the bed and try to think of something she was going to do that day that she hadn't done before. She was so lonesome at school. She couldn't think of a single reason why she should want to go on living.

At breakfast Dad was cheerful about everything, with some news from the paper he thought would be interesting. He would say, "Why so glum, chum? It's a wonderful life. Let's have a smile from my girl." She tried to smile for him. He didn't know her at all, and she knew it wouldn't do any good to tell him how bad she felt.

The summer after she graduated, he spent a lot of money with an architect and a contractor to open her whole north wall and enlarge her room out over the garage until it was bigger even than his bedroom…so she could have a "private studio."

There were drawers full of all her supplies and a table for still lifes, even a sink for cleaning her brushes. She had Randy move her bed so she could wake up in the morning and see whatever canvas was on her easel and lie and look at it and decide what to do next. The walls were white to set off all her paintings.

Her life seemed better for a couple of years after that. Dad didn't let her have a lock on the door, but it was a place that was hers alone…she bought her own alarm clock. And there was college. Art classes. It wasn't until the past year that she started to wonder again why she should go on living.

"Randy, I'm so cooped up all week in that little tower, let's *drive.*"

"OK by me. Where?"

"Oak Creek Canyon?"

"I can't go far, I might get a fire dispatch and not hear my pager."

"How about Walnut Canyon? We haven't been there for *years.* I can see part of it from my tower, but I don't know which part. Do you suppose it will be too crowded?"

"We don't have to go down in and compete with tourists. We can walk out along the rim and find a place on the edge where we can sit. But no dogs, we can't take Venn." He rubs the dog with his foot. "She'll have to stay here and keep Mom company. S'awright? We're outa here."

It's only ten minutes out of town toward Albuquerque on I-40. They take Randy's truck, he turns on the air conditioning and snaps in a tape. "I've been on so many fires this summer I feel like a lemming— everybody go here, now everybody go there."

"Does the smoke bother you?"

"*Bother* me? You should see the black stuff I cough up every morning. The price I pay for saving the world, you wouldn't believe it."

"You *look* good."

"Solid muscle. I can hardly wait for winter so I can go to flab."

She didn't know there'd be an entry fee, but Randy pays it and jokes with the Parkie on duty in the little drive-by station. Around the curve the parking slots are *crammed* with cars and vans and motor homes. Randy sings, "Oh, we'll all go together when we go."

A child is screaming in the visitor center. They turn away on the rim trail. There's hardly anyone there, it's quiet and peaceful. Now and then through the trees to the right they can see into that sudden gash four hundred feet deep into the ground.

At the last overlook there are German tourists translating the interp signs for each other, so she and Randy wait, looking down at the swirling bottom level…old sand dunes, she remembers, turned to stone.

When the Germans leave, Randy whispers, "Go for it." They hurry past the sign that says Stay On Paved Path. Behind juniper and around a bend, and they are away from rules all of a sudden. There are elk beans on the ground. A big squarish pile of stones has a sort of hollow in the center…a ruined ancient house? Rusty-colored lichen is growing on it.

At a flat place they sit down. A raven sails above the canyon. A swallow flashes past. She wishes she had remembered to bring a hat to keep the sun out of her eyes.

Randy says, "Here we are, American youth, hangin' out."

"Is it all right, though, for us to be here?"

"No worries, we're golden."

"I don't see Woody Mountain. It must be just the first section of the canyon that's visible from up there."

She can see colored shirts below on the island trail, but no voices come through the air. There are fir trees a hundred feet away on the opposite side.

Randy points. "Habitations all along the canyon in the cliff face, the limestone layer. Right across from us, follow that layer, see? Probably some below us on this wall too, but we can't see them. With any point of view you lose something. Ah, I'm so philosophical."

She feels close to the past. "Imagine being the person who discovered this place. Hidden for centuries. Silent. It's awesome. I hope whoever it was felt, you know, respect for the people who lived here."

"How old were we when Dad brought us the first time? I barely remember it."

"I was only eight or so. He was always trying to expose us to education. I remember…" she begins to laugh, "…he was trying to tell us about ancient culture and how it would have been to be children here. He turned around and you were peeing off the cliff."

"And Mom was horrified."

"But Dad laughed and told you to stop showing off."

"Good old Dad. He's always cheerful when he can take us some-place good for us. Never saw a man so hot for uplifting influences for somebody else."

"I know. He just doesn't seem to see how *suffocating* it can be never to let a person be free to find things alone."

"Wonder how he got to be that way?"

"I thought maybe tomorrow I'd go see Beste, take her out to dinner with my own money. Maybe she has some ideas. At least she won't ask about Jake."

"Poor old Jake, he sure was hard to like. Not that anybody made much of an effort. He was always thumping his chest or spreading his tail feathers. I've got a plan to divert Dad at dinner tonight if he wants to bring it up. Brilliant, if you'll excuse the modesty. Absolute genius. In other words, fab. Smart as that raven up there."

"Are ravens smart?" She *knew* it.

"Apparently the most intelligent of the bird families. They solve problems. Use tools. Mate for life. Hikers say they can figure out zippers and get into packs. Also, they can count."

"Like in numbers?"

"Put five hunters with shotguns in a blind, let the raven see you do it, send four of them out, and the bird won't come down to the nuts you've scattered until the fifth hunter leaves. I don't know whether anybody's tried it without the guns."

"Do they ever try to be friends with humans?"

"You mean like they fed Elijah in the wilderness? I don't know…all the rumors are anecdotal not experimental. Not science, not proof."

"Do they talk?"

"Depends on what you mean by talk. They definitely communicate with sixty-four different calls."

"No, I mean to *people.*"

"You have one on the mountain who's trying to start a conversation?"

"It seems like it to me."

"Good answer. Subjective reaction identified as such."

"But is it possible?"

"I won't say it isn't. Just that nobody's proved it yet. There's probably a lot that we suspect but we'll never be able to prove. And a lot we'll never even suspect. The human mind is a mediocre guide to reality."

She loves to talk to Randy. She learns stuff but he doesn't treat her like she's dopey or anything…doesn't ridicule her questions or use big words she doesn't know. They sit there being part of the world for a long time. Two hours at least, talking. She feels like a whole person sitting on the ground and being part of the world and talking to Randy about anything they want to.

*M*eg drove away from the tow truck, west on the road that got into rocks of all sizes on either side. Uncle Matt had been old and slow to get off his horse, no longer good for much body work around the ranch. "Look at them close, Meggie. How did they get here? Did the volcano shoot out bombs? Glacier moved them around? Or would you say it's an old lava flow breaking up?" Lichen was growing on the surface, making its own kinds of change, taking what they needed, sometimes adding, making no noise doing it.

"It's pretty dry in here, mostly pines and grass, we're in the mountain's rain shadow. Take a look at the mullein, see all those tiny hairs on the leaves? That's to help the plant reduce evaporation. Now over here's lupine and clover and paintbrush. Can you tell which plants are native and which have been introduced? Look for evidence that might show they adapted a long time ago to a dry climate—narrow leaves or waxy ones—to animal predation: barbs or stickers. How about these butter and eggs plants?" With P.J. and the boys to do most of the work, he had time to study things he was curious about.

Four miles farther on she reached the edge of the three-month-old Hochderffer burn. Her first look at it—she'd been on the highway that week working traffic roadblocks. "Yes sir, it's a wild fire out of control, we'll hold you here a while until it's safe for you to proceed. Enjoy the show. Pretty spectacular, isn't it? We're expecting that big tanker up there—see it?—to drop retardant any minute."

She'd spent four years as a Hot Shot: she could read the signs, smell the smoke, hear the sounds as if they were still happening. It had been intense—the small trees rooted close together in dog hair thickets were dead and black clear to the top, understory ladder fuels that had carried flames into the crowns of the big trees. An occasional yellow pine looked to be still alive amid the destruction. Fire, nature's favorite thinning method—take out the little trees, leave the big ones more room.

Hill, home after an exhausting week: "The fire wanted to go east or back uphill into the wind, but we managed to turn it. Textbook demonstration of what stand treatment can do—every place there'd been thinning to separate the crowns and broadcast burns to clear off the understory, we saved the trees or held the spread, lost very little where there'd been fuel reduction."

Evidence was clear as a map. Left side of the road black and dead. Right side, look at that, green and untouched except for a few spots started by wind-blown sparks—they'd been able to hold it at the road. It was a mosaic, all right, as they'd said, what the time of day and air currents and terrain had dictated. And wind: there'd been high wind and a Red Flag Warning.

Half a mile later the left side was green. On the right side trees were black eight feet above the ground, probably from a back fire started there at the road to widen the fire line. They'd needed aggressive techniques, but back firing was tricky, no room for error. RH and time of day were critical.

It must have been close to chaos at times. Burned 16,400 acres, 1,100 people from several states fighting it. For four days fire had run ahead of the wind, north and east, fanning out across the land from the point of one lightning strike until it had died for lack of fuel in the grass-lands. Plotted on the map it looked like a lava flow.

Jake had sized up the Hochderffer briefly—right at first when it wasn't much more than a single tree burning—and gone on to look at other starts from the same dry lightning storm. The next day he'd been I.C. on the fire out by the Humane Society, 97 acres burned, two neighborhoods evacuated. It would have been the big show if Hochderffer hadn't grown out of control, and he made sure everybody knew how he'd caught it before there was structure damage.

Other people had caught Hochderffer's spread and saved the north side of the Peaks. The haunting places were groves of aspen, beautiful and clean in the sunshine, that had grown up where fires years in the past had turned conifers into dead sticks and left room for aspen—early in the succession line. Years in the future there'd be new aspen groves along 418, if deer and elk could be fenced out to let trees get established. Probably there'd be re-hab seeding.

The White Horse Hills, dead as a battlefield, could have some serious erosion problems. Fire had run uphill, crowned half-way and made air eddies, burned most intensely in the saddles and on southwest slopes. Before too long the hills would draw tourists in October, gold and white clear to the top, and cars would be parked along the road while people photographed the seasonal beauty, radiant every autumn for a century. Growing out of Hochderffer destruction, *right* out, through ash, charred branches, shriveled grass.

Nobody was on that stretch of road—there'd be no recreational use in there for a long time. Probably some days it was crawling with foresters from NAU studying and monitoring. Maybe she'd run into Chuck McHugh, he was developing a technique to predict survivors that could be saved from salvage sales. Complex data—DBH and height, aspect, percent of scorch, soil compaction, insect damage—he was really into it.

After the road turned, 151 was a cathedral aisle of aspen impossibly tall. The stand was decadent, well past maturity, doomed by Douglas fir growing up, crowding elbow to armpit too close for tree health—aspen didn't tolerate shade—but it felt spiritual to drive through. She'd have to move to the left to get past a little car parked ahead.

One glance made her hope they had a permit. Couple in their twenties, boy about five—they had dug up and were kneeling on the earth carefully balling in burlap the roots of a fir a foot tall. Removing resources without a permit, big fine. She stopped behind their car.

The boy ran toward her, his little face excited. "We're saving a tree! There's no room for it to grow here."

His parents were also aglow with good intentions. "We got every inch of the root. Should transplant all right."

She sat on a boot heel to look. They'd done a fine job, careful, concerned for the life of the tree. And they smiled at her, so proud.

The boy leaned against his mother. "We're going to give it a good home where it can grow big and strong for birds to make nests in. It will be my job to water and take care of, we have a book from the library that tells how."

She nodded. "It's a beautiful little tree. And you're right, it wouldn't have a chance for enough sun in here. Or rain. The big guys would grab everything for themselves."

The woman was modestly pregnant—not hugely, just modestly.

She put her arm around the boy. "We saw it when we drove through here last week, and it just broke our hearts, how brave and hopeless it was, so we came back to rescue it."

"It's my present to my new brother. When he's old enough to take care of it himself, he can. Then maybe we'll get another one for me."

Crumb, it got worse with every word.

> Unauthorized cutting or removal of timber or other forest products from National Forest System lands is normally a violation of law or regulation and the responsible party is criminally liable; consequently, action is necessary to bring those responsible before a court of law to answer for their crime.

Crime? These people? Idealists, OK, but criminals for adopting a tree a foot tall? A present for his new brother?

"It's a decent thing you're doing, caring for life. I wish everybody would.: She extended her hand to the woman. "Meg Pederson, Coconino law enforcement."

"Maybell Morris." Maybell, it fit.

"Ms. Morris, this job requires more paperwork than you'd believe. Would you mind taking a break, leaving the boys to finish up here? I need you to give me some information for my daily log."

"Information?"

"Your names, things like that, proof I wasn't joy-riding out here."

Maybell Morris stood, her hand on her son's shoulder. "Of course. I'd be happy to."

Kids were up front with the world. "Why are you so big?"

"Zach!"

It happened often. "Why are you so little?"

"I didn't grow yet."

"*I* did. But once I found the OFF button, I stopped."

"I'll grow lots more."

"Maybe we'll be the same size some day."

"But you're too big."

"*Zachary!*"

"Too big for what? I can reach things on top shelves and get on a tall horse with no trouble at all. *I* think I'm a very good size."

She took Maybell to the far side of her truck. "I wonder, did you get a permit for that tree?"

"Permit?" The blank look was answer enough.

"We try to protect the forest as best we can, partly by asking people to get permission before they take anything away. You're doing a fine thing, saving a life, but there are—well, some folks think it's fun to rob and vandalize. You understand, I hope?"

Maybell was afraid she did. "We didn't mean to break any laws."

"I don't think you did. I'm not going to write a citation—I wouldn't spoil Zach's present for anything. But I wanted you to know that if you do come back for another tree, you should go to the ranger station first and get a permit. Now, let's get you into my log. I know you and Zachary, what's your husband's first name?"

Waving goodbye, driving away, knowing she'd deliberately ignored regulations—crumb, one little tree when she'd just driven through hundreds burned and dead: no brainer. She hoped it wouldn't come back to bite her.

*L*ittle cumulus clouds were scattered all over the sky, some dark on the bottom already. Too early yet to predict a storm, but they looked possible. As a rancher, Grandpa cheered every cloud and hoped for enough rain to green the grass and fill water holes, rode his range with one eye on the sky. She couldn't count the times he'd told her that when Hopis said "good weather," they meant wet.

There was a photo of her great-grandmother with her friend Ada Nelson and Jo Boren, the woman from New York, standing up to their ankles in water, holding their shoes in their hands and laughing at the camera. On the back someone had written their names and "Celebrating the end of drought." Great-grandmother Green was taller than the other two. It was good to have a happy picture of your great-grandmother—people usually weren't laughing in old photos. And a great-grandmother meant a lot, especially for someone alone, the whole family evaporated out of Arizona.

Going through Mill Park she didn't look east to where the vultures had been. Nope. Kept her eyes on the road. That didn't stop pictures in her mind though. A sleeping bag with flies and the top of a blonde head. Jake's hair had been stirring in that little breeze.

Evan had been too weird that morning, but what he'd said was true. Buck had been alone down at Fernow Thursday night, and that wasn't far from Bob's Tank. It didn't prove anything, but Buck was no doubt wishing he'd had his wife overnight in the cabin or gone into town and taken her out for pizza or something.

It wouldn't take long to check it out. She went on to the old cinder pit where the power line brushed 231 and took the Crater Sinks road a couple of miles to 535, another mile north to Kathy Tank.

So close to Bob's Tank, it looked about the same—basalt rocks, pines. A two track wandered away around a clump of trees; she drove along it until the tank was out of sight. A truck wouldn't be noticed there unless someone drove right to it.

Bob's Tank was only a mile away, with mostly flat ground between. It would have been no trouble at all to walk it in moonlight. Even going carefully and watching where he put his feet, Buck could probably have done it in, what? at most an hour round trip?

She looked up from the map and stared into the trees toward Bob's Tank. Evan must have been figuring this, or he'd tested it for himself one evening last week. Driven down after work and taken a chance there'd be no one to recognize him. Rain had washed away tire tracks and foot prints. For that matter, *anybody* could have done it that way, anybody who knew the forest at all.

She and Meg both had days off Friday. Maybe Meg would like to take a hike, Kathy Tank to Bob's Tank, on to Woody Mountain and back to prove Sarah couldn't have done it, eight miles, another mile to Kathy Tank—ten miles round trip. They could start early and do the whole thing by noon. Bailey couldn't object that a couple of friends out for a hike would prejudice his investigation.

In the middle of the week, even in Archery Elk season there weren't many campers in the forest, and she'd already talked to most of them. A little before noon she turned into Howard Pocket. Hey, she needed a final check on the Buzz fire. Standing on the rim, she looked down to the blackened spot which had been a fire a week earlier. Nope, no smoke. Call it out and erase it from the board.

She found a flat-topped rock big enough to sit on and made herself comfortable. Opening her lunch box, she started with carrots. If she was correct, the rock she was sitting on had been—she turned pages in her book–sand on the shore of a shallow sea. The cross-beds in the opposite cliff swirled and dipped and showed which direction wind had blown. That made it, wait a minute, Upper Paleozoic, 265 million years ago. If it was Coconino Sandstone instead of Toroweap, it was even older.

The Toroweap was 300 feet thick at Sedona. Add the Coconino and there were 800 feet of white aeolian sandstone deposited through eight million years. They lay on top of more than 100 million years of older deposits. Millions of years above them had already eroded away. The plunging cliffs she was looking at had just started to be exposed about two million years before there were any volcanos around Flagstaff, before there was much of an Atlantic Ocean even.

She unwrapped her sandwich. It would be great to be back in school studying geology. She wasn't too old, there was no such thing; thirty wasn't old. The life she was living was going no where. Parts of it were good–there were people all over the planet who never in all their lives could find a place to be alone as she was on a beautiful cliff– Bombay, Brooklyn, Los Angeles, they never got away from the city. What she had in that one hour was a luxury that was becoming extinct.

She had pushed open the door and walked out of the Administration building into a radiant day. There'd be no problem! In front of her were Old Main and the Ashurst building–they had been there solid in the background every year of her life. The campus art gallery was in Old Main. Paintings, sculpture, a show of colored textiles and two foot tall stonewear vases. Minds working, studying, hands creating. She'd stood in the middle of an empty gallery and spread her arms, catalog in one hand and papers in the other, and turned a slow circle to the colored pictures.

A gust of wind blew up out of the canyon, ruffled pages in the book, lifted her hair. Sky above the old Buck Mountain volcano twenty miles away had filled with cumulus. Clouds made invisible air currents visible–a warm moist river of air flowing up out of the Gulf of Mexico.

Behind her, thunder rolled across the trees. She turned on the rock–a solid black cloud loomed high. Lightning streaked down. Obviously she was going to have to take rapid action or her book would get wet. She closed it into her lunch box, pushed off the rock and hurried through the ferns toward her truck. Jeesh, lightning was striking all around. She switched off the radio on her belt.

Rain spotted the windshield, then wet it, then *flooded* it. She couldn't see out, not even to the side, could barely see trees through it. She might as well stay right where she was. Summer storms were often heavy right on the rim, but inside the truck was safe and dry as a cave.

Using her book for a pillow, she lay down across the seat and ate a cookie. Always, all her life, she'd cared about why Agathla in Monument Valley was a different color than the other towers and what violence it had been that showed in the cliffs around Mexican Hat. Things like that. Why one side of Oak Creek Canyon was different from the other. Why there was no northeast wall to the Inner Basin. What made natural arches and bridges.

By the time she'd reached college, she enjoyed bringing surprises to her parents. They said they came to the dinner table excited about what they were going to hear. Just imagine! All that under foot.

The estate they had left, such as it was, had gone into a trust fund, one for her and one for her brother, to be held until each of them was thirty, which meant she could finally draw on it. Maybe there'd be enough with ten years worth of interest to see her through a graduate degree. In July she'd made an appointment with the trust officer at the bank and arranged a transfer to her checking account to cover tuition.

Rain seemed to be letting up, moving off along the rim to the west. She sat up and started the engine. Mist was rising from the ground and drifting through the trees. Wet as they were, they were darker than usual. Ground was black. After a rain the forest always looked soft and lush, even the pines. Sun would hit it in a minute—little diamonds sparkling in the branches.

"Flagstaff, Turkey Butte. Fire Flash."

That one would probably be in her area—better get moving.

*D*riving south after leaving Maybell's family and their tree rescue, Meg had come out of the pines at Fern Mountain. Taking a lunch break, she'd stopped in at the Nature Conservancy preserve to say hello to Edward and ask how the scarlet gilia were doing. There were two species of flowering valerian there on the prairie, fringed gentians, purple delphiniums, wild iris of course, the rose-family prairie smoke that made the meadow look reddish in June. But the gilia, a kind of phlox, was what she found fascinating.

Not because of its scent—the leaves smelled like a skunk when they were bruised. Or sensational beauty—there were hardly any leaves and the stems were spiky and sticky. Or because it was rare—it was common in Western mountains and meadows. But on Hart Prairie the trumpet flowers changed from red in June, when hummingbirds were the main pollinators, to pink to white by August when hummers had left and moths were attracted in the evening. Probably a local adaptation to a lot of factors.

In June Edward had walked out to show her what was going on. "The population's been in decline for over a decade—we suspect because the seeds need fire to germinate and fire has been suppressed out here. We're thinking of conducting a prescribed burn to see whether we can reverse the trend. Otherwise we might see another local extinction, like the wolves and grizzly bears."

Bebb willows were the big issue on the preserve. They weren't particularly beautiful—not much more than big shrubs with multiple twisted trunks, leaves kind of dull green, no flowers as such, just wind-pollinated catkins. But there were only twenty places in the world where Bebbs grew in wetlands communities, and the Hart Prairie group was the largest known, 1300 trees. It was rare to find them as the major canopy, sheltering an understory with birds and wildflowers.

"Reproduction is poor because settlers in the last century diverted water to their fields with dams and ditches, harming the riparian communities. You know what water means in Arizona."

"And how occasional a riparian area is."

"This summer volunteers will demolish the earthen dam upstream. We want to fence elk out of the willows so they can't graze them down, deer and elk *love* willow sprouts. We'll try thinning and controlled fire, study the system for wetland diversity."

Standing there that day talking with him about plants had been natural as breathing, the way she'd felt with Uncle Matt years before. Calm and content, feet on the earth. Still thinking about kids using cars to grow up, she'd planned to walk out to look at them again, but cumulus were towering high above the mountain, turning black, and Edward had work to do. First drops were hitting the roof of the lodge by the time she reached the porch.

Rain was falling hard on the aspen grove across Hart Prairie, a heavy curtain—the west side of the Peaks was a ghost. Rain hammered the roof and dripped from the eaves. Wonderful smell of wet earth and green plants. Wonderful shelter: the deep porch of the lodge at the preserve was as good a place as she knew to wait out a summer storm, especially with Boatman Bob sitting in the next chair telling stories.

"There were a lot of Germans out here: Hochderffer, Michelbach. Mrs. Michelbach was the doctor—when anybody was having a baby or kids had measles, they came and got her. The Freudenbergs home-steaded in 1883. Frank Hart had stopped earlier with his sheep; later the stage line to the Grand Canyon ran right past, y'know. The Freudenbergs grew potatoes as a cash crop—at least Lina did. Gus was always off around the country working here and there, blacksmithing and such. Once she traded a shot gun for a cow. Stayed out here one winter, which must have been a trial. After that she moved into town before snow fell–they had a house near the brewery where Gus was working. I've sometimes wondered if she was relieved when she sold to the Wilsons after forty-five years and took a rest."

The radio: 6-4 and 1-4 were responding to a campground in Oak Creek Canyon. Young males had been slashing tires with a knife. "If you can hold off, I'll be there in fifteen minutes."

She'd give up LEO in a minute if there were a job in a place like Hart Prairie she could go to. But ten years ago she'd been tired of going to school, tired of taking orders that were pointless half the time, and she didn't have a degree in anything. You had to be able to wave that degree if you wanted doors to open.

A fresh, after-the-rain smell is coming through the windows. They're not half through dinner when Dad begins to ask. "How is the investigation going?"

Randy answers. "What I've heard is that they can't find any evidence. Law Enforcement's been hanging around the station questioning everybody."

"That's to be expected."

"Looks like they think we're all suspects. They're probably right. Jake isn't exactly being mourned. We're thinking of having a medal made for whoever did it: outstanding service to the community."

"Deliberate murder is not a light matter."

"No, it's not. There's a question, though, whether it was a one-time thing. Jake provoked just about everybody who worked with him to consider violence." He puts his hand on his chest. "And the verdict is 'Served him right'."

"A clever lawyer might have some success using provocation as a defense for violence. With a jury. Not with the law."

Randy smiles like he's ready with something good. "Well, sometimes law can't see all the circumstances."

Dad smiles too. "You feel that there are deficiencies?"

"Bound to be. It's an evolving human creation. For example, science is usually several years ahead of law. The concept of interaction in any biological community and the necessity of all the organisms in it was at least a generation old before law began to recognize it."

"Ah, biology again."

"What else? Another lag: legal standing catching up with public opinion. For example, rights in law for other species."

She can see that Dad's interested…he folds his arms on the table. "Can you cite precedent and opinion for such an idea?"

"It's a slow development toward recognition of the value of all life, not just our own. We're this short," he pinches his thumb and forefinger two inches apart, "from reaching it."

"Anything in the literature?"

"There's the evolution of laws relevant to women and blacks and Asians. There was a time not so far back when those groups didn't have equality, weren't even legally persons. We heard all kinds of dire warnings about the collapse of society, and we got past that." Randy is like a different person now, older somehow.

Dad beams, you can see how proud he is. "First give me a definition of a legal right."

"A claim, entitlement, privilege—choose your word—conferred by legislative or judicial action or action by an agency under enabling statute with judicial review. Natural right is a shifting social consensus based on custom, religion, morality, sympathy, hysteria sometimes. Occasionally even by reason. I would think you'd have to be very careful using it."

"I'll accept the distinction. You're confining yourself to legal rights?"

"Hey, I'm not stupid."

It's the hardest she's seen Dad laugh for a long time. Mom is smiling at Randy.

Randy is smiling too. "I'll admit up front that I'm biased. But that's allowed, I think?"

Dad nods. "Expected."

"And I haven't got the language down. Excuse the common touch."

"We don't have all night."

"I'll be brief." Randy chuckles. "That's a pun. I'm shameless." It's the first time *ever* that Randy has dared to tease about law. "Last month we established a basis for federal action?"

"We did."

"OK then, forging ahead. We had a nationwide system of refuges for waterfowl for such human interests as hunting. Protected creatures were always referred to as 'game,' food for humans, even in the international Migratory Bird Treaty."

"When?"

"That was in 1918, I think. Odd treaty for a war year, but never mind. The term 'interstate commerce' cropped up in that debate. I'm much taken by the image of ducks engaged in interstate commerce."

She looks back and forth across the table. Dad is not interrupting at the moment, so Randy, like, *surges* on. "By 1934, which I'd like to point out was a Depression year…"

"What's that got to do with it?"

"Well, you'd think we'd have had our minds on other things. By 1934 a different language began to creep into law as it referred to wildlife. The word was still 'resources,' the rationale was still 'contribution to the national economy,' meaning human priority, but the Fish and Wildlife Coordination Act held, and I quote, 'Wildlife conservation shall receive equal consideration with other features of development programs.' That was significant language, but it wasn't an overnight conversion."

"Law is conservative and should be. Legal conversions never happen overnight."

"Well, whatever they *should* be, they're not. Overnight. But people were finally aware of abuses perpetrated in the name of economic progress and mad enough to have some effect."

"Examples?"

"In 1937 the Wildlife Society joined the Sierra Club and the Audubon Society as organizations of citizens. U.S Fish and Wildlife Service was organized in the Interior Department in '39. Bald eagles and wild horses were protected as important American symbols by acts in 1940. That introduced new values onto the scene. You know, animals as something besides food. We were moving toward the concept of animals as a public trust. Defenders of Wildlife was organized in 1947.

"All right. Your point is made."

"Society for Animal Rights came along in '59. Do you discern a trend in public opinion?"

"Quite definitely."

"The word 'rehabilitation' appeared in an act of 1960 and 'wildlife' was separated from 'game' and given equal consideration, especially if it was threatened or endangered. That was in accordance with The Multiple-Use Sustained Yield Act that year. Multiple use by humans, I might point out."

It said that forests were to be administered for wildlife, among other uses. You had legislation in '66 and '69 concerned with protecting habitat—leave the other guy a place to live, that kind of thing. Also in '69 the National Environmental Policy Act which didn't mention wildlife as such, but people read that into it. What hurts wildlife, hurts humans— we're all in this together. About the same time there were at least two federal laws that prescribed guidelines for animal welfare, especially in research and experimentation."

She sees the scene as if she were deciding to draw it. Dad's arms strong against the white table cloth, hands on his elbows. His shoulders large, leaning in…full light on his face. Randy in profile, elbows on the cloth, numbering points on his fingers. Although they were so close together, she would draw Dad a little larger. Randy would have shading on his shoulders and back.

"Now, right in there the Forest Service granted Walt Disney Enterprises a permit to build a ski resort in Mineral King Valley, and the Sierra Club sued for an injunction, and a District Court ruled that the Club had no cause to bring the suit."

"I remember that case. It was appealed to the Supreme Court, which upheld on the ground that the Sierra Club indeed had no personal stake in the outcome and thus no standing."

"Exactly. But a professor of law at U.S.C. got into it with an essay in *The Southern California Law Review*. The title was 'Should Trees Have Standing? Toward Legal Rights for Natural Objects.' He was talking about forests and mountains and lakes, not wildlife, but it was pertinent. In his dissent Justice Douglas cited it; Blackmun and Brennen concurred. Douglas had already written a book urging a wilderness bill of rights."

"And what was the gist of the *Law Review* essay?"

"That we ought to make a systematic effort to develop a body of law that would question our historic attitudes toward property and allow for the rights of non-human life. He said it would be a struggle, but we could do it."

"The recreational complex was built by Disney?"

"The Forest Service had second thoughts and denied a permit to build the necessary roads. Begged the question and delayed a real consideration of the issue."

Dad laughs. "I'd say that was a political maneuver, not a legal one."

She thinks she's following Randy's history. It's not the kind of thing her mind velcros *onto*, but he's telling it so that it's kind of a drama.

"OK, so the Marine Mammal Protection Act of 1972. Very important. The central feature was a complete ban on harassing, hunting, capturing or killing. Limited exceptions for science and Eskimos. And it didn't cover walruses, I'm not sure why."

"And what was its effect?"

"There were ambiguities in the act. The protectionists weren't completely satisfied. But it said that marine mammals have recreational as well as commercial value. It talked about the marine ecosystem. In *Committee for Humane Legislation vs. Richardson…*" he grins, proud of himself for knowing the name. "…the judge found that the interests of marine mammals come first, before human interests, I infer. I haven't located that case yet, but I will. I think it would have damn near stopped all purse seining in tuna fishing if there hadn't been appeals."

"As I remember it, you're probably right."

"By the time Nixon signed the Endangered Species Act of 1973, we were definitely talking about animals as more than just food for humans. They were, I quote, 'of aesthetic, ecological, educational, historical, recreational and scientific value.' The Act limited human action in a big way."

"I'd say so, yes."

"I see it as Congress reflecting pressure from the public, which was showing some pretty strong support for wildlife, land protection, ecosystem integrity, clean air, clean water. The Wilderness Society was thirty-five years old, the Nature Conservancy twenty. Friends of the Earth and the National Resources Defense Council had just been organized. There were forty-one wildlife conservation associations by then and thirty animal welfare groups."

"I follow your thinking." She wishes Dad would let Randy talk without putting himself into it all the time.

"But damn if the shit didn't hit the fan, 'scuse the French, Mom. ESA had teeth. It was a mandate to federal agencies to prevent activity that would imperil any species on the verge of extinction... and it was interpreted to authorize interfering with jobs and businesses and use of private property. And—an important change—the act specified that citizens and citizen organizations would have standing to bring suit. Cynics have been saying ever since that neither Congress nor Nixon realized what they had done."

Dad laughed. "I'm one of those cynics."

"Environmentalists used the courts to make hostile administrations enforce the law. I looked up those cases in the *U.S. Code Service* and the *Federal Supplement*. You are wildly impressed, right?"

"I am. I definitely am."

"Terrible writing. Little tiny print. I can't believe you want me to do that for a living."

Dad's laugh is more of, like, a sputter. "Legal writing has to be precise. But you're right, it's formal."

"For a while I thought I was onto just what I needed. Check this out, starting in 1979 cases brought under the ESA had non-humans as plaintiffs. Birds, deer, grizzly bear, the Mount Graham red squirrel. Northern Spotted Owl versus the Secretary of the Interior, for example, twice. An owl didn't actually walk into court and file the case, it was done for him, but the language was allowed. The owl won, in case you hadn't noticed. Last year a sea bird in California sued Bruce Babbitt."

"Hard to miss that one."

"It looked like standing to me, and I damn near whooped right there in the NAU library. For a while I was feeling good. By the time I got to the law library in the court house, I realized that the critters were just the first of the listed plaintiffs. The 1988 spotted owl case had twenty-two environmental organizations as fellow plaintiffs. Mount Graham red squirrel had eleven."

"People have to be involved."

"'Fraid so. Palila versus Hawaii was the earliest, and I thought maybe it would say what happened, you know, what it was that the others followed. But all I could see was a finding that the Sierra Club and the Audubon Society had standing to sue in their own names as next friends. Under ESA, I suppose.

"Wait now." Randy raises his hand to stop Dad. "I finally gave up and asked a professor. Short cut to legal research, I'll bet it happens all the time. I gather that the Supreme Court still hasn't gone for animal standing."

"Correct."

"Humans have to bring suit. And animals aren't accepted as parties to cases. BUT you can list anybody you want in a caption, and usually there aren't motions to dismiss a non-human, so if you put it first, you get your case identified by the eagle or deer or grizzly bear that it's about. Psychological and publicity advantage but not a strictly legal one."

"Indeed."

"OK, so you had the Sagebrush Rebellion. The God Squad. Bitterness. Social turmoil. Judicial decisions and challenges to them. Biology versus statistics. Environmentalists versus loggers. Also books like *The Case for Animal Rights* and *The Evolution of National Wildlife Law*."

"I'm not familiar with them."

"I'll bring them to you. Anyway, what a battle! Twenty years of controversy so intense Congress couldn't pass new wildlife legislation for making somebody mad. Amendments to ESA were proposed, one of which required scientific data as a basis for decisions."

"You see the situation as fertile ground for evolution of law?"

"Well, look at the numbers. Remember, ESA authorized citizen involvement, which opened the process up to the interested public. Within twenty-five years wildlife conservation groups had more than tripled–from forty-one to one hundred and thirty. Animal welfare groups were up from thirty to one hundred and twenty."

"Numbers make convincing arguments."

"There were six organizations devoted purely to animal rights. You had the Animal Legal Defense Fund. People for the Ethical Treatment of Animals was founded in 1980. So was Activists for Protective Animal Legislation."

"All citizen groups, not legal bodies."

"In 1990 Rutgers University Law School founded an Animal Rights Clinic. Law schools all over the country, Detroit and places, set up courses in wildlife law. And—get this—in California there's a political action group titled PAW PAC. Is that great? By 1995, membership in all the groups was somewhere between eight and ten million. All within twenty-five years."

"It's become a political issue, part of public debate. To at least some degree the idea of legal standing is already working through the pipeline. Ecosystems and species as well are assumed in some quarters to have legal rights—the idea is no longer shocking. If that's not being this far"—he pinches his thumb and finger two inches apart—"I don't know what is."

*W*alt's car was there when Josy pulled into the driveway. It was *his* house, as he had told her often. He opened the door before she turned the engine off and stood dark against the room behind him. As she started up the steps, he came out to meet her and put his arm around her. "Hi, Sweetie. Busy day?"

He wasn't fooling her—she'd read enough to know classic abusive behavior: first they slam you and then they apologize gracefully, sincerely. Tell you they love you. She didn't believe in that kind of love. "We had a fire down by Turkey Butte."

"Tomorrow's a day off, isn't it?"

"Yes. Why?"

"I have to drive out to Wupatki and Cameron in the afternoon to check the new systems. If you can break away from housecleaning, I'd like to have your company. We've hardly had any time together since fire season started."

It didn't mean he realized he'd finally gone too far and he was afraid he'd lose her. Being nice was just his way of stringing her along, as Grandma said. If he wanted to pretend nothing had happened, she'd go along with it a little longer.

*D*inner is a social activity—everybody knows that—a time for talk, when you can put your elbows on the table and be honest. "Hill, I need to talk."

"We haven't been talking?"

"I mean serious."

"What've I done now, left my socks in the corner? Talked in my sleep?"

"No, you're perfect. It's me. I've got a problem and I need your ideas."

"That's my favorite kind of request. Almost." She loved the way he smiled, the sound of his voice, his eyes—she flashed on pins stuck into them. She hadn't told him about that.

"Proceed."

"OK, so are there people who went out on a limb to get me the LEO job?"

"Mitch, probably—Raleigh, the good ol' boy network. Sure, there'd have been people recommending you."

"Did you have anything to do with it?"

"I wasn't putting any pressure, if that's what you mean. There were the years you worked in Fire. You're tall and everybody likes you, strong, you don't go to pieces in a tough spot. They were looking for a woman, and you were the best." He pushed his chair back and put a bare ankle across his knee. "Why? What's up?"

"I was wondering how many people look good if I'm good."

"Somebody complaining?"

"No, I get pats on the back now and then."

"You don't satisfy your own standards?"

"Of course I don't, who does?"

"I'm hearing good comments, if that helps."

"Thanks."

"Then what?"

"For the first time in my life I have medical insurance. Full benefits. I'm finally a full-time employee, conditional, but that could change soon. Even my brothers take me seriously."

"But..."

"But I'm...I've got reservations. Look, I'm beginning to dread going to work in the morning. The job's so stinkin'...so *ugly* most of the time. Now and then I get to help people or do things I think are moral. But check it out, I'm wearing a Sig Sauer everywhere. For good reason. Two days in a row I've delivered teen-agers into the hands of furious fathers who may have beaten them for all I know. I just don't like what I'm doing most of the time."

"And now there's a homicide."

She leaned back. "It's getting to me. It doesn't frighten me that I might be working with a murderer. That's *always* true."

He nodded. "You never know."

"Bailey came in this morning with a list of twenty-five people who can't prove where they were Thursday night. He wanted to know what I had to say, if I could tell him anything about those people."

He tipped his chair back and hooked one foot on the table leg. "Is Jake an important reason or just the latest one?"

"Both. I've been feeling bad right from the beginning about the kind of people I confront. Somebody has to be out there keeping them in line, they run amok as it is. But I hate doing it day after day, it never lets up. Finding fault, writing citations, arguing, listening to threats. Seeing the worst and dumbest. What if I get so pissed off that I learn to like hassling them?"

"It could happen."

"I don't want to turn into that kind of person. And now I have a list of people I'm supposed to speculate about. Josy's on that list. Bob Dalton. Buck. Duvenek."

"Duvenek?"

"He says he was working on his car in the garage all evening. See what I mean? He's your friend, could you tattle on him to a detective?"

"He wouldn't have done it."

"Are you sure? Are you sure *I* didn't?"

"Did you?"

"What good would it do to say no? That wouldn't prove a thing. Why didn't Duvenek?"

"I've known him a long time, fought fire with him."

"That's not going to be good enough for Bailey."

"All I have to go on is feelings."

"Exactly. And how does that make you feel, huh?"

"We have a problem here."

"Tell me about it. Bailey could send somebody else in if he were personally compromised, but I'm the only LEO on the district and I'm supposed to cooperate with other agencies on an investigation—I can't very well refuse. I can't quit without letting people down. And I don't *care* who killed Jake. This job is gonna ruin my disposition."

He moved to stand behind her chair and put his arms around her. She clutched his hands—she loved how strong and hard they were. "And if I wimp out, the good ol' boy network will think women can't hack it. It isn't women, it's me."

"You're not a natural cop."

"No. I'm not. I'm trying to force myself, but I'm not. It bothers me more than it should."

"Don't say that, don't even think it. *Should* has nothing to do with it. You're not other people, you can't judge yourself by them, you don't have their brain chemistry. Anybody who says it bothers you more than it should has his head too far up his ass to think straight."

He went back to his chair and held one finger up. "When I'm in a quandary, I say, 'I shall apply masculine logic.' Hold on, don't throw something, I'm kidding. What would feminine logic do?"

"Separate the problem into parts and attack the worst first."

"Brilliant. And the worst is…"

"Right now? Bailey's list."

"You have it with you?"

She stared at him for a second. "Divide it into separate headings. I've been letting Bailey control the process."

"Let's do it."

Half an hour later they had a page of arrows and cross-outs. 'I Don't Know Enough About This Person'—six names: lookouts and newbies. 'No Way' was a blank. 'Maybe'—nineteen names.

"Stink, half the maybes are my friends or yours. We haven't made what you'd call progress."

"Helluva a note. I say we think about this in the shower."

"Sing hey for the bath at the close of day."

*A*fter dessert, Randy helps her carry clean clothes and groceries out to the truck and puts Venn in the back. Sarah hugs him. "You were absolutely *awesome.*"

"Piece of cake. Gimme five." He holds out his hand, palm up. She claps her hand down on it.

"Challenge is good for me: remember the human brain quadrupled in size during the Ice Ages. And my own survival is at stake here." Randy makes jokes, but he's as much a fish on a line as she is.

She's through the gate on the tower road with it locked behind her while there's still light in the sky and she can see to drive. When the road circles up to the east side of the mountain, there are the colored lights down in town shining through trees that move across them as she drives past. It's like they flicker off and on in the pines.

Half an hour later, in bed, she opens her book. She's reading about an artist named Kate Cory, wishing she could be as brave and adventurous as that. Cory was thirty-three in 1904 when she met Louis Akin in New York and decided to come to Arizona to live at Oraibi and Walpi. She's reading that part now, how Cory painted and photographed for seven years and made a valuable record of Hopis in case that life changed forever. It was a challenge, everything being so different. That was even before Lillian's first trip to Rainbow Bridge.

Venn is restless, wanting to go out, wanting to come in. The minute the book gets interesting, she's at the door again. "Oh, Venn. Make up your mind." She puts down the reading light, gets out of bed and opens the door. "Stay out a least ten minutes. This is getting boring."

Reading isn't easy for her. Sometimes she can't remember what the letters mean, or they scramble into words she doesn't recognize at all. She actually sees a *b* and thinks it's a *d*. It makes her tired to read, but she does it if she wants to find out about artists.

In April she read a biography of Georgia O'Keeffe, carrying it up and down the tower every day. The painful part was what Alfred Stieglitz did to her because he thought he knew best. Trying to control her, run her life.

He was violent about murals Georgia had agreed to do for a ladies' room at the Rockefeller Center Music Hall…carried on for months… went into the office and told the designer that Georgia was a child, not responsible for her actions, and he was her manager and the contract she had signed wasn't acceptable. She was thirty-five years old then.

Finally Georgia thought she was losing her mind, she was so afraid to go out onto the street. She could barely breathe or speak or walk or eat. She had blinding headaches and pains in her chest. Worst of all, she cried a lot. Who could imagine Georgia O'Keeffe *crying* all the time?

She moved into her sister's apartment to get away from Stieglitz and then for two months she was in a hospital and he was restricted to one ten-minute visit a week. He said he felt like a murderer.

She read that part of the book over and over. It was like her father. Once he burned a sketch of a male nude she had copied from a book…not even from the front, from the *back*. Took it from her and tore it into pieces and threw them into the fireplace. "Indecent," he said. "I expect better from my daughter."

Until she read about Stieglitz, she thought something was wrong with her, she was selfish or immoral not to be grateful. Crazy to be so upset when nothing much was wrong. She had everything she needed. Like Georgia had fame and money because Stieglitz promoted her paintings, but she was sick anyway.

She had thought she was the only one, but it had happened to Georgia O'Keeffe. She copied lines from the book. "Squeeze all the life out of me." "Most people don't have the chance to develop as people let alone as artists."

"*Engine* 3-2 departing Flagstaff. ETA two hours." Randy's going somewhere on a fire.

Sarah opens one eye. It isn't even light yet, just kind of *luminous.* Not dark. Sky is pale behind the tree tops, which aren't moving for a change. Dawn coming or is it moonlight? At June solstice the sun was already up by now.

When you live in town, the moon doesn't matter. You don't look up...you can't see out. Here you see by the moon and tell time by it, and it's part of life. She's just discovered that.

Randy's engine must be going off forest. She wishes the dispatcher would say where. Last month the engine went to a scrub fire on the South Rim of the Grand Canyon, over by Peach Spring. He said it was awesome to look up from dousing a burning juniper and see the Grand Canyon spread out in front of him.

She curls onto her side. Private. Free. Except for Venn, who isn't moving yet, no one will try to wake her up. Laundry is done, a week's groceries are bought. She can spend the day any way she likes. Stay on the mountain and find things to sketch? Carrying a drawing pad is a good way to see...the world is *rich* when you're wandering with a drawing pad. Shapes. Light and shade.

But she'd rather drive, which is freedom too. Georgia O'Keeffe said she needed to be private and free, and being an artist meant she could do as she wished. She was middle-aged by then, just before she made a trip to Monument Valley and the Hopi mesas. It's harder to be free when you're young.

This summer she's learned to see things new. It's amazing the difference clouds make when a hundred miles of country is below you and the sky is most of what you can see. Clouds can move so fast...they make shadows across miles and miles, ragged shadows that slide across tree tops and bend over ridges, down into canyons. She's learned so much stuff this summer.

Not all of it's nice. One thing is about Dad. She applied for the lookout job without telling him...Randy took her to talk to Mitch without telling him. When the letter from the Forest Service came, Dad opened it first.

> We are pleased to offer you employment on the
> Coconino National Forest. The position we have for you is
> a fire lookout. Your official duty station will be Woody
> Mountain. Quarters are available and will cost approxi-
> mately $18 per pay period. Cost of quarters will be

deducted from your check. This position is from 3/31 to 9/30, or until further notice. Continued employment beyond that date will depend upon ceiling restrictions, finances, and the weather. We are pleased to have you with us and hope you will find the work both enjoyable and rewarding.

Dad said he didn't want her to take the job, it was too dangerous. "I'd worry about my girl out there alone miles from help."

Always before she's done what he wanted. He's put his arm around her and hugged her against his side. Told her how good she is and how proud he is of her...she hasn't argued with him. But she said she was going to say yes to the letter.

He didn't believe her at first. Then he was furious. But she and Randy stood side by side and faced him together. Finally he realized the way to be in control was to pretend he'd practically arranged it. He laughed and went out and bought the Toyota for her "first job." But she didn't forgot the scary look she'd seen on his face.

She throws back the covers. She wants to be in sunrise in the Painted Desert. "Come on, Venn. Let's go to Tuba City." No time at all, and she's headed down the road with Venn beside her in the truck because they'll be on a highway and going fast.

With a dog on the mountain she sees things that might hide from her, and she would never know. One evening in July after she locked the tower, she and Venn walked down the road a mile, past the gate. The shadow of her mountain stretched out on the land, across green trees toward Fort Tuthill and the airport. Venn was running back and forth, nose to the ground, but *she* looked up at a milky half moon radiant in high late sunlight.

Venn turned an invisible corner and rushed up a slope. Disappeared in the trees. Then there was a piercing ringing sort of call, and Venn began to bark. The sound moved back and forth up on the hill, the piercing scream and the barking.

Over her left shoulder she heard heavy thudding and turned. A huge cow elk was running toward the fracas...at least, she *looked* huge. Randy said they could weigh six hundred pounds, and maternal anxiety made them even bigger.

The barking was coming down the hill. Through the trees she saw Venn running at the shoulder of an elk calf. Not going for the throat, just having fun. Something warned that dog brain ...Venn looked up to see an animal as big as a horse coming fast and veered off, ran straight to her human...and hid *behind*.

The baby elk went on running. The mother turned and started after Venn. There wasn't time to do anything, move or run or get behind a tree or even wave an arm…barely time to be afraid. The big mother elk suddenly saw a person just *standing* there and changed direction so fast she skidded and nearly fell. Kicked up a great cloud of dust into the late sunshine…ran off after the calf. Venn moved then, out of safety, and walked to the side of the road looking after them.

If Jake had been there, he'd have cursed that he didn't have a gun or a bow to shoot with. She didn't understand why killing was so important to him.

She knew him a month before he kissed her. He had been south to check on the engine crew at the Fernow guard station and stopped by on his way back to town to see if she needed anything…so he said. Just before he left the tower, he moved close to her. Ran his fingers along her jaw and raised her chin and bent to put his lips on hers so soft and gentle. She was surprised…thrilled all over. He kissed her again, and she felt like she was falling a long distance, so *romantic*. She thought about it for days.

Three weeks later he arrived one evening at sunset with a chocolate liqueur. Venn barked and barked, but Jake was calm about it and talked to her. Finally she stopped barking.

He sat on the doorstep pouring tiny sips of the liqueur into one cup for both of them, sang silly songs and joked and made her laugh. When it was dark and cold and she was a little dizzy, he picked her up in his arms and carried her inside.

"You're shivering," he said. His voice was deep. "Let's bundle on the bed to warm you up."

He whispered romantic words and stroked her hair and kissed her neck and held her until she felt *cherished*. It was wonderful to feel cherished, to feel so close to someone else. No one had ever held her before.

He was tender and sweet…it was like opening a door into sunlight. She put her hands on the muscles in his upper arms and felt how hard they were and the wonderful *surging* curves and hollows of his back. His body was a treasure under her fingers.

It was a long slow night, nothing hurried or rough. He loved her with his tongue and his fingertips and his voice. Very softly, a piece at a time their clothes came off. He was beautiful, he made *her* feel beautiful. She had never been in love before.

For a few minutes he slept on top of her, so heavy she could barely breathe, but she didn't mind. She touched his silky hair. When he woke up and moved to one side, she realized he had on a condom. She'd never seen one.

She began washing her hair every two days, just in case he should come back. She didn't want to smell like oily hair to him.

Sky is brightening…pink is just beginning in a few little clouds, kind of a peachy-pink. She finds the Flag Ranch Road and drives up the ramp onto I-40. There's no traffic at all, just now and then a big truck. It's exciting to have the highway all to yourself…you can see the land for what it is. She *sails* past Flagstaff and makes the turn onto 89 north before people begin to clog the road going to work.

*J*ake. His back, but Josy knew the hair, the shoulders. He turned a face of horror—black, swollen, covered with crawling flies. There were no eyes in the sockets. She tried to scream but couldn't make a sound. Her heart pounded.

Pale white light on the ceiling. Sun was not up yet, but she could see the clock on the opposite wall—quarter to five. Walt was asleep on the other side of the bed.

In the shower her heart calmed, and her mind stopped whirling. Pouring hot coffee into a mug in the kitchen she felt almost rational. Jeesh, what a dream!

Out on the back steps, warm cup between her palms, she looked up for the usual signs. Little clouds just becoming visible, then turning pink. Tops of the tallest pines strong orange as the sun rose. Shadows stretched long across the ground. Full light, and another day started.

Walt surprised her with his arms around her waist, a kiss against the side of her neck. "Morning, Sweetie. Looks like another beautiful day." He hummed as he turned back into the kitchen and went to the coffee maker. So she wasn't a frigid bitch at the moment, and he was trying to put an ugly scene "behind them."

Walt was cheerful as he hadn't been for weeks. Usually he was distant at breakfast and read the paper and refused to talk; usually she was getting ready to go to work, so it didn't matter. She tended the washing machine, cleaned the refrigerator. It felt good to wear shorts and sandals for a change.

"More coffee? More toast?" Perfunctory offers.

"No thanks, Sweetie. You certainly take good care of me."

How could he be so dense? Or maybe he knew how she was feeling and believed he could charm her out of it.

"Glad you're coming with me to Cameron this afternoon."

There were geologic formations visible out there that dated from the Quaternary all the way back through the Cenozoic. She'd see whether she could recognize the big north-south monocline near Doney Crater—she'd never tried to find it. Walt didn't like to talk while he was driving. She'd be free to look.

"What's your program this morning?" It had been a long time since he'd asked.

"The usual around here. And I thought I'd go in to the NAU library and see what I can find on the Toroweap formation."

He laughed. "Oh Sweetie." What a talent—he could turn that one word into a sneer. "You have such curiosity about completely useless things." Nice hadn't lasted half an hour. She didn't know why people tried to turn each other into nothing.

She was so angry she turned her back so he couldn't see her face. "That's me, all right. I'll meet you outside your office at 13:00."

"Ah, military time. My sweetie's a toy soldier."

It exploded out of her. *"Don't call me Sweetie!"*

"It's just an affectionate term." His voice was full of superior amusement—oh ho ho, you're so cute and childish.

"Not when you say it, it isn't."

"Look, dear…"

"Don't call me *dear* either—that's worse. It isn't the words, it's the way you say them, as if I were just barely above contempt. If you think I'm not smart enough for a genius like you, I'll leave. I've got two days off, I can pack."

He pushed back his chair and came toward her. "No no, you don't see the picture." Put his arms around her like a duty. "This murder at work has you upset, that's all, and I've been too busy lately to focus on you. I'll try to adjust the parameters. Let's have no talk of leaving. You belong here with me, can't you see that?"

A year ago he was the most exciting man she'd ever known, and she was alive in her mind all the time. Now everything he said was so banal it was embarrassing. Had he changed that much or had she?

The, like, *forehead* of the sun is just above the eastern horizon as Sarah drives down the long hill and out of the pines into a bowl of light. Hills miles away on the west, taking the full intensity, are *radiant* like they were formed of light instead of rock. There's color everywhere…rose and peach and gold, carmine and cadmium and vermillion, the glowing warm tones. She can barely see edges, the light is so full of color. To the east, hills in front of the sun are blues and mauves. Air vibrates and sings all around her, away into the distance, everywhere.

Earth turns very fast, you see that at sunrise. In only a few seconds everything changes…now there are shadows hundreds of feet long across the earth and edges have turned sharp. The land *rushes* away in all directions, so huge, and not a building in sight, only one truck far ahead. The world is bigger than you realize when you're in town. Town makes it smaller.

Being out on the road like this, moving through the open morning and the light, it's *escape*. She drives past weird eroded formations and sees them change shape as she moves, like they're alive. Everything she sees…it's all alive. She just *knows* Lillian felt like this, going slower on a horse, the big city world left behind on another planet or something.

In May the forest was so dry, human-caused fires broke out everywhere. Josy put up Road Closed signs across 231. Patrol units on every district were doing the same or locking gates. Randy said it was about as effective as a paper airplane for keeping barbarians out. She loved it, though…without people the forest was safer. After it was closed, all the fires that had been starting every day, mostly along roads, disappeared completely. For weeks there was no smoke anywhere.

Everybody who could be spared from offices went out to stations on the barricades to stop people from driving into the forest. On her radio she heard patrolmen hurrying around to find the ones who had parked and walked in, especially on weekends.

"A report has come in here of violation of the closure below Kachina Village. Check on it."

"We've got hikers on the Elden Trail. Clear them off." "There are tons of folks on the Snow Bowl Road. Can we lock the gate?"

"We've had a report of gunshots inside the closure area south of the airport. How do you want to handle it?"

"Patrol 3-4, a caller from Equestrian Estates says a horse got away from its owner and ran into the closed area. Tie in with the folks there and see what you can do about it."

The next time Josy came up, she laughed. "That horse was dumb as a chicken, I don't care what the owner thinks. I found it on the power line road and just herded it slowly without getting out of the truck. It made a right turn on 532 and trotted in front of me all the way to Fort Tuthill. If it had gone cross country I'd have lost it, but no, it tried to run away from me on the road."

People didn't get twenty feet away from places where they could drive. For days Law Enforcement and patrolmen ran after them, trying to keep them from spoiling everything. She thinks it's because people don't know how they should behave when they get out of their usual lives and into the forest. Were the first explorers from the East just as thoughtless? Was Lillian? Zane Grey? Did they go on acting and thinking the way they had before?

Early last March not long after she got her new Toyota truck, she left home one morning and drove all the way to Kayenta. The Wetherills had been gone for fifty years, but she wanted to find their old trading post, the one they built after 1909 in a place that was wild and free. The one Lillian and other people knew for thirty something years, so wonderful on the edge of Monument Valley that they never forgot it. Maybe at Kayenta she could, like, find Lillian.

It was a gorgeous day, the sky was full of clouds that actually reflected the colors of the land below, pink mostly. Shadows moved across miles and miles of ancient shapes. Remains of old sea beds, Dad had said. She drove through unimaginable time and felt, you know, *enhanced* to be there.

Kayenta had gas stations and a Holiday Inn. There were cars and trucks everywhere, pavement, stores. On the road that started out toward Mexican Hat she saw a sign that said Wetherill Inn. The woman at the desk asked a Navajo woman who was working on books and said to turn at the next left. They thought the old trading post had been down there behind a store.

It was an important place, a wonderful place, one of the best, the most magical in Arizona history. Discoveries. Lives changed forever. How could they not *know*? Famous people had come there. The walls had been covered with paintings and Navajo blankets.

Down the hill was a boarded-up little old sandstone building. There was no romance, no beauty, just a little old building, worn and neglected, surrounded by newer houses not especially nice. *Grass* had grown there once. Louisa Wetherill had been proud of her yard.

Up on a nearby hill she found the red, dusty graves of John and Louisa Wetherill inside a fence. When they were buried there, the country lay open around them for miles out of sight. But last March there was a church nearby and plain square little houses were in the way of the view. Navajos drove past and slowed to look at her standing at the fence. She felt she didn't have a right to be there.

It was one of her saddest memories. All those people not just dead and gone, the whole history, like, crushed to powder with nothing good to take its place. Nothing beautiful or romantic or even hopeful for *any*body. Just plastic bags blowing in the wind and cars going by.

Driving toward home, aching for something lost, she stopped by a motel at the entrance to Tsegi and walked out to the edge, trying to imagine Lillian and Zane Grey and John Wetherill and the rest of them on their horses riding by and up the canyon out of sight. Packs, bedrolls behind saddles. Hats with brims. White shirts on human backs, taking form, *materializing* as they had been eighty years before. Sound of hooves. Voices. Maybe laughter. There were big trucks roaring past, and the vision wouldn't come.

At Betatakin a cold wind was pushing clouds across the plateau. She couldn't find a place at the overlook to be alone where she could listen for the past for a minute. Tourists never stopped talking or shouting at their children to get off the wall. She went behind some trees where she at least couldn't *see* the tourists, and a man came with a camera and crawled around on the edge of the cliff in front of her snapping pictures of the awesome ruin in the cave opposite, violating everything. He probably thought he had *seen* it.

After Betatakin, she stopped at Tuba City to find the old trading post Lillian saw first in 1913 and lived in more than ten years later. She knew what it looked like, a stone octagon with a hogan shape on top to let in light. But there were paved roads and cars going in all directions, and she was so hurt already that she couldn't see anything really clear.

S he thought so. Hill's forehead was against hers, his nose pushing her nose. When Meg opened her eyes, his were open staring at her all one big eye.

It was comfort to sleep close to him. "Bet a cookie you were a little boy once." She raised her hand to his cheek.

"How long can you go without blinking?"

"Watch—see, four seconds. My brother timed me once."

His arm lay across her arm. "Look deep into my eyes..."

"...eye..."

"...eye and repeat after me: 'I'm not going to work today...'"

"...so I'll sleep until noon."

"That's not the way it goes. You're supposed to say, 'So I'll get up and cook breakfast for my noble husband.'"

"...so my lazy husband who isn't enough bigger than I am to matter will bring me breakfast in bed."

"...noble husband who loves me..."

"You're unscrupulous." She moved her hand across his back, down his side. She loved to feel his bare flesh against her palm, loved the bulge of muscle behind his armpit.

"I'd use any trick."

"...for my pancakes."

"I don't want you to forget how."

"What's it been, since...?"

"...since April when the season got off to a rousing start."

"Suppose it will ever end?" She kissed his mouth, a small, soft kiss.

"Maybe when it starts to snow, and most of the trouble-makers go back to Phoenix."

"We'll have our days off together."

"We'll be in the office doing paperwork instead of risking life and limb outdoors."

"We'll get out of the station at 17:00 every evening."

"And go out of town if we want to."

"Whoop-ti-doo...Sedona for dinner if I don't feel like cooking."

"Speaking of cooking..."

She loved the way muscles in his back made a groove where his spine was. "I want you to know if I do get up, it will be because I have an appointment to have my teeth cleaned at eight. What time is it?"

"Six, so you have no excuse for neglecting me."

"...except how sleepy I am." She closed her eyes. "I'd probably put in too much salt."

"I'll stand right there and watch you."

"Then why don't you do it yourself?"

"My pancakes don't taste as good as yours."

She groaned. "My mother warned me marriage would be like this."

"She wouldn't have, she likes me."

"...just because you're polite to her."

"I talk to her. She's liked me ever since I told her I'd read Spinoza. Which happened to be true."

"Show off."

He walked his fingers up her cheek. "If you'll do the pancakes, I'll serve up my famous and faultless soft-boiled eggs."

"I tell you right now, I suspect you of something devious."

"I want to be in the kitchen with you. Got a problem with that?"

"All right. OK." She turned onto her back. "What a negotiator. I accept your terms."

He raised his knees. "Ready?" Together, kicking, they pushed the covers off.

While she measured flour and such into the blue mixing bowl, he poured orange juice and started water to boil. "I've been thinking."

"About last night? The list?"

"That's one thing."

"You've decided who did it? I need an egg."

He handed her the carton. "Does it have to be on your district?"

"No. I kinda think Bailey is looking in other directions too and not mentioning it. But given what he's hearing from us about Jake's lack of charm on the job, he shouldn't ignore us."

"Did anybody see Jake outside of work hours?"

"I don't know of anyone."

"That part's Bailey's job." He leaned against the frig.

"Move. I need to get the milk."

He shifted to the table. "What you said about not caring who did it—does everybody feel that way?"

"I haven't heard anybody express any grief. I guess not caring isn't something they'd say to me, I could ask Josy." She looked at him for a clue to what he meant.

The water was boiling. "Eggs'll be done before the flapjacks. Your griddle hot?"

"Go ahead with the eggs." She turned to the stove and poured oil on the griddle. "You have a brilliant guess?"

"Not a thing. Just prowling around."

"Prowl on your side of the stove, I need elbow room here."

"What I was thinking was, do you want to resign?"

There it was, in the open. "Now that you mention it, sometimes I do. Quitter is a bad word, but yes, sometimes I do." She kept her eyes on the griddle. "Sometimes I don't. That's part of the problem—it isn't all horrible. Most of the situations I'm in are shitty: I'm developing a very bad attitude toward young males, and I don't like it. As a matter of fact, I don't feel too positive when I encounter males of any age out in the forest: they lie like high school kids when I catch them in violations."

"Like this?" She looked up—he'd put on a wide-open smile.

"You got it. I also run into good people of all genders who need my help. I like helping. They make it hard to decide—that's why I wanted to talk with you."

"Are you concerned about the money?"

"Well sure."

"I don't want you to be. This summer's been overtime for both of us and fire time and night differential—we'll end the season with more in checking than we've ever had. If you want to resign and hunt for another job, this is the year to do it. You'd still be on my medical benefits."

"Congratulations."

"On…?"

"You've now reached ten thousand reasons why you're the most loveable man in the world."

"I mean it. Don't let money be the heavyweight."

"Hand me down two plates, please. One thing that weighs heavily is that I can't stand whiners, and I'm whining. Another is that I'm the token female in law enforcement, the show female, and there's more than just me on the line. If I wimp out, it might be years before another woman gets the chance."

*T*his time in Tuba Sarah finds the right road to turn on, probably a road that didn't even exist when Lillian lived here. Power poles string out everywhere. A swap meet is going on. She tries to hold onto the idea of the past, 1870, 1913, and not see anything else, but it's hard. Was the past ugly too? Did it look so *meaningless*?

She's looking for the trading post standing alone in Navajo country and realizes she's been looking right at it without recognizing. There's a Macdonald's across the street. Where Shekayah was is a Quality Inn and an RV Park. She stops between white lines next to a tour bus and turns off the engine. Shekayah is covered *over*, obliterated. It would have been really shabby by now like that low building against the wall of the post. Nobody would have wanted to stay. But couldn't they have left it for a memory of other lives and built farther back?

The inside of the trading post though, that's *enchanting*. Light pouring down into a big room with no square corners. Through windows all around the top clouds are visible in a blue sky. The pillars that support the roof are polished trunks of trees that must have been brought from far away. They didn't grow around *Tuba*.

But it doesn't matter, the old room is so beautiful. There are Navajo blankets and kachina dolls. Baskets and pottery and jewelry, some old, some new. It wasn't just like this, of course, when Jess and Jot Stiles were the traders here, but maybe the *light* was the same and the rising happy feeling. Lillian moved through it in 1926, came in to talk with Jess. For two years it was part of her home.

Driving back to Flagstaff toward storm clouds above the Peaks a hundred miles away, she reaches out and rubs behind Venn's ears. It was so long ago...all that was happy, all that was sad is gone. For a few minutes in the trading post she'd imagined that the feeling in her chest was what Lillian felt.

*A*mid the familiar, there were changes on campus: the Geology department had grown so much that it had moved into its own building next to Administration. Josy had walked through it that day two months earlier with her hands full of catalog and papers, up all the stairs and along the halls, past offices and lecture rooms. The walls were covered with maps, different colors for different formations—geology maps were so beautiful.

In the new library building she'd walked through the stacks, trailing her fingers along the spines of books, every one a possible adventure, looking for geology. The section, *her* section was still in QE. She'd touched the books with her fingertips. The whole building had echoed with mind. There were study carrels at the ends of the stacks, and only twenty feet away tables at windows where she would look up and see snow falling on pines in February.

The card catalogue had disappeared since she'd left, and computers were everywhere. A woman working the desk had been slow and patient teaching her how to use them to locate books. She wrote notes: it wasn't hard once you understood how it worked. She'd know that library cold by October—bound periodicals, microforms, rest rooms—she'd make it hers.

With classes starting in three days, it was time to go into the book store to buy the texts she'd reserved—she headed for the east side of campus. Textbooks were in a big room all the way at the back, row after row, stack after stack. Two months ago she had prowled until she'd found geology and resolved that another thing she'd buy was that big wall map of the Colorado Plateau. Writing a check, she was glad she'd come to get acquainted before students crowded in, when she could see what was there. Computers: she'd probably need to buy one.

Through the big windows in the back she looked across the street to Citizens Cemetery. At such a time, hey, she ought to go and visit.

It had been ten years—her parents' funeral—but she remembered the turns into the old section under trees and found the family plot, all her people with numbers that bracketed their lives. She hated the numbers.

Green		Owens		Kirkman	
Richard	Ruby	Roger	Emily	Daniel	Rose
1849	1852	1880	1886	1911	1915
1915	1941	1960	1979	1986	1986

Virginia
1913
1986

All in pairs except for Aunt Virginia and Ruby's two children who had died young.

She sat on the low stone wall around the plot. Wind in the pines overhead was the only sound, the only movement. And cars going past out on the road. "Know what, you guys? I came to tell you I'm going back to school. When you were all gone, I was alone, pretty unhappy. I guess I'm embarrassed to say it, but I dropped out, although at the time it seemed like it didn't matter. I sort of hoped you'd be proud of me. So I came to tell you because it's the only place there is."

Well. She stood and looked into Meg's family plot for the woman she'd been named for.

	Friendly		
John	Margaret	Matthew	Josephine
1842	1851	1889	1892
1920	1936	1979	1980

	Scheffler	
Paul	Daisy	
1895	1885	
1975	1983	

In pairs, all in pairs. Lives over and done with, but that didn't make it any easier to accept. "I'll be back to tell you guys how it's going." You always had to walk away and leave your people among the graves.

The Lockwood plot was nearby. Looked like the Wong sisters had put up a new marker for Dew Yu. She liked the Chinese characters cut into the stone and the flowers and the one word–Mother.

At a little table in the front window at La Bellavia she spread out her books and paged through them, just to get a feel. OK, they were pretty dry and academic, but you know what, learning about anything you liked was a thrill.

"How are you today? Are you ready to order?" She was young and wholesome, maybe a PE or an Elementary Ed major.

"Today's quiche and a glass of Flagstaff's best."

"Water?"

"That's it."

"Ready for classes to start? Looks like geology."

Obviously both quick and observant. "Yep. Yours?"

"Molecular Biology. I'll finish my B.S. next spring. Be right back with your quiche."

OK. So scrub the grade school coach stereotype. Actually, she was ashamed of herself. What would people decide looking at her? Grade school coach, probably. She forgot the world going by out on the street, she got so interested in looking at the tables of contents.

"Here we are." The biology major waited while she moved books out of the way and then set the plate down. "Anything else? Shall I bring ketchup or salsa?"

"No thanks. Hey, maybe I'll see you on campus next month–our buildings are next door. Will you go on working once the semester starts?"

"Have to. I live at home, but the family can't afford to cover tuition. My grandfather drove a taxi in this town back in the 20s and 30s, we never had much money."

"You're a native? No kidding! So am I–how did we miss knowing each other?"

"Who knows? Kids are pretty preoccupied with themselves."

"You were probably just far enough behind me for it to seem like another generation."

"And since the war the town's grown so much you can't know everybody. Not like it used to be."

"I know. Isn't it too bad? Maybe our grandparents knew each other."

"Meg." She looked up from *People*. Even across the waiting room Annette Wong looked dainty. Neat in her white uniform, pretty as a doll. Only a foot shorter, but Chinese women always made her feel about ten feet tall and clumsy.

"How's it going? Still working as a policeman?"

She followed down the hall. Chiming voice, concealed strength– that was another thing; she bet a cookie Annette was tougher than she looked.

"It's been six months. Any problems or changes?"

"Lots, but not with my teeth." She leaned back in the chair.

"Oh, Meg." It was an adorable little laugh.

"Law enforcement is problems enough for anybody. Hill says hello." He knew her younger brother.

"I'll just clip this around your neck. Hello to Hill. Tell him we're having a family gathering next month and Winton will be in town."

"Many people?"

"Eighty-five–a lot of them will stay in my house."

"Eighty-five! All Wongs?"

"Sixty Wongs."

"Your grand-parents have multiplied."

Another dainty laugh. "They really have."

"Your mother's coming from San Francisco?"

"She's bringing family records to go over them with my aunt Pinky." Annette had graduated from NAU, licensed RDH by the state.

She put on a paper mask and latex gloves. "Tip your chin up a little so I can have a look."

Annette's grandmother had known Grandma. Not that they were friends—that didn't happen in Flagstaff seventy years ago. Mrs. Wong had been busy, always working, children, home, the laundry: she knew people in town by their clothes. Grandma said when she'd come back from China, Mrs. Wong had looked carefully at the silk robe she'd brought home.

"Not too bad, no cavities, no trouble spots. You must have been taking care of yourself."

"My teeth anyway. Annette, do you think you'd like being in law enforcement?"

"Oh no. Goodness, I've never even thought of it—all that adrenaline. Turn your head away from me a little."

Mrs. Wong had died years ago, they all had. Great-grandmother had gone when Mom was just a baby. The year she was eleven, Grandpa had died. But he'd lived to be eighty, long enough for her to know him and hear his stories about courting Grandma. "I used everything New York was in those days. You wouldn't believe how many ferry rides we took: she loved the water. Plays, concerts, galleries, shops, just walking the streets. She soaked up the city, and I loved showing it to her, finding new sights. I'd never known anyone who was such pure joy to be with, there was no doubt in my mind that if I could persuade her to marry me, the rest of my life would be wonderful. So I poured days into her hands like jewels and dazzled her. Been doing it ever since, so she'd keep me."

Grandma would laugh—she did that, danced when she walked and laughed as she talked. "You should have seen him when he got off the train with me. I had such fun showing him Arizona. He's never been one of those people who thought he was too good to enjoy things."

"Now turn your head toward me." Annette's eyes above the paper mask: no history in them, at least none that she could see.

Wong Dew Yu was still running the laundry when Grandma brought her big-city fiance to Flagstaff. Great Aunt Jo had stepped down from the train with them—almost down, Uncle Matt had lifted her off the little stool the porter had put there and swung her around he was so glad to see her. She had hugged Josy's grandmother Ruby and Ruby's friend Ada and great-grandmother Margaret and the taxi driver, crying because she was so happy.

"Now lift your chin please, Meg."

Grandpa said, "Showed me off like a trophy."

"You *were*. I was so proud."

"No prouder than I was of you."

He'd transferred what the town considered an astonishing fortune into a local bank. The first night at the ranch he'd sat at the table and proposed a partnership to Matt and Great-grandma: his money invested in drilling deep wells and putting up windmills on the east side close to the Little Colorado, his experience in banking, and a house built right there so Grandma wouldn't have to leave home except to go traveling now and then. They'd shaken hands on it, and that was enough contract for him, Grandpa had said. The extra wells and windmills, trucks for hauling water to sections where water was too far down for windmills to lift—that was what got them through the drought and depression in the 30s.

Later when Great-aunt Jo had married Uncle Matt, they'd used some of her money to build another house, and all of them had been close together. Uncle Matt had lived to be ninety and taught her all he knew about everything as if it was what he'd had to leave to the future. He'd died two years after Grandpa.

Aunt Jo had lived only a year beyond him. That last winter there was a terrible storm. Grandma had stood at the window and looked across at Aunt Jo's house a hundred feet away but almost invisible through blowing snow, and when she couldn't wait another minute, she turned to the boys.

"What good are grandsons if you can't send them on rescue missions? That little woman is eighty-seven years old and alone. I want you two big strong college boys to go over and get her, tell her we're having a blizzard party. Get your sons a rope, P.J."

Everyone called him P.J., even his children. He had brought a long rope and tied it to the porch. Her brothers had stretched it, leaning against the wind, and disappeared into the storm. She'd stood between Grandma and Mom, watching for them to come back along the rope, while P.J. built up the fire and put coffee on and went out onto the porch. It seemed forever, staring into white nothing until she saw their moving shapes, one carrying Aunt Jo wrapped in a blanket and the other following with a suitcase, turning their faces away from the stinging flakes. Grandma had rushed to the door and shouted "Yay!" when P.J. took Aunt Jo into his arms.

"OK, Meg, now we'll polish, and your teeth will be ready for another six months of policing. I've been reading in the paper about a man in the Forest Service who was shot. Did you have to do anything about that?"

"I was the first law enforcement on the scene."

"That must have been awful." She envied Annette's thick dark hair, the way it moved and never looked messy.

"Uh-huh." The polishing compound tasted like cinnamon.

"No, I don't think I'd like to do that job, but I admire you. You must be very brave."

*T*he new books Josy had left in her car—no need to start *that* argument yet—but when Walt saw the old geology book she'd brought, he laughed. "Going back to your hobby, I see."

She put the book solid on her lap and fastened the seat belt. "I guess." *Hobby!* "Men have careers; women have hobbies."

He patted her hand. "You've got the picture, Sweetie. A woman's career has always been house, husband and children."

What a Neanderthal. She found the pages on Elden so she'd know what she was looking at when they passed by. Partly extrusive and partly intrusive—jeesh, one paragraph and she was already turning to the glossary to be sure. OK, rock from magma that had come to the surface and magma that had pushed up but solidified below the surface. She knew that: the northeast side of Elden had domed up Paleozoic sedimentary layers. You could tell by how steep the slopes were that the extrusive lava had been thick.

"Care to share with the group?"

"I thought you didn't like to talk on the road."

"I thought you liked to listen to me and learn about my job."

That had been last year. "I did. I haven't heard much lately."

"I've been busy, as you know, too busy thinking to talk much."

"Of course. Thinking." The Peaks were composite too, formed by layers of different kinds that erupted over a couple of million years, burying earlier vents. The Inner Basin might be a caldera that collapsed after underlying magma had been ejected, or what was left after a violent sideways explosion that blew off the top, but it definitely had cirques that were carved by seven active glaciers during the Ice Ages. You could still see the terminal moraines. She liked it that the surface of the planet she lived on was always moving and changing and leaving records of what it had done.

"Are you looking at me?" Walt was smiling.

"Past you. Into the Inner Basin, and thinking about it."

"Shall we take the loop road?"

"Yes. I'd like that." It would give her a good look at O'Leary. A *cluster* of volcanic domes had pushed up nearly a quarter of a million years ago. Magma had bulged out at the surface and hardened before it could go far. That was why O'Leary was so steep. Sunset Crater, on the other hand, right next but less than a thousand years old, had the thirty degree slope that was the angle of repose for cinders.

She put a marker in her book and closed it to watch for the first sight of the Painted Desert and the Little Colorado valley and in the distance a hint of Monument Valley. What could you say about a view vast as a big-screen movie, delicate as a watercolor, and older than dinosaurs? Every time she'd seen it since she'd been, oh, six or so, she'd fallen on her metaphorical knees. It was not the kind of spectacle you got used to. Walt didn't seem to notice, his face was impassive as a potato.

The Wupatki visitor center with its displays and plate glass windows had been built in the late 1940s. She left Walt with the ranger and walked along the paved path to the bench where anyone who wanted a long slow look could see the pueblo opposite. The red sandstone rock of which it had built eight hundred years earlier were Moenkopi formation, laid down in the Triassic and broken into slabs along natural joints.

A dark ridge loomed behind it—was that a monocline or basalt? The whole Plateau had risen slowly from sea level millions of years earlier, folding the crust while it was at it and leaving all kinds of evidence. Out there somewhere Paleozoic sedimentary strata tilted and dove beneath the Mesozoic.

Storm clouds were massing above the Peaks, swelling out minute by minute and darkening on the bottom. Her grandmother had said it was at Wupatki that Boren had fallen in love with northern Arizona.

*I*n late May Jake had asked if on her day off she'd like to go along and help his father move cattle into corrals so they could be trucked up to his permit land in the forest. Sarah was excited…it would be an adventure.

Randy was on a fire. Dad was on a case. Mom was lying down with a bad headache. She went without telling anybody where she was going. Maybe if she got home early, if nobody asked, she wouldn't have to say. Venn stayed with Mom.

Mr. Holding was large and loud with a stomach that covered part of his belt buckle…his shirt fit tight across it. She didn't like the way his mouth turned down at the corners, and she didn't like his loud voice.

"We need more pretty girls around here. The place has been kinda masculine since we lost Jake's mother."

She hadn't heard about his mother. *Lost* could mean anything. But he was so rude to Jake that she shrank away from him...nasty, right in front of her. "I don't want half the meat run off, way you did last time, hot-doggin' like some dumb kid. Are you too young or just too stupid to take 'em slow? I'm tellin' you, I mean it. You hear me?" She thought it was *rude* to humiliate anyone like that in front of a friend. Embarrassed, she saw Jake's face go hard and red, but all he said was, "Yes, sir."

On the way to the corral she stopped at his truck and took out a little pack with her sketch pad and pencils. Jake's voice was mean. "Whadda you think you're gonna do with that?"

"There might be a time when I'm waiting. So I won't be in the way. I thought maybe I could..."

"This is a working day. We won't have time for any damn fool crap." He jerked the pack out of her hands and threw it back into the truck and slammed the door. "Get on over to the corral."

She knew he was acting that way because his father had shamed him, and she could sympathize. But he put his hand on her back and pushed her. She knew right then he was *not* her Jesse Smith.

All day he was cruel and insulting. "You can't even sit the saddle right. Who taught you to ride a horse, for god's sake?"

"Nobody. I never had any..."

"It sure shows."

Her leg hurt. If she tried to ease it a little he shouted, "Hey, dumb ass, keep your feet in the stirrups."

"I need to rest my leg."

"I don't care. Git it back in there."

He called her names every time he talked to her. Lame Brain. Nit Wit. Dip Shit. It was such a horrible day she was numb with the pain of it. Dropped her reins, turned the wrong way. The more he yelled, the more mistakes she made and the more he called her names.

In the truck on the way back to Flagstaff, he put his arm around her. "I guess you noticed working with cattle is pretty tense. Things can go wrong in a minute and somebody can get hurt." He teased her into a weak smile, but she knew he would be mean again whenever he felt mad.

He was a good fire man, that was one thing you could say about him, and he had plenty of chances to show it early in the season. Most of June was hot and dry day after day like there would never be any rain, ever again. Up on the reservations Navajos and Hopis were doing prayers for rain. *Everybody* was. But there was just a trace now and then, a few drops at a time, with sun shining on them. They looked like silver streaks against the pines.

On Solstice a fast dry-lightning storm moved across fifty miles or so of the Coconino and started a dozen fires. Ground crews rushed around trying to put out the little fires before the wind blew them into big ones. There'd been *record* drought in northern Arizona…extreme dry conditions in the forest. Wind hadn't really dropped for two months. Nobody wanted to take chances and ignore a little one-tree fire that could spread into a big problem within minutes. So they tried to put them all out.

There was a smoke right at the top of Hochderffer Hill, a single tree struck by lightning. From sixteen miles away it looked like a little white thread. Jake drove out to make decisions and give orders, but crews had trouble getting in to it because there were no roads, and initial attack was by helicopter. Then Crew Five got there.

Myrna reported smoke above Friedlein Prairie on the Peaks. It was under cloud shadow with a strong wind that kept it lying down across a ridge…sun had to come out before she could find it for a cross. Jake drove back to look at that one.

At 06:00 the next morning she heard lookouts on the Kaibab reporting smoke south of East Pocket. In her robe and slippers she climbed up into the tower…no smoke was visible from Woody Mountain. Sedona units were dispatched to look for whatever was burning, but it was Josy who went out onto the rim an hour later and looked down and located it near Vultee Arch and Lost Wilson Mountain in the wilderness.

A Red Flag Warning was declared…winds were expected to be above twenty-five and humidity was very low. The tiny white thread at the top of Hochderffer had blown over the ridge into layers of dead trees and turned into huge clouds of dark smoke. Four hundred people had been assigned to that fire overnight. In the middle of the morning they began to call for help, "any help you can send us."

Elden's wind was fifty by then, hers was strong enough to rattle windows. Smoke on the Friedlein fire was building, but the crew's request for a slurry drop was denied because high wind made it dangerous to fly so close to the mountain.

It was the most gnarly possible day. Right after noon Myrna reported smoke inside the city limits, south of the Little America hotel. Jake was the first to arrive…he described half an acre burning, fire climbing trees and threatening structures. Everybody who wasn't already fighting a fire rushed out there. By then it must have been *anxiety* in the dispatcher's office. Half an hour later smoke from the Vultee Arch fire was rising high behind East Pocket and blowing to the northeast. The Sedona fire boss said he was afraid it would run up East

Pocket Knob or over into Oak Creek Canyon, and that was "political" too. Category Two crews were everywhere…which meant only partly trained firefighters from all over the state.

Jake's fire near Little America was huge and black already, spotting out ahead…units pulled back behind a road. Voices on the radio were *urgent.* From eight and a half miles away she could see huge red flames. The band of smoke was a mile wide. The first air tanker to arrive began to drop slurry to stop fire short of a subdivision, if possible. The lead plane pilot told the tanker pilot, "Drop on the head of the fire."

Smoke behind Hochderffer just kept getting worse. At 13:15 the Air Attack observer above it told the dispatcher: "There's been deployment on the Hochderffer Fire." Randy was up there. Somebody was being burned over and fire shelters had been opened. She felt sick. Randy.

The fire was working on a radio frequency she couldn't reach, so she didn't know what was going on…she just stood and stared at that evil black smoke. Half an hour later ambulances were staging down on highway 180 and road 151. She guessed from what Air Attack said that it was a crew from off forest that had deployed shelters, but he didn't say who, just "We still haven't got those folks out."

That was enough trouble for *any* day, but the Baker Butte lookout south on the Mogollon Rim reported a dark grey smoke on the north side of West Clear Creek. Flames were forty feet high, she said…two other lookouts crossed it and south end units were dispatched. It was so much to handle that the forest switched to a unified command system that coordinated everything.

Jake ordered two Type Two Crews for his fire in town and eight more engines, "any type you can get." Neighborhoods were threatened…he estimated more than thirty acres burning with spots in back yards on the Herold Ranch Road. Spot fires had reached the Rio de Flag. Butler Avenue was closed, but he thought they could hold it if conditions didn't change.

"Task Force One" was called up, a new voice on the radio identified itself as "Air Ops". Air tankers were ordered to return after loading in Prescott, not Winslow where wind was too strong. At 14:00 smoke on Jake's fire in town, with so much slurry, was smaller and lighter in color. Smoke from Vultee Arch didn't actually look too bad. Gusts of wind were so strong they were blowing her trap door up and letting it drop with a bang.

The Hochderffer Fire was the biggest, its smoke rose high above the Peaks. Air Attack reported "all people out and accounted for." They were taken to the Flagstaff hospital emergency room and treated for smoke inhalation…one had serious burns. She began to cry. Oh, Randy.

It was awful. Baker Butte's fire had been named for Pot Hole Tank…the report from there was that it had grown from four acres in heavy fuels to forty acres. She could finally see the smoke, more than fifty miles away. The Prescott Hot Shots were responding.

A helicopter had arrived from San Bernardino, a "heavy." Randy told her later it was an Erickson, a huge tanker designed to siphon up two thousand gallons of water through long tubes and dump it on a fire wherever it was needed…there were only half a dozen in the country. The big Erickson worked the Vultee Arch fire, fighting wind down in the canyon, fighting for air time on the radio.

At 15:00 the Hochderffer fire boss informed Flagstaff in the calmest voice, "everything is lost," out of control. Spots were burning in Kendrick Park, the crews were falling back to highway 180, which was closed.

Jake refused to release any of the engines on *his* fire. He said, "There's too much potential, you won't get anything from us." Eighty acres had burned, two neighbourhoods had been evacuated and two more were on evacuation watch, with the country club on stand-by.

It went on like that the rest of the day, drops of slurry from air tankers, voices so thick on the radio they were covering each other. There were voices all night, calling, requesting, reporting. Hundreds of people with hand tools and planes, dozers, engines…support teams for food and water, and overhead personnel and caches of equipment. The radio was layers of overlapping voices. Wind diminished a little after midnight, but never died.

The next morning all five fires were burning with no containment. Jake's fire in the city limits, which had been held at ninety-seven acres overnight, was only eight per cent contained. Acreage on the Friedlein fire was twenty with a handful of people fighting it. The Vultee Arch fire had grown to 200 acres, but it hadn't spread into Oak Creek Canyon yet. The Pot Hole Fire was up to 500… Clear Creek Pines subdivisions were threatened. The I.C. down there started calling for air tankers by 06:00. The big one, Hochderffer, was over 1500 acres with hundreds of people on it and White Horse Estates north of the Peaks had been evacuated. One firefighter was still in the hospital.

That day was almost as bad as the day before, wind was just as strong, at least where she was. Black smoke on the Hochderffer *boiled* up behind the Peaks to twenty thousand feet when the fire made a run and got into something burnable…through her binoculars she could see half a dozen distinct colors. Black smoke *churned* down on the Pot fire, which closed the road between Stoneman Lake and Clints Well. Television helicopters requested permission to fly over the fires and film them. Hot Shot crews reported in from all over the place…Globe, Rock Point on the reservation, New Hampshire, Washington. Mendocino and Stanislaus crews from California, Negrito from New Mexico.

Bruce Babbitt was there from the Interior Department to go out on the line for two days…Randy said he was certified so he did that sometimes and worked as hard as anybody else, even if he was so old. He had his fifty-eighth birthday on that fire, and in base camp they gave him a cake with candles.

It was almost a week before most of the people were released and sent home. Hochderffer grew to more than twenty-five square miles. That made *it* the biggest fire ever on the Coconino. The Pot Fire was 8000 acres before they could get it stopped. But nobody was killed. "*This* time," Randy said. "You know, I'm getting a bad feeling about this job."

The district silviculturist said those two big fires north of the Peaks had been so hot in places that the ground itself would be sterilized for years. You know, all the organisms in the soil destroyed, little fungus and stuff that helps pines to grow. Unless they plant seeds, some areas will be barren for several human lifetimes.

P.J. was on the hill at the big corral with the mares and foals. Meg saw his blue Dodge up there and turned off the road. It wasn't half a mile from the house but what the hell, he liked to say, a rancher never walked when he could ride and kept his horse and his truck in good condition so he wouldn't have to.

The landscape grew as she drove up the hill until finally the Painted Desert and the Little Colorado valley spread wide in front of her with Grandma's magic cliffs beyond. South west, cumulus were building high above the Peaks, but the colors of the Painted Desert lay in sunshine as it had all the years of her life.

When he heard her coming, P.J. stopped work on the gate and waved. She closed the car door and walked toward him. "How's my girl? How goes the battle?" He wore working clothes—boots, jeans, hat. You wouldn't guess to look at him that his manager did most of the hard chores while P.J. kept up with the money.

She went through the gate, pulled it shut. A pretty little filly stood against the far fence, ears up, watching. She walked out into the corral. "Hey, Clover, come say hello."

The filly came to meet her and touched her hands with a soft nose. "Hi, cupcake, is the big bad man scaring you again?"

P.J.: "Haven't lost your touch, I see. She won't let me get close."

"Sweetheart, you've grown. You'll be tall as I am first thing you know." She kissed the little forehead. "I treat her like a person."

"She's a *horse*, she'll always be a horse."

"That's your mistake right there, not all of us girls are alike. She's a person to me." The filly trotted back to the far fence. "Whatcha doin'?"

"Fixing the latch here." He hugged her shoulder. "Glad to see you."

"Just had my teeth cleaned. See—are you blinded?"

"I *thought* you looked unusually brilliant."

She kissed his cheek. "You haven't lost your touch either."

He laughed. "Well, a compliment never hurt a girl's feelings. Been thinking about you."

"Good or bad?"

"Remembering what you said about the Fourth of July, what you told us about underage drinkers, arson fires, illegal woodcutters, cattle on the roads, injury accidents, all those campers who ignored restrictions. Wondering if Labor Day would be just as active."

"Probably. I'm beginning to dread holidays. Gives me a bad attitude about campers, which is fair—they have a bad attitude about me."

"Was that body the other day, the shooting, on your district?"

"It was. The county has the investigation, but I was the first response. Awful smell, he'd been there for days. My first human corpse. It was creepy, being alone with it."

He leaned against the gate. "Care to talk about it?"

"I would, yes, but you're busy."

"Nothing that won't wait."

He listened while she told him—Josy, tire tracks, photographs, pistol, paperwork and then Bailey's list. P.J. was an attentive listener, watching her face as she talked.

"Well, that's quite a situation. No tracks, no trace, no clues—somebody was smart enough to think ahead. It wasn't a passer-by. Nor a spur of the moment. Certainly not an accident. Had to been somebody who knew him."

"I think so too. Had to been. What kind of person would you say could plan like that?"

"Hmmm." He pushed his hat back with a thumb. "That's a good question, the kind of person. I'd say somebody who keeps secrets inside himself, doesn't show his emotions—very cool customer. You'd never know what he was thinking. Your Jake Holding, now, he wouldn't have done it like that, he'd have been more likely to provoke a fight and then beat a man to death with his fists. No, this guy, you're after a thinker."

"Could it have been a woman?"

"A woman?"

"Some of the women don't have alibis."

"Now that's a different angle entirely. I suppose it could have been—it wouldn't have occurred to me though. But they do call a gun an equalizer. Do you think one of the girls did it?"

"No. Not that one of them might not have thought of it, but a windy night out there alone, chance he'd wake up, chance somebody would see her—it doesn't seem likely."

"None of that would've have scared *you*. You'd have handled it easily. I don't mean to say you would have, just could have. Josy too, I think. Lots of girls in this country." He moved his big hand around a half circle—cinder cones and lava ridges, mile after mile, gullies in the valley, clouds turning dark above them. "We've got girls to match the mountains. I believe it."

"That's a wonderful compliment, P.J."

"I mean it as such. This land doesn't tolerate sissies, never has."

"Plants, animals, or people."

"Right, they don't last. The people, though, you can't always tell by looking. You have to give 'em time and watch what they do."

"OK, then tell me, what should I do about Bailey's list?"

"What's there to do?"

"I could snoop around, ask questions, pick up hints and gossip, really play detective. That's not exactly what Bailey asked for, and it may not be any of my business, but I could."

"You could just give him brief opinions on everybody."

The little filly was still watching. "Would that be right? I know those people—like Josy."

"That's the kind of thing your mother would ask."

"I'll ask her, but what do *you* think? What would you do?"

"Oh boy." He rubbed the back of his neck. "Given what you've told me, I think I'd keep my eyes open and say as little as possible."

"What would you be looking for with your eyes open? What was this mystery person *like*? Somebody who hated that much, somebody who didn't see any other way?"

"There'd have to be a strong reason. You think eliminating Jake from job competition would have been cause enough?"

"Not unless you added something else: hatred, resentment, revenge, outraged ego."

"Fear?"

She hesitated and leaned against the gate, looked across the miles. "Fear. Like a preventive act?"

"Suppose someone wanted to stop him from doing something. I've read that abused women, the kind that put up with it for years, finally leave or fight back when their kids are threatened."

Startled, she searched his eyes. "That hits pretty close to home. There's something…" She told him about the photo with pins stuck into the eyes. "I suspected Jake. I haven't told Alan about it. P.J. don't…I didn't want to make you mad."

He piled obscenities up—she hadn't ever heard him talk that way—and turned and kicked the fence post. The horses blew and shifted. "God damn sneaking crawling coward. Slimey bastard, what sonofabitch would do a thing like that? Anonymous. God damn."

"I second *that* motion."

"You do all you can for years to keep your kids safe and healthy, love them, and some psychopath comes along…I'd have gone after him with a gun myself. Done *something*. A father would have to."

"I know."

"That leave it to the law bullshit cuts fathers out."

"All of us—makes us all helpless."

"Meggie, honey, are you OK?" He put his hands on her shoulders.

"P.J., to tell you the truth, I'm…it's…I don't know."

"Oh, honey."

"All this with Jake, it's just the worst of it. What happens every day, what I walk into, the people—I don't know—it's like the world is full of awful. I can't keep it, you know, separate from *me*."

"I was afraid of that."

"I haven't told anybody, just Hill a little. I feel like a failure."

"Not a bit of it, no sir."

"Other people can do it, women, good people with families and friends. They still laugh. What's wrong with me?"

Sitting on the second floor balcony wall at Cameron, Josy looked down at a sheer cliff of hard red stone on the other side of the Little Colorado and tried with the book on her lap to figure out how old it was. If the surrounding land was Triassic, what did that make the cliff? Some kind of Permian sandstone?

They had come north across—far as she could tell—a fault, an anticline, a monocline, and three descending sedimentary layers that had once been sea bottom. Looking from the pages to the land and back had made her a little car-sick. If she'd been alone, she'd have stopped at every turn-out to figure the clues, but she didn't bother to ask Walt to drive slower—she knew he wouldn't.

She'd wandered around the new motel for a while and found a quiet corner on the balcony where she could see out into the landscape and down into the river canyon. The dark red-brown sandstone cliff across on the other side was fractured into blocks in places. It was obviously sedimentary, but a different color from the cliffs visible miles away. Green tamarisks at the water's edge made an accent.

They were early enough in the dining room to have a seat by one of the big windows where she could see out across about a zillion years. After he had ordered, Walt closed the menu and opened his notebook computer on the table in front of him

"I need to enter some comments while they're still fresh in my mind. Be with you when the food comes."

"Fine." *Maybe* he would. More than once he'd worked all through dinner without saying a word. "I've got a book to read."

He didn't look at her through the whole meal, just watched the computer screen and typed and forked up food from the plate, which he had moved to the side. Finally he snapped the notebook closed and slipped it into the briefcase at his feet. "There. How's your book?"

"Very interesting."

He reached across the table and took her hand. "Sweetie, I've decided I'm ready to marry you." He smiled broadly. "You just say when and where."

She pulled her hand away. "That's not very romantic, Walt."

"Romance is for beginnings. Beginnings and winnings. After that practical takes over."

"Once I moved in with you, I was won and you didn't need to be romantic anymore?"

"Well, it's not quite like that."

"I've been lonely for months, living with you."

"That's why I think we should get married. So you can have a baby and be fulfilled."

Fulfilled? Was it Walt or an evil twin? That idiot word was too much, even for as full of cliches as he'd been lately.

"You know, your biological clock is ticking."

"That's a crocodile."

"What?"

"Captain Hook."

"You're not making sense."

"Never mind." Meg would have known what she meant.

"Dear, don't you see," he flung his hands out, "if you had a baby, you wouldn't be lonely."

"Walt, I'm not won any more. You've un-won me." Left a vacuum she'd filled with a dream.

"What are you talking about? You've been irrational ever since you found that body." There were the beginnings of bags beneath his eyes–strange how clear details were.

"Don't shout. No, it goes back before that. A lot has happened to me lately that you haven't noticed. But it's made me different."

"Have you been screwing around with somebody at work? While I've been earning money to support you?"

"I support myself. And that's an ugly thing to say."

"What's got into you?"

She put her napkin on the table and pushed back her chair. "You're attracting attention–people are looking at you. I'll wait in the car while you pay the bill. Here's ten dollars for my share."

Seven feet tall at least walking out of the dining room. Proud that she'd behaved so quietly. But he caught her arm in the gift shop.

"Wait a minute, you. Where do you think you're going?"

"To the car. I don't like being part of a public scene."

So he pushed her outside–did that make sense?–and hauled her to the car and shoved her against it. "Now, what's this all about? *What's* happened to you that I don't know about?"

"Walt, this isn't helping. You can't force me to marry you."

"I can drive off and leave you here."

"I'll call Meg. She'll come and get me."

He unlocked the car door, pushed her inside, slammed it. In one movement he came into the driver's side and shoved his face so close she couldn't focus on it. "Were you fucking that guy?"

"What guy?"

"The one you found dead."

"Oh, jeesh, give me credit for a little taste."

"Were you?"

She lost it finally. Shouted, "*Back off!* And quit shouting insults at me. You make me more unwilling every second."

It was an instant change. His whole body relaxed, and he moved back behind the steering wheel. That patronizing little laugh. "Look how you've got me upset. All I did was ask you to marry me."

"You didn't ask, you *announced.*" It was a revelation: she could out-bully him if she was willing to act like a harpy. Who wanted to do that the rest of her life?

*T*he house smelled wonderful. "Is that apple strudel you're baking?" It was childhood, coming home on a cold day.

"Just ready to take out of the oven." Mom hugged her. "Come on into the kitchen. I'll cut a piece for you when it's cooled a little. Have a seat, it won't be a minute."

From the time her feet hadn't reached the floor it had been special to sit in Mom's big chair in front of the window.

"Want your favorite plate, the little one with wildflowers?"

"Please. If it ever breaks, I'll never be able to eat a thing again."

Mom laid a knife beside the pan cooling on a rack. "Milk in the flowered cup?"

"Does anyone else ever use it?"

"No one. It hangs there forlorn."

She moved to a chair at the table. "Aren't you having any strudel?"

"Oh, for heavens' sake, I forgot to get out a plate for myself. Which one, do you think?"

"The daisies."

"Of course, your grandmother's favorite. Aunt Jo bought it for her. I think this strudel is ready to cut now. Big or little?"

"Two little pieces, maybe three."

"Here you go, luv, to your good health. Oh, I forgot forks."

"Mom, I've got a question. Do people have a responsibility to participate actively in communal society? Is it unethical to concentrate on personal interests?"

Mom's fork stopped halfway to her mouth. "You're speaking about yourself."

"I didn't expect you to catch me on the first sentence. But yes, I'm wondering about what I should do. I need to talk to you."

She set her fork on the plate and described her growing discomfort, irritation with people, sense of falling short—she hoped objectively. "It's an emotional thing, I guess, feeling wrong for your job. Should I go on as an LEO and try to find a way to do it that I can live with or quit and look for something else?"

"You're not eating—malnutrition is not conducive to thought."

"Look, I'm eating, I'm eating."

"You wonder whether it would be selfish to leave a job that's necessary to social order and public welfare?"

"And protection of natural resources, not to mention life and safety of the law-abiding public."

"But damaging to your own personal welfare."

"That's the way it feels."

"Another small piece? More milk?"

"I'll get it." She went to the refrigerator.

Mom sat looking out the window. "I agree about the necessity of social order—law or custom, whatever, has always been a basic principle. Agreement about, participation in, communal goals and behavior were absolutely essential to any life in the West, and that was long before people from Europe got here. Certainly to people like the Hopi, to humans from the beginning—no survival was possible without a cooperative group. Is there any argument about that?"

"No." Wise of Mom to talk and let her eat strudel.

"From what I've read I'd say it's a nearly universal position. Plato said all moral questions revolve around the good of the whole. Spinoza: action should fit the perspective of the whole."

"I'll have another small slice, please."

"But you can't be much good to the group if you're miserable. And trying to fit yourself to a job you're not suited to is miserable."

Mom pushed crumbs together with her fork, tidying up the pan. "You remember last year when I questioned whether the job was right for you? An important job, but maybe not right for you. People are not interchangeable units."

"I do remember. Don't put that away yet.."

"Victorian ideas about duty are ebbing. I'm not sure I'm comfortable with the current dogma that duty to one's self should be primary, it allows a scope for self-indulgence that worries me. However, I do think it can be dangerous to take either your values or your estimate of yourself from people who are different from you, places very different from your own. Am I boring you?"

"Of course not. You're talking about *me*, how can I be bored? OK, one more slice."

Mom took her hand. "Unhappiness isn't good for you either, there's clinical proof. Self-defense is a well-recognized principle."

The tang of outside air behind him, P.J. came in through the kitchen door. "Looks like more rain any minute. I smelled strudel clear up at the corral. Came to get some before you girls ate it all. I'll just take what's left." He opened the drawer and took a fork. "How's it going in here?"

"We're solving Meg's problems for today."

"Good, good. I have something to say about that." He pulled the pan toward himself, sat down, tasted. "Been thinking while I worked on the gate. This is without a doubt the best strudel I've ever smelled or tasted." He saluted Mom. "Meggie, I have a suggestion. See what you think."

"Can you talk and eat at the same time?"

"You know I can. But have your mother explain our wills while I get a running start."

Mom was still, looking at him for a minute. "Equal division between you and your brothers. I can guess where you're going P.J. Provision for cash settlement in case one or two of you aren't interested in running the ranch. We hope that will prevent quarrels."

"Right. You see where I'm going, Meggie?"

"I think so."

"This place has been in your mother's family four generations. You're the fifth. Are you interested in living here, owning the place?"

"I've thought about it, but you and Mom will be around for years.."

"Yes or no."

"Yes. I am." It was where she belonged, her place in the world.

"I'm not sure about your brothers, they're so busy being pro-fessional. Could you fix up Matt and Jo's house and live in it?"

Her chest felt tight. "Yes."

"Like to?"

"Yes."

"How many years until Hill can take retirement?"

"Fifteen."

"I've been thinking it's time for another change around here. The management Matt and your Grandpa set up in the 40s and 50s—pipe lines from the wells and tanks they could turn off so stock could be moved around—that let us control grazing, allowed some grass recovery, blue and sideoats grama mostly. In the 60s we increased our cattle rota-tion, kept some places free from grazing for a couple years."

"Uncle Matt had those experimental plots, trying to grow clover and wheatgrass and black grama near the water lines."

"You already know most of this."

"He said the cool-season bunch grasses out here weren't nutritious."

"Helluva guy, your Uncle Matt. But this situation can be harsh, rainfall can vary from two inches annually to eighteen. When I took over the day-to-day…"

"…you began raising registered quarter horses with six breeders you got from Driftwood Ike in Chino Valley."

"Smartest horses in the world, resourceful, *reasonable* animals you can practically talk to. I love 'em, but they need supplemental feed. The operation still just about breaks even. How would you feel about helping me experiment with breeding the mares to a registered donkey and training the mules we'd get?"

"Mules?"

"I've been reading. You know anything about mules?"

"I did a report in high school."

"That's right, you did. I'd forgotten."

"They're a cross-breed from donkeys, which originated from wild asses in North Africa, and horses, hybrids with big ears and short manes."

"Mules, so I've read, are superior to both parents: steady, surefooted, intelligent, hardy. You can train them to anything a horse can do, and they're stronger. Be interested in seeing what you could do with them?"

"I've been curious."

He looked at Mom. "Your mother'd like having you here. I kinda think her Uncle Matt would too. Thanks to your grandpa and your Aunt Jo and my interest in the market, there's money to try it if we want to. That money's been through some hard times the last seventy years, but I think we could swing it."

"P.J...."

He raised the hand that wasn't cutting strudel. "It's selfish of me—I haven't had anybody good with horses since you left. Talk to Hill, think about it, decide whether you'd be letting other folks down, what you want to do about that murder investigation. There'd be some legal changes to make, some conversations with your brothers. I'm kinda excited about it myself."

*S*unlight is golden through a light rain, the end of the afternoon storm. It's the earliest possible time for dinner, so early that every other table in the old Cottage Street house is empty. She loves listening to Beste say things like, "I played bridge in this house not so many years ago."

Once, maybe she was twelve or so, she came away from looking at the paintings in the bedroom. "Beste, tell me about Lillian. What was she like? Where did you meet her?"

Beste was stirring a chocolate sauce. "I didn't know her well, of course, I was just a child. My parents stopped at Tuba City, Shekayah. I don't remember where we were coming from. In those days there weren't many paved roads—a car had to be tough—and any excuse to stop was welcome. I think it was the middle of the day, lunch time. We went in and my mother said, 'Why, hello, Lillian.' My mother knew her from Flagstaff, I think."

"What did she look like?"

Beste laughed. "She looked quite large to me, but everyone does when you're a child. I can't have been more than eight."

"Was she pretty?"

"I suppose so. She was, let's see, almost fifty, I should think. Maybe a little younger. I was very taken with the way she smiled at me. As if I were as important as my parents. I was such an awkward, shy little thing, and she quite won me with that smile."

"It's hard to think of you awkward and shy, Beste."

"Of course I was. Weren't you? People who say childhood is a time of innocent happiness have poor memories. Or they're dolts."

She lifted the spoon and let the sauce run off. *"I incline toward the latter. This is about ready. Do you want to dip the biscotti? Then a few years later, not many, a couple, I saw Lillian in Flagstaff going into the Monte Vista. I think she was staying there. She stopped and talked with my mother."*

"Did she smile at you?"

"She did. And she remembered my name. Can you believe it? I've heard people say that she didn't like children, but that was not my experience. She recognized me as a person, not a pet or an idiot. Here's a plate to put them on."

It was the big creamy platter with the golden border, perfect contrast for chocolate cookies. She began to lay them in a careful pattern so the plate showed through.

"I don't think Lillian ever stayed long in Flagstaff. She traveled about painting. I'd have a glimpse of her now and then, that's all. Then I married an engineer and I was gone for a long time myself. I heard the last part of her life was sad. That was when I bought the paintings."

She decides on schnitzel and sets the menu aside. "Beste, I need to talk to you."

Beste closes her menu. "The shrimp, I think. Of course, Sarah."

"Dad's so good to me, and I don't want to hurt him, but I feel like I'm in prison."

Beste takes off her glasses. "It's comfortable, but it's prison."

"*Yes!* It's all him. Everything is *him*. Even my room, it's because *he* wanted it. If I ever have children, I'm going to try to find out who they are and give them a chance to *be* it."

"Will they let you know, I wonder? Children tend to hide from their parents."

"Then I'll let them find out who they are. Beste I don't even *know*. I'm, like, *choking*." She can hear her voice, too loud.

"Will you let them find out who *you* are? Maybe not. Maybe they won't care. Parents are often not real to their children. That is, children don't want real people as parents."

It's a relief to turn the topic away from herself. "That's what I want to talk to you about. I thought maybe if you could tell me how he got this way, then maybe, I don't know, maybe it will help."

The waiter fills water glasses. "Are you ready to order, ladies?" His elbow makes a sharp bend inside his sleeve.

After he's gone, she looks down at the painted flowers on her plate. "I didn't mean to get so excited." She's afraid she's going to cry.

Beste is wonderful. "Of course you're agitated. You're fighting for your life. An appeal for information is an intelligent approach." She clasps her hands on the tablecloth. "We moved often when he was a child. And he hated it. He'd plead each time. It was never an adventure for him to go to a new place, being the new boy."

It's odd to think of Dad as a little boy with no control.

"But his father—his father loved his career. It meant a great deal to him. As I saw it, Randolph felt it meant more than he did. It's probably impossible ever to know your own deepest reasons. Definitely impossible to know someone else's. But that's what I think is going on. Do you understand what I'm saying?"

"I think so."

"Children are quite self-centered, you know. I suppose they have to be. He wanted to be important to his father, but he was a very small part. I tried for years to compensate by being interested enough for two." She smiles and shakes her head. "Oh my, how I tried. It quite wore me out. But I used to ache for that boy. His father didn't even hear him when he talked."

That's sad. She can see a boy telling something, see his eyes when his father doesn't answer. "You think he's trying not to be that way with Randy and me."

"It doesn't fit your image of him, I suppose. That's part of what living is, changing your images, or what's the point of doing it for so many years?"

The waiter comes with a tureen of soup on a cart. Ladles it into bowls, places them on the table. Goes away.

Maybe Beste's right. But she still thinks it's about power too, Dad wanting to control. Like a gnarly sickness deep inside of him. His mother's never seen how he is when she's not around.

Beste lifts a spoon to her mouth. "Oh, that's tasty." Then, "You don't realize yet, Sarah, that some people can't separate their children from themselves. They try to give themselves the childhood they wanted. Usually it doesn't work."

"But you couldn't *ever* make it up to yourself."

"You go on trying anyway. Randolph doesn't see what he's doing. I honestly think he doesn't mean to sacrifice you."

After the waiter changes the plates, sets shrimp and schnitzel in front of them, after they begin to eat, Beste says, "To return to a fascinating subject, next spring you'll be graduating with a B.F.A. What do you want to do then?"

Her mouth is full, she pats it with her finger tips. Beste smiles.

"I'd..." she swallows. "I'd still like to go to San Francisco."

"The Art Institute?"

"I could get a Master's there. The library has twenty-five *thousand* art books. It's really, really awesome."

"That would be a thrill. Have you talked with your father?"

"I'm afraid to. I *know* what he'll say. Why should I leave home when I have everything I need here or something like that. But Beste, what do you think? I looked the Institute up at the library. It says financial aid is available. Sixty-eight per cent of the students get assistance. I should have about six thousand dollars saved by the end of this summer and maybe six thousand next summer. That's not enough for even one year's tuition, but maybe I could get a scholarship. My art grades are high."

"So! You're having independent ideas. Good for you."

"I was wondering...if I write for an application, may I use your address? Have it mailed to your house?"

"So your father won't see it?"

"He might throw it away. And if he didn't, it would be a year-long argument. And he'd want to do everything if he *did* decide to let me go."

"I see no harm in keeping it between us two for a few months."

"Thank you *so* much. It won't be *my* dream anymore when Dad finds out about it."

"Wouldn't he have fun, though, taking on San Francisco?"

They laugh, looking at each other. It's the most wonderful feeling to have Beste for help.

"And Sarah, keep this in mind. My graduation present to you could be, I've just decided, rent for an apartment near the Institute. Wait now—the Institute is close to the waterfront, I think. Somewhere near North Beach? Rents might be very high in that neighborhood. You might have to find a place out in the avenues and ride the bus in. I'd love to go and search with you, if you'll have me."

"Beste, you're *awesome*. I'll just *die* if I can't get away. Only for a little while, you know, time enough to get to be me instead of Randolph Findlay's daughter."

*M*eg went out to the highway through Wupatki, planning to turn onto the long slope of 89, a straight line through miles of enormous land. A gunbelt and a hand-held radio were on the seat beside her. Even in her own car on her day off, as the people in Georgia had advised, because you never knew. The radio and the pistol gave her choices in case of trouble, and trouble was part of her job.

> The responsibility to bear firearms carries with it an obligation and responsibility to exercise discipline, restraint, and good judgment in their use. The Forest Officer must keep in mind that when firing a weapon, there always exists a danger to innocent parties.

She'd left Wupatki behind and climbed up onto Antelope Mesa, loving everything she saw, every scrubby little juniper, every cinder cone on the horizon, every cloud in the sky. Some people could look at that landscape and call it barren. Crumb, some people could see only what they were used to.

Somewhere in the dark beneath her tires were hidden faults, old cracks in the earth. Doney Fissure was supposed to be five hundred feet deep. She'd never gone down to see for herself, but her brothers had tried it once, with headlamps, and found an old ladder made of timbers no sawmill had turned out for years. They'd stopped finally when a slope ran down to a sheer drop-off with nothing but black below and come back up saying it didn't matter enough to them to try to go on down.

She lifted her foot from the gas pedal. On the right a pronghorn antelope was running full-out, back among the junipers parallel to the road, cutting closer at every tree in its path until it was just off the shoulder. She held her speed to twenty-five, and it stayed with her. Whoop-ti-doo! a pronghorn race!

It sprinted across the road, a blur of tan with a white rump, and ran along the left shoulder, watching her: the big eyes gave it good peripheral vision. She loved antelope, smaller than deer by a few inches but heavy-muscled, powerful runners.

Uncle Matt had admired them. "There's a reason why you find antelope around here. Well, two reasons. One—they have excellent vision so they can see a predator coming a long way off, especially out in the grassland where there's nothing to block the view. And two—nothing can catch them if they have a good start and a clear run." She judged by the size of the horns that her racer was either a female or a young male.

Pilots of small planes claimed they could herd antelope from the air. Maybe so. It was possible, though, that the pilots didn't know a race when they were in the middle of one.

A sense of play showed up now and then in every creature she'd ever known. She whooped out the open window. "Go, darlin'! Go!"

The antelope pulled ahead, crossed in front of her again, and ran along the right shoulder, having fun, she just knew it. The black and white bands in its neck looked close enough to touch.

Once more it sped across the road, teasing her, maybe even saying something for all she knew. Still running full-out, it disappeared among the trees. She called after it. "Thank you."

She was elated—it filled the landscape from one horizon to the other. The antelope touching her life like that had made her part of something bigger and older, given her a quick glimpse of the long sweep of life and kinship. Lucky to have such animals for neighbors, such country for home. Anybody who didn't like Northern Arizona was way too different from her.

She thought of Grandma's brother Luke, the one who'd married Aunt Jo's cousin Gertrude and gone off to live on her money in New York City—way too different. Grandma said he stopped off in Flagstaff fifteen years later to see his mother: a thin, sad, aging man who left the train with a suitcase that had seen better days and found someone who'd drive him to the ranch.

"Gertrude had taken the starch out of Luke, we barely recognized him. High life in New York had lasted through the Jazz Age, and they'd hit every possible note, but most of what they had left had disappeared in the Crash. Gertrude lost her money and Luke lost his looks, and that was about all they'd liked about each other."

"How did your brother lose his looks, Grandma?"

"Along the way somewhere in what was called riotous living, he probably didn't notice until it was way too late. For five years they'd been staying in a room at her Grandmother's house. I gather Gertrude blamed Luke personally for everything up to and including the Rape of Nanking; Jo said her cousin could be a knife in the ribs, and Luke had no doubt paid heavily for his years of all-night parties."

"So he was poor?"

"In every way you could think of. Mama cried and touched him and told him he'd always have a home with her if he wanted it, but two days later he was off for Hollywood to see about work in the movies. I don't know if he got it, we didn't hear from him after that nor any word about him. Mama never stopped grieving. A lot of mothers had lost their sons, but she mourned her own."

"Grandma, what happened to Aunt Jo's cousin?"

"She was alcoholic by the time the fun ended—she died of cirrhosis. I'll bet a cookie most families have that kind of bad example."

*T*hey were in Flagstaff's neon again before Walt spoke. The whole hour and a half from Cameron, she'd sat silent. For the first time in her life, she knew what she wanted. It was a good thing he'd become so creepy that she saw what would happen if habit and biology tricked her into giving it up.

At the first traffic light, he turned to her and said softly, "I need you. Will you marry me?"

"You know what, Walt?" She looked at his face as kindly as she could. "You don't want to be married, not really. You just want a woman to run the house for you, and you don't want to be alone at night. That's not what I'd call a marriage."

"Is there somebody else?" Anything but admit there might be something wrong with him.

"No. In fact, I've been thinking lately that I might not ever marry."

The light turned green—he slammed the gear lever up. "So what are you saying, you've decided you're a lesbian, is that it?"

She was tempted to say she was—it might make things easier. "I just don't think marriage would fit with what I have in mind."

"And just what do you 'have in mind'?" There was the sneer again.

"Some ideas I've been considering while you were too busy to talk to me. Nothing that would affect you."

"Is it because of the things you said have happened to you lately?"

"Partly. Partly because we aren't really friends—it's been like living with a stranger. You weren't that way when I first knew you; I'm afraid to think what you'd be if I married you. Maybe you gave me a preview back in Cameron."

"You women are so fucking strange."

"How would you know? You haven't ever got far enough out of yourself to see anyone else."

"Look, I'm not going to argue with you about it. You're sneakier with words than I am—if I argue, you'll turn everything upside down. I made a fair offer, and I'll give you a few days to consider it. That house is pretty comfortable—take a look around and see if you want to leave it and go back to a seedy little apartment."

*F*rom the outside, people said, there had been a big difference between Uncle Matt and his brother Luke, not how they looked so much as how they acted, and outsides were clues to insides. Raising didn't make people alike.

"Now look at this, Meggie, it hasn't been so obvious for years. What do you see?" Matt had taught her through his last years.

"What?" She was all of eight, still riding the little old mare.

"Here's the fence between us and Wupatki land. See the difference?"

"Yellow flowers on us and none over there."

"Good eyes! Now why is that?"

"Why?" She looked hard, trying to please him.

"Well, what about those plants with the yellow flowers—snakeweed, it's called—what do they look like?"

"Little round bushes."

"And the leaves?"

"Narrow, not wide."

"What might that mean?"

"The plants trying to keep moisture? They've been here a long time?"

"Good thinking. Probably native, not introduced. What's different about the other side of the fence?"

She loved it when he praised her. "The ground is the same. It gets the same rain, same sun."

"Your mind works just right, eliminating possibilities."

"Cows?"

"That's my girl! Cattle graze on our side, but there haven't been any on Wupatki for years. Now that Peshlakai sheep are excluded, there won't be anything but antelope. Think, why does that make snakeweed here and not there?"

Back and forth, back and forth. "There's more grass on that side."

"Your big brothers wouldn't have seen that. Why would grass have made a difference?"

With every compliment, she was more sure. "Cows don't like snakeweed. They eat the grass and the snakeweed gets rain."

"And over there?"

"Grass gets the rain."

"Exactly right. Native species do pretty well in this harsh country. They're long-term strategists, that's where their energy goes: narrow leaves, small flowers. They can even hide for years underground in what's called seed banks. Like we'd put money away to keep it safe, they bank their seeds. If nothing comes along—cows or a new road—the soil will be stable, undisturbed, for years."

"If we built a fence and kept cows out, what would happen?"

"I've been curious about that myself. Wouldn't it be interesting to build a fence and watch? Leave the ground alone and watch? I'd also like to see the effect on piñon and juniper."

New plants were like ranchers who had come to dominate land once used by the Indians. Like new-comers who were beginning to drive out the old pioneer culture. Some of them had taken advantage of Western ideals and then betrayed them. Driven the frontier families out to the edges or wiped them out, as they had Josy's grandparents. Thriving in disturbance like introduced plants.

Jake was the worst possible example of a Westerner. Last spring she had stopped in the door of the shop and seen him talking to Buck in a loud ugly voice, the kind she thought of as Eastern.

"You do what you're told or you're out on your ass. You want a transfer out of fire money to timber markers, I can put you there tomorrow, don't bet I can't."

She wouldn't talk to a criminal in a voice like that. Buck's face had been full of choked-back hatred, and she'd felt so much sympathy for him that she'd stepped away so he wouldn't know anyone had seen. Buck, who had stayed alone at Fernow cabin Thursday night last week, less than ten miles from Kathy tank…

*S*un is below the horizon but clouds remaining in the west are every color. Sarah hurries to get to Rogers Lake and out of the pines and stop so she can see it all before it fades. It's finally the most *royal* sunset she's ever seen, purple and gold…radiant. Then peach to pink to lavender half up the sky. Venn stands in the back of the truck, nostrils twitching at the smells in the air.

On one of her first days off, in late April, she drove her new Toyota down through Oak Creek Canyon, loving the way it felt on the curves. Lillian had been there once with Zane Grey when there was barely a narrow dirt road…maybe lots of times with Jess later when they had their Shekayah guest ranch.

She was looking everywhere for Lillian. It was so important it hurt. Like Lillian had to be someplace…she had been so alive once.

She tried to push aside Now, erase it, to see Then. When she could do it, Sedona was the most inspiring place. No flashy stores…no purple jeeps for tourists. No shoppers walking up and down. No noise, no traffic, no hotels. Just cliffs and trees and creek and sky and clouds. Little ranch houses very far apart.

If you could push aside the ugly stuff people had made, you could see what it had been. Lillian had lived there ten years "in the big park," she said, "at the mouth of the canyon." In a stone house on a little rise above the creek. Sedona wasn't full of pavement and cars then. Rushing water in the creek but no rushing people.

It was the closest she had come. But Los Abrigados was all wrong. It looked like money, like making money and spending money. Love and art had been there once.

She found a place close to the little stone house and looked up above the tops of old sycamores at the cliffs. And knew how happy Lillian had been there…something good and true to paint every day. It had been a whole ninth of her life.

The door of the stone house was open with cleaning supplies inside. She stepped in like you would into a church, expecting that happiness would wash over her. It had all been changed… the walls weren't pink anymore, and Indian designs weren't around the fireplace. Everything was new. A steel kitchen. A skylight.

A woman turned and looked at her. "Miss, I can't let you walk in here sight-seeing. If you want to look at the house, you'll have to check at the front desk."

She went away numb. There was no place on what had been Shekayah that wasn't built on or paved over except for the old trees and flower beds tended by a commercial service, probably. Lillian had lived twenty-five more years after she and Jess drove away from Sedona, and their guest ranch became a made-up place.

She wanted to sit by the creek where she could try to honor them in her thoughts. But there wasn't any such place. Maxfield Parrish said people in paintings of the Southwest were an impertinence because they spoiled the sense of space and loneliness. He should see Sedona.

The longer Jake knew her, the more he found wrong with her. When she smiled it was a silly grin, when she laughed she sounded like a horse. Her feet were skinny and he didn't like that pink paint on her toenails…she held her hands like a chipmunk. Why did she do that to her hair, it was dumb.

He made fun of everything she said like she was some kind of joke that was too stupid to take seriously. She already *knew* she was a fool, but it hurt when somebody she loved treated her like that. She hoped he'd think everything about her was wonderful or at least enough to make him love her, but he never said a single nice word, no compliments even, just criticism all the time, like he couldn't see anything about her that was as good as *he* was.

Not all the time at first, just now and then. But he could see it made her feel bad, so he did it more and more often. Once she said, "It hurts me when you say things like that," and he said, "No it doesn't." With scorn in his voice. Like that was stupid…"What's wrong with you?" For a little while she went on loving him anyway.

She *felt* like loving. One of her days off in early June when she was going into town, off to the left, a completely black chow dog was limping through the trees. When it saw her it turned and sat down and watched her drive by. It looked so hopeful, *pathetic*…like "Maybe this person will *help* me." Randy had said there was a lion on her mountain. He showed her a kill that Venn had found, a little deer carcass stuffed under a fallen tree and covered with branches. She turned around and went back…the black chow was still there, watching her.

First she petted Venn's head and talked to her. "Look, Venn, here's somebody who needs us." Then she whistled. The dog limped toward her slowly. It was matted and grungy on one side, like it had lain on something wet. It had a red collar.

"You poor thing, you look *awful*. Are you lost? Have you been out all night?" She checked the collar for tags. There was one for rabies vaccination, no ID or phone number. A female, the dog looked up at her…she couldn't just drive away.

It wouldn't jump up into the back of the truck, because of the lame foot maybe, so she struggled to pick it up and lift it in. Venn growled. "No, Venn. Don't be mean. We have to help."

She watched in the mirror. There was no fighting in the back as she drove to the Humane Society. Would someone have already called, trying to find their lost chow? She was such a nice dog.

*T*hey'd been awake half the night talking in the dark about P.J.'s proposition, turning it over like something they could hold in their hands. A change like that would have to be good for both of them.

"One thing that worries me is that living out on the ranch you'd feel like an intruder into my family."

" I haven't felt like an outsider yet. I like being there, like your folks, working with P.J. on projects. Who's autonomous anyway?"

"We haven't been there more than a Christmas overnight. Could you live in the house Uncle Matt and Aunt Jo built?"

"I like it, the way it belongs where it is. The design suited them and what they cared about–I'd want to keep all Matt's books right where they are, all Jo's paintings–but it would fit us too."

Lying together, they'd drifted into thought. For her, below the surface was a photograph with steel circles instead of eyes.

Finally into sleep. Just as well: she was due to pick up Josy early to drive out to Woody Ridge so they could hike before it got too hot. And the suggestion wasn't something that needed a quick answer–P.J.'d probably take weeks figuring out arrangements, financing, incorporation. There'd be evenings at the ranch discussing details. Letters to her brothers. P.J. didn't do anything in a hurry.

They discussed it in the morning while Hill was shaving and she was sitting on the side of the tub brushing her hair. "We haven't any idea what my income would be, what our expenses would be. If you were to get the AFMO job on Blue Ridge, you'd be driving two hundred miles a day round trip."

"I haven't decided yet whether I want to apply. You're talking negative, all the objections I could have. Did it occur to you I might want to quit Fire and be a partner in this new corporation?"

"Would you?" He was so experienced as an engine boss.

"I might. I'm not as good with horses as you are, but I'd probably be OK at the business end of it once P.J. had trained me. It could be a better future than turning into an old fart with bad knees still driving an engine and trying to climb up-slope as fast as college boys. And I've got some ideas myself. I'd like to talk with P.J. about experiments with fire intervals for conversion of brush back to grass. And maybe Israeli techniques, drip irrigation in selected spots."

They'd talked about it in the kitchen cooking breakfast. "You wouldn't feel like a quitter?"

"Heck no. I've been in Fire since I was twenty, I'm under no obligation to stay until I'm fifty. The chances that I'd move up are pretty slim the way the Forest Service is going."

At the table: "Would you miss being in charge of all those people and machines?"

"You don't think there'd be plenty to be in charge of? Come on. Would you miss the power the Sig gives you?"

"Some days I think I do as much harm as good. I like the possibility of helping people. But I'll tell you: I'm the law, I'm the enforcer. If I follow the rules, I'm going to win every argument, and I can come down heavy on people who irritate me. What if I learn to like it?"

"The job could change anybody."

"Anyway, I've got to brush my teeth and get on the road so Josy and I can play detective. I hope it'll ease my guilt about not doing enough as Bailey's sidekick."

First she called the cell phone at the ranch. "We're talking about it, P.J. So far we're positive. I'm hesitant because it's too wonderful to be true, but we're talking."

"Good, good. Your mother's already wondering whether she could go through Wupatki and get phone lines out here for e-mail and a fax. Sure would change this old place. What's wrong with that, she wants to know."

In the bedroom she opened a drawer and took out the little box that had been hers for thirteen years. A gift from Grandma before she died: a fragile chain and a golden daisy painted on a ceramic disk. The old hands had caressed it one last time.

"I want you to have it, Meggie. It was a Christmas present from your Aunt Jo sixty years ago. Since the day she gave it to me, my life has been beautiful, all my dreams have come true. This little flower has gone around the world with me. To Paris. To China."

"It's a treasure, Grandma."

"Now I'm passing it on to you as a talisman. When you were little I could keep you happy with love. When you were in school, I could be a refuge where your sorrows could heal."

"It's true. You did that."

"But now you're seventeen, and grown-up grief and pain are harder for someone else to help you with." She whispered. "So I've put all the magic I know into this tiny thing, and now I promise it's more powerful that it looks. It carries love that grew through a lifetime of happiness."

"Oh, Grandma." She felt tears in her eyes.

"If you'll try, bet a cookie you'll find it works. I'm leaving you a powerful charm to keep you safe in your spirit, which is the most important safety there is."

*O*ne day on the way home from high school Sarah had stopped at Beste's house. She was feeling so freaky, out of place everywhere, like she never would belong. Sometimes talking to Beste made her feel better. She tried to say how it was.

Beste sat on the couch beside her. "You feel lonely because you're different from the others?"

She picked up a throw pillow and hugged it to the unhappy place in her chest. "I always have, that's the trouble. It isn't just now."

"I've wondered about that. I'm glad you told me. Had it occurred to you that perhaps the difference is in your mode of perception?"

She just stared. She didn't know what that meant.

"Some people are verbal minded. They think in words most of the time. Since school and the society it reflects both emphasize words, those people are quite successful. They can be forgiven for thinking of themselves superior."

"They *do*. They really do."

"Other people are visual minded. The words they hear are less real to them than the pictures they see around them. It's an inherent trait, born with them, but verbal people tend to consider it a weakness, and they make the visual people think so too. I've suspected you're one of the visual ones. The mind of the painter is visual by definition. That makes sense, don't you think?"

She nodded…she supposed so.

"Your father is verbal, of course, or he wouldn't be a successful lawyer. Randy obviously thinks in words. So do I, I'll confess. But you, don't colors mean more to you than words?"

She nodded again. It was true.

"By its nature your mind does things our poor blind minds can't. I hope, my love, that one day you'll recognize your worth, and different will feel much better."

Beste stood up and rubbed her hip. "And then there are people whose minds work in numbers. We often call them geniuses. Or in movement, the superb athletes. I'm completely baffled by the people who invented computers. Their minds must operate in ways alien to me. I suppose we all think our own way is the smartest."

*J*osy was out of bed before Walt could wake up and decide she was irresistible. By the time he came into the kitchen and lifted the coffee pot, she was combed and fed, dressed in shorts and hiking boots. He looked surprised.

"Where are *you* going? I thought you had another day off."

"Meg is picking me up. We want to hike around in the south end and check some theories on Jake's murder—you know, before it gets too hot. Or rains."

"Since when were you a cop?"

She didn't answer. It was no fun feeling defensive every time he walked into the room.

"And after that what?"

"Grocery store." And she had to find a place she could move into right away. "I thought I'd go to the library and find something to read— figured you'd be working late again."

"It's Friday. Maybe I'll come home early and take my Sweetie into town for a movie." Jeesh, now it was Mr. Hearty. "And dinner."

She was wary. "We haven't done that since last Fall."

"Then it's about time."

"OK. Sure. Tell you what, I'll meet you at the library. That would be easier for you." She'd been left sitting at home before if "something came up" and he "couldn't make it."

"So, have you been thinking about my proposal?"

"Yes, I have, and don't pull at me. You said a few days."

"Well, I'm anxious to sew you up."

Gawd. "Sounds like a body bag."

"You know what I mean. Come on, say yes."

"Walt, I don't think I'm the woman for you. Some other kind would make you happier, you know an old-fashioned woman who'd make you the center of her life."

His smirk changed into a very ugly expression, and he opened his mouth. She grabbed her car keys—"See you this evening at the library"—and ran. *Fled* was how it felt.

Meg wasn't due for an hour. Plenty of time. She'd rather drive to town and leave from there than have Walt back her into a corner of the kitchen and then get mad because she didn't love him. Love wasn't an obligation, something he had a *right* to. When she parked in front of the house, Meg was just coming out. "I thought I was supposed to pick you up."

"Walt's gone to round-the-clock scenes, so I booked."

"Same old?"

"He's decided I should marry him, and he'll be unpleasant until I say yes, you know, insults and accusations. Go figure."

"And it's all your fault, I bet a cookie."

"You got it. If I were properly feminine, I'd capitulate at the first sign of a frown." She opened the passenger side door. "Pair dynamics is not his field. Can't see past the end of his nose, Grandma used to say."

Meg started the engine and shifted into reverse. "I gather you're not buying it."

"I'm going to have to move out right away." Relaxing into the seat, she realized how tired she was. "I thought maybe I could keep the relationship going when I went back to school, but no way. I've been thinking you never know a man until you live with him; I'm beginning to suspect you don't really know him until he decides he loves you."

She told Meg all about it—well, not *all*—until they were across I-40 and headed south on 231. "Classes begin next week, and I need to find a place to rent right away. Do you know of anything?"

"What can you afford?"

"You know, Meg, you always go right to the most important thing. When my parents were killed, the will converted everything to cash and set up two trust funds that Tim and I couldn't touch until we were thirty. That was last month's birthday. Just in time too: tuition and fees are over $1000 a semester. I've been living pretty much paycheck to paycheck—I wouldn't have been able to afford even one course. The trust administrator arranged for me to draw the interest for living expenses and raid the principle for big costs like tuition."

"Good. I've been wondering how you were going to swing it."

"On the way in this morning, I was calculating. If I can take first-and-last-month's-and-deposits from the trust money to get into a place right away, I can probably manage $500 a month rent, plus utilities. That's not much. I don't have any idea what's available or what I could find for that. When we get back this afternoon, I'll look around. I have a very bad feeling about spending even another week with Walt—he'll escalate to Mach 2 the way he's going."

"Then you ought to leave immediately. That he hasn't hit you doesn't mean he won't."

"Or I might hit *him.*"

Meg grinned. "Either way, not so good."

"I've been trying to be fair, looking at the problem from all sides: how much of my feeling has been because of Jake? You know how unpleasant he's been this summer. And that day a couple of weeks ago—when I doubled up with him because my truck was in the shop—that was the bean that over-loaded the mule, as Grandpa said. I won't take any crap from any man any more. And that includes Walt."

"Everybody downstream had better look out. Grandma."

The laugh was a surprise, the way it exploded out of her. "I'm loaded for bear. Grandpa. I have what you'd call an *attitude.*"

She was laughing, but it was no joke. Since they'd pulled into the shop that night after the fire in L.O. Pocket, she'd hated so much it scared her.

*C*umulus clouds are beginning to build. With the windows open there's no barrier between Sarah and miles of landscape. She isn't afraid of falling out. And she loves being able to be right *in* it…better than any feeling she could ever get hiking on the ground.

She isn't doing anything. Not reading or drawing, not even thinking, just sitting and being in the air, the same air that birds and trees and clouds are in. Maybe it's good for her. A lot of the time lately she thinks there must be invisible *wounds* in her that make her cry so much…pain in her chest that lasts for days. And maybe the wonderful air that pines breathe out will help.

Her freshman year at NAU she had to do a research paper. As soon as the teacher assigned it, she knew she was going to find out about Lillian if she could. There was nothing in the university library, not even upstairs in Special Collections. Nobody had even heard of her. Nothing in the city library except two pages in a magazine printed by the Museum of Northern Arizona about painters who had worked on the Colorado plateau. John at the reference desk found it for her.

That was where she started. She checked out a copy and kept it for three weeks. Awesome painters, most of them men. Some really brave about color…Holmes and

Leigh and Akin and Groll. Gunnar Widforss. Lillian and Mary-Russell Ferrell Colton were the only women. Did people know about those painters at all? The names anybody knows are artists who lived somewhere else.

But Barbara in the research library at the museum was very nice and brought out boxes full of slides and letters and photographs and watercolors. She spent all day there with things spread out on the table, so excited she didn't notice when it started to snow. Lillian! Her face, her living face. Her handwriting, not a copy, the original paper. Sketchbooks. So many years ago. Lillian's sister and a grand-daughter of John and Louisa Wetherill had given them to the museum after she died. It was like exploring and discovering for herself. She got all the bibliographical numbers right for her research paper, but they didn't seem important compared.

Some of Lillian's paintings were locked in a separate building. Barbara helped her fill out an application for permission to see them. Things she hadn't imagined, faces of people and places in old Arizona, donated by the same Wetherill grand-daughter. She stood alone in a room with no windows and looked at them and saw Lillian's hand as she painted them.

Dad said she would go over to the Sharlott Hall Museum in Prescott if Randy would go with her and drive. In the library there she opened more boxes with more things, newspaper clippings, diaries, photographs of Lillian as a child and an old woman. Randy read a biology book while she went through everything. If he hadn't been there, she'd have cried. How awful…to do so much and see so much and then get old and die…and be forgotten.

Randy helped her with the technical part and she got an A on the paper. Dad was very proud, it was her first A in an English class. As a reward he took her and Mom to Catalina that summer, across on the ferry from Los Angeles…there were dolphins in the water. The island grew and then Avalon was visible. They stayed two nights in Zane Grey's actual house, high above the cerulean bay. She saw a Yei figure Lillian had painted above the fireplace in the study and sat for hours on the terrace and pretended she was seeing what Lillian saw. Looking at the ocean, she vowed that the first thing she would do when she got to heaven would be to find Lillian and tell her she cared.

It's a quiet morning. Wind blows, of course, and makes an awful noise in the tower, but not much is going on over the forest radio, just crews talking about where tools are and stuff like that. You can tell early whether clouds will turn into a storm. The bottoms of these aren't flat and black enough and the tops don't tower up hundreds of feet. It has something to do with invisible water in the air.

She's afraid she's ruined "Woody Autumn." Working with the board on her knees, she finished all the pencil work and loved the delicious color showing through. But when she put all three panels together and stood back as far as she could, she saw there was no contrast. Everything was the same blah…no intensity.

It wouldn't be so bad to start over. Consider this one a study for identifying the problems. At least with pencils there's no preparation or clean-up. She wants to get started again. Her fingers *yearn* to be on the paper. They feel like that a lot, no matter what else she's doing.

Georgia O'Keeffe said if you could only reproduce nature and always with less beauty than the original, why paint at all? At the beginning of "Woody Autumn," she didn't mean it to be realistic, but maybe she hadn't been original enough. She did the mountains in dull blues because they *are* and because objects far away are supposed to diminish in intensity. Copying and following rules, not creative at all, *that* isn't art.

She jumps to her feet and pulls her box of pastels from under the windowseat. She doesn't even *like* Prussian blue…the rich plum pink, that's what she'll use for the mountains. On a sheet of paper she begins to mash it into powder.

Since the Artists Gallery on San Francisco opened, she's gone in now and then to see what Roberta Rogers has been doing lately. Her watercolor landscapes *glow* with color that most people don't even see. All those colors are in northern Arizona for an artist to work with, whether anyone else sees them or not.

They spread topo maps out on the hood of Meg's car. "OK, here we are, Kathy Tank. It's a mile in a straight line northeast to Bob's Tank—he was just south of that. No change in elevation between here and there. Let's take it casual and time ourselves. It'll be a stroll, not more than half an hour."

Air was cool and heavy with a smell of trees growing. She rolled the maps and slid them into her pack. "Ready?" Sun was not far above the tree tops.

"Bet a cookie anyone who knew where Jake would be and knew the South End, even a little, could have figured out how easy this would be. Evan is accusing Buck, but I say at least a dozen people fit."

"You heard about that stand-off Wednesday morning? We were all there—Evan made his scene in front of the patrol units and most of the engine people."

"What's your opinion?"

She walked on for a minute, considering. It wasn't smart to blurt out any old thing and besides, Meg was asking for thought. "Evan is usually hard to get along with, critical and sarcastic, always complaining. But he surprised all of us. There wasn't any real provocation—he just

started shouting. Maybe he's unstable. But it seemed to me he was trying too hard to direct blame toward Buck. I'd like to know why he's so anxious and agitated."

"Do you know anything about him away from work?"

"Not much. This is his first year on patrol. I think he was on the Blue Ridge Hot Shots last season—I don't know why he transferred. Mitch put him on leave Wednesday to keep down tension in the shop. It was that or transfer him to timber markers."

In twenty-two minutes of easy walking they'd reached the place where she'd found Jake's body. The yellow tape was gone. All the tire track and footprints had been erased by rain.

"You know what? If you knew what you were doing, you could drive out from town, walk over here, drive back to town: three hours. Give yourself an alibi till midnight and pull it off, no trouble."

"Nothing like expanding the list."

"Well, jeesh, you could."

"You're right, you're absolutely right."

They unrolled the maps again. Connecting two-tracks wandered across the paper all the way to Woody Mountain, with a deviation from due north of not more than a mile. The only obstacle was the ridge south of Auza Tank—a road angled across its face on either side.

"What would you do? Go straight cross country in the moonlight or use the roads and count on rain to wipe out all the tracks?"

Meg moved her finger on the map. "You mean, if I had a weak leg and I wasn't used to walking? I'd use these logging tracks from the mountain to Auza Tank and then follow the road over the ridge, hoping it got so little traffic that it would be hard and wouldn't show footprints. Then right here, just before Black Tank, I'd walk beside it a few yards away, past Bob's Tank until I found Jake's truck."

"The east side?"

"That would be more likely."

"OK. It's 08:35. Let's go see how that would work."

Usually she drove through the forest—it was a pleasure to walk, right out in breeze and bird songs. A narrow road curved away from the bite Black Pass took out of Woody Ridge. Not a ridge really—it was created when the east side of the Oak Creek fault was downthrown by crustal reaction to the uplift of the Plateau, a few million years in the past. Another few million years of erosion, and Oak Creek Canyon might reach north all the way to Flagstaff. Which wouldn't be there any more, no matter what happened, and wouldn't be in the same place on the globe either. By then it wouldn't matter who had killed Jake.

"Meg?"

"Hmmm?"

"Does it really matter?"

"What?"

"Finding out who did it. I'm curious—it's a puzzle and a challenge. And I don't hold with murder in general. But that doesn't mean it *matters*. Whoever did it might not ever be a danger to anyone else."

"I have to admit it's an intriguing puzzle to me too, more than a desire for justice."

"I wouldn't say this to anybody else, but I don't *want* to find out. I like most of the suspects—if one of them has to go to prison, I'll feel terrible. Jake did vicious things to people: life was worse for everybody around him. Not one of us is sorry he's out of the picture. It's an awful thing to say, but I'm *glad* he was shot."

"Probably not the only one. You're a good person, Josy. Everybody is working to find out who's guilty, and you're trying to show who isn't."

They climbed the ridge without talking. Woody Mountain had been visible now and then through the trees almost the whole way. When they reached the top, it stood clear before them with its little tower. A lava cone on the edge of Woody Ridge, its dead roots far below in some magma chamber opened by faulting. It had poured a blanket of lava over miles of country.

"See, it's just down this slope to the tank, cross the power line, and then an old track right to the base of the mountain. It's rocky all the way but not hard."

"What kind of time have we been making?"

She looked at her watch. "More than a mile every half hour. A little over another mile to the mountain, give it an extra fifteen for getting up the slope. Make it two and a half, five hours round trip—allow time for fatigue and resting her leg, if she needed to, moonlight that would have kept her slow over rocks, staying out of sight. I'll bet the walk would have taken Sarah at least seven or eight hours. The whole night."

"It's a stretch to imagine her doing it."

"It is for *me*." What a relief—she smiled and nodded.

"Is she up there now?"

"Yes, she's in service across the week-end. Oh *no*!"

"What?"

"She's off on Thursday."

They looked at each other before Meg said, slowly, "She'd have had all day to walk down there. Even if she went into town in the morning, she could have been out here late in the afternoon to start."

"Take her time in daylight. Find a place to hide for a few hours, until midnight."

"The moon would have been bright by then."

"Five hours until sunrise. Jeesh, this is awful."

"She could have walked back with no rush."

"Alone. In the wind."

"It was possible."

"Oh Meg, this isn't what I wanted." She sat down in the middle of the road. "I *still* can't see her doing it."

"But it was possible."

*H*er raven is walking up the driveway. Not hopping, walking, one foot in front of the other like a person. Sarah laughs to see it. Sometimes she sees two ravens at a time…have they had a nest close by on top of the mountain all summer?

After two and a half months of *gales* in the spring, air didn't move at all, not a breath. She didn't know why it had to be one or the other. The weather report was that moisture was streaming into Arizona from Mexico and summer storms were starting. At first she didn't see any difference except there was no wind. A completely naked sky in the morning, then a tiny speck of white cloud appeared above the Peaks. She could *see* it ballooning out of nothing, higher and higher, like a tree grows from a seed…up and up. She couldn't stop watching…a miracle that happened every day. Clouds are always moving and changing shape, *always*. Ballooning up, growing sideways. Fading away. You can't sketch fast enough to do any cloud at one exact moment.

She didn't know she would like lightning so much. In town you shut yourself in a building and look *up* at one stroke at a time, but in a lookout tower you are in the middle of a storm It's all around you, you can see everything through the glass. So you don't look up at lightning, you look *out*, sometimes down. It's in the same plane you are. It's jagged, never one straight line from top to bottom, and she's pretty sure it's never curved. It's very fast, you have to be looking at the right place even to see it, especially to see how it repeats itself a few times on the same path, like it's flickering.

In the last week of June, after the big fires, Hurricane Alma off the Baja coast threatened more lightning, maybe even rain. But all it ever produced was beautiful white clouds *ranked* across the sky. Days of absolutely awesome clarity when she could see every shadow on the Mazatzals eighty miles to the south, colors across the Painted Desert, shades of pink and peach, with blue buttes here and there. Every detail in the cliffs above Oak Creek Canyon.

"So much for trying to prove who didn't. Meg, you know what, I feel awful. Sarah does such beautiful drawings, you should see. Intense colors but they're delicate too. I don't believe a person can create beauty out of nothing."

"It's crumby, the whole affair."

"We've let her down, is what it feels like."

"Look, we walked it, we also proved either of us could have shot him. I don't think you've let *me* down."

"But you know what, Meg, we should think about this from some new angles. I've been thinking from my point of view, how I'd have felt or why, and trying to imagine the killer. Which may be a mistake. Evan wouldn't think the way I do."

"Or Henry."

"Or Sarah or Duvenek."

"Or any of them. You'll make this even harder. We know how and when, we haven't a clue to who, and you want to complicate why."

"Well, I like the idea. What else do we have to work on? If you had killed Jake, why would you have done it?"

"Hatred, anger and fear."

"That was fast. Why fear?"

"Oh stink-ink. I don't want to talk about it."

"Meg!"

"What reasons would *you* have?"

"Hatred, anger and outrage. The outrage part is another secret. Josy, I'll tell you—I'm a law enforcement officer. I'm supposed to cooperate in the effort to find out who performed a public service act, and I don't want to. Does that make me an accessory?"

Drought had lasted too long, and it was too late for most grasses or forbs to get started for the season. The animals were in trouble. Sarah put out a third bale of hay. Hordes of hummingbirds came at dawn every morning to sip sugar water at the feeders and stayed all day. Squirrels, chipmunks, she fed them all.

By July 4th there had been a few storms from the hurricanes off the Mexican coast. One day over half an inch of rain fell on Woody Mountain. But it was always just spots here and there...in one direction bright sun and blue skies, in another black clouds and lightning...white cumulus over Mormon Mountain, long curving lines of dark rain over

Flagstaff. Among dark shadows cast by clouds, streaks of fiery green where sun shone through onto the pines. In town all the weather you have is over your head.

So no place was really *wet*. The forest closure was still on, no public allowed in most places. Which didn't stop some people. Barricades were ignored or torn down or stolen—signs, chains, locks, everything. Patrol units were busy day and night. Citations were issued. The public was everywhere, trying to camp and hike and ride bicycles. And *smoke*.

On the 4th of July everybody working together managed to exclude most of them from the forest. Randy said there were fewer deaths and associated outrages than they'd had in years. At one campground some people went hiking and when they came back *everything* was stolen…their tent, their food, everything.

But on the Fourth no ten-year-olds drove ATVs into trees. No shouting, shooting fights in campgrounds…no roll-over accidents on dirt roads. Randy said he didn't know where everybody was instead of the Coconino, but he didn't much care.

Two weeks after that night when she knew she loved him, Jake came up to the mountain in the evening and shut Venn outside the cabin. Hurt her lips and stuck his tongue into her mouth and bruised her back pressing her against the door frame. It was like being attacked, not like love at all. Outside the door Venn barked and barked.

She tried to push him away. His voice was angry, "What's the problem?" He rubbed his hips against her, rubbed his chest against her breasts, stuck his tongue into her mouth again.

Then he forced his knee between her legs and put his hand down and started to unzip her jeans. She tried to twist away from him, but he held her against the door with one shoulder while he fumbled with himself. Then he pulled her hard against him and rubbed a few times and walked her backward toward the bed and threw her onto it. Jerked her jeans off, pulled his down, rammed into her and pounded and pounded as if he hated her…it was *degrading*. Suddenly he pulled out and got up and left. The next morning she found a completely dry condom at the edge of the trees.

Through the next six weeks he arrived now and then with no warning. Sometimes she thought he must surely love her, he was so sweet and kind. But there was no telling when he was going to be sullen and mean…she was always off *balance*. Once she told him she didn't like it when he jammed his tongue into her mouth. He hissed, "Don't tell me how to make love," and stepped back and stood with his legs apart and slapped her three times with his arm full out.

One day rain was falling all around the cabin when she woke up. Fog was so thick she couldn't see off the mountain. The forecast was for heavy rain and damaging wind all day. She loved it...you don't have to worry about floods when you're on top of a mountain.

She stayed in bed, safe and dry, and read a murder mystery. She'd never read any. After that day she checked a lot of them out of the library, but she didn't like the ones where women were killed horribly. That kind of book should be against the law or something...what if it gave men ideas? Before she took a book, first she looked to see whether there was a picture of a pretty dead woman on the cover. Then she read a little to find out whether *men* were the ones killed, that was the only kind she'd read. She stopped checking them out when she realized most of the murderers made her think of Jake.

*D*ay off, but after a shower Meg put on a clean uniform: neat, well-pressed and not overly worn, as the handbook specified. A uniform wasn't strictly required for court—conservative business attire would be acceptable—but she preferred to look official.

Pre-trial had been three months earlier on the regular Forest and Park Service docket for northern Arizona. This would be a second appearance for a man who'd been caught cutting oak—live as well as large dead and standing—with no permit. He'd been angry when she'd told him the Coconino considered it theft of forest resources: insolent, aggressive, threatening. "You just try writing out that citation, and see what happens to you."

She'd recited the situation...

> United States Magistrates...may try and sentence persons
> charged with violations of the regulations contained in 36
> CFR 261, relating to the protection, occupancy and use of
> the National Forest lands...

and tried to be courteous, reminding him that assault was a felony under Title 18 of the Code of Federal Regulations, and he could be in bigger trouble if he didn't calm down. In pre-trial he'd pled not guilty and challenged the regulation. "What's a dead tree worth anyway?" What indeed? Judge Stephen Verkamp had requested the Forest Service to prepare a document that answered the question and continued the case for trial.

U.S. District Court was in the old Babbitt garage across the corner from the county court house, old but remodeled. While a U.S. marshall was conducting her live-oak-sawyer through the metal detector—"Please put your keys, belt, calculator, billfold, glasses into this container"—she handed off her Sig to another marshall for placement in the lockbox and went into the courtroom wearing her belt with its baton and pepper spray. Hand techniques would be used if he became violent in court, but crumb, the guy was volatile.

Since she was to testify, she nodded to the other LEOs on the benches to the left of the door and went through the swinging gate to sit with the district wildlife biologist behind Raleigh, who was spokesman for the Coconino. She'd been impressed by him in the courtroom three months ago: deep-voiced and professional about driving on forest roads without a license, careless operation of a vehicle, trash left at a campsite, attempt to establish residence in the forest, possession of an alcoholic beverage by a minor—ordinary shabby little misdemeanors. Most of the violators stood before the bench, admitted guilt and paid their fines.

The best moment of the day had been a big sullen kid who had refused to comply after three warnings about parking restrictions in Oak Creek Canyon. He had come to court wearing old sweatpants. Judge Verkamp, elegant in his black robe, had said, "You figured the rules didn't apply to you?" and then, after the boy muttered something she couldn't hear, "Don't get smart with me." Yay, Steve. Her family had known his family for about a century.

Now, three months later, the small misdemeanors had been cleared away, there'd been a short break, and they were ready for the trial. There was no jury. Wearing a suit and tie, Raleigh conducted himself as efficiently as any lawyer, better than some, Steve had told P.J. It was her first stint in the witness chair, but she'd been coached: sit comfortably without slouching, preferably with both feet flat on the floor and hands folded in your lap...give as short, simple and direct an answer as possible and then wait for the next question.

OK, short and simple. Patrolling in early May, alerted by the sound of a chainsaw, she had come upon John Bursage illegally cutting oak two hundred yards south of forest road 231C, Township 20, Range 6, northeast quarter of Section 9. One six-to-nine inch diameter green oak had been cut, also one sixteen-to-twenty inch diameter dead oak. In early May oak leaves were not yet apparent, so Mr. Bursage had insisted that the small tree was dead. However, because oak was last to leaf out and so easily stressed by fire that it might not do so for a year and still be alive, a standing tree could not be taken for firewood at any time.

Raleigh introduced Exhibit A, a copy of permit regulations, which he showed to her for verification and then handed to the judge. Exhibit B was an enlarged map of the location where the violation had occurred, mounted on a poster-sized board with photographs which she had taken at the site. She'd even done one of Bursage holding his chain saw and looking furious, but Raleigh hadn't used it.

That was all—she was excused. For the record Raleigh stated the question of the monetary value of the trees which had been cut and called Sandy Nagiller, wildlife biologist.

The result of cutting oak was an adverse cumulative effect on twenty-one mammals and sixty-one bird species in the forest. Well! That got Mr. Bursage's attention. Living trees provided high protein, complex carbohydrate acorns which were a principle food source that contributed to reproduction and winter survival. Both live and dead trees provided such habitat needs as hiding and thermal cover as well as roosting, nesting and granary sites. Sandy offered a thick stack of pages, a Wildlife Habitat Damage Assessment.

Raleigh asked whether she had determined the monetary value of that effect. She had. Oak regeneration was rare and growth slow. Replacement and maintenance costs included planting. Value lost over the estimated seventy-two-year life of the young green tree was $7,146; value lost to wildlife in acorn production was $4,764. Long-term habitat damage for loss of the dead tree would be $1350. Add to that the long term value of Wildlife and Fish User Days (WFUDs) to hunters as well as such non-consumptive activities as viewing, photographing and nature enjoyment. Green oak: $30,782. Dead Oak: $3,300.

Mr. Bursage no longer looked aggressive. Judge Verkamp questioned Sandy: "You've documented these claims?"

"The three authors of the damage assessment requested peer review from eight professionals, Attachment C. We have cited seventeen examples from relevant literature and three precedents—U.S. vs Scarry, U.S. vs Franz, U.S. vs Tauber."

Sandy'd clobbered Bursage, and he knew it. Steve Verkamp ruled guilty of defiance of regulations and allowed the fine to stand. He looked at Meg with no expression, and she gave him the slightest of nods, but whoop-ti-doo! Phooey to Mr. Bursage.

*L*ast month she was walking down the road with Venn one evening, noticing how different just being on the ground made the landscape look. On the east side of the mountain Venn rushed over to the shoulder of the road and looked down the bank with her ears up. Then she plunged out of sight...right away there was that piercing scream.

When she hurried to the spot where Venn had disappeared, she saw a *tableau*, perfectly still for a minute. Venn was standing only ten feet down. Below her was a doe looking up and a fawn at her side. Only a few feet away was a second doe, also looking up.

For just a moment more they all stood without moving. Then the second doe began to move slowly away from the doe with the fawn. Venn followed right past the other two, who turned and ran away as soon as the dog couldn't see them.

It was awesome...the deer were *thinking*. She didn't know they could be so smart...smarter than Venn, anyway. She saw for herself how they worked together to save the fawn from a dog.

That was a lucky fawn. The poor crippled elk calf wasn't. It was in the middle of the road when she drove around a corner in her truck. Its right back hip was hardly there it was so deformed, and it could barely walk...the poor little leg splayed out to the side. She stopped so she wouldn't frighten it and watched while it struggled over to the bank and got off the road. But you knew it was going to be caught and killed by coyotes or a lion before much longer.

Thinking about it makes her fierce with her drawings. She'd used a little brush to cover the mountains with magenta powder, and as soon as she started, she knew it was all wrong. She kept on anyway, like, *murdering* "Woody Autumn." Now the mountains come out in *front* of the trees, that pink is so intense. But it doesn't matter, it's only a study to learn on. At least it isn't blah anymore...not subtle, but not blah.

She sighs. What will happen if she tries to take some of the powder off? In her art box she finds a big gum eraser. *Draws* with it on the mountains. Oh, so cool! You can make shadows just by what you leave. It's a discovery she's made by herself. If you use a wet brush, will the powder work like watercolor? She laughs...the world can be any color, *every* color.

One evening she was standing at the cabin window watching male hummingbirds trying to scare each other away from the feeders. They were so tiny, and they acted so tough. Sun shining on the glass must have made it reflect. One of the little birds zipped up in front of her face and fanned his tail feathers out to scare his own image. And there was something she never imagined...feathers above his eyes lifted straight out and exposed bright red underneath! Just for a second. She'd been watching hummingbirds for weeks, and she hadn't seen that at all.

She needed to get away from Walt, but moving out when he was gone, no warning—that would be a cheap trick. Josy wanted to think she could behave well. She really ought to talk with him, maybe tonight at dinner. She wasn't looking forward to it, but she really should tell him. That is, if he came without his laptop. If he came at all.

She drove to the east side of campus. Modest old neighborhood there, some shabby student rentals, run-down and cluttered, tenants who didn't care because they wouldn't be staying long. On other blocks, houses were neat and painted; they looked like they were lived in by people who had owned them for years. The lots were at least twice as deep as they were wide. On some of them, small houses were behind at the back fence line.

On south Leroux only five minutes from the geology labs, a man with thick white hair was setting up a FOR RENT sign in front of a white stucco with neat blue trim. An apple tree shaded the front door; wooden tubs along the sidewalk were full of yellow and orange flowers.

She parked at the curb and ran across the street. He looked up and watched her come, glancing at her shorts, her hiking boots.

"Hello. You have something to rent?" She thought his grandparents had probably been from Mexico.

"I do, but I won't rent to just anybody."

"Fair enough. What kind of tenant do you have in mind?"

"I don't want any kids. They're too destructive. Are you the one who's wanting to rent?"

"I am. Thirty last month."

"Student?"

"Geology." It was a thrill to say it.

"How many more years to go? I'd like to have somebody who plans to stay a while."

She hadn't counted ahead. "At least, let's see, three years, maybe four or five. I have a summer job with the Forest Service, so I'd be year-round."

"Don't mind me giving you a personal third degree. It's right behind the house here; I have to have somebody I can stand to live next to. So does my wife."

"No, that's all right. I'd feel the same way."

"Well then, I'd like to know if you have a steady income."

"So the rent will be on time every month—sure. My parents' estate set up a trust fund. I'll be drawing on that."

"Your parents died?"

"Killed in an auto accident ten years ago."

"Sorry to hear it. My mother died just last year. It's hard to lose your parents, however they go."

"You're right, it is."

"So, the rent. I want $500 a month not including utilities, first and last plus a $500 deposit, $1500 up front. Some people don't have that."

"I can swing it."

"Well, you might do. Want to see the place? It's back here. Just one driveway, but there's parking for your car." He stopped walking. "I forgot: no pets, no roommates, no loud stereo, no big parties."

She laughed. "That's me."

"OK, come on back. I built it myself after I retired. Took me five years. Thought maybe one of my grandkids would like to live in it while they went to college, but not one of them did. I had it rented to a kid who changed his mind yesterday and went to California. I'd rather have a young woman anyway, they're cleaner and quieter and easier to get along with."

They rounded the corner. "Oh!" She stopped. "Is that it?"

""You like it? I designed it myself. I like working with wood."

"You're an *artist*." The walls were golden brown boards fitted in a geometric pattern. There was a small deck. Big windows. A bright blue front door. Who would have expected?

"It's kinda small, just two rooms and bath. That's why I want only one person. But it's cozy."

He unlocked the door. "See, one room is kitchen, dining and plenty of space for a sofa or something. Electric appliances are new, small but big enough for one person. Morning sun comes in this window. This other room is the bedroom, I figured space for a bed and a big chair and a desk for studying. Bathroom in here, no tub but a good shower. Never been lived in. I just finished it this spring."

The paneled walls were the same golden brown. So were the wooden floors, every detail perfect. "You must be very proud of it."

"Took my time and did everything right. Windows fit tight. Good insulation. You have furniture?"

"In storage." She turned to face him. "Will you rent it to me? I can move in right away."

While she was writing a check—"I'll go straight to the bank and have funds transferred to cover it"—he talked on.

"I've lived on this street for fifty years. Bought the property when we got married and raised my kids here. Seen some changes."

She signed her name. "Flagstaff native?"

"My grandfather came here to work at the sawmill."

"My great-grandparents came in the 1880s and homesteaded."

"No kidding. Who were they?" He took the check.

"Richard and Ruby Green."

"You're Ruby Green's great-granddaughter? Well, I'll be doggoned. My grandmother used to work for her, doing laundry." He put out his hand. "Name's Armenta. You're…?"

"Josy Kirkman. Roger and Emily Keeling's granddaughter."

"I knew them." He shook her hand and then put his other hand over it. "Your grandpa was a good man. When I was a teen-ager he hired me to work summers on his ranch. I remember when he died, I felt real bad about it. Well, if this isn't something. I'm happy to have you here, never thought I'd get somebody I'd known so long. Come on in the house and meet my wife."

There was just time before closing to see her trust officer and arrange for $2000 to be transferred to checking and get to APS to have electricity turned on and city offices to pay the deposit for water connection.

*A*fter court, Meg went home to change out of her uniform and drove back to the NAU library. You didn't have to to to college to educate yourself—Uncle Matt had taught her that. Crumb, she was about to make a big decision, and she needed information.

She hadn't looked at the ranch before as *hers*. Her place, yes, but it had always belonged to someone older: Grandma and Grandpa, Matt and Jo, Mom and P.J. Uncle Matt said "we" and "our" not "I" and "mine." So did his sister. So did Jo and Grandpa, whose money made them partners. They all belonged there; even the grandchildren were included in decisions.

"Here's the picture," Grandma had said. "We've got to stop thinking in old ruts unless we want to run this ranch as a hobby."

She'd been ten years old that day, excited, like seeing an adventure coming. She liked the idea of thinking out of old ruts.

"Grass on the place is scanty in a dry year and it's bunch grass mostly, not as nutritional as some others. When we get grassy rains, you've seen how the range greens up, but we can't count on reliable rain one year to the next. Even with pipelines from tanks to drinkers, even hauling water to the west side, the Friendly ranch hasn't been really profitable since the 1920s.

"Money from your Grandpa and Aunt Jo kept it going, but ranching isn't recreation. We've put in internal fencing and moved cattle around. We've tried rotating yearly, growing our own feed by irrigation. But we still don't make as much money as we'd like to."

None of them had talked to her about money before, about the ranch as a business. She'd felt grown up, important.

"So it seems to us and to your parents too that we need to make some changes. Bet a cookie you can come up with some suggestions."

Her brothers had asked about how much it cost per head to run cattle and how much they'd averaged in sales over the past five years, and she could see how proud P.J. was of them. She'd asked the same questions about horses and everyone had smiled at her.

"If we raised quarter horses, could we sell them for more per head? Would they be easier to manage on the range?"

Uncle Matt looked proud. "Good questions, Meggie. Branch out into quarter horses." He was the best man in the whole world—he'd probably been thinking that all along.

Grandpa and Uncle Matt being so old, P.J. had done most of the work with the horses and made enough to offset expenses, and they'd held on. It hadn't all been lost to a bank like Josy's family ranch had.

Now her father was talking about bringing her into it to tend and manage. She needed information about range grasses—not that P.J. and Uncle Matt hadn't read everything there was to know, but she wanted to investigate for herself. If she were to take a bigger part and give up a sure job to do it, she'd better know whether there was a chance of managing the range, technical stuff: growth cycles, grazing systems, educated kinds of things. Couple of hours and she realized she needed to see whether Uncle Matt had made any notes on his experiments. There were a dozen different grasses that might be worth trying, but she wasn't sure exactly what he'd done. Had he seeded rye? Rice grass, tabosa? How about adding phosphorus?

Probably P.J. knew what Billy Cordasco was doing on the CO Bar, it was pretty much the same kind of conditions, and the Babbitts were keeping working cowboys busy. She really ought to go see for herself. Course, the Babbitts had a *lot* more land. Well. She'd take her notes out to the ranch and confer with her parents.

But while she was in the library, she'd check what it had on mules. There was an idea growing in her mind. If mules were hardy and calm and gentle and long-lived and patient and careful and sure-footed and intelligent....if they could do anything a horse could do only better....if they had an understanding affinity for humans....if they could be bred for riding and jumping and showing....if they *thought*....well, then, how about......

Sarah hears a truck coming beyond the bend in the road. At first she thinks it's Jake, and she's frightened. She starts toward the bank...she'll slide off and get behind a tree. But Venn runs down the road, excited, and then Randy comes around the curve. She starts to shake and tears choke her throat.

Randy's face is smudged with ash. He stops beside her and sings out the window. "Hey, good lookin'. Whatcha got cookin'?" Venn is whining and standing with her paws on the side of the car and he's scratching her head. "What's up, kid? You look like a bad night."

She's crying now. "I thought you were Jake."

"Jake's dead." He gets out and puts his arms around her. Sings, "Put your head on my shoulder. You need someone who's older."

"I can't reach your shoulder. You smell awful."

"Wood smoke. It's organic. I came right from work without a shower or nuthin'."

She steps back. "Have I got soot on my face?"

"Some—congratulations." He shakes her hand. "You are now a member of the fire organization."

She and Venn ride back to the top with him. "Why didn't you go home first? What's wrong? Is it the investigation?"

"No, no. In fact they've let up on us a little. Or so it seems. At least they're not out on the fire line asking questions. Most of us have got an alibi, including me. I told them I was debating with Dad all evening, and they found out who he was and didn't bother to ask him." She starts to laugh and chokes in her throat.

"I'm here because I got off work on time, and I hated to go home. Dad can't let go of the animal rights idea. He'd come into the shower with me if there was room. Have I looked into *Corpus Juris Secundum* and the index to the United States Code? How about Title 9 of the Code of Federal Regulations? Have I read *Taub vs. Maryland* or the LeVasseur case in Hawaii? What's in the literature about property rights? I gave it pretty much all I had Wednesday at dinner. I'm about maxed out."

"Oh, Randy."

"Yeah, I thought I was being so clever. Pride goeth before destruction. That's not a song."

"I know. Have you had anything to eat?"

"Can you feed me?"

While she makes sandwiches, he talks. "Yesterday I stopped at Beste's and killed an hour. Told her I wanted her to see me in my working clothes. She was out front looking at an empty cicada shell. Who knows how long it had been there."

"Beste's cool."

"As is my wont, I explained the whole process thoroughly, metamorphosis from larval stage to mature insect. She said kind of a sad thing. 'Humans need to change into a mature stage too, but we have no instinct as a guide. Usually we're so old when we figure it out that it doesn't do much good. We have too much to be ashamed of.' She seems so wise it's hard to think of her struggling to become a grown-up."

"You know, sometimes I wonder whether she had a hard time once."

"Who hasn't?" Venn's head is on his knee. He rubs her ears.

"Yes, but you know what I mean. In school or with her husband or something. Something unhappy in her life."

"If she did, she made good use of it. I hope I can do the same. Turn difficulty into understanding. I'll have to remember that when Dad's interfering with my digestion."

She puts the plate in front of him, sits across the little table in the other chair. "So Dad doesn't approve of legal equality for animals?"

"I don't think he cares one way or another. He's just using it to get me into legal thinking. I figured I'd push him back a little. Spent a lot of time collecting that argument. But he sees an opening, and it's made him worse."

She props her elbows on the table, her chin on her hands. "You didn't really mean that about animal rights?"

"Oh, sure I do. It's pretty clear, at least to me, that law is evolving in that direction." He puts his napkin on the table. "Whether that's ethical or not is another question. I happen to think they go together. Sixty years ago Aldo Leopold wrote that law is based on philosophy and ethics and that *our* ethic should concede rights to wildlife outside human economics: we need to admit that other creatures exist for their own sakes rather than purely for our use. Darwin said moral development is a widening extension of human sympathy. Those aren't legal arguments, I'm sorry to say, compelling though they may be."

"Can't law and ethics go together?"

"If it's widespread long enough, public discourse can affect the development of ethics, and ethics can affect the development of law. Despite my brilliant argument, we're not there yet. The LeVasseur case, for example. The judge said he didn't care how intelligent a dolphin is or whether it knows symbols represent things, it's not legally a person. So an experimental dolphin that was dying of neglect wasn't in involuntary servitude, and the men who freed it were guilty of theft. The defense wasn't able to get the judge disqualified for prejudice, which I thought was a good point. Hell, law regards corporations as persons. Why not dolphins?"

"*I* think they are. Venn is. They don't talk like we do, but they *think*, and they're good as often as humans are."

"Right on. They're conscious. They make choices. Last fall some biologists with Game and Fish ran transects up on Anderson Mesa and baited live traps with peanuts so they could determine Abert squirrel population by vegetation type. It seemed like good project design—squirrels need as much food as they can get before winter—they go in after the peanuts and trip the gate and you've got 'em. You can weigh and measure and tag them and let them go. But those little buggers figured out the game in no time. Damn if they didn't tip the cages over so the peanuts would fall out through the wire right down a whole trap line. At the end of the day, no peanuts and no squirrels."

"And are you going to say anybody that smart isn't a person? That she isn't worth as much as we are?"

"My point exactly. We have interests in common, shit, *DNA* in common. What else do we need? I just can't talk about animals as property in which humans have ownership rights."

"I think we're pretty slow, you know, to change our ideas."

"Right now we have a volatile controversy, and animals are caught in the middle. You've got people like Jake who want to kill everything in sight. Activists who want to stop all human use of animals. Industries that work with animals, farmers and ranchers and researchers and zoos and rodeos and movies. People who like to live with animals, keep them as pets. People like you who want to love every animal in sight."

She takes her chin off her hands. He thinks she's wrong to help by feeding them? Taking care of them?

"I don't mean you're as bad as Jake. It's nice of you to feed them. You're a nice person, love is a good thing. But they're wild animals, not just pets running loose. They deserve respect more than love. The best thing we could do for them would be to give them room to live and leave them alone. Life, liberty and property, Fifth Amendment."

Randy looks unhappy. "I mean, think about it, Sarah. Give them everything, not let them do anything of their own. It's treating them like children, not creatures of worth like Dad treats us."

*T*he city library closed at 7:00 on Friday nights. Josy spent two hours checking the books on Arizona geology—not as many as she'd hoped, but they were shelved where Walt could see her as he came through the front door. At five minutes till, she checked out the two books that looked most interesting and went to sit on the lawn.

An hour later all the cars were gone but hers and half the lights had been turned off. Too late for the start of any movie in town, and she was hungry. Air was getting chilly.

When she drove into the parking lot behind Walt's office building, she wasn't surprised to see that his car was the only one there. His window was lighted, but he'd been adamant: "*Never* bother me at work." OK, she wasn't hanging around any longer.

She was finishing a sandwich at the kitchen table when he stormed in and slammed his briefcase down on top of her book. "I've *had* it with you. Not even the decency to wait for me when I've invited you out for the evening." He leaned into her face. "I want you out of my house *now*."

She retrieved her book and stood up. From a bottom cabinet she took a box of garbage bags.

"What are you doing?"

"Packing. I'll be gone by midnight."

He stood in the bedroom door watching her dump things into black plastic bags, fill one with shoes, another with coats and jackets. "I didn't mean tonight."

"You said *now*."

"Well, not right now. I haven't had anything to eat."

"I don't live here anymore."

"Josy, come on. It's ten o'clock at night. Where will you go?"

"You didn't care about that when you yelled in my face."

He followed her to the bathroom door and watched her sweep things off the shelves into a bag. "I was hasty. Come on."

"These towels are mine—I'm taking them. And you are now out of shampoo and toothpaste."

He tried his jeering laugh. "You're too sensitive. Come on, you've paid half the expenses for eighteen months. You should demand at least a week's notice."

"It's your house, as you've often told me. I'm outa here."

Another laugh. "Don't be a silly goose. I lost my temper, but that's no reason to stomp out of here at midnight."

Her hand flat on his chest, she shoved him hard and went back into the bedroom to load books, a dozen to a bag, and tie the tops tight. "Try losing your temper to an empty house."

He took her arm. "Come on, Sweetie, you can't do this. I love you. I asked you to marry me, didn't I?"

"So I could have a baby and stop being lonely. Let go of my arm." She looked around the room—it was amazing how little of her was in it. No wonder she hadn't been happy. "Let *go*."

"I won't let you leave like this. You owe me better treatment."

"I owe you *nothing*." She grabbed his little finger and bent it back, wrenched her arm free. "Remember, Mr. Big-City-Slumming-in-the-Sticks, my people were tough Arizona ranchers. You don't want to get physical with me." She began moving garbage bags through the door.

"OK ok. You're calling my bluff, and I'm backing down. Look, Sweetie, I don't want you to go. I like having you here when I get home."

"Say hello to your microwave. *Get out of my way.*"

"Josy, please, I was wrong. God damn it, stop and look at me."

She set four bags down at the back door and straightened. "Am I supposed to see something new?"

He tried to pull her into his arms. "See a man who's in love."

"I see a man who's in love with *himself*. Any woman would do, Walt, we all look the same to you."

"That's not true. Who do you think you are, talking to me like that?" He raised a fist into her face.

"I'm not your wife, that's for sure. Are you going to hit me now to prove I should want to stay with you? Try it, and I'll come up off the floor swinging."

"Well, I want to show how much I love you."

"*Bullshit.* You've been proving how much you *don't* since I moved in here." She opened the door and threw out two bags full of clothes. "You're way too late."

"I want to change."

She threw out two more bags. "Good. Maybe you'll be able to keep your next woman."

"Josy, you won't get away from me."

"Pew. You can't take the time from work. But thanks for the warning. Tomorrow I'll buy a gun." Two more bags went out.

"Listen, you." He grabbed at her arm again. "You're not leaving."

She leaned into *his* face, furious, just furious. "The thing is Walt, I get maniacal when I'm being held so I can't move—unless you want to find out how an Arizona native fights when she's maniacal, you'll *keep your hands to yourself.*" He stepped back.

She grabbed the last of her things. When she drove away, he was standing in the doorway watching her go.

*H*ey, she worked as a Forest Service patrolwoman—if anybody knew good places to camp overnight, she did. Twenty minutes after she'd pulled out of Walt's driveway, she'd parked, locked her doors, and curled up in the front seat. Punched her ski jacket into a pillow. If you couldn't make do for one night, you didn't deserve to call yourself a Westerner.

Waiting for sleep she'd replayed that last scene. Walt was an ordinary cheap bully, but not evil, not an actual villain. *Jake* was evil–he did awful things to people and relished their horror. A real villain went out of his way to cause permanent damage. She'd probably hate him the rest of her life, dead or not. Walt she'd forget after a while.

That night, coming in from the fire in L.O. Pocket, they'd been only a few minutes ahead of the other units, but it had been enough. Jake had parked in dark shadow under a tree in the yard, and when she started to walk away, he grabbed her from behind with his feet apart and his knees bent and rammed his pelvis against her.

Two weeks. Two weeks of remembering every move, every word like a scarifying flame. Some men deserved removal from human society.

She hadn't slept badly on the front seat, considering the day before. Stopped for breakfast at one of the cafes along the tourist approach to town, reached the shop before anyone was around, washed her face and changed into work clothes in the women's room. To hell with Walt and Jake anyway, she had things to do.

"Mrs. Armenta? I hope this isn't too early to call? Good. I need to ask–would it be all right for me to move in a bed and stuff this evening? If I'm not on a fire. Oh, that's wonderful. It's kind of abrupt, I know, but things are tight, what with school starting day after tomorrow. That's great. See you tonight."

By the time people began to arrive in the parking lot, she'd stashed yesterday's clothes in her car. There, who could guess last night she'd been homeless? They wouldn't find out–feelings that went the deepest with her, she couldn't talk about to anybody.

Since that night she'd avoided walking past the place. Jake's left arm had pinned her elbow to her side; his left hand was a vice on the other one. She'd kicked, but his feet were too far apart. She'd tried to spin away from him but his right arm was tight on that side. It was as if he'd rehearsed it–she couldn't move her hands far enough to scratch, her head far enough to bite.

"Morning, Josy." Abby was coming down a row of cars.

"Morning. How you doin'?"

"Could be better. Things were hairy on your days off."

"The Jake Holding Murder Mystery hasn't calmed down any?"

"It's worse. Friday Duvenek was prowling around trying to find out who tattled to Bailey about the things he's been saying. He was accusing Jill and me. Turns out Jake had been hinting he'd screwed all three of us, which given the way I felt about him would have taken some heavy-duty bondage. And he'd told the other guys Bob Dalton could be had too. Bob's so mad I think he'd kill Jake if he weren't already dead."

They stopped at the corner of the shop—she was having trouble with breathing or her heart rate or something. "You know what? You don't say things like that unless there's something wrong with you."

"Yeah, it's my theory Jake was a big prick with a very small one, and he was so dumb he didn't know he was advertising the fact. Probably couldn't get it up half the time. I gotta go out back and get my truck. See you in a minute."

Rage was a taste in her mouth. That fascist Jake, that stinking *thug*, he'd unzipped her Nomex pants and jammed his hand inside her underwear. "You like this, you know you do," he'd fingered into her. "I'll have you wet in no time."

Engines had turned off the highway, their headlights flashing across the pines—the others coming in from the fire. He'd pulled his hand out, and she'd scrambled away from him, shaking, fastening her clothes, and run toward her car. He called after her. "See you tomorrow."

She'd been ashamed as if it had been *her* fault. Left without saying a word to the people climbing down from their engines and driven away hating Jake like she'd never hated anyone in her life. She probably hadn't got out of the parking lot before he was bragging to the other men, waving his hand under their noses.

The Forest Service was tough on harassment: she'd heard of rangers being relieved and transferred if complaints were treated like jokes, including complaints about girlie calendars. She knew Mitch would have taken it seriously if she'd told him what Jake had done, and she definitely should have. He had gone way beyond harassment—it had been *assault*.

But she couldn't think of how to tell Mitch without feeling humiliated, and when she tried to report in writing, she froze and couldn't put a word on paper. She couldn't even tell Meg, it was so horrible.

And she could just see herself standing in front of a committee, telling about it, and Jake denying it and laughing and saying it was all wishful thinking, and the other men thinking hey, he hadn't *hurt* her.

For a week she'd been numb with the shame of it, hardly able to talk to anybody. Then Jake had turned up dead, and she didn't have to worry anymore about putting it into words for everyone to know.

*I*t was as if she'd been gone a long time—the office looked familiar, but every detail was strange. Nothing like two days off and the possibility of a major change to sharpen your eyesight, let you see the real spirit of things like chairs. Meg flicked on the scanner: Rim Country Rescue was responding to a motorcycle accident down by Blue Ridge. Welcome back to the real world of Saturday morning.

She turned on her computer and settled down to write two reports. The Wilson boy who had marooned Daddy's new 4WD up a cinder slope, that one would be easy, she'd followed regulations to the letter without blinking. Pretty straightforward account, photos, citations, signatures. But how was she going to describe the Morris family rescuing a little fir without getting a reprimand for ignoring the absence of a permit? An LEO had no business being sentimental about which rules she enforced.

> Prepare a narrative summary of the case which gives reviewing officials or attorneys a brief, broad picture of the case and aids in understanding the details of the case. The narrative summary should include the following information: geographical location of violation (State, county, legal description), type of violation alleged, amount of damage or loss necessary to determine felony or misdemeanor, and the name of the principal(s) involved.

Was there a law that federal handbooks had to be writtten in the worst possible style?

She was typing—Wilson jr. and the tree that got in his way—when Sergeant Bailey knocked on the door frame. "All right if I come in and sit for a few minutes?"

"Morning, Bailey. Be my guest." She swung her chair to face him.

"Am I interrupting something?"

"Reports. What's up, the same?"

He sat down like a tired old man. "We're no closer to charging anybody than we were Wednesday, and it isn't for not trying. We've interviewed everybody here at least once, some of them twice. Confirmed all alibis. Run background checks."

"Hours of leg work."

"You know it. Lots of fun. The names on the list, any reactions?"

"My husband and I went over them." She pulled the papers from her notebook. "We're pretty much buffaloed too."

He didn't look up. "You don't have anything you could pass on about *any* of these people?"

She told him the brief scene she'd witnessed between Jake and Buck and felt terrible about doing it. "Most of the people who've worked engines had encounters like that, it wasn't unusual."

"Know the Navajo?"

"Henry? No better than anybody knows a Navajo."

"Off hand would you suspect him?"

"Off hand, no. I worked an engine with him two years ago. He seemed a decent man."

"Duvenek?"

"Alan's sure he didn't do it—they've been friends a long time. Always making smart cracks, Alan says, likes to shock and roil the waters but no record of violence."

"Hard to make a smart remark stand up in court. But I'll tell you, one of these unlikely folks might be our perp. You don't know much about the others?"

"I've known Josy all my life, I'd call her my best friend. If she had any reason to shoot Jake, I don't know about it."

His eyes when he glanced up were intense. "She temperamental?"

Why did he ask that? "No more than run-of-the-mill. Ten years ago her parents were killed in an accident—she was distraught about the drunk high school kid who ran into them. If he hadn't been in the hospital, she might have pulverized him. Then she was so depressed for a while she could barely function. I wouldn't call that temperamental."

"Senseless unnecessary death, sounds like a normal reaction, I've seen it a lot. What do you know about Evan Franklin?"

"Not much. Josy says he's always pissed off about something, bitching, unpleasant to be around. She told me about the scene in the shop with Buck, which she called irrational. To be accurate, she said wacko. But I haven't ever talked with him. Bailey, have you found anybody who knew Jake away from work?"

"We tracked down an old girl friend. She said he was a sadist and she was glad somebody'd killed him, he had it coming, but she has an air-tight alibi. Otherwise, a complete zero. If he made friends, we haven't found any."

"You talked with his father?"

"Now that the first shock is past, he's being disagreeable. Accusing us of incompetence, being as loveable as his son was."

"So Jake had a role model at home."

"By the way, the lookout's pistol wasn't the murder weapon. No record it had been used in a previous felony. You want to tell her?"

"I'll do it, I've been wanting to get up there again." She didn't mention the hike she and Josy had taken Friday morning. Thought of it but didn't, she wasn't sure why. Gender loyalty had no place in a murder investigation.

"Tell her I've released the pistol to her brother since it isn't evidence. We lifted some prints from it in case we need them later."

She hoped she hadn't been outright uncooperative. "Anything you'd like me to watch for? My job takes me away from the station usually, so I don't see much of the people."

"I don't quite know where to go from here, but I'll think about it. Labor Day coming up, we're all going to be swamped given the public tendency to get into trouble. A fresh homicide has high priority though, capital case with no statute of limitations, we could keep it for years. We'll get him."

"Could I ask you a question, Bailey?"

His eyebrows went up. "Sure."

"When you were new to this work, you were young?"

"Fresh out of the army and needed a job. That was a long time back. I sure was a green rookie for a while."

"Did you have trouble getting used to it?"

He nodded slowly. "It bothered me a lot the first couple of years, I almost didn't stick it. Smell of a body stayed on my hands for days. I joke that one reason I got married was to have somebody to talk to, but it wasn't far off the truth. It can be lonesome out there trying to help when all you see is bad, half the people you deal with hate your guts. The job getting to you?"

"I'm not sure I'm the right type. Why did you stay?"

"I learned little tricks to keep myself separate from it. You know, kept a core and built a shell around it. Dropped the curtain when I could. Concentrated on the times I did somebody some good. But it took a while. For a long time I wasn't sure I was the right type either. Couldn't sleep, had recurring bad dreams. Didn't eat well, drank too much. One of the first cases I was on was a murder of a child. Still haunts me, that's the one thing I can't handle."

"Did it change you?"

"Can't help but change you. I used to be afraid I'd turn into a hardass that hated the world. You know what happened instead? I developed a bad case of compassion. Felt sorry for everybody. First crazy I had to shoot…" He looked down at his hands…"I cried. That kind of thing can get you killed. *Then* I turned into a hardass."

On the scanner a Flag PD officer was responding to a house where a woman had overdosed on drugs, not breathing, CPR directions being given by phone. On forest net Crew Two was being dispatched to a fire on the Kaibab, 5-4 to a multiple vehicle party that was tearing up a riparian meadow with ATVs. It wasn't becoming a hardass that she worried about, it was being so disgusted with humans that she learned to like shooting one now and then just to clean up the gene pool.

*C*unning little birds with white chests and dark caps flutter around the tower. Nuthatches, Randy said. They travel in flocks and eat small spiders and bugs, you can tell by the shape of the beaks. Their feet make scratching noises when they land on the roof. Why would they be pecking away all over the metal, even on the windows?

Just today and tomorrow left before she'll close the tower for the season. For the past week she's carried things down…water and kleenex and art books and stuff. It's going to seem so *claustrophobic* in town. She'll miss the huge spread of the view and watching weather approach from a hundred miles away. Three and a half months she's been part of it.

It was exciting weather for a while. Black clouds, lightning, she loved it. In the first two weeks of July Woody Mountain had almost four inches of rain. That wasn't enough to break the drought, but it made grass come up all over the place. The meadow at Rogers Lake was green clear across.

Then a high or something moved down through Utah and there was a low someplace…moisture in the air was crowded back into Mexico. Whatever. Anyway the days were *blasting* hot in the tower and she stayed on the shady side. Even in the mornings it made her skin feel burned if she sat in the sun for five minutes. It went on like that for only a week and a half, but it felt like *forever*.

Three times a day she filled the hummingbird feeders, about fifteen cups of sugar water. The little birds moved too fast for a good count, but she thought there were at least three dozen of them flying around her when she lifted the feeders up to the hooks. They zipped past but never once bumped into her.

The swallows too…tiny, but so fast she couldn't really see what they looked like, just their white breasts and the V shape of their wings. There must have been two dozen at a time zipping around the tower *slicing* the air, with no apparent pattern. It was so fabulous. Probably they were catching insects so small she couldn't see them… living with Randy had taught her to look for biology reasons.

Hawks are some kind of marvelous engineering. They coast on invisible currents so fast she can barely follow them with the binoculars…and suddenly stop still right in the air and hang there facing into the wind without moving–"stylin'," Randy would say. It's absolutely awesome, the way they can do that without falling and then turn one shoulder down and slip off into the currents.

She worried that the storms wouldn't come back, but every day there were a few more clouds and finally on July 25th they were like a gnarly black *wall* beyond Anderson Mesa. There was lightning every-where every minute.

At 14:20 Myrna on Elden reported top smoke beyond the Dry Lake Hills, estimated distance four miles. Myrna's impressive how accurate her distances are, but there was nothing showing from Woody Mountain. For eight minutes she scanned back and forth across the hills and Schultz Pass and Doyle Saddle. It was frustrating, most of that stretch was under shadow and all one color.

She moved farther and farther out. Suddenly there it was near Friedlein Prairie, two miles beyond Myrna's distance. She reported her cross, and it changed the legal, and Jake was responding along with Engine 3-2.

"Thanks, Sarah." She was surprised to hear Myrna's voice come over the radio. She didn't know anybody knew her name, especially somebody she'd never seen. What a warm feeling, like having an invisible friend. She cried a little, of course. She cries about *everything,* it's so *disgusting.*

By the time she went out of service she could see four smokes…by sunset there were twenty-three fires all over the forest. Timber markers and archaeologists were cutting lines around some of them because all the fire crews were busy. She ate dinner looking out through the open cabin door watching rain falling.

Air was full of moisture. Next morning the first thunder rumbled at 10:30, when humongous clouds were already towering above the Peaks. In no time they appeared above her and all around her, thick and black, so heavy they looked like they would fall of their own weight. Lightning started in every direction …thunder came from everywhere. It was like she was in a big dark room with echoes. When she went down the tower stairs at noon, holding the wood part of the railing but not the metal, hail was pinging against the legs of the tower.

This morning a storm is off the Baja coast. Air is so *saturated* that the light is actually blue…it's the most magical sight. There are the trees as usual and mountains and cumulus piling up and shafts of sunlight streaming down and patches of sky…and everything seen in this soft blue enchanted light. She doesn't know *how* she would paint it. There won't be time to try, clouds are building fast.

There was some kind of problem on the scanner about an accident on Milton, collision involving a pick-up pulling a pontoon boat. It had left the scene, and the city had issued an Attempt to Locate. The Long Valley LEO was delivering an injury patient to the hospital–the motorcycle accident, probably. Whoop-di-doo.

Meg finished her case report and sent it to Raleigh over the DG computer. After she'd retrieved a hard copy from the printer down the hall, she called him.

"Coconino Law Enforcement."

"Raleigh, it's Meg."

"Hey, Meg, how's it going?"

"I'm still breathing. Can you check your mail? There's something I want you to look at."

"Hold on, I'll get out of this."

She closed her eyes while she waited and thought about the ranch, the plants that had bloomed since rains had started. "OK, I've got it. What's the problem?"

"The first one—tell me if I've used the right words."

There was another pause while he read. "Looks OK."

"Now tell me if I did everything wrong on the second one, the judgment call."

Another pause. "You're safer going by the book. I strongly advise it. *Strongly.* You could let yourself in for an internal investigation. I'll have to think about how to handle it. I'm not saying you were wrong. We didn't want an LEO who couldn't use her head."

The Mormon Lake LEO was calling Flagstaff: they both stopped to listen. No explanations needed, it was selective hearing. She'd seen half a dozen Fire people stop talking at once and turn toward the radio, caught by a word no one else had heard.

"5-4, Flagstaff."

"I've located the truck and boat on the ATL at Marshall Lake. I'll be making contact with the driver."

"Copy, 5-4 making contact. We'll notify the city."

Raleigh went on from the break. "So what I'm saying is, every situation is different and sometimes you have to make decisions based on what you can see."

"If you'd been there…"

"But you have to be careful. Cut some people slack and they take advantage of you—then you get into an investigation, and it's hard to defend your actions. My advice would be to go by the book. You won't last long unless you do."

Two young males were being reported on the Woody Mountain Road overpass throwing rocks down at vehicles on I-40. Reported by a trucker whose windshield had been broken.

$\mathcal{F}$leeing town and all the people in it, Josy turned her truck onto the Woody Mountain Road. Did any woman make it through life without disfiguring scars on her soul? Or men either, maybe. Cumulus clouds, blinding white on the top where sun shone on them, were already ranked above the Peaks. To the east sun behind the clouds made them luminous as light bulbs. Maybe there'd be a storm by afternoon, a good cleansing rain. She hoped so—she needed a natural day with natural problems: like a lightning-struck tree across a road, like something to do with elk or lion or bear. An earthquake. A washed-out trail. Just the patterns of an ancient earth. She wasn't up to human nastiness at the moment. So what did she see within half a mile, before she'd even crossed over I-40, but an abandoned camp fire back in the trees, burning cheerfully. Litter and trash left by somebody who'd probably pulled away no more than an hour earlier, headed for California. She turned off the engine and sat there for a minute taking deep breaths before getting out.

It was all inside the rock ring. Ground for yards around had been so hammered by campers' feet that there wasn't a blade of growing grass. Even if a wind were blowing, there wouldn't be a threat to the forest. "Flagstaff, Patrol 3-4. I'm on an abandoned camp fire between 66 and I-40. It's non-stat. I can handle it."

She pulled the Pulaski hoe from the side box, gloves, hard hat, fire shirt. The small diameter hose on the live reel would be adequate for a campfire—she released the brake and set the nozzle for a fine mist.

Using the Pulaski and the side of her fire boot, she tipped the ring rocks back out of the way to expose all possible coals and began the tedious stir-and-spray that she could do without thinking. Back bent. Stir. Straighten up. Spray. Three or four times, till there was no smoke and water didn't hiss when it fell on the ashes.

Finally she pulled off a glove and held the back of her hand to the surface. No heat. Dragged her fingers through the ash—no heat. OK, out. She turned the hose onto her hand and washed it clean. All in a day's work. When the live reel was rewound and all the switches and buttons were in proper position and equipment was back in the side box, she pulled out a garbage bag and filled it with cans and bottles and plastic. Jeesh. Some people had no couth.

Another half a mile farther she made the turn-off to the Party fire behind the old dump and bumped along past the rotting furniture and rusting refrigerators. It was not being her favorite kind of day. Crouching beside the dead ashes, testing for heat, she was hit by the same fear she'd felt on Wednesday. Ran to the truck and locked herself in.

Of course there was nobody in sight, just thickets of close-growing pines and bare earth and garbage. So why the big panic attack? Combination strain of the last couple of weeks, maybe. Walt. Jake. Flies on a dead face. Going back to school. Visiting the cemetery. Sleeping in her car. Then put her alone in a place she associated with ignorance in a crowd and mindless drunkenness and the strange idea some people had of fun. Enough to frighten anybody.

When she drove through Mill Park, she could see a solid black wall all across the east. It wasn't symbolic, not rising evil or anything. Far as she knew, evil had always been rising. The usual storm was building over the Hopis and Navajos and Apaches, that was all it was.

At Phone Booth Tank she turned west. It had been more than a week since she'd checked the trail heads into Sycamore Canyon, all the springs—Strahan, Kelsey, Dorsey. Nobody was in the Turkey Butte tower; she could go up and look for smoke in the canyon the other lookouts wouldn't be able to spot. Then drive south to Dave Joy Point, see if anyone was camping there, look for smoke in Loy Canyon. Come back past Lost Lake through Barney Pasture and eat lunch overlooking Secret Mountain Wilderness.

The rim there was lower than at Howard Pocket, and she wanted to look at the cliffs. Everything below the rim was sedimentary, Upper Paleozoic, 280 to 220 million years old. Erosion had begun to expose it about twenty million years ago. But if she remembered correctly, the Secret Mountain Wilderness was red-orange quartz sandstone, dunes cross-bedded, but older than the Toroweap or the Coconino formations. It would be restful to sit there eating her deli sandwich and decide. With luck she wouldn't see another person.

*T*he first thunder of the day rumbles from over by Elden. Then there's a funny knocking sound overhead, and Venn opens her eyes. Small *hail* begins to bounce off the windows…Sarah leans close to the glass and looks up. Well! There's a pile of clouds right above her she didn't even see. What fun! She loves to watch hail jump when it hits the ground down there. Where are the little nuthatches hiding? And the hummingbirds?

It looks like three gnarly rain cells are coming at her from the southeast, like in *waves*. She hopes there'll be time between them for her to get down the tower stairs for lunch…it's scary to be on the stairs when they're wet and lightning is striking all around.

She just can't concentrate on anything for very long, her mind is jumpy all over the place. It didn't used to be like that, you know? She was unhappy or not wanting to go on living. But she never cried so much and she could be calm inside. Painting or doing her paper on Lillian, she could concentrate. Now she can't even focus on "Woody Autumn" more than half an hour at a time.

She's still the same person, only…she's a failure. She can't stand up to Dad. She couldn't stand up to Jake. Both of them, they've turned her into a *zombie*.

Jake began to say, "I'm not going to let you do that." Dad read that there was a big exhibit in Santa Fe, "Independent Spirits: Women Painters of the American West, 1890-1945" that was traveling out of Los Angeles. There were 120 painters in it, and one of them was Lillian. They could fly over and stay in a hotel and spend the weekend looking at paintings. Jake said, "I'm not going to let you do that. You tell your father you're moving in with me. I love you too much to let you go away from me." She didn't think it was love at all.

Everybody gets so upset when a bomb explodes in an airplane or at the Olympics and people are killed, but nobody even mentions all the ways there are to kill a person and leave the body alive. If there are murders, those are the worst ones.

When she was in high school, Beste's house was her favorite place to be. She didn't have any friends, but she could stop and talk every afternoon and eat cookies. Mom and Dad thought she was doing it to be nice, but that wasn't it at all.

"Beste, what was it like growing up in Flagstaff? Did you, you know, ever wish you were someplace else?"

Beste put her feet up on the big blue ottoman. "Not at first. I don't remember much before the Crash, just little snapshots. That was the Twenties. There were flappers even here. Grown-ups danced a lot and played cards. Children ran loose like cows did, all over the place, the whole town to play in as long as they stayed away from Front Street and the railroad tracks."

"Didn't you know kids from the other side?"

"Not many. It was mostly mill workers over there. Forbidden and therefore exciting country. But our side gave us plenty of scope. There were still original settlers here, pioneers. Al Doyle had died not long before. The first of the Riordans and Babbitts were still living. And the old cowboys, my, they were a colorful bunch. Most were over sixty by then, some were old and frail, but they seemed heroes to me. I loved to hear the stories about them. One wonderful woman lived right down the street. I never pass that old white house without thinking of her. Ruby Green, isn't that a wonderful name? Full of color."

"Was she old?"

Beste laughed. "About as far along as I am now. When I was eight years old that seemed ancient. Now it's just advanced middle age."

"Was she a pioneer?"

"She came here with her husband to homestead when there was hardly a town at all. It required courage and intelligence and the ability to work hard without feeling sorry for herself. Until almost the day she died, she was straight and true as a two by four, her mind and eyesight and hearing acute. I was too shy to visit her house, but I used to imagine all the adventures she must have had. She couldn't have been more important to me if she'd been a queen in exile."

"How did she die?"

"Just wore out, I suppose. It had been a hard-working life. She didn't really fail...they used to say things like, 'She'd been failing for months'...but Ruby Green was just tired for a few weeks. Her hands had become very thin, as if the cushions in them had shrunk. There was something about her, people said, hard to tell what, and they knew she wouldn't linger. I thought my heart would stop when I heard that. I was only, let's see, eleven or so, still young enough to think about something other than boys. Two nights later she died asleep."

She loved to hear about Beste when she was young. *"Were you sad?"*

"Oh, I took it hard. It was the first person who'd been part of my life, you see, the first one to go. The next month Fred Breen died, that witty man who was the publisher of the Sun. He'd stop and talk with me for a moment as if I were someone important. I couldn't say the words 'died' or 'death' for a long time. It seemed so tragic, so unjust. I thought climbing a mountain and walking on up into the air away out of sight made more sense. I guess I still do."

She knew, she felt that way about Lillian...death made everybody's life seem so wasted. For a long time she remembered the pain in her throat that day, when she realized Beste too would...it was too awful.

*T*raffic on Milton was super bad–the ants go marching one by one. Summer tourists trying to reach the Grand Canyon, funneled under railroad tracks. The town council couldn't put off a solution much longer.

Josy had reported an abandoned camp fire; just past the Woody Mountain Camp Ground Meg saw the green pumper truck back among the trees. By the time she reached the malicious mischief at the over-pass above I-40, city police had the kids in custody. Citations for reckless endangerment and damage to property. Wasn't quite as funny as it was a while ago. No use to stick around.

The Long Valley LEO was reporting five people being transported by ambulance to the Payson hospital. Injured in a one vehicle accident just within the forest boundary–"It's on us."

Clouds were building early, dark masses. If she were up in the air like Sarah, she'd probably be able to see storm cells here and there. Some rain had fallen already, brief hard rain that her wipers had trouble keeping up with. The road was still passable, but it could get sticky with more precip.

Across the south side of Rogers Lake there was a band of bright yellow. She'd noticed it Monday when she was driving out to meet Josy and wondered whether it was a variety of sunflower, it was the right time for them to be blooming. There was no particular hurry—she drove down to the south shore and got out to look.

A mass of flowers. Coreopsis, maybe, common name tickweed. She'd read that it grew in moist fields, which they didn't have out at the ranch. Bloom was right for the sunflower family, height, stem. Yay. She'd guessed right.

A raindrop hit her back just as a brilliant light flared around her with a deafening crack of thunder. She flinched and looked up. In the few minutes that she'd been bending over flowers, all the black of Mordor had developed over her head. She could lie flat to avoid attracting lightning or run for her truck where there were tires to conduct it down. She ran for the truck, which would at least be dry. The meadow could turn boggy in no time—she got back to 231 before rain could be flood and drove back to the tower road. Out of the open, into trees where traffic would be light.

Someone on the Sedona district was requesting law enforcement to conduct an eviction from site five at the Cave Spring camp ground. Someone being a nuisance or a threat? Someone trying to defy the stay limit? When Mormon Lake and Sedona LEOs were dispatched, she was relieved.

*W*aves of rain cells are still coming. Others begin to form all around her. They spread until they join. Lightning strikes are *everywhere*. Hurrying, Sarah closes the windows and tells the radio, "Woody Mountain out of service for lightning," and sits in the lookout chair. It has insulators on all four legs. She wishes she could pick Venn up in her lap to be safe too.

Rain begins to hit the roof hard, *furious* rain. There's no visibility in any direction, rain as thick as fog on all sides Brown *rivers* of water are flowing down the driveway. The mountain is wearing away.

All the birds and animals must be soaked. Plants are happy for the rain and ground squirrels can hide in deep burrows. But deer and elk have no shelter. She looks down at Venn, sleeping dry and comfortable on the floor…at least *one* animal on the mountain isn't miserable.

Venn hears it first…lifts her head and listens, gets to her feet. Then the sound comes through the window…a truck is driving up the east side. Where the road curves in to cross a ravine, the sound is clear. It disappears going around the old lava out-crop. Ten seconds later she hears it again, coming up through the clearing in the mountain's old crater. Venn growls.

Somebody's coming up the road, a truck from the sound, not a car. Venn stands up and stretches and points at the trapdoor with her nose. She strokes the dog's head. "Yes. Somebody's coming. Can you tell who it is?" It doesn't sound like Josy.

Looking down through the trees, she sees a green Bronco with a cop package. Meg? Is that who it is? She doesn't know Meg very well but maybe she'd like to.

Venn rushes down the stairs and begins to bark when she reaches the ground. Meg steps out of the Bronco and holds her hand out for smelling. "Oh, come on, you know me." Calm and strong, not frightened at all. She looks up and waves. "Hi. May I climb?"

Meg comes through the trapdoor behind Venn. "Well! That's real exercise. Maybe we could turn tower climbing into a competitive sport. Did you ever time yourself?"

She's forgotten how nice Meg *looks*. "I'm pretty slow. I'm always watching my feet. Would you like to sit down? The chair has insulators on the legs because of lightning. I'll sit here on the window seat."

"Thanks. This is quite a chair. Guess you need one this tall so you can see out."

"I love being able to look so far. When I'm in town now, I feel closed in, all I can see is down the street."

"I know a Hopi man who grew up at Shongopovi. He says he went back East once and didn't like it. He couldn't see out, couldn't see the bones of the land."

"My Best—my grandmother says that's a big reason why Easterners are different from Westerners, geography. You know, space and air. It's made us what we are if we've been here since the early days."

"She has a good point. My family has been right here since 1885. I was named to remind me that my great-grandmother Margaret was a homesteading pioneer. Sometimes I feel so different from people from the east coast. Even when I don't like or approve of Westerners, like Jake, I think I understand them."

She stares a minute. "Yes! I know what you mean."

"Sarah, your view is magnificent. My great-aunt Jo would have loved it, she was an artist who did a lot of landscapes."

"Did she paint from firetowers?"

"Not that I know of, but she did like to work from high places where she could look down into the land."

"My grandmother used to know a woman who painted like that, but her name wasn't Jo."

"Here in northern Arizona?"

"She died twenty-five years ago. Lillian was from New York…her cousin was married to Zane Grey. She went with him a lot of times when he went to Rainbow Bridge."

"That sounds like a story my grandmother told me. I wonder if my great-aunt Jo knew your grandmother's friend. She was from New York too, lived with Josy's great-grandmother"

"I can ask Beste, my grandmother."

Sarah was so pale and solemn, but when she smiled her sad little face was alight and almost beautiful. "Wouldn't it be special to find a connection?"

"Yay!" She puts her hands on her knees, "Anyway, I've brought you good news. Your pistol, the one I took, is not the one that shot Jake. So you're cleared on that score."

"Yes. Thank you. I didn't think it was."

Movement in the air—she turned to look. Four large black birds not more than thirty feet away, weaving and floating around each other, making curving patterns in the air. "Oh, see!"

No wings were flapping; the birds made no sound turning their tight figures. She moved to the window and Sarah came to stand beside her. "It's like they're dancing, like they know they're creating something beautiful."

"The most graceful thing I've ever seen."

"They *know*, they have to know. It's art."

A bird sailed off away from the others, turned and rode the wind back, entered the dance again. If they were pursuing insects, there was no sign. Movement looked to be for its own sake.

"I haven't seen more than two ravens at a time all summer. I wonder if they're young ones that were in the nest until now?"

"Good question. Could be."

"It's like they're showing us a secret we should know." The pattern loosened into long curving lines, closed in toward an invisible center, loosened again.

"They may know we're watching—it feels that way, doesn't it? Performing for an audience."

"I'll tell Randy, he might know."

As if at the end of music, the birds fell softly as autumn leaves into the trees and were gone. Sarah turned a radiant face. "We saw it together. They've never done that for me alone."

Something sad there. Something vulnerable. On impulse she hugged Sarah's shoulders.

The forest is full of bow hunters. At every possible spot along the road there are tents and trucks. You know what? There are lots more places to camp back on the two-tracks.

Rain cells had been coming across the forest in black waves all afternoon. Josy'd been hit with hail and downpours, startled by lightning, and deafened by thunder overhead. Now *that* was the kind of weather she liked—when she wasn't out on dirt roads in a heavy truck.

Last season she'd responded to a smoke reported by Volunteer lookout, and crossed by Turkey Butte, right on the edge of Sycamore Canyon below Dr. Raymond's lily pond at Poison Spring. Before she'd reached the head of Volunteer Canyon, the road was getting slick with wet clay and she was looking for a place to turn around. Shaeffer had joked that the right maneuver in a situation like that was to accelerate so you wouldn't get stuck, but last time he had tried it, he'd slid into a tree and bogged down. It had taken Engine 3-2 all day to pull him out, and the accident report had been a major issue. Under "cause" he'd written "pilot error." A sense of humor wasn't appreciated in government documents.

So she hadn't been *about* to speed up. But she'd driven that country before in wet weather, and she knew mud was likely to get worse. She'd evaluated every foot of the road and the edges, trying to find something rocky enough for a turn-around. It had been a tense ten minutes. She'd radioed Engine 3-4: "Buck, I'd advise you to stand by at the intersection of 527 and 527B. I'm going to bail as soon as I can."

"Copy," he'd said. "Standing by." She was grateful that he hadn't said they'd be on the scene with assistance if she needed it.

Finally there was a short stretch of what looked like limestone pavement wide enough to allow jockeying a few feet at a time, and she was headed back into that muck. It looked inches deep. When she'd finally got back to Engine 3-4, it didn't take a minute for them to decide to ask that the lookouts monitor the Poison Spring smoke. Three days later it had become a fifteen acre burn, and they could get in to take action.

*S*canner again: the county was responding to a roll-over accident on the Hart Prairie Road, also an ambulance and Ranger 3-2 helicopter. Whoop-ti-doo. Chances were good somebody had come down off the hill near Crater Lake too fast. Her district, she'd have to go.

Meg left Woody Mountain with clouds moving in again from the east. Road surface was already soft with mud, but she'd probably be back on pavement before more rain fell. Not that it mattered a whole lot: she'd been driving on muddy dirt roads out on the ranch since she'd been tall enough to reach the pedals—about age twelve.

P.J. had been patient. "Your hands will follow your eyes, look where you want to be going."

"OK."

"This is a little fast for that curve coming up. Brake before you reach it and then let up—if you keep the brake on through a turn, you could throw the back end into a skid, wet road or dry."

"OK."

"When you can't guarantee how the tires will grip, it's a bad idea to drive as fast as you think you can."

She'd never had to walk home for help because she was stuck in the mud. But the driver of a Jeep coming up fast behind her would most likely be in trouble. In the mirror she could see he was all over the road. Idiot would kill somebody driving like that.

A quick glance when they passed: two men in their thirties. As they pulled ahead, the passenger threw something out—an empty beer can intended to hit her. It bounced off her windshield. No damage, but the insolence of it, the nasty provocation, brought anger up into her throat. Throw something at a clearly marked law enforcement vehicle, how dumb could you get?

She turned on her lights and siren. "Flagstaff, 3-4. Notify the county that a Jeep, driver possibly intoxicated, is on 231 headed toward pavement. He went by me too fast for me to read his plate."

"Copy, 3-4, we'll let them know. Will you be following?"

"Affirmative."

Skid marks were obvious all the way through the S curve that turned away from Rogers Lake. Several violations to cite him for as soon as she caught up with him, which she did in half a sec. He'd hit almost the first possible tree, slid off the road and slammed head-on into a big pine before he was out of sight of the lake. The pine hadn't budged, but from the look of things, there was one adventurer who wasn't going anywhere right away. She loved seeing immediate justice— couldn't have happened to a nicer guy. She stopped.

> Within Forest boundaries, 36 CFR 261.13e allows Forest
> Officers to enforce Driving Under the Influence of
> Intoxicants. State and local law enforcement officers have
> primary authority...the Forest Officer should detain the
> driver until a State or local law enforcement officer can
> arrive or transport the driver to the county jail.

"Flagstaff, 3-4."

"3-4, Flagstaff."

"Requesting county response ASAP to a one-vehicle accident on
Forest Road 231 just east of Rogers Lake, Jeep collision with a tree, the
driver who had been moving at reckless speed."

"Any injuries?"

"The passenger is getting up now. The impact sprung his door and
threw him out. Nose is bleeding and his arm might be broken, the way
he's holding it." His right arm, the one that had thrown the beer can.
Oh frabjous day. "Inebriated or concussion or both. He doesn't seem to
be able to stand upright without support." Also, he was vomiting, and
he'd wet the front of his pants. Charming.

"The driver?"

"He's still in the vehicle, maybe pinned. I'll check."

"Copy. We'll notify the county Code Three and send an ambulance."

She was reassured by the heavy items on her belt. The can-thrower
was leaning on the back of the Jeep, staring across the road with eyes
that didn't seem to be in focus. Old beer was a foul smell

"Here, sir, why don't you sit down?" Feeling for a concealed
weapon, she eased him to the ground, pulled her handcuffs out of their
holster and snapped his left wrist to the spring shackle. "Just wait there
until the county arrives, there's a bright boy."

As she rounded the left rear tire, the driver stumbled out with an
automatic pistol that looked big as a cannon, huge chamber, aimed more
or less in her direction. Her Sig was in her hand before she thought
about it. Feet braced apart.

"Forest Service Law Enforcement, drop it. *Drop it.*"

"Women won't shoot." Creep got his philosophy from television.

"Drop it."

"Mind your own business, or I'll blow you away." The threat alone
was an offense.

The Sig felt good in her hands. "***Drop it!***"

He lurched toward her off balance. Enough; her bullet hit his
shoulder and knocked him backward. As he fell, a dozen shots stitched

an arc up and across the pines and down. He hit the ground hard, screaming–the automatic finally stopped moving five feet from his hand. He rolled over and scrambled to reach it. There ahead of him, she kicked it into the ditch, and he grabbed at her ankle. Okay, creep. She fired off another shot, and there were two nice new red holes in his shoulder. The man cuffed to the jeep was shouting. "Tom! God damn, Tom!" She stepped back. "Lie right there on the ground, Indiana Jones, where you're a good target."

Panic: "I'll bleed to death."

Remains to be seen.

"Help me, honey, I didn't mean anything."

I did.

He began to vomit too.

She backed off until she could cover both of them and reached into her truck for the cell phone. Glad for her Sig, *glad* that she'd shot him, glad that they both were injured. And not one bit sorry about being glad–a girl needed some job satisfaction.

"Coconino Law Enforcement."

"Raleigh, it's Meg."

"Hey, I heard your call for the county. What happened?"

"I shot somebody."

"You *did?*"

"Self defense. I didn't kill him."

"I'll be there right away. Don't move, don't touch anything, don't *say* anything." He hung up before she could answer.

Bet a cookie there'd be a major investigation. Those years she'd driven patrol, every scrape the size of a nickel to the paint on her truck, she'd had to wait in place while people came rushing out from town to investigate. It was humiliating, a responsible adult treated like a delinquent kid. A bump or a dent and her government driver's license was yanked for three days and she'd had to double up with someone else. This was going to be a hundred times worse.

On the radio Abby was reporting a man who was claiming that his ex-girlfriend and her family were chasing him and trying to kill him, acting 10-16, maybe an addict. She was requesting city back-up. Schaeffer was trying to locate a runaway juvenile. Rain began to fall again.

*F*or more than an hour Sarah hasn't been able to see off the mountain. Finally Elden is visible, and the land to the southeast. But they're faint and hazy. As the rain moves off toward Volunteer lookout, air clears, and it's clean and beautiful! Except for places where black rain is falling, she can see practically to Mexico. The dark, wet forest looks so soft. Sun shines through the clouds, actually sends *rays* down to turn some spots to gold and emerald. She opens the window and hears the soft sound of rain falling from trees. Wet branches of the oak trees are a lovely red-brown color.

There are water dogs everywhere, almost as white as smoke. They rise and twist and fade like ghosts and begin again someplace else too fast to get a good reading on them. In July she was excited thinking they were all fires from lightning strikes. Now she knows water vapor when she sees it.

There *should* be fires, there was so much lightning. She doesn't see any yet...maybe later when air dries a little. Sky is reflecting silver in little pools of water in the lowest places in the meadow down at the lake. Maybe some of it came from her mountain.

Even after the forest was opened when rains began in July, she didn't have many visitors. Most people probably don't even know there's a tower up here. She's glad...maybe there are more good people than bad, but you can't tell from their faces. This summer she learned from Jake that men can be just plain evil when it comes to women, and she doesn't want any strange ones up here. The few who've come alone or with other men, she won't let them climb inside her tower room.

"It's too small," she tells them. "As you can see. But there's as much visible from the top landing." One man stood down there and shouted awful things, and she was *glad* she hadn't let him in. There's something about some men, they like to hurt what they think is helpless. And how do you know by looking at them?

She'd rather be alone with art, that makes her happy. Now that the mountains in "Woody Autumn" are magenta and she's added more pink to the shadows on the aspens, she's rubbing the cadmium sky with q-tips. It's so *neat*! It makes the most glowing golden green, like sun shining. It makes *light* in the picture, who would have guessed it would do that? Sky can be green sometimes, she's seen it low in the evening between clouds. So she's never seen the *whole* sky this particular color, so what? She likes it a lot.

She wrote letters to every art museum in the southwest and not one had even heard of Lillian except the Amerind Foundation southeast of Tucson...they didn't know much but they had paintings. And a woman in Cochise who was the daughter of the people who started Amerind remembered Lillian. Dad said she could go down there if Randy was willing to go with her and drive so she would be safe.

Lillian had never driven on the 17 highway…her traveling days were over before it was finished. It was packed with people in cars. She watched the land go by, still empty, still looking as it did when Lillian and Jess were moving around Arizona on bumpy dirt roads. She ached because it was a part of Lillian's world that wasn't changed much yet.

They drove around Scottsdale trying to find the place where Lillian's citrus grove had been but it was all built up with condos and town houses. On the way to Tucson I-10 was, like, frantic with hurrying cars that dodged back and forth from one lane to another. They crossed rivers with no water in them and passed mountains of rock jutting up from the desert floor. Arizona is like an old story.

Southeast of Tucson was kind of nice…she had never seen that part of the state. The San Pedro Valley was inspiring the way it swooped down from the Chiricahuas and up again to the Dragoons. It looked huge and ancient. Lillian had painted "In Old Cochise" there somewhere.

When they drove into the Amerind grounds, the pink buildings and the granite boulders and the oaks, Randy said "This is it. This is where I want to live. Oh, so cool!" Lillian had lived there for a while after she and Jess left Sedona. Lived in that peace and beauty and painted all day if she wanted to. It was good to know that she went to such a beautiful place when her heart was bruised.

The woman in Cochise didn't remember much, just that she had liked Lillian and Jess. But she had photographs. They turned through her albums together finding a few pictures of Lillian looking kind of stout and wearing old-lady shoes…grey hair. She didn't want to see her looking like that.

A gnarly black storm front stretches from O'Leary to Hutch Mountain—forty miles or so—with clouds that look very low, just above the tops of the Cinder Hills. Myrna on Elden says her visibility is only fifty feet. More black is rising behind Humphreys and Hochderffer… masses of dark cumulus stretch out ahead. Above her, clouds are moving fast, but there is no wind yet, not much thunder. It looks evil and threatening, but that's to say clouds are like humans.

When Josy was near Phone Booth Tank again, and Scott on East Pocket reported what looked like a lightning-struck snag near Buck Ridge cabin, Josy drove up to the Turkey Butte tower for a cross—it was probably in a blind spot for Woody Mountain and Volunteer.

She could see the smoke clearly enough; it was only a couple of miles southwest of Turkey Butte. But she was amazed that Scott could have picked it out against the water vapor boiling up out of Sycamore Canyon and West Fork and Casner Cabin Draw. After Flagstaff acknowledged her reading, she locked the old tower again and drove off to make a stab at reaching the burning snag. Not that she had much hope, but at least she could try.

Buck and Henry in Engine 3-4 were also responding. Henry would know exactly how to get there, of course; he always did—"I think maybe it's this way." Buck would say, "*This* turn?" and Henry would say, "Maybe so," but he was always right.

At first it was solid going, bumpy with rocks as the ground fell off toward the canyon. She didn't trust it though—she watched ahead for mud or puddles. "Engine 3-4, Patrol 3-4. Your location?"

"We're down here at Power Tank, Josy, but it's really sloppy. We're not gonna be able to get anywhere near Buck Ridge. Where are you?"

"Turkey Tank Number Two."

"We're just south of you. Hang tight, we'll be back in a minute. We'll request permission to confine this one."

That particular jargon word always amused her: "confine" like put in a cage. Technically it was supposed to mean there were natural fire breaks all around, so they could let it burn itself out with no widespread damage. She guessed mud made as good a fire break as anything.

"Engine 3-4, Flagstaff. As per 3-34, permission to contain."

That startled her for a minute, 3-34—like Jake was still running things. But the numbers referred to jobs not people and with Jake dead, Bob Dalton was acting engine specialist.

Heading back to town, she avoided even *thinking* about Fry Park. That meadow, and Mill Park too, both of them were truck traps in rainy weather. You bogged down there, and you might as well walk home—nobody could get close enough to get a cable on you.

The blackest clouds she'd seen in years were moving west across Woody Ridge, villainous looking. Myths and legends could be based on clouds like that. She supposed they were ominous. She should be afraid, but they were so dramatic it was exciting more than anything else. On the built-up roadway through Mill Park, she pulled to the side and stopped to watch them. Would Navajos call those *male* clouds?

As she watched, they began to glow like phosphorescence with a green light, dark green around the edges, brilliant green back inside. She tingled all over. She hadn't seen such a thing, ever, but she'd read that a green light meant tornado conditions and there she was exposed with nothing but meadow for a mile in every direction. It would probably be prudent to haul ass out of there.

So what did she do? She got out and stood in the road and laughed. Raised her face and her arms to that wild shining green and laughed. Hey, she was an *Arizona* girl. She didn't need exercises to get rid of panic when the sky was full of magic and she was Free!

*T*he black wall is still rising to the east, but there's not much of anything happening right above Woody Mountain. Sarah hopes the storm comes this way. Afterwards the forest will make soft murmuring noises—air moving, water falling from the trees and running away down the slopes. Tonight she'll be safe and warm in bed. In the morning maybe shreds of clouds will sail past on a cold wind and the whole changeable world will be clean and beautiful. Right now, with a storm coming, she loves practically everything.

By the end of July she realized something bad was wrong. The tender nights of cherishing hadn't happened for a long time, although she kept hoping for them. Jake would arrive late and *attack* her with hardly a word…it seemed *angry*…and he didn't care if he hurt her. Usually afterward the condom was dry. Sometimes he couldn't get hard enough to put it on.

He blamed *her*. "I can't get excited if you don't get excited." But how could she? She *wanted* to love him, but he made her miserable. She tried to talk to him and tell him, and he slapped her.

If she was so bad, why did he begin to say that she was going to marry him? Didn't even *ask*. He said, "At the end of the season, we're getting married."

He wasn't even romantic…"You'll do it. I'll make sure of that. How would your father like to know his little daughter has been fucking her head off up here?" There was the most awful smile on his face when he said that. She was frightened to think of what Dad would say, and he knew it, and he *liked* doing that. "And don't forget Randy works for me. I can put his engine anywhere on a fire I want to. Be a shame if a fire blew up and ran right over him, wouldn't it?"

Why did he want somebody he had to hold on to with blackmail? "That's *sick*."

He hit her on the jaw with his fist and knocked her against the refrigerator. Then he pinned her there with his left hand and pulled the right one back, doubled up. "That was just a little love tap. Won't even bruise your face. Just a hint of what I can do if I'm provoked. You don't ever insult me. Ever. Understand?"

The back of her head stung. His face looked like some kind of snarling monster's. "Understand?" He pulled his fist back farther.

She couldn't breathe…she nodded.

"Say it. You understand?"

All she could do was whisper. "Yes." She started to cry with the helplessness of it. Helpless is awful.

"That's my girl." He pulled her into his arms like he wanted to comfort her for what he had just done. "You're learning. You'll be a good little wife."

The two weeks after that were the worst nightmare she had ever had in her life. She listened to the forest radio…if he was on a fire, she stayed in the cabin, but if he wasn't she left the mountain as fast as she could after work and went home to spend the night. She didn't ever *ever* want to be alone with him again.

She couldn't *eat* and she was numb, she was so scared. The first night she was in town she looked out of her upstairs window and saw Jake's car turning around in the cul-de-sac…her truck was in the driveway, so he knew she was there. She felt, like, hysterical.

Twenty minutes later he called the house and talked to Dad and told him she and Randy were doing a fine job and they were kids to be proud of. Randy said, "Now, what was that all about? Jake never gives anybody an attaboy. No way. I don't get it."

But *she* knew what it meant, it was a threat. How could she tell Dad and ask him to help her? It would be awful…he'd call it proof. He'd make her quit the lookout job and that would be the end of her freedom forever.

Those days she cried most of the time…she was trapped between them, *trapped*. That's when she began to think of shooting herself with the pistol. Her life was ruined anyway.

One day Jake came up to the tower in the middle of the afternoon. Lowered the trapdoor and folded his arms across his chest and stood with his legs apart. He scowled. "You were gone every night for the last two weeks."

"I was in town watching the Olympics." She didn't want to show him she was afraid, but she didn't want to act defiant either, he'd hit her. "With my family."

"You didn't ask my permission."

His *permission*! Like he *owned* her. "I didn't leave until I'd gone out of service at 17:00. It wasn't as if I was taking off. It was my own time."

"Your own time." He *sneered*. "What did you do on your own time, watch half-naked men wrestling and jumping around?"

"I didn't think the wrestling was too interesting. But the gymnasts were *beautiful*. I wish I could do those things. Did you see the girl slip and hit her head on the balance beam? She didn't even touch the floor. Just climbed back up and went on. It was really awesome."

"The titless wonder? Spreading her legs for the whole world to see? Most of the men watching were thinking of banging her. That's what you want?"

She couldn't even answer him, it was so awful. She didn't believe all men were so nasty that they couldn't think about anything but sex.

Just thinking of it still makes her cry. Jake's dead, and he can't threaten her any more, but she'll never get over what he did, never. Never forget. Never forgive him.

The big black storm to the east is thinning, she's sure of it. She can see the outlines of mountains through it. The sky behind Kendrick is blue-black now. If that cell moves south too, she could get a storm yet. She checks overhead, you know, to see if clouds are moving above.

They're green! Very dark and dense and heavy and *boiling*, with the most erie green light shining from somewhere inside…like there are green angels back in there somewhere. Lower edges of the billows are blue-green and gnarly. "Then God spoke to Job out of the whirlwind." She can't help it, she starts to cry.

The green light lasts only about five minutes…then the clouds break into two parts with tangled skeins trailing and move off in opposite directions along Woody Ridge. What an awesome, awesome thing.

In no time at all she isn't crying and it is a beautiful afternoon everywhere she looks. Now that the black wall has moved south, and eastern clouds have faded away, she can see the salmon-pinks of the Painted Desert brighter than they've been all summer, it must be more than thirty miles away, maybe fifty or more. There's no *hint* of fading into blue or grey, no atmospheric perspective at all. The hills beyond Cosnino are pink-magenta.

*W*alt was leaning against her car when she went out into the parking lot. "Hello, Sweetie." A superior, you-can't-get-away-from-me smirk.

Some men took more discouraging than others. "Stalking is a crime these days." She unlocked the door.

"I wanted to see you."

"And show me you know where I work. And scare me."

"And take you home again. I realize I can't live without you."

"Oh, Walt, be honest." She opened the door. "You're not fooling me, even if you're lying to yourself."

"Come on. Don't act like that. Let's go get something to eat and talk about it.'

She looked at him, seeing every flaw in his face, places she'd ignored when she thought she loved him. "Funny. Yesterday that's what I decided I should do, talk to you. Tell you how I was feeling and what I wanted. Be *fair* to you, was the way I put it."

He thought he'd won, she could see it in his face. "Right. Let's have no more nonsense." And he was back in charge. Mad that she'd inconvenienced him. It was chilling. "You follow me, and I'll choose a place." He even expected her to be obedient.

"You just don't get it, do you? You blew it big last night." She thought of spitting at him, but there were people all over the place. "How dense can you get? I don't even *like* you any more."

He drove out of the lot behind her and hung on her back bumper through three traffic lights. In the mirror she could see the hard jaw, the tight line of his mouth. OK. Far as she was concerned, she had the advantage: she was leading.

At the pawn shop she pulled into the only parking slot in front. By the time he'd found a place on the back of the lot, she was inside.

"What can I do for you today?" The clerk looked weather-worn but hey, what did you expect in a pawn shop?

"You can sell me a small light-weight pistol."

"Sure thing. What do you want to use it for?"

Walt came in through the door fast and angry, grabbed her arm. "What the hell do you think you're doing?"

She smiled at the man behind the counter. "My former boyfriend is making an ass of himself. Again. You might have to identify him."

His grip loosened, but he didn't let go. "Sweetie—"

"Don't call me Sweetie. I don't like it." To the clerk, "I'm going to dictate his name, address and phone number. Please write them down."

Walt flung her arm away. "You won't get away with this."

Gawd. Who wrote his lines? "You know what, Walt? You've been watching too many dumb movies."

He slammed through the door. The clerk acted as if it were an everyday situation. "You don't know something about hand guns, you've got no business with a semi-automatic. Otherwise you're better off with a revolver and the kiss approach. Know what that is?"

"Keep It Simple, Stupid. Good advice. I've lived around firearms all my life, but I'm no expert."

"Then I suggest this little Smith and Wesson .38." He broke it open and handed it to her. "Holds five shots in the chamber. Aim at the man's chest, and you ought to be able to stop him with that."

It fit her hand nicely, and it wasn't too heavy. "Is there a wait?"

"We have to do a criminal record check with the state, takes about ten minutes on the phone. I'll need your driver's license for the information. You over twenty-one? Arizona resident? Legal citizen?"

While DPS was confirming it had no record for her, she filled out federal forms that would establish ownership. "Do I need to register a new gun with the police?"

"Nope. Everything's done right here. You need ammo?"

"You bet—I want to walk out of here with it loaded."

He showed her what she needed to know about using and cleaning. "Now, you have to take a course to be certified for a concealed weapon. Here's information on a couple. Otherwise, in Arizona you can carry it loaded in a holster, long as you have it at least partly in plain view. Be a good idea to take gun safety training."

It was remarkably easy. When the DPS check came back clear, she bought a leather holster, a cleaning kit, and *The Arizona Gun Owner's Guide*. Walked out with a loaded pistol in her hand, holding it high where Walt could see it from his car.

When she turned out into traffic again, there he was behind her. She sighed, "You're getting to be a bore, Walt. Let's see what it will take to get some kind of protective order that'll require you to stay away from me."

He stuck close until she turned into an open space across the intersection from the police station on Beaver Street. There were no other spots to park in sight. He pulled up beside her, hesitated, gunned his engine, and peeled past. Ran a red light and, only fifteen feet in front of her, slammed into the back of a pick-up truck in the intersection. A large, rough, and very angry man exploded out, shouting obscenities.

Really, she couldn't help the laughter that bubbled up. "Redneck to the rescue. Try bullying *him*, and see how far you get." Walt's door had sprung open. He stepped slowly into the street, and a blue heeler launched out of the back of the truck and sank its teeth into his leg. In the shouting, screaming and barking, she started her car and drove away.

It was just too delicious. She probably wouldn't need that restraining order for the rest of the day, Walt being occupied and all for quite a while—there in front of the police station. She could get to her storage locker in peace and load up enough to get her through the night in Armenta's little house.

*C*leared away: two drunks transported to Flagstaff Medical Center, both in custody; a smashed Jeep towed off. She'd stood for a wet hour while three men had measured skid marks, photographed everything, dug into a tree across the road and retrieved a bullet.

Raleigh had been friendly enough. "Congratulations. It's been a while since I plugged anybody."

"It's my first. Don't know that I like the feeling." At the time she had–that was not so good.

"We'll put you on admin leave with pay coupla days until we finish the investigation. Standard policy, nothing personal."

"Yeah, maybe."

"You're lucky this came after that episode with the little tree, it'll give the mucky-mucks at headquarters a different take."

"Not too female to put a drunk in the hospital if necessary."

"Something like that. Bound to influence their review. So treat the time off like a vacation."

"OK. I need a vacation. Sure, why not?"

*T*he walls around Josy were beautiful in the morning light; she might not hang any pictures. Well, maybe the ones that had come down from her great-grandmother: a bedroom with a blue rug, a watercolor of women cooking titled "View from My Corner of Ruby's Thanksgiving Kitchen," a small oil of the house on Verde in strong afternoon light. The big one was radiant, Wupatki as it had looked in 1925. They were all signed simply–Jo. Walt hadn't liked them, so she'd put them in storage with everything else.

Come to think of it, the hell with Walt–she *would* hang them. When she was little, she pretended she could walk into them and be there in the past, stand at the end of that kitchen table and listen to the women talking. Pretend they could see her faintly if they looked hard. Those pictures had always made her feel good, and hey, she had a right.

She stretched. Her life had turned an important page. Tomorrow she'd be putting on jeans and sandals, filling a book bag, stepping out the door to a whole new chapter. She threw back the sleeping bag she'd used for the first night and got started. Lunch box packed. Fire boots laced. Door locked. A wave to Mrs. Armenta at her kitchen window.

There was no sign of Walt in the parking lot. She drove out to the back of the yard and hid her car behind a stack of empty propane cylinders. Her new .38 was in the glove box; she sat for a moment deciding whether to transfer it to her truck. Strictly against the rules; she could lose her job. Better just rely on an attitude.

She walked into the shop. "Hi, guys. I see they've rounded up the usual suspects."

"That's us." Abby grinned. "I keep suggesting they follow the money, but they ignore me."

Jill stood up from the computer. "The clue is the dog that didn't bark." She high-fived both of them.

Warren and Randy were making a hose pack on the frame—they already had a hundred feet of inch-and-a-half trunk and the Y in: they were curling in the lateral hose. Randy stopped and sang, "A policeman's lot is not a happy one." Warren repeated in the deepest bass he could manage: "Happy one." When Randy turned to stare, he shrugged. "My momma raised me right."

Shaeffer said "Hot damn, but you people are witty this morning."

Henry smiled, "Pretty good, OK. I kid you not," and everybody began to laugh. She couldn't answer for the rest of them but it was the first time they'd all laughed since heck was a pup, as Grandpa used to say, and it felt good.

Everybody except Buck. He was testing the hose fittings, not looking at anyone. Jeesh. It had been dense of them to forget that Evan had made that big scene Wednesday. Buck must be taking it hard—*he* obviously didn't think being a suspect was funny. She searched for something to say to him, that would bring him in without offending.

Randy had noticed. "Hey, Buck, can you give us a hand here? This hose'll have to go in tighter than we've got it, and you're the man with the experience."

Buck looked up. "Sure." His eyes—what a shock. Four days of suspicion had done a number on him.

She moved closer. "Going to keep your engine out at Fernow?"

"Hunting season for the next couple of months. Plus end-of-the-summer campers." He was stiff about it. Poor guy, he must really be hurting, probably thought they all believed Evan.

"I'm back in school tomorrow, but I'll work the next few weekends to help you chase any smoke that shows up." She turned away like you do from a horrible scar and then forced herself to look back. "Think you and Henry can get along without me?"

"We'll try."

Henry was watching. "We'll save some fire for you." Everybody there deserved better than they'd had with Jake. Well, a lot of people deserved better than they got. Some days it was a chore to keep smiling. She fled.

Mitch was coming across the parking lot. "Got a minute?"

"Sure. Better out here than in the there. The sight of you might send Buck over the edge."

"Bad?"

"Jake dead is hurting him worse than Jake alive. Are you pushing him?"

"*I'm* not. I don't know about Bailey. Evan is missing—does anybody in the shop know, do you think?"

"*Missing!*"

"Gone. His housemates don't have a clue—his room is empty, his car's gone, nobody saw him leave. Bank account's closed out."

"You know what, it doesn't look good."

"Are you surprised?"

"At first. Now that I've had ten seconds, I guess not. Evan was always apt to explode in any direction. It doesn't necessarily mean he's guilty. Just, it would be in character for him to react to pressure with something off the wall."

"His parents say they haven't heard from him."

"Evan's disappeared. Buck looks like he's fallen into a black hole. Most of us are furious for one reason or another. I've just left Walt; he'd be sure to tell you I'm irrational. I hear Duvenek's agitated."

"You hear right. Better give me your new address and phone number. You don't want to be out of reach at a time like this."

"*D*ay off with pay—how does it feel this morning?"

"Instant weight loss, most of it in my chest. Forget what I said last night about humiliation as policy, now that I'm past the resentment, I'm happy as a cow in clover, as Grandma said. Thought I'd bake caramelized french toast for breakfast, OK?"

Hill hugged her hard. "What's on your agenda for the first day of freedom?"

She took eggs and milk out of the fridge. "Work around the yard for a while. Go to the library and get a book, take it to the old Clark house for a leisurely lunch." She cracked eggs into a bowl. "Drive out to the ranch to take a look at Uncle Matt's and Aunt Jo's house as a prospective resident. Here, slice the bread, two slabs an inch thick. On the way home I'll stop at a grocery store and buy ingredients for meals that take hours to cook. As long as the investigation lasts, no short order."

"Whoo-ee. If I run into Raleigh, I'll thank him for saving my marriage. What's your plan for day two?"

Adding vanilla and cinnamon: "I don't know yet. But it's going to be something wickedly self-indulgent, something I've wanted to do for six months and haven't had time for."

"Hope it doesn't make you hard to get along with." He dropped bread slices into the batter.

"Bet a cookie I enjoy every minute. If this goes on for a week, I'm going to be on leave through Labor Day—if Raleigh calls and wants me to come back to work, maybe I'll tell him I'm not home. Turn the oven on 350, please."

"You're not going to be excavating in the forest trying to find the murder weapon?"

"Nope. Not my problem. Move that big bod, I need to get out the little casserole."

Her scanner and Forest radio were sitting in the corner of the counter with her belt. A dozer operator on his way to work was reporting an apparently inebriated driver who had rear-ended another car at the Humphreys intersection and driven away east on 66. The city was responding to a neighborhood where two shots had been fired. There was a fist fight in progress outside the Research Center at the Museum of Northern Arizona.

Hill stepped over and snapped off the scanner. "I don't know of a reason why we should spoil our breakfast with that crap."

"Yay!"

But on the Forest radio there was a call from Engine 5-4 reporting a fall injury and requesting an ambulance. "I gotta go." It might be one of his people.

"Sure. I'll save your toast," and he was gone. The dispatcher: "All stations clear channel one for emergency traffic." She listened to the Ranger 3-2 helicopter pilot coordinate evac of "the patient" with Engine 5-4 and the Pinewood ambulance.

*M*onsoons went back and forth to Mexico like a see-saw, gone the first few days of August…back again…gone again. Something about highs and lows. Humongous clockwise currents in the air and stuff.

A couple of times there was fog around the mountain when Sarah woke up. Air was cold and heavy, and water dripped slowly off everything, the grass, the tower. Condensed on the insides of windows. She loves being able to see weather forming two hours away and the landscape, like, sliding away, but in zero visibility fog she loved the dry safety of the cabin.

Sometimes mornings were beautiful and soft and clouds at sunrise were saffron, peach, apricot, persimmon and for a few minutes in that light the whole world was those colors. Later the clouds either burned off into a bare blazing day or grew white and grey with sunlight shining on them. They looked like they'd feel silky if you could touch them. By noon they were turning black, and lightning struck all over the place.

One day it started three fires so far down in Sycamore Canyon that she couldn't see any of them.

The really impressive fires were in other states, Utah and Nevada and California, forty gnarly fires all over the West. *Millions* of acres had been burned so far in the season. All of the Coconino Hot Shot crews were gone to those fires and even some of the engines. Districts were making up Regulars crews out of practically anybody "Get your red packs together and be at the cache at 1600." So few people were left on the forest that if they had more than half a dozen starts a day, there were no resources to send to them.

Randy was still on forest, but Jake had flown out with some other people to be overhead in Oregon. There were seven huge fires up there. There wasn't much hope that if he was overhead he'd be hurt.

She was glad he was gone, *glad*, and she didn't have to worry that he'd come up to the mountain. It's terrible to be afraid all the time…she didn't really know how terrible until he was gone.

She hadn't dared say anything to Randy about how Jake treated her and how bad she felt for fear he'd fight with Jake and get hurt. Or killed, Jake was so strong and mean. Mom was good for food and flowers, but you didn't talk to her about problems…she'd tell Dad. Beste might be all right though, she might not criticize.

But she was ashamed to say anything, even to Beste. On her day off she stopped to talk, and the only thing she could do was ask about Lillian. Venn settled down with a sigh at her feet.

"Beste, was she a great painter?"

"If you mean 'competent,' yes, she was that. Especially in pencil and watercolor. Some of her early oils seem a little stiff to me, as if she were painting by trendy ideas rather than her own. If you mean 'original' or 'unique,' which wasn't highly prized until fairly recently, I would say that her choice of subject, Arizona before it was fashionable, put her in a rather small group."

"But was she *great?*"

Beste thought a minute. "That's often a matter of publicity. The art world tends toward the bizarre. Georgia O'Keeffe is a case in point—I admire her later work, but would she have been 'great' if Stieglitz hadn't exhibited those nude photographs right at the beginning? She was always such good copy, especially after the move to New Mexico.

"So what *is* great?"

"The important question is, do you like the paintings? But 'great,' I suppose is whatever we say it is at the time. Here in Flagstaff we had Viola Babbitt, who was an enthusiastic amateur…if there's any kind of civic organization for art in Flagstaff, it's thanks to her and Mary-Russell Colton. Viola thought art was important and she painted for years, but not for money. 'I paint and donate," she used to say. Gene Foster did marvelous portraits of Viola's children, but Gene was interested in so many things she didn't stay with it. Neither had big-city gallery promotion."

"What do *you* say great is?"

Beste's voice was quiet. "I'm quite self-centered, I'm afraid. And subjective. If I look at or listen to or read a piece of art and feel changed. Moved emotionally, enhanced. Alive. Convinced because of it that I can go and create something myself. Then for me that piece of art is a glimpse into the Real, the Best. It's great, not just decorative or a good investment. So is the artist who made it."

"So was Lillian great?"

"For me, I suppose she was. I don't know how much of my reaction is influenced by what I know of her life. Her willingness to break with convention and do work that had meaning for her. Her forty-year love for a man like Jesse Smith. The friends, the adventures all over Arizona before it was built upon. I suppose I can't separate her work and the art of her life. But then, why should I? It's all a tangle that can't be untied. How can art be separate from life? There are many good painters but few great lives. She and Mary-Russell Ferrell Colton…both women surpassed what most of us even attempt. What do you think? Was Lillian great?"

"Oh, *yes!* I mean, I've *always* loved looking at her paintings. But when I found out about her, I loved *her* too. Practically nobody knows about her. She didn't make much money, and she died poor and forgotten. But what does *that* matter?"

*E*very place Meg went, the present was a layer on top of the past. Today would be another layer covered over in fifty years, and she'd be saying, "I remember that old house when it was a French restaurant; my grandmother remembered when John Clark built it."

"The first stone-wall Craftsman bungalow in Flagstaff, it was at the southeast corner of the farm. The town bought it in the early Twenties."

"A farm in the middle of town—it must have looked funny"

"Oh, Meggie, town didn't reach that far. Humphreys was a dirt road that ended at the Clark house. It was dirt for years."

"Flagstaff must not have amounted to much."

"It had grown in the forty years since its beginning. By the Twenties land was needed for new schools, and the council thought a big park would be nice. Also houses for a growing population. Bet a cookie you can't tell me how big the farm was."

She had seen it all clear as a picture. "The high school I go to?"

"Was once a farm where John Clark harvested his hay."

"The baseball fields?"

"Hay fields."

"And all those houses north of the school…"

"Once fields. The property extended to the Fort Valley Road. I remember when the town bought it and the paper published a map."

"Did Mr. Clark sell the house too?"

"No, they kept that. John died three years later, and Agnes lived on there another twenty years. As I remember, it was not sold until the early war years."

"And it was turned into a restaurant?"

"Oh dear no, not for years, not until the 1980s. I'm glad the place has been kept up, too much of my past has been demolished to make room for buildings that have no memory attached."

She was the first person there for lunch. A waiter in a white apron and a black bow tie led her to a table in the corner of the old living room, next to the fireplace, and left her with a menu. Walls were dark wood, the tablecloth was white—what a classy place. There were books on shelves. Light reflected from glasses and wine bottles, even the wood paneling. From a loudspeaker over her head, someone was playing the Pachelbell Canon on a guitar.

Waiters were showing other people in, a lot of older people. She watched faces for signs that they remembered the families, the furniture, parties maybe, card tables, but they sat at their white tablecloths and talked as if it were just another restaurant. She ordered a salad with a fancy name and opened the book she'd brought, a biography of Florence Merriam, C. Hart's ornithologist sister, one of the first of the women scientists in Flagstaff. She had stayed only a few months in 1894, but that was long enough to cure her of "a complaint of the lungs."

Her husband had been Vernon Bailey, whose name was on plants and animals all over the West. But she was worth reading about for other reasons. One of the first naturalists to study live birds in the field, an important nature writer—that was significance enough. An adventurer who rode horses astride when that was considered "eccentricity of conduct." A major campaigner in the battle against loading ladies' hats with dead birds. Yay for Florence.

She made of her life what she wanted it to be despite the "obliga- tions" that burdened women in that century. From childhood on, she was interested in birds. She reached the age when she was supposed to devote her life to a husband, and she went on doing what she cared about. Women always had to defy "should" to follow their own desires. Still true, but "should" had changed: like sticking to a job you didn't like so you wouldn't let other women down. The story hit close to home.

When her salad arrived, she was thinking of her tiny Aunt Jo, who'd have taken such a restaurant for granted, sat there as if she were in her own home, telling stories to a little girl. "The Family was furious when I defied them and came out to Arizona. They blamed me when your grandfather escaped the banking fate they'd planned for him and moved here to live as a rancher."

"Didn't they like Grandma?"

"Well, horrors, she not only wasn't German, they knew nothing of her background. The Girl of the Golden West and all that but not their sort. They made some high voltage scenes. If Paul had given in to them, I'd have kicked him."

"I'm glad you would have."

"Didn't do them any good to be mad, they couldn't touch his money, nor mine either. Oh, you should have heard the Upper Crust sniffs when we took Matt and Margaret and Ruby and Ada back to New York for a visit. My cousin Gertrude actually looked Matt over and said I didn't have to be that desperate. Our contingent was having too much fun to notice, which put them in a worse snit than ever. My mother finally fled to Santa Fe and lived Happily Ever After in her own studio taking painting lessons from her friends."

She loved talk of the old days. "That was brave of all three of you, Aunt Jo, you and Grandpa and your mother."

"Well, my cousin Lillian had blazed the way. It's a pity she didn't have the money we did, life would have been easier for her."

"Was she sorry?"

"No, I don't think so, she married a fine man who was good to her. And she lived free. One thing my family never did understand is that a woman needs to live her own life, not everyone else's."

*T*hings got scary out there in early August, about the time Jake left. The public schools would be starting on the 16th, so summer vacation was almost over for some people. There was so much trouble, you'd have thought the ending was making them reckless, especially on weekends. One Sunday there was a motorcycle accident with head injuries near Turkey Butte…two cars broadsided at Fort Tuthill with a child injured…six cows were loose on Highway 180. And a man who had to stop so fast that the fence posts loaded in the back of his truck came right through the window and hit him.

A pickup slid off the Snow Bowl Road and hit a tree, probably taking a curve too fast. The worst accident, though, was the school bus that rolled over four times on I-17 the first day of classes. With her binoculars Sarah could see it down there all morning and the flashing lights and the highway south of the airport jammed *solid* with cars and trucks, hardly moving.

Law Enforcement was busy all the time, campers cutting down green trees for firewood and stupid stuff like that. A horse trailer broken down in the middle of the road, could someone come for traffic control? One night at 22:30 Meg and the Mormon Lake LE went into service at the same time, but she never found out why.

There were gun shots in every direction...probably people practicing for fall hunting season. She could see some of them with her binoculars down at the pond setting up beer cans on the high side and walking around to the other bank to aim. Even if you couldn't see them, you could tell they were target shooting by how regular the sound was, one two three four five. Some were small sounds, but some made her jump they were so loud. One thing you can say about bow hunters, at least they don't make a lot of noise.

*T*hree times before Josy got to Rogers Lake, she stopped to talk with campers. The forest was full of them, and every camp had a fire going. Hey, a cold Sunday morning—what could you expect? She wondered what it looked like from a lookout tower, all those little smokes everywhere along the roads.

"Morning, folks. Hi, kids, how ya doin'? I stopped to be sure you understand fire regulations. I see you've got yours all inside a rock ring and the ground around it's clear of fuel—you people know what you're doing. I wish all our visitors did."

"Are we supposed to put it out or something?"

"No no, you're fine—we're not in any kind of restriction. But the rain we've had lately doesn't mean fire couldn't spread in a wind. Please be sure you don't leave it unattended; you don't want to come back from a hike and find that sparks from your friendly little campfire have set your tent to blazing. That happens a couple of times every summer."

They agreed they wouldn't like that at all. There was plenty of water and a shovel. They'd be careful.

"Most human-caused fires in the forest aren't deliberate. People don't always realize what can happen, and they get careless. But you look like experienced campers—no garbage thrown around, I see—so you'll take proper care. Please be sure your fire is dead and out when you drive away. It'd be a shame if this nice spot was ruined because you didn't spend an extra five minutes. That would be a good job for you kids: use the shovel to turn the ash over and wet it, turn it again, wet it, hold your hand close to test whether there's heat left in it. Then cover it with dirt. A supposedly dead fire can come to life fast in a strong wind."

They assured her they wouldn't think of leaving it alive. She wrote out a contact notice. "This tells my boss I've been on the job. I'll fill in your names and car license number and the location so if we get an attempt to locate from your relatives, we'll know where you are." It would also help to assign suppression costs if they started a fire, but she didn't say that, just tore the notice off its pad and handed it to them. "Have a great time—we're glad to have you here."

She waved to the children as she drove away. Most campers were decent. It was touchy to approach them not knowing—like the man camped at Poison Spring who invited her into his big tent for tea and she declined and found out later there was a warrant out for him—he'd kidnapped two women tourists, then pushed them out and stolen their car. But she was all the Forest Service some people ever saw.

It never took more than a few minutes. Everyone was casual, happy to be out of the city for a night or two. One man joked that she was a tree pig, not knowing how often she'd heard that, but she smiled and agreed. "Yep, that's my job, taking care of the forest so it'll be here for a long time. You wouldn't believe how destructive ignorant people can be. As bad as lightning, some of them—half of the fires on the Coconino are caused by John Q. Public out for recreation."

She stopped to talk with a bow hunter camped at the turn-off to Woody Mountain, a nice older man who said he'd been walking for three days looking for elk without seeing any, and he was "one tired boy." There were probably other people on the tower road, but she wanted to drive up to see Sarah in the afternoon—she'd wait to contact them.

Clouds to the south were shining glorious in the sunshine, sailing along in the wind happy as you please. They looked so free and delicate it was hard to believe they could merge into something as threatening as that huge black storm on the eastern horizon. The tops of it seemed to be leaning to the south; maybe it would stay along the New Mexico border and leave her to work without interference.

Hunters were camped back in the trees on the south side of Mill Park in the same place they were every year. She drove over to talk with them and go through her Smokey Bear routine. From the smell of things, they'd poured whiskey into their coffee at breakfast and decided to wait until evening to go out with their bows, but they were courteous.

At Phone Booth Tank, jeesh. Talk about *guilty*: way too close to a water source for wildlife; firewood was piled next to the rock ring with a rifle on top of it and a can of gasoline along side; empty beer cans were all over the place; a man in camo clothes was passed out on a cot right in the sun. You know what? Some people were too dumb to be running around loose.

*M*eg stood in sunlight and wind on the black basalt ridge that towered above Wupatki and the Friendly Ranch buildings. Not all of their land was visible—what with gullies and lava flows, there was no place where you could see it all. On the southeast side it dropped steadily down, treeless, away from the volcanic field to the Little Colorado River, what there was of it in late August.

It wasn't the best land for cattle, but it would be hers—*could* be. Sky and space and light, the Peaks off to the southwest. Shadows that changed every minute. Clouds back-lit by afternoon sun. She'd ridden over every part since she was a child.

The ranch had to make money; she couldn't live on P.J.'s investments, not and have any self-respect, and neither could Hill. Only someone like her great-uncle Luke could do that. And she had to have something useful to do with her life.

She couldn't market the way she felt when she came down from Sunset Crater and saw the Painted Desert spreading until the whole colored world was magnificent beyond words and her soul surged up and out, so beautiful she wanted to sing, and life was glorious again despite what other people did to make it mean and little.

Think creative, that was the ticket, think out of old ruts. P.J. had suggested raising mules. Quarter horses hadn't brought in a fortune but they had paid their own way—it might be worth a try. Might require extra barns and corrals, another well for the water they'd need. Couldn't have many mules at any time: it was a rule of thumb that stock needed a tree every fifty yards summer and winter for shelter, and they were short of trees.

She'd like to try training mules, learning how an animal reputed to be so intelligent would respond, what it understood. Whether it would return friendship and be a good companion. Would there be a market? The difference in muscular structure was intriguing—would a mule make a better jumper?

P.J. would keep detailed breeding charts; she'd keep detailed daily diaries about feed and training and human contact. You sold a horse for its manners—what kind of manners would a mule have if you sat down and talked to it half an hour a day? The study could keep her engrossed for years, and after all that effort, she wouldn't want to sell to just anybody who had the money. Could she require applications and interviews and a get-acquainted time, make her animals something people had to be worthy of?

While they were at it, how about llamas or vicuñas? Were they hardy enough to take advantage of high desert conditions? Could you shear them and sell the wool? Back to the library.

Off to the southeast there was a cloud shadow over Roden Crater—a cinder cone standing at the edge of the volcanic field. That section had been theirs, but twenty or so years ago they'd swapped it so that James Turrell could—crumb, how would you say it?—turn it into art. Some people thought his idea was off the wall, but she liked it. Not sure she had it right: light was his medium, not paint or marble; he wanted to construct rooms and tunnels inside the mountain and use light from the sky to create effects that would bring viewers to see light differently, see the sky differently.

It seemed to her that Turrell's idea might be appropriate to country that had attracted Aunt Jo and Lillian Wilhelm, all kinds of artists for more than a hundred years. The best part of it was the view anyway.

*U*sually Sarah has slept with all the windows open to let wind blow right through the cabin. Last night was so cold she shut them and loved her cozy warm room. There's a hurricane off the Gulf coast of Mexico that's feeding moisture into Arizona.

Looking for Lillian, she drove over to Prescott by herself. Through Ashfork and all that high open country. Through Chino Valley. Past the Phippen Museum of Western Art that hung a dozen of Lillian's paintings in a show last winter with four other women painters of Prescott. Past the Granite Dells. That country must have been beautiful the way it looked sixty years ago when houses didn't cover the hills and make them look small...all sky and space.

Driving is fun. But in a strange town the street signs go by faster than some people can read. She was so confused by the turns and merges that twice she had to stop in a parking lot and look at her map before she could even find the Sharlott Hall Museum.

For a few years Lillian lived nearby, in a tiny house on Beach Street when she was eighty years old or so. Alone because Jess was in the hospital and then he died.

It was an all right street, but shut in with no view...not like the other places she had lived in her life, open and free. The Pioneers' Home was better, on a hill above town. From the porch you could see all over Prescott. A breeze blew. She hoped Lillian had been in a front room with windows where she could sit and look out and remember her wonderful life.

Inside she found the office, and the secretary photocopied Lillian's records of admission...and then death. The whole place was full of old people who could hardly walk. Most of them were just sitting. It's awful that lives end like that. Lillian rode to Rainbow Bridge five times...she was the first white woman who hiked to Havasu. She lived at Amerind and Shekayah and sailed on Zane Grey's yacht and rode horses all over Arizona. It wasn't right that she became old and helpless. It didn't make sense.

The turn into Fort Whipple was hard to find...she drove past it twice. But then she was off the highway where she could go slow enough to read the signs, and finally she found the big white Veterans' Hospital. She walked all the way around it, looking up at the windows, wondering which one was the room where Jess died.

Inside the front door in the lobby, there it was, the Rainbow Bridge painting Lillian gave to the hospital because they were so good to Jess. It was different from the one Beste had. She stood and looked at it for a long time. After thirty years it was still there. She hoped they knew who painted it and cared why they had it, in memory of Jess and his wonderful life.

A man in the office told her how to get across the highway to the National Cemetery and where to look for the grave or she'd never have found it...rows and rows of identical white stones flat in the grass. Finally there it was. Jesse R Smith. She had been looking for that name, but it was a shock anyway.

She crouched down and touched his stone with her fingers. One of Randy's songs: "Go to sleep, you weary cowboy," and she began to cry. She was at the ending. His bones were down there. Lillian's ashes were buried above his heart. She sobbed for a long time, crouching, touching the stone, touching the place where the ashes were. They were right under her hands. All that they were should have come to more.

Jake was *definitely* not her Jesse Smith. For days before he went out to Oregon she didn't even open her sketchpad, she felt so hopeless... what had ever made her think she could be an artist? You have to be a *person* to be an artist, and she was a blob of jello.

But when Jake left she didn't feel so bad anymore. "Woody Autumn" looked really pretty good for being away from it for a while. She could see what needed to be done next. One day when the country around her was brilliant with light and shadow and Beaver Creek was flooding because of storms the day before around Apache Maid lookout, she started adding more color to the magenta mountains behind the trees, little strokes of everything she wanted to put in.

She may not ever be any good, not so that anybody would want to buy her work. But it makes her feel alive and free when she's doing it, strong. Glad to be who she is. It's a feeling in her chest, all over her, to be in touch with art. The people part of the world can be so ugly you have to make whatever beauty you can.

By noon Josy'd worked south past Casner Cabin Draw and West Fork to Fernow. Good time to drive up to TV Knob to eat lunch and look out over the Secret Mountain Wilderness. Ed Piper had told her about that particular place, it was a good lookout point—in June she'd spotted smoke from TV Knob, seven miles away near where Vultee Arch nestled in a tributary to Sterling Canyon.

She'd sat there all day as a spotter watching cypress and oak burn and the big Erickson helicopter fighting winds. Fire'd been spreading in all directions, but the crews had caught it before it could run across the ridge and down into Slide Rock. As it was, it burned along part of an ancient Indian trail that went up Sterling Canyon to its head and up and over and down to Indian Gardens.

She didn't get there often enough. A lunch stop would give her another look at that canyon country, and she just happened to have her geology book on the seat beside her. With her truck locked and chocked, she walked out to the view and chose a rock, unwrapped a sandwich, opened her book.

The sandstone layers up in Four Corners country—red because of iron oxide—were deposited, gosh, during the Mesozoic, was it? Before there were Rocky Mountains, while the North American continent was still pretty much part of Pangaea and Arizona was not far north of the equator. The continent traveled, and the sandstone was covered by more deposits a mile thick, and that eroded away, and canyons were cut beginning along about two million years ago. Hundreds of natural spans formed by erosion where the rock was just right—she hadn't realized there were that many. Rainbow Bridge was the biggest.

The Bridge was only 150-60 miles away from Vultee Arch; was the red sandstone in Oak Creek Canyon the same strata as red sandstone in the Colorado Plateau? Sand dunes on the shore of the same ancient ocean? She turned pages, trying to make the connection. The Schnebley Hill Formation was maybe a few million years older than Navajo sandstone, just two shakes of a lamb's tail, as Grandma said. Maps showed sand dunes through the whole area for millions of years, but she couldn't find a definite answer, sedimentary layers seemed to have different names in different places.

Ok, she had it: Vultee Arch was in Supai sandstone, 300 million years old, just above the Redwall layer, Paleozoic; Rainbow Bridge was in Navajo sandstone, Mesozoic, Upper Triassic and Jurassic, about 200 million years old. The sandstone of Vultee Arch was about 100 million years older than the sandstone of Rainbow Bridge.

A geologist could spend her life working on the Colorado Plateau. Half the history of the earth was there, on half of Arizona and Utah and a good part of Colorado and New Mexico—a huge tableland, a raft on a violent sea, as Halka Cronic said. There must still be secrets.

*N*o one had lived in the house for sixteen years, not since Aunt Jo had died there, alone and asleep in her bed, the book she'd been reading under her hand. In the room she'd used as a studio, a painting she'd been working on—a great sweep of the Painted Desert in the last brilliant light before sunset—waited on the easel. Meg opened the curtains. Still there, almost finished. She'd have it framed.

She'd wondered, driving out, whether memory would make living in the house painful. She'd taken the key from P.J. with, as Jo would have said, A Lump in the Throat. Those people, the years, the life—gone forever. Her mother had said, "I envy you the possibility of living in that house, full of knowledge and beauty."

Canvases were stacked against every wall in the studio. She knelt and turned through them. Aunt Jo had loved light and color, more so the older she grew, as if every year had freed her a little more. Aunt Jo had loved almost everything she saw. She had a very wide scope: cliffs and clouds at all hours, plants at all seasons, rocks, storms, you could see she'd loved them by the light she'd used. She'd lived the same way, happy to be alive. No wonder she and Grandma had been such friends.

Uncle Matt's natural history books wouldn't need much more than dusting. The Navajo rugs lay flat and strong, in the twilight of pulled drapes their colors were still true. She opened the glass case that held "treasures" and lifted out a little old Hopi bowl. Nampeyo. Bet a cookie it was worth a bundle.

Her mother was standing in the open doorway. "Well? What do you think?"

"I think I've always been the luckiest person there ever was."

"You've handled it with grace and good humor."

"Runs in the family."

"Bet a cookie." They laughed together. "Oh, Meggie, I miss them ."

"Me too. If they were still here, I'd probably know what to do without even thinking about it."

"Having trouble deciding?"

"Let's go talk to P.J."

Sarah loves the way her pencil box looks open on the bench with all the colors showing together. And the way "Woody Autumn" looks next to them, bright and *singing* with its green sky. A dozen colors in the mountain tops, pink yellow blue lavender lime. The mountains are jewels in a magic country. She loves the way it's turning out, free to be what it is instead of what it's *supposed* to.

To think she almost died. When she went down into the aspen on the north side of the mountain to choose a place where she would lie down and shoot herself. Crawl under a tangle of fallen aspen and shoot herself in the head. On the last day of the fire season because after that she might not be able to get away from Jake.

She hadn't known he was back. There'd been snow in Oregon… she'd heard on the radio that a plane was coming in to the Flagstaff airport, but his name wasn't one that was told to the districts. So she was trying to sketch the swallows and watching clouds build up, how beautiful they looked, and their shadows sliding across the forest. Feeling sort of happy. Then she heard a truck coming up through the trees and knew by the sound it was Jake.

Her heart felt like it was going to stop and her whole body went numb all over. "Oh no." Venn raised her head and looked up. "Oh no oh no oh no." She'd never heard anything so awful as the loud heavy sound he made climbing the stairs. Her chest and throat were so tight that she began to cough.

"I don't know why you let this mutt come up here." He pushed Venn down the top flight before he closed the trap door. "Thought I'd surprise you. See if I could catch you with somebody else up here. Did you miss me?"

Her breath was short little gasps. She couldn't make a sound. Venn was barking and barking on the top landing.

"S'matter. Cat got your tongue? I said, did you miss me?" He knew how she felt. He *knew*. And he liked it. "I expect a better welcome." He grabbed her arm and shouted in her face. "**I expect a better welcome**." He jerked her arm and pulled her off balance. "Smile like you're glad to see me, little miss lawyer's daughter."

She couldn't. How could she smile when she wanted to die right there? Her two wonderful weeks were over.

"Well, I can see you're overcome with passion. I'll just fix that for you." He backed her around the firefinder and pushed her onto the window seat. "Give you the thrill of your life."

Her head and shoulders were clear out the window, the metal sill a hard line on her back. She was hanging forty-five feet above the ground. Her hands scrabbled for something to hold on to...she couldn't see anything but sky.

He was pulling off her jeans. "You'd better wrap your legs around me if you know what's good for you. If I feel like it I can shove them up and tip you right out the window."

He would. She knew he would. He pushed her knees apart as he was kicking his pants down and pulled her hips to the edge of the bench. She tried to reach the underside.

"Here, I'll give you something to hold onto." He put her hand on his, his *thing*. "Grab it. I said GRAB IT." He bent her fingers around it and pushed them up and down.

It was stiff and naked. "I'm not messing with condoms any more. Can't get a good hard-on." He threw her hand aside and forced his thing inside her.

She thought she was tearing...a long line of fire. He held her hips between his hands and began to pump back and forth. Behind her eyes everything shrank to a pinpoint.

The next thing she knew she was wet and slimey down there and stinging inside. The bench was slimey under her. Jake was saying, "Nothing like good balling to make a man glad to be home. Right? I said RIGHT?" He put his hands under her knees. "Answer me, or out you go on your head."

She didn't care. It would be escape. Her life was finished anyway.

"Hey, can't you take a joke? What's wrong with you?" He swung her around until her head was inside and she was lying on the bench. She hurt too bad to talk. Down on the top landing Venn was still barking.

He stroked her hair back from her forehead and kissed it. "Don't get spooky on me now. I guess I should've given you a little more fore-play. A surprise like that didn't give you time to work up to it. Come on. Open your eyes, that's my girl." His voice was low and gentle. "Give me a smile." He kissed her forehead again. "You haven't said a word since I got here. I'm glad to see you again." His fingers were soft, brushing her face. "You're so pretty, I just plain lost control. Two weeks away from you. I couldn't help myself."

He patted her cheek. "Hey, wake up. I didn't mean to scare you. I'll make it up to you. What do you say we go into town to dinner tonight?"

She's glad he's dead. She should probably feel sorry for him, maybe he was nice when he was a little boy, soft and shy, but there's no excuse for what he turned into. He raped her that day. She's glad he's dead, and she doesn't feel one bit guilty.

It's just, like, sometimes she shakes...wraps her arms around herself...curls into a ball. Cries in painful gulps and can't stop. She doesn't ever know when it will start.

*T*ime was getting short: Josy wanted to be away from the station an hour early in case Walt had decided to get cute again about showing up. And she wanted to stop by Woody Mountain. She could take a swing close to Turkey Butte and then go north.

A family was camped at Flag Tank. "Afternoon, folks. Hi, kids. I stopped to be sure you know about fire safety. And I'm sorry to tell you, but here on the Coconino we have a strong feeling of courtesy toward our wildlife. We try to avoid interfering with their basic necessities—right, kids, bare necessities—like drinking water. That might seem odd in the middle of hunting season, but it's part of an idea we have about natural ethics.

"You bet, that's Aldo Leopold all right. You've been reading—he was a Forest Service man in eastern Arizona and New Mexico.

"So anyway, these little tanks are the only source of drinking water for all kinds of creatures—deer, elk, turkeys, squirrels. Bear too. Lions. Yes, we have them, all over the place. When you're camped right at the tank, the little ones are afraid to come in for a drink. And you probably don't want to get in the way of the big ones. May I ask you to move your camp back a quarter of a mile?"

No problem, they said, happy to. They didn't realize. Where they came from there was water everywhere, but it figures in a dry country, sure, they could see that.

She unrolled her forest map and showed them how to get to several good spots on down the road where they'd have killer views out over the red rocks. And she asked the children to be in charge of the camp fire, be sure it was built right, be sure it was out when they left. "Your children do you credit, folks. It's a pleasure to see such good manners." She meant it.

At Norris Tank she made the pitch to four hunters who should have known better and reminded them it wasn't considered sporting to stake out a tank at dusk. "You could get away with it, maybe, but you couldn't be proud of yourself—*bow* hunters who don't know about sportsmanship?"

They blustered and made loud noises and implied she didn't know what she was talking about, so she pulled a copy of the regulations out of her truck to show them. Teased, flattered their vanity. Two of them told the other two to shut up and listen to the little lady. She thanked them all for their cooperation and drove away dreading rifle season. Maybe she'd plead heavy homework and quit before it started. Pew to men who were showing off for other men.

"Well, what do you girls think of the house?"

"Sound as the rock it's built on. Probably last as long." She slumped into the big tweed chair and hung her legs over the arm.

"Is it livable?"

"When my grandchildren are ready to move in, it'll still be livable. No, now stop that—you two look like a dog that sees food coming. I'm not, not yet. How are we going to keep the ranch in the family if I don't provide another generation, that's all I meant. And I want to be here then, want my children to grow up here as happy and free as I was."

Her mother went to the kitchen. "Talk loud so I can hear while I brew coffee."

P.J. moved to stand in the doorway. "We called your brothers this morning to get their reaction to changing the wills and making the ranch over to you—they had some questions, but they were positive. I'm going into town tomorrow, got appointments with my lawyer and accountant to explore the possibilities. How are you and Hill feeling?"

"We're waiting to hear details about practical matters like whether the ranch could support us and our fifteen grandchildren, what changes would have to be made. But so far we want to go ahead with discussions, and we have a ton of ideas. Hill says he'd consider leaving the Forest Service and working out here full time."

"Tell him I'd welcome that."

"I've been reading about mules, that seems like the kind of project I could throw myself into."

"Thought it might."

She pitched her voice into the kitchen. "You remember I was talking about social responsibility?"

Her mother's voice: "I was very impressed."

"See what you think of this. What if I were to take a handicapped child or two every summer to work with the colts?"

P.J. looked blank. "What kind of handicap?"

"Deaf, blind, retarded, crippled, abused."

"What age?"

"Ten or so. Young enough for it to make a difference."

"Boys or girls?"

"Wouldn't matter. Riding's been tried on kids with cerebral palsy and head injuries in California and Texas—seems to help. In Europe children who've had polio are treated that way with some success. Down in Sierra Vista there's a facility, but nothing I've found so far in northern Arizona."

"Well, now, that's quite an idea."

"There's a little boy on our block in town, eight years old, who struggles along with crutches. I see him in the mornings waiting with his mother for a bus to pick him up and take him to school, and I've thought what a shame it is he can't have the kind of childhood I had. Fantasized about taking him in front of me on the saddle and showing him the world."

Her mother came in. "Meggie, you do us proud."

"So far I haven't found anybody who's using mules. What I thought was, if mules are as smart as people say they are, we could buy a good donkey, maybe a smallish one? And breed to one of our smaller mares. Find a kid whose parents are interested in having him or her here right from the birth, pair them up, you know, a partnership with the colt. Have him or her out here week-ends, all summer for years."

Mom stroked her hair. "I say yay for you, Meggie."

Sarah wants that humongous black wall of storm to come west and cover the mountain, like, *rage* around her. Lightning hail wind. And she'll be safe inside the tower, hidden from everybody, stroking colored chalk into the golden leaves of "Woody Autumn." But it's moving around the Peaks and south across Mormon Lake toward Hutch Mountain. She's disappointed. There's been plenty of hot sunny weather this summer...too much nice. Nice doesn't get you anything.

After that day, she hated Jake. She was going to shoot herself, but then she was just *mad*. She'd never felt like that before...all she could think of was how awful he was. For a while he tried to make her feel cherished, but it was too late, she already knew. Maybe he could feel it...he wasn't quite so mean. He came by one evening with his bow so she could admire it and took her south to Black Tank to show her where he was going to sleep so he could start hunting at sunrise.

Sometimes though he'd reach out fast and grab her breast and pinch the nipple hard enough to hurt. Then he'd laugh, "Just teasing. Can't you take a joke?" Once he kicked her bad leg and said it was an accident, but she didn't believe him, even when he made her sit down to see if he had broken the skin. She knew he hoped he had. And she knew he'd kill her someday if she was ever so dumb as to love him again. Just, she was afraid to say anything.

She's tired of being everybody's good little girl. Of never getting praise except when she does what somebody else wants her to. People pick on you if a good little girl is all you are.

She cried that whole week after Jake came back for fear she might be pregnant. He actually patted her cheek and said, "You better be nice. I know when your monthly period is, I know when you can get knocked up. Your father wouldn't like to hear about that. And I'm not going to let you get rid of a baby of mine."

When she felt cramps starting and then the first drop of blood, she was so relieved she cried even harder and shook and curled into a ball on the windowseat.

The thing was, after the engines came back from the Los Padres fire, Jake got weird with them, weirder than usual. Randy said he had them doing stuff that didn't make any sense. "He accused us of sloppy hosepacks. For two days we were unrolling them and washing them all over again and drying them and rolling them up. I mean, we all had repairs to make after that fire run, the tranny on my engine was beginning to growl, and he wouldn't let us get to it. Buck told him we had a potential safety hazard and he got red in the face and shouted about insubordination.

She remembered what Jake said…"Don't forget Randy works for me. I can put his engine anywhere on a fire." What if he *wanted* Randy to tell her?

"You know that fire you called the other day in the Sycamore drainage? We're so short we can't put together a hand crew on the district, so Jake called for two engines and two patrol units. Pete was off, so Engine 2-2 was newbies. Jake put them at the head on the slope above the fire with wind blowing in their faces. Buck said 'I don't think so.' He didn't say anything on the radio, he just ran over there and moved them. Jake was shouting at him dumb things about countermanding an order, but I had the impression he was enjoying himself playing to the audience. Guy's gone over the edge if you ask me."

"Can't you do anything about it?"

"Finally half a dozen of us went in together to talk to Mitch, tell him we have a problem, Jake's gonna get somebody hurt. Buck said he was going to make up his own mind from now on whether to follow orders."

"Did it do any good?"

"Mitch said yeah, he knew, he'd have to do something about it. But it takes time to fire a GS 7 and you can't transfer a guy with Jake's reputation, who'd take him? Mitch called him in and talked to him, and he came back smooth as oil, patting the women on the shoulder and calling the men 'Dude.' Nobody trusts him—that's bad news on a fire. I'm thinking of quitting at the end of the season."

A huge bird is, like, coasting on the wind above the steep western slope of the mountain...bigger than a raven or a hawk, big as a vulture at least, but with wings that fit to its chunky body all on one long line, not a V shape like a vulture. Alone, not in a group like vultures are...a wonderful rich brown color. She manages to find it with the binoculars and follow it. Short hooked beak, *fierce* eyes, powerful legs with long talons held against its body so they look like they're folded away.

It's a golden eagle! Randy asked her to watch and told her what to look for. He thought he saw one in the top of a pine down by the pond, but he wasn't sure.

"There aren't many around here. Goldens are specialists in small mammals, so any one part of a pine forest can't support much more than one. If it's a female, I'd like to see if I can find a nest."

It circles and glides back until it's below her. She's looking down on the *back* of a beautiful golden-brown eagle. Maybe it's lived here on the mountain with her all summer, in the very same air, and she's never once seen it before. It drops out of sight below the tree tops. She lowers the binoculars to watch for it, but it doesn't come up again. Sitting on a branch, maybe, holding with talons that are its weapons, not minding being alone. She'll draw it from above with its wings spread, sailing past the trees outside the tower windows. It's a killer and all, but she'll never forget how it came so close.

There's a *wonderful* mass of white cumulus clouds shining in full sun beyond the Prussian blue slopes between Hochderffer and the Peaks. *Towering*, with grey nimbus far behind them. And in the left foreground Hart Prairie is the most vivid emerald green and swirls of wheat yellow.

She hears a heavy truck starting down at the gate. Winding slowly around the mountain, coming up the road. It sounds like Forest Service...a heavy sound, maybe the big pumper truck   she hopes it's Josy. Ten years older, but they both grew up in Flagstaff, they're both Western. Maybe they can be friends. She hopes so.

She slides her pencils into the box, closes the drawing pad. Through the trees she can see Forest Service green, a square hood, then the equipment in the back...it's Josy. Venn begins to bark and moves off the trapdoor. Stands with her nose pointing to the place where it will open, scratches with her foot.

"Okay, okay. Go see."

Venn *spills* nose first down the steep top flight and stands barking on the landing. Echoes ring back from the trees. The truck turns around and comes back. Venn dashes down the stairs.

Josy steps out of the truck. Closes the door, looks up and waves. "Hi! Well Venn, hello hello hello." An elkhound nearly *talks* sometimes, you can almost hear the words. Josy bends and pets with both hands. "Yes, I'm glad to see you too. How are you? How are you?"

*J*osy eased up onto the tall lookout chair, three feet above the floor, and hooked the toes of her boots into the circle that bound the legs. Sarah was smiling at her with a look she couldn't read. Had she been that young when *she* was twenty?

"You got your truck back."

"A few hours of being a passenger was all I could stand. Do you need anything I can bring you next weekend? Batteries? Window cleaner?"

"Oh no, this is my last day—classes start again tomorrow. I'll be a senior, you know—art."

"Hey, I start tomorrow too, but I'll be in geology. Tell you what, we'll be on the same campus. Let's keep in touch, have lunch."

Now what did *that* look mean? The kid was almost beautiful she was so radiant. All for a suggestion about lunch—hadn't that ever happened to her before? Given what Randy said, maybe not. "I don't think I've ever been in the Fine Arts building. How about a tour some day and a look at what you're doing? If we can both work it in. I can show you the Geology set-up, if you're interested."

Sarah sat there nodding, as if she didn't trust herself to speak. You know what, this could turn into *responsibility*. "So are you glad to be getting back to it?"

A deep sigh. "I hate to leave the mountain—I *love* it. I'll be living at home again, and that's not the freedom this has been. But it is exciting to be where so many people are working. I like being part of it."

"I know what you mean—that's how I feel. All the sediment in my brain stirred into circulation."

"Do you live at home?"

She shrugged. "Only in memory. My parents died in a car crash ten years ago. No, it's OK, I think maybe I've learned to take them back into my life, if that makes any sense. I've just moved into a little place of my own near campus—left Walt finally."

"I'm glad. The things you've said, I wondered."

"Emotional violence is hard to defend yourself against. You know, insults and criticism and accusations. Sneering and jeering. Shouting. Mad about everything. I got sick of it."

"Was it hard to break it off and move out? I'm afraid my father will be a problem. He won't want to let go."

"The hardest part with Walt was making up my mind to do it, and then deciding how I was going to tell him." She described the scene at Cameron on Thursday and then what Friday night had been. "Yesterday when I walked out of the shop, he was waiting for me in the parking lot. Major bummer, as we used to say when I was in grade school. But listen to this—" She acted out the car chase and the pistol and the blue heeler that jumped out of the pickup truck.

"Do you think he'll leave you alone now?"

"I don't know. I don't know whether I'll need a lawyer."

"My father's a lawyer, but if you go to him, he'll use it as proof that the world is dangerous for girls and that's why he should keep me close to home. You could go to the woman who's in his firm though, he might not even hear about it."

Jeesh. What had life been for her? "Thanks. I know where the office is, I've seen the sign. I'll do that if it looks like I need legal help. There's not much chance of enlisting the police unless he attacks. Sort of leaves me on my own."

"Yes." Sarah glanced away. "It's terrible when there's no help anywhere." She looked down at her hands.

"Hey, it could be worse, I could be a ninny. But I'm northern Arizona for more than a hundred years, great-grand daughter of pioneers. I'm a pretty poor descendant if I can't scare off a varmint. Or shoot him if I have to."

Without raising her head, Sarah looked up, into her eyes. Like an electric shock. Gawd, slammed back, hit by something invisible. *She* did it! Sarah killed him! Limped down there alone in a howling wind and put a bullet in Jake's head and limped back in the moonlight, hid the pistol somewhere. Stunned, she floundered through another minute. Sarah had shot him—it was real as a rock.

Finally she slid off the lookout chair. "Well, I've gotta leave so I can be outa there before five o'clock. Are you in the phone book? Shall I call in a couple of weeks? OK, see you soon." And she was down the stairs, driving away through the trees, shaken right down to her toes.

Sarah's face, the eyes, the shock of it. Sweet and mild and then wham! a jolt of electricity so strong it crackled. Look how her heart was pounding. "But that's not proof of anything. What would I say, 'I just know'?" Jeesh, feel like a fool.

Where'd Sarah get the pistol? Was Venn with her, or did she leave the dog in the cabin? At the gate Josy got out and opened the lock, swung the bar back. Killing is killing. And what if she were to go on doing it? That would make me an accessory. But Jake must have done something horrible and left her no way out." She said, *It's terrible when there's no help anywhere.* Poor kid.

But what a thing to carry, the memory, all of it. "Chances are, she'll never get over it. I just know how it would feel. And who could she tell, who would understand why she gets stranger every year? What'll happen to her? You know what, she's going to need a friend in the worst way."

She drove through and got out to close the gate again. "Take the long view, the time of the earth. All the living and trying and then the dying."

Downhill a hundred feet, then she engaged the gear. "Hey, nobody lives without wounds, nobody. As Grandma used to say—what gets us through is propping each other up the best we can." OK, she'd try that.

Sources

Published

Archer, Lou Ella. *Sonnets to the Southwest.* Los Angeles: Times-Mirror Printing and Binding Co. 1930.

———*Canyon Shadows.* Los Angeles: Times-Mirror Printing and Binding Co. 1931.

Bernheimer, Charles L. *Rainbow Bridge.* New York: Doubleday, Doran & Co. 1929.

Boswell, Payton, *Modern American Painting.* New York: Dodd, Mead and Company. 1980.

Boswell, Payton, *Modern American Painting.* New York: Dodd, Mead and Company. 1980.

Chapman, Arthur. "Out Where the West Begins," *The Home Book of Verse.* New York: Henry Holt and Company. 1912.

Chase, Katherine. *Brush Strokes on the Plateau.* Flagstaff: Museum of Northern Arizona. 1984.

Chronic, Halka. *Roadside Geology of Arizona.* Missoula: Mountain Press Publishing Company. 1983.

Clymer, Floyd. *Henry's Wonderful Model T.* New York: Bonanza Books. MCMLV.

Coffin, Charles, *The Story of American Painting.* Garden City, New York: Garden City Publishing. 1937.

Coffin, Charles, *The Story of American Painting.* Garden City, New York: Garden City Publishing. 1937.

Comfort, Mary. *Rainbow to Yesterday: the John and Louisa Wetherill Story.* New York: Vantage Press. 1980.

Davidson, Harold G. *Jimmy Swinnerton.* New York: Hearst Books. 1985.

…Editors of Time-Life Books. *American Painting, 1900–1970.* New York: Time-Life Books. 1970.

…"Elizabeth Oldaker," *Arizona Women's Hall of Fame.* Arizona Historical Society and the Arizona Department of Library, Archives and Public Records.

…Editors of Time-Life Books, *American Painting, 1900–1970.* New York: Time-Life Books. 1970.

Gibson, Arrell Morgan, *The Santa Fe and Taos Colonies.* Norman: University of Oklahoma Press. 1983.

Gibson, Arrell Mogran, *The Santa Fe and Taos Colonies.* Norman: University of Oklahoma Press. 1983.

Gilmore, Frances and Louisa Wetherill. *Traders to the Navajos,* Albuquerque: University of New Mexico Press. 1934.

Grey, Zane. "Down Into the Desert," *Ladies Home Journal.*

———*The Rainbow Trail.* New York: Grossett and Dunlap. 1915.

———*Tales of Lonely Trails.* Flagstaff: Northland Press. 1986.

———*To the Last Man.* New York: Harper and Brothers. 1922.

Griffen, Joyce. "Electricity and Steam Heat: Co-generation in Flagstaff, 1920-1966." *Journal of Arizona History.* Arizona Historical Society. Summer, 1985.

…Guide to the United States. New York: D. Appleton and Company. 1890.

Haftman, Werner, *Painting in the Twentieth Century.* New York: Frederick A. Praeger. 1965.

Jones, Courtney Reeder. *Letters from Wupatki.* Tucson, Arizona: The University of Arizona Press. 1995.

Kant, Candace. *Zane Grey's Arizona.* Flagstaff: Northland Press. 1984.

Mangum, Richard K. and Sherry G. *Flagstaff Album.* Flagstaff, Arizona: Hexagon Press. 1993.

———*Flagstaff Historic Walk.* Flagstaff, Arizona. Hexagon Press 1993.

———*One Woman's West.* Flagstaff, Arizona: Northland Publishing. 1997.

McElfresh, Patricia Myers. *Scottsdale: Jewel in the Desert.* Woodland Hill, California: Windsor Publications. 1984.

McDonald, William F. *Federal Relief Administration and the Arts: the Origins and Administrative History of the Arts Projects of the Works Progress Administration.* Ohio State University Press. 1969.

McNitt, Frank. *The Indian Traders.* Norman, Oklahoma: University of Oklahoma Press. 1962.

———*Richard Wetherill, Anasazi.* Albuquerque, New Mexico: University of New Mexico Press. 1957.

…"Past Present At the OW," *Phoenix Home and Garden.* October 1994.

…"Pueblo Bonito," Southwest Parks and Monuments Association

Ranney, Wayne. *Sedona Through Time.* Flagstaff, Arizona: Red Lake Books. 1993.

Reilly, P.T. *Lee's Ferry.* Logan, Utah: Utah State University Press. 1999.

Rinehart, Mary Roberts. *The Best of Tish.* New York: Tarror and Rinehart. 1937.

Robinson, Roxana. *Georgia O'Keeffe: a life.* New York: Harper and Rowe. 1989.

Rulon, Phillip, with Speer Morgan et. al. "The Letters of Zane and Dolly Crey." *The Missouri Review,* Volume XVIII Number 2. Columbia: University of Missouri. 1995.

Ryan, Frank. *The Forgotten Plague: how the battle against tuberclosis was won—and lost.* Boston: Little Brown. 1993.

Smiley, Terah L., J. Dale Nations, Troy L. Pewe, John P. Schafer. *Landscapes of Arizona.* Lanham, Maryland: University Press of America, Inc. 1984.

Stragnell, Robert. "Five Ladies of Prescott and their Art." Prescott, Arizona: Phippen Museum Gallery Guide, 1995.

Tagg, Lawrence V. *Harold Bell Wright: storyteller to America.* Tucson, Arizona: Westernlore Press. 1986.

Thybony, Scott. *Walnut Canyon National Monument.* Tucson, Arizona: Southwest Parks and Monuments Association. 1988.

Trenton, Patrica, ed. *Independent Spirits: Woman Painters of the American West, 1890–1945.* Berkely: University of California Press with Autry Museum of Western Heritage. 1995.

Vail, Karole. *Peggy Guggenheim: a celebration.* New York: Solomon R. Guggenheim Museum. 1998.

––––Zane's Grey West Society Publications. *ZaneGrey Quarterly, Zane Grey Review, Zane Grey Reporter.* Fort Wayne, Indiana:

Primary

American Artists Professional League. New York

Amerind Foundation; Dragoon, Arizona; Allan McIntyre, Collections Manager

Arizona Department of Library, Archives, and Public Records; Phoenix, Arizona; Carol Downey, Reference Librarian

Arizona Historical Foundation. Arizona State University; Tempe, Arizona

Arizona Historical Society Library and Archives. Tucson, Arizona; Deborah Shelton, Librarian

Arizona Historical Society; Yuma, Arizona; Carol Brooks, Curator

Arizona State University Special Collections Library; Tempe, Arizona

Bank One Corporate Properties; Phoenix, Arizona; Ro Sipek, Art Curator, Walter Bimson Collection

Center for Anthropological Studies; Albuquerque, New Mexico; Albert E. Ward, Director

Coconino County Recorder's Office; Flagstaff, Arizona

Department of Veterans Affairs Medical Center, Fort Whipple; Prescott, Arizona

Flagstaff City-Coconino County Public Library; Flagstaff, Arizona; microfilms of *The Coconino Sun,* Flagstaff City Directory–1920, weather bureau records

Guilford Free Library; Guilford, Connecticut; Nona Bloomer, Historian

Grand Canyon National Park Service Research Library; Grand Canyon, Arizona; Sara Stebbins, Librarian

Heard Museum Library and Archives; Phoenix, Arizona; Nick Klimiades, Manager

Historical Society of the Town of Greenwich, Connecticut

Hunter College of the City of New York Library; New York; Reference Services

Maricopa County Recorder's Office. Phoenix. Civil Actions

Museum of Northern Arizona Harold S. Colton Memorial Library; Flagstaff, Arizona; MS 158, Lillian Wilhelm Smith; Museum Archives, Box 57, A90,610, Arizona Artists Arts and Crafts Exhibitions

National Academy of Design; New York, New York
National Watercolor Society; Rosemary Macbird, Historian
New York Art Students League. New York, New York
New York Public Library; New York, New York; Research Library: maps of
    Manhattan
Northern Arizona University; Flagstaff, Arizona; Special Collections: oral
    history tapes; Coconino National Forest Service/CCC work diaries of
    Edgar B. Raudebaugh
Old Trails Museum. Winslow, Arizona. Janice Griffith, curator
Prescott National Forest; Prescott, Arizona; Ken Kimsey, Curator
Ruff's Gunshop. Flagstaff, Arizona
Sharlot Hall Museum Research Library; Prescott, Arizona; Michael Wurtz,
    Archivist; Album 4 Box 2 (photos), Document boxes 123, 33, 169,
    150B
Soroptimist International of the Americas. Lisa Mangiafico, Archivist
William Wrigley Corporate Library. Wrigley Building, Chicago, Illinois
Zane Grey Museum; Lackawaxen, Pennsylvania; administered by the
    National Park Service
Zane Grey Museum. Payson, Arizona; Mel and Beth Counselor

Correspondence with:
Virginia Baker, Arizona native
Jerry Bradley, Range, Coconino National Forest
Jan Klehfoth, Model T Ford Club of America
Harvey Leake, great-grandson of John and Louisa Wetherill
Kay Manley, friend of Lillian Wilhelm Smith
Ray and Ruth Manley, son and daughter-in-law of Kay Manley
Ruby Perkins, Arizona native
Virginia Terrell, daughter of Claire Wilhelm Carlin
Carolyn Timmerman, Zane Grey's West Society
Thomas Way, writer of northern Arizona history
Richard Williams, nephew of Lillian Wilhelm Smith

Conversations with:
The Babbitt girls, daughters of Viola Babbitt: Emma Jean Bader, Elizabeth
    D'Mura, Mary Eleanor Bilby, Rayma Sharber
Mary May Stiles Bailey, daughter of Jot Stiles
Ron Bales, Law Enforcement, Coconino National Forest
Katharine Bartlett, anthropologist and librarian, Museum of Northern
    Arizona, retired
Louise Black, long-time resident of Flagstaff
Tom Cain, biologist, Coconino National Forest
Johni Lou Duncan, granddaughter of John and Louisa Wetherill
Joe Feller, Arizona State University

Rita Gannon, granddaughter of Mary and T.A. Riordan
Henry Giclas, Flagstaff native and historian
Alan Gordon, internist
Elizabeth Fulton Husband, daughter of W.S. Shirley of the Amerind
    Foundation
Bob Jensen, Nature Conservancy, Hart Prairie Preserve
Larry, caretaker at the OW Ranch
Dorothy Lillian Leake, granddaughter of John and Louisa Wetherill
Scott Lederman, former forest firefighter
Mark Leitterman, Flagstaff City Library
Ted Leighton, Sedona
Margaret Low, daughter of Wong Dew Yu [Dear Yu Wong Jun]
Richard and Sherry Mangum, Flagstaff historians
Edward Miller, Nature Conservancy, Hart Prairie
Rick Miller, Arizona Game and Fish, Region Two
Mary Lou Morrow, granddaughter of Ed Raudebaugh
Barbara Ohlwiler, daughter of James Albert Smith
Rob Olson, Briar Patch Resort, Oak Creek Canyon
Leona Pouyama, Hotevilla
Kent and Mary Rethlake, Coconino National Forest
Joe Richards, Coconino County Sheriff
Phillip Rulon, Northern Arizona University
Teresa Schalow, survivor of pulmonary tuberculosis
Edward Smith, Nature Conservancy, Hart Prairie Preserve
Marie Stilley, long-time resident of Flagstaff
Paul Wilkerson, Law Enforcement, Coconino National Forest
Annette Wong, granddaughter of Wong Dew Yu [Dear Yu Wong Jun]
Billie Williams Yost, native of Northern Arizona
Loree Williams, research in the New York Public Library
Mark Zummwalt, Law Enforcement, Coconino National Forest

Index